PLAGUED, WITH GUILT

MICHAEL JASON BRANDT

CASUS BELLI
BOOKS

This is a work of fiction. All of the characters and events portrayed in this novel are either fictional or are used fictitiously. Any resemblance to actual events or persons, living or dead, is entirely coincidental.

PLAGUED, WITH GUILT

Library of Congress Control Number: 2015909609

ISBN 978-0-9964984-0-1

A Casus Belli Book

www.CasusBelliBooks.com

Happy Times lyrics used with permission from Alfred Music.

Praise for *Plagued, With Guilt*:

"A fierce academic thriller and a powerful meditation on humanity... A striking, powerful debut that heralds the start of a promising career."

— KIRKUS REVIEWS

10th Annual National Indie Excellence Awards Finalist

Join The Kings Club

Michael Jason Brandt's Kings Club members are always the first to hear about new books and publications, and receive free books and unique items to accompany the *Empire Asunder* series.

See the back of this book for details on how to sign up.

PREFACE

Whenever the scope of a novel extends to multiple countries and cultures, the author must make a decision regarding the use of language. In this book, the majority of dialogue is conducted in English, and the few uses of other languages should be clear enough from context. In cases where a conversation would logically be conducted in a different language—for example, a dialogue between two native Arabic speakers—I use English as a convenience to readers with the understanding that it is a translation of the actual language being spoken.

Additionally, for reasons that will become clear in the narrative, some speakers will have errors in grammar and pronunciation. Once again, context should make those occasions clear, but it can be jarring to those of us who tend to fixate on proper language.

In what I know is an unorthodox approach, each chapter is prefaced by a short account of science or history relevant to the narrative. These introductions cumulatively tell a story of their own, one I hope is both entertaining and educational—and a little bit thought-provoking, because this fascinating existence we clumsily navigate is an inescapably complex and treacherous one. My reason for including these accounts is partly to provide deeper context to the ongoing story, partly to spark interest in hopes that each reader might find a new topic or two to investigate further. I appreciate that some readers will desire to go straight back into the narrative, and for that reason these introductions are fully italicized for clear identification. While I believe they contribute significantly to the overarching storylines, they are not absolutely necessary to following them. The same may be said for the novel's Prologue, which is centered around a fictional account of an actual historical king and his time and provides several clues about the story that ensues.

Thank you for reading, and enjoy the journey.

Michael

For my parents

PROLOGUE

A KING FORGOTTEN

Excerpt from *Lost Legends of Sumeria*, author unknown, date of publication unknown, English translation 1961:

> Before Nebuchadnezzar, before Hammurabi, before the Sargons of Assyria, ruled Ushpia of Ninive, first of his line. Though he defeated mighty Assur, he is not known as Ushpia the Conqueror. Though he unified Assyria, he is not Ushpia the Uniter. Though he erected the most magnificent structure of his time, he is not Ushpia the Builder. Though he did all these things and more, he is not Ushpia the Great. Curiously, the records list him only as Ushpia the Martyr. The reasons are lost to time.

Excerpt from *Kings of Assyria* by Allesandro Migliomori, published 1897, English translation 1938:

King Ushpia and the Rise of Assur

He was a slave who became a king, then founded an empire. He constructed the foremost wonder of the age. Yet these are not his greatest accomplishments. Ushpia should be remembered not for conquest but forbearance, not determination but reflection, not longevity but brevity. So much that happened during his reign had the utmost significance. Why then does history not immortalise Ushpia as the greatest of the early Assyrian rulers?

To understand the story of King Ushpia, one must first understand the rivalry between Assur and Nineveh, twin cities of Upper Mesopotamia. The Akkadian Empire was crumbling. It was a time of petty tyrants, each city a kingdom, the settlements between exacted of tribute. Tributary rights were a frequent cause of fighting between rulers. The losers of these conflicts, soldiers and farmers alike, were often bonded as common slaves.

Such was the case with the family of Ushpia, caught between the warring kings Mektiara of Nineveh and Belu of Assur. Ushpia's father and kinsmen cultivated the lands around the Zab where it fed the Tigris. They paid in grain each year to Assur, until Mektiara swept through, defeating Belu in battle and asserting dominance over the region. Ushpia's father fought on the side of Assur and died defending his home. Ushpia's mother and all her children were enslaved by Mektiara and taken to Nineveh.

The people of the city devoted themselves to the goddess Ishtar, to whom Ushpia became a faithful acolyte. His mother prayed for her children at Ishtar's shrine whenever she was not working the kitchens of Mektiara's palace. The child Ushpia, full of curiosity and boyish charm, wandered the halls despite all attempts to keep him restrained. Soon he became a favourite of servants and lords alike. The palace flowed thick with the children of the gentry, and Ushpia was allowed to spend his limited playtime with them. For better and worse, his playmates included the king's own children, for Mektiara had many wives. Although Ushpia was merely a slave, the higher classes took to treating him as one of their own—all except Hazbetta, Mektiara's bright and headstrong daughter, who never missed an opportunity to remind Ushpia of his low station. As he grew older, less governable, and ever more resentful of his bounds, Ushpia yet abided Hazbetta's harsh commands. The elders took notice and felt sympathy for the boy. Even Mektiara, informed that his daughter had taken to reed-whipping Ushpia when he failed to obey her commands with sufficient alacrity, intervened by warning her and moving the slave's chores to a different wing of the palace. Nevertheless, Hazbetta found occasion to defy her father's orders and torment the boy with her childish persecutions.

Naturally proud, treated by most less a servant than a distant cousin, Ushpia did not learn the boundaries of his station. Although weapons were forbidden to slaves, Ushpia was allowed to practice-spar with the sons of lords. He began to dream, as other boys did, of becoming a warrior in Mektiara's triumphant army. No one saw fit to disabuse him of this notion, and from unbridled ambition sprout the seeds of discontent.

At the age of thirteen Ushpia was appointed attendant to the king's royal guard. This duty was the highest honour accorded to slaves, yet not without risk, for it was Mektiara's habit to participate in the forefront of the fighting wherever he waged battle. He frequently rode, with scant escort, ahead of his army to scout the terrain and enemy. Although he ached to fight with the soldiers, Ushpia was determined to use the new position to prove his value to king and master. It was years before opportunity came, and in a form far more perilous than Ushpia could have wished.

On campaign against Nineveh's persistent rivals, the Drushites, Mektiara's vanguard was ambushed well ahead of the bulk of his army. In the chaos of battle, Mektiara fell senseless to an enemy stone. Discerning their singular opportunity, the Drushites made repeated and urgent attacks on the position, hoping to kill the hated ruler before the main contingent of his army came upon the field. Ushpia and the other young attendants watched Mektiara's guard fall one by one, until too few were left to prevent a last wave of attackers from overrunning the camp. In violation of Nineveh law, Ushpia rallied the other servants, arming them from the dead and wounded and taking places beside the remaining soldiers. Ushpia personally stood over the fallen body of his master as the fighting reached its apex. Just then Mektiara's main army arrived and chased off the remnants of the Drushites. Few of Mektiara's guards and none of the servants—save Ushpia himself—survived the battle.

Upon his recovery, Mektiara went on to utterly defeat the Drushites in a brutal campaign. When they returned to Nineveh, Mektiara summoned Ushpia for a special honour. He granted the young man his freedom, an act of the greatest generosity. Yet Ushpia dared ask more of his master. He wished to become an official member of the king's guard. Considering the circumstances which had led to this moment, Mektiara saw fit to not merely grant the request but appoint the young man commander of the rebuilt unit. But Ushpia was not yet finished. He brazenly asked for a father's blessing to marry Hazbetta, an absurdity which elicited laughter. Because he saw with his eyes and not with his mind, Mektiara expected Hazbetta to mock the young man cruelly. Instead, the king was astonished to see tears of happiness on his daughter's face as she embraced the new commander.

From that day on, lord and former slave were seldom apart as the bonds of respect and family developed between them. Ushpia had found a place in the world few slaves could imagine. Within a few years, Hazbetta bore him two sons, Bala and Apiashal. Ushpia was proud of his eldest, who grew up strong and charismatic like his father, but disappointed in the frail body and gentle temperament of the younger. When he came of age, Bala would join his father in the army, but Apiashal seemed destined for the mundane duties of the household.

Meanwhile, the competition with Nineveh's neighbors continued to flare into frequent war. The greatest challenge came from the south and the city of Assur, resurgent under Belu's successor Azarah. Assur was blessed with great wealth and population, and each year its armies inexorably expanded its dominion. Mektiara had the utmost disdain for the people of Assur, for they worshipped not Ishtar but the god Ashur, from whom the city derived its name. Furthermore, Azarah of Assur had proclaimed himself king of all the north and considered Nineveh and all its tributaries subject to his rule. Hazbetta warned her father and husband that Assur had grown too strong to resist, but the aging Mektiara led his armies south one last time to fight for the independence and beliefs of his people. As always, Ushpia took his place at Mektiara's side. Marching to war with his father for the first time was Bala, still a youth but already possessed of skill and zeal.

Alas, as Hazbetta had warned, the strength of Assur was too great. In one grisly day, Mektiara was defeated in battle near the overflowing banks of the Tigris, the long ruler of Nineveh killed, his body desecrated by

Azarah's men as befitted a common brigand. Ushpia rallied the few survivors and fled into the hinterlands. Azarah dispatched a pursuing force while he marched on to Nineveh itself with the rest of his army, intent on conquering the city and forcibly subjugating its people.

Ushpia and his men were chased farther and farther into the wilderness. Each time they paused to regroup, they lost more men in skirmishes with their pursuers. So Ushpia pushed his band on with little rest or mercy, losing even more to desertion. His sole remaining hope was that, as they distanced themselves from the south and drew nearer their homeland, the land and people would become more accommodating to them and less to their enemies. Sadly, Ushpia was cruelly awakened to a harsh reality: that strength trumps loyalty, for the people of the north closed their doors to him rather than face Azarah's wrath.

A despondent Ushpia and his few remaining followers camped one night on a lonely hill overlooking a desolate and uninhabited land. Alone, his men sleeping off their exhaustion, Ushpia stood silent watch on the trail below. They numbered no more than a score—including Bala, who remained with his father to this last extremity. Ushpia's greatest regret was that his son, so full of potential, would not experience life as his sire had. It was too much sorrow for Ushpia's heart to bear.

There on the rock Ushpia turned away from Ishtar, who had abandoned him, his king, and his city. He renounced her and called for help from any god who would listen. To his astonishment, a solitary lion approached Ushpia and spoke to him. This was Nergal, the God of war, to whom Ushpia would owe his future triumphs and sorrows. Nergal offered the opportunity for salvation from his hopeless circumstances, for Ushpia would be given the strength and ferocity of the lion. And this power could be passed on, to all Ushpia's men and beyond. But it must always grow, or wither. The lion told Ushpia he must never stop spreading the word of Nergal.

So Ushpia accepted the favour of the god, and the god gave Ushpia his blessing, and empowered him to bestow it on others. Ushpia shared the blessing with his men, who became like lions themselves—stronger, tougher, and fiercer than before. Their wounds healed, their vitality not simply restored but enhanced. Feeling this newfound strength coursing through him, Bala was never prouder of his father.

Soon their pursuers came upon the site and surrounded the hill. These men were tired of the chase and eager to return home, and so eschewed concentration of numbers in favor of preventing any further escape. It was a fatal mistake. Ushpia's men set upon them with animal ferocity. Most of the enemy were killed outright, but many were taken. Some captives accepted the blessing of Nergal and swelled Ushpia's ranks. Those who refused were made to dig deep pits in the hard earth for their own sacrifice. No one was permitted to escape and report back to Azarah. All the while, Bala observed and learned.

Ushpia constructed a rudimentary shrine to his new god marking the site of this conversion and first great victory. They named the location Nergashala, birthplace of the lion. Ushpia intended to lead the survivors home, but the men had other ambitions—to take the fight back to Azarah. Ushpia looked to his son for support, but Bala was taken with the furor and desired vengeance as much as the others. Ushpia sent a messenger to Hazbetta, then marched his small army of death back across the inhospitable countryside towards Assur. This time he did not allow the inhabitants to refuse him succour. Upon all willing able-bodied men and boys he bestowed Nergal's blessing, whilst upon the unblessed he bestowed merciless death.

Ushpia's band grew in numbers as it marched nearer Assur. Hearing of this growing menace, Azarah marched his own army to confront Ushpia outside the walls of his city. Ushpia's small force numbered not a fifth of the Assurians, yet the outcome was never in doubt. It was Bala who took off the head of the man responsible for the downfall of Mektiara. The battle of Assur was over, but the killing had just begun, as once again the ritual of blessing and sacrifice followed.

Ushpia was now undisputed ruler of the lands of the Tigris, and declared himself Azarah's successor as king in Assur. The city itself was the largest of the era, and he was in awe of its size and grandeur. Events had overtaken Ushpia. He felt himself inadequate to his new responsibilities, and he needed the council of his wife more than ever. For the moment, he kept the army outside Assur for the safety of its occupants. Already, with no enemy remaining as outlet for their lusts, the men began to quarrel amongst themselves.

Ushpia's worries did not abate when his wife and younger son arrived in Assur. Hazbetta was visibly disturbed by her husband's conversion. She told him to renounce Nergal and suffer the consequences, but he reminded her that kings rule through strength. Yet Hazbetta pointed out that lions need prey to survive, and asked what would happen when the prey was gone. Ushpia did not know the answer, but did know he had a kingdom to rule, and asked her again to accept the blessing of Nergal. She refused not only for herself but for their second son, as well. The customary penalty was death, but Ushpia sentenced them to chambers until he decided how to proceed. He felt abandoned by his wife, yet remained determined to rule justly.

Unwilling to end his devotion to the god responsible for his victories, but equally unwilling to lose a wife whose wisdom knew no peer, Ushpia issued a decree to discontinue the practice of sacrifice. Not wishing to turn the populace against his rule, and seeing how the favour of Ashur had brought grandiosity to the city, he began construction of an immense temple inside the walls where followers could congregate openly. Ushpia appointed Bala commander of the army and ordered him to continue the campaign of subjugation started by Azarah. While his son waged war, Ushpia dispensed justice in his new capital. Years passed, all the lands of the Tigris were conquered and unified, trade was renewed with the kingdom of Egypt, and a flourishing Assur became the beating heart of a growing empire.

Ushpia longed for the return of his wife's esteem, for although she remained in Assur they seldom spoke. Apiashal, too, was wary of his father and king. Ushpia believed the prosperity of the city was evidence of his benevolence, and that the new temple he was constructing proved his fairness towards all. He waited in vain for Hazbetta to admit to her own folly. Finally, as the temple neared completion, he received word that Bala was returning with the army to participate in the ceremonial consecrations. When he could wait no longer, Ushpia summoned his wife to demand her apology.

Instead, Hazbetta gifted him the last of her wisdom. She warned that he had lost power over his own subjects. Outside the city, not he but the army ruled, turning the country into a wasteland, the sacrifices of the unblessed not merely continued but increased a hundredfold. Nergashala had been transformed from a shrine to a necropolis, the pits dug so deep they reached the path of Inanna's descent. The people of the kingdom lived in perpetual fear of Ushpia, of the army, and of Bala in particular. Their son quenched his thirst on rivers of spilt blood. And now he marched back to Assur not to join in a ceremony but to seize power for himself.

Ushpia listened to his wife's admonitions, then recalled Nergal's warning. Yet he had been born a slave, was now king of Assyria, and had seized triumph from adversity before. He told Hazbetta he would learn from his mistakes; he would stop what he had inadvertently started. His wife replied that he could sooner stop the flow of the Tigris with his palm. Ushpia believed Bala would listen to reason, but Hazbetta believed their son was now less the man than the lion. And so Ushpia's brow darkened, and he accepted that he too was the lion, and would fight accordingly.

Afterward, Ushpia seemed not himself. He canceled completion of the city temple and outlawed open worship of Ashur. He sent word that Bala was to be welcomed into the city with honours, then had Apiashal arrested and imprisoned in the dungeon. Upon hearing the news of her husband's decrees, Hazbetta swallowed poison. If the king mourned her death, he showed no sign.

Bala arrived at the city with an uncertain mind, ready to fight at the slightest provocation. Instead, he was received at the palace with great fanfare. Ushpia embraced his son, openly praised the blessings of Nergal, and resumed his previous place at the head of his soldiers. Moreover, he wished to correct the mistake of tolerance he had made so many years before. He announced a return to Nergashala for a ceremony restricted only to the blessed. He would take all the followers of Nergal with him, including the entire army, leaving the citizens of the city to fend for themselves.

The night before departure, Ushpia visited Apiashal in his cell. The father expressed his disappointment in a son who had not lived up to expectations. Apiashal listened in respectful silence. Taking his leave,

Ushpia knew they would not speak again. Without a sign of hesitation the king issued orders to the boy's guards, to be carried out the following day.

The return march to Nergashala was a time of great joy for the blessed of Nergal. Always beloved, Ushpia was once again celebrated amongst the ranks and officers of the army. There were fights between the men that often turned deadly, but Bala assured his father that this was merely how the men now expressed themselves. When Ushpia saw firsthand how the shrine he built had swelled in magnitude and importance, the walls aboveground paling in comparison to the labyrinthian depths of the sacrificial pits, he was moved beyond words. He closed his eyes, hung his head reverentially, then faced skyward to utter an invocation. Then he led his men inside the temple and into the pits, the only area sufficiently capacious to accommodate all the followers of Nergal. There they engaged in an excess of drinking and festivities lasting well into the night.

As the torches burned low, Ushpia again addressed his army. The men cheered—none louder than Bala, who was again proud of his father. Ushpia told them that wherever they marched, no man could stand against them, that absolute obedience or death followed them everywhere. Then Ushpia's manner and tone changed. He said he could not allow these things to continue. By the time his audience realized what was happening, it was too late—for all of them. Apiashal's force had arrived, overcome the sentries posted outside, and sealed every means of egress from the temple. Ushpia announced to those few still listening that the temple was being buried, hopefully lost for eternity. As Ushpia began to pray to Ishtar for forgiveness, he was struck down by Bala even as the enraged men fell upon one another, violence having long since become their only catharsis.

Ushpia's final orders to Apiashal had been to complete the temple in Assur. Apiashal's own reign was dedicated to preventing any recurrence of the cult of Nergal, who was transformed in the pantheon from a god of war to one of plague. Sadly, this meant the obscuring of Ushpia's accomplishments, both the great and the terrible. Unwilling to see his father's legacy completely forgotten, however, Apiashal gave full credit to his predecessor for the grand temple named for god and city, and for which the empire of Assyria was ultimately named.

From the professional email account of Dr. Maxwell Middlebrooke:

```
Sent To: Schwarzvogel, Adolphus [Universität zu
Wesel]
Sent From: Middlebrooke, Maxwell [University of
Cambridge]
Attachment: legends_of_sumeria_ss0207_eng.pdf,
kings_of_assyria_ch17_eng.pdf
```

Dear Herr Doktor Schwarzvogel,

An amusing story, is it not? Ever since you sent the first batch of cuneiform pics, I've tasked my research assistants with digging up everything they can find related to Ushpia. So far these legends are all they have found, as not much seems to be known about him. Although one cannot take these tales seriously, the mention of the temple of Ashur reveals at least a modicum of veracity, as it is generally accepted that construction did occur during his reign. Due to the dearth of primary sources from that time and place, all we can do is glean what little we can from these mythologies. Perhaps there is a kernel of truth to every story, but there is no telling which particulars have merit. With luck we will learn more from your discovery and the wealth of text yet to be translated. The pictogram of the lion reminds me of the story from *Kings*. What else will we find? This is an exciting time, truly.

.   .   .

In response to your request for additional resources, I have contacted several colleagues on the continent and in America. Not surprisingly, Ancient Mesopotamian Languages is not the discipline of choice amongst most students today. I was referred to a certain Ben Appelstein at Catoctin College who has a background in Akkadian and Sumerian and some exposure to other ancient Semitics. He chairs their Ancient Studies programme, which has a reputation as one of the best in the States. I understand he studied at Oxford around the same time as you. Are you familiar with him? Of course, going with Dr Appelstein does raise an obvious concern with respect to Arab reception, but in der Not schmeckt jedes Brot.

No word on additional funding, alas. Also, no luck on extending the visas of the students currently on site. The Iraqi government seems to be a touch sensitive about this project now that it has actually found something. I believe they worry the vile Europeans are going to steal all their artifacts again. And of course that province has been known to have some friction with Baghdad in the past. We will continue to work our channels here. In the meantime, you should be especially respectful in your interactions with the authorities there.

Best,
Max

PART I

Exposure

1
VALHALLA

SPRINGTIME in northern Maryland is a gift of natural artwork, a vivid display of shapes and colors on a boundless canvas of earth and sky, where the eastern reaches of the Appalachians form a series of rolling ridge lines alternating with green valleys far richer in foliage and farmland than people. In places the ridges rise high enough to form forested peaks, smaller than their brethren to the west yet impressive for this low-lying region. Due to the area's proximity to the sprawling megalopolis of the east coast, the freshness of the land is all the more striking. Not that indications of modern civilization are altogether absent. Intermittent service stations and lonely market plazas dot the grassy lowlands, while above artificial cuts tear through the tree-covered slopes like disfiguring scars.

To the south the city of Frederick finds itself inexorably racing toward destiny as a suburb of Washington, and the traffic flowing between the two has grown to rival the busiest beltways. Yet just north of Frederick, traffic remains a trickle in comparison. Because the communities of south-central Pennsylvania remain relatively uncrowded, there are no bustling interstates connecting them to the nation's capital. Instead the smaller, solitary US Route 15 skirts along the mountainsides, bisecting the Mason-Dixon Line at its midpoint,

providing view after glorious view of the topography. The route
continues northward toward the historic town of Gettysburg,
unabashedly proud home of the deadliest battle ever fought on
American soil. The highway of today traces the same path as marched
a hundred thousand boots of General Meade's army on their slow
trek to victory on the bloody rise of Cemetery Ridge. Not a few of
those soldiers remarked in journal or homeward letter that it was the
prettiest country they had ever seen.

Perched along this stretch sits Catoctin Mountain, unremarkable
in size but blessed with peaceful grandeur. A traveler pulling off US-
15 onto one of Catoctin's back country roads will no sooner lose sight
of the highway than be transported to a universe of rustic tranquility,
surrounded by the scent and shade of old wood and the soft music of
gentle streams.

Roughly a mile inside the tree line, nestled along the mountain's
lower slopes and serenaded by the ubiquitous quiet trickling of Black
Bear Branch Creek, sat the sleepy campus of Catoctin College. These
days the campus was even sleepier than usual, for its six hundred
students were largely absent, at home to rest or vacationing for
recreation. This was spring break at Catoctin, and rarely had the label
been more apt. In this region it was not uncommon to see snow fall
intermittently into April and linger in the shady depressions even
later. But this year was refreshingly different. New snowfall had not
been seen in weeks, and the cooler temperatures of February had
been appreciatively replaced by day after day of warming March
sunshine.

Here was an ecosystem well suited to many forms of life, and so
the spring weather was enjoyed by more than just students. This
season, the hours before dawn belonged to the insects. The night gave
way to an interlude of quiet tantamount to a calm before the storm. At
first began a chirping here, a droning there, joined by one then greater
numbers, swelling to a symphony and then a cacophony. It was the
daily performance of a melody repeated throughout time. It was a
celebration of life.

Hear us. We are here. This earth was made for us, and we for it. We are perpetual. Here before. Here after. Long after you are gone.

Four pairs of headlights pierced the predawn fog. Four cars drove by in quick succession, the roar of engines discordantly disturbing the chorus of nature. In their wake, all was silent, like a collective sigh. The moment passed; the singing resumed. Undaunted, nature would soon forget the passage of man and return to its routine, tireless and eternal.

To all this the occupants of the cars were, quite naturally, completely oblivious. By and large they were thinking about making the most of this final day of their break. All except one. In the back seat of the last car in the group, a girl was thinking about the unlikely intersection of peer pressure, hangovers, and Greek philosophy.

The ability to prioritize anxieties, she decided. *This is what distinguishes man from beast.* Aristotle said that the mark of a man was to entertain a thought without accepting it. Of all God's creatures, mankind alone possessed the mental capacity to choose between many responses in any situation. To override instinct. Nature behaves through stimulus-response, but a human injects analysis into the process.

This morning Christine was developing her own corollary to Aristotle. To her, the concept boiled down to anxieties. An animal gets scared, so it runs away. It gets hungry, so it eats. It is overtaken by a distinctive impulse, so it copulates. Or perhaps the truth was even simpler than that. Perhaps animals did not experience anxieties at all, only basal urges such as the need for food, sleep, and sex. Maslow's first tier. But humans...they knew all about anxieties. Sometimes it seemed that was all they knew. Certainly, she seemed nothing but a bundle of them today.

A walking testament to Aristotle's theory, Christine had overridden every instinct she had felt thus far this morning. First she battled her alarm through three separate snoozes. Not only was five o'clock a full four hours before her usual wakeup, but she had been out much later than normal the night before. Both body and mind craved more rest, yet from the first moment of consciousness she was aware of a social duty that beckoned stronger. Eventually, she had summoned the wherewithal to force herself up.

Even before rising from bed, she was aware of another sensation, more distressing than mere sleepiness. The hangover had started slow, just a feeling of dehydration mixed with a mild dull throb. Nothing but a teasing reminder that she drank too much last night, faint enough to allow her to hope that she was going to get off easy. Alas, it was not to be. By the time she had put her hair up rather than showering, the throbbing had become a constant sharp ache. No stranger to migraines, Christine's instinct was to pop one of the powerful pills that her doctor prescribed. But that was a drug that numbed not only her pain but also her mind, made her stomach queasy, and cramped up her muscles. Those were not side effects she could allow herself today. Instead she had settled for accepting a few aspirin from her roommate Tempest and forcing herself to guzzle two glasses of water. The most irritating thing about her condition was that she had not wanted to drink so much last night. She had done so for the best of reasons, so now she felt like a martyr. It did not help that Tempest had drunk even more than Christine and yet seemed completely untroubled this morning.

The hangover would also have been more tolerable if she had had any reason to look forward to today's excursion. True, she would be spending more time with James, and a certain part of her was excited. Another part, however, dreaded the tension that she felt in his company. It stemmed partly from a desire to impress him, although perhaps impress was not the right word. A desire to meet expectations. He and his buddies, not to mention many of her own friends, were among the most popular of the college's students. She felt a perpetual pressure to prove that she belonged with them. To be fair, none of them had ever displayed the slightest indication that she did not. It was something generated purely from within, but that did not make it any less real. As a result, Christine persistently felt on display for their evaluation.

She wondered if every nineteen-year-old felt the same pressure.

She supposed they probably did to varying degrees, some more and some less than she. After all, Aristotle also said man is a social animal. *Different from beasts, but still an animal.* Perhaps her idea was not so clever after all. She would need to give it more thought.

In any case, she could not really help but feel anxious around James. He elicited mixed feelings within her. Built like a linebacker but smart as a professor, he was also moody and volatile and always seemed to carry a weight the size of their mountain on his broad shoulders. While she was with him, she not only felt the need for acceptance but a desire to keep him in good spirits. That was easier said than done, because it did not take much to flip his switch. It had partly been his quick temper that had gotten her into trouble the night before.

Still, there were far worse things than spending more time with him. Despite his flaws, he was probably the most appealing guy she had ever dated. And despite her self-inflicted apprehension, Christine was confident that she could make almost any situation an enjoyable time for the both of them. Today, however, she had her doubts. This was the source of her greatest anxiety of all, for she, James, Tempest, and Donny were on their way caving.

Christine knew nothing about caves. She did not want to know anything about caves. She assumed they were cold, dirty, dark, and completely without interest to a young psychology student. Moreover, the impression she formed last night was one of crawling around, barely able to move, sometimes unable to turn, and generally feeling the enormous mass of the earth looming precariously above. It held no appeal for her. In fact, she was instinctively repelled by the thought.

Her mind drifted back to a time when she was nine. Her brother Anthony was only two years older, but in those days had effectively functioned as a babysitter for the hour between the end of school and the return of their parents from work. They grew up in a Philadelphia suburb that seemed safe in retrospect, but they had been told to stay indoors until the first parent got home. So she and Anthony would pass the time with games like Parcheesi and checkers. Anthony invariably won, but Christine still enjoyed playing just for the pleasure of his company.

On this occasion they had played hide-and-seek. He told her to count to twenty from inside their parents' closet while he hid somewhere else in the house. She had no reason not to play along. At the time, the prospect of being inside a closet aroused no particular fear inside her, and she trusted Anthony with childish naiveté. She dutifully got in and counted, unaware that he had just learned a new trick—that a chair could be wedged against a door to seal it more effectively than a lock.

At first she had giggled at the joke, allowing herself to see it from his amused perspective. But it was not long before giggles and smiles turned to yelling and panic. When there was no sound coming from the other side, she became convinced that he had forgotten she was there. She pounded hard at the door and yelled his name over and over, just wanting him to come back and rescue her, hugging her and apologizing profusely. Fifteen minutes of pleading, begging, and finally crying eventually convinced him to let her out, but the damage had been done. Ever since that experience, she worried that she might be claustrophobic.

It was the first time Christine remembered thinking about the complexities of her own mind. It was the start of the long road that led her to Catoctin, where the psych department was top-notch. She was a serious, disciplined student who had worked hard to get accepted here. And she came fully prepared for four years of heavy studying. The relentless run of social activities had come as a surprise, albeit mostly pleasant. Today was an exception.

The way caving had been described the night before brought to mind unwanted recollections of the closet all those years ago. She found it incredible how the memory could still conjure the smell of her mother's dresses after this much time had passed. She knew a cave would not smell the same, and yet she worried that the dark, cramped spaces would bring back the small, crying child. Perhaps it was a spectacle of shame she feared more than anything. But it was her own intervention that had led to this trip, and not coming was never really an option.

So there it was. She was tired, hung over, and stressed, yet willing to go through it all because her social anxieties trumped all others. If this was what it meant to be human, she was not entirely sure that she would not be better off like her father's Golden Retriever.

"Turn it up," said Tempest, and Christine was stirred from her reverie.

James turned the knob on the Audi's radio. He and Donny had been bantering, but they paused so everyone could hear.

"...yesterday, another thirty cases of Duck Flu were reported in Maryland." The newsman's voice spoke in a calm, composed baritone that belied the gravity of the message. *"This brings the total for the state to over six hundred, while the death toll from influenza-associated complications remains at twelve. For the entire country, total cases topped the eleven thousand mark with two hundred twenty deaths. In last night's press conference, a spokesperson from the Centers for Disease Control in Atlanta reiterated that the mortality rate for those contracting the disease remains quite low, and that every available resource is working to minimize the impact of H5N1—"*

"Good luck with that," James said.

Tempest shushed him, but Christine silently agreed with him. The new influenza strain had already proven itself to be vaccine resistant, so she doubted there was much the CDC or anyone else could do except let the disease burn itself out. She opened her mouth to make a comment, but stopped when Tempest flashed her a look.

"Shh!" Tempest repeated. "I'm listening."

"...other news, law enforcement agencies nationwide are sending representatives to meet with the Justice Department and Attorney General Dewey to discuss ways to counter the recent rash of mass shootings in America. This on the heels of the attack in an Iowa shopping mall that left six—"

"Never mind," said Tempest. She sank back into the seat.

James flicked off the radio, and there was a moment of silence in the car while four minds thought of something appropriate to say.

"Who would have guessed we'd all die of the stupid flu?" Tempest asked rhetorically.

"We're not going to die of the flu," James responded. Christine thought his tone sounded overly condescending, but she still quietly agreed.

Tempest was looking out her window. She did not reply.

Christine had known Tempest back in high school, but they had not really associated with one another until college. Now that they were roommates and constant companions, Christine believed she understood the other girl as well as anyone. Probably better than Tempest knew herself, since her friend was not inclined toward self-reflection.

There were three things Christine envied about her roommate. First and foremost was the distinctive streak of white through her otherwise jet black hair, a pigmentation anomaly caused by a minor disorder known as Waardenburg syndrome. It drew the eye to Tempest in a way that naturally made her the center of attention everywhere she went.

A second thing was her impressive lung capacity. Some girls had all the luck.

But the thing Christine most admired was how Tempest wore an air of invulnerability like a second set of clothes. She always seemed to take bad news in stride. Her typical cure for any setback was "a witty quip and a shopping trip," as she put it.

Which made her reaction to this bug so out of character. Back in their room this morning, while Christine was dosing her hangover with aspirin and struggled just to get ready, Tempest had good-naturedly teased her. Then Tempest had coughed a single time and her entire demeanor changed.

"Do you think I might have Duck Flu?" she asked.

"No, silly. I don't think one cough is a reason to panic."

"Maybe I should stay in today."

"Don't you dare."

"They said the cave is muddy and cold."

"They said it's *cool*, not cold. Wear a sweatshirt and you'll be fine."

Tempest had followed the advice and put on an extra layer—a fashionable sequined pink pullover that put to shame Christine's gray college hoodie—and her mood soon returned to its chipper norm. Yet here it was again, this disproportionate concern.

Everyone has their anxieties, Christine reminded herself. She had just learned Tempest's. Apparently, her friend was a bit of a hypochondriac.

Christine tried to think of something to say to lighten the mood. She was saved the trouble by Donny. Whenever conversation became labored, he had a wealth of jokes and stories to fall back on. His humor often transcended the appropriate, but he was undeniably the funniest guy she had ever met. Clever and indefatigably optimistic, he practically radiated good times. There was no question why he appealed to Tempest.

"Okay, here's one. My basketball team had this guy named Leroy. He started out the season like gangbusters, but he seemed to get worse as it went on. He made mistakes, didn't listen to instructions, and stopped giving the same level of effort. One day during practice Coach said 'Son, what's wrong with you? Is it ignorance, or apathy?' Leroy looked back and said, 'Coach, I don't know and I don't care.'"

Christine understood the joke, but could not bring herself to laugh. Tempest said, "I don't get it."

"Think about it. You will," Donny responded. "Jokes aren't funny if you have to explain them."

Tempest's expression soured a little more, and Christine worried that Donny's humor was having the opposite of the desired effect.

"Okay, T, here's one for you. There are ten types of people in the world. Those who understand binary and those who don't."

This time Christine did not get it, but did not care. Tempest smiled, and that was the important thing.

That smile was fleeting, however. The four of them rode on in silence for another minute before Donny and James started talking. Christine only listened long enough to discern that it was nothing to concern her. They were talking about sports, which interested her even less than caving.

Then her ears perked up again when Donny said her name. "Christine, you're from Philly, right? *Te gusta?*"

"Huh?"

"Do you like it?" he explained. Then hesitated. "Wait, you don't speak Spanish? I thought you were Latina."

"What? No! I'm Italian, you goof."

"Oh. Oops. Sorry!" He laughed good-naturedly. She shook her head a little, then glanced at Tempest, who was rolling her eyes.

The mistake would have been easier to overlook if Donny's nature had not kept him talking. "That's too bad. Latinas are hot."

Tempest rose to her friend's defense. "Italians *are* the original Latins, you dork." Donny and James chuckled, and even Tempest appeared on the verge of laughter.

James made a comment that Christine did not hear. Donny laughed. Tempest joined their conversation, allowing Christine an opportunity to be back alone with her thoughts. She leaned her head against the window glass and stared out. Her head was feeling a little better, and with that slight relief she became more hopeful about the day ahead.

Through the window she saw the sun coming up at last. She could begin to make out colors in the passing foliage. They had driven out of the heavily forested region where the school sat, though there were still patches of woods all around. This was one of the grassy valleys divided into farm plots by wooden fencing. She could tell the fences had been around for years from the way plants grew into and curled around the posts like ivy on latticework. Compared to Philly, everything here seemed so *green*. She admitted that the country had a few things going for it over the city. It certainly was more scenic.

Christine's head thumped against the glass as the car swerved. James hit the brake hard, then the gas again. Looking ahead, Christine was surprised to see a flock of untended sheep milling about. One of them had gotten close enough to the road to panic James into evasive maneuvers.

"Don't run over the sheep," Tempest called out.

"That's helpful," James snapped back. He was clearly annoyed by the backseat driving, but Christine guessed he was even more annoyed at himself for needlessly jerking them about.

"Well, you're going pretty fast."

"I have to. The others are going over a hill. I don't want to lose them."

"We're in the middle of the country, dumbass. There aren't any other roads for miles. We're not going to lose them," Tempest retorted. Donny laughed. James didn't respond, but his expression turned a little darker.

That's not a good sign.

Another moment of silence set in.

Finally Tempest broke it. "I'm kind of looking forward to caving," she said.

"Spelunking," said James.

"What?"

"It's called spelunking."

"Ernie called it caving."

At the mention of the cute guide's name, Donny's expression turned as sour as James'.

"Ernie's a redneck," said James. "I'll bet those guys didn't get past tenth grade."

Now Christine was concerned that irritation was starting to take over the whole conversation. It was astonishing how volatile and contagious moods could be. She was about to ask Donny if he knew any more jokes, then she saw him point ahead through the windshield.

"Looks like we're here."

The others cars were parked in a clearing between the road and tree line on the right. James pulled into line and put the car in park. As he cut the engine, Christine felt a rising wave of apprehension. She really did not want to be here, but there was nothing she could do about it now.

All four vehicles disgorged passengers to the staccato rhythm of car doors slamming shut. There was a moment of stretching, yawning, and general milling about. Within a few seconds everyone was face-down on their cell phones. The age of casual conversation had long since died in an explosion of electronica.

There were no new messages on Christine's phone to distract her. She put it away. Now that she was back out in the chilly morning air, she found herself shivering. It did not help that the grass was both tall and damp. Her sneakers and socks were rapidly soaking through to the point of discomfort. Around her a few low conversations were breaking out, but she could not hear over the noise of crickets chirping all around them. She was reminded again of how different life in the country was from her home in Philly.

The two guides were busy getting equipment from the back of the Jeep, so she studied some of the other cavers. She counted thirteen of them in all, including her group of four and the two guides. There were four more girls and three more guys. She thought she might recognize a face or two—Catoctin was not a particularly large school —but she did not know any of them.

She expected James to come join her. Instead, she saw him and Donny move closer to the guides' Jeep to take a look at the contents. Then she expected Tempest to stand with her, but her friend followed the guys. *Fine, let them deal with his mood.*

Christine glanced around. She saw only one other person standing alone like herself, a girl with a short bob haircut and a friendly expression. Christine took a step toward her, intending to introduce herself and start an idle conversation. It never hurt to get to know more of her peers. One never knew when it might spark a new friendship.

The girl smiled at someone. Christine followed her gaze all the way to James. He smiled back and his head gave a little nod. Christine changed direction. She moved up to stand beside him, and slipped her hand inside his arm.

The guides had pulled several large cardboard boxes from the Jeep, then one started pulling what looked like white hardhats from one box and stacking them on the lowered tailgate. The other guide faced the group. "All right, people. Gather around," he said in a voice loud enough to get everyone's attention. "I'm going to go over the gear real quick. This is kind of important, so please pay attention."

His name was Ernie, Christine recalled. She had forgotten it until the exchange in the car. In the light of day, she realized the two guides were a little younger and considerably less scary than they had seemed last night. Ernie was certainly the handsomer of the two, with his chiseled features and distinctive green eyes. She decided to make an effort to remember his name for the remainder of the day. She probably should learn his friend's, too, although she hoped to avoid conversing with either of them.

She realized she was not paying attention the way he had asked, so she tuned back in.

"Everyone gets a helmet. We have two types. These are caving helmets. They have lamps attached. These are regular climbing helmets. They don't have lamps." He held up one of each for everyone to see. "Tuck this strap under your chin and make sure it's tight. You must keep the strap secure the whole time, even if gets uncomfortable. Which it will. The whole helmet will be uncomfortable, and you will find yourself bumping into things with them. Doesn't matter. Everyone must keep their helmet on at all... Good Lord, what are you wearing?"

Ernie was looking at Tempest as though seeing her for the first time. "I thought we told everyone to wear clothes you don't care about."

Christine felt defensive for her friend, but Tempest appeared to remain nonplussed. "I don't care if this gets dirty."

He looked a little doubtful. "I'm not sure you realize what 'dirty' means in a cave. You will literally—and I do mean 'literally'—be covered in mud. Your shirt might get ruined."

"If it gets ruined, it gets ruined."

Ernie shrugged and moved on, but Christine knew her roommate better. Tempest would not be happy if that shirt were ruined. Christine hoped the mud was not as bad as he had suggested, not only for her friend's sake but for her own. But how bad could it be? She knew there would be some crawling through a pipe to get into the cave, but once inside the cave things should be better.

"All right, so keep your helmet on all the time. Actually, that goes for everything. Whatever you are wearing or carrying, don't put anything down. People who put things down forget to pick them back up. You don't want other people tripping on loose items in there. And, trust me, you do *not* want to try to find something you lost track of. It is almost impossible to find a small item inside a cave. A few of us are taking backpacks in with some food and drink. If we have time, we'll have a little caving picnic for lunch. That will be the only time we stop and put things down."

"Moving on. I mentioned these helmets have headlamps on them. This is how you turn them on and off. Don't turn them off until we're back outside. I wish we had more of them so we could give one to everyone. But we've never had a group this big before, so some of you are getting *these* helmets instead. Those of you with the lampless helmets are going to get flashlights. I feel sorry for you, because it is really inconvenient to carry a flashlight inside a cave. Particularly this cave. You will want to use your hands to feel your way around and maneuver through tight spaces."

"Those of you with flashlights, remember both rules. Do not turn them off until we come back outside. And do not put them down or drop them. Trust me, the last thing you want to happen inside a cave is to be without a light."

"Dude, we're not children," said Donny.

Ernie stopped. He looked at Donny, who glared back. *Oh nuts,* thought Christine. *Here we go again.*

Last night she and Tempest had gone to *Bacchus Bluff* with James and Donny. It was exciting because it was her first time in a bar. When James suggested it, Tempest had quipped, "We're not twenty-one, genius." But the guys knew the bouncer and, sure enough, they got in without being carded.

It was darker and noisier than she expected. And one other thing: smoky. Christine had expected that even less. She had grown up in a world where smoking only ever happened outdoors. Even though she saw very few cigarettes, the effect on sight and smell was dramatic. It did not really bother her, however. If anything, it reinforced the atmospheric sense of a new, more mature world than the one she was used to.

Unsure how to behave in the new surroundings, she and Tempest took their cues from the guys. James saw a table being vacated by another party and immediately staked a claim. Then he pulled a chair out for Christine. It was one of those little acts of consideration that renewed her appreciation for him.

Saturday night at the *Bluff* was karaoke night, and as soon as the girls found out they tried to talk the guys into joining them at the mic. It was a lost cause. James and Donny were not the type. Instead, the four of them spent the next hour polishing off a pitcher of beer and failing to get much going in the way of conversation. The noise made it hard for Christine to hear what was being said, and it was embarrassing to ask the others to keep repeating themselves. So she spent most of her time people-watching. There were perhaps thirty patrons in the bar when she arrived, and more flowed in every few minutes. She was glad that her group arrived when it had, just in time to snag a table. Most of the occupants appeared to be students, with maybe a dozen older folks scattered about. A few of them looked like they might even be middle-aged.

The foursome was in one of its lulls when she heard Donny suddenly say, "That's bullshit," in a loud voice. Apparently, it was directed at the two guys sitting behind him, for he and James turned away from the girls to face them. Christine was immediately concerned. These other two looked older. At least a few years too old to be students. James and Donny were not small guys, but the others were bigger. One tall, one broad, and both intimidating. She knew James had the type of ego to get in a fight just to impress her. A fight was bad enough, but his mood would be unbearable if he lost.

The taller guy with the dark hair and red plaid shirt turned around. Even in the modest lighting of the bar, his eyes shone like emeralds. He made a threatening look at Donny. "Come again?"

"I said that's bullshit. Your little story about the cave."

Rather than replying, the man looked back at his companion, a shaggy blond in a solid black long sleeve tee. His features were not particularly remarkable but for his wide chin, which she thought gave him the look of a thug. Christine could not hear what was said, but the companion only shrugged. Brighteyes eased back into his seat as they resumed talking, leaving her group staring at his back. Apparently, the two men were not terribly interested in Donny's opinion.

"Is he ignoring me?" Donny looked at James.

"Looks like it."

Christine tried to intervene. "Donny, tell us—"

But James cut her off. "Sorry, Christine, but we have some assholes to deal with."

The next few minutes were tense. The general volume of voices in the bar was too loud for her to overhear the exchange, but she could see it getting more and more heated. Most of the arguing was between Donny and Brighteyes, who seemed to be getting under Donny's skin and enjoying it. The two of them seemed to be matching each other insult for insult. But what worried Christine the most was the way Shaggy was reacting. She watched him discreetly slide his chair back from the table, push his mug of beer to the side, and roll the fingers of the right hand as though loosening them. Even to Christine, inexperienced at such things, it did not seem like a good sign. His gaze was locked on Donny and James. He looked like a snake that might strike at any moment. His expression did not appear eager so much as prepared, but she still worried that he might intervene in violent fashion.

Meanwhile, Donny and Brighteyes were still in each other's face, and neither looked likely to back off. Christine decided that James and Donny did not know what they were getting into. She felt compelled to do something. Neither knowing nor caring what the argument was about, Christine got up from her chair, touched James on the arm, and said, "If you don't cut this out, we're leaving." For support she looked over at Tempest, who shrugged.

"You should listen to the lady, friend."

They all looked at Shaggy. It was the first he had spoken during the entire incident.

Brighteyes gave them an amused grin. *Now you've done it*, his expression suggested. He nodded. "Yeah. In fact, why are you wasting time with us when you're sitting with two beautiful women?" His gaze drifted toward Tempest.

James looked down at Christine. Maybe the logic clicked with him. "Come on, Donny, forget these assholes. Let's pay a little more attention to the girls." Donny hesitated, but clearly did not like the idea of pressing the matter further without backup. He turned back to their table.

Relieved, Christine returned to her seat. Everyone did their best impression of acting as though nothing out of the ordinary had happened. A few minutes later they were surprised when another pitcher was delivered to their table. "Courtesy of those gents," the waitress told them. They looked over to see the two men raise their mugs in salute.

Christine felt a weight lift when James returned the gesture, and the rest of the night progressed without any further fireworks—although not uneventfully. The banter between the two tables resumed, friendlier than before. At some point the tables were pulled together and the two groups became one. The guys introduced themselves and shook hands all around, but between the noise and the effects of the beer Christine missed their names. More pitchers were ordered. She let the men do most of the drinking, but even so she probably drank more in one night than she ever had before. She became aware that she was starting to slur her words, and her brain seemed to operate a few seconds behind everyone else. As the others talked and laughed, she felt herself drifting into the background. Even James was barely talking to her, as though she were less interesting than the newcomers. It was an uncomfortable sensation, and her natural apprehensions rose to the forefront of her mind. She began to worry that she did not belong.

The beer must have loosened up some vocal cords, or at least relaxed everyone's inhibitions. Several of the others tried their hands at karaoke. Christine was not surprised when Tempest sang *Wrecking Ball*, was a little more surprised to watch Donny and Brighteyes set aside their differences to sing a duet of *I Am Woman*, and completely astonished when Shaggy got up to perform a solo rendition of *My Way* in a singing voice that sounded amazingly similar to Frank Sinatra's. No one wanted to follow that up, so the group settled back down to idle banter.

The conversation returned to the subject which had first sparked the argument. Something about a cave close to the campus. Sitting right under one of the back country roads, if the two guys were to be believed. Christine did not catch all the conversation and frankly had a difficult time seeing how it could be worth arguing about. They were talking about crawling through a drainage pipe, cars driving overhead, to get in. Donny again did not believe it, albeit in a less belligerent tone than before.

"If you don't believe us," Brighteyes said, "why don't you see for yourself? We're taking some friends there tomorrow. You should join us." As he said it, his eyes again flicked over to Tempest.

Christine's companions glanced at each other for a second. With that opening, her fuzzy mind decided it would be a good idea for her to reassert herself. "Sounds like fun," she announced, and flashed a bright smile at the others. *Still here*, she was reminding them.

James looked at her and chuckled. "I thought you were falling asleep," he said. "I was about to carry you out." He looked at Donny and Tempest, both of whom shrugged. He turned to the newcomers. "All right. Where do we meet?"

Now, in the light of day and without the benefit of alcoholic conciliation, it seemed some of the masculine animosity between Donny and Ernie was again rearing its ugly head. The two of them stared at each other for a moment. Tempest shook her head at them, but did not look altogether upset.

Ernie was about to say something, but his companion put a hand on his shoulder. "Just go on with the instructions, Easy," he said. Christine believed she was seeing a hierarchy playing out before her eyes.

Just like that, Ernie winked at Donny and resumed the speech.

"Okay, moving on. It's very easy to get turned around in a cave. There are quite a few places where tunnels branch out. Some caves have chalk arrows on the walls to point the way back out. This one doesn't. We prefer not to mar the walls. In fact, we want to have as little impact on the cave as possible. It may seem illogical, but caves are fragile. It takes hundreds and thousands of years to build even small rock formations. Just by wiping your hand across a wall you can undo a thousand years of nature's work. Some of it is going to be unavoidable, but please be careful and mindful of your impact. Particularly with the smaller stalactites and stalagmites, which can be more fragile than they appear.

"Anyway, getting back to the point... It's easy to get turned around and lose your sense of direction. We're going to move as a group, so no one should be able to get lost. Still, it's a good habit to glance behind you every so often. Especially when you pass a fork in the tunnels. This is in order to see how the cave looks coming from the other direction. If you don't do that, you will swear up and down that you haven't been there before, even when you're going back out the same way you came in. You'll see what I mean when we get in there.

"There's another reason to stay together in a group. Sound behaves strangely inside a cave, so it will be hard to hear each other from any kind of distance.

"I guess that's about it." Ernie glanced over at the other guide. "Halfus, anything to add?" The other shook his head, so Ernie finished up. "Okay, come up and get your gear. I hope everyone is ready to do some caving."

The group formed into a couple of makeshift lines.

"I thought it was called spelunking," asked a girl standing ahead of Christine.

Ernie shook his head. "You can always tell an amateur because they call it spelunking," he said. "Cavers call it caving." The girl nodded, and accepted her helmet from him.

Christine watched Tempest deliver a look toward James, who was carefully not looking back. A little bit of red crept into his neck, however.

The four of them moved up as a group. Halfus was handing out the helmets, and Ernie gave flashlights to each person who needed one. Christine was pleased to receive a helmet with a lamp. James got one without, then took his flashlight without a word. Christine assumed Donny would get one of the lampless helmets as well, an unspoken reproach for trying to initiate another pissing contest. But she was wrong. He got one of the good ones also, and instead it was Tempest who received a climbing helmet and a flashlight.

"May I have one with a lamp?" she asked with a flirtatious smile.

Ernie shook his head. "We're giving one of each to each couple. You can always ask him to trade with you." He nodded his head toward Donny.

Her smile wilted. "Never mind. It's no big deal." Tempest plopped her helmet onto her head, hiding the prominent white streak. She fiddled with the strap, then turned to Christine. "Help me." Christine adjusted it for her.

Ernie was already heading out of the clearing along a path through the tall grass. "Follow me," he said over his shoulder. The others started filing out behind him.

When Christine finished with Tempest's helmet and then her own, she looked for James. It took her a second to find him. She was a little surprised to see that he was already walking along the path behind Ernie, the bob-haired blonde just behind him and chatting away as though he was an old friend. Christine stood there, cocking her head, feeling a little put off.

"Everything all right?"

She turned. Shaggy was looking at her. *Halfus*, she recalled. She supposed Ernie was taking the lead, and Halfus bringing up the rear. It made sense.

She nodded, then moved quickly to catch up to Tempest. The grass was shorter along this path than the field all around, but even so was almost knee-high. And it was still wet with dew. Now not only her shoes and socks but the lower half of her legs were slick and uncomfortable. Along with James leaving her behind, it was not a good start to the experience.

I should be home, studying.

The path stayed parallel to the road for thirty or forty yards before turning in. Ernie was across the road already and others were in the process of crossing. When she reached it, Christine instinctively looked both ways. And immediately felt foolish. Not only were there no cars to be seen—in fact, there had been none since they arrived— any that did come would be heard long before posing a danger.

"You're from the city, aren't you?" asked Halfus from just behind her.

She nodded. "Yeah."

"Me, too," he said. "It took me a long time to lose the city instincts, too."

That was odd. She was under the impression that he was a redneck. She felt a little awkward talking to him, although he seemed nice enough now. At least he was being civil, which was more than could be said for Ernie. And Donny and James, if she were willing to admit it.

She finished crossing and saw that the others had followed the path past a solitary oak tree and into a gully of sorts. She joined them by running down the five foot drop to keep from slipping on the steep, slick path. She pulled up at the bottom, nearly colliding with Tempest in the process, then noticed that everyone was standing still. They were all looking at a culvert under the road where they had just crossed. She realized that this was the cave entrance itself. It looked innocent enough, if more than a little dirty. It was hard to imagine anything but solid earth on the other end. She wondered if the guides were not simply pranking everyone.

"The pipe is about ten yards long," said Ernie. "The opposite end opens up into a chamber we call The Gatehouse. That room isn't really big enough for all of us, so we'll pass through into the tunnels. There are three main tunnels coming off The Gatehouse. We call those Tom, Dick, and Harry."

He paused for a moment. "Does anyone know why we call *three tunnels* Tom, Dick, and Harry?" He looked around. "Any movie buffs in our group? No one? Oh, well.

"We should have time for all three tunnels. We'll take Tom first, and he'll lead us down to the first room we'll all fit in. You're probably all tired of listening to me, so I'll stop for now and pick up again at that point. Any last questions?"

There were none. Ernie tightened the straps on his backpack and climbed into the culvert. It was about four feet high, so Christine had hopes of walking through it hunched over. Ernie, however, immediately went to hands and knees and started crawling. Soon he disappeared and the next person behind him followed his lead.

Here, staring at the entrance, Christine was confronted with some last doubts. No one else seemed nervous, but she was. If she went in there, would it be the closet all over again? Was she willing to find out? She had to decide right now.

She forced herself to replay the memory. It was not a pleasant one, which was why she had avoided thinking about it too hard all these years. Part of it was that she had never been put in a situation like the one she was in now, with the threat of claustrophobia looming ominously before her. But deep down she knew there was more to it than that. There was a stronger reason why her thoughts avoided this particular memory.

She still remembered the layout of her parents' bedroom, the colors of the dresses in the closet. The darkness. There had been a little light coming under the door. The darkness had not really scared her. Something else had. *Abandonment.* She visualized the scene when the door reopened. The first thing she saw. She had already been upset, but the worst part came next. Her brother had been laughing as he let her out. Worse than the sense of being trapped was the disbelief that her brother had actually enjoyed upsetting her. He had been there the entire time, listening to her cry. It had still taken him fifteen minutes to let her out.

It was a harsh lesson for her nine-year-old self: finding out that others did not always see you the same way you saw them. If her beloved brother could be a monster, was there anyone who could not?

Was it a flaw inside everyone? That night she had lost a piece of her childhood. But it was not for herself that she had cried, it was for him. It was not only the complexities of her own mind that had driven her to study psychology. It was also the defects in her brother's.

She felt a twinge of regret at the realization that that had been the last time they played together. What had been such a big part of her childhood had ended in fifteen callous minutes. She had gone on with the pretense that they remained close, smiling at dinner time, laughing at jokes, but there had always been excuses when it came to playing together. Soon he hit the age where a boy stopped palling around with his little sister. It had come as a relief as much as anything. It meant she could stop pretending. To her brother, to her parents, and to herself.

Ten years later it still hurt. She was ready to stop thinking about it. She had dwelled on the memory enough for now. For the moment, all that mattered was the knowledge that the incident was less about the confines of the closet than she had assumed. Being inside a cave still did not exactly thrill her, but neither did she believe it would cause her any irrational panic.

Most of the others had climbed in already. She waited her turn, then joined them.

Once she was inside, Christine's first impression was that she hated caving. It was because of the little things. Things that started before she got to the cave itself. Her attempt to walk hunched over through the pipe failed about halfway, when the stress on her back and knees became too uncomfortable. She had hated to get down on her hands and knees, exposing them to the dirt and cobwebs and whatever else lurked in the pipe, but she had no choice. Then she reached the cave itself. She was initially relieved to be able to stand up straight, but in moments became aware of other annoyances.

First and foremost, the cave was muddy. Ridiculously muddy. Everything she touched—the floor, the walls, the little rock formations—was coated with a layer of moisture. It appeared to be water, but felt thick with minerals. It was more like liquid stone, and whatever touched the substance came away caked in the stuff. Before long it seemed that her arms and legs were encased in a thin layer of clay, and it made bending her elbows and knees feel clunky. But it was not just on her arms and legs. Once it got on her hands, the mud found its way to other parts of her body every time she touched anything. She scratched an itch on her cheek and left a cool wet streak on half of her face.

The other thing that she noticed was the awkwardness. There was not a flat surface to be found anywhere, including the floor. Walking involved more than putting one foot in front of the other. Most of the time she kept one or both hands on a wall or protrusion to balance herself as she moved along angled channels and over difficult outcroppings. She felt sorry for those who were forced to hold a flashlight in one hand, because she had enough difficulty even using both. When she watched her feet, she bumped her head. When she kept her eyes up, she tripped on one of the many irregularities. The helmet was a big part of the problem. It added a few inches to the head that she was not used to, throwing off her sense of clearance. No sooner had she emerged from the pipe into the cave's first room then she stood up straight and banged her head on the low ceiling. Tempest laughed at her, turned to follow the others into the first tunnel, and promptly banged her own head. They were complete klutzes down here.

Yet somehow seeing her friend bump around just as awkwardly changed Christine's outlook. Her revised impression was that she loved caving. Once again, it was the little things. The mud and tripping around was actually a big part of it. The mud took some getting used to, but it was neither painful nor particularly uncomfortable. Once she accepted that they were all going to get filthy, it stopped bothering her entirely. She certainly understood the warning to wear old clothes. It was the same story with the awkwardness. Once she got used to it, it was much less annoying and actually sort of fun. It added to a sense of adventure she was beginning to feel. It was like a whole new world in there, a place where only a handful of people had ever been, and was totally unlike anything she had experienced before. She felt like an explorer. Even with thirteen beams of light swinging around, the cave was always extremely dark. She had to concentrate to make out people and objects, and felt dependent on touch and sound to maneuver without mishap. The heightened reliance on her senses made her feel that she was pushing her own limits, and she enjoyed the challenge.

Moreover, even though the cave was smaller and tighter than she had imagined—much different from anything she had seen in movies —she felt not the slightest pang of claustrophobia. Not even in the narrowest spaces where she had to turn sideways to move. There was no sense that the earth could shift, or that the ceiling would collapse. Now that she was inside, she wondered what the worry had been about.

Tempest did not seem to be embracing the experience in quite the same way. Just ahead, Christine heard her crash into yet another rock, eliciting one of the strongest curses she had ever heard her roommate utter.

"Tempest, what's wrong?"

"I think I broke my flashlight." She flicked the switch on and off with no effect.

"It's probably just the batteries. Ask Ernie if he has extras."

Tempest harrumphed. "I'd rather not. He already thinks I'm an idiot."

Christine wondered when her friend had started caring what Ernie thought. "Okay, just stick close to me, then."

It took a few minutes for the group to slowly progress to the end of the first tunnel. They emerged into a wider area with the first relatively flat floor they had seen so far. Most of the group was ahead of her and had formed a semicircle around Ernie, who stood facing the entrance. Behind him was a smoothly curving wall. At his feet flowed a slow shallow current of running water, not more than a few inches deep.

Ernie waited until he saw Halfus bringing up the rear, then he resumed his narrative. "This is The Wash. Since we are in the underworld, this mighty torrent is called the River Styx. Be careful not to be swept away. Also, I don't recommend drinking it unless you enjoy the taste of rock."

"Normally, when we bring only a few people down here, we all take a minute to turn off all the lights. You've never experienced darkness like being deep in a cave without light. With everyone completely silent and stationary you can just hear the slight sound of this stream and nothing else. It's a way to commune with the earth. For those of you into that sort of thing. I'm looking at you, Aaron and Mindy.

"Anyway, we're not doing that with a group this size. I'll take special requests to bring two or three down sometime, though. Or one, if she's cute and single.

"Now we're going to go back up Tom and take the second tunnel, Dick. That will take us to the biggest room in this cave system. If you let me get through, I'll lead the way there."

It took some time to get a group this size moving back up the tunnel. Christine found herself waiting with Halfus and a few others. It seemed like a good opportunity to ask a question that had been bothering her. She hesitated a moment, not wanting to sound ignorant. Then she decided to risk it.

"Why is it so muddy down here? I thought since the cave is made out of rock it would be pretty dry." One of the girls nearby seemed interested and moved closer to listen.

"Good question," he said. "Well, you live your life aboveground, where buildings and streets use gutters and pipes and drains to flow all the water down and away from where it's not wanted. But out in the open country there is nothing like that to direct the flow. Some rolls down to rivers and streams, of course, but a lot of it just seeps into the ground. Rock isn't as solid as you think, and water does all kinds of interesting things to it. Once water gets underground, it carves out these big holes in the rock that we call caves, it makes underground streams, it drips for thousands of years to form stalactites and stalagmites...and it gets caked on cute young girls' cheeks."

He did not speak like someone who had not finished the tenth grade. She found herself full of curiosity borne from mistaken first impressions. She did not even notice the other girl heading out, leaving the two of them alone in The Wash.

"What do you do, Halfus?"

"Ancient Studies."

"You're a student? At the college? You seem a little..." She stopped herself.

"Old? As in, 'College was the best ten years of my life?'"

"I'm sorry." She was embarrassed. "I didn't mean to sound—"

"It's all right. I am a little old. I'm a grad student."

"Oh. Oh!" She laughed, mostly at herself. She felt a little flush to her cheeks and was glad the lighting was too dim for the color to show.

"They'll be waiting for us," he said. "Let's get going."

They caught up to the others back in The Gatehouse. Along the way, Christine learned that Ernie had spoken true about one thing. Even though the tunnel to The Wash had been relatively straight and without branches, it did not look like the same tunnel now that she was moving in the opposite direction. If she had not known better, she would have sworn it was an entirely different passage. It was not until she reached the first room and recognized the end of the drain pipe that she knew exactly where she was.

Ernie and most of the others were already well down the second tunnel. Christine moved close behind a big muscle-bound guy in what had been a white sleeveless shirt. His impressive shoulders were completely covered in mud, and the shirt had turned more gray than white, the writing on the back illegible.

They rounded a bend and were forced to stop. Ahead, the tunnel was thick with people. Their movement had slowed to a crawl. She heard Ernie's voice echoing back, a little distorted but intelligible. "...coming up to my favorite part of the cave. I know everyone is tired of crawling and squeezing through tight spots, so you'll be glad to know that this room is spacious. All right, follow me."

The line began to move forward again. Christine had to crouch to work her way around a low-hanging obstacle. As she got past it she saw the others spreading out where the walls widened. So far she had enjoyed the tricky navigation, but now she was ready for a breather. She looked forward to having room to stand up straight and stretch out her arms a little. She hoped it would be a room at least twice the size of The Wash. She stepped into it, looked around, and gasped.

"Ladies and gentlemen, welcome to Valhalla." Ernie held his arms out wide in presentation.

So far everything in the cave had been small and tight. For most of their length the tunnels were barely wide enough to move through in single file, and even the relative immensity of The Wash was only by comparison to the entrance.

This place, on the other hand, was positively enormous. A hundred people could have moved about this room without bumping. The ceiling was high and covered with stalactites of all sizes. Likewise the floor was a maze of stalagmites. The largest of these was close to the center of the room, stretching upwards and merging with a stalactite to form one impressive column. Around the perimeter were a few more tunnel openings, and those were just the ones she could see. Most of the far side was too shadowy from this distance to make out with any clarity.

"We'll take a break here and have some lunch," Ernie said. He unslung his backpack and dropped it to the floor, then unzipped it. Halfus and a skinny guy with unstylish glasses joined him and dropped their own. They spent a few minutes organizing the plastic bags and small Tupperware containers, holding each close to their headlamps in order to read the labels.

Christine realized how hungry she had gotten, though it was strange to hear him call this lunch—on normal days, she would just be starting breakfast now. Caving burned a lot more energy than she had expected, and she had skipped eating earlier because of her hangover. A hangover which was now completely gone. She decided that she was really glad she came.

"Enjoying your flirting?"

She saw a big bulky form in front of her and recognized the voice as James. Suddenly she felt both defensive and offended.

"Me?" She was a little uncomfortable knowing that Donny and Tempest were close enough to hear, if they cared to listen. Which they almost certainly did. But Christine had to defend herself from unfair accusations. Besides, she had been annoyed with him before they came in. The excitement of the adventure had wiped the annoyance away, but being confronted like this conjured it back up. "We weren't flirting. Unlike you."

"Excuse me?"

"You seemed more interested in that girl who was flirting with you than you were in me, so you can't blame me for talking to other people. You want me to talk only to you, but you can chat up anyone you want?" She knew her volume was rising a little, but thankfully other groups were talking as well so she did not think they were making a spectacle.

James stared at her for a moment. "Whatever." He turned away. "Hey, Donny. I'm going to explore a little. Let me borrow your helmet."

Donny seemed reluctant. She could see him glancing back and forth between herself and James because the light beam moved with each turn of his head. Then he loosened his chin strap, pulled off the helmet, and traded with his friend. James donned it and wandered toward the far side of the cavern.

Christine did not feel like dealing with any judgmental talk from the other two, so she headed toward the array of food that the three men laid out. She approached the one she had not met. He was spinning the plastic lid of a cup on his index finger. She stuck out her hand. "Hi, I'm Christine."

He put down the lid and shook her hand. "Aaron. Nice to meet you, Christine."

She had a brief conversation with the three guys as the rest of the cavers came up, perused the food parcels, and took their choices back to wherever they were sitting. For herself, Christine took a plastic fork and a small container of macaroni salad that she ate standing up. The guys were also handing out half-sized bottles of water and repeating the refrain, "Please bring the trash back to us for disposal." All in all, it was a fairly efficient little picnic the guides had arranged. Especially for a group of thirteen.

Except they seemed to have misjudged the number of servings to bring. As she set her empty salad bowl down in the used pile, she noticed two uneaten sandwiches and a container of what looked like potato salad. One of those might be for James, whom she had not seen claim any food. *Come to think of it...*

"Where are your friends?" Ernie asked.

"What?" But she was already looking at the spot where she had left them. They were not there.

"Your hot friend, and the troublemakers."

She looked around the chamber. "James is over there, exploring." She pointed to a solitary beam of light moving around in the distant darkness. "I don't know where Tempest and Donny are."

"Hey, Halfus?" Ernie raised his voice to get the other's attention. "We're missing two."

The broad shoulders sagged. "*Jesus.*" She could not tell if he sounded annoyed or worried.

"You think they wandered off, Halph?"

"Probably."

Christine saw James returning. She moved toward him as the guides consulted. James saw her approaching and started to angle away from her.

She cut him off. "Not now, James. We have a situation."

"Did something happen?"

"T and Donny are missing."

James stopped. "That fucking idiot." Christine did not like harsh language, and James knew it. Her first thought was that he meant to offend her. Then she realized he was genuinely upset. He nodded his head in the direction of the guides. "Have those jerks come up with a plan?"

"They're discussing it now. We just found out. Come on."

As they rejoined the picnic area, Christine watched Ernie turn to the group for an announcement.

"Listen up, folks. We have two cavers who went AWOL." There were murmurs in the crowd. "It's like this. There's a chance they're just pranking us, and will show back up any minute. It's more likely they wanted a little privacy, and will wander back when they're done." Christine did not appreciate hearing Tempest characterized in that manner, but she had to admit it was the most likely explanation. "The third possibility is that they wanted a little privacy, wandered off, and got lost. There are a lot of tunnels leading from this spot and we didn't show most of them to you yet."

"So we could wait for them to come back, which they will probably do. We could split up to look for them, but we only have two guides and that runs the risk of someone else getting separated and potentially lost. So what we're going to do is have everyone stay here with Halfus while I go look for them."

"I'm going, too," James announced.

Ernie sounded agitated. "Look, buddy, we don't have time to argue about this—"

"No, we don't. He's my friend, and I'm worried about him. Both of them."

Christine expected the argument to continue, wasting valuable time. Yet Ernie conceded quickly. "All right. But keep up."

The two of them moved toward the first tunnel on the left side. It was the one closest to where Tempest and Donny had last been seen.

"The rest of us are stuck here?" Christine asked out loud. No one answered. Halfus and Aaron were discussing something, and she did not know any of the others. Suddenly she felt very alone in a group of strangers. And she would not blame them if they were none too happy with her at the moment. After all, it was her friends who were ruining this trip for everyone.

Until now, being inside the cave had not felt oppressive at all. She began to realize that was because she had not felt trapped. It might have been embarrassing, but there was no reason why she could not have left the cave early if she had felt the need.

But now she could not. Nothing else had changed, but the air suddenly seemed stale and uncomfortable to her lungs. She gasped for heavier breaths, but it felt as though there was not enough oxygen down here for all of them. She realized she was panicking, and fought to control her breathing. She took a few steps away from the group and hoped that no one could see her struggling. But it was getting worse, and she was beginning to feel a strong impulse to scream and tug on her hair. She had convinced herself that she would be fine, but now her worst fear was happening after all.

"Are you all right?" It was Halfus.

She tried to nod. She wanted to smile and reply in a calm voice that everything was fine. But she desperately wanted to be back outside, breathing fresh air, and she did not think she could wait. She looked away from him.

She heard him say, "Hey, Aaron. Keep an eye on things, will you?"

She felt his hand on her shoulder. "It's going to be fine. You're just feeling a little panic. It will pass in a minute." She was not sure whether to believe him or not, but his tone was reassuring, as though he knew what he was talking about. "Why don't you sit down?"

She sat on a little outcropping that made for a convenient bench. He sat beside her. A large stalagmite blocked most of the others from view.

They sat in silence for a minute. She focused on her breathing, attempting to slow it back to normal.

"You heard Ernie call this chamber 'Valhalla,'" he said. "Do you know what that is?"

She shook her head. "Not really. Something from mythology." He was trying to give her something to think about, she was sure, but was not off to a good start.

"You're right. In Norse mythology, it's the hall of the gods."

"Like Mount Olympus," she said.

"Yes, like Mount Olympus. I'm impressed." She appreciated the compliment, although she assumed everyone knew Mount Olympus. But it was better than looking ignorant. "But with one important difference," he continued. "The bravest warriors who die in combat are brought to Valhalla.

"You've heard of Valkyries?" he asked, and she nodded. "Odin is the father of the gods in Norse mythology. Valhalla is his drinking hall. The Valkyries are the ones who choose which warriors are brought to Valhalla. They fly over the battlefield and scoop up the most deserving, because it's an honor to sit at Odin's table. Once they're in Valhalla, the warriors get to party with the gods until Ragnarok comes.

"It's a good system for a warrior society like the Vikings. It gives warriors that extra reason to be brave. It must have been very appealing to be picked as one of the very best, to go drink mead with the gods until the end of time. Sometimes we need that little extra push, that little extra help. After all, we're human."

He stopped talking, and silence settled between them. She became aware of the rest of the cavers engaged in talking and eating with little or no regard for her predicament, for which she was grateful. Her breathing had calmed a little, and she felt no more impulse to pull her hair out. That had been a weird—and scary—sensation.

"What happens on...what did you call it? Raga...?"

"Ragnarok." He seemed to hesitate a second, as though unsure how much nerdiness to pile on her. "Ragnarok is sort of like Judgment Day in Norse mythology. It's the time when evil rises up against the gods like Odin. There is another god named Loki who turns against his brothers and sisters and leads the attack against them. The gods and the forces of evil destroy each other, and at the end an inferno is unleashed that consumes the world. In the end, everyone dies. Realists, those Vikings."

She really did not care about any of that. She was very caught up in the present.

"I'm embarrassed," she said at last.

"Why?"

"It's irrational, I know. I got worked up over nothing."

"I've had it happen to me. It can be scary."

"My friends always say I worry too much."

"That sounds familiar." He sighed. She detected something more than assuagement in his voice. It sounded like real empathy.

She sensed an opportunity to turn the conversation away from herself. "That sounds interesting." She looked over at him. He was staring ahead, not looking at her. It was hard to tell if he was genuinely engaged with her or not. She pushed him a little. "Let me guess, Ernie tells you that." Ernie seemed like the type. "Or a girlfriend does." Even in the poor light, she saw a slight reaction in his face. "Ooh, a girlfriend. Tell me about her."

He shook his head. "I'm not much good at stories."

"Please?" She did not want to use her panic as an excuse, but she hoped he would take it into consideration. She wanted something to distract her.

Perhaps he realized it himself. After a moment his shoulders seemed to sag. She sensed he was giving in. It was hard to understand how a guy could be willing to sing in front of a crowd but resisted talking about his girlfriend.

"I wouldn't know where to start."

"What's her name?"

A pause. Then, "Shauna."

She waited. When he did not continue on his own, she prompted him.

"Keep going."

He seemed a bit reluctant, but finally opened the door for her. "What do you want to know?"

"Tell me about how you met."

He took a breath. "A few years ago I went rock climbing with a group of friends. One of them brought his girlfriend, who I had met before, and her best friend, who I had not. The friend was Shauna. I remember when we were introduced I didn't really give her a second thought. Maybe because Easy was with us. Girls usually go for him. So we start climbing, and I doubt if we said more than two words to each other. But then it went from being one big group, where you talk to the people you know the best, to smaller teams. Most of that climb was relatively easy, but there were places where we had to partner up. She and I wound up being a team for a stretch.

"It wasn't my first climb but it was hers, so she was a little slower than almost everyone else. Me being the exception. I climb slowly. I have a fear of heights—"

"You have a fear of heights yet you were out climbing?" Christine interrupted, a little incredulous.

"Well, at the time I believed you could conquer your fears by persistent exposure to them," he answered. He shook his head. "It doesn't work. At least not for me."

Christine smiled. She found it interesting that he was willing to talk about a weakness to a girl he just met. She could not imagine James doing that.

"Anyway, it's because of my fear of heights that I'm slower than the others. It's the result of double-checking every little thing. Every hold. Every nut and cam and carabiner. So Shauna and I sort of found ourselves watching the others get farther and farther ahead. As happens so often, circumstances thrust us into each other's company, like it or not. Or maybe it was planned all along, I'm not sure. It's the sort of thing some of my friends would do. I never asked them.

"So, you know how sometimes you meet someone and just click right away?"

Christine nodded, because she did. Then she realized he was not watching her, so she said, "Yes."

"Well, that's not what happened with Shauna. It's the opposite of what happened, actually. It took most of the climb for us to exchange more than a few words. You wouldn't know it based on today, but I'm not usually a talkative guy. And, to be honest, she intimidated me a little. More than a little. Not that she was too pretty or anything, she just had that air about her. Someone good things happen to."

"It was intimidating in another respect. Like I said, it wasn't my first climb and it was hers, yet she picked things up so easily that soon she was outpacing me. Just a little, but I started noticing that she could move faster when she wanted to. I was just too cautious to ever be particularly speedy. It was a little embarrassing, to be beaten by a first-timer like that."

Christine noticed that he said 'first-timer' rather than 'girl.' She wondered if that was because he was talking to one now. Surely that was part of it, though. It would bother most guys she knew.

"Of course, I found out later she had practiced on those REI walls quite a bit, which helps. It's not the same thing by any stretch, but it works out the right muscles. Anyway, it was obvious she was just a really good athlete. I figured she would catch up to the others. After all, I wasn't much fun to talk to. She did an interesting thing, though. As she got better she actually seemed to slow down. She would still climb faster, but take longer breaks. At first I thought she was tiring and needed to rest her muscles, but then it seemed to me she was pacing herself to my speed. I thought about telling her she didn't need to, but to be honest it was nice having someone else around. Even if we weren't really talking.

"Then one time she reached a ledge we were climbing to about a minute before I did, and she leaned out over the edge watching me, holding the side of the rocks like this." He reached back with one hand and grabbed a pretend projection. Clearly he was intending to make it appear to be a tenuous position, and Christine supposed it would be at a height. "It made me even slower, not because I disliked being watched but out of concern for her safety. Of course the reason she was going faster than I was all along was because she took little risks that I wouldn't. But this was the first time it was so blatant. It's irrational, but my mind visualized her falling, and then me falling, and then I had to just hold on a second for the disorientation to end. When I finally could start climbing again I was even slower than before.

"Do you know how sometimes embarrassment becomes annoyance, and the annoyance is really with yourself, but your emotional mind blames someone else? Well, I was embarrassed to be going so slowly despite having more experience than she did, and I found myself annoyed with her for making it worse. In retrospect it's pretty silly, but at the time I blamed her for making me panic.

"I didn't want to embarrass myself any further and I didn't trust myself to not say something inappropriate to her, so when I reached the ledge I just started collecting my gear for the next leg of the climb. To my surprise she told me to say it. I looked at her and realized she was partly poking fun at me, sure, but she was mostly making us put this little friction behind us. So I asked her not to hang off the side of a mountain with one hand anymore. As soon as I said it I felt like a jerk for trying to tell her what she could and couldn't do. I had thought it was for her own safety—and there was a little of that, to be sure—but I also knew it was mostly because of the tricks my mind played on itself.

"She didn't get mad. In fact, she was amused, as if she could watch my conflicting thoughts duke it out. At that point my annoyance with her just deflated, and I admitted that it was as much for my own good as hers. I said that I was worried about her safety, of course, but I told her how my mind got fixated on her falling and it made my own balance more precarious.

"She smiled and said, 'You worry too much.'"

Christine felt him looking at her. She still had trouble reading his expression in the limited light, but his features now seemed far more appealing than they had been just the night before. It was remarkable that her first impression was to think of him as a thug. Appearances aside, he now seemed like one of the nicest guys she knew.

As though aware that she was studying him, he turned away, facing forward again to continue the story.

"She poked a little fun at me on the rest of that climb. Pretending to be about to fall with her feet dangling six inches from the ground, little things like that. Before you get the wrong idea, though, she did it only when it didn't matter. When either of us was in a situation that required actual concentration, she used the same techniques she had watched me use, even though it slowed her down. I caught her glancing over at me a lot to make sure I was noticing. So I knew she was only doing it for my benefit. Still, it was nice that she did it.

"Climbing isn't conducive to lengthy conversations, so we still didn't talk all that much. So I'm not sure exactly how it happened and how we both knew, but by the end of the climb when we caught up to the others we were pretty much a couple. We were already planning another climbing trip together, just the two of us. When she found out I was a caver she wanted to join me for that, too. But caving was never as thrilling for her as climbing.

"I did fewer climbs, but she did more and more and got better and better. I stopped going with her, because I felt so slow. No guy wants to look bad in front of his girlfriend. She and my friends started doing tougher climbs than I could ever do. And my acrophobia got worse. It was bad enough when it was just me, but having a second person to worry about frayed my nerves even more than before. Besides, two people need their separate activities, anyway. Not that I didn't have second thoughts. I found out that one of the other climbers from our group, a guy named Greg, had once gone out with her. He was with us on the day we met and apparently he wanted to get back together with her then. Naturally, he was not happy with me. I was a little uncomfortable at first seeing her keep climbing with those guys, knowing he was around. But clinging doesn't help, especially with a girl like Shauna. You just have to trust people."

Christine thought of her little argument with James earlier. What did it say about the two of them? Did he trust her? Did she trust him?

"I even stopped telling her to please be careful. Every time I did, she told me I worry too much. It was a running joke for a while, but we grew out of it, I guess."

He paused, and she wondered if the story was over now that he made the connection. He had certainly answered her question, and it had worked. She had been distracted enough by the story to forget all about her panic. She was about to thank him, but he started talking again. He had not looked over at her in a while. Judging by his tone, he was a little lost in his own story, and she was not sure he even remembered she was there.

"I think the scariest day of my life was the first dinner with her family. Mister Hostettler has this really thick black mustache and it makes his expression come across as incredibly dour. When I shook his hand it seemed like disapproval was a foregone conclusion."

"They love you, don't they?"

"I guess so. They're great people. You know how some folks are really slow to warm up to you, but once they do they're worth the wait? That's them to a T."

"For our one year anniversary I planned out a trip for the two of us to hike the Grand Canyon. I thought a relaxing hiking trip would give us more time and energy to just enjoy each other's company. She had another idea. There was another climb scheduled just before, and she asked me to come along for a change. She joked that Greg was going to be there, and he would leave her alone if I was there. But I couldn't, I was too deep in classes." He shook his head. There was a pause, and then he scratched his cheek.

"I still think of her now and then."

There was a commotion at the far end of the chamber. Christine looked up to see three beams of light coming toward them.

Halfus was already up and moving toward the others. Ernie and James were followed by Donny and Tempest. As the groups converged, she saw James turn to Ernie and shake his hand. Then Ernie headed toward the backpacks, where Halfus met him.

It was obvious that the caving trip was over. The packing was completed and they filed into the tunnel leading back to the entrance with noticeably less chatter than on the way in. Christine took a place in line behind James, but they barely spoke the whole way out. Both of them were clearly preoccupied with other thoughts.

Even though her panic attack was long gone, she appreciated being back out in the fresh spring air. She took a second to breathe it in deeply. She looked around at her fellow cavers. The mud made everyone look like statues with patches of color showing through.

James was looking down at her from above the gully. She looked at him curiously, worried that he was still in a foul mood. But his expression was gentler than she expected. He reached a hand down to help her up. She accepted it. When she was up he put both hands on her arms and looked at her closely. He had dried mud caked on his forehead, and she became aware of the mud on her face and probably all through her hair. The effect made him look rugged, but she doubtless looked awful.

"I'm sorry we argued," he said.

"Me, too." She smiled at him.

He wrapped a hand around her shoulder and they walked side-by-side across the road and up the path. It was not really wide enough for two, but he placed himself in the position of pushing through the taller grass. The benefits of being a big guy.

Tempest and Donny were already at the Audi. They looked sheepish. It was an unusual look for them.

"What happened?" Christine asked.

"We got lost," replied Tempest. "Donny decided to scare me by turning off his flashlight. It worked."

As the two of them began to talk, James and Donny started a separate conversation.

"I don't care. He had no right to talk to me like that." Donny sounded agitated.

"Yes, he did. You fucked up."

Donny must have realized he had no support. His body language indicated surrender.

"Did you two get yelled at?" Christine asked Tempest.

The girl nodded. "Big time. He said we ruined the trip for everyone else."

"Well, I still had fun." Christine hugged her roommate. This was as close to contrition she had ever seen on the other girl. It felt kind of nice to be able to comfort her for once. "Don't worry. No one is going to be mad."

Tempest shook her head. "I don't think he likes me."

"Who?"

"*Him.* Ernie."

Christine let go of her roommate. They were in dangerous territory all of a sudden. She put her hands on Tempest's arms and looked into her face, the same way James had done to her a few minutes earlier.

"Of course he does, T. He can't take his eyes off you. But listen to me. Donny's a great guy. Don't mess that up."

Tempest looked over at the boys. Christine did, too. She realized that what she had just said could also apply to her.

The two guides, bringing up the rear, entered the clearing. They opened up the Jeep and pulled out the big empty boxes.

"Everyone, throw your stuff into these. We'll sort it out later." Ernie sounded a bit tired, but not particularly upset.

Christine wanted to speak to Halfus, but he took charge of collecting and sorting gear and was surrounded by people. As she removed her own helmet and dropped it in the box, she looked at him. She expected him to look back and smile, but he did not notice her.

Ernie was talking with another guy at the side of the clearing. As she watched, the other boy shook his hand and went to one of the cars. Christine walked over to the brash guide. "Hey."

He took a swig of water. "Hey. Christine, right?"

"Yep. Do you have a minute?"

"Sure. What's up?"

"I have a question. It might be a little unusual."

"Okay. Fire away." He seemed approachable enough.

"What happened with Shauna?"

Ernie visibly stiffened. "He told you about Shauna?"

"Well, he told me a little. I asked how they met. He started to tell me the story, but... Well, it just stopped. I guess we got interrupted when you all came back.

"Did she get back with her ex?" She felt certain that was it, and was prepared to act suitably outraged. She had gotten to like this girl from what little she had heard. On the one hand, Shauna seemed so ill-suited to Halfus. On the other, she seemed to have a zest for life that Christine sometimes wished she possessed for herself. If, however, the girl had broken Halfus' heart, Christine was prepared to instantly dislike her.

Ernie shook his head sadly. He lowered the water bottle. "No. There was an accident. She took a fall while doing a climb. She and some others were racing, and apparently it had rained recently and, well, she fell pretty far. I heard she was conscious when they got to her. Then she went into a coma."

"Oh, my God, I had no idea." Christine felt terrible. "Was this recent? Is she still in the coma?"

"No. She died a few months later, if I remember right. It happened a few years ago."

Christine fell silent. She had nothing left to ask.

"Look, I need to help with the packing up. Will you excuse me?" She nodded, and he turned away.

A little in shock, she went over to the Audi. Two of the doors were open, but no one had gotten in yet. James and Donny were still talking, and Tempest was sitting on the rear bumper, watching a group of horses in the distance. Or perhaps just staring in that direction. She looked as though she was thinking.

Christine was thinking, too. *I still think of her now and then,* he had said. That must have been quite an understatement. She felt incredibly sad for Halfus. And more. She knew this was a bad idea, but she was going to do it anyway. She knew she would regret not doing it.

Christine opened her door and reached into the bag she had left in the car. She removed a ball point pen and a small flip notebook. She wrote a number on a page of the notebook and tore the page out. She dropped the pen and notebook back in the bag and closed it up, then folded the page she had torn out inside her palm so it was concealed.

She glanced over at James. He was still engaged with Donny. She started walking over to where Halfus and Ernie were closing up the boxes and lifting them into the Jeep. One of the cars was already pulling onto the road. She had to let it pass before she approached the two men.

"Halfus," she said. He looked up. "I'm sorry for making you tell me that story."

He shook his head. "Nothing to apologize for. I enjoyed talking to you." She was not sure whether he was being genuine or merely being polite. She hoped it was the former. She stepped closer to him and stuck out her hand with the piece of paper showing.

"Call me sometime. If you want to talk some more." She felt more awkward than she had expected. He took the paper and nodded. She found out it was not just the bad lighting below that made his expression hard to read.

She heard Tempest calling to her. "Christine, are you ready?"

Christine thanked Ernie and shook his hand before returning to the Audi. Donny and Tempest were getting in, but James waited so he could open the door for her.

"I wanted to thank them for letting us come," she told him as she climbed into the back seat.

Tempest and Donny seemed to be in a better mood already. They were talking about possibly going back to the bar that evening. The thought of more beer made Christine's stomach turn over, but she knew she would probably join them if they went. *Unless I get a phone call tonight.*

Thank goodness I didn't stay home to study.

James started the engine and pulled out onto the road in the direction of the college. Christine did not want to be obvious, so she let the natural turn of the car bring the Jeep and the two people beside it into view. She saw Halfus shut the tailgate and secure the boxes, then James was accelerating up the road and the image was gone.

She looked out the window at the scenery. They drove past the horses, who seemed oblivious to them. She felt happy. Considering how the day had started, she was glad she had come. She really appreciated that people could prioritize anxieties. It was a way to get the most out of life. She also thought about how suddenly and unpredictably momentous events can happen. How one moment you can not know a person exists and the next they are all you can think about. How sometimes the most important people in your life come out of nowhere to completely blindside you.

Of course, sometimes people who seem important disappear before you ever get to know them. She never saw him again.

2
TRIANGLES AND CIRCLES

IN 1947, speaking before the House of Commons, Winston Churchill famously called democracy, "The worst form of government, except for all the others that have been tried." The same idea applies to capitalism as an economic system. Democracy and capitalism, twin pillars on which precariously perches modern America; fair, efficient, and beautiful at times, yet fundamentally flawed.

Democracy may be a Greek concept, but these pillars are not styled Doric or Corinthian. Nor are they even circular. These pillars are triangular, for only in that shape does each side intersect and interact with the others. Moreover, these triangles should be equilateral, for only equality between each of the complementary forces prevents domination by any one.

Owners, Workers, and Consumers form the sides of Capitalism's grand column; Government, Media, and the People that of Democracy. Government regulates the People even as it remains beholden to them. The People have the power to shape Government. They have the right to demand equality, integrity, and morality from their leaders. They have the responsibility to be involved and informed enough to make this happen. Only a populace that is fully educated and invested can effectively execute this function. The role of a free and fair Media is not to shape public opinion, but to inform it.

In contemporary democracy, each of these three segments is highly flawed. The Government comprises leaders who place self and party above country. It is in the best interest of the opposition party to prevent any actual good from happening, for fear that the ruling party will claim and receive credit—which indeed it will, whether deserved or not. For much the same reason, effective policies are regularly torpedoed—turned into inefficient farces to provide fodder for the endless polemics that political sharks feast upon.

In a perfect world, this transparent behavior would backfire. That is where recent developments in the media come onto the scene. With few exceptions, the members of the media have withdrawn to their separate corners and entrenched. Because news is a business, and a highly profitable one at that, news providers are incentivized to tell their viewers what they want to hear—and what they want to hear is how terrible the other side is. The selective customization of the news means consumers no longer get to hear an objective analysis of opinions they do not already agree with, nor have their perspectives challenged by facts that do not support their preexisting worldview. Market share trumps silly conceits like principle and responsibility.

The People have the power to correct these abuses, of course. With rare exceptions, they choose not to. Each person perceives the world through a prism. The fragmentation of the media causes these prisms to become more and more distorted. Very few people seem to recognize this, or at best believe it taints only those on the opposite end of the spectrum. For all the improvements in education throughout the centuries, schools still do not teach critical thinking. Rather than providing motivation for reform, the problems in the government and media lead only to further divisiveness amongst the most political and a mounting apathy among the rest. Having thus abrogated their own responsibilities, the People are as guilty as the other two.

Whether these flaws are beyond repair remains an unanswered question.

For her part, Wendy was not hopeful. Just thinking about it drove her into a tailspin of frustration. She took her role in the triangle seriously, but it seemed no one else did. The most exasperating thing was the disparity between what the citizenry was capable of and the disappointing reality. For most of history, regular folks like her had no voice in how their country and community were governed. Wars had been fought, and countless lives lost, for them to gain this voice. Now all people cared about was sports or the royal couple or the latest cop show.

She did her best to pay attention to the vapid conversation she was in. "Didn't you see the news last night, Mrs. Fields?" she replied to the chatty middle-aged woman sitting to her left. "There was a special report at nine."

"Oh, no, dear. I watch *Celebrity House Makeover* at nine."

Wendy did not trust herself to respond, so she sat back and watched the activity on the stage. A technician wearing a tucked polo shirt over his impressive gut and a box with wires on his hip was conducting a sound check on the standing microphone that Representative King would be using. "Check, check, check," he said, and a high-pitched feedback noise ensued. He went to a knee, adjusted a knob, and repeated the phrase. The feedback faded out, and the man stood up and walked off the stage.

Wendy gave a quick glance at the wall clock. It showed five minutes before one. Things would be starting soon. She fidgeted anxiously with the notebook on her lap, purposefully ignoring the older woman, wishing she would find someone else to bother.

Mrs. Fields was one of Wendy's mother's neighbors, a busybody who showed up wherever there was activity, but with little to contribute herself. Wendy had taken a seat beside her because the woman had seen her come in, and to sit elsewhere would have been rude. She doubtless would have heard about it from her mother on her next visit. It might have been worth it, though. Mrs. Fields was not someone Wendy had time or patience for. While the older woman was probably here just to socialize and gossip, Wendy was all business. She opened her notebook and pretended to read it until Mrs. Fields began conversing with someone else.

Reprieved, Wendy slid the notebook under her chair, looked up, and saw a genuinely welcome face entering the room. She stood up and waved. Her friend Rich saw her and came over to take the seat to her right. Wendy immediately felt a little better. Calm, friendly, and insightful, Rich was the implicit leader of the little group that had formed from Catoctin's Ancient Studies program. He was probably the smartest, most confident person she knew, and she drew strength from his presence.

As the only black person in the room, Rich stood out from the crowd. A little distressingly, but not surprisingly, she noticed the seat to his right remained vacant while more residents of McGahey shuffled in. The town was small, rustic, and overwhelmingly white. Although the people were generally nice, it was a far cry from the cosmopolitan atmosphere of the big cities. Nevertheless, Rich did not seem bothered. To be fair, Rich seldom seemed bothered about anything. Still, she was relieved when a white-haired older gentleman finally took the empty chair beside him.

They were there for a town hall meeting. Representative King liked to meet with his constituents a few times each year, and usually timed it to correspond with newsworthy events so he could take the pulse of the communities he represented. It was one of the things Wendy liked about him, and one of the reasons she had volunteered to work on his last reelection campaign. Normally, she attended these events enthusiastically, but tonight's town hall was about gun control, so it was less with enthusiasm and more a sense of purpose that she was here. This was a topic in which Wendy was quite emotionally invested, and not only because of last month's school shooting in Iowa.

She had a second reason for coming, however. With graduation on the horizon, she was beginning to worry about finding a job. Because she had little faith in her history degree to get her one, she was coming around to the idea that she might turn her volunteer work into a full-time position. She was aware that King kept a permanent small office running in Frederick. She knew it functioned as the brain trust during campaign season, but had little idea what it did the rest of the time. She did not know whether her skills and background could serve any use in that office, so she was hoping to use today's event as an opportunity to impress the Congressman.

Bob King represented Maryland's Eighth District. It was traditionally a rural, conservative district, but a decade earlier the growth of Frederick turned the demographic tide. King was a Democrat, and if he sometimes took more moderate or even conservative positions on issues than she would have preferred, she presumed it was to appease his mixed constituency.

The turnout today was good, as Wendy had expected. The timing of this event was scheduled to coincide with the completion of local church services. The auditorium, inside a middle school, was within walking distance of the church—in a town the size of McGahey, everything was within walking distance of everything else—so many of the worshipers had simply grabbed a quick bite for lunch before migrating to this gathering.

At one on the dot the representative was introduced to a pleasant round of applause. "Thank you, McGahey," he told them, being careful to pronounce the 'h' in the town's name with the hard 'k' sound that the locals used. He followed with the briefest of opening statements, then opened the floor up to the crowd. "I'll do my best to answer any questions you might have, but this is really more about you than me. I'd like to hear what you all think."

For Wendy the next hour was a combination of head nodding and shaking, of alternating agreement and consternation. The mood of this crowd was evenly mixed. Many of them felt, as she did, that guns were a public hazard, while others still clung to ideas that she believed were better suited to the nineteenth century. Each time an argument was made against gun control, Wendy thought of a rebuttal, then waited to see if anyone else would make it, prepared to jump in herself if no one did. The discussion was generated more by emotion than critical thinking, most of the opinions little more than stale, rehashed slogans.

"We don't need more laws, we should worry more about enforcing the laws already on the books."

"Ninety percent of Americans are in favor of universal background checks."

"The only thing that stops a bad guy with a gun is a good guy with a gun."

"The NRA is more interested in selling guns than saving lives."

Things became slightly more interesting when there was discussion of how other countries handled gun control. Most European states have much stricter laws and correspondingly fewer gun deaths, evidence of direct proportionality between firearms and violence. A few exceptions, such as Switzerland, seemed to prove the counterpoint, that gun proliferation is what led to fewer crimes. The complicating fact was that Switzerland had nearly universal military conscription, something that would be completely unpalatable in the United States. There was some contention about Israel, with some people proclaiming it a gun-lover's paradise and others arguing that it is actually stricter than America.

The argument shifted to the realm of whether citizens had any need for guns at all. When the deterrence of crime was mentioned, even Mrs. Fields got in on it. "That's what policemen are for," she offered. "We should leave enforcement to the people who are trained for it." Wendy silently approved, pleased at the unlikely ally.

The arguing went on.

"A gun registry will reduce the likelihood of guns getting into the hands of criminals."

"The only purpose for a gun registry is so they can take our guns away."

The crowd debated the Constitution. It never ceased to amaze her, for all the attention it received, how little people actually knew about their country's foundational document, and how much less they understood it. Some people thought that a gun registry would somehow shred the Constitution. A girl that Wendy recognized from the college spoke up in response. "No, it says you can have a gun in order to form a well-regulated militia." She asked what part of a registry conflicted with 'well-regulated.'

This led to a nasty retort. "I don't need some little schoolgirl to teach me the Constitution." A bit of inane bickering ensued. Wendy tuned out and allowed her mind to wander. Bob King was nodding along with each speaker, but she imagined he was as bored as she. There was nothing groundbreaking being said here. The only real take-away so far was that this district was as mixed on the issue as the country at large. McGahey was their own local microcosm of America.

"Guns don't kill people, people kill people," said a tall man several rows behind her.

Wendy squirmed in her seat. She wished she had been tuned out for that one, too. She felt tremendous revulsion at this expression and its deceptive assignment of blame. It unjustly absolved people—like the speaker—who were responsible for the proliferation of deadly weaponry, and placed guilt solely on the perpetrator of the act. But nothing was ever that simple. It was like blaming the river for a collapsed bridge. The engineer played a role, since he designed it. The suppliers played a role if they used substandard materials. The government played a role, since they failed to inspect it adequately. The public played a role, since they voted for the people who prioritized cutting taxes ahead of funding the necessary maintenance.

This man felt perfectly fine about putting weapons in the hands of people who should not have them. And when the inevitable accident occurred, this man would shrug his shoulders and claim that he played no part.

Wendy was working herself up. She listened for a rebuttal, but the next person to speak went back into the same old rhetoric she had heard half a dozen times already. To Wendy, it seemed that the topic of conversation was shifting away, allowing an unchallenged air to linger on what the man had said. If no one else was going to address it, she would do it herself.

She stood up and impatiently waited her turn to speak. She did not have to wait long. Representative King noticed her with a nod of the head and pointed to her next, without using her name or otherwise indicating that he knew her.

"I'd like to address the point the gentleman made a minute ago," she said. "That guns don't kill people, people kill people. Let me explain all the ways that is wrong."

She dove right into it. She spoke of the role of people like those in the room. She used the analogy of the bridge. She gave examples of people from all segments of society who became involved in gun deaths more through the fault of gun availability than their own agency. The husband who drinks and gets angry. The woman who has never fired the gun in her purse. The child who emulates what he sees on TV. All of them could kill with a gun, and each of them was partly to blame. Partly, but not entirely.

Wendy was a good speaker and she knew it. She often felt the jitters beforehand, but they disappeared once she got going. Her mind moved at the same fluid speed as her words, not too far ahead and confusing her thoughts, not falling behind to cause pauses and stutters. The message flowed in an easy cadence that conveyed confidence, often more valuable in swaying a crowd than was any actual insight.

But she did not want to come across as pedantic or pretentious, so she did not insult the man directly or waste time repeating herself. She felt a natural break point to her thoughts and cut her speech short there, although she could have continued for longer. Then she nodded to the Congressman and sat back down. His expression revealed no indication of what he thought about her oration, but she imagined that was gamesmanship on his part. She was pleased with what she had said and how she had said it, and assumed he would be as well. As Wendy sat back down, Mrs. Fields patted her shoulder and flashed a reassuring smile.

For a moment, she heard mumblings in the audience, but no one seemed to want to directly challenge her statements. She took that as a good sign. An even better one was when Rich stood up. "If I may, I'd like to make a comment," he said. He looked at King, who nodded.

Wendy smiled. *I wonder if he thought of a way to reinforce what I said?* She had seen it happen before. Rich was excellent at that sort of thing.

"As you can tell by my accent, I'm not from around here. I grew up in England. I've been in the U.S. for six years now, and although I don't yet have a vote I believe strongly in being involved with the community. As most of you probably know, most civilians do not have guns in England. Compared to America, the English are rather more dependent on authorities for many things, including crime prevention. Americans tend to be much more self-reliant.

"This is one of the things I most admire about the U.S. From a practical standpoint, it makes sense for rural communities to rely on themselves simply because police cannot be everywhere at once and take too long to respond from a distance. But I believe it goes well beyond the practical. In my opinion, the self-reliance of Americans makes for a much healthier society than what we have in England.

"I'm not suggesting there shouldn't be some gun control. If it makes sense to have universal background checks, then by all means do that. It might help. I don't see how it could hurt, provided it can be done cost-effectively. If guns need to be registered, do that, too. But it appears that some people think those things will solve the problem of gun violence. They won't. There is no point of delicate balance between gun control and gun ownership where crime and accidental deaths drop to zero. To get there you would need to ban guns completely, which is something no one wants...because it would fundamentally change what it means to be American."

Wendy's smile was long gone by this point. She was not pleased with her friend, and did not look at him as he thanked the audience and sat back down. Maybe she was being a little irrational. He was entitled to his own opinion. Yet she had assumed, given his background, that he was as liberal as they came. Plus her hopes had been raised when he stood up, making his little speech that much more disappointing.

She tried not to be angry with him. Rich did not understand how strongly she felt about the issue. Her personal connection. Her little brother and a loaded gun in their parents' room. The accident. That was something she did not talk about. Only one other person at Catoctin knew, and she intended to keep it that way. But without that knowledge, how could Rich understand her?

"Well, we've run a little over our time, so I believe I'm going to have to leave it there," said Representative King. "But I want to thank everyone for coming and sharing their thoughts."

The noise in the room increased. Some people got up and began to file out, while others congregated around the room in small groups. Wendy gathered her notebook from under the chair, stood up, and pulled out her cell phone. One quick glance told her she missed a call. Checking it would give her a convenient excuse to ignore Rich. Her thumb was poised above the button when a voice stopped her.

"Wendy?"

She looked up to see the smiling face of the Representative.

"Mr. King," she replied.

"Bob," he told her. "I wanted to let you know I was impressed by how well you expressed yourself. You're quite articulate."

"Thank you," she replied. And she meant it. She had really needed that. It brought back to the forefront her primary reason for being here today. And on that note, she suddenly realized what an opportunity this was. Presuming he was being genuine and not just polite, perhaps she could get him to intervene directly in the hiring process. "May I ask you something?"

"Of course."

"I will be graduating in a few months," she told him. She paused for a moment, unsure whether to come right out with it or gradually build up to the request.

"I'd be glad to give you a reference," he said, detecting her hesitation and taking a guess at her intent.

"Thank you, that's very nice. But I was actually wondering whether I might continue working for your staff in Frederick...in a more permanent capacity."

"I see. Oh." He stoked his chin for a moment, and she felt a twinge of panic that she had somehow overplayed her hand. "Well, I have an office manager who is responsible for hiring decisions. I wouldn't want to step on her toes. I'm also not sure whether we have any open positions."

Wendy's hopes began to deflate.

"But I tell you what," he continued. "I'm going to be talking to her...tomorrow, I believe...I'll have a word with her about it. Why don't you call the office later this week and ask about potential openings then? In the meantime, my offer to be a reference still stands, should you decide to use it."

His engaging smile conveyed nothing but goodwill, and Wendy smiled back even as she silently chastised herself for getting too hopeful. Of course she would need to go through the normal process. What had she thought? That he would hire her on the spot?

No sooner had the rep excused himself to greet some other constituents than Wendy became aware of someone hovering beside her. She turned and saw Rich. He had not left yet. He was clearly waiting for her. He looked down on her, his face radiating concern. He had handsome, expressive features that she easily could have fallen for, if she had not known he was gay.

Wendy sighed. She had not had time to organize her thoughts, and was unsure just what level of low-key hostility to adopt.

Always forthright, Rich challenged her politely but directly. "Wendy, you're angry at me. I'd like to know why," he said in his typically calm tone.

She shook her head. "No, I'm not."

He just stood there, waiting. She did not want to let him off easy, but neither did she wish to fully explain why she was so annoyed. She decided to use a word that her mother used to use on her, one that was measured yet could sting like a barb.

"Rich, I'm not angry. I'm just disappointed in you," she told him.

His brow furrowed, and she felt a little better at seeing him affected. For a moment he seemed to struggle for a response, and she felt a perverse satisfaction at knocking him out of his unflappable demeanor. A part of her also felt guilty for feeling that way. Now she was not only disappointed in him, she was disappointed in herself.

Her cell phone beeped in her hand, and she glanced at it.

"Rich, it's my mother. I need to take this."

"Of course."

She turned away and pressed a button on the phone. "Yes, Mom?"

She began heading toward the exit. She would be able to hear better outside.

"Hi, Sweetie." The voice of her mother was pleasant, and the timing made it more so. She almost wanted to thank her mother for rescuing her from what was rapidly becoming an uncomfortable conversation.

"Did you speak to Mister King?" her mother asked.

"Yes, he was very nice about it."

"Did he offer you a job?"

"No, Mom...it doesn't work like that. I need to interview with his campaign manager. But he seems to like me well enough to put in a good word."

"Well, of course he would do that. You're very likable. I'm sure they'll find something for you, but I'll add to it my prayers."

Her mother's talk of divine intervention always made Wendy a little uncomfortable. It was not that she did not believe in God—she did, in fact—she simply believed that God had bigger fish to fry than helping her find a job. Her mother, on the other hand, seemed to believe that prayers were a sort of wish list. If God ever really did fulfill a wish, Wendy wanted to save it for something really big.

"Are you coming over later today?" her mother asked.

"I wasn't going to. I have...a lot to do before classes resume tomorrow."

Lately Wendy had been hesitant to go over to her mother's small apartment. The visits were exhausting. They always began with her saying she could not stay long, and they always ended hours later with a stomach full of home cooking and a laundry list of worries.

"I understand. Don't worry, it's not important."

Wendy recognized the disappointment in her mother's voice. "Do you need something, Mom?"

"No, I'm fine... Well, I need to get a prescription filled, but I can do it myself."

Wendy sighed. McGahey had a small drugstore, but it was mainly for over-the-counter merchandise. They could fill some of the common prescriptions, but they simply lacked the inventory to satisfy any but the most basic requests. The nearest real pharmacy was in

Frederick, so that was where her mother generally had hers filled. It would mean almost an hour round-trip for Wendy, but she really did not have anything scheduled for the afternoon anyway.

"Did you phone it in to the pharmacy yet, Mom?"

"They said I didn't have to any more. They did something on the computer. It's an amazing age we—"

"Okay, Mom. I'll drive down to Frederick and pick it up for you. Is there anything else you need while I'm there?"

"Oh, thank you. No, nothing else. Well, I could use some more aspirins. And I'm almost out of cough syrup."

"All right, Mom. I'll pick some more up. I'll bring it by later this afternoon."

"Thanks, Sweetie. Don't rush."

Only partially listening now, Wendy started walking toward her Toyota. Recently her mother was complaining about her health much more than usual. This week she was fighting bronchitis. Wendy was not so much worried about any actual illness, but she did worry about the older woman's increasingly frequent cries for attention. Wendy's father had died two years earlier, and her mother had never attempted to fill the vacuum with new friends. There were neighbors like Mrs. Fields who sometimes stopped by, but Wendy felt like she was really the only important person remaining in Miriam Weald's universe. When she enrolled at Catoctin, her mother had moved to McGahey to be close to her last remaining family member. Whatever friends she had back in Providence were out of the picture now. For a time Wendy's ex-boyfriend had been there to help shoulder the responsibility, and he had seemed to actually enjoy their visits, even going so far as to bring treats for Truman. Ever since their breakup, however, she always came and went alone. And although her mother's spirits always seemed high, especially considering what she had been through in her life, Wendy often made excuses not to visit. The trips never failed to make her feel a little sad.

She realized she had lost track of what her mother had been saying.

"Mom, you can finish telling me about it when I get there."

"Oh, I was just rambling again. I guess that's all for now. Well, I did
want to thank you again for the flowers you brought last time. They
make the kitchen look just grand. Well, they did until Truman got to
them. That little rascal managed to knock them off the table. Soil
everywhere. Took me all morning to clean it up."

"Mom, you need to teach that cat some boundaries."

"Oh, I do. He just likes to ignore them."

"Mom, I'm getting into the car now, so I need to hang up. Love
you."

"Love you, too, Sweetie."

Rich rented half a house not far from the middle school where the
town hall meeting had been held. The weather was pleasant and he
still had a few hours before the game, so he covered the distance in a
leisurely walk. It gave him a few minutes to think about what Wendy
had said. He hoped his face had not betrayed just how much her
words had stung. Her annoyance perplexed and distressed him, and
he knew it would gnaw at the tendermost fragments of his ego until
he figured it out.

He prided himself on being coolly rational. The ironic thing was
that he was an extremely emotional person. As a child, his emotions
had often gotten the better of him, until one day his logical mind
caught up and decided that it would reign supreme. Ever since then,
Rich wore a mask of stoicism like a suit of armor. It hid his inner
conflict and gave him the reputation as a reliable decision maker,
which was the one attribute he prided himself on the most.

The problem was that a constant battle raged within. He was
human, after all, and humans were nothing if not emotional. He had
tremendous respect for his friends, including Wendy, and he liked to
think he had earned their respect in kind. So it bothered him to be
told that he let her down. It was also confusing, because he did not
fully understand her reaction. Demographically—being gay, black,
and English—he was about as liberal as they come, so he and Wendy

tended to see eye-to-eye on most political topics. But they had disagreed before without her taking it so personally. He instinctively knew that there must be something more to it.

As he rounded the last corner and turned onto his block, Rich saw a man washing his car with a sponge and soapy water, a hose stretched from the side of the brick building across the small front yard to the street. As Rich approached, the man looked up and their eyes met briefly. Then the man looked back down, pretending not to have seen him.

Rich was used to it. He had long since resolved to be civil. "Hi, Jim," he said as he passed.

There was a grunt in response but his neighbor did not look up. Rich walked by and up to his own front door. A second later he heard the spray of the hose. Water ricocheted off the side of the car about halfway up the short walkway Rich had just taken. He was not sure whether Jim was deliberately trying to get him wet, but he *was* sure there would not have been an apology if it had happened.

Rich had lived here since he started postgraduate studies at Catoctin the previous autumn. The neighbors had always been a little less than friendly around him, but initially he had simply chalked that up to being the stranger, along with the customary disdain townies felt toward college students. Still, he was from a small town not completely unlike this one. He believed things would change once he got to know them, and they him. That impression had changed a few months ago with the coming of winter.

It was not exactly the Arctic, but the snow in northern Maryland was heavier than what he was used to, and there were a few items he had not thought to bring with him to McGahey. An ice scraper for his car was one. Another was a snow shovel. He was made keenly aware of their absence the morning after the first snowfall. He had been making breakfast and glanced out the window of his kitchen to see the Swishers at work outside. Jim was shoveling the walk, his heavyset wife scraping the ice off their car. Because their homes shared this stretch of sidewalk, Rich simply assumed Jim was clearing all of it, and decided to express his thanks. He also thought of his own car and intended to borrow the scraper to clear its windshield. He sensed an opportunity to get to know his neighbors a little better, to break the ice figuratively while doing it literally.

By the time he threw on some heavier clothes and grabbed a thin coat—his only preparation for the winter—Jim's wife had finished clearing the car and returned inside. Jim was still shoveling, however, as Rich walked out.

"Good morning, neighbor."

The man nodded to him as he continued his work.

Rich was about to explain a little of his own history, moving here from England with an intermediate stop in Richmond, when he noticed the ground. The walkway to his door had not been cleared, of course, but neither was his part of the sidewalk. It was clear that his neighbor was shoveling only the portion directly in front of his own half of the building. Rich's little ten foot stretch remained covered, while to the left and right the walk was clear.

Change of plans, then. No need to thank the man for his generosity.

"Your name is Jim, correct?"

The man looked at him a moment. In his eyes Rich saw that it was not shyness that explained his neighbor's reticence. There was animosity here.

Jim nodded faintly. "And you're Rich."

"I am. I was hoping to catch your wife so I could borrow her ice scraper for my car. And would you mind if I borrowed your shovel for my part of the sidewalk? I'll pick up one from the store this afternoon, but I have class in an hour. I don't want to leave it like this." The man still had not replied or displayed any reaction at all, so Rich pressed on. "The next time it snows, I'll do the sidewalk for both of us."

Then Jim smiled. "I think you better get your own shit. You're not in England any more. And stay away from my wife, pervert—she doesn't want you touching her stuff, either. Whatever weird diseases you people have, we don't want." Some smiles convey goodwill, others spite.

That had been the longest conversation the two of them ever

shared. It had been all grunts and nods ever since. It was not the first time Rich had faced discrimination and it was certain not to be the last. He could not control the behavior of others but he could his own, so he made sure not to return Jim's ignorance in kind.

He unlocked his front door and entered the house. He was not particularly hungry, but he would need plenty of energy for the game this afternoon. He half-filled a small saucepan with water from the sink and put it on the stove top. Then he measured out enough steel cut oats to make a large bowl of oatmeal. It was one of his staples—a meal that would fuel him for hours. It would also take a while to cook, so he went up to his room to change into his uniform.

Catoctin and the other conference schools were experimenting with a split season of soccer. They played a few exhibition games in the spring and the regular season in the fall. This afternoon was the last of the exhibition matches, against the rival that Rich was most personally invested in, Bowie State. The Bulldogs finished last season with the most goals scored in the conference, while the Catoctin Bears defense had allowed the fewest. This afternoon would be Rich's toughest test since taking over as the Bears' starting goalkeeper.

The half-house was narrow, his bedroom directly above the kitchen with a bath and utility closet above what passed as a living room. The place was small, but Rich was used to that from his time growing up in England. Even after five years in America he still sometimes marveled at the size of things here—buildings, roads, vehicles, meals. He had not been to Boston or New York City yet, and heard they were more European in that respect, but thus far the scale of everything he had seen in the States put his own country to shame.

The house suited him perfectly. It was the first place in America that felt like a real home—his residence in Richmond had merely been a dorm room. So it was with a certain pride of ownership that he moved about the five tiny rooms. He had everything he needed here. In fact, the only thing he would change about it was the neighbors.

The partition between sides was not nearly thick enough, and he could hear them almost constantly. Often this meant listening— whether he wanted to or not—to Jim yelling at his wife or young daughter. The man was clearly a bully, and Rich felt sorry for the women in the household. But as long as he did not hear any violence, he considered it none of his business. If he thought he could help he might feel differently, but he knew that any involvement on his part would simply make the man angrier.

He was reminded of all this now because it was happening again. Judging from the wailing, it sounded as though Jim had yelled at his daughter until she cried. Forcing himself to pay as little attention as possible, Rich poured his oatmeal from the saucepan into a bowl, stirred in a liberal quantity of syrup for flavor, and sat down to eat at the little fold-out table that functioned as his dining area. He allowed his mind to wander ahead, past the game, to the return of classes tomorrow and the big announcement Doc Appelstein had scheduled for the afternoon. They had all received an email and a Facebook invitation, and the tone made it seem like big news. He wondered if the professor had gotten his long-anticipated job offer from Harvard. If so, Rich would have mixed feelings. He would cheer the well-deserved recognition, even though he would miss the man who had been both a mentor and a father figure. Although Doc was happy at Catoctin, Rich knew that his highest goal was to follow in the footsteps of his father and teach in the Ivy League.

A crash next door interrupted Rich's thoughts. More yelling. He was nearly done with the meal anyway, so he wolfed down the last few spoonfuls and placed the bowl in the sink. He would wash it later. He liked to get some peace and quiet before a game, and he clearly was not going to get it here. But there was a spot along Black Bear Branch Creek that never failed to calm him, and he had time to drive to campus and walk there before heading to the football field.

A few feet below his perch, the creek peacefully trickled over smooth black rocks, the sound of perpetual percolating enveloping and soothing his troubled mind. Rich was annoyed at himself for having carelessly upset his friend. Upon further reflection, her reaction made sense. It was not simply that they had disagreed, it was that he did it publicly. Right in front of the congressman for whom she used to campaign. Even so, Rich was certain there was more to it than that. He was not surprised by her anger, but he was surprised by its intensity. He had seen the hostility in her expression even before she said she was disappointed in him. He always thought of her—as with most everyone he met—as an open book. It unsettled his confidence each time he rediscovered that people are more complex than he gave them credit for. Now he felt that he was paying the price of complacency.

At the same time, he reminded himself to be thankful for these learning opportunities. He was only twenty-five, and neither believed he had the whole world figured out nor wanted to. Life was a constant learning experience, and as far as he was concerned that was as it should be. He understood that he was blessed with intelligence, and never wanted it to go to his head. For better or worse, any time it started to, some incident like the one today would bring him back down to earth. Humility was not owned but leased, and it seemed one never stopped paying rent.

He looked forward to his next meeting with Wendy. They would see each other at the announcement tomorrow. It was possible that whatever friction there was between them would have faded by then, that she would wear her winning smile and act as though nothing had happened. She would not apologize, of course—that was simply not her way. But even if the friction lingered, he felt confident that they could work it out with a little determined effort on his part.

It would bother him until then, so he was thankful for the upcoming distraction. Not unlike the serenity of this creek, there was always catharsis in the vigor of sport.

Rich and his teammates were all smiles and laughs as they went through their ritual pre-game warm ups. They had their work cut out for them today. Bowie State fielded some of the conference's best players, but because this match was only an exhibition it evoked much less of the usual solemnity and stress. Not that any of them were not taking it seriously. The spirit of competition was strong at this level of athletics, and the chance to prove their skill against a quality opponent motivated each one of them.

Of course, Rich had particular incentive to play well today, even before one of the other guys came in with an announcement that electrified them all. "DC United has a pro scout here," he told the team, speaking over his shoulder while dialing out his locker combination—an effort toward nonchalance that belied the significance of the words. The news was a bit of a bombshell, for the scouts normally keyed on the bigger programs such as the Universities of Maryland and Virginia. But it was not unheard of. Just as in soccer's seasonal cousin, American football, the small schools would get one or two chances a year to showcase themselves to scouts looking for diamonds in the rough.

They all knew the scout would be there to see Tre'Andre Bryant, Bowie's star striker and last season's conference scoring leader. It was Tre'Andre who dominated Rich's thoughts and motivated him to play with extra intensity in this match. One could measure respect based on performance against the best, and Rich hoped to earn a little today. He had all the attributes of the best goalkeepers—length, reflexes, athleticism. Perhaps he could catch the eye of the onlookers with an amazing save or two. It was not uncommon for pro careers to be born from one timely demonstration.

Warmups were held on the practice field beside the playing field, separated by a few sets of sparsely filled bleachers. A few fans were still shuffling in, but between the absence of students for spring break and the relative unimportance of this match, they all knew turnout would be low.

Coach Schneider called them together for one last strategy review. There was little chance they could compete in a shootout with Bowie's forwards, so instead they planned a collapsing defense, always keeping men between the ball and their goal, challenging the dribbler and filling the passing lanes. "No open shots on goal," the coach emphasized. With that, he scooped up his clipboard and left them alone for the last few minutes before taking the field. It was customary for the players to use the time to fire themselves up.

The best player on the team was a junior midfielder named William. His quickness and ball handling skills were elite, and he easily could have played for one of the more prominent schools in the area. However, like many of the student-athletes at Catoctin, he was primarily here for the education. That earned him Rich's respect. The two of them shared captain responsibilities for the team, which on most days meant that William would give the pre-game speech to pep them up. Today, however, was going to be different.

As they huddled, Rich caught William's attention. "Do you mind if I say a few words?"

His co-captain showed a brief expression of surprise, then smiled. "Of course not. We'd all like to hear what you think."

Rich thanked him and looked at the others. He put his own arms around the two nearest him, signaling everyone to do the same. Soon they formed a close-knit circle of twenty, a physical attachment that matched the emotional one. On a scale of importance, there is no comparison between soldiers and athletes. But in terms of affinity and communion, the bond that forms between teammates is very much like that between brothers in arms. For a few hours every day, they pushed themselves to their physical limits, driven less by a desire for personal glory than for mutual respect. The coaches always emphasized team above individual, and the players bought into it without reservation. This team had no real stars, but their chemistry as a cohesive whole made them the equal of many of the more talented squads they faced. It was a self-reinforcing cycle, for success had only brought them closer together.

Rich felt another, more personal connection to these guys. Being the gay man in a group of alpha males could be an intimidating circumstance. It had been difficult enough finding acceptance amongst his family and friends in England, and everything he saw about America had prepared him for worse. But he had been unwilling to pretend to be someone he was not for two years while he played here, and resolved to tell his teammates and coaches sooner than later.

The decision was easy, but following through had been harder. They had all been together after the very first practice, and Rich knew there would never be a better opportunity. For one of the very few times in his life, the words came out awkwardly as he cleared his throat and addressed the group.

The build-up had been so much worse than the execution. When he had finished, he was literally met by nods and shrugs. Coach Schneider stepped up and said, "Thank you for telling us, Rich, that must have been hard for you. I think I can speak for everyone here when I say that it doesn't matter. Work hard and put the team first and you'll be fine. It's if you don't do those two things that we'll have a problem." The others nodded agreement.

Of course, those had merely been words, and Rich waited to see if their behaviors matched. He was determined not to give them any reason to doubt him, so he worked as hard as they asked and let his play on the field speak for itself. By the end of that first season, a curious thing was happening. He went from being one of the guys to being looked to as a leader. He was already used to it in his academic life, but this was the first time it had happened in athletics as well. Even when he began a relationship with a player from another team, his sexuality never seemed to have any effect on his teammates. Except indirectly, when they teased him for consorting with the enemy.

Now the whole memory raced through his mind in a flash, and Rich's heart caught in his throat for a second. He was not prone to showing emotions, but that did not mean he did not feel them. At times like this he felt as close to them as he had to anyone in his life. That included his family, and especially his brother Marvin. In some ways these guys were more his brothers than Marvin had ever been.

They were all leaning in, looking at him expectantly. Moments such as this used to elicit a touch of stage fright, particularly when he had first switched countries and felt that his speech stood out as much as his orientation. In the intervening years, however, he had adopted most American mannerisms, if not the accent, and become far more comfortable in his own skin.

"Guys, I don't usually wear my heart on my sleeve, but I think you all know this game means something special to me. I want to ask a favor of you all. Forget about the scout watching the game. Forget that this is just an exhibition. Forget that Bowie State has stars and we don't. Forget that everyone expects us to lose. We want to be known as a team that plays harder than everyone else. Make them earn every yard. No pass goes uncontested. If you care about me, you'll leave it all on the field today. We'll measure our success today by effort, not goals. Win or lose, that team is going home today feeling as though they were in a real punch-up. All hands in. Bears on three. One, two, three—"

"Bears!" Their hands flew up, and the circle broke. A few teammates patted him on the back.

As the starters trotted out to their positions, Rich was flanked by his fullbacks, Joey and Chad. "I hope we don't let you down, man," said Joey. Chad nodded.

"You guys won't let me down," Rich quickly responded. This was an unintended side effect of his speech. He had been so worried about sounding daft that he had forgotten how much his defenders looked up to him. They all felt discouraged enough after a loss, he did not want them feeling any worse on his account. *I should have thought of that before I opened my damn mouth.*

The game played out true to form as a defensive battle. With Catoctin committed to four defenders against Bowie State's three forwards, Rich rarely faced a credible threat. Of course, that same game plan prevented any real threats of their own, as the hoped-for counterattack never materialized. The result was not just a scoreless game at halftime, but one that appeared likely to remain scoreless to the final whistle. The already mellow crowd seemed on the verge of falling asleep.

Still, the tempo played into Catoctin's hands. The longer Bowie

State went without scoring, the more confidence Rich and his teammates felt. The game's few observers could sense the momentum slowly tipping toward the home team. The opposing sideline must have felt it, too, for they put renewed energy into the attack from the instant the second half kicked off. Catoctin was pushed back on their heels, but Joey and Chad each continued to make play after play to keep the heat off Rich, who found himself needing only to make a few trivial saves. As Bowie State's energy abated so did their intensity, and the game slowed back down to a sustainable rhythm.

Sensing that their opponents had tired themselves, Coach Schneider called in some new instructions to his players. The midfielders were directed to press farther forward when given the opportunity, exchanging a little defense for a little more offense. If the team could put some pressure on the opposition for a change, the momentum swing could be completed. To the casual observer, the shift was subtle, but the impact on the game was enormous.

Bowie State seemed about to take advantage when a failed steal attempt at midfield allowed them a two-on-two break. Tre'Andre brought the ball up the field to Rich's left, his speed threatening to leave Chad a step behind. Desperate, Chad made a sliding attempt to steal the ball. Tre'Andre anticipated the move and crossed the ball to the other attacker, who made a beautiful trap with his left foot, sidestepped Joey's interception attempt, and used his right foot to fire a rocket toward the left corner of the goal.

Rich flung himself toward the corner, stretching his long frame to its limit. He managed to get a few fingers of his hand on the ball. It was redirected just enough to deflect off the goalpost and back in his direction. Never touching the ground, the carom of the ball was about to take it just over his body as he crashed to the ground, but Rich managed to get his left hand up to stop it even as his right helped ease his landing. Then he scrambled after the ball before it could roll too far away. He was able to scoop it up a split-second before Tre'Andre could get there to tap it in.

No sooner had he secured the ball than Rich saw his own midfielder, William, streaking into an open space on the right. Rich jumped over a player on the ground, took a few steps to get some room to maneuver, then expertly placed a drop-kick ahead to where William could catch up to it. One of Bowie State's fullbacks raced against him, but William beat him to the ball, leaped over the man's attempt at a sliding tackle, and broke into the clear where he was one-on-one against the opposing goalkeeper. Behind him, most members of both teams sprinted to catch up to the action. The crowd was reacting as well, yelling and cheering with spontaneous fervor.

Rich felt that jolt of exhilaration that athletes live for. Fans feel it, too, when they realize their favorite team is about to win a championship. There was the briefest flicker of sympathy for the players of the other team, one of them in particular, but that sensation was overwhelmed by the thrill of victory. His teammates felt it, as well, and he saw a few of them jumping in anticipation and shouting encouragements.

These moments are when soccer is at its best. In no other sport does so much excitement stem from the mere chance of a score. Often, the excitement fades in a chorus of disappointed cries. Such was the case now. William telegraphed his shot, the opposing goalkeeper made a brilliant save, and optimism instantly turned to dejection. The same players who had jumped one minute were caught flat-footed the next as play rushed back toward and beyond them. The game's long, steady buildup of momentum deflated in an instant. Before the sequence of events had fully registered in his mind, Rich saw Tre'Andre bursting away from the pack in midfield, coming right toward him like an arrow in flight. He had only one tired defender left to beat. With a halfhearted lunge, Joey stuck one foot out as he sped by, but their opponent sidestepped and dribbled past without losing speed.

Rich snapped out of it, unwilling to concede a goal after coming so close to scoring one. His instincts took over, his knees flexing, his arms stretched out to present the largest possible obstacle. He focused on reading Tre'Andre's hips and stepped forward a few paces to shut down the shooter's angles. At the last instant Tre'Andre's hips pivoted, and Rich sprang left as the shot was unleashed.

One thing that made Tre'Andre a prolific scorer was the ability to use his body movement to feint one way and shoot in another. If the kick had been a rocket off the instep the way everyone expected, the ball would have collided with Rich's outstretched arms. Instead, Tre'Andre eschewed power for finesse, pushing the ball with tempered velocity right beneath Rich's legs. The slow pace of the ball only intensified the drama for a few seconds as it rolled over the line and into the back of the net.

From the ground, Rich looked back and watched the ball go in with pained disbelief. Just like that, they were down a goal and staring at defeat. The missed opportunity to score themselves made the pill that much harder to swallow. It showed in the body language of his entire team, who looked dejected even as their opponents rejoiced. For the next few minutes, Tre'Andre was hugged and tackled by his teammates in a celebration that contrasted sharply with the tepid applause of the onlookers.

To Rich's way of thinking, leadership required sometimes stepping out of oneself for the good of the team. He picked himself off the field, clapped his hands together, and did his best to rally the troops. He waved his teammates closer. Most of them came, but a few seemed unable to pick themselves off the grass where they had collapsed. Rich could not worry about them now, he simply had to work with the ones who still possessed a modicum of spirit. "Tip your caps to them, they made a good play there. But it's only one goal. We have ten minutes to get it back. Remember that you promised to leave it all on the field today. Bears on three..."

Bowie State was back on the field and the referees were positioning the ball for the kickoff as his teammates went jogging to their places. Those who had not joined the impromptu huddle simply picked themselves up and walked to their spots. Rich felt a stab of disappointment when he saw that Joey was one of them, his long hair soaked with sweat and plastered to his neck and cheeks. The fullback glanced once at Rich then looked away, as though embarrassed. Rich wanted to say something encouraging, but play had resumed and Bowie State was already pressing forward again, buoyed with newfound energy. Joey charged back into the action and made a nice play to dispossess an attacker of the ball and clear it ahead.

It appeared to Rich that the team had taken his words to heart, for he rarely saw as much hustle from them as they showed in the few minutes that remained. But the comeback was not to be, as he had expected. When the final whistle sounded, it came as something of a relief. Everyone was already running on fumes.

As they dejectedly walked off the field, he gave it one last try. "Don't hang your heads, guys. They came here expecting an easy win, and they're going home knowing they barely escaped. It's not as good as a win, but it's something we should be proud of."

As always when he spoke, he read the faces of the guys around him. Some of them nodded, and one or two actually seemed to cheer up. Some clearly did not, but you could not expect to influence everyone equally. If his words helped a few of them, he would consider that a success.

Coach Schneider called them over for a quick roundup. He clapped his hands aggressively, smacked a few on them on the back, and grunted out some encouragements.

"Guys, I'm proud of you. We could have drawn with them if I hadn't made that last shift. This loss is on me, not you. We got a lot better today, and we'll get these guys next time. All right, hit the showers. See you Tuesday."

Some of the guys headed straight for the dorms, but Rich joined most of the others who showered and changed in the locker room. He was hoping for a chance to talk to Joey, to judge whether he needed a pat on the back. Until he could gauge how upset his teammate was, it felt like unfinished business. Rich was a firm believer in not allowing potential problems to fester. As they headed up the slope to the gymnasium, however, Joey peeled away from the group to engage a few of the spectators, presumably his friends, in conversation. Rich went ahead with the others, assuming he would get another opportunity later.

Joey still had not rejoined them by the time Rich finished

showering and dressing. He was in no hurry to go home, however, and lingered a few more minutes just in case.

Unfortunately, sitting alone after a tough loss was conducive to negative thoughts. Wendy. His neighbors. The goal.

An alarm sounded in his mind. As he matured, Rich had picked up the habit of not dwelling on the negative. Between the rejection of his family and his own inner turmoil, negativity would have consumed his childhood if he had not developed a defense mechanism. He would make sure to deal with Joey the next time he saw him, just as he would with Wendy. Until then, he would find something more positive to occupy his attention. Classes were resuming tomorrow and he had plenty of work he could be doing, but schoolwork was not exactly the thing to distract his mind the way he needed. What he was really in the mood for was a drink or two with friends. He thought about calling Halfus or Kevin. Those guys were usually up for an hour of relaxation and good conversation. Or maybe he would go ahead and try Wendy, to repair the damage he had done earlier in the day...

"Hey, handsome." The voice brought him back to the here and now. He looked over.

This was a surprise. His boyfriend was standing at the entrance, gym bag in hand, grinning like a fool.

"Tre'Andre, what are you doing here?" Rich stood up.

"Checking on you. You look upset."

"I'm not upset."

Tre'Andre's expression changed. *Don't give me that*, it evinced. "Come on, man. I know you don't like to show it, but I'd like to think I know you well enough by now—"

"Shouldn't you be on a bus back to Bowie?"

"I asked coach if I could drive separate. I thought I'd surprise you. Maybe stay the night."

Rich hesitated. On the one hand, he had just been hoping for some good company tonight. No one fit the bill better than Tre'Andre. On the other hand, the loss still stung. Rich liked to be master of his emotions, but he was human.

"I don't know about that. I've got a lot of work to do. Classes resuming tomorrow..." He crossed his arms over his chest. "And you probably shouldn't be in the opposing team's locker room. If coach came in and saw you—"

"He wouldn't care," replied Tre'Andre with a smile.

"He's right," said a voice. Joey finally walked into the room. His hair had dried but remained caked to his skin. It looked terribly uncomfortable, and Rich did not know how he could stand it. "It's just an exhibition game."

Joey took a seat at his locker, opened it, and pulled off his shirt. He appeared unperturbed about the enemy—the deliverer of defeat—standing here. Probably, they had all seen Tre'Andre with Rich often enough by now that he had an unofficial guest pass.

Rich felt Tre'Andre's gaze, challenging him, an unspoken query to clear the air between them. One of the things that drew Rich to him was that they shared the philosophy to attack problems head-on. That they were both confident, assertive men often caused friction in their relationship, but thus far the very same dynamic had forced them to smooth things over before resentment had time to build. It did so again.

Rich was unhappy with his boyfriend, although he had done nothing wrong. Scoring goals was what he did. And he had cared enough to search Rich out, to make sure he was all right. His motives were good, his priorities in a healthy order. It occurred to Rich that it was a little silly to begrudge others for not putting him ahead of themselves. Silly and illogical, but completely understandable. Suddenly he began to understand Wendy a little bit more. *Never stop learning.* Rich appreciated how these people challenged him, taught him, made him a better person. Since coming to Catoctin, the circles he moved in—his friends and his teammates—had given him everything he missed back home.

Rich dropped his arms and nodded. "You're right. It's been a long day. Let's get a drink. I was thinking of calling the guys to see if they wanted..." He left the sentence unfinished. It occurred to him he did not know whether Tre'Andre preferred to be alone or not.

"Okay with me," his boyfriend replied. "You want to invite him, too?" He jerked his head toward Joey.

Joey had finished showering and now wore a towel around his waist. He did not appear to be listening. He was standing at his locker, from which he retrieved a pair of black trousers, a two-tone shirt, and dress shoes. The outfit was less casual than Joey's typical street clothes, which Rich took to mean that he already had plans.

Still, in order to be sociable, Rich decided to ask. "Hey, Joey," he called. "Want to come out with us tonight?"

Rich could immediately tell from his teammate's expression that he had overstepped. He might be a leader on the soccer pitch, but that was the extent of it. His teammates may not hold his sexuality against him, but that did not mean he was really one of them.

"No offense, Rich, but when we hit the bars, it's usually to pick up girls." Joey was not being deliberately malicious, he was just pointing out facts the way he saw them. Rich would not be interested in girls, so he would be uncomfortable. Or make them uncomfortable. It was the story of his life writ large.

"Yes, of course," Rich replied reflexively. "No worries, mate." It sounded more apologetic than he intended.

Joey had finished pulling on his clothes. As he tied the shoelaces, he gave them a quick farewell.

The two of them watched him go. When the locker room door swung closed behind him, Tre'Andre turned back to Rich. "Hey, fuck him, man."

Rich shook his head. He was not mad. In a way, he appreciated the irony. He had been concerned about Joey's feelings, and instead had gotten his own hurt. As with Wendy, he would not let it get him down. It was always good to be reminded of the general inconstancy of people. Some circles were tighter than others.

3
ANNOUNCEMENTS

THE TEMPLE of Angkor Wat is the largest religious monument in the world. Like the Hagia Sofia and Mezquita de Córdoba, Cambodia's most famous structure has experienced a spiritual conversion—once Hindu, it is now Buddhist. Built in the twelfth century, Angkor Wat is the foremost of many temples populating the province. Some of the ruins date as far back as the ninth century, when across the world Charlemagne ruled a continent and the Golden Age of Islam was fast approaching. The towers and statues of Angkor have witnessed the relentless progress of man for a thousand chaotic years, but now their days are numbered. Thieves carry away priceless artifacts by the hundreds. Vandals ravage beauty for the sake of hatred and spite. Behind the resurgent overgrowth of vine and leaf in the nether regions of Angkor one finds headless carvings and empty pedestals, a testament to the universal truth that there is no masterpiece man can construct from his own fertile imagination and the blessings of the earth that he cannot also nihilistically destroy.

The Great Pyramid of Giza, one of the tallest, largest, most awe-inspiring buildings ever made, was constructed an almost-inconceivable four and a half thousand years ago. It is one of three grand pyramids on the site, which is also home of the quixotic Sphinx. There is an apocryphal legend that the nose of the Sphinx was shot off as target practice for Napoleon's rowdy troops during his Egyptian campaign. While almost certainly false, the fiction has a decidedly believable ring to it. In any case, Sphinx and Pyramid both lie helplessly vulnerable to a new form of the onslaught of man. For all the boundless expanses of the Saharan desert, urban sprawl from Cairo has already reached out to encompass this small plot of land. What was once a camel-borne pilgrimage from civilization is now a brief cab ride from the city center. Soon the magnificence of five millennia will become little more than an inconvenient obstacle to the relentless growth of a thriving modern city.

It is not only the grand structures that are threatened. Smaller artifacts and relics of Ancient Egypt and other early civilizations are equally at risk. Whereas Westerners are accustomed to museums possessing mechanical and electronic security measures, in many locales around the world museums are little more than open repositories akin to trash dumps. Security is typically human, and easily bribed. Corrupt officials line their own pockets and those of their kinsmen and supporters with proceeds from the sale of treasures. Where corruption is not a problem, negligence often is. A visitor to many smaller museums can, with a modicum of ingenuity, contrive to walk out with any relic diminutive enough to fit in a pocket or handbag.

But poor governance, ineffective rule of law, and relentless population growth are not the greatest threats to antiquity. That distinction belongs to mankind's unceasing propensity for conflict. When war comes to a region, one of the first and most defenseless casualties is the treasure of history. Armed conflict both exacerbates existing conditions and creates new problems all its own.

Countless sites of varying importance were destroyed in total or part during the chaos of World War II. The throne room in St. Petersburg looted by Germans. Another in Kronberg Castle looted by Americans. A Raphael masterpiece stolen during the Nazi invasion of Poland. The Allied bombing of the abbey at Monte Cassino. No side was completely free from guilt, although America should be credited for not dropping the atomic bomb on Kyoto, a Japanese city with transcendent historic and negligible military significance, which at one time topped the list of targets.

In the summer of 2012 a coup d'état in Mali sparked a vicious civil war. The resulting fighting brought a group called Ansar Dine to the historic cities of Gao and Timbuktu. Amongst other atrocities great and small committed by the fighters was the destruction of world heritage sites guilty of violating their particular deeply held religious sensibilities.

More looting and destruction characterized the U.S. invasion of Iraq in 2003. The great mosque of Samarra, so famous it is proudly depicted on Iraqi currency, was bombed by insurgents during the occupation. In Baghdad, while the Ministry of Oil was famously secured as the highest priority of the liberating invaders, museums and government buildings were looted of thousands of artifacts dating back to one of the earliest civilizations known to man. Thieves took advantage of the ensuing chaos to smuggle these relics out of the country. In the decade since, many have been located and returned, yet incalculable numbers remain missing, likely gone forever.

Mankind is quite literally losing its history. Historians and archaeologists are the warriors serving on the front lines in this entropic war against time. Theirs is a losing struggle, for unlike with the living, the erosive effects of time on history lack a process of replenishment. Their work is essential and valiant, if unappreciated and doomed.

～

Ben held in his hands the manifestation of his hopes and dreams. It had come unexpectedly, which made it all the more satisfying.

Dr. Appelstein, it has come to our attention that you recently applied for a travel grant for overseas study. While we are unable to comply with your specific request, we are pleased to inform you of an opportunity that may serve much the same function.

"Not the same," he said aloud to the empty room. "Better."

A German project team is currently conducting ongoing archaeological work at a newly established site in northern Iraq near Mosul. Visas for the student members of the current field team are expiring, and they have requested additional resources with a familiarity of Sumerian scripts. According to your grant application, your students match said criterion. Current funding is adequate for four students and associates in addition to yourself. Availability is a priority...

There was no question that he would accept the offer. Iraq was a part of the world that historians had been desperate to get back into for decades. The regime of Saddam Hussein had never been as welcoming to the academic community as it had been to certain business interests. Following the First Gulf War in the early 1990's, even that modest trickle of activity came to an end. Now it seemed things were changing for the better. It was exciting to think about how the American invasion had brought renewed opportunities.

Yet he was not without reservations. There were several serious concerns that he could not push out of his mind, even if they were overshadowed by the excitement of the news.

First of all, he would be responsible for the students he took along. It was a very serious consideration. Whereas his initial application had been for field study in the relatively comfortable confines of Israel, northern Iraq was a much different story. Since the withdrawal of American troops following the invasion, a quiet stability had settled over the ravaged country. But there was a certain tension to the peace, an expectation that trouble could brew up at a moment's notice. New to power, the Shia majority pursued a policy of repression and revenge over the emasculated Sunni minority, which were perceived as complicit benefactors of the years of Hussein's misrule. For the time being, the Shia government had the not-insignificant vocal and monetary backing of the Americans, but the easing of tension would come only with years of quiet.

Until then, there was a small measure of danger for Americans traveling in Iraq. Or nearly anywhere in the Middle East, for that matter. Kidnappings, ransoms, and even beheadings were an infrequent but terrifying occurrence. Americans were probably the most at-risk of any nationality, although the relative chances of anything happening remained quite low. Moreover, as a man with a conspicuously Jewish surname, there was the possibility that Ben made an even more appealing target than the average American.

Nevertheless, one had to put these things into perspective. The risks were not nonexistent, but they were negligible, and the benefits of the opportunity substantially outweighed them. The expedition would not only be exciting and elucidating in its own right, but it would look very impressive on his own CV and those of his students.

And it would be an adventure they would all remember for the rest of their lives. He had no doubt that his class would see it the same way.

Yet there was one more issue his class would not be aware of, a problem uniquely his own. As enthusiastic as he had been as he progressed through the letter, he was equally disconcerted by the final paragraph.

Overseeing all aspects of the expedition is Herr Doktor Adolphus Schwarzvogel of Wesel University...

He and Adolphus had been colleagues at Oxford when Ben started working on his doctorate. Colleagues was probably not the best word. Rivals was more appropriate. Ben actually remembered the first time he tried to strike up a conversation with the Swedish-German, at an orientation session for all the doctoral candidates. The man had been standoffish at best, condescending at worst—his accent and manner of speaking had made it a little difficult to interpret. Soon thereafter, Adolphus developed a reputation for being brilliant and hardworking, but also arrogant, conniving, and devilishly lucky.

Ben recalled the time that several of his fellow students were involved in a paper-writing scandal. Oxford was a prestigious, academically rigorous school. Many of its undergraduates were the scions of affluent English families. Most of the doctoral candidates, however, were not. They tended to come from the working classes of England and abroad, from which they rose through inspiration and sheer hard work. Few of those keeping up with the demanding workload had time or energy for a regular job on the side. But one thing they could do, practically in their sleep, was write with purpose and flair. It was inevitable that the two groups—wealthy, privileged underclassmen and gifted, strapped writers—would come together in an economically advantageous, if slightly nefarious, manner.

A group of his peers formed a consortium that wrote undergraduate papers for fee. The sums of money involved were never extravagant, and the group refused to get involved in final exams in any way. In that manner, they hoped to remain under the radar of the college authorities. Several of his friends became involved in the group, but Ben himself was fortunate to have resources of his own, and so avoided temptation. He first learned of the enterprise when one of his friends asked him to join. The friend had accepted an assignment that netted a worthy sum of several hundred pounds, but which had begun to interfere with his own studies. So he asked Ben the favor of taking the assignment for himself. "The Theoretical Viability of the Schlieffen Plan" was the subject of the essay, Ben recalled. "The Inherent Asininity of Doctoral Students" would have been a more appropriate title, he thought with regret.

He had not only refused the favor, he begged his friend to get out of the group. The sums involved were too trivial to risk expulsion from the school. Instead of heeding the advice, his friend asked Adolphus for the same favor. A few weeks later the doctoral students involved were quietly dismissed from their respective programs.

Somehow, Ben's own name had come up as associated with them. He remembered the time he was interrogated by the Dean and Chancellor. Dismissal from the school at that time would have ruined his life. He was so nervous he could barely form complete sentences, and cold sweat made a mess of his back and armpits. He staggered through his version of events, aware all the while of how unconvincing he sounded. *I wouldn't believe myself,* he had thought. Ultimately, it was only the admission of guilt and corroboration of his story from his friends that had saved him from banishment.

It was impossible to know for certain that Schwarzvogel had gone to the authorities, but everyone assumed it. Certainly, he had never gone on trial like the rest of them. Ben had thought it best to avoid Adolphus as much as possible after that. Surprisingly, however, the resentment seemed only to go one way. The few times they had interacted since then, Schwarzvogel had been politely respectful, bordering on familiar. It was as though the Dean's exoneration had also marked Ben as worthy of friendship and respect, as though they were partners in obedience. Nevertheless, it had been a relief to Ben when Adolphus got his final degree and left for a teaching position back on the continent. The two of them had not stayed in touch.

And now the Herr Doktor is running the show. He wondered which aspect of his capricious nature would show. Disloyal lordling, or capable director. One way or the other, he supposed he would find out soon enough.

All the stressful contemplation was beginning to take its toll. Despite his excitement at the news, Ben felt his regular afternoon headache materializing. They were consistent in frequency but not location or intensity. This one began to form in his temples, and thus far seemed tolerable. Yet he knew from past experience that they often started mild but grew into full-fledged zingers. He wished he had the willpower to ride them out, but long experience had taught him that treating them early was the best way to stop them from becoming debilitating. In the old days he would give them time, and was occasionally rewarded by their disappearance on their own. Too many times, however, his inaction had only allowed the headache to increase in magnitude. These days, with little confidence in his body's natural processes, he tended to dose himself right away.

Unfortunately, he was noticing a disturbing trend. It required more pills to have any effect. He had heard of such things amongst drug users, and the parallel was disconcerting. He sometimes wondered whether this was how addiction began, where one was not certain whether he was addicted or not and did not want to find out, since that would involve quitting. He preferred to believe that he was not abusing the painkillers. He had enough to worry about already, and the painful headaches felt real enough. Still, he made a token effort to use his pills sparingly.

He exhaled deeply and pulled open the drawer of his desk where his Vicodin sat waiting. He held the bottle in his hand, considering. In a few minutes he would be spending time with a handful of his favorite people, and they generally had a positive effect on his head. He smiled to himself just thinking of their reaction when he read this letter out to them. If ever there was a time for forbearance, this was certainly it.

He glanced at his watch. Five minutes to six. It was time to head down to the classroom where they would be waiting.

He stood and walked out of his little second-floor office. As he turned and locked the door, he became aware of someone walking down the hallway. The footsteps were moving away from him, hard clacks of heel on stone. His subconscious mind registered that they seemed to speed up just as he had exited his office, but his consciousness had not fully processed that fact as he looked to see who it was.

He reacted without thinking. "Brenda!" he called.

Her shoulders stiffened as she stopped. Then his young peer turned to face him. With the evening sun almost down, most of the corridor was cast in shadow. There was insufficient light to read her expression. She stood still, neither coming closer to engage him nor beating a hasty retreat.

"What?" she asked, with a hint of impatience.

There were signs here to be read, but as typically happened around her, his brain stopped processing information at regular speed. When a quarterback makes his first start in the pros, they talk about the game needing to slow down for him. The same expression could apply to a man who is hopelessly infatuated. The brain is constantly digesting inputs from a million sources at once. Words are the easy part of interaction, but there is also body language, facial expressions, background stimuli, and mood. Under normal circumstances, the mind has a pretty good idea how to prioritize these in order to function effectively. But like a linebacker blitz that drowns out everything else, Brenda's irritation rendered him ineffective. Even in his forties, he was a different man around a woman like this.

"I have news," he stammered. "Big news." He felt the need for something to justify stopping her.

"Ben, I have night class. Is this important?"

"I'm going to Iraq."

She said nothing at first. Then she walked toward him, stepping into one of the diagonal beams of early evening sun that checkered the hall. She wore an ivory blouse with a pattern of blue and red, the sun making the shapes on it shimmer and dance.

She scrutinized his face. "You're serious, aren't you?"

Now that he had her attention, his heart and mind at last calmed down to a manageable level. He nodded. "That's right. A research grant." He held up the letter in his right hand. "Four students plus me."

He smiled, but she did not. "I thought you were going to Israel," she said at last.

"They want us at a site in Iraq. Visas expiring for the crew there now."

"What do you mean, 'a site'?"

"A dig site. An archaeological dig."

Her brow furrowed. "You don't know anything about archaeology."

"They need us for translations and research. And we can help with some of the grunt work around the site. But the archaeology itself is in the hands of an old friend of mine from Oxford." *An old friend of mine.* He silently cursed himself. He had said it to brag about Oxford, as though that would impress her. He was disappointed in himself. He thought he had long since matured from this kind of behavior, but apparently not. Perhaps one never did.

She began to nod. "Good for you, Ben. I mean that." She paused for a moment. "But I do need to get going."

"I thought maybe you'd like to hear more about it. We could get some coffee tonight..."

Her shoulders slumped, and he registered the annoyance on her face. When she spoke, it was in a tone of tired monotony. "We've been through this. I'm with Trevor now."

She turned and continued back in the direction she had been going before he stopped her.

He stood motionless for a minute. That had not gone well. It had started out promising, but went south quickly. He rarely felt so impotent as after a brush with her.

It was not fair. She had liked him first. She started teaching at Catoctin the previous semester, and he had been the first coworker she connected with. It had started innocently. A few lunches, a few cups of coffee. He taught her the ropes. Introduced her to others. He had been comfortable with her, slightly attracted but mostly just enjoying the prestige that came from being in her company. She was pretty and ten years younger. It did not hurt knowing that several of the other professors had crushes on her.

Just before Christmas break she invited him to dinner. Looking back, he understood that that should have been the night. She almost seemed to be expecting it. They shared a bottle of wine, and he imagined that it was her way of signaling to him. His analytical mind considered, but ultimately had not wanted to risk what felt at the time like an ideal situation. In his memory now he saw her flash of disappointment when he walked her to the door of her house, only to merely kiss her cheek. But her warm, easy smile had quickly returned as they said their good nights, and he had felt good as he got back into his car. It was the last time he remembered feeling good about much of anything.

Whether he had liked her more than he understood, or that had come later, he still was not certain. What he did know now was that it had been a disastrous decision on his part. Once they returned from the break she was already dating Trevor, and her relationship with Ben quickly declined. It was not her fault, it was his own. She had continued to treat him as a close friend, but their talks together became increasingly infrequent. Soon he no longer felt the pride of his coworkers' jealousy. That may have been the first thing he missed, but it was replaced in importance by something he missed even more. Her companionship. The more desperately he tried to win back what he had lost, the more she pulled away. Now their relationship was a sad remnant of what it had been. Longing on his part, polite tolerance on hers. There was no trace of her earlier affection for him, as he was reminded each time they saw each other. Warm genuine smiles had been replaced with curt nods. In his mind's eye, he recalled when she laughed at his lame attempts at humor, swaying forward and playfully touching his elbow. The phantom sensation of memory still brought an electric charge to his skin. Now, on the few occasions when they talked, she always kept a respectable distance. He felt like an inmate talking through a glass barrier. He found himself wondering how someone could lose interest so quickly. It broke his heart, knowing what could have been, but was no longer possible.

The ache in his head was beginning to rage out of control now. He would need that Vicodin after all. He turned back to unlock his office.

As Ben finished speaking, he lowered the sheet of paper.

He was not sure whether he had really expected whoops and high-fives, but if so he was disappointed. He should have realized this was not a whooping crowd.

What they did instead was wait quietly and patiently for him to finish—then applaud. The clapping of six respectable young adults never sounded so loud and inspiring as in this moment. The sourness that had crept into his mood during the encounter with Brenda was instantly abolished. He beamed at them. *God bless these kids. They keep me young.*

Rich stood up and approached him. Ben put out his hand, but the tall young man wrapped him up for a powerful hug. It was not the typical professional interaction between professor and favorite student, but it was completely understandable in this context. It was quite out of character for someone as calm and restrained as Rich, but that only made Ben even more pleased by the gesture. In order to maintain a modicum of a professor's authority over his students, Ben could never admit to Rich just how much he admired the young man's opinion and judgment. This hug meant a lot.

The others picked up on Rich's cue and followed suit. Wendy playfully nudged Rich aside to hug her professor as well, with even more enthusiasm. When she wanted to, she had a radiant smile that was utterly contagious. He grinned down at her like a proud father. He wished she could be so happy all of the time. Sadly, he knew it was not in her nature. There was a sadness within her, some unspoken burden that clearly weighed heavily upon her.

Tracy followed Wendy with a hug, less vigorous than the previous but untarnished by any hint of melancholy. If Wendy carried an inner sadness, Tracy carried an inner joy. She had less of the serious student in her than the others, and was clearly less enthralled by their chosen field of study, but her persona was a welcome addition to any group. He felt a twinge of regret about what was coming next.

The other three guys—Kevin, Halfus, and Ernie—were satisfied with handshakes over hugs.

"Congratulations, Doc," said Halfus. Ben thanked him. Like Rich and Kevin, he was in a combination Masters and Ph.D. program with the goal of becoming a professor himself. Halfus was quieter than most of the others, but not unsociable or difficult to approach. He simply let others absorb the spotlight, much like Ben himself. Presumably, the trip would give them the opportunity to know each other better.

Kevin took Halfus' place. "Felicitations," he added with a toothy grin. He was Tracy's boyfriend and very much the male version of her. They even shared the red hair gene, although where Kevin's was light and subtle, Tracy's was fiery and intense. Ben could see why they worked so well together. Tall, muscular, and confident, Kevin hardly looked the part of an Ancient Studies student. None of them did, for that matter. But Kevin the least. Appearances aside, he was an excellent student, with a particular knack for languages. It was Ben's understanding that Kevin had been fluent in five languages even before starting his studies at Catoctin. These supposedly included Hebrew, although Ben had never had a chance to confirm this personally. He was someone else Ben looked forward to having on the trip. Those language skills might turn out to be incredibly useful.

Kevin stepped back to allow Ernie a turn. The dark haired young man met Ben's eye and nodded as they shook hands, but remained silent. He was probably the hardest of any of them to figure, perhaps because Ben had known him the shortest time. Unlike the others, who were all in their second year of the program, Ernie had been there less than one. He was clearly very intelligent, if perhaps a little too anxious to show it off. But he was a great kid, full of potential. Ben wished he would have been able to take him along as well. Instead, he did not look forward to telling him the bad news.

Now the six of them stood around him in a semicircle, looking at him expectantly. There was a moment of relative silence as he attempted to resume his professorial countenance.

"All right, Doc," said Halfus. "We're ready for the bad news now. The letter said four. Which ones are you taking?"

And there it was. The one part of this he had been dreading.

"I want you all to know I would take everyone if I could," he began. "If it were just the money, I think I could cover it myself so that everyone could go." He hesitated, realizing he was being a bit presumptuous. "Everyone who wanted to, that is."

Tracy laughed. "As if any of us would turn down a chance like this," she scoffed. Ben winced a little. Part of him had been hoping she would not even want to go. That would have made this much easier.

"Well, it's not just the money. There are visas that need to be negotiated with Baghdad. Escorts. Accommodations. And, of course, the whole project is under the management of the Germans. So it has to be just four."

Even after years of teaching, his instinct was to look down when delivering bad news. He caught himself this time. He forced himself to be their leader, and a leader had to exude confidence. He looked directly at their faces, each one in turn.

"I'm going by seniority of how long you've been in the program. Rich, Halfus, Kevin, and Wendy."

He forced himself to look at the other two. "Tracy, Ernie—I'm very sorry."

Kevin had his hand on Tracy's shoulder. At the news, he used it to pull her into his chest for a hug. She appeared bitterly disappointed, her face contorting into something that resembled a pout. It was a foreign expression to her, however, and it could not really take hold. A moment later she playfully pushed her boyfriend away, saying "I don't want to talk to you, Mister." But he started rubbing her shoulders and smiling down on her, and she began to shake her head and mockingly laugh at her own bad luck. "You'd better be careful over there and not do anything stupid, you big idiot." Then she sank her head back into his chest as he swayed her back and forth comfortingly.

Then she sneezed right into his shirt, a slimy spot of mucus appearing on the flannel. "Gross, woman," Kevin said, and Ben found her spontaneous laughter reassuring.

He peeked at Ernie, who had not said a word. It was impossible to read his expression, but Ben was worried. If he had to guess, he would have said it looked like shock. But surely the boy would not have expected to be one of the finalists. He should not have, anyway. Well, part of life was dealing with disappointment. Ben consoled himself with the belief that he was teaching the young man an important lesson.

The conversation among the students was turning into a bit of a free-for-all, but Halfus stepped closer to Ben. He lowered his voice. "I'm sure you thought about this already, but are there any...considerations?" He hesitated and Ben saw his eyes briefly glance toward the others. "Particularly for women?"

"Jesus," Wendy exclaimed in a loud voice that quieted the others. Apparently she had heard despite his precaution. "Will you mind your own business? You're not responsible for me any more. You never were."

Halfus nodded, not attempting to argue. Ben felt sorry for him, but he understood her point. There was a lot of history between those two, and he believed Halfus' question probably exceeded the responsibilities of an ex-boyfriend. But he had no doubt it was coming from a place of genuine concern. He tried to think of a way to pacify the situation without hurting the feelings of either.

"I understand the concern for safety, but it's being taken care of. Wendy, I wish it weren't the case, but it might be a little more uncomfortable for you. In Baghdad there wouldn't be any issues, but where we'll be you might need to wear the *hijab*. We'll be there at the discretion of the locals, so we follow their customs."

"Fine, then I'll wear a *hijab*." She looked at Halfus indignantly.

"Well, as I said, I'm not yet sure it will be necessary. We have a few weeks to prepare. I'll know more before we leave. Don't worry about safety, though. I wouldn't take any of you if I didn't think it was perfectly safe."

He wished he felt as confident as he pretended.

Fuck my life, Ernie thought. *It's happening to me again.*

The others were now asking Doc whether he thought this was going to be the stepping stone to that position at Harvard he coveted. Ernie did not join them. He really did not care, being none too pleased with the professor at the moment. Not that he did not understand the rationale for leaving him behind, but that did not make it any easier to swallow.

Ernie had lived most of his life as an invisible person. He believed he was capable of greatness—felt it with every fiber of his being—but no one else seemed to. And every time he thought he had an opportunity to prove himself, to touch greatness, it beckoned and tantalized only to draw away and leave him empty-handed. But his life was more than just a series of disappointments. He could live with that. What was worse was feeling that he never had any control of events that directly affected him. His family had made sure of that. He had spent most of the past decade in his younger brother's shadow. Just like this decision to be left behind, that too was understandable. Yet in both cases, it still hurt deeply.

Every day, every interaction with his parents had been all about Jackie. At school it had been his defining characteristic. Everyone wanted to be polite, so they always asked about his brother, rarely remembering to ask about him as well. The environment was suffocating, so he had studied extra hard to give himself the opportunity to get away to his choice of colleges. But his parents saw it differently. They had wanted him to stay home. There was a local junior college, why was that not good enough for Ernie? His most important function was not to chase some wild adventure, it was to help his family. And they were right. He did not want to be selfish, to be one of those guys who was all about himself. He did not want to let them down.

So he had not. Maybe he could have wished for a little more

gratitude when he told them his decision to stay at home like they asked, but at least he knew in his own heart that he was being a good son. And there was an upside. He spent each afternoon on his studies, learning, and each evening with his brother, bonding. The two of them grew closer together as only brothers can. It was a connection he sorely needed, for he was a boy with no real friends but too much feeling inside to remain contentedly alone.

Things had worked out in the long run. He wound up being glad that he stayed home those years. It was a selfless deed being rewarded. During his last year of undergraduate study, on the advice of a kindly academic counselor, he had begun to send out feelers to postgraduate programs he was interested in. The replies were overwhelmingly positive, and he had become encouraged. That period of his life, when he felt that the world really was his oyster, now seemed almost surreal.

It was then that he had applied to Catoctin. He had been on the fence about it, because it was a more exclusive school than the others, and—ironically, considering current events—he was not sure how well he could deal with rejection. In an uncharacteristic display of openness, he had shared his dilemma with his brother. Ernie had all but decided against applying, and it had been Jackie who convinced him to go for it.

But he had not told his parents, mostly from a desire to defend himself from embarrassment. His father was a good man, but not above the occasional "I told you so." Anxiety had lingered in the back of Ernie's mind the rest of that semester, but he preoccupied himself with imagining the life that awaited if the response were positive.

The day he received his acceptance letter to Catoctin was one of the most vivid memories of his life. His heart had started racing from the moment he saw the address on the envelope, and he forced himself to breathe deeply before tearing it open. As he started to read the letter inside, he tried to force his mind to temper its expectations. He failed. He was expecting good news. Could feel it in the air around him. But that did not make it any less sweet when he saw the words.

We are pleased to inform you. He was looking at his chance to prove to everyone that he could be exceptional.

It felt as though a lifetime of hard work, self-sacrifice, and commitment to family was finally paying off. That the gratification was delayed only made it better.

He hurried home to break the good news. He had been extraordinarily eager to share the moment with others. Not unlike how Doc was behaving today. But did his family clap for him? Did they hug him, or shake his hand? That was not how his family operated.

He could still picture his mother at the sink, yellow rubber gloves up to the elbows, rinsing dishes as he entered the kitchen. She did not turn to face him even as he announced that he had big news. As always, she listened with one ear, her attention focused elsewhere. He had hoped his announcement would change that, and it did. She listened to him, and he knew when her shoulders slumped that he would not be receiving the effusive praise he craved. Instead, she slowly lowered the plate she was scrubbing into the sudsy water and turned to look at him. "You would do this to your family? To your brother? Knowing that he needs you?" Ernie should not have been surprised by the disapproval, yet he was. Nor by the parental command that came next. "Go and tell your brother. Tell him that you're leaving him."

So he did. His heart had not yet stopped pounding from the encounter with her as he climbed the stairs. He became fixated on his brother's reaction, the disappointment crystallizing in his mind like an inevitability. He hesitated at the door. It took an act of will to force himself to knock, to face what would come next.

"Come in." The response was too immediate. He was not prepared yet. How could he look his brother in the eye?

He pushed the door open, knowing his brother would be in one of two places—in bed facing the ceiling, or in his wheelchair looking out the window. Those were the only two places Jackie could have been, because Jackie could not move. He had not been able to move on his own for ten long years.

He was in his chair at the window. Strapped in tight, the chair was angled so he could see inside and out. He was dressed in his favorite blue and gold pajamas emblazoned with the buckskin-wearing, rifle-brandishing mountaineer of the state university. The pajamas were all Jackie ever wore at home, although he reluctantly allowed himself to be dressed up for the rare occasions on which they took him out. Ernie loved his little brother, but he hated those pajamas. They were more suitable for someone half Jackie's age, as though he had stopped maturing on the day he broke his neck, suspended in time while the rest of them got older and sadder. The mountaineer logo was virile and dynamic, a stark contradiction to the invalid inside the clothes. Ernie had owned similar pajamas when he was younger, but had grown out of them by the time he was twelve. Now he hated that mountaineer, the school it was associated with, and the state it represented. Hated them all with a passion that was no less strong for being so illogical. He knew that he should have loved the state for all its beauty, but instead it simply felt suffocating.

The window pane was open just a crack, the scent of copious growths of dogwood around the house permeating the stale air in the room.

"Hi, Ern. I saw you come in a minute ago. You seemed excited." Jackie's voice was a little more cheerful than usual. His own world never changed, so he fed off the animation of others. Seeing the excitement evident in Ernie's gait must have gotten him worked up himself.

Ernie went in, softly closing the door behind him, and sat on the edge of the bed. "Well, that's what I came to tell you. I got my letter today from Catoctin. They accepted me."

"Really? That's great!" The pleasure was so genuine that Ernie felt tears rising up.

"Do you think so? I...was worried that you would be angry with me if I left."

"I'll be angry at you if you don't. It's too good an opportunity to pass up."

"That's...that's what I think, too. But, I thought maybe...I mean, you won't miss me?"

"Of course I will. But you'll come home on breaks, right?"

"Right. Promise."

The relief had been so overwhelming that Ernie stood up behind the chair, where his brother could not see him shake. Jackie interpreted it differently.

"You gonna take me for a walk?" Jackie hated to feel like an imposition, so he rarely asked. He must have been truly excited to break from custom.

Ernie recovered. "Sure am. How about once up and down the block?"

"Sounds great. Make sure it's okay with Mom, first, okay?"

"No problem."

And so Catoctin had become the first place in his life where Ernie got to completely be himself. In fact, here he had learned what it even meant to be Ernie Zolak. It was here that he shaped a reputation—no, an entire persona—as though from soft clay. It was kind of fun in an odd sort of way, starting from scratch, making himself into whatever kind of man he wanted to be.

It had not always been smooth, of course. After the first good-natured ribbing he had learned to mask the most obvious parts of his accent. And he told only his closest friends where he was from. Catoctin was in the sticks, but most of its students were not. It was not long before discomfort about his West Virginia roots drove him to action. He had modernized his hairstyle and wardrobe, and in so doing felt changes happening within him, as well. Most notably the confidence to express himself with less reservation than ever before.

It was gratifying when he came to realize others actually found him appealing. He had been as shy as a teenager on his first date here, with a cute little blonde named Rachel who liked dancing. Later he discovered that everyone liked dancing, so he made sure to become good at it. The first time Rachel called him handsome had sent a shiver of pleasure up his spine. That was last semester. By now he had come to take it for granted, knew that his country-groomed looks plus a smile and a little charming, suggestive conversation could get him in with almost any girl but the ones most devoted to a boyfriend. Naturally, there were still a few that he thought of as out of his league. Girls that possessed a certain *je ne c'est quoi*, like Tracy and Wendy. He sometimes avoided really getting to know the ones he went out with, because the more he respected them as a person the more he placed them on a pedestal, and that made it harder to maintain his confident pretenses. It made rejection far more possible and much more difficult to accept.

There were things he wished he could take back, of course. At first he had been shy and jittery, fearful of drawing too much attention to himself. But soon he realized his intellect was sufficient to hold its own, even here with the brightest of the bright. After so long being invisible, he became aware of a tendency to overcompensate by showing off. He was not proud of it and resisted the urge when he could. But there were two types of people in the world, those who behaved instinctively and those who were thoughtful. Ernie was one of the former, and recognition of his braggadocio usually came only in hindsight. Thankfully, his friends were a good influence. He knew it, even if he could never vocalize it. Ernie admired the calm confidence they possessed, especially Rich. These guys were great role models at a time in his life when Ernie really needed them most.

He knew he had changed for the better. With few exceptions, Catoctin had been an overwhelmingly positive experience. For the first time in his life he was not only succeeding, not only heading toward some worthwhile destination, but enjoying the journey. Recently it felt as though it had been building with the momentum and inevitability of a heat-seeking missile, arcing toward some explosive end.

And now this. To come so far, only to be left out now, was more than he could take. Even though he understood the decision to leave him out, it still felt as though the man upstairs was playing a cruel joke.

His friends were all smiles and laughter, and he had already assumed a fake smile to match their mood. He knew that people never wanted to be around the guy whose bad mood brought them down, so he was used to pretending. But inside he was aching.

His eyes locked in on Wendy. When she had entered the room earlier it had been with her usual gravity. That had only been exacerbated when Rich pulled her aside for some private discussion that she clearly did not want to be a part of. The discussion had ended in a hug between the two of them, leading Ernie to wonder what it was all about. But it had not seemed to lift her spirits at all. When she had taken her seat she looked even more stressed and haggard than usual.

Now she was grinning and giggling and babbling away without restraint. It was all too infrequent an occurrence, but she looked radiant when she was happy. At moments like this, Ernie could just sit back and admire her all afternoon. Not for the first time, he thought about how much of a fool Halfus was for throwing their relationship away. If Ernie was ever in that situation, he would do anything to keep her.

The hour allotted to their meeting was nearing an end, and the group was beginning to gather their things to vacate the room.

Wendy picked up her notebook and textbooks and turned to face the group. "Anyone want to celebrate with a beer?" she asked. She looked each of them over, passing by Rich before lingering on Halfus with furrowed brow. Then she looked at Ernie and flashed him a warm smile. "Ernie? Celebrate with a beer at the *Bluff*?"

Ernie felt his face flush. His expression soured before he could catch it.

"Probably not Easy," said Rich, putting a hand on the younger man's shoulder. Rich looked from Wendy to him. "That's a tough break, mate." His face showed genuine sympathy.

"Thanks, Rich." Ernie really appreciated it. It felt nice to have someone acknowledge his emotions.

Wendy looked mortified. "Oh, Ernie, I'm so sorry. I wasn't thinking."

He forced a smile. "No worries. I'd love to come out. I'm happy for my friends."

She looked hard at his face, however, and he wondered how well she could read his thoughts. She must have detected the pain behind the eyes and worried that she had been the cause of it, for she reached up and touched his cheek. "No, it was stupid of me. I'm really sorry you aren't going on the trip. It would be so much better with you there."

Her touch felt electric, enhanced by the meaning of the words. He worried the flush in his cheeks would burn brighter. For once, he was speechless.

Halfus saved him from needing to reply. As Rich had done, he put a hand on Ernie's shoulder. "She's right. It won't be the same without you, Easy."

Wendy shot Halfus a look of irritation. Things were clearly still not right between those two. Ernie was glad he was not in Halfus' shoes just then, although he was more than a little disappointed that her attention had shifted away so abruptly.

Rich broke the tension. "Tre'Andre is in town for another day. I'll see if he's up for a beer. He'll want to see you guys, I'm sure. We'll meet you over there."

"Kevin and I have plans. We'll take a rain check," said Tracy. Kevin stood beside her and nodded along, quite used to letting her dictate his social calendar.

Halfus looked at Ernie. "You're in?" Ernie nodded.

There was one more person in the room. "Doc?" asked Halfus. They all doubted he would join them, but they wanted him to know he would be welcomed.

"I need to send an email to an old friend. Lots of preparations to start working on."

"Suit yourself."

They began to shuffle out, Ernie behind the others. He wondered why he had agreed to go. The last thing he wanted to do was pretend to be happy. It was not fair that they were going without him. It was not fair that every time he thought something good was going to happen, it turned into fool's gold. It was not fair that his parents loved

Jackie more than him. All he had ever wanted was to make them proud.

Bacchus Bluff was crowded for a Monday night. Apparently, the first day back from break was a good time to put off the end-of-semester grind just a little longer. There were friendly faces to greet after a week-long absence, debauched stories to share, an unending river of alcohol to imbibe.

They were lucky to get a table as soon as they came in. There turned out to be six of them in the group. Wendy had invited her friend Matt, a recent graduate whom Ernie had never warmed up to. His presence was not a surprise, but it was disappointing.

Ernie needed to feel better about himself. He had hoped for a recurrence of what transpired earlier with Wendy. The touch on his cheek still lingered in his mind. It was the only thing that happened all day to feel good about. But her attention was focused on Matt, so Ernie turned his own to the other ladies in the bar. There was no shortage of them. A few he recognized from around campus, but most he did not. Being a graduate student meant he walked in different circles from the majority of students at Catoctin. It set him above and apart, and could be a useful subject of conversation once flirting was in full swing, but it also meant he lacked the easy icebreaker so many others could use.

"I wonder if the girls from yesterday will be here?" he asked Halfus.

"Who?"

"The girls from caving." Ernie noticed from the corner of his eye that he had Wendy's attention now, as well. He did not mind. It never hurt to plant a tiny seed of jealousy. Besides, she had all but ignored him since their arrival at the bar, and he could not stop from allowing a hint of annoyance to affect his behavior. "Tempest and Christine. I wouldn't be surprised to see them here."

"Oh." Halfus seemed unmoved. "Pretty sure those guys they were with are their boyfriends."

"Don't give me that. I saw Christine give you her number."

As soon as he said it, Ernie regretted it. Without looking, he was aware that Wendy's attention was now focused intently on their discussion. But her gaze was not directed at him. His plan was backfiring. He had made her jealous all right, but not for him. He kicked himself for failing to see that coming.

Halfus started shaking his head. "She was just a little upset, that's all."

Now Matt, realizing he had lost his conversation partner, joined in. "Did something happen?"

Halfus was conspicuously taking a long pull of his mug, leaving Ernie to explain. "Just some caving newbs got lost." Suddenly he felt torn between downplaying the incident or highlighting his own role in it. "Two of them wandered off from the group and we had to rescue them."

"The two of you rescued a couple of girls?" asked Wendy. Her question was aimed toward Halfus, but Ernie answered.

"No, it was a guy and a girl who got lost. It was no big deal, really, but the girl's friend had a panic attack. Halfus talked her through it."

Wendy nodded, and Ernie waited with some trepidation. She was known to be a little on the contentious side, especially when it came to Halfus. It had been that way since their breakup last semester. Not that her bitterness was completely unwarranted. Ernie did not know exactly what happened between them, but it seemed to him that Halfus had never showed her the affection she deserved.

As it turned out, they need not have worried. Her reaction was surprisingly mild. "That was nice of you, Halph."

Halfus shrugged. "I didn't do anything special. Mostly just sat beside her until she calmed down."

Ernie knew that was not true. *You told her about Shauna, buddy.* But he agreed that discretion was the best approach. He decided it might be best to cut his losses on this botched attempt. "Yeah, you're probably right. I think they are with those guys." *Which is too bad*, he silently added. *That Tempest was gorgeous.*

Thankfully, the subject changed as Rich and Tre'Andre returned to the table. They had seen one of Rich's soccer teammates and left the group to visit him for a few minutes. Now they were back, and brought a convivial mood with them.

Ernie was still a little uncomfortable around the two of them. They were the first gay friends he ever had—or at least they were the first friends that he *knew* were gay. He had enough respect for Rich to not allow his own instinctive squeamishness interfere with their friendship. Tre'Andre, however, had a louder, more aggressive personality. It made Ernie feel awkward, and he masked it with aggressive banter of his own.

"I think I'm going to get a couple more pitchers for us," he announced to the table. "Apostrophe, some Zima for you?" He knew that Tre'Andre hated that nickname.

"Suck my balls, Redneck," Tre'Andre replied. "I'll drink you under the table any day."

"I'm not interested in your balls," Ernie quipped as he stood up.

"Right, you're more interested in your cousin." It was a stale dig at his country roots, but Ernie chuckled anyway. At least the joke showed a growing level of camaraderie between them.

That went well, he decided as he headed to the bar.

Ernie laid two bills down on the bar, then picked up the heavy pitchers. Next came the tricky balancing act of getting through the crowd back to their table. Along the way, a short brunette with pronounced dimples caught his eye. She caught him looking her way and smiled, and cute became adorable. He lifted the pitchers to display his preoccupation, while nodding to signal his interest. She had a taller blonde friend who was talking into her ear, and the brunette looked away from Ernie to respond. He had little to go on but his instincts, but had long since learned to trust them.

He arrived at the table where his friends were engaged in conversation of their own. Ernie had lost the thread in his five minutes at the bar, but did not much care at the moment. He set the two pitchers on the table and sat down beside Halfus. "Sorry,

Apostrophe, no Zima." He glanced over at Wendy, saw her occupied with Matt, and lowered his voice.

"Halph, I could use a wingman."

"What?"

The bar was noisy so he assumed his friend had not heard. He leaned a little closer, still trying to be discreet. "I need a wingman."

"I heard you. I meant, now?" He seemed a little put off.

Ernie was a bit surprised at the reaction. What he was suggesting was not an infrequent occurrence when the two of them went out for drinks.

"It would be best." Then, "Thanks." He nodded to Rich who was refilling their mugs.

"Go for it, guys." It was Rich who spoke. He spoke naturally, not looking at them, focused on the pouring. It took Ernie a moment to even realize he was referring to them. "She needs to understand that you aren't together any longer. And so do you." Rich looked directly at Halfus as he set the pitcher down.

Halfus looked a little sheepish. For a moment, Ernie thought he was going to protest. But then his friend nodded, picked up his own mug of beer, and bade Ernie do the same. "Loser has to break the ice?"

Ernie grinned and nodded. They chugged, caught the attention of the others at the table, continued through the giggles and wisecracks, and slammed their empty mugs down at the same time.

"The Redneck won," said Tre'Andre. Ernie flashed him a smile. Tre'Andre winked and raised his own mug in salute.

"Hmm." Halfus stroked his stubble. He seemed doubtful. "All right, whatever. You can tell me what to say on the way over."

They got up, ignoring the questioning looks from Wendy and Matt, leaving Rich to explain however he thought best.

"So, you guys are grad students?"

Halfus had struggled through the introductions. Now came Ernie's time to shine.

"Well, I am. Halfus is my bodyguard."

The blonde laughed. "He is, is he?"

"That's right, ladies." Halfus touched his ear and nodded the way that they imagined secret service agents would do. "Careful not to get too close, ma'am." He used his palm to gently move the brunette back an inch.

She looked at him oddly. Her companion laughed. "So, you're famous?" she said to Ernie.

"Not yet. He's preemptive. You never know when it will happen. One day you do something exceptional, the next day you find yourself without a bodyguard."

"No one to protect you from all the groupies, eh?"

Halfus chimed in. "That's correct, ma'am."

She looked him up and down, then back at Ernie. She cocked her head toward Halfus. "He doesn't scare me. I think I could take him."

Ernie laughed, and even Halfus chuckled.

"I don't recommend it. He's a boxer."

"A boxer?" She looked doubtful.

"Not any more, I'm not," interjected Halfus. He looked at Ernie. "Dude, where in the handbook of meeting young ladies did it say to talk about beating them up?"

"It's an interesting approach," agreed the blonde. "Anyway, I'm Laurie. This is Deanna." The brunette waved her fingers at them without pausing from sipping her orange-colored drink through a straw. Her eyes darted back and forth between Ernie and her friend. Thus far, the two of them seemed to be the ones clicking, even though she had been the one to catch his eye.

"So what brings you to Catoctin?" asked Ernie. "The opera or the fine dining?" He could always tell a lot about a girl by how she reacted to sarcasm.

"Neither," replied Laurie. "The beach."

"The beach?" He raised an eyebrow. "We're on a mountain."

"I was misinformed," she said dryly. Matching grins broke out on both of their faces.

Halfus nudged Deanna with his elbow. "How about you?"

She hesitated a moment. "Oh, um, English Lit." It was as though she had been programmed to respond to "What's your major?" and did not know how to deviate from script.

To his credit, Halfus continued as though that was the exact question he had asked. "American or British?"

"British. Mainly nineteenth century."

"Have a favorite?"

"I'm on a Lewis Carroll kick right now." Since that initial hiccup, she seemed moderately more comfortable. Seeing Halfus nod, she asked, "You know him?," then resumed sipping nervously.

Ernie nudged Laurie. "Watch this," he whispered.

Halfus nodded. "'Twas brillig and the slithy toves."

Deanna giggled with her mouth still on the straw. Her orange drink bubbled up and spilled over the side of the glass. She stopped sipping and replied with delight. "That's the one!"

"Okay, that's a little weird," said Laurie. "Did you guys rehearse this or what?"

Ernie shook his head. "Nope. That's just him. Halfus knows everything," he said. "Go on, quiz him on something. Ask him the capital of Shitzganistan, or what year William Faulkner became a commie."

"Hardly," Halfus disagreed. "Our friend Rich is the one who knows everything." He hesitated a moment. "Also, I think you mean Ernest Hemingway. Or maybe John Steinbeck."

Ernie just shook his head at his friend.

Halfus chuckled a little at himself. "Easy's just trying to embarrass me. He knows I won't punch him with ladies present."

"He wouldn't dare," said Ernie with a grin. "Besides, Halfus and I could never fight. I owe him too much." He really meant that, too. Halfus had been his very first friend at Catoctin, and had introduced him to the Ancient Studies clique into which he had settled quite comfortably. Nevertheless, he wished he had not made the comment. It sounded a little too serious for the circumstances, when he should be keeping things light. "So, how about a round of drinks? What's everyone's poison?"

Halfus bought the first round and the four of them settled into a relatively quiet corner. It started as four people talking, but soon divided into two separate groups of two. Ernie had been quickly enthralled with Laurie, and was only slightly discouraged when she mentioned a boyfriend back home, some sweet guy who gave her the necklace she was wearing, just this past Valentine's Day. Ernie imagined the romantic scene and wondered why she was flirting with him now. In his experience, there were two types of girls: those who remained true to a guy even when he was not around, and those who seemed to feel if you cannot be with the one you love, you should love the one you are with. To be more accurate, he *assumed* those were the two types of girls. He had never actually met one from the former group. Generally after a little attention, a few compliments, and a bit of dancing they seemed to forget they even had a boyfriend. He sometimes marveled at how easily people could turn off the relationship switch, to take for granted something that had probably taken a lot of time and effort to build up, to risk its loss on a whim. Maybe it was just college kids sowing their wild oats, but he doubted it. He assumed real grown-ups did it, too. He wondered how many couples made it through decades of marriage without either of them cheating, and he guessed it was fewer than commonly believed. After all, people are people.

Although the back of his mind pondered such things, he never let it interfere with the job at hand. Even while he was enjoying the banter, the logical part of his mind focused on three simple steps: figure out if he liked her, find out if she liked him, then make her want to leave with him. That definition did not do the process justice, however. It was more an art than a science, and quite a fun one at that. Good talk, good laughs, the need to think fast, the chance to exercise wit, topped off with great dancing. That was his favorite part. Even when he decided he really did not like the girl enough to leave with her—or vice-versa—the dancing was always a good time. For him, it was the best way to spend time with someone that was not intimate.

There had been occasions when he had been on the fence about someone and let the dancing decide for him. This, however, was not one of those nights. Long before he asked Halfus to take Deanna home he knew how the night was going to end with Laurie. She knew it, too, for while they were dancing he watched her eyes notice the other two leaving. She said nothing, but their dancing took on an anticipatory intensity. They swayed and swung, dipped and juked, until exhaustion made them stop. On an unspoken signal they mutually decided that this step of the ritual had gone on long enough. As they walked out shortly before closing time, she slipped her hand inside his arm. "You're a fun guy, Ernie," she told him.

He looked at her and smiled. It had been a rotten day, but it was going to have a pleasant conclusion. It was just what he needed.

4
HAPPY TIMES

The deadliest pandemic in human history, both in terms of total deaths and as a percentage of population, was the Black Death that struck Europe during the fourteenth century. Records from the era should be taken with a grain of salt—as is the case with most historical records—but estimates range as high as two hundred million people dying over the span of several decades. Some historians estimate that over half the population of Europe perished.

There is no consensus on what exactly initiated the plague, but the most likely culprits are Eurasian trade ships and the vermin infesting them. As merchants aboard increasingly larger sailing vessels plied farther afield, it was only a matter of time before they brought a little something extra back with their salable wares—a minuscule bacteria known as yersinia pestis. *Even seven centuries ago diseases liked to use the latest improvements in human transportation to introduce themselves to new hosts. It is nearly unimaginable the damage that little Y. pestis would have done in the age of airplane travel.*

With such extraordinary numbers, a disturbing abnormality becomes apparent. Whereas nearly all diseases target primarily the most vulnerable members of society, during the Black Death even young and healthy adults succumbed to the horror. The effects on every aspect of human society— social, economic, military, even religious—were staggering. With half of an entire continent dying off in the span of one generation, the resulting upheaval was far greater than any war, famine, or natural disaster. The Black Death's effects on Europe likely qualify as the second-worst in human history. Yet, in a macabre display of ironic resilience, within a mere hundred years Europe recovered sufficiently to inflict a similar, even greater, cataclysm on their distant neighbors to the west.

The deadliest pandemic of today is HIV/AIDS, achieving a total death toll exceeding twenty-five million worldwide. Although capable of striking down the young and otherwise healthy, HIV is not as indiscriminate as the Black Death was in its penetration to every segment of society. Nor is it as untreatable. Treatments are expensive but effective, and the world appears committed to the research and development required to drive costs down and increase availability. The disease remains rampant in many developing nations but is on the decline in the developed world. With continued effort and a little good fortune, the eradication of this scourge may achieve results similar to the smallpox miracle of the 1970s.

Terrible as HIV/AIDS is, however, it is not the deadliest pandemic of the twentieth century. That grim honor goes to the Spanish Flu, which circumnavigated the globe two times over between 1918 and 1919. As much as a third of the world population became infected, and between fifty and one hundred million died. A convenient comparison to World War I, which raged during the outbreak and aided the spread of the disease, shows that at least three times as many people died from influenza as from the war. It is an impressive statistic, considering this was simple flu—a disease which strikes humans in modified form year after year.

What made the outbreak of 1918 particularly unique were its victims. Rather than striking down children, the elderly, and the infirm—the elements of society usually most vulnerable to disease—the Spanish Flu actually wreaked the greatest havoc on the young and strong. It was not the disease itself that performed the majority of the killing. Rather, it was the body's own immune system, waging its own existential war with the virus, deploying microscopic weapons and tactics to such heroic effect that it destroyed the very battlefield itself. The Spanish Flu was a sobering example of the delicate balance a body requires with respect to its own defenses and the threat posed by infection.

~

In the morning, Wendy received a phone call that would change her life. She got the job working for Representative King. It was a staffer position, starting in late summer when his reelection campaign would begin to ramp up. Her exact duties were to be defined later.

The offer came as a surprise to her, since she had convinced herself to not expect it. She had driven down to Frederick to meet with Sandy Kesmet, the Frederick office manager, a few days after speaking to the congressman at the town hall. They spent most of the morning together in a surprisingly informal interview that concluded with lunch at a Japanese restaurant on the Golden Mile, the small city's famous commercial stretch.

The woman had given Wendy a funny vibe. She was perfectly polite, but still seemed to be holding something back. The impression she gave was that she really did not like Wendy, who had spent the rest of the day wondering why. Perhaps Sandy had been coerced into the interview by the congressman against her will or better judgment. She made it clear enough during their discussion that there were not any immediate openings to fill. She also said it would be a few days before Wendy would hear back from them.

That had been more than two weeks ago. Wendy considered calling the office to remind them that they owed her a response, but she feared it would be interpreted as unprofessional and nix whatever slight chance she had at a position. Instead, she simply spent the intervening time convincing herself that a rejection would not be the end of the world. She knew she was bright and likable. There would be other jobs.

And it was not as though she did not have plenty to keep herself occupied with. The trip to Iraq was approaching quickly, and there were many things to do before they left. Foremost among them was to make sure her mother would be taken care of during her absence. With that in mind, she asked one more enormous favor from the guy she already had dumped on time and time again.

Matt had been her first friend when she came to Catoctin. He was also her closest and most dependable. Even when she and Halfus were dating, she spent almost as much time with Matt as with her boyfriend. Halfus had not seemed to mind. He had, in fact, encouraged it, never showing the slightest hint of jealousy. That was something that had both surprised and, if truth be told, annoyed her. Not that she wanted him to get upset, but it would have been nice if he had shown just a little possessiveness. It might have made a difference in the outcome of their relationship.

In any case, she had come to trust and rely upon her old friend. She had still been mourning the loss of her father when she met Matt, and he immediately provided a sympathetic ear. He had been there again during the breakup, never pressuring her, always willing to listen. On occasion, he had been known to give her advice—albeit nothing she had followed through on. In her mind, his role was akin to the statue of Jesus she used to pray to in the church back home. She would vent her frustrations and hope that things worked out in the end.

Today was as much celebratory as serious, however, and she was pleased to have some good news to share with him for a change. The two of them had already made tentative plans to meet soon. Then the job offer added a sense of urgency to the meeting. She was eager to tell a friend all about that stroke of good fortune.

Matt had graduated the previous year, but lived between here and Baltimore. It was close enough that allowed them to meet in person a few times each month.

She sent him a text message. *Still up for meeting today?*

Although graduated, he was working as an intern at an affiliate of Johns Hopkins University. It was neither a paid nor a full-time internship, and allowed him plenty of opportunity to socialize. More than he wanted, she knew. His replies were usually immediate. In this case, however, she did not hear back until she had showered, dressed, and spent an inordinate amount of time on her troublesome blonde hair. She was in a good mood, and decided her appearance today should match. She was glad it was warm enough now for the summer blouse and skirt outfit that had become her favorite for special occasions. The top was white with just enough blue to bring out her eyes, the skirt cut just right to show off the best part of her legs. She had lost much of the dancer's figure she had maintained in high school, but her calves retained just enough muscle to remain shapely.

She was about to send a follow-up message to Matt when her phone beeped back at her. *Of course*, the message read. *I have a surprise to tell you.*

That made her twist her lips in consternation. She had been thinking of today as her big day, and now he had something that would preoccupy his thoughts. She had to remind herself to be happy for him, whatever it was. They could surprise each other.

Me 2, she texted back. Then she sent another. *What's good 4 U?*

I'm going to be in McGahey this afternoon, he replied. *How about lunch on campus?*

Well, that certainly was convenient. They typically met somewhere between their homes, so this saved her a drive.

What time are you thinking? she texted. Matt was one of those people who could eat whenever convenient. An hour early, a few hours late, a handful of peanuts instead of a meal—it did not seem to matter to him. But Wendy liked to eat lunch at the same time every day. She hoped he would take that into consideration.

She saw by the clock on her phone that it was already after eleven. As though on cue, her stomach gave the first inkling of a growl.

Her phone beeped. *I'm thinking all the time*, it read.

"Very funny," she said out loud. She twisted her lips in thought, considering how to reply. Her instinct was to fire back, but she knew she would lose any battle of smartassery.

Then her phone beeped again. *Noon. I know you.* With a winking emoticon at the end.

So now she had almost an hour to kill, and campus was only a minute away. She lived in one of the apartment buildings exclusive to wealthier students located on the campus side of town, where she was within walking distance of classes. Her unit, on the second floor, was a modest little one bedroom for solo living. Above her, the third floor had two bedroom apartments for students who shared. Wendy knew she paid too much to live there, but her life during the period when she matriculated at Catoctin had been terribly stressful, and signing up for this through the school's accommodations program had been easier than trying to find something on her own. She could have volunteered to split rent with a roommate, but she had been concerned about getting someone hard to live with. Besides, she felt that a graduate student should be on her own.

With nothing to do but think for the time being, she allowed a whirlwind of ideas and emotions to get the better of her.

What exactly would her job be? What was it about Sandy Kesmet that bothered her? Would they get along?

Now that she had future employment, she began to have second thoughts about the trip to Iraq. It had seemed like quite the addition to her résumé, but all of a sudden that was less of a concern. There was still plenty of excitement swirling around her mind, but as the departure loomed closer so too swirled doubts and misgivings.

How miserable will six weeks in the middle of nowhere be? Will I be the only woman? Will I need to cover myself head to toe, all day, every day, in the summer, in a desert?

Since finding out she was going, Wendy had started paying more attention to events in Iraq. She saw plenty of women dressed in Western garb, going about their business the same as men. Participating in government, mostly, since that's all that the news showed. But always in Baghdad, where the national government and American presence held the most sway. And Wendy's group was not going to be in Baghdad. They would be in the north, far from Western influence. She was not without concerns.

Why am I even going?

This was a more difficult question to answer. She enjoyed Ancient Studies, but it had not been her original pursuit. She was a European history specialist who had gone through the unorthodox—and not altogether simple—process of changing her program of study after enrollment. She did it partly because of Halfus. When they started dating she had instinctively centered her life around him and his interests. One of the manifestations of this had been to change her major. She did not tell him she was doing it, and when he found out he had been against it. But she had gone through with it anyway—because *he* was not her only reason.

It was all of them. Halfus had introduced Wendy to the others in the Ancient Studies program. Kevin and Tracy, Rich, even Doc. She envied the relationship Halfus had with them. She had friends of her own, of course, but they began to seem shallow by comparison. This was more like a family. And considering the difficulties her own family had, it was a structure and stability that she had never fully experienced before. She had not realized until then just how meaningful a close-knit circle of friends could be.

As soon as she got to know them she knew she wanted to be a part of their group. And not just as Halfus' girlfriend. She wanted to be one of them on her own. And now she was. Even though the two of them were no longer a couple, she felt accepted for herself. It was a decision she did not regret at all.

More than any other, they were the reason she was going to Iraq. It was going to be the ultimate experience for them. Soon they would be graduating and going their separate ways. Of course, they would all stay in contact, modern technology being what it was. But there was a sense that this was a golden age for all of them, and this trip would be their crowning achievement. Despite the hardships she knew would come, she was proud to be sharing this moment with them.

"So, you're going to cure the flu?" Wendy asked.

"Not exactly," replied Matt. "There's no cure, but we're studying both preventive measures and new methods of treatment. It's pretty frustrating. Thousands of man hours and millions of dollars in testing, and so far the best remedy is still bed rest and a lot of water."

Within the past few days the number of Duck Flu cases in the United States had crossed the fifteen thousand mark. It had also caused over three hundred deaths. Perhaps more tellingly, the national media continued to cover the story with the same reckless fervor now, months into the epidemic, as it had when the story first broke. The attention and uproar led to a shifting of resources in the health care community, particularly those portions of government that researched communicable diseases and the private organizations they interfaced with. A sudden influx of funding to Maryland State Medicine, a partnership between Baltimore's most famous university and hospital, had led them to upgrade Matt's position from internship to full-time.

He was clearly excited about the promotion. "We have some of the leading doctors in the field," he went on. "I'm getting contacts in both the CDC and USAMRID. This is a huge step for me this early in my career."

Wendy listened patiently, feigning interest in a topic she did not understand and was frankly a little disgusted by. She loved Matt dearly but she found his fascination with disease to be a bit morbid. She nodded along with what he was saying, anxious to get to her own good news.

Finally he asked her. "So, enough about that. What did you want to tell me?"

"I got the job with Robert King's campaign."

"Wendy, that's great. What will you be doing?"

"I'm not exactly sure, yet," she admitted. "But it's a huge relief. It was quite a big monkey on my back."

"Tell me about it," he agreed. "I remember being terrified about graduating without a job waiting for me. I was thrilled just to get the internship."

"Well, it worked out for you," she said, reaching out to touch his shoulder reassuringly.

"And this will work out for you," he replied with matching optimism.

They both paused to take a few bites of their meal. The beautiful weather had compelled them to eat lunch outdoors. They sat on the low stone wall that encircled the campus fountain, paper plates precariously balanced on their laps. Their meal was a strange but delicious vegetarian concoction, served gratis to students by a generous trio of Seventh Day Adventists who came to the campus

with a different delicious dish once per week throughout the spring
semester. Young men and women found the lure of free food and
warm weather irresistible, and the line to the food carts was steadily
growing. A few others joined Wendy and Matt at the fountain, and
she found herself nodding distractedly at the occasional faces she
recognized.

The courtyard was located in the center of the grassy campus, with
narrow walkways heading off in each direction. They were cement
arteries running through a body of green. The courtyard was filled
with a steady stream of students moving to and from the academic
and administrative buildings like an enormous, ceaselessly pumping
heart. For such a small college, Catoctin felt overcrowded at moments
like this. It seemed that the entire student population was out for a
walk this afternoon.

Wendy wondered whether Halfus would happen by, possibly with
Ernie or Rich. Although not without reservation, she looked forward
to sharing her news with him. He would be supportive. Whatever had
happened between them, she knew that he genuinely wanted the best
for her. It would be nice to let him know she was thriving. Buried
beneath her conscious thoughts, a part of her ached to show that she
was thriving *without him*.

Right on cue, Wendy traced her eyes along one of the streams of
people and saw him. He did not see her, because he was distracted by
the person walking beside him. Wendy recognized the little brunette
girl he had met at the bar a few weeks earlier. Wendy did not know
her name. Halfus and Ernie never rejoined her group the rest of that
evening. She had not been altogether happy about that.

Wendy looked away. She did not want to get caught looking at
him. In fact, she suddenly hoped he would not even see her and Matt
sitting there. Her brain was a rush of thoughts, many of them
unpleasant. A four-way conversation with him and this girl was the
last thing she wanted. It would seem too much like two couples.

She risked a sidelong glance and was relieved to see them passing
by without reaction. She had dodged a bullet. She began to relax, then
realized she was not paying enough attention to what Matt was

saying. She tuned in and nodded her head in a gesture of agreement, hoping that her distraction had not been noticeable. She met his eyes, then watched them glance toward the crowd. Recognition registered in them.

"Hey, Halfus!" Matt called before Wendy could stop him. She cringed. Then she pursed her lips and looked back at her ex.

It took him a moment of looking around, but when Halfus saw the two of them sitting there, his face lit up. Wendy knew she had not been entirely pleasant with him the last time they talked, so she was both surprised and relieved at the reaction. It was always nice to know someone was genuinely happy to see you. She reminded herself to never stop appreciating that.

Halfus looked down at his companion and said something. From this distance, Wendy could not hear what he said, but she watched the dark haired girl nod and motion in the direction they had been heading. *Good*, Wendy thought. *She won't be joining us.* The girl flashed Halfus a bright smile, and the effect on her features was dramatic. Wendy could see why guys would find this girl attractive. Halfus leaned down for a quick kiss and the girl met him on her tip-toes. Then she turned away and walked on contentedly as Halfus came over to join his friends.

Well. That was fast. Wendy had not realized they were a couple. Just like that, her world began to spin. It was unfair that he should find a new companion before she had.

Her head swam as greetings were exchanged, so she let Matt do the talking while she collected her thoughts. It was the first time she had seen Halfus with another girl since their breakup six months ago. She was over him and had been for a while. So why was she upset? Was it simply because she was caught by surprise? Because she had not started dating someone else first? Or maybe it was because she had liked believing that the reason he was not dating anyone else was because he was not yet over her. Given her justification for breaking up with him, she supposed that had always been unlikely, a fantasy of the mind to make herself feel better during a difficult time.

Most likely her unease stemmed from a little bit of all three.

Whatever the cause, she knew she did not want to seem upset in front of the two guys. Wendy composed her face into a practiced smile and nodded along with whatever Matt was saying.

He must have just finished telling Halfus about the new jobs, because the newcomer said, "Congratulations. To both of you." He spoke in that usual calm, measured tone that often drove her crazy. Would it hurt the guy to show a little excitement from time to time? His eyes locked with hers. "I know that must be a big relief."

She downplayed it with a shrug. "We'll see how it works out. I don't even know for sure exactly what my job will be."

But Halfus was shaking his head. "I know you. You'll take it and run with it. Soon you'll be running that whole office." She flushed a little, appreciative of the compliment but not wanting to show it.

Meanwhile Halfus had turned back to Matt. "And you. I won't pretend that I understand exactly what it is you do. In my imagination I see you pushing slides under a microscope, but I don't know if people even still do that."

Matt swelled with pride. He seemed to like it when others showed actual curiosity in his work, probably because it happened so infrequently. "Well, there's still a little bit of that, but most of the time I work on the computer. I'm hoping to eventually get trained for a Level 3 suit. That's when they wear the spacesuit and work in a lab like you've seen in the movies. It's for the really dangerous stuff like Ebola. Things that you accidentally rub into your eye one day and drop dead the next. Very few people get to work with that stuff. But with Duck Flu getting all the attention right now they pretty much diverted everyone to that. I just hope we don't have any outbreaks of anything else any time soon. We don't really have the resources to tackle two at the same time."

"Well, I can see how excited you are, so I know it's a huge step."

"Why are people so upset about the Duck Flu, anyway?" Wendy asked, now wanting to express curiosity of her own. "Isn't it still just the flu?"

"Well, the flu is not usually so deadly in the United States," Matt admitted. "But around the world it can be quite a bit worse. Most countries still have substandard health care systems for much of their population.

"But even here there is a risk. Some strains are worse than others. Just a few years ago a few hundred thousand people died from Swine Flu. And a hundred years ago the Spanish Flu killed millions."

But Wendy was skeptical. For better or worse, once the gears started turning inside her head, she began to analyze out loud. "It just seems like more of the usual overreaction to me. The media takes a story and whips the masses into a frenzy, and then the politicians pass some new bill that's either ineffective or counterproductive, just to make it look as though they're doing something."

Matt opened his mouth, then closed it. He seemed not to have an answer to that. Or—another thought occurred to her—perhaps she had offended him. She had not intended to make it sound as though his job was a waste of time. She wondered if she had just made an ass of herself to her best friend. And right in front of Halfus. She was trying to think of a way to clarify her remark to take some of the sting out of it when her cell phone sounded a peculiar melody.

"Is that...Animotion?" asked Halfus with an amused grin. Her ring tone was *Obsession*.

She nodded at him as she pulled it from her bag, not at all surprised that he recognized the tune. He had a fairly eclectic taste in music. She had heard him listen to everything from classical to modern industrial metal.

She glanced at the display as she stood up. The incoming call was a convenient excuse to extract herself from a conversation she did not really want to be part of.

She excused herself and walked a short distance away, onto the grass where she had some distance from the tumult of walkers. And from her friends. She did not want them to overhear her conversation, preferring the mystery of doubt to mundane reality. Perhaps Halfus would think it was a new beau.

Feeling a little on display, she composed her mouth into a wide smile as she brought the phone to her ear. "Yes, Mom?"

~

The two of them watched Wendy converse with her unknown caller for a minute. Finally, Matt asked the question that had been plaguing him for months.

"You two aren't getting back together?"

Halfus shook his head. "I don't know how you ever got the impression we would, Matt. Things aren't good between us. Sometimes we manage to get along like friends, but most of the time she seems to hate me."

"She doesn't hate you, dude. She's just a little bitter."

Halfus nodded without protest. "I guess I don't blame her."

"I don't either. I still think you should have your head examined for letting her go. You two were perfect for each other."

"I don't know about that," Halfus demurred. "Part of me sees it, but there's more to it than an outsider can see." He looked at Matt earnestly. "You know how sad she can get, Matt. She should have someone who can help her with that."

Matt snorted. "It's because of that that you were perfect for her. Yes, she got sad sometimes, but I've never seen her happier than when she was with you. I can't believe you didn't see it."

Halfus sighed. "I didn't. I had my own problems. She was right, you know. I never should have gotten started with her to begin with. I wasn't ready for another relationship." He stared vacuously at the crowd. "I'm still not. I wonder if I ever will be."

"Well, it sure seems like you're in one now. Looks like you have a new girlfriend."

"Deanna? I don't think I would call her my girlfriend. We've gone out a few times, but it's nothing serious."

"Dude, she is crazy about you. It was obvious to me, and I only saw her for fifteen seconds."

"Matt, my friend, you see things no one else does."

"Halfus, my friend, you know nothing about women."

"No argument there."

"It's a shame," Matt went on. "If you had stuck with it, I think you would have learned to really appreciate her." He was referring to Wendy again, as though this other girl were insignificant to the real issue. "She's got some prickles, but there's a flower there that's worth the effort."

"I know. We had our moments. But it wasn't a matter of my not sticking with it. She broke up with me, remember?"

"That's bullshit and you know it. How much of a fight did you put up? Any at all? Have you considered that maybe that was what she was hoping for? A sign that you cared enough to fight to keep her?"

Halfus was still staring ahead. When he spoke, it was quietly, more to himself than Matt. "I cared. Just not enough. Part of me knew I would regret it, but I still couldn't summon the impulse to argue with her." He looked disappointed in himself.

"Maybe next time you should."

Silence ensued. Matt had spoken his piece. Maybe too much. He considered Halfus a close friend, and believed the other felt the same way about him. He was glad they could talk so openly, but even so he kept an eye on his friend's expression, searching for any clue that he was going too far. Thankfully, Halfus appeared thoughtful, but not particularly disturbed by the prying.

"I'm sorry, Halph. I don't mean to sound so harsh. It's all a learning experience."

Halfus nodded agreement. "It certainly is."

A moment later Matt had it thrown back at him. "So what about you, huh? How come you two never got together? You seem to understand her better than anyone else."

It was Matt's turn for self-reflection. "I thought about it. You know I had a crush on her at first. But she wasn't interested. By the time she might have been, I realized it would never work. It takes more than understanding. I love her to death...in manageable doses. You don't get to manage doses in a relationship, though. I'm not a patient guy."

"I can respect that. Not many guys could do that."

Matt was only being partially honest, however. He *was* a patient guy. No doubt he and Wendy would have their issues, but he knew he could have worked through them. No, the real reason that he did not get involved with Wendy is that he understood how people operated. They consistently compared their new partner to their old, whether they realized they were doing it or not. No one knew this more than the guy sitting beside him. Just as Wendy did not like being compared to Shauna, Matt would have hated to follow up Halfus. He pitied the man who did.

In their field of view, they saw Wendy excitedly wave to a passerby. Her phone was still at her ear and she made no move to return yet, but the guys watched Ernie detach from the stream of walkers and head their way.

Halfus greeted him. "'Sup, Easy?"

"'Sup, Halph?" he said to his buddy. Then, with noticeably less levity, "How's it going, Matt?"

"Heya, Ernie."

Matt was sure that Ernie was a decent enough guy, but for some reason the two of them never really clicked. They got along well enough, but probably would not associate with each other if not for their mutual friends. Matt never felt less witty than he did around this guy. He worried that the conversation might be a little awkward if Halfus did not do most of the talking, which was roughly akin to hoping for a blind man to do most of the driving.

To his relief, Halfus immediately said, "I've been waiting to see you today. I hear congratulations are in order. I'm excited."

"Me, too," replied Ernie.

Wendy rejoined them. The end of her call seemed to have coincided with Ernie's arrival. She hugged him in greeting, eliciting a broad-grinned reaction.

"Why? What's going on?" she asked.

"You haven't heard?" asked Halfus.

She looked back and forth from him to Ernie. "Obviously not," she answered curtly. "What's going on?" she repeated. She stared curiously at Ernie, who was just standing there, beaming.

Matt wished he would not keep her waiting like this. Wendy possessed a short fuse in the best of times, and she seemed even edgier than normal this afternoon.

Finally Halfus answered for him. "Ernie's coming," he said simply.

"Coming?" She sounded confused. "You mean to Iraq?"

"To Iraq," Ernie affirmed. He grinned even wider.

"What... How?" she stammered.

Matt wondered, too. The way he heard it, it sounded unlikely that the Germans would alter their plans to accommodate an extra student.

"Kevin's sick. Duck Flu. Got it from Tracy."

"That's...terrific!" She let out a little scream, then threw her arms around Ernie in a flashy show of affection. Ernie basked in it, and even Matt felt a momentary jolt of jealousy.

Wendy let go and regained her composure. "I mean, it's terrific for you. Not that Kevin and Tracy are sick. But it's going to be so much fun having you on the trip."

Matt felt his jealousy diminish. He had no doubt that she was genuinely happy for Ernie, but her reaction seemed a little too over-the-top to be completely genuine. He wondered if it had something to do with Halfus sitting there, watching her hang all over his friend. Matt also wondered whether she was even aware that she was doing it.

"We're going to celebrate, right?" she asked.

Halfus nodded. "I think Rich is already organizing something tonight. A last night out for the whole crew. He said that Doc might even join us."

"Really?"

"I'm not sure I would hold my breath on that, but it would be kind of nice to see him in different surroundings."

"We'll see him in much different surroundings soon," Ernie observed.

"True."

"Matt, can you come?" Wendy asked.

He hesitated. This sounded like an Ancient Studies affair. He was friends with most of them, but it still might feel a little awkward.

Then Halfus reassured him. "You should come, man. I think Rich said Tre'Andre is coming up from Bowie. Should be the whole clan."

"Kevin and Tracy, too?" Wendy asked.

"I believe so. I talked to Kevin yesterday and he said he's pumping himself full of medicine. He says he doesn't feel too bad. I think they're both tired of just laying around the house."

"Yeah, but isn't going to a bar a bad idea? Aren't they contagious?"

"Probably. I think we'll need to send them home after a round. But it's the last chance we'll all get to be together until after the trip. I couldn't bring myself to tell them not to come."

Wendy nodded.

"So... What do you say, Matt?" They both turned back to him.

He smiled at them. "I think I can stick around."

"Great," said Wendy, flashing him a warm smile of her own. He could not tell if she was more pleased or relieved. "You can crash at my place until tonight, if you want."

Matt did not have so many friends that he could not still appreciate these. It felt good to be accepted. Life was about to get very busy for him with his expanded job. They would feel the same way about their trip and really cut loose tonight. It promised to be a fun evening.

Miriam Weald lived in a four-story brownstone apartment building on the opposite side of McGahey from Wendy's student accommodations. Wendy estimated she would be here for less than an hour, so she had asked Matt to meet her at her place at two o'clock.

There was a small parking lot for residents behind the structure, but she never had any problem finding available street parking nearby. It was one of the benefits of living in a small town. She parked in front and glanced up at a window on the top floor. It was the window of her mother's bedroom, and Wendy had learned to use it as a predictive barometer of her mother's mood. Happiness was represented by open curtains, melancholy by closed. Perhaps the sun had a benevolent effect on her mother. More likely, Wendy was confusing causation and correlation. Good moods welcomed the light and bad ones shunned it.

The apartments were nice inside, but Wendy always felt the edifice of the building was a little on the dreary side. It was probably the normal hue of the stone, but this particular color made the building appear perpetually dirty. The effect was most pronounced during sunny days like today. It seemed to have a bad condition that made her want to scrub it clean like she would her own skin.

The lobby did nothing to alter that impression. Most of the smooth stone floor was covered by an old red carpet, thirty years old if it was a day. There was an elevator just past the lobby, but Wendy headed past it to the stairs. The elevator was small and inconceivably slow, while the stairwell was wide, clean, and inviting. Large, well-positioned windows at each landing made this the brightest part of the building during the day.

A year ago, Wendy could climb the six flights to the fourth floor without becoming short of breath. Today she found out that was no longer the case. It depressed her a little, reminding her that she was slacking off on the workout regimen she had adhered to for most of her college career. She used to make time for thirty minutes of stretching and exercise each day, but recently she was lucky to do it twice a week. Being tired out by these stairs was one obvious reminder of her lack of commitment, and she shuddered to think what she would discover if she stepped onto a scale. She made a mental note to get back to it as soon as they returned from Iraq.

As usual, she encountered no one on the way up. But one thing was different. She noticed the door to the adjacent apartment was hanging open, and she heard voices inside. Perhaps her mother had new neighbors. Turnover in the building was fairly regular. She was tempted to sneak a peek through the open door, but reminded herself that she was on a schedule. She could not afford to waste time and still make it home to meet Matt.

She did not knock on her mother's door. She had her own key and was long used to letting herself in. Usually she did so silently, in case her mother was sleeping. She doubted that would be the case today, since they had spoken on the phone less than thirty minutes ago. But habits are habits, so she opened the door without announcing herself.

The first thing she noticed was how dark the place seemed. Normally, her mother kept the curtains in the living room drawn back to allow in as much sunshine as possible. It was part of her morning ritual, so seeing them closed like this came as a surprise. The windows of this room faced the side of the building rather than the front, so Wendy had not observed these curtains from below.

The second thing she noticed was the smell. She wondered when the kitty litter for her mother's cat, an adventurous tabby, had last been cleaned. Judging by the unpleasant aroma in the stale air, it had been too long.

As her eyes adjusted to the dimness, she began to see objects on the floor. A few parcels of clothing, some envelopes and papers, and a toppled knick-knack that normally resided on the coffee table. It was one of a pair of tiny cats shaped from porcelain. The other, a kitten toying with a ball of yarn, remained on the table. The fallen one was a cat with one paw in the air, usually positioned to seem as though it was playing with the other. Now it pawed at the air as though crying for help.

Taken individually, the signs were nothing to get upset about. Taken together, Wendy was unnerved. Her mother had always been a fastidious person, so the slovenliness was remarkable.

Wendy glanced down the short hallway. The bedroom door was closed. She would peek in on her mother in a minute, but first she had to clean up the worst of this mess. It would not be the first time she took it upon herself to do something her mother should do for herself. More and more often, Wendy felt that their roles from her childhood had reversed. Now she was the responsible one and Miriam the infantile.

She replaced the porcelain cat figurine first, relieved that the fragile item appeared undamaged. She tossed the papers onto the dining room table, then began folding the clothing one piece at a time over her left arm. As Wendy was hunched over, she heard a loud thump on the table behind her. The sudden noise caught her by surprise. She gasped and jumped before her mind registered that the source of the disturbance was only Truman, greeting her in his own mischievous fashion. Her reaction caused the cat to hurriedly scamper away, knocking the papers she had just placed on the table back onto the floor and recreating the mess.

"Stupid cat," she muttered. She stooped over to recover the papers.

Then she heard a noise from the bedroom. Loud coughing, clearly audible through the closed door. Wendy lost interest in cleaning and went to check on her mother.

The bedroom was too dark to see, so Wendy flicked on the light. Her mother turned away, but Wendy saw her for long enough to see that the woman looked awful. It was the first time in many years that Wendy had seen her without makeup, and her face appeared drab and colorless. *Lifeless* was the first word that occurred to Wendy, but her mind instantly repelled that thought.

Her mother turned back and looked at her with supplicating eyes. Then she brought a fist to her mouth and burst into another fit of coughing.

"Mom, how long have you been sick?" Wendy regretted asking as soon as the words left her mouth. She realized her mother had been telling her about the illness for weeks, but she simply had not taken it seriously.

"Oh, I'm just a little under the weather, dear." As usual, now that Wendy was here in person her mother tended to downplay the same ailments that she talked up on the phone. That was why Wendy had gotten into the habit of dismissing them as hypochondria.

Her shoulders tightened. She realized this visit was going to take much longer than expected. She needed to let Matt know that she was not going to be home to meet him, after all. She excused herself to make the call, wondering what she would tell him.

In the end, she asked him to meet her here instead of going to her place. He had promised to check in on her mother during Wendy's absence anyway, so it seemed logical to go ahead and get the two of them used to each other now.

She began cleaning while she waited for him to arrive. The first thing she tackled was the kitty litter, which was stale and overloaded with excrement. The foul smell remained, so she searched the kitchen for additional droppings. Naturally, she found them in all the hard-to-reach places. As she worked, she wondered if her mother was even still capable of looking after a pet.

She tried broaching the subject indirectly. "That cat is becoming a troublemaker," she said as she brought a light snack to her mother's bedside.

"Oh, no, he's my protector," was the reply. "He looks out for me. Don't you, boy?" Truman chose that moment to hop onto the bed with his owner. He sat meekly on her frail chest while she cradled his chin with one hand and scratched his head softly with the other. He was as docile for her mother as he was troublesome for Wendy. "I wouldn't know what to do without him in the house."

Wendy understood that her mother was attached to the animal, and she certainly did not wish to deprive her of its companionship, such as it was. She did not press the issue.

When Matt arrived, she got the two of them talking and left them alone in the room. If she had stayed with them, they would each default to speaking more to her than each other. This way, they would become acquainted much faster. Not that she doubted Matt would have any trouble being friendly. He was too nice for his own good.

She thought about him at length as she vacuumed the living room carpet. He was probably the nicest guy she had ever known. And she knew that he was interested in her—or at least had been. Months had passed since he had last shown any of the telltale signs every girl learned to pick up on. Still, she did not doubt that he would be again if she expressed interest in him.

So why did she not? She did not buy into the nonsense of a friend zone. She had boyfriends in the past who had started out as friends. In fact, she considered friendship a requirement for any successful relationship. When the fire of attraction burned down to a low flame, there needed to be something else to fall back on. She had seen enough girls burn out on a cute guy within a month or two, then try to keep things going through mere inertia. Those relationships never ended well.

She could see herself with Matt. He was not hard on the eyes. She could imagine a little flame developing between them. But it would always be little. She did not think she could fall madly in love with him. Part of it was that he allowed her to take him for granted. She did not want to, but it was human nature. There needed to be some sense of challenge to keep things interesting.

The other problem was Halfus. She hated herself for it, but as long as he was around, she felt hope. She did not want to, but she could not control it. It was incredibly frustrating. She could start dating Matt, and things could begin going well. And if Halfus suddenly wanted her back she would resist. But she would lose. In time, she would unquestionably go to him. She knew in her mind that it would not happen like that. He would not suddenly want her back, and she spent most of the time trying to convince herself that she did not want him to. Until today she had even thought she succeeded, but seeing him kiss that girl at lunchtime had finally dropped the scales from her eyes.

She knew the others thought of her as spoiled and selfish. She did not doubt that they liked her anyway, but they simply liked her despite these flaws. And she could not argue that it was not true, at least some of the time. But at moments like this she felt good about herself. She had too much respect for Matt as a person to let him become a poor player in her own confusing drama. She did not often pretend to know what was best for other people, but this time she believed she did. And she knew he was better off without getting involved with her. She would be the end of him.

She switched off the vacuum. She could hear him chattering away in the other room, along with the sweet sound of her mother's laugh. It was music to Wendy's ears. She could at least feel confident that things would be all right here while she was away.

∼

Professor Benjamin Appelstein maintained office hours between two and four on Friday afternoons. On this day, he hoped no one would show.

There were a million little things yet to do and not much time left to do them. When he had first received approval to join the Schwarzvogel Expedition, he knew there would be a ton of work involved to prepare himself and his students. Not only was there coordination with Wesel University, but there was even more with both the American and Iraqi governments. At this point, well into his career, he still was not proficient at maneuvering through academic red tape. Now he found himself trying to navigate foreign and domestic government bureaucracy, as well.

Nevertheless, when he started working on this project several weeks ago it had seemed that there would be plenty of time. If anything, he had been anxious for the trip to get started. Now he would have paid money for a few extra days of preparation.

The burden of responsibility was taking a toll on him. He envied the carefree nature of the students. They had invited him out for a drink tonight, one last occasion for everyone who was and was not going to spend an evening together. He desperately wanted to join them. Had, in fact, led Rich to believe that he would. But now he did not see any way it could happen. Perhaps that was for the best. It ran against his instincts. He could not very well discipline a student for missing a deadline because of a night out when he was himself guilty of the same infraction. Well, he could—he certainly knew plenty of professors who did exactly that—but he would feel like a hypocrite.

Better that he work late and hope the work got done. The only problem with that plan was that most of the unfinished business required waiting for responses from other individuals and institutions. So he might be denying himself a little fun for no real purpose. He was simply pragmatic in trying to avoid being seen behaving inappropriately, just in case some snafu led to trouble down the road. Maybe he tended to be a little too conformist, but avoiding reckless decisions had gotten him this far in life.

Ordinarily, the stress would have a detrimental effect on his mood.

He could at times be a little snappish, although his sense of professionalism usually prevented it from occurring with students. Counterintuitively, however, that was not happening to him this week. He remained in good spirits despite the anxiety. He probably should not have been surprised. On the scales inside his mind, worry remained far outweighed by the mounting excitement of the expedition. He should have been a frazzled wreck, yet when he walked around campus, he still felt as though his shoes did not touch the ground.

His mood was not the only beneficiary. The headaches seemed to be getting better in both frequency and intensity. He believed the constant focus on preparations—the relentless racing of his industrious mind—was the critical factor. He might even have had some mild headaches without realizing it. Simply put, he did not have time to think about whether his head hurt.

However, he noticed a peculiar thing happening recently. He had gotten used to the feeling of relief that ensued from taking the painkillers. Perhaps to the point of counting on it. He had underestimated what that feeling meant to him. He likened it to recovering from an illness. It was horrible to go through, but it made one really appreciate being healthy again. Thinking back on the few times he had ever been sick, he remembered never feeling quite so energetic as those first days afterward.

Now that he had gone a while without experiencing the discomfort of the headaches, he began to miss the relief. It was all bundled together. His mind had learned to associate the relief with the pain. Without even realizing it, he had gotten to the point where he rather enjoyed—even looked forward to—those first headache pangs. The pain became a necessary prelude to the soothing numbness that followed. He supposed this was addiction, but the realization did not particularly bother him. It seemed an innocent enough vice amid all the depravities he heard about every day. Not that he would not continue trying to resist temptation. He certainly did not want it to get worse.

There was a knock on his door. He sighed. Nine times out of ten, no one visited him during office hours, although normally he would have welcomed it as a break in the monotony. Naturally, someone would disturb him now that he needed every precious minute.

"Come in," he called out. He attempted to clear his mind of distraction. Students deserved his full attention.

It was not one of his students, however.

"Brenda," he said in surprise. He felt his brain begin to race again, as always. This time he let it. Today he would not be on his A-game no matter how hard he tried, so he did not bother with the attempt. "Would you like to sit down?" He gestured to one of the two padded chairs in front of his desk.

She shook her head. *Of course*, he thought as he assumed his professorial pose, propping his elbows and clasping his hands. *These days it's too much to expect conversation to last more than a minute.* He wondered what she could possibly want. *When was the last time she came to see me?*

"When are you leaving?" she began.

"Next week."

"How are preparations going? Are you ready?" Although she was asking the questions, her body language proclaimed disinterest. She seemed unfocused, possibly even nervous, which was unusual for her.

He shrugged. "They're going. Not ready yet, but I will be." Then he added, as a sort of feeler, "But thank you for your concern."

She smiled. He could see it was fake. It pained him more than a little. He really wished it had not come to this between them. Not so very long ago they had gotten along splendidly. Now she was uncomfortable just talking to him. It would not do.

"Brenda, whatever it is, just say it." It came out sounding a little more abrupt than he intended.

"Ben, Trevor asked me to marry him. I said, 'Yes.'"

"I see." He nodded. His first thought was that it was good timing for him. Normally this news would have destroyed his world. It would be all he would think about day and night. But right now his mind had too much going on to fully dwell on this. "All right. Thanks for telling me. Congratulations." It all came out sounding very natural.

She stared at him a moment. She seemed to be waiting for him to say something else. When he did not, she appeared a little unsettled herself. "Okay, well, I don't want it to interfere with our work relationship—"

Ben shook his head. "No, not at all. I'm sorry that I've given you the impression it would. When I met him, I thought Trevor seemed like a very impressive man. I'm very happy for you."

Is this me speaking? he wondered. *Are these words actually coming out of my mouth?*

She looked at him a moment longer, then slowly began to nod. "Well, I... Thank you, Ben."

"Anything else? I wish I had longer to talk, Brenda, but I still have quite a few last minute details to resolve."

"Of course," she said. It sounded as though her tone had a hint of resentment. "Good luck on the trip, Ben." She turned away, stepped outside the office, and eased the door shut. The latch audibly clicked. He was alone. It seemed he always would be.

He stared at the door for a moment. *How am I feeling?* He was not sure.

He realized now that he should have asked when the wedding would be. He wondered whether she would be married when he returned from Iraq in late summer. Probably not, he decided. Brenda was an impetuous girl, but even she would want a little more time than that to plan a ceremony.

I can't think about this right now. He would have to do his best for the next few days to pretend this had not happened. He told himself it was an unneeded distraction and nothing more. In his experience, a good night's sleep was often the best salve for a troubled mind. But he needed to make it to tonight first. Being alone all evening would invite unwanted reflection. *Maybe I will join the kids for that drink after all.*

He felt the faintest of twinges in his temple. It was just what he had been waiting for. There was no enthusiasm, only a sense of inevitability. He opened the drawer of his desk, welcoming the excuse.

~

"You didn't bring Deanna?" Ernie asked as Halfus took a chair at the table.

Ernie had been the first to arrive. He had wanted to stake a claim on one of the few tables that was large enough to accommodate their group. Friday nights always brought crowds to *Bacchus Bluff*, and their last outing together would be a lot less enjoyable if they had to stand all night long. In the back of his mind was the possibility that Wendy might think of it as a sign of his consideration. There was an excellent chance she would never even find out—he never tooted his own horn, so someone else would have to mention it—but life comprises many simple gestures, and not every one needed to be noticed in the greater scheme of things. It only took one to get yourself noticed.

Halfus shook his head. "With exams coming up, she needed to study."

Ernie nodded, but he had his doubts that was the full story. He might buy that excuse Monday through Thursday, but not on Friday night. He suspected it had more to do with her being out of place amid this group. That, or perhaps Halfus did not want to risk irritating Wendy. It made sense, and it seemed like the kind of martyr behavior that Halfus was good for. Ernie also believed it would not do any good. She would find something to snap at him about anyway. Ernie did not envy his friend's bad breakup, even as he was considering a throw of the dice with her himself.

It was not long before others began to arrive. Wendy and Matt showed up next. They took their places at the table and Ernie filled their chilled mugs from one of the pitchers he had already ordered. There was a minute of friendly greetings all around before the four of them promptly split into two separate conversations. It was awkward, and every one of them hoped more people would show up soon to make it less conspicuous.

Then Rich, Tre'Andre, Kevin, and Tracy all arrived together. Tracy explained that they had bumped into each other on the way in. During greetings, Ernie examined her and Kevin closely. They did not look too bad, although their eyes were a little red and Tracy kept wiping her nose from a pack of tissues she kept perpetually in one hand.

"So, what are we talking about?" the affable redhead said as she took her seat. Ernie breathed a sigh of relief, and assumed the others were doing the same. Tracy would pull everyone into one group.

No one answered at first. She gave them all a curious glance, and when her eyes met Ernie's he felt compelled to speak. "Halfus and I are having a bit of a debate. Maybe you all can help us settle it."

"Oh, what about?"

"The Great Schism."

"The what?"

"The Great Schism," he repeated.

"Oh, something about history. Your specialty, dear." She touched Kevin's arm to draw his attention away from the two black athletes and the sports conversation they were engaged in.

Kevin took the chair beside his girlfriend. "What's up?"

"Help these two nerds settle their argument."

"Okay." Kevin looked at Ernie inquiringly.

"One of us is saying that the Great Schism is the period when there were two Popes," said Ernie. He watched Kevin's face for any reaction. Their friend was bright, but Ernie was not completely sure that he would know enough about this to be any help. "The other is saying it's the split between the Catholic and Orthodox Churches."

"Gotcha." Kevin nodded at the explanation.

"How incredibly...boring," said Tracy. She feigned a yawn, which turned into a sneeze that she nearly failed to catch in a tissue. Now Ernie understood why she never let go of those things.

Kevin flashed her a quick grin, undeterred by her derision. He faced Ernie and Halfus. "And what's riding on it?"

"Boilermakers," said Ernie.

"It just got more interesting," Tracy said.

"Indeed," Kevin agreed. "The answer you're looking for is...is..." He drew it out for dramatic effect, then stopped to take a swig of beer. He set his mug down and gave a satisfied *ah*. "Where was I?"

"I forget what we were talking about," said Halfus.

Kevin laughed. "Anyway, it's the second," he said. "The time when there were two Popes is called the Avignon Papacy."

"Help! Help! My boyfriend is a nerd," cried Tracy in the general direction of the bar.

Ernie smiled. He had been pretty certain about his position, but it still felt nice to have it confirmed. He did not often win disagreements with Halfus.

Tracy leaned forward. "Now that that's settled..."

They looked up at Rich, who was joining them while his boyfriend stepped away. "Wait a minute," he said. "The Avignon Papacy is also the Great Schism."

"Oh, wonderful," Tracy said, and sank back in her chair.

They had gone from one-against-one to two-against-two, but the sides were still deadlocked. The four guys began to chuckle. The conversation had gone from eccentric to absurd, but that was not at all surprising. It was one of the things Ernie loved about this crew. You never knew where you were going to wind up next.

"It was the Orthodox split," Wendy said from the far side of the table. Ernie had not even realized she was listening. For a second he wondered how she would know. She did not usually strike him as the authoritative source of information to resolve their debates.

But Halfus seemed to accept it without protest. "If anyone knows about this, it's Wendy. I'm satisfied." That remark caught Ernie by surprise. Then he remembered that she had switched her major to Ancient Studies. Perhaps her previous field had been religious history. Or European, more likely.

Ernie saw Wendy meet Halfus' eyes, then look quickly away. But she seemed pleased by the compliment. An idea occurred to Ernie. He could do her one better.

"I'm impressed," he announced. "It's not every day someone corrects both Rich *and* Halfus." He raised his mug in a playful toast. "Here's to Wendy."

The others raised their mugs also. Her name sounded in a chorus as glass clinked loudly.

Ernie caught Wendy looking at him. She silently mouthed something to him. *Thank you.*

Although outwardly he simply nodded, inside he swelled with pleasure.

Halfus stood up. "I'll get the drinks. Four? Me, Easy, Kevin, and Rich?"

"Make it five," said Matt. Ernie was surprised, but not unpleasantly. Maybe Matt would loosen up tonight. It was shaping up to be a night to remember, and Ernie did not want anyone holding them back.

Kevin counted. "One, two, three. Go!"

Each of the five of them dropped a whiskey shot into his full mug of beer, then gulped down the mixture as quickly as he could.

It was not a race, but Wendy paid attention to the order anyway. Kevin, Halfus, and Ernie all finished without a pause. Rich needed an extra breath and a moment longer. Then everyone watched Matt struggle through to the end, laughing and tapping the tabletop in encouragement. His neck waggled in the final moments, and Wendy worried that beer might start spilling out of both sides of his mouth, but to his credit he did not lose a drop. He slammed the mug down and smiled in happy embarrassment at their cheers.

Ernie patted Matt's shoulder. "Ready for another?" he asked with a grin.

Matt did not hesitate. "I am if you are."

"In that case, maybe not." Everyone laughed.

"Whew." Matt exaggerated a sigh of relief.

Kevin rubbed his nose with one of Tracy's tissues. "Good call. Those things are deceptively strong."

Rich refilled their mugs from another pitcher of beer. Wendy saw Ernie lift his glass to Matt, who clinked his against it. Then they both took a sip.

Ernie is a good guy, she decided. She was pleased to be getting along so well with him. Until recently, he had always seemed more like Halfus' friend than hers. Part of it was intuitively understanding that, following a breakup, mutual friends remained loyal to the person they knew first. It had seemed a matter of taking sides, and Ernie would naturally side with his closest buddy.

But it no longer felt as though they were taking sides. Now she felt a friendship developing directly between them. She was beginning to see him more for himself than for his connection to Halfus, and she wondered whether he looked at her the same way. Or maybe he never had that perspective to begin with. Perhaps she was the only one who had ever taken sides.

She was still glad Matt was there, but it no longer felt that she needed to attach herself to him. Not for his sake, nor her own. Whenever he engaged with others, she could turn to Rich or Tracy. And now Ernie. Her boundaries were expanding, and it felt good.

The evening settled into a typical outing of good beer and good talk. And, for a brief period, good and not-so-good music. They saw an employee of the bar clear off the stage and set up the karaoke machine. Previously, the *Bluff* had done this only on Sunday nights, but popular demand compelled them to do it more often. Karaoke was usually a big hit with the college students, and college students dominated the Friday crowd.

Of course, many of the amateurs could not carry a tune, and the alcohol only made things worse. More often than not, songs were performed more for comic relief than musical quality. Which was fine, as far as Wendy was concerned. Everyone was there to have fun.

There were exceptions, of course. One girl was clearly an admirer of Beyoncé and conducted her renditions in an impeccable replication of the popular singer. Much the same could be said of a gangly, bespectacled boy with a prematurely receding hairline who sang *With or Without You* with an intensity that would have made Bono proud. And no evening of karaoke was complete without the ensemble of drunken students belting out the chorus to *Wanted Dead or Alive*, a song that could only be improved by mockery.

Wendy was thrilled when the guys from her group went on stage together. She wondered what song they would choose. Then she recognized the Beatles, although not the name of this particular song. She and Tracy sat and clapped through the performance, and at the end Tracy put two fingers to her mouth and whistled loudly. Then the whistle exploded into a paroxysm of coughing. Wendy inched her chair away, trying not to be too obvious.

As the men stepped down from the stage, Wendy flashed her brightest smile at Matt. She was pleased that he was becoming more comfortable with everyone. She felt the same about Tre'Andre, who was quickly securing a place in their little community. She was very happy for Rich, who was clearly in love. Wendy caught Ernie looking at her and flashed him a smile, as well. She would not have been surprised if he turned out to be the ringleader of that little escapade.

Then she noticed that Halfus was not with them. She looked around until she spotted him. He was still on stage, alone, microphone in hand.

Wendy frowned. She had seen this once before when they were dating, and it had delighted her then. He was usually an unassuming kind of guy, so seeing him emerge from that shell had been a pleasant surprise. She had worried that he would embarrass himself, only to find out that he knew what he was doing. He could sing like Sinatra. She had been so proud of him at the time.

Now she was simply annoyed, although she could not understand why. There was a stool on the stage, and she watched him pull it over to sit with an exaggerated slump, like a man burdened by the weight of the world. Then he shifted, giving his shoulders a rigidity that conveyed defiance. A trumpet or French horn—it was difficult to hear through the crowd noise—sounded through the speakers, suggesting some kind of old jazz or blues.

He raised the microphone, and the brassy intro was complemented by a melodic voice far deeper than his conversational one. She had no idea how he did that, but it was captivating. So was the song. There was not much to it, but he sang very slowly, a pause after each phrase, as though giving the listener time to think it over.

Wish on the moon...and look for the gold in a rainbow
And you'll find happy times.
You'll hear a tune...that lives in the heart of a bluebird
And you'll find happy times.

Halfus had a peculiar stage presence that suggested he was aware of nothing but the music behind him and the microphone in his hand. Every other performer had played to the other patrons, often encouraging them to sing along. Halfus, on the other hand, seemed oblivious to the audience, which was slowly turning out to be most of the bar's occupants. Some of them had seen him before and nudged their friends to watch. By the time he reached the second verse, those in the bar who had not been paying attention now began to. The volume of background noise diminished noticeably.

Though things may look very dark, your dream is not in vain.
For when do you find a rainbow? Only after rain.
So wish on the moon...and some day, it may be tomorrow
You will suddenly hear chimes
And you'll have your happy, happy times.

The music was contemplative, the lyrics hopeful. Wendy saw a handsome man near her slip his arm around the shoulders of a girl. The two of them began to sway together.

Wendy loved, and hated, every minute of it. It was shit like this that made it so hard to get over him.

There was a lull while the instrumental bridge played on unaccompanied. Halfus waited it out, his head slightly bowed, microphone at his lap. Then he brought it back up for a final repeat of the chorus. This time with a little more head gesturing for effect, as though finally convincing himself. He was acting, of course, and she wondered how he managed to make it look convincing. She knew from personal experience that he did very little on impulse. She decided that he must practice. Even so, she had to give him credit. For he was very good.

He repeated the chorus one last time, ending on a happy note. Then the music trailed off, and he received an appreciative round of applause. As he returned to the table, the others patted his back and complimented his performance. Wendy wanted to tell him, "Nice job," or, "I liked it," or something equally banal. She wished she could acknowledge things like this without betraying the whole tangle of emotions she really felt. Instead, she looked around for someone to be talking to when he sat down, just in case he looked her way.

She picked out a receptive target. "Ernie, was that Beatles song your idea?"

She was relieved when he smiled and replied instead of falling all over his friend as the others were doing. She really did not pay close attention to what he was saying, however. She paid more attention to the conversation breaking out between Tracy and Halfus. "Who was that?"

"Bob Crosby."

"Bing Crosby?"

"Bob Crosby."

"Bing?"

"Bob."

"Bill Cosby?"

"Tracy, I love you, but I'm going to ignore you from now on."

He sat down a few seats away, and Wendy could stop pretending disinterest.

The longer the night went on, the more Ernie revised his earlier impression about Kevin and Tracy. Whatever little spark of energy they had when they came in was long since gone. They both looked very tired, and even Kevin had to borrow a few of Tracy's tissues. They also sat themselves at the end of the table, a little apart from the others. They wanted to be involved in the conversation while exposing their friends as little as possible. None of the others begrudged them their time at the bar, knowing how nice it was for them to get out of the house, but no one argued when Tracy announced that they would be leaving soon.

Meanwhile, Ernie ordered another pitcher from a passing waitress. She smiled broadly at him as she returned to set it on their table.

"Thanks, Flo," he told her, having no idea what her actual name was.

"Sure thing, Sugar," she replied in a mock country accent.

Ernie watched her walk off. *Maybe*, he thought. She was only semi-cute, but sometimes they looked better once you found out they had a nice personality. Despite what the shallowest of men would say.

"I think she likes you," Wendy said to him. She was smiling at him mischievously.

It was not exactly what he wanted to hear. He had hoped that Wendy was starting to come around a little herself, but a girl who was interested would be unlikely to push him toward another. Unless she was being tactically deceptive. Girls did often play hard to get. Maybe a part of that was the art of deflection.

He shrugged. "Not really my type."

"Oh, what's your type?" Wendy inquired. She was still smiling, and her expression suggested that she was enjoying herself. Prying into his private thoughts.

Ernie looked hard at her. He had a mind to reply with a perfect description of her. *Blue eyes. Curly blonde hair. Light complexion, light makeup. Smart. And a little self-absorbed.*

No, it would not do. That was too direct. Even if she would be flattered—which was not at all certain—it would not be long before she lorded it over him. It was always better to keep them guessing.

"There's no one thing," he said. "It's easier to know what you're not into than to list everything you are."

"Oh." She looked a little disappointed. He was not certain what that meant, but he decided to take it as a small but encouraging sign.

They looked back at the others, and he became aware of Tracy prodding Halfus about something. She did that a lot. She tended to identify the person in a group who spoke the least, then asked them questions to draw them out of their shell. She liked it when everyone shared the spotlight. Which was somewhat ironic considering that she was herself almost always at the center of it.

"I'm just curious what a phobia feels like," she was saying. "It seems so irrational."

Curiously, Halfus was patiently trying to explain something about himself that many people would have found embarrassing. "Irrational, maybe, but not illogical. It depends on what the mind perceives as pressure," he said. "Different people are fixated on different things. Who knows why, but there it is."

The others were watching and listening. They all seemed content to allow Tracy to do the questioning and Halfus to do the answering.

"Yes, but it's one thing to worry about flunking out of school. That's normal. It's another thing to lose basic motor functions just because you're up high. You said you can't even stand up straight. I don't get it...doesn't that make it worse? Why would your mind do this as a defense mechanism?"

"Maybe it's telling me to avoid the situation entirely. It's like being burned by a flame. You quickly learn to stop sticking your face in it."

"But that's pain. This is just..." She fished for the right word. "Anxiety."

"It depends on what the mind perceives as pressure," he repeated. When she shook her head in frustration, he tried again. "There's more than one kind of pressure. Imagine carrying that pitcher of beer across this crowded bar without spilling a drop. Easy, right? You could do it while talking to a friend about a movie you just saw. You don't really even need to pay attention.

"But that's the crux of it. Now imagine someone was going to pay you a million dollars if you can do it without spilling a drop. The equation changes. Maybe you could still do it. But what if your friend wants to keep blathering on about this movie while you're trying to do it? Do you think you might ask her to shut up so you could concentrate?

"Now imagine that instead of your friend talking movies, it's a man with a gun pointed at your head. Spill a drop and he pulls the trigger.

Unless you are exceptionally relaxed—which, knowing you, Tracy, is probably true—your mind is going to obsess a little about that pitcher of beer. Every step, every twitch of your wrist, every sign that your fingers are getting tired, or your grip is loosening...everything gets magnified. To the point where you can't trust your basic motor functions any more. You could easily overcompensate to the slightest jiggle and shake your hand too much. Or lose just enough sense of balance that you don't keep the pitcher level, and you see that it might spill over the rim, so you jerk your hand the other way, and—"

"Okay, I get it," she said.

"For me, heights are like that. No matter how hard I try, my mind gets overly fixated. I know my knees will overcompensate for the slightest brush of wind. And knowing they will makes me not trust them. And not trusting them turns them to jelly. So I can't stand up straight."

"Well. Sucks to be you," said Tracy, abruptly resigning the topic of inquiry. She finished the last sip of beer in her mug.

"I hate to say it, kids, but we should go," said Kevin. He pushed back his chair and was about to stand up.

Ernie saw someone approaching. "Doc!"

Everyone looked up. A moment later the table erupted into cheers and laughter.

For that split second before announcing the newcomer, Ernie thought he was looking at the face of a troubled man. Any sign of that was quickly extinguished in a cascade of handshakes and hugs. Doc seemed to bask in the attention of his students. As well he should. He was more than a regular professor to them. Not exactly a father figure, although there was some of that. He was both a mentor and a friend. Ernie was not as close to the man as most of the others, but he had no doubt that Doc would bend over backwards for him as much as any of them. He was guiding them through this most critical period of their lives, and he was just as invested in the result as they were themselves.

But there was something more to it than that. For all his intelligence, for all his authority, Doc came across as vulnerable. The way he clearly appreciated the attention he was receiving now was a sign of it. Maybe that was what drew them so close to him. Not only was he good for them, they were good for him. It was an appealing notion.

"Well, I'm glad we waited this long," said Tracy. "I would not have wanted to miss this." As she spoke, she rubbed one of her tissues over a spot on the pocket of Doc's shirt, where she had left an embarrassing drip of mucus when she hugged him.

"Someone get the man a mug," commanded Kevin.

"Thank you, Ernie," said their professor when Ernie complied.

Everyone was standing with drinks at the ready, staring somewhat expectantly at Doc.

"Speech," said Wendy.

"I, uh, well..." Doc stammered. It was unlike him to be inarticulate. But then again this situation was quite unlike giving a rehearsed lecture in a classroom. Finally, he shrugged his shoulders. "Thank you for inviting me. You all...well, you know how I feel."

It felt a little sappy, amplified by the alcohol already in their systems. But no one minded.

Still, Ernie took it upon himself to rescue the shy man from the predicament.

He raised his mug. "To Iraq," he called out. *It's going to be quite an adventure.*

"To Iraq!" Nine mugs clinked.

It was the last time they were all together.

5

THE CRADLE OF CIVILIZATION

In 1588, the English navy defeated the Spanish Armada in a climactic battle whose results portended an end to any future fears of invasion. Thus puffed with pride and seeking new worlds to conquer, the small island nation began to stretch its mercantile tendrils outward. Within a decade, English vessels were sailing around the coastlines of India and the course of history was forever changed.

In 1600, the Honourable East India Company was formed. It began as a modest endeavor, trading pepper from Java, but within a few hundred years accounted for half the trade of the entire world. The company garnered monopolies on commodities such as cotton, silk, saltpeter, tea, and dyes. And it was directly responsible for drawing England into a war to force drugs on the people of China.

The East India Company serves to illustrate the particularly incestuous relationship between business and government. Although the crown issued the company's royal charter, the British government itself officially owned no shares. Instead, ownership was entirely in the hands of the wealthiest aristocrats and merchants of the day. Those owners who were not already a part of the English bureaucracy simply informed the crown and ministers what was best for the company, and England acted accordingly.

In many cases, the involvement of the English state was not really necessary. The company financed its own private armies and handled administrative matters in the locations of their branches, effectively governing without Government. Only when it encountered difficulties beyond the capabilities of its own troops and directors did the East India Company enlist the aid of the English crown.

One such crisis happened in the early nineteenth century. The company had already cornered the market on the production side of opium, but Chinese authorities bit into East India profit margins by outlawing importation of the destructive drug. When China went so far as to order the execution of opium smugglers, England was forced to step in on behalf of the company, fighting two Opium Wars against the Chinese until that country acquiesced in legalizing the substance—and handing Hong Kong over to the victors for good measure.

The experience of the various East India Companies—many European countries had their own version—sheds light on contemporary international relations, for those willing to look. The influence of business on government affects the daily life of every global citizen in surprising and manifold ways. More ominously, it is one of the primary shapers of foreign policy, where merchants are enriched and soldiers sacrificed. The mushrooming conflicts of interest between business leaders and governments at every level is something of which every individual should be aware. These conflicts should, in fact, be obvious. Yet in many cases the efforts to keep them shrouded in shadow are increasingly sophisticated. In others, their longstanding presence is so ingrained as to render them acceptable. They are, in essence, invisible in plain sight.

The founders of these earliest trading companies were among the first to figure out the great game, then subsequently how to rewrite the rules in their own favor. As the world evolves, so too does the game. But the reward for winning never changes. International relations, both yesterday and today, is less about the betterment of man than the enrichment of men.

Iraq was completely different from what he expected.

No, that was not quite right, for he had not really known what to expect. Since learning that he and the others would be joining this expedition, he had paid a lot more attention to news stories pertaining to the Middle East in general, and Iraq in particular. But the stories had a peculiar slant to them, always pro-Western and pro-business, leaving him wondering whether censors were still at work even though the war here was long since over. The editorial pages, on the other hand, had a lot more variation in their depictions of the situation. But they were also, by definition, skewed toward the opinion of the writer.

That said, he had come with an open mind, eager to learn about the country first-hand. And what he was learning so far was surprising.

For one thing, his initial impression was that Iraq was surprisingly full of Westerners. The first clue had come when they boarded the second leg of their flight path, an Iraqi Airways jetliner from London to Baghdad full of blue and white collar workers, mostly middle-aged white men. Absent on the plane were the families he was used to seeing on every other flight he could remember. He did not think through the ramifications until their arrival at Baghdad International Airport. At first glance, the only obvious Iraqis were the employees, busily serving their white patrons with pleasant smiles. All the travelers appeared Western in complexion and garb.

Apparently, he was not the only one to notice. "I wonder...are there any Iraqis in Iraq?" quipped Ernie.

"Yeah, you're right," agreed Wendy. She, too, was standing still, looking all around, taking in their new surroundings.

Rich and Doc were ahead, moving toward the Transportation signs. The other three hurried to catch up before they were lost in the crowd. Baghdad International seemed to be doing brisk business.

In this respect and several others, the airport seemed like any other. Signs were posted in Arabic and English. The five of them claimed their bags and passed through customs with no greater rigmarole than if this were a vacation in Paris or Madrid. Possibly less, considering the lack of scrutiny given to their American and British passports.

The group had one more flight to go, from Baghdad to Mosul. But that would come tomorrow. For now, they were to spend the remainder of this evening getting to their hotel, getting something to eat, and getting a good night's sleep for the long day ahead. In the morning they had a meeting scheduled at the American embassy, followed by the last flight and drive to the dig site.

As they stepped outside the terminal, he was overcome by a different and entirely unique sensation. Ahead of them stretched the bustling, modern city of Baghdad. But behind the noise and commotion he saw a much smaller, quieter ancient city. Allowing the others to walk on without him, he stopped and took a deep breath, attempting to commune with it. It was difficult to filter out the dynamic sights and sounds crying out for attention. When he relaxed his eyes, allowing the background to drop out of focus, he could easily imagine he was standing in any large city back home.

But inside him the feeling remained, growing in intensity. *Hammurabi may have stood on this exact spot. I am standing on ground where kings walked, slaves toiled, and chariots clashed. Here, empires rose and fell thousands of years before Christ was born. The residue of five millennia—fifty centuries—fills the air around me. I am breathing it in. It is now inside me. Whatever is happening in this place today, it is but a tiny fragment of all that has happened here.*

It was exhilarating and humbling at the same time. As a student of history, he was intoxicated. *No matter how mundane life becomes when we return, we will always have this.* He felt blessed.

"Halfus, our shuttle is here," Rich said beside him. Halfus had not seen the large black van pull up. Now a side door opened, revealing two rows of comfortable seats.

They piled into the vehicle, a shuttle bus belonging to the hotel. Their driver was a young man with close-trimmed beard and a crisp white shirt that would have looked sharp if not for the sweat discolorations under the arms. In very good English he welcomed them to Baghdad and asked politely about their trip. Halfus allowed the others to answer. He was more interested in the activity outside the shuttle than the conversation inside.

They were heading into the famous Green Zone, the section of Baghdad where most of the international community lived and worked. The drive was not long, but somehow brilliant day turned to shadowy evening during the brief trip. They passed a checkpoint manned by Iraqi soldiers who paid them little mind, then immediately passed into a different universe. Outside the perimeter, small dirty homes and modest establishments dominated the backdrop, while the streets were occupied by a mix of sober-looking pedestrians and frolicking children. Outdoors in the summer heat, it was hard to decide if they looked more tired, parched, or dusty. He knew better than to feel sorry for them, however. Just because their lives were different did not mean they enjoyed them any less.

Inside the zone, the city looked to be all business. The volume of traffic increased, pedestrians diminished, and buildings appeared large and immaculate in relation to those outside. Their hotel emphatically solidified the impression. It was a towering structure of glass and lights, and Halfus knew before entering that it would be the nicest place in which he had ever laid head on pillow. The lobby conjured visions of an oasis, complete with bubbling fountain. The contrast with the dry and thirsty people he had seen earlier was striking.

His companions seemed to be as moved as he was, to judge by their expressions. As well as their comments.

"Well, I'm impressed," said Rich.

"Me, too," Ernie echoed.

"This is a very nice hotel," said their driver as he wheeled in their baggage. He unloaded it onto a porter's trolley. "You will like it very much." Halfus watched Doc thank and tip the man. Then, as an awkward afterthought, shake his hand. The driver flashed a bright smile and gave him a nod before returning to his vehicle.

"Can we just stay here for the next six weeks?" Wendy asked jokingly.

"I doubt Herr Doktor Schwarzvogel would be too happy about that," replied Doc.

"Besides, this place would get old very quickly," added Halfus. He found it interesting that Rich nodded at the thought, while the others did not. *Different strokes.*

"Come on," Doc said, taking charge and leading them to the bank of hotel clerks. "Let's get checked in. We can talk in the rooms."

"Or over dinner," said Ernie. "I'm starving."

The next morning they visited the gargantuan complex that was the American Embassy in Iraq. Located on the bank of the Tigris, the quasi-military compound was fittingly impressive for a conquering nation. Halfus could imagine Genghis Khan building something on this scale—if he had been born eight hundred years later, and in a modern hospital rather than a yurt.

The main building was a yellowish sandstone, four stories high and stretching broadly in either direction. Halfus wished there had been time to explore the site—not just this building but the entire area —but their flight schedule would not allow it. Nor would the soldiers with automatic rifles. The mood of the compound was officious and dour. At least that was the impression given by the armed guards patrolling outdoors and manning the security check which the group cleared upon entering.

Halfus had been to one other embassy in his life, the Japanese embassy in Washington. He remembered it as a quaint building built for two purposes—to conduct the official business of the Japanese government in the United States, and to showcase some of the important aspects of Japanese tradition. Halfus had attended a tea ceremony there. At the time, it had surprised him with its whimsical ritual, but he later realized it had taught him that a culture could place great importance on things both utilitarian and ornamental.

Now he wondered what aspects of American culture this embassy illustrated to curious Iraqis. He recalled the pundits on television at the time of the invasion who seemed genuinely excited about bringing freedom and democracy to the Middle East. They claimed that Iraqis were desperate for America to bring their ideals to their country. Who better to teach them? Sometimes messy, sometimes glorious, the circuitous road to democracy was etched deeply in the history of the United States. The embassy could showcase some of that road. Perhaps a museum in one wing devoted to the trials and tribulations of the fight for American liberty, to show interested visitors that obstacles are inevitable, but surmountable.

It now seemed naive to wonder whether such a museum existed. For all the lofty rhetoric about Iraqi eagerness and gratitude, the sight of this embassy made clear that those who paid for this monstrosity understood the way Americans would really be perceived in Iraq. No, not paid for—because of course taxpayers had paid for this. Those that *designed* this compound had one thing in mind—security from a hostile populace.

The five of them spoke little as they were ushered to a tidy interior conference room and told to wait for their contact. They took seats around an oval table with room for twenty. They looked and felt minuscule in a place like this.

Ernie spoke what Halfus was thinking. "Is it just me, or is this place scary big?" Heads nodded.

"I researched it," Rich announced. "The embassy is the size of eighty football fields. It cost seven hundred fifty million dollars to build."

Ernie whistled. The sound seemed incongruous with this authoritative, intimidating structure. He immediately stopped himself and they looked around as though expecting guards to arrive.

Rich cut through the awkward silence with his continuing narrative. "Apparently, before this place was built they used one of Saddam's palaces as the embassy. I guess it wasn't big enough for them."

The next thing he said surprised Halfus. "I rather like it."

"What?" Wendy sounded painfully chagrined.

Rich nodded. "It reminds me of the cathedrals in England. Not in a religious sense, naturally. Many people see them as a huge waste of money, but others see them as the Houses of God. They should be splendid." He was looking at the others, reading their dubious expressions. "Authority works better if it conveys a sense of awe. I think this place accomplishes that."

Now their faces registered a mixture of understanding and dissent, the two reagents that alchemically combined in students to form heated debate. This seemed neither the time nor the place, however, and even Wendy slumped her shoulders and let the matter drop.

Ernie changed the subject. "I think whatever I ate last night is trying to claw its way out of me."

Halfus had wanted to go out on the streets last night in order to experience some authentic Iraqi cuisine, but the others voted to stay in and eat at the hotel's own fancy restaurant. Based on the number of Americans not only in the hotel but all around the Green Zone, he guessed that the menu would cater to that patronage. Instead, he was pleased to discover that they offered an array of Arabic and even a few Persian dishes as a complement to the standard American fare.

Ernie had wanted to order spaghetti with meatballs, but Halfus and Rich had urged him to try something new and exotic. He had remained reluctant until Wendy joined the prodding. Then he relented and told her to pick something for him.

They ordered a variety of mezzas, soups, and rice dishes to share. Halfus particularly liked the *falafel* but was disappointed in the *dolma* he tried. He could not remember the names of most of the bigger dishes, but nothing had stood out one way or the other.

Just for Ernie, Wendy ordered a *kibbeh* that he picked around for a few minutes before finally mustering the courage to try. He asked what he was eating, and Wendy's face brightened with humor as she told him, "Yak penis." It was clearly a joke, but Ernie contorted his face in disgust. Halfus sampled the dish himself and thought it delicious, but Ernie overdramatized the ceremony of eating for theatrical effect. His friend liked being the center of attention. Halfus did not know if it was something that came natural to him, or simply something that made him feel better about himself. Either way, it suited Halfus fine. Considering that he seldom wanted the spotlight on himself, theirs was a symbiotic friendship.

He could believe that the exotic food and spices might have really had an effect on Ernie's digestive tract, unaccustomed as it was to much more than hamburgers and beer. He was not without sympathy, but the others seemed more amused than anything.

Ernie fidgeted in the large padded, yet somehow uncomfortable chair. He did look a little pale, but Halfus suspected the anxiety of this meeting had as much to do with it as a troubled digestion.

"You look like you're turning into a yak," Wendy joked.

"Or a penis," Rich added dryly.

"Knock it off," said Doc.

Their good humor was cut short when the door opened and a man with pristine charcoal hair and a suit to match entered the room. He took a seat across from the five of them. He opened a folder full of paper forms on the table. He had not so much as looked at them. Halfus had been brought up to look people in the eye, and this man's behavior already struck him as impolite. The man radiated self-importance.

As he examined the top sheet from his file he distractedly said, "Good morning, gentlemen," to the room.

"And lady," asserted Wendy.

The man looked up from his pages. He raised an eyebrow in confusion. Then he caught himself. *Wouldn't want to show your feathers ruffled*, thought Halfus.

"Apologies. And lady." He looked at Doc. "Excuse me, I was not aware that you had a girl in your group."

Doc reacted with a nervous twitch. He seemed to shrink away from the man. "Did I miss a form? There were quite a lot of them."

The man shook his head. "No, there is no separate form for girls. Someone on my staff simply should have said something to me."

Halfus could imagine how much Wendy was enjoying being talked about as though she was not in the room. She squirmed in her seat, but kept her mouth shut and allowed Doc to handle this.

"Is there a problem?"

"No. No, of course not. There are simply certain...sensitivities that must be taken into consideration. In fact, that leads me into the purpose of this meeting. We—"

"Pardon me," said Rich. "I'm Richard Lewis."

"Yes. And?"

"Might I inquire your name?" Halfus noted that Rich was trying not to sound condescending. He was always considerate of the feelings of others, even if consideration was not being returned.

Halfus wondered where Rich found the courage. It was not always easy to speak up like this. There is a curious intangible quality to some meetings, spoken in the language of confidence. Typically one party would dominate, while others would shrink. Balance was rare, but Rich came close to accomplishing it. The embassy representative had authority on his side, but they had numbers.

The man was momentarily flustered. This meeting was probably not starting the way he expected. He put down the sheet he was holding, and took a moment to look them over.

"Scott McGammon. I am your liaison for your time on the Schwarzvogel Project."

He reached across the table to shake Rich's hand, then each of the others in succession as they introduced themselves to him.

"Wendy Weald."

"Ernie Zolak."

"Halfus Lonagon."

"And you are Doctor...Benjamin Appelstein?" McGammon inquired, glancing back at the top sheet.

"Yes."

"Pleased to meet you all." It did not sound particularly convincing. His voice was stiff, with a hint of irritation. He was rediscovering his authority. "Now, pleasantries aside, let's get to business. I am on a busy schedule, as I'm sure you are, too."

They quickly learned the purpose of the meeting. This was no formality expected of all visitors, nor a courtesy extended to an honored assemblage. This meeting was a strict admonition to behave by a rigid set of rules during their time in Iraq. They were not to call attention to themselves—particularly Wendy, who was to keep her head covered anywhere she could be seen by the locals. They were not to explore on their own. They were not to leave the immediate environs of the dig site for the duration of their time in country, except by special request of officials. All for their own safety, of course.

"One other item that I'm sure you will understand," McGammon finished. "Europeans do not have a great track record when it comes to taking artifacts away from the country where they found them. The Interior Ministry is particularly concerned to see that this does not happen here. This expedition is here to gather knowledge, not souvenirs. Is that clear?"

When Doc assured him that it was, the officious man smiled at last and wished them a pleasant time in Iraq. He stood and shook their hands a second time, then held the door open for them as they filed out of the room. The whole meeting had lasted less than thirty minutes, but the entire mood of their group had changed in the meantime.

"Well, that was terrifying," said Ernie as soon as they were outside the building and headed for Al Kindi street. Wendy nodded.

Doc stepped ahead to flag down two taxis. The four students stopped and waited, looking at each other without speaking. They were clearing their heads of the surprisingly disturbing encounter.

Halfus' eyes met Wendy's. Neither looked away. "I'm proud of you," he told her. "You displayed more patience than I would have."

"Thank you."

"I am, too," said Ernie. She looked at him and smiled.

"Cabs are here," said Rich.

A few hours later they were back in the air on a flight to Mosul, their penultimate destination. Mosul was the largest city of Nineveh province, which bordered Syria to the west and reached almost to Turkey in the north. The ruins of Nineveh, the ancient city that gave the province its name and the initial location of the Schwarzvogel dig, were located within the city's perimeter. But the expedition had apparently found something more intriguing and relocated to a secondary site a few dozen miles to the south. Halfus was not sure how they would be getting there. He doubted they could easily take another shuttle or taxi the way they had in Baghdad.

Halfus sat beside Rich. Doc sat quietly alone behind them, while across the aisle Wendy and Ernie chatted away incessantly. Ernie was a theatrical gesticulator and seemed to be doing an effective job entertaining her, judging by the frequency of her giggles. Halfus was pleased to see her in a good mood, even though he felt a pang of regret. Not so very long ago he kept her entertained like that. It was not just that he missed her company. There was also the feeling he got from making her smile. Matt was right. He had been pretty good at it, and it had made him feel like a better man. What he missed the most was feeling good about himself.

He did not speak much during the flight, and Rich was the type of neighbor who respected his silence, so Halfus found himself with plenty of time to contemplate those around him. The plane was sparsely occupied. Other than the five members of his group, there was only a handful of other people aboard. Three looked like businessmen *sans* business attire. Instead of suits they wore khakis and sandals, but carried the ubiquitous laptops that were the hallmark of their class. As soon as the plane was airborne the laptops came out and all three men stared at what appeared to be spreadsheets. Possibly it was the same spreadsheet on all three computers, for the men continuously engaged in hushed discussions animated by frequent finger-pointing at their screens.

Seated in the row ahead of him were a pair of young men wearing jeans and tight-fitting pullovers. Halfus' first impression was that they were some kind of engineers or mechanics. He had seen plenty of those so far in Iraq. It had been a little disturbing to witness first-hand how many jobs in the country were performed by imported Westerners. Surely, there must be Iraqis who could do much of the work. And more could be trained. The plethora of jobs would be far better for the economy and stability of a country recovering from war and occupation. Not to mention it would give a tired people hope. Halfus could think of no better way to make certain the changes in

Iraq were more readily embraced. Sadly, it had not happened that way.

On reflection, however, he did not think these two men were here for work. At least not work of that kind. Now he was leaning toward military. What threw him was their clothing, and the unkempt goatee worn by one of them. But their lean frames were heavily muscled and their posture stiffer than normal. One wore his light hair in a buzz cut, while the one with the goatee kept the top of his head shaved bald. Halfus found himself wondering about them and felt the temptation to ask for their story, but he was not the type to engage with complete strangers unless events dictated otherwise. Which they currently did not.

"Guys, I have a favor to ask of you."

Halfus turned to see Doc leaning forward in his seat to a spot between their shoulders. He spoke in a reserved voice. Clearly, he was using Wendy's and Ernie's distraction in each other as an opportunity to speak to his two senior students. He seemed nervous. Halfus could not remember ever seeing him like this before.

Rich and Halfus exchanged a glance. "Anything, Doc. You know that."

"I don't think I mentioned something to you before. I have...a history with Herr Doktor Schwarzvogel." He hesitated before continuing. "It's kind of a bad history. He is a hard man to figure out, and I don't really know what he thinks of me. But I get a little anxious thinking about him."

Rich wore a look of concern. "What can we do?"

"This is hard for me to ask of my students. But I trust you two. I remember the Herr Doktor as a very particular, exacting man. He will have a very low tolerance for mistakes. Or unprofessionalism. Or humor."

They nodded, and Halfus glanced across the aisle at the other two. They were still chatting away obliviously.

"I'm not worried about you two, but I'd like you to help me with the others. I want everyone to be able to enjoy this trip. But we're here first and foremost to do a job, and if anyone looks as though they're having a little too much fun—"

"We got it," said Rich. "You can count on us."

Doc sat back, leaving Halfus and Rich to chew things over for themselves. Halfus could see where their professor's concern was coming from, but he doubted it was necessary. Wendy and Ernie sometimes came across as having chips on their shoulders, but everyone had their idiosyncrasies. They were all serious, hardworking students when they needed to be.

"Hey, buddy. Got a map of Mosul?"

Halfus looked up to see one of the young men from the row ahead speaking to him. It was Buzzcut. He had twisted around on his seat, and now Halfus could see the long tail of a snake or dragon winding up the length of his forearm and under the sleeve. Halfus also noticed the arm was rippled with muscle. His amateur boxing instinct immediately evaluated the man. Based on arm length and build, Halfus was glad he did not have to face him in a ring.

"No, sorry."

Unfazed, Buzzcut looked at Rich next. "How about you?"

Rich was already reaching to his bag under the seat. "I do, yes."

Halfus' curiosity was piqued. "You're not going to the army base?"

The man looked amused. He snorted. "Heh. No."

Now that they were talking, Halfus could not resist probing further. "I had you pegged as military."

"Yes and no." The man looked at his companion, who shrugged. "We work for Pax America. We're private contractors." He had a noticeable affectation to his speech, as though he had learned to talk by watching old mobster movies.

"You mean mercenaries," said Rich as he handed over a folded map.

"If you prefer."

"You fight for money, yes?"

"So do security guards. And police, for that matter."

"Fair enough."

"Lee and me, we were in the Army. I Corps. I did two tours here. We liked it, and there's not exactly an abundance of new jobs back in the States. So when Pax America offered to bring us back here for five times what we were making before, it was a no-brainer."

"Can't say I blame you," said Halfus.

"Goddamn right," said Baldy.

"Only problem is my girl doesn't much like it. She wanted me to stay home when I left the Army."

"My wife, too," said Baldy. "Although she doesn't complain about the money."

Halfus never understood how military families could stand spending so much time apart. He supposed it was a matter of getting used to it.

"So what precisely do you do?" Rich asked.

"Shit, what don't we do?"

"You don't fight beside the garrison troops, I presume."

"Sometimes. Been part of a few convoys that got attacked."

"You escort military convoys?"

"Sure, why not?"

"Well, doesn't the Army do that themselves?"

"They don't have the manpower to be everywhere at once."

"And you do?"

"Not Pax America alone. But all the contractors? Yeah, I guess so."

"How many mercs...contractors are there?" asked Halfus.

A shrug. "Now that things have quieted down? I'm not sure."

"How many were there during the war?" asked Rich.

Buzzcut looked at his companion. They grinned. "At least ten thousand."

"More like twenty," Baldy said.

Halfus exchanged another glance with Rich. "Jesus." His head attempted a quick calculation of how much money that must cost. Tens, maybe hundreds of millions. Oil companies, building contractors, food caterers. And now mercenaries. Iraq was no desert —it was an ocean of money. And the companies that took advantage were swimming in it.

Buzzcut was chuckling now. "Yeah, man. Uncle Sam likes to keep his footprint small when it comes to the public. It's better politics.

And we're more efficient. They can send us to hot spots at a moment's notice."

"Hot spots?" asked Rich. "What are you gents doing in Mosul, anyway?"

"Not sure yet."

Halfus felt a slight knot of concern constricting inside him.

This time, Baldy chuckled.

"I wouldn't worry about it," said Buzzcut. "There's still some troublemakers out there, but they're getting fewer and farther between. And we're ten times better trained and better equipped than them. My biggest fear is that the country is going to get too peaceful and the contracts will dry up."

"Amen, brother," Baldy agreed.

The plane was hitting turbulence and Buzzcut bounced around a bit while he talked to them. He seemed not to notice. "We got reassigned yesterday. They said to catch the next plane to Mosul and they gave us some address where their local HQ is. It's less impressive than it sounds. Probably some guy operating a *falafel* stand. So we don't know much more than you. Never even been to Mosul before. I wasn't with them when I Corps was here back in oh-four."

"Say, thanks again for the map, buddy."

"Welcome," said Rich. To judge by his expression, he was less concerned about what they were hearing than Halfus. But Halfus had learned *not* to judge Rich by his expression. He was sure the wheels were turning.

Buzzcut sat back down, disappearing from view. Halfus sat there, shaking around from the turbulence. Despite his acrophobia, planes never really bothered him. That did not mean his thoughts were not disquiet, however.

The turbulence continued for the remainder of the flight. When they touched down, it came as a relief to bodies and minds weary from the travel. Soon it would be coming to an end.

Halfus was a little surprised when Buzzcut and Baldy shook his hand on their way out of the plane. He wished them good luck, which they returned. He watched them step off and wondered what their lives must be like. How very different to seek out danger and excitement in a foreign country every day. It put their six-week research project into perspective.

Soon after debarking he learned how they would be getting out to the dig site. A young woman in *hijab*, tunic, and blue jeans stood in the arrivals section holding up a sign that read "Dr. Appelstein." Doc led their party to her and introduced himself, followed by all the others.

"Lisa," she repeated to each of them as she shook their hands while smiling broadly. Halfus could not help but notice how very blue her eyes were, much bluer than any he had seen before. When their gazes met he was so taken by them that he felt a little embarrassed. She noticed something in his expression and her smile seemed to widen.

Then, turning back to their leader, she said, "Please follow me." She led them not toward the exit, but to a lounge area occupied by three mustached Iraqi men. One was dressed in a sharp business suit, the others in uniform. The writing on the uniform jackets was in Arabic, and Halfus did not know Iraqi heraldry well enough to tell if they were police, military, or something else entirely.

"Greetings, Doctor Appelstein," said the suited man in a friendly tone. "My name is Ahmed Shalhoub. I am the Cultural Minister for Nineveh Governorate." His English was excellent, and he politely took the time to shake all of their hands before continuing. Halfus was relieved that he paid no more attention to Wendy than the others. Apparently, word that one of them was a woman had reached this far.

"I will be traveling with you to the site. I hope you don't mind." Halfus noted the use of the singular rather than the plural. Either the two uniformed men would not be joining them, or they were merely an extension of Ahmed Shalhoub. Halfus guessed the latter, which would make them security. It seemed a reasonable deduction considering everything they had seen so far. Security seemed to be a significant priority in post-war Iraq. That was both a good and a bad sign. Good that it was taken seriously, but bad that it needed to be.

"Come. We can speak as we go." He motioned with his hand, and they set out toward the exit.

"I visit Herr Doktor Schwarzvogel once per week. The Iraqi government is very interested in his discoveries. We understand that we have a very rich history in this country, and we are proud to work with our partners for the erudition of everyone."

Ahmed lifted a hand toward the exit. "Please, after you." Halfus thought he was going to hold the door for them, but instead one of his sidekicks performed that function. They stepped back out into the dry heat of late afternoon. Most of their time in Iraq so far had been in air conditioned vehicles and buildings. It now struck Halfus just how warm the days were going to be. Things might be uncomfortable over the coming weeks. The adventurous part of his soul reveled in it.

The airport was located south of the city, so he presumed they would be heading north. Instead, they took a trio of taxis to a depot too small to be called a bus station. Lisa joined Halfus and Rich in one cab, giving him an opportunity to learn that she was from Stuttgart and was one of the last two of Schwarzvogel's students remaining on the expedition. She spoke freely about herself and the dig, answering every question he and Rich posed to her with articulate English and abundant liveliness. Halfus wished they had had more time for conversation than the brief taxi ride accorded. Lisa was jauntily finishing one anecdote about her own first day in Iraq as they stepped out of the car. Halfus glanced at the others and saw Wendy watching with a disapproving scowl.

Ahmed led them to a small weathered bus and informed them that this was to be their transport to camp. They repeated their seating positions from the plane, Halfus and Rich on one side and Wendy with Ernie on the other. Doc sat in the front with Ahmed, just behind the bus driver. The uniformed men sat behind them. Lisa sat alone toward the back. Rich had offered his seat to her, but she declined with the explanation that she had some reading to do. Halfus saw her pull out what looked like a paperback novel. As the door of the bus closed and they started moving forward, she pulled off her headwear and absently ran fingers through her straight blonde hair.

"Hey, Halph," Ernie called. "Beautiful view, isn't it?"

Halfus looked over at his friend. Ernie was grinning mischievously at him. Then he nodded at the windows, beyond which a dusty, desolate landscape stretched out as far as the eye could see. Perhaps Ernie was being sarcastic about the terrain, perhaps he was being deliberately provocative. Either way, Halfus looked away before his thoughts could betray him with a healthy dose of red in the cheeks.

He found himself staring out at the landscape with increasing interest. Dusty and desolate it was, but for all that still possessed a form of beauty. No doubt he was influenced by the knowledge that five thousand years of history had transpired on these plains and those hills. He closed his eyes and allowed himself to imagine farmers and slaves, horses and war chariots. He was communing with history again, and lost track of time.

He snapped out of it when Rich prodded him. "I think we're close."

He looked out at the darkening sky. "I hope so. It's getting late. Is that the camp?" In the distance he saw several tents growing larger as they drew nearer.

The bus was slowing down. Ernie was now standing in the aisle. He leaned across the two of them to look out Halfus' window. "Either we're here, or Ahmed's selling us off to a tribe of Bedouins."

"It's 'Bedouin,'" Wendy corrected. "And don't say that. I think he's nice. He reminds me of my Uncle Charlie." Halfus noticed that she had removed her own headscarf at some point during the trip. He knew wearing it must have bothered her. She was rightfully proud of those golden curls.

Halfus did not know her Uncle Charlie, but he doubted there were many similarities. Ahmed Shalhoub's behavior had been impeccably polite so far, but Halfus sensed a harder edge below the surface. One did not become a minister in a brutal place like Iraq without a certain toughness of character.

Halfus saw Lisa getting up and grabbing her things. He swallowed, and realized how uncomfortably dry his throat was. He had been drinking bottled water all day, but neglected it during his little reverie. Already he was feeling dehydrated, and their physical exertions had not even begun. He made a mental note to force himself to keep water handy at all times.

Ahead, Ahmed stood up and called back to them. "Ladies and gentlemen, we are here. Welcome to the Schwarzvogel Expedition."

Ernie felt a little ashamed for the comment he had made to Halfus. It was one of those spontaneous acts that he should have thought through. He knew that Wendy got irritated when Halfus showed interest in other girls, which he supposed was a natural reaction for an ex-girlfriend. He also noticed that his friend seemed a little taken with the German girl, Lisa. Not that Ernie blamed him—she possessed many of the qualities highly regarded by the superficial male. Ernie had wanted to call Wendy's attention to the fact, believing that a little jealousy might instinctively draw her closer to him.

It was petty and manipulative, and had been borne from frustration. He and Wendy were getting along as well as they ever had, but it was still unclear to him whether she actually *liked* him. With any normal girl he would have pushed hard enough to find out by now, but she was different. She was not someone he just wanted to have some fun with for a little while, the way he did with most. He wanted her by his side all the time. Time felt wasted when she was not around. He supposed what he wanted was a real relationship with her. His mind danced around the L-word, twisting and hiding in its attempt to avoid confronting reality.

In any case, Halfus did not deserve to be drawn into Ernie's own problem. He had shown no lingering interest in Wendy for as long as Ernie could remember. It was perfectly clear that whatever their past, neither Halfus nor Wendy wanted to be back together. Affection had been replaced by barely suppressed hostility. Ernie doubted that they would have even remained friends if not for the fact that they shared the same academic field and social network.

He was relieved that his friend had basically ignored him. And his thoughtless joke seemed to have had the desired effect on Wendy, who had talked his ear off for the entire trip. It had been refreshing to be able to listen for a change, instead of feeling the pressure of steering the conversation himself. He was good at entertaining girls, but it did get tiring.

As they stepped out of the bus, he turned his attention to the camp. He saw five dark green tents erected around an unlit campfire. In the sweltering heat it was difficult to imagine needing a fire, but they probably used it for cooking. As he perused the sight, he noticed that one of the tents was smaller and a different shade from the others. Most of them appeared to be two-man, but this one was large enough for only a single person.

Seeing the tents made him ponder the sleeping arrangements. He wondered if they would be allowed to chose their own. If so, he was very curious whether Wendy would choose him. Then he realized how ridiculous that was. This was no couples vacation. She would berth with Lisa, of course.

A short distance away from the bus sat a faded blue sedan with tires that looked older than he. Back in the States he would have taken it for a junker, good for nothing more than spare parts. On the way here, however, he had seen any number of people driving cars in even worse shape. He supposed this jalopy was their lifeline to civilization, such as it was.

He watched a short man with a ridiculous straw hat and ruddy complexion approach the bus from the direction of a low ridge a quarter-mile away. Ahmed and his followers walked over to greet him. They did not shake hands. Sadly, they were too far away to be overheard, so he could only use his interpretation of their faces and body language to follow the conversation that ensued. Ahmed had seemed to drop the courtly act. It was clear that he was in charge and had something of great importance to say to the man.

Ernie assumed this was the Herr Doktor Schwarzvogel he had heard a little about. He was about to ask Doc for confirmation, but noticed that his professor was staring at the exchange with great attentiveness. In fact, all of them were. Halfus, Wendy, and Rich all stood quietly, focused on the barely audible dialogue. Ernie wondered what language they were using. English, Arabic, or possibly even German. It was difficult to tell.

"*Nein!*" They heard that word clearly enough, although it seemed more like an expletive than a part of the discussion. Schwarzvogel had listened calmly to this point, but now his already red face grew a shade darker. He began to shake his head and gesticulate behind him, toward the ridge line and whatever lay beyond. A back and forth that appeared to be some sort of negotiation ensued. Ernie could hear syllables that sounded like Arabic.

"*Ithnaan,*" Ahmed said emphatically. That seemed to be the end of it. Schwarzvogel shook his head as he turned away from the minister. Ahmed returned to the bus. As he passed Ernie and the other students, he acknowledged them with only a curt nod. He looked to be in no mood for any further pleasantries, so they let him walk by unmolested. He stepped into the bus, followed by his two silent companions. They heard him bark an order to the driver and watched the door of the vehicle swing shut. In moments it was pulling back onto the primitive road.

They approached Schwarzvogel, Doc leading the way. The angry man was shaking his head to himself, seemingly oblivious to the newcomers. "*Zwei Wochen. Zwei Wochen,*" he repeated distastefully.

Ernie tapped Halfus' shoulder. "Two weeks," his friend translated.

Two weeks? What did that mean? Suddenly, Ernie felt a sick sense of disappointment in his stomach. *No, it can't be for us. We're supposed to be here for six.*

Only when they were within a few yards did the German professor take notice of their presence. A smile appeared on his face, but it seemed both forced and uncomfortable. The Herr Doktor was a man unaccustomed to smiling. "Benjamin," he said in a voice that was more reassuring than the expression accompanying it. "It is a pleasure to see you again, *mein Freund.*" He spoke with a thicker accent than expected, not only in pronunciation but also in cadence. Each consonant came out crisp and abrupt, without any of the lazy slurring from one syllable to the next that most people acquired with familiarity. It gave the man an intimidating air, despite his smallish frame.

He held out his hand in greeting. "It has been many years."

"Adolphus." Doc took the hand. "I hope you are well."

"Passable. Please introduce me to your children." Ernie was not sure whether that was a typical German way of referring to students, but he could not help but bristle at the insulting implication.

Doc obeyed. The man barely seemed to pay attention, and did not offer his hand to any of them. Ernie was unsure whether this was the Herr Doktor's usual disposition or if the news he had just received from Ahmed was affecting him. Ernie had a feeling it was a little of both.

"You are too late to do anything this evening," Schwarzvogel was telling Doc. "You may use what light remains to get situated in camp. You must sleep early. We start at sunrise. Benjamin, please oversee your children as you will. When you have a minute, come see me." With that, he turned from them and walked toward one of the five tents. They watched him in silence until he disappeared from view.

Halfus, too, appeared to be annoyed. "Fuck that," he said quietly in Ernie's ear. "I'm checking out the dig now. You with me?"

"Hells, yeah."

Rich put a hand on Halfus' shoulder. "Be quick, mate, all right? We have to get settled in, and we don't want to start out on the wrong foot."

Halfus glanced at Schwarzvogel's tent, then back at Rich. "You think it makes any difference? He had his impression of us since before we arrived. We're laborers."

Rich nodded. "Maybe so. Just don't do anything to make it worse. Got it?"

"Deal. We'll be back in thirty."

The two of them walked up the long, gradual incline of the ridge. After the better part of two days in planes, cars, buildings, and buses it felt good to be out and active again. Ernie felt his muscles warming and stretching. It gave him a burst of energy that was sorely needed.

Somehow, traveling seemed to take more out of him than actual exertion did.

They walked in relative silence, which was nothing unusual when hanging around Halfus. It gave Ernie the opportunity to study their surroundings. There was not much to the landscape, only parched earth and stunted foliage spaced intermittently. Then a couple of shapes appeared on the horizon ahead. Two people were coming over the ridge, heading toward the camp. One tall and one short. Soon it became apparent that one was a man and the other a child.

The two pairs veered directly toward each other. As they drew nearer, Ernie saw that the man was young and Caucasian, most likely another student. The other was a boy of perhaps twelve or thirteen. He looked like an Arab. Each of them carried a backpack bursting at the seams.

"Good evening," said the student. His accent was much milder than Schwarzvogel's, but not nonexistent like Lisa's. "You are the Americans, yes?"

"Yes," Ernie replied. "Good evening back."

"*Guten Abend*," said Halfus.

"You speak German?"

"I don't," Ernie said quickly. He did not want the two of them launching into an exchange that he could not follow.

"Ah, I see. I am Michael." He pronounced it oddly.

"Ernie."

"Halfus. And who is your friend here?"

"This is Mahmoud. He is from a local family. He is become...how would you say...our good luck charm."

"Does he speak English?" Ernie asked.

"Probably better than you," the boy responded.

Michael chuckled. "Be careful. He is a sharp one. I will not be surprised when he rules the world one day." As he spoke, he tousled Mahmoud's hair, which elicited a giggle. Ernie guessed that Mahmoud had joined the expedition out of boredom. Perhaps there were few kids his age around this desolate area. But much more likely, he enjoyed the company of adults more than those his own age.

He would be persistent in showing off his own intelligence—which, if the students of the expedition had accepted him, was likely considerable.

"Probably so," Ernie said back to him, and the child grinned.

"Are you heading up to the dig?" Michael asked them.

"We were planning to. Is that okay?"

"Of course. Come, I will show you around." He unshouldered his backpack and handed it to Mahmoud. "Will you take these to my tent?" The boy took it and started off in a jog. His pace was impressive for his lack of size and the obvious weight of his burdens.

"He is a good boy," Michael told them as he led the way. "He is very smart. And very curious. Be careful, because he will ask many questions."

"He looks strong."

"Yes. He says he is fifteen but of course that is a lie. Probably closer to eleven or twelve. But he does everything we ask without complaint. He runs very fast, so we use him to go between the camp and the site. He carries things without tiring. We are all very fond of him."

A few minutes later they were standing on the edge of a wide pit, perhaps twenty feet wide in each direction, dug to a depth of five or six feet. A second pit of similar proportions lay some small distance away. The light was now too poor to see anything with any detail, but there looked to be white string roping off sections below. All he could see was dirt and stone, but Ernie presumed there would be more to observe in the light of day.

"You cannot see it from here," Michael was telling them, "but there is another, smaller pit over there." He gestured toward a small rock formation. "Behind those rocks. We believe the main structure is located here, so this is where we have concentrated our effort. With your help, we hope to get to the other in a few more weeks."

"You might not want to get your hopes up," said Ernie.

"Pardon me?"

Halfus flashed Ernie a look, then looked at Michael. "They didn't tell us anything official. But we think we might only have two weeks here."

"Two? I was told you would be here for six. Why would you leave so soon?"

"We don't know. It's only a guess. But I have a feeling it isn't just us that will be leaving in two weeks."

"Oh." Michael stiffened. There was a moment of shared silent disappointment. "Well, my new friends, I hope you are wrong."

"So do we," said Ernie.

Halfus had a lot of trouble sleeping that night. Part of the problem was the time change, but a bigger factor was his restless mind. The eternal chatter of the soul, as he thought of it. It often happened when he was in new and exciting circumstances, such as he currently was. The others had all gone to sleep early, the stress and activity of recent days hitting them with greater efficacy than the best pharmaceuticals. But tired as he was, Halfus could not get his brain to cease its infernal prattle. It meandered between Iraq, Ahmed, Lisa, Wendy, and the mercenaries, never bothering to complete one thought before chasing the next.

Whenever this happened to him, Halfus used a technique to slow his racing thoughts. Others counted sheep, but he had long since learned that method did not work for him. Counting sheep took too little concentration, allowing his mind to quickly drift back to whatever had brought on the restlessness. Instead, he mentally painted the alphabet on a blank canvas, taking the time to imagine each letter form with deliberate precision. The exercise required enough concentration to prevent his thoughts from drifting, yet was boring enough to induce sleep. Most nights he nodded off somewhere before 'M'. This time he had to repeat the entire alphabet several times before drifting into slumber.

Despite being the last one asleep he was still the first one up. He awoke to darkness, but could sense the break of day approaching. He heard Ernie's peaceful breathing in the tent with him. The two of them had taken one tent, Rich joined Michael in another, Wendy went with Lisa, and Doc with Schwarzvogel. The smallish tent was for the boy, Mahmoud, but apparently it was the rare evening that he slept on site. His family's domicile was supposedly about thirty minutes away on foot. No one could say for sure because no one had ever visited. There was speculation that Mahmoud may have been lying about his family and was possibly homeless, although Michael believed it was more likely that his father simply did not approve of his son spending so much time with foreigners. Just in case, the students made sure to feed the boy every chance they could from their own supplies.

All this was according to Michael and Lisa, who had shared stories last night around the campfire. It had been a fun but brief evening. The night brought a drop in temperature that made the fire welcome, and the newcomers found the German students to be agreeable company. They cooked up some beans and vegetables, which they ate on paper plates with plastic utensils. Everything was meticulously cleaned and discarded in garbage bags for later disposal in town.

Now Halfus was too warm in his sleeping bag, which was probably what had awakened him. He unzipped and pulled himself out as quietly as possible, then opened the tent flap and stepped outside. The air was still cool, but refreshing after the stifling heat of the bag. His first impression was that he was the first one up, for there was no one else in camp. But the first glimmer of a sunrise was appearing on the horizon, and as he looked toward it he noticed the figure of a man walking away in the direction of the dig site. Schwarzvogel. He was up early. Whatever the man's profusion of flaws, laziness was clearly not one of them.

No one else was in sight. Before they arrived, Halfus had expected there to be a few soldiers watching over the expedition. He was pleasantly surprised to find none. He wondered whether Shalhoub was a proponent of security by ignorance. As long as no one knew they were here, they should not have anything to worry about. They were, after all, in the middle of nowhere.

Because he and Ernie had visited the site last night and returned to camp late, Halfus had been the beneficiary of a dinner ready and waiting for him. He decided to return the favor by preparing breakfast for the others. He was no stranger to the camping lifestyle and went about his work with eager efficiency. If anything ever happened to the world such that all the conveniences of modern life suddenly disappeared, he believed he would be right at home.

Breakfast was enjoyable but brief. The others had thanked him for getting everything ready, and even Wendy had a smile for him this morning. It was a good start to an important day.

Halfus thought they might go to the site as a group, but as they each finished their meal, they proceeded directly up the slope alone or in pairs. As the unofficial cook for breakfast, Halfus waited until everyone else was done. He resigned himself to going it alone this morning, but was pleasantly surprised to see someone had waited for him.

"Thanks for waiting up, Easy."

"Sure thing."

Just as they started following the others, they were joined by a third. Mahmoud came jogging into the camp from the direction of the dirt road, and they stopped to wait for him. They greeted him and accepted his company without complaint. Soon Halfus was glad they had, because he proved another useful source of information, and his impressions were not skewed by any bias for the dig to be a great success.

According to Mahmoud, not much of value had been found. The locals had known of this site for ages, so any objects of any monetary or functional value had long since wandered off. From a research standpoint, he did not know how much had been learned, but he believed that the initial excitement of the find was wearing thin and the expedition members were going through their routines with growing frustration.

In their briefings, Halfus and the others had been told that the site was the ruins of a temple or shrine of some sort. Very little of the foundation remained, and nowhere were as many as two blocks stacked together. There was nothing so intriguing as a statue, which is what Mahmoud had been hoping to see, but there was writing and pictures carved into the stones, including a few mid-reliefs. One of these Mahmoud was eager to show them, because it depicted a battle scene he found intriguing.

They arrived at the site to find Doc already in the process of doling out assignments to the students. Mahmoud wanted the two of them to follow him, but Halfus explained—as much for Ernie's ears as the boy's—that their first priority was to get to work. There would be plenty of time to look around later.

Lisa and Michael were archaeology students, and as such assisted Schwarzvogel in all of the sensitive work. The five newcomers were there for research, translation, and menial tasks. Much of the writing and carving was too faint to show up on digital cameras, so the expedition was using the old-school method of taking rubbings. Lisa showed them how to do it without risk of damage, and Michael showed them a paper chart he had created to keep track of their progress. Scattered about the site were many small markers and areas roped off by the white string, each corresponding to an entry on the chart. Halfus and Ernie were charged with taking the rubbings, Rich and Wendy with organizing them and updating the chart.

It was slow and tedious work, but Halfus felt energized by the knowledge that he was amid ruins that dated from the beginnings of history itself. Mesopotamia was the location of the earliest known human civilization, dating at least back to 3000 BC and possibly earlier. If these ruins turned out to be Old Assyrian as believed, he could be looking at writing well over four thousand years old. Some of the earliest writing in human history, in fact. Even if they learned nothing from what little remained, simply being here was an experience of epic proportion.

Ernie, on the other hand, appeared to be less fascinated. He kept glancing away from his work and over toward Wendy and Rich. Halfus thought that Doc had been smart to keep her and Ernie separated like this. As distracted as his friend was now, it would be much worse if he was in a position to keep her entertained.

Halfus had mixed feelings about the two of them. He had

reconciled himself to Wendy hooking up with someone new, but he honestly did not think Ernie was a good match. Their personalities were too different for a relationship to be likely to last. He knew from personal experience that Wendy was a demanding companion, and he was not sure that Ernie fully appreciated that fact. His friend was more of a playboy. He had really blossomed in the years that Halfus had known him, breaking out of his unassertive shell to grow into a magnetic socialite. But that process had involved building confidence through a series of girls, each of whom wound up as discarded and forgotten as this morning's trash. Halfus still cared too much for Wendy to see her go through that.

But it was not any of his business. Even if he believed either one of them would listen to him—which he did not—he would not presume to say anything about it. Wendy would surely take offense, and Ernie would probably believe it was just lingering jealousy on Halfus' part. Thus anything he said would accomplish nothing and probably make matters worse for himself. In any case, the two of them were adults. He was their friend, and he wanted them both to be happy, but that was the extent of it. He would simply hope for the best.

Besides, perhaps he was wrong. Perhaps Ernie was getting tired of shallow relationships and wanted to settle down. Perhaps he genuinely liked Wendy enough to do so. But Halfus had a suspicion that the main reason Ernie spent so much time with Wendy was that she was the only girl on this trip. Or had been, until Lisa showed up. It might be a lot better for everyone if Ernie decided to shift his flirtations in that direction. She was certainly attractive enough, and Halfus would not be at all surprised to see it happen. The more he thought about it, the more he came to expect it.

"Is it lunchtime yet?" asked Ernie. He was on his knees nearby, carefully settling tracing paper over a crumbled stone with half-destroyed markings.

"Dude, we just had breakfast. It's not yet nine."

"I should have eaten more."

"You, my friend, are hungry like the wolf."

"Tell me about it."

. . .

"The unusual thing is there aren't really any historical records of a settlement near here," Lisa was saying. "There is an oblique reference in some fairy tale, but nothing else that we can find. We're still looking. That's part of why you're here."

They were taking a quick lunch break, each of them holding a simple sandwich in one hand while they talked.

"We'll have more than fairy tales when we're done," Rich told her. "Even the small amount I've seen so far, even without translating...I can tell there is something here. I can see why the Herr Doktor relocated the expedition. By the time we're finished, I believe we will have another chapter for the history books."

If we have time to finish, Halfus thought. He did not say it out loud. The work was tedious enough that every bit of optimism helped, and he did not want to dampen spirits.

Rich finished the last bite of his sandwich. "I'd better get back to it," he said, excusing himself.

Halfus noticed Lisa looking at him. When he looked back at her, she looked down at her sandwich. There was a slightly awkward pause. Then she said, "I told you about my background. What about yours?"

Halfus swallowed his last bite. "What do you want to know?"

"Everything. I mean anything." She blushed a little. "Excuse me, sometimes I mix up my English words."

Halfus said nothing while she regained her composure.

"Where did you grow up?"

Halfus was about to answer when they were interrupted by Mahmoud. He ran right up to the two of them, slamming on the brakes just shy of a collision. "Excuse me, Lisa. The doctor wants you."

She was immediately all business. "Where is he?" She glanced around the site. So did Halfus. The other students were around, some of them watching Mahmoud, curious why he was running around a site that everyone else treated as fragile.

"Down at the camp. He said to hurry."

"I'll go now. Thank you, Mahmoud." She looked at Halfus, opened her mouth to say something, then simply smiled and walked off.

"He wanted the other girl, too," Mahmoud said out loud. He began looking around.

"He wanted me?" asked Wendy. Halfus had not noticed her nearby.

"Yes. He said to hurry."

"I'll go right now, too," said Wendy. She briefly looked at Halfus. Then she, too, turned and started toward the ridge.

"Thank you, Mahmoud," Halfus said for her. The boy grinned at him, then turned to follow the girls.

A thought occurred to Halfus. He had originally intended to use this trip as an opportunity to improve his German. He had studied it for a total of six semesters, but had never really felt comfortable with the language despite all it had in common with English. Now he sensed a different opportunity.

"Mahmoud?"

"Yes?" The boy turned back to face him, returning Halfus' gaze. He certainly seemed confident. Halfus could see why Michael had spoken so highly of him.

"They say you're a smart man." Mahmoud's face lit up with pleasure. "Will you teach Arabic to me?"

"You want me to teach Arabic...to you?"

"They said you were smart, Mahmoud. Don't tell me I need to repeat myself." He was curious whether the boy could take it as well as dishing it out.

Mahmoud laughed. "Ha! No, you don't need to repeat it." His face assumed a suspicious, or perhaps mischievous, smile. "What will you pay me?" he asked.

"Only my gratitude and respect. I won't twist your arm." Halfus turned away.

"Okay. I will do it," the boy said quickly.

"Great. Thank you, Mahmoud."

But the boy was already shaking his head. "No, not 'thank you.' '*Shokran.*'"

. . .

Before dinner that evening, they learned two things—why Schwarzvogel had wanted to see the girls, and precisely what Ahmed had told them last night. It was not good news in either case.

"This fucking sucks," said Ernie. Both professors had gone into their tent to continue talking about strategy, leaving all the students together to commiserate.

"At least you don't need to go into hiding," Wendy retorted with genuine irritation.

"You're right. I'm sorry," he told her. He put an arm around her shoulder to comfort her. He wanted to turn it into a hug, but her posture seemed uninviting. It was more of the unspoken resistance he sensed in her. Every time he believed she was coming around, something happened to remind him that they were still just friends. He told himself that it was all right. For her, he could be patient.

Schwarzvogel had not told them exactly why they would be departing in two weeks, but it was not hard to put the pieces together. Especially after today's incident. Ernie learned from the others that a group of men had been seen in the area. Several of them had come close to the camp, where the good Herr Doktor confronted them.

That much was known, the rest was guesswork. Ernie assumed the men were armed. No one knew exactly what they said, but it was immediately afterward that Schwarzvogel told the women to keep out of sight. Both Wendy and Lisa had long blonde hair that would draw stares from a hundred yards. In this highly traditional region of the country, women were not supposed to walk around uncovered. If the men came back, the sight of two pretty girls could provoke trouble. From now on, they would wear the *hijab* during the daytime unless they were somewhere prying eyes would not see them. To that end, Wendy was being reassigned. They would find things for her to do down in the pits.

It was a tough pill to swallow for all of them. They had just gotten here, and already their trip was being severely truncated. Moreover, they were now acutely aware of the sense of danger that had hitherto been pushed to the back of their thoughts. No one had any idea just how seriously to take the threat, but the strangeness of the surroundings and the foreignness of the people made their imaginations run wild.

It was worse for the girls, of course. Ernie sympathized as best he could, but he could not truly understand what they were feeling. To go from a society with short skirts, tank tops, and a debate about birth control to one where you could not speak to men or show your own hair was difficult to wrap one's mind around. Yet that was exactly where they found themselves. They had been led to believe that the war had brought Western liberties to Iraq, but now it seemed that was merely an illusion in many parts of the country.

Lisa seemed to take it in stride. She announced that she would start preparing dinner and busied herself without another word. Wendy, on the other hand, was headstrong. She was unsuited to this kind of restraint. He made a note to keep an eye on her. He did not want her getting herself in trouble, and he wanted to be around in case it happened.

Fortunately, the next few days passed without incident. The slow progress of the expedition continued, the stacks of tracings accumulating far faster than Rich could translate them. In an attempt to capture as much raw data as possible in the time remaining, Doc decided translating could wait and put Rich to work down in the pits with the others. Mahmoud continued to visit the site daily, and Halfus' knowledge of Arabic improved from nonexistent to merely very poor. As the impending deadline loomed nearer and nearer, they all eschewed any type of relaxation time during daylight hours. Mahmoud made and distributed sandwiches for them to eat while they worked. Only when the last faint slivers of light faded to oblivion did they finally return to camp, the campfire, and a highly anticipated evening meal.

On many occasions Halfus found himself walking with Mahmoud. He did not mind, and not just because of the language practice. The boy was a good enough teacher for his age, although he tended to teach Halfus whatever words occurred to him without any real sense of organization. They were not working toward a goal, but Halfus supposed it really did not matter given the shortage of time they had left.

Lessons aside, Halfus found himself really enjoying the kid's company. His clever charm had been on display from the start. But he also had a good heart, and a natural curiosity about things that reminded Halfus of a younger version of himself. The boy had a bright future, and Halfus believed his time with the Germans and Americans was likely to be a real formative experience. With luck, he would get the chance to study or work overseas. It was nice to know that there was no longer a political obstacle preventing that opportunity. Whatever else the war had brought, the future was looking brighter for the young people of Iraq. It was yet another layer of complexity that complicated Halfus' impressions of what America had done to and for this fascinating country.

For his part, Mahmoud seemed genuinely upset that the team would be leaving soon.

"What will happen to the site when you go?" he asked Halfus one evening.

"I don't know. I presume Minister Shalhoub will decide what to do."

Mahmoud muttered something under his breath.

"What was that?"

"Halph, you and the other Americans and the Germans...you do not understand our country at all. You think it is like your home, but it is not."

Halfus knew this was true enough, but he did not want to interrupt. Mahmoud had something on his mind.

"The people here steal. I don't mean the bandits. I mean the people in charge. The people in Mosul, and in Baghdad."

"You mean the government."

"Yes. Anything that is valuable, they will take. In school I hear that the English came and took our things, the French came and took our things, and now the Americans come and take our things. And I say,

'Good.' Come and take our things. Put them in a museum in your cities. It is better than what will happen to them here."

"Mahmoud, my friend, be careful who you say things like that to. You are a smart boy, but you think too much for your own good." Halfus worried that his words might sting, so he softened them. "In eight years when I am teaching at Catoctin College, look me up. We'll have a place for you."

On the day of exposure, Halfus awoke with a bad back. He must have done something to pull a muscle, although he could not remember it happening. He stepped out of the tent and went through five minutes of stretching as he used to do during his boxing workouts. He felt the tension ease, and he breathed a sigh of relief. Their days were quickly running out, and there remained a lot of work to be done. He did not want to be hampered by soreness.

He instinctively finished his stretching routine with a series of shadowboxing moves, delivering a flurry of punches to an unseen attacker, crouching left, crouching right, then punching again. His hands were a tad slower than before, but not too bad for being three years removed from the ring. He dropped his arms to his sides and hopped on the balls of his feet a few times.

"Did you beat him?"

He spun around. He had thought he was the only one up, but apparently his boxing pantomime had been observed. Lisa was watching him with a toothy grin.

"Yep. TKO in the third. Didn't you see him go down?"

"No... But I have astigmatism." She giggled.

He changed the subject. "Quite a setup you have here," he said, nodding toward the campfire.

"You should have been here when we roasted a goat. Really, we did. You would have loved it." She was still smiling at him, and it seemed to him as though it was going on a little too long. She must have felt the same, for she suddenly looked away in embarrassment. This time she changed the subject. "I was about to start breakfast. Help me?"

"*Natürlich.*"

They chatted while they cooked up a giant batch of oatmeal. Lisa pointed to a collection of packaged fruits and asked him to get some raisins. He did not find any, but there was a bag of medjool dates. *Even better.* He grabbed them and fetched a large knife to hack them into raisin-sized pieces.

Lisa saw what he was doing and laughed. "Resourceful," she teased.

"I have my moments."

The others were stirring from their tents. Michael was the next one out, followed by Rich. They came over.

"Oatmeal. Just like home," said Rich. "I like mine with loads of brown sugar."

"You know where the supplies are," Lisa responded. "Get your own if you want some." She had caught on to the playfully disrespectful banter of the guys, but was much too nice to take seriously. Rich winked at her and went to look for some sweetener.

"It's been a while since I made oatmeal. How thick should I let it get?" Halfus asked.

"How thick do you like it?"

He shrugged. "I wouldn't know."

"Here," she said. She stuck a finger into the pot and brought it up with a glob of gooey oats. She held it in front of his mouth. Her radiant blue eyes twinkled. He obediently opened his mouth and she slipped her finger in. "Do you like it?"

He felt a little embarrassed. Others were watching. He swallowed. "*Ja. Das ist gut.*"

"Then it's ready," she said, withdrawing her finger and looking away as though nothing had transpired.

Halfus stirred the batch once more and cut off the heat. He looked up. Directly into the face of Wendy. She did not look amused.

He spooned out a bowl for her. "Rich has got some brown sugar, if you want." She said nothing and walked away with her bowl.

· · ·

Halfus assumed Lisa wanted to walk to the dig together, but he decided that would be a bad idea. Instead, he returned to his tent to look for something that had thus far remained stowed. He found it buried beneath a pair of unopened paperback novels.

Music was an important part of his life, so he traveled everywhere with an iPod. He had anticipated listening to it a lot during this trip, but that had not turned out to be the case. Thinking about it now, he realized that he had been spending much less time by himself than he was used to. The fact that everyone got along so well was a pleasant surprise, so he had not missed the music or the seclusion.

Now he figured it was a good time for both. Depending on his mood, music could either energize or soothe him. At the moment, he wanted the latter.

Lisa saw him emerge with the wire running from his hands to the black rubber buds in his ears. She took the hint and left him alone. She did not appear to be mad. He presumed she was probably a lot like Ernie—someone who took things in stride.

Yet he did not make it the whole way up undisturbed.

"What is that?"

Halfus pressed pause as Mahmoud approached. The boy had jogged to catch up, so the least Halfus could do was talk to him.

"This is an iPod. Have you never seen one?" Not for the first time, Halfus wondered where the boy had learned to speak English so well. It was particularly puzzling if his father was as anti-foreigner as they speculated. In any case, Mahmoud's proficiency had led Halfus to subconsciously assume a familiarity with American commercialism. In a way, it was refreshing to discover that was not the case.

"No. What is it?"

Halfus plucked the buds out of his own ears and placed them in Mahmoud's. Then he pushed play and adjusted the volume to something that would not scare the kid out of his shoes.

His face said it all. Halfus could empathize. He still sometimes felt that way himself, depending on the song. It was a good time to be alive.

"What am I listening to?" The boy reached for the device.

Naturally, he would be curious about the controls. And he would learn quickly.

"Leonard Cohen," Halfus said, then pointed to the name on the display. He found it mildly ironic that he was playing a Jewish musician to an Arab child. Of course, music was larger than any boundaries.

"It's amazing."

"It's yours."

It was a spontaneous decision, but it felt right. He might miss it on the flight back to the States, but he could easily buy another when he got home. The bigger concern was to figure out a way to charge it. He did not even know if they had electricity at the boy's home.

"Really? Do you mean it?"

They had reached the top of the ridge and were within sight of the dig.

"I do. Go ahead, listen to it a little bit today. But not too much, and not when the Herr Doktor is watching, okay?"

"Okay."

Halfus wondered whether the gift might make Mahmoud a little more willing to open up. This might present an opportunity. Halfus had not intended to be manipulative, but he had a genuine curiosity about the boy's background.

"Mahmoud, tell me about your father."

"Father is *ab*." He was changing the subject, as was his wont. Halfus went along with it, for now. But he would not give up quite so easily.

"Ab," he repeated. It was similar to some of the other languages he had studied.

"To be possessive you add an 'E' sound, so 'my father' is *abi*."

"Got it."

"Mother is *om*."

"Om."

"Brother is *akh*. Sister is *okht*."

"Do you have any sisters, Mahmoud?"

The boy did not answer right away. His face assumed a look of suspicion, as though Halfus were trying to trick him into revealing his innermost secrets. "I might have one."

Well, that was a start. "Do you have any brothers?"

Mahmoud's suspicious expression became a smile. Halfus had no doubt that in a few years, that smile would be charming the socks off girls. "I do now."

In the afternoon they heard gunfire in the distance.

Halfus was in one of the main pits. He scrambled out and scanned the horizon. Several of the others were doing the same, but there was nothing to be seen.

Ernie joined him. He had come from the direction of the smaller auxiliary pit, where Wendy was working.

"See anything?"

Halfus shook his head while he continued to scan.

"I hated finding out we only had two weeks," Ernie said. "Now I'm starting to think two weeks is too long."

"I know what you mean."

Not far away, Schwarzvogel was yelling something at Doc. Their professor listened obsequiously. Even with the warning they had received on the plane, Halfus was surprised at how deferential their professor was to the imperious little man in the funny hat. He wanted to slug Schwarzvogel for treating someone Halfus respected this way. And he wanted to slug Doc for taking it. He turned away from the sight and faced Ernie.

"How's Wendy doing?"

"She's in a bad mood. She feels like they gave her some busy work just to keep her out of sight."

"What's she doing?"

"Brushing dirt. With a tiny little brush. So we can go in later and take rubbings. I don't blame her. It takes all day just to clear a minuscule area."

"Well, it's not busy work. It needs to be done."

"You tell her that."

Halfus did not think that was a good idea.

The sun was well on its way down when Halfus finished his last rubbing of this particular stone. It was in a sunken hollow away from the main site. He had chosen it in order to have a little time to himself.

He was putting his supplies back into a small pack when he saw movement from the corner of his eye. The gunshots must have had more of an effect on his nerves than he realized, because his head jerked up in a panic, and it took a second to calm down when he saw who it was.

"Hi, Wendy."

She came down into the hollow with him. She was wearing the *hijab*, but he could see her face well enough to tell that she was bothered by something. She crossed her arms and stared at him. He braced himself.

"Aren't you at all ashamed?"

He was taken aback. This was a stronger rebuke than he had expected. "Ashamed of what?"

"You and that German girl. Lisa. While you have a girlfriend back home."

He shook his head. "There is nothing between me and Lisa." *Not that I should have to explain myself to you.* "I think she has pretty eyes, but that's hardly the same as jumping into bed with her." He moderated his reaction. It would not do to get into an argument here. "Look, I barely know her. Do you really think I would fall for someone without giving it far too much time and thought first?"

Wendy did not seem pacified, so he continued. "Besides, I don't have a girlfriend back home. Before we left I told Deanna that we could only be friends."

"You what?" Wendy seemed to grow more agitated. "Why? She was...cute. And she seemed really nice. What happened?"

He was not sure what to say. This was awkward territory. But he lived by a simple rule. *When uncertain, tell the truth.*

"You did."

She stared at him. *Well, now I have her attention.* He supposed this was as good a time as any to get some things off his chest.

"Listen, Deanna was the first girl I dated after you, so it made me do some thinking. About you. I'm sorry that we turned out the way we did. I know I shouldn't have gotten involved with you when I still had feelings for someone else. And...I guess I didn't want to make the same mistake again."

Her expression clouded. She was clearly conflicted about something. Exactly what that was, he did not care to speculate. He was just relieved that she had not started yelling.

"Are you saying...you still have feelings for me?"

"Of course I do. Feelings don't end overnight."

"But I thought...I mean, the reason we broke up...that I broke up with you, I mean." Wendy was normally a very articulate speaker. Her thoughts were obviously racing faster than her mind could handle for the words to come out like this.

Apparently she overcame the confusion with anger. Her brow furrowed. "I broke up with you because you weren't over Shauna. And now you decide to tell me you have feelings for me? A year later?"

He had to cut this off before her volume rose after all. He tried his best to explain. "Look, Wendy, I always did. You wanted someone who could give you one hundred percent, which I couldn't. But that didn't mean I was zero percent, either. I had feelings for both of you. My mind knew I needed to move on, but my heart moves slower. The way I lost Shauna..." He shook his head remorsefully. "It was tough to get over that. Maybe it wasn't fair to you, but you were helping me get past her... I just didn't appreciate it at the time. I didn't appreciate you." He paused, then just came out with it. "I took you for granted."

The whole time he spoke, she appeared to be on the verge of another eruption. Now she went back to merely staring at him. He could not tell whether her anger was lessening or getting worse.

"Anyway, I learned that it's not fair to the new girlfriend when you aren't completely over the old. Look how bad it turned out with you, and I was ten times crazier about you than I am about Deanna. So it seemed best if I ended it."

He felt that he had explained it as well as he could. He had spoken his piece. If she was still mad at him, at least he had told the truth.

She leaned in, and his mind was not aware that they were kissing until his arms were already around her waist. He had pulled her in instinctively, and now he raised a hand to her neck to make sure she did not go anywhere. He reached up, under the headscarf. As his hand brushed her hair, he remembered what it felt like to fondle those captivating curls. He found himself massaging them against her temple with the tips of his fingers, just like old times. Their mouths found a rhythm that was both familiar and supercharged by a year of frustrated absence. It was highly inappropriate and a bit scary, but he also felt an extraordinary relief wash over his body. An overwhelming sense that things were suddenly going to work out. This was how it should have been all along. Why had they waited so long to talk?

Don't think about it. Just enjoy it. Don't think about it. Don't think about it. Yet he could not help himself. They had to stop. His hand tightened on her hair and he pulled firmly until their mouths reluctantly separated. They stared at one another in silence, his hand still clenching her hair. Her eyes looked wild, and he suspected his own matched. With a force of will he dropped his hand and shook his head, just once. "Wendy. Not here. Not right now."

He expected disagreement from her, or possibly more anger. But her expression coalesced back into an amazing smile. She nodded. "Okay. Tonight?"

He was so relieved that he felt himself grinning stupidly. He took her hand and squeezed it. "Tonight. It can't come soon enough."

He dropped her hand and they stepped apart. Over her shoulder a shape became visible. It had been blocked from his view until she moved. He felt an instant of panic, then calmed himself as he recognized his friend. It was only Ernie, standing at the lip of the hollow. *Thank goodness it isn't Schwarzvogel.*

"Hey, Easy. You looking for me? Anything wrong?"

Ernie had a strange look on his face, but Halfus was much too distracted to think about anything but the impenetrable whimsy of love. In a moment, Ernie's usual smile appeared. "Both of you, actually. It looks like everyone is assembling for some big announcement."

Halfus helped Wendy out of the pit and then followed. The three of them walked side by side, Wendy between the men. She engaged Ernie in some jovial banter, leaving Halfus with his manic thoughts. He did not make eye contact with her for the entire walk, and slowly his heartbeat returned to normal.

"I have decided we need to leave right away."

Herr Doktor Schwarzvogel had waited for everyone to assemble. He had never learned any of their names except for Rich, and now it seemed he did not even know exactly how many students there were. He had waited for Doc to nod that everyone was present before launching into his speech.

"Clearly, the little automobile will not transport all of us and our work. Michael and I will go into the city tonight. I will speak to Minister Shalhoub and return tomorrow morning with the bus. Use the remainder of this evening to finish your current assignments. And pack your necessities for early departure tomorrow. Doctor Appelstein will be in charge tonight. Listen to him as you would me. That is all. Now back to work. Michael, come with me."

Doc looked disconsolate. Wendy attempted to comfort him by rubbing his shoulder. But her question probably did not help matters. "I don't really need to finish brushing dirt, do I?"

Doc ignored her. "I'll be in the tent if anyone needs me." He walked away, head cast down.

Ernie was barely aware of any of this. His mind was in turmoil. He still had difficulty accepting what had happened. And it had nothing to do with the announcement.

When he had seen the two of them, his first reaction was confusion. *Did I follow the wrong girl?* After all, they both wore head coverings to hide their hair. He had closed his eyes and prayed. But when he reopened them, he saw that there was no mistake. Now he felt as though he was in shock. The world made no sense.

He wandered away before anyone noticed his condition. It was embarrassing, and he absolutely hated being embarrassed. Why had he thought she would like him? Had she only been using him to make Halfus jealous? How long had it been going on? Were the others laughing at him behind his back? If not yet, would they when they found out?

No one was in the second pit. He jumped down and found a rock to sit on, not noticing its carvings and marker. He bent his head back and stared at the sky, then toward the waning sun. He no longer wanted to be here. He wanted to be home. Not Catoctin. Home. Little old Bakerville, West Virginia. It had been a mistake to leave. It had filled his head with delusions of grandeur. He had been so proud, and he had dared believe he would make his parents proud, too. They would surely ridicule him for going away these past few years, but it was no more than he deserved.

"Easy? You okay, bro?" Halfus hopped down into the pit. "Dude, stand up. You're sitting on a marker."

Ernie really did not care, but he stood up anyway. Halfus was his friend and compass. Ernie always listened to what he said, and he followed directions obediently when given. The habit now kicked back in.

"Come on, let's walk a bit," said Halfus, and Ernie fell in beside him. They exited the pit and began making a circuit around the site.

"I know it looks grim right now," Halfus said, and Ernie nodded along. "But don't let it bother you so much. We have almost five more weeks on our visas. Maybe they'll let us stay until things quiet down again."

"Huh?" Ernie was confused by this comment. Then he realized Halfus was talking about abandoning the dig. *I don't fucking care about the dig, you bastard.*

He stopped and looked at his friend. Halfus meant well. He had done nothing on purpose. It did make sense, after all. He would assume that Ernie viewed Wendy as another conquest. Why would he not? How could he know how Ernie really felt? Besides, the two of them were better suited for each other. *The better man won*, Ernie thought with immeasurable sadness.

He collected himself. "Thanks, Halph. I'm better now." He was not, of course, but all he really wanted was to be alone.

They heard yelling. It was Wendy. "Guys! Guys! Come here!" They were not standing far from the auxiliary pit, which they reached in a matter of seconds.

She was standing over a dirt-covered stone that looked about six or seven feet long. It was difficult to tell for certain because the stone slanted down into the earth. At first glance, it did not look significantly different from the many smaller stones lying around in disarray.

Ernie followed Halfus into the pit to stand beside her. Wendy's smile was uncharacteristically unreserved. She was clearly excited about something. Halfus crouched to inspect the large stone more closely, and now Ernie saw carvings etched into it. It looked more like a picture than writing, but there was still too much dirt to be sure.

He saw Rich and Lisa join the little gathering. They stayed up on the edge of the pit, looking down. Halfus stood back up and looked at Wendy. "It's another carving. Nice find."

"Not that, you idiot. Watch." She got to her knees beside the end of the stone that dug into the earth. "I saw that carving this morning, so I started clearing off the rest of this rock," she explained patiently. Ernie wished she would hurry up and get to the point. "After the break I started brushing here. And this happened."

She started brushing dirt away from the stone, toward the sunken end. The dirt collected at the base. She stopped and looked at the pile, as though expecting something to happen. She started brushing some more. She paused again. This time she got visibly frustrated and put more energy into it.

"Careful, Wendy," Rich warned.

"There!" she cried.

The accumulation at the base had grown into a pile several inches deep. They watched as it slowly shrank before their eyes. The dirt was leaking like the sand of an hourglass.

"Holy shit," said Halfus. "I can see it. It looks deep." He looked at Wendy. "You tricky minx. You covered it back up before we got here."

Her eyes gleamed as she returned his gaze. *She never once looked at me that way*, thought Ernie.

"I wanted you to see it the way I did," she explained in a voice filled with happiness.

"I'm proud of you."

Somehow Wendy's smile grew even larger, and she hugged Halfus. Then, when he released her, she turned to Ernie and hugged him, too.

"Me, too," he said awkwardly.

Rich took charge. "Mahmoud, go get Doctor Appelstein." The boy took off running. Ernie had not even noticed him arrive, he was so easy to overlook. "Lisa, do we have a flashlight on site? Yes? Go get it, please. Halfus, Ernie. See if you can clear a little more of that. Carefully. We don't want to damage any carvings."

"We don't want the ground to open up beneath us, either," said Halfus. "You can't see it from there, Rich. This looks big."

Several large stones around the hole prevented them from widening it more than a few inches. Most of the stones were too bulky to move, but one looked as though it might not be too heavy if they worked together.

"Halfus, want to help me with this?"

"Sure." Halfus tried to find a suitable position to get a grip on the end opposite Ernie.

"What the hell is going on here?" roared a heavily accented voice. Ernie and Halfus stopped in mid-crouch. Wendy took a step backwards toward them, away from the Herr Doktor. He looked more upset than they had ever seen him.

Michael stood behind him, and Ernie saw Mahmoud returning with Doc. Their professor came up to stand beside the expedition leader.

"Benjamin, what are your children doing?"

Doc opened his mouth, but the angry German did not give him the opportunity to answer. He turned back to the three of them in the pit. "Get out of there. Immediately. Everyone back to camp. Everyone. Right. Now."

~

They stood in sheepish silence as they listened to the expedition leader berate them. Had they not been ordered to do nothing without speaking to him first? He did not care if they struck oil in that hole, he would be damned if he would have rebellion on his project again.

Halfus had been through stern lectures before, so the castigation did not particularly bother him. What did bother him was what the man went on to say. Even if they had time to come back in the future, any new find would need to be registered with the cultural ministry. It was up to the minister to decide how to proceed. They may want to send an Iraqi team. If so, that was their prerogative.

It sounded like CYA to Halfus. The team members did not even know what they had found. It might just be a hole with nothing in it. *No, it's not*, he told himself. He had glimpsed a tiny shaft of sunlight glinting off something several meters below. *It's too big. Something is down there.*

For now they were commanded to stop all activity on the site save for cleaning and packing. Schwarzvogel saved his nastiest reprimand for Doc. He mockingly asked if the professor could make sure the team could do that much without more trouble.

Halfus pitied Michael for needing to spend the evening with the odious little man. The two of them climbed into the old sedan. Michael started the engine and pulled onto the makeshift road as a cloud of dirt rolled over the rest of them. They dispersed to sullenly finish their chores.

"Halfus." Ernie came up behind him and spoke quietly, as though not wanting to draw attention. "I left some things at the site. Help me carry them."

The two of them walked up the slope alone. Halfus knew

something was up, but he waited patiently until they were well out of earshot of the others.

Eventually his friend broke the silence. "Halph, we need to go in. Tonight."

"I had a feeling you were going to say that."

"It's right there. In front of us. Don't tell me you aren't tempted."

Halfus did not reply.

"We don't know what's down there. What if this is the tomb of someone important? This could be the find of the decade."

"Or it could be empty. We'd be taking a big risk for nothing."

"You don't want to?"

Halfus sighed. "Yes and no. If things go wrong, it will be the devil to pay."

"What could they do to us?"

"I'm not worried about us. It could be the end of Doc's career."

"Oh. I hadn't thought about that."

"It's all I'm thinking about." *Because I want to go in, too,* he thought. *And I'm trying to talk myself out of it.* He was conflicted. Vivid in his mind was the conversation with Mahmoud. *The people here steal,* he had said. *Anything valuable, they will take. I don't mean the bandits. I mean the people in charge.*

What could they do about it? They could not take things for themselves. Besides the impracticality, it would be just as bad. Maybe he could take a camera. Catalog anything down there. Then what? Even if things disappeared, he would not know how to stop them.

But at least he would have *seen.* He and Ernie, the first to set foot below for thousands of years.

They walked on in silence. Eventually, Ernie changed the subject. He wanted to know what Halfus' plans were if they returned home early.

"Hadn't thought about it. Work on my dissertation, I suppose."

"In McGahey?"

"I guess so."

"I think Wendy is going to be moving to Frederick."

"Yeah."

There was a pause. Halfus was not sure if Ernie was leading up to something, or if this was just idle chatter while they thought about the real issue. "What about you?"

"I...don't know. I'm not sure if I want to stay in McGahey, or maybe go back home."

"You should stay in McGahey. We like having you around."

"Cheers, mate." Ernie sounded tired.

"Cheers."

There was another long break in the conversation as they gathered anything they could find and started back down toward the camp. As they drew near, Halfus knew he had a decision to make.

"Hey, Easy?"

"Yeah?"

"Okay, I'm in."

"An hour after dark?"

"Let's make it two. We need to make sure everyone is asleep."

Wendy would be hurt and unhappy when he did not make an appearance tonight. But he could not explain anything to her, either. He did not want to implicate her, or anyone else. With luck it would not matter. No one would ever know. He would make it up to her tomorrow.

6

TOMB

IN 732 A.D. the Battle of Tours, also known as the Battle of Poitiers, was fought in central France. It was a grand clash between Christian and Muslim armies. The Christians emerged victorious and the Muslims, who hitherto had expanded across North Africa and southwest Europe without pause, at last withdrew into Spain to consolidate their sizable gains. Although parts of the Iberian peninsula remained under Muslim domination until the conclusion of the Reconquista in 1492, the rest of west and central Europe was spared the threat of Muslim conquest until the Ottoman siege of Vienna eight hundred years after Tours.

The leader of the Christian armies was one Charles Martel, or "Charles the Hammer." Martel's son Pepin became king of France and founder of the Carolingian dynasty. Martel's grandson, Charlemagne, became the first emperor in Europe since the fall of the Roman Empire. The empire of Charlemagne was the most impressive of the Middle Ages, extending beyond the lands of modern France and Germany, although he never succeeded in reclaiming Spain for Christendom.

The Song of Roland is one of the earliest works of French literature. It is an epic poem about Charlemagne's foray into Spain to battle the Saracen king Marsilla. Fearing defeat, Marsilla agrees to convert to Christianity and reward Charlemagne with treasure if the French ruler withdraws from

Iberia. Charlemagne agrees and leads his army north. His rearguard is led by Roland, Charlemagne's greatest knight. Charlemagne and Roland are betrayed by the latter's own stepfather, Ganelon, who informs Marsilla how to ambush the rearguard in the Pyrenees mountain passes.

Roland possesses a horn that he could use to summon the rest of Charlemagne's army. At the sight of the enemy, however, Roland believes his honor and courage are at stake and refuses to blow the horn. Only when his men are slaughtered and his own death imminent does he relent. He calls for revenge, blowing the instrument until his temples burst. His soul rises to Paradise. Charlemagne returns to do battle with Marsilla, whom he kills in personal combat. Marsilla's wife is taken captive, and Ganelon brutally executed for his treachery.

Most of The Song of Roland *is, of course, sheer fabrication. As do most works of literature and history, it tells us more about the age in which it was written than it does the age of which it speaks. Yet it is not wholly without historical accuracy. Charlemagne did war with the Muslims of northern Spain. He did withdraw, his rearguard was led by a knight named Roland, and that rearguard was indeed destroyed in battle. The rest is simply fiction inspired to some degree by actual events, which themselves will never be known. Such is the limitation of all legends.*

This rule more or less applies to history in general. Much of what we call history comes to us through the words of a select few sources of dubious veracity, leaving us with a host of unanswered questions. Were Emperor Constantine's pagan Roman soldiers really inspired by the Christian God at the Battle of the Milvian Bridge, or did Constantine's Christian biographer add this episode for reasons that are obvious? Did William the Bastard really lift his helmet during the Battle of Hastings to reassure his men that he was not slain? Was Christopher Columbus really Genoan—or Greek, Catalan, or Jewish? Was Davy Crockett killed during the Battle of the Alamo, or executed afterward as a prisoner? What should one believe in the absence of a trustworthy account? For that matter, are any accounts truly trustworthy?

History is a slippery pursuit, truth an elusive reward. We must accept that there are things we will never know, and things we think we know that are quite wrong. Some events were simply never recorded. Others were written about poorly. This does not mean that one should dismiss all primary sources as worthless, however. For all their flaws, they remain the best connection to our past. One should simply acknowledge the regrettable folly of interpreting them as gospel, revel in the chaos of uncertainty, and make the most of whatever rare opportunities arise to extend our understanding of truth.

Once upon a time, the jackal witnessed greatness. He had known light. His home had been a world of men, gods, and miracles. These things were all one and the same, for the men came to experience the miracle, and were transformed into gods. In ever increasing numbers they came, some for the miracle, some to pay homage, others to die. This was the first era. The jackal did not know when it began, for he was himself born during this period.

Now the jackal's home was crumbling. The worst damage had happened at once, entire sections of ceiling collapsing not far from where he stood guard. The passage of men came to an end in that cataclysm. The jackal forgot light. The chamber around him continued to suffer deterioration and decay in the countless years since. This was the second era.

The jackal was unmoved. He did not miss the light. Or the men. Nor did he worry about the rubble forming around his feet, crowding his home. Since the cataclysm, the jackal experienced naught but timeless oblivion.

Tonight, however, for the first time in many centuries, stars appeared overhead. This was new. A third era was dawning.

The tail end of a rope dropped to the stone a few yards before the statue. Ernie slid down first, quickly. He placed his feet, let go of the rope, and executed a confident landing. Halfus came more slowly and cautiously. By the time he detached himself from the line, Ernie was already sweeping the room with his flashlight.

"Tell me this doesn't remind you of the Well of Souls from *Raiders of the Lost Ark*," he said. "Except I don't see any asps."

"This isn't a movie, Easy."

As Ernie's beam encountered the statue, he lifted the angle so he could see the head more clearly. The lupine grin did not appear to perturb him. He grinned back at it.

He lowered the beam to the base, where wolfish feet merged with the floor, which was composed of large, cut, interlocking stones. The walls, where they remained intact, were more of the same. The workmanship was not impressive, but it proved that whatever they were standing in was man-made.

Halfus stopped watching Ernie in order to unsling his pack, placing it carefully in the center of the floor. Then he pointed his own flashlight toward the wall that appeared to have experienced the greatest destruction. In fact, it was not a wall at all.

"This would have been the entrance passage," he said.

Ernie joined him in the examination. Whereas signs of collapse appeared on every side of the chamber, obscuring parts of each wall, in this direction there was nothing but debris. No wall lay behind, and enough of the ceiling remained visible to show that it had once been a tunnel.

"Looks like this place has seen better days," said Ernie.

"Yeah. See anything noteworthy?"

"Just our friend here." Ernie shined the light back on the statue. It looked normal from neck to ankle. Only the head and feet were inhuman. It reminded Halfus of Egyptian statues he had seen in books and museums.

"Is he supposed to be a god?" Ernie asked.

"Not any one I know of," Halfus said absent-mindedly. He was not worried about a statue. That was not something that could easily be removed. He began to scan the rest of the chamber. "I suppose there could be things beneath some of this rubble."

He began to walk in a slow circuit, mentally sectioning off the room into a grid. Then he began methodically gliding his beam slowly across the first sector. He hoped they would find something after all they had gone through. It had taken far more time and effort than expected to open a hole on the surface large enough to accommodate them. Their hands were raw from moving the stones they could lift, their bodies nicked and bruised from squeezing between those they could not. He felt beaten and battered, and the exploration had barely started. Thank goodness for adrenaline. At least he was feeling strength creep back into his tired muscles. And his mind was clear. The climb from surface to floor had only been about twenty feet, not quite enough to trigger his acrophobia.

Ernie was continuing to study the statue. "Hey, Halfus. There's writing here," he said.

"I have rubbing supplies in the pack," said Halfus. So far he was underwhelmed. The statue was an interesting find, but his hope of discovering something truly impressive was rapidly diminishing. He supposed that was both good and bad news. If there were nothing down here, he would not have to worry about anything being stolen.

"No need. I recognize it. It's all over this place outside. 'Bala.' I think Rich said it's a name."

"Hmm," Halfus replied. He wished they had not been so rushed since arriving at the dig. They were supposed to be here for analysis as much as collection, but because of the unexpected time constraint had spent almost all their time on the latter. "Now what are you doing?" Halfus was hoping that Ernie would help with his search of the debris, but instead his friend was swinging his light around the perimeter.

"Checking the walls."

Halfus left him to it and went back to his own job. *Now, where was I?* He found the last spot he had inspected and resumed the scan.

"A-ha. Halph, over here."

Ernie had indeed found something. Halfus had to hand it to his friend, so far he was proving to be the superior explorer.

"How far back does it go, I wonder."

"Only one way to find out," Ernie replied.

"You think you can fit between those stones?"

"Only one way to find out."

He could. Halfus picked the pack back up and followed him.

The rubble that nearly blocked access to this tunnel did not extend far. Once they crawled past it, they were able to stand upright and admire a corridor at least seven feet high and wide, extending as far ahead as they could see. The stones here were cut smaller and more carefully fitted. A few had fallen to the floor, but the tunnel seemed to be in fairly good shape. Halfus was impressed.

"I'd say this place is holding up pretty well, considering it must be thousands of years old," he said. He noticed that he was instinctively speaking in a hushed voice. The acoustics down here called for it, but there was more to it than that. He felt that he was violating some religious sanctum. He reshouldered the backpack, which he had pushed ahead of himself through the rubble.

"True, but any idea what this place actually is?" asked Ernie.

"Good question. My money is still on a tomb, but that's only a guess."

They began moving down the tunnel, which seemed to be perfectly straight. Halfus thought it might not be level, however. His hunch told him it was angling down at a very slight angle. He wished he had brought a leveling tool along.

"A tomb, eh? Think we'll find mummies?" Halfus could not see his friend's face, but was sure it was grinning.

"No, Easy, I don't. This isn't an episode of Scooby Doo." He wished Ernie would be a bit more serious. Normally he appreciated when his friend kept things light, but this was an exception. There was a disconcerting sense of enormity about what they were doing. It gave the experience a surreal quality. He wanted to stay focused.

Ernie caught on to Halfus' mood and stayed quiet for the next few minutes. They moved deeper into the labyrinth. Their footing was not treacherous, but they moved slowly nonetheless. The walls were marked at intervals by mid-reliefs, pictorial scenes carved into the stone. The two of them cursorily examined the carvings as they passed. The images depicted men praying, fighting, and dying. These last were the worst. All the carvings were crude, devoid of any sense of perspective or realism. Even so, there was no mistaking what they represented—human sacrifice.

"Bloodthirsty, weren't they?" Ernie said.

"Mmm." Halfus nodded and kept moving. Ernie gave up on conversation for the time being.

Something loomed large in the tunnel ahead. As they approached, the shape of a lion formed from the darkness. A giant stone lion. At first it appeared to fill the entire passageway, blocking any further progress, but then Ernie saw the walls veer outward, widening. The lion was in a new chamber, or perhaps antechamber, for now he saw an archway beyond. The statue was guarding something important.

"We'll call this room the lion's den."

Halfus did not reply.

They were close enough now to get a better look at the animal. Just as the earlier statue had mixed some qualities of beast and man, so too did this. Only in reverse. The lion's head bore human features. It was a grotesque combination. The expression was savage. Feral. The teeth were oversized incisors, too large for the gaping mouth. It was only stone, but unnerving nonetheless. Ernie paused for a deep breath. Then he followed behind Halfus, who had not slowed down.

They examined the archway. There was another relief carved into the stone above. This one was less disturbing than the sacrificial scenes. Here, men approached what seemed to be a holy site of some sort. Holiness was represented by lines radiating magically from an object. A chalice, perhaps. Because of the limited light and poor workmanship, it was difficult to make out. There were supplicant men on hands and knees to one side of the object. Powerful men with animal heads stood on the other. Floating in the sky above, a half-man, half-lion figure watched the events unfold.

Maybe we'll find that chalice down here, Ernie hoped. That would really be something.

Halfus lowered his beam from the relief and approached the aperture, but Ernie shone his light around. He saw something else interesting.

"Halfus." His voice was now barely above a whisper, as though there were something blasphemous about speaking down here.

Halfus looked at him, then followed his gaze. They both angled their lights into another tunnel, branching off from this main one. It was smaller, and there was no question that it angled down. Ernie estimated ten or twelve degrees.

"Which way?"

"There's something in here," Halfus replied, indicating the archway. "Let's check it out first."

That was not the answer Ernie had been hoping for. For some reason he was not eager to go in there. But he did not argue.

The opening was only wide enough for one at a time. Ernie let Halfus go first. Then he took another deep breath and followed him in.

This chamber had a different feel to it. His first impression was that it felt somehow cooler, although that did not make sense. It seemed more like another tunnel than a chamber. The walls were only slightly wider than the passage they had just come down, and it extended forward as far as they could see. As the two of them swung their beams around, they saw that the walls were rough and unfinished. Natural. He looked down at his feet. The floor was uneven.

"This is a cave," Ernie said incredulously.

"Looks that way."

It was disorientingly out of place. "Did they build the tunnels to this, or did they find it while they were building?"

"I don't know." Halfus sounded as surprised as Ernie felt. "If I had to guess, I'd say they found this first, then built the tunnels to give this place greater grandeur." He looked around their surroundings. "Assuming there is something grand in here," he said doubtfully.

"Is or was," said Ernie. A new surge of bravado seized him, and he took another step forward. "Come on. Let's check it out."

They marched slowly ahead, Ernie now a step in front. He kept his beam on the floor, while Halfus swung his from side to side in steady arcs. It was a tactic they had practiced before, giving them optimal coverage with their limited light.

Suddenly Ernie's heart skipped a beat, and he froze in place. A second later, he began to laugh at himself.

"You gonna tell me what happened?" Halfus asked in an edgy voice. He had stopped as well.

"It's a fucking beetle," Ernie said. He felt strange, and had to force himself to stop laughing. He was becoming hysterical.

Halfus put his hand on Ernie's shoulder. They looked at each other, but said nothing. Then Halfus nodded reassuringly and dropped his hand. He looked ahead and took a step forward, prepared to resume the lead.

Ernie stopped him. "I'm all right." He took a step. Then another.

He saw another beetle. He ignored both it and the implications. Food. Water. He did not know enough about beetles to make sense of it.

At least some of their questions were answered. They saw shapes ahead. Three more statues, spaced about fifteen feet apart. These were much smaller than the jackal or the lion. They were also completely human. On their knees, arms outstretched. The three of them together held the rim of a giant stone basin.

"Mahmoud would love it down here. Lots of statues."

"Mmm-hmm."

They stepped closer, and Ernie heard his shoe make a different noise. As if he had crunched something. He froze in place, fearing he had just stepped on a beetle. He did not want to look down.

Halfus shone his light into the basin. It was empty, and the bottom was a gaping hole. Ernie watched Halfus crouch and shine his light under it. "Interesting," was all he said.

Now Ernie forced himself to look down, and discovered that there were small pieces of earth on the ground. And, amazingly, a tiny leaf. He looked around. A withered-looking vine or creeper ran along the stone. He followed its course with his beam, until he was looking at the same place as Halfus, beneath the basin.

It was too small to be a pond, but the dimensions of the hole were large enough to accommodate one. It covered nearly the entire area between the statues, under the ruined basin, growing deeper toward the center. A small pool of brackish water filled the bottom. It was about two feet wide, of indeterminate depth.

"You thirsty?" Ernie joked.

"Not anymore."

"How did water get down here?"

Halfus shone his light toward the ceiling.

"Hard to tell. There must be some small opening up there. Probably need to be here in daytime to see it."

"I don't hear any dripping."

"When was the last time it rained?"

"Good point. I don't think I've seen a cloud since we've been here."

As far as oases went, this seemed a poor one. Nonetheless, it was a bit marvelous to behold. When they first climbed down, he had been hoping for buried treasure. Then, when he saw the lion in the antechamber, his imagination had run wild. This seemed more like the world's oldest practical joke.

"Well, this is not what I expected."

"Me, neither," Halfus agreed. "Come on. We still have a little time. Let's check out the other tunnel."

Ernie started to follow. Then he had a thought. He wanted to be sure.

He stepped into the dry edge of the hollow, then crouched to reach toward the pool of water. He used one hand to disturb the disgusting layer of slime on the surface while he aimed his flashlight with the other. His pulse quickened a little. Somehow he was certain he would find something. *Come on, chalice.* But the water was still too dark to see into. He edged closer and thrust his hand down into it, then patted along the bottom. There was nothing. Naturally. If there ever had been a chalice, several dozen centuries in a pool of scummy water would have done quite a number on it.

Ernie stood back up, irritated. The excitement of exploration was slowly being tempered by disappointment. He did not wish to come away from the night empty-handed.

· · ·

The side tunnel was not only smaller, it was rougher. Either the centuries had been less kind to it, or the workmanship had been poorer to begin with. Footing was not exactly treacherous, but both of them repeatedly caught themselves from stumbling on uneven ground and hidden protrusions.

It did not help matters that they were completely exhausted. The work of recent days had been physically demanding, the summer heat draining. Moreover, the excitement and stress had caused a serious mental fatigue, and they were now halfway through the night without a wink of sleep to refresh them. The adrenaline of adventure had long since faded, and the strangeness of the little grotto had done little to bring it back.

Ernie was disappointed that they had not found a single relic. Not that he intended to keep anything, but it would have been nice to receive credit for a find. He envisioned taking friends—or even family—to a history museum on some indeterminate day in the future. There he would proudly display the dazzling object he had found in the rocky wastes of Mesopotamia. He would pose beside the display while his mother took a photo, Jackie looking on in excitement, his father with pride. Ernie realized he was smiling to himself, then shook off the daydream. His mind was drifting when he should be concentrating. He knew from past experience that underground tunnels were no place for carelessness.

He stopped to take a swig from the bottle of water he was carrying. He noticed that his fingers still carried a little slime from the water. He tried ineffectually to wipe them off on the wall. The skin was already raw and nicked and the roughness of the stone was irritating. He sighed and wiped them on his shirt instead.

Halfus was getting farther ahead. Ernie took a few quick steps to catch up to him, nearly tripping in the process. He was glad his friend had not seen that.

They followed this passage for a few more minutes before it began to widen. They were entering another chamber. A big one, it seemed.

From here they could not see the opposite side, the beams of their flashlights simply trailing off in darkness.

"You take the left wall, I'll take the right?" suggested Ernie.

Halfus shook his head. "Better stay together."

A little annoyed, Ernie did not reply. He began to follow the wall to his right. If Halfus wanted to follow him, so be it.

The construction of this chamber was the equivalent of the tunnel that led them here. Rough and uneven, but still definitely man-made. It was a wonder that it was still so intact after all this time. Ernie began to appreciate that they had found something truly remarkable, even if there was not a single relic to be found. He may not get an exhibit in a museum, but he still might get his name in a book.

Ernie's foot came down on almost nothing. Only the back end of his heel found purchase. Then this, too, slipped off an instant later. His wandering mind suddenly raced back to the present, but too late. He was helplessly falling forward into terrifying blackness. His hands opened as he instinctively reached out for something to stop his fall.

A hand grabbed his shirt at the shoulder. The fabric began to tear, but it slowed his fall long enough for Halfus to get his other hand on him as well. Ernie felt his legs dangling as he clutched Halfus' arms in horrible desperation. The world had literally gotten much darker, and for an instant Ernie's panicked brain believed the apocalypse was nigh. Then he realized he was no longer falling, but being lifted instead, and overwhelming relief washed through him. He kicked out with his foot until he could get a leg up on the broken floor. Even with one leg still dangling, he felt safe again.

"Fuck." Never had he needed to say that so much.

"Ernie, mind easing up a little? Your fingers are ripping my arms to shreds."

"Yeah, sorry." But Ernie had some difficulty doing it. His muscles seemed to have locked in a vise grip. Then, as calm returned to his mind, his hands slowly obeyed his will. He pulled himself into a sitting position beside Halfus, who seemed to be catching his own breath. They sat side-by-side for a moment.

"Damn, I'm glad you're strong," he said at last.

"You okay?"

"Yeah. Dropped my fucking flashlight down there, though."

At the mention, Halfus reached back to pick up his own. Ernie realized he had dropped it in order to get his second hand in on the rescue. It was a damn good thing that it had not gone down the hole, as well.

Ernie watched Halfus run the beam along the floor near them, then along the edge of the hole. The floor was not broken, after all. The edge of the hole was smooth and even, not at all haphazard as Ernie had expected. It was a perfect circle built into the floor. And it was huge, perhaps thirty feet in diameter. He had assumed the opening was the result of a collapse, but now he realized it was there by design.

"What is this, anyway?" he wondered aloud.

"Looks like a pit. For what purpose, though, I have no idea."

"A trap, maybe?"

"Back on *Raiders of the Lost Ark* again?" Halfus said dismissively as he stood up.

Ernie changed the subject. "Halfus, I can see my flashlight down there. Shine your light down."

"Hang on." Something in Halfus' voice drew Ernie's attention from the gaping hole. His friend was a few paces away, stepping slowly and carefully toward the center of the room. In the distance, Ernie saw that the floor was elevated. He stood up to follow.

"Careful," warned Halfus. He pointed his beam in another direction. "There's another pit." Without a light of his own, Ernie would have to step only where Halfus did.

They approached the elevated area. It was a large circular stone platform, or dais. It was four feet high and roughly twenty feet in diameter. On it was a smaller platform, perhaps two feet high and four across.

They climbed onto the dais to use as an observation point. They peered out on four large pits spaced evenly around the chamber. There was enough room to walk between the pits to the dais, but not between the pits and the walls. That had been their mistake, and it had very nearly been a costly one.

"So what are they for?" asked Ernie.

"I'm wondering the same thing," Halfus responded.

"You have more rope in the pack, right?"

Halfus did not answer right away. "I don't think that's a good idea," he said at last.

"You don't have to go down. I'll check it out while I recover my flashlight."

Halfus sighed. Ernie knew his friend was torn between fear of heights and a love of adventure.

"Seriously, Halph, you should stay up here. I just need to kick this place in the butt for scaring me."

Halfus unslung the backpack from his shoulder.

They tied the rope around the topmost platform. Its outline was round, and they worried that it could slip, but the surface was rough enough that it seemed unlikely. And Halfus would stay up here to keep an eye on it.

Standard climbing rope was sixty meters, so they had no concern about its reaching the bottom. Judging by the distant light of his fallen flashlight, Ernie guesstimated the pits were sixty or seventy feet deep. He wished he had brought gloves. His hands were sore and his fingers tingling, and the climb would make them much worse.

"We're starting to run low on time," Halfus said. He had taken out his cell phone to see its clock. Ernie saw the bright glow of its display illuminate his friend's serious expression. Then Halfus slipped it back into his pocket. "Just get down there, punch the wall or whatever makes you feel better, get your flashlight, and climb back up."

"And if I find treasure down there?" Ernie asked with a smile.

"Then I'll join you."

It took him several minutes to reach the bottom. Sure enough, his hands were aching by the time he let go of the rope.

The first thing Ernie did was recover his flashlight. Then he examined his eerie surroundings. He was standing on unfinished earth. The walls were framed with cut stones, but the builders had apparently ignored the floor.

There did not appear to be anything worthwhile at the bottom. Ernie was getting used to disappointment, but he looked around anyway. Besides, he wanted to give the muscles of his hands a minute to recover some strength. He knelt and worked his light around the ground. He was no geologist, but he knew from caving that the rock here seemed soft, looser than expected. With no digging tools available, he used his heel to gouge a little cavity. Then he shone his light in.

He stood up, his heart suddenly racing.

"Halfus!" His voice sounded disturbingly loud down here, but he had to yell to get his friend's attention.

"What is it?" The response was clearly audible. Perhaps he was not as far down as he thought. He looked up. Halfus' light was maybe fifty feet above.

"You need to see this."

"What is it?"

"Bones. Lots and lots of bones."

By the time Halfus was beside him, Ernie had gouged out a few more holes. The bones were everywhere. Many were in pieces, and often they were nothing more than small flakes mixed in with the earth. But some were nearly intact.

The two of them stared at the ghastly scenery, a terrible understanding dawning.

"The dais is for the sacrifices," Halfus speculated. "Maybe the victims placed on the other platform. The smaller one, where we tied the rope."

Ernie nodded. "And the bodies tossed into these pits."

"Yeah." Halfus seemed less than thrilled at their discovery. "At least I hope it was just bodies. I wonder if they killed everyone before throwing them down here."

"If anyone was alive when they were tossed, they were dead when they hit bottom."

"Yeah. You're right. What a place to die." There was a sadness in his voice, and Ernie wondered how Halfus could feel sympathy for people who lived thousands of years ago.

They stood at the bottom of the pit for a moment of silent reflection. Ernie waited for Halfus to say or do something. It was unspoken, but Halfus had assumed authority—as he always did, whether Ernie liked it or not.

At last Halfus spoke again. "We really need to be going. On the way back we can talk about whether to say anything to the others." He looked at the clock on his phone again. "Lisa might be up soon."

Lisa. Ernie wondered whether she would say anything to her boss if she found out. He doubted it.

"Okay. Who's first?"

"I'm slower. You go ahead."

Ernie began climbing. Almost immediately his hands screamed out in pain, but it was nothing he had not dealt with before. Then his mind visualized the platform where the rope was tied. With no one there to watch it, it might slip off at any moment. He pushed himself to keep going at a faster pace than normal. He felt Halfus holding the rope steady for him, which helped. He made good progress and soon neared the light above, where Halfus had left his flashlight pointing across the top of the pit. Ernie pulled himself up and out and breathed a sigh of relief.

Then he watched Halfus climb. His friend was about halfway up now. His pace was slower, for several reasons. His fear of heights naturally had an effect, of course. Ernie was impressed that he could even force himself to do things like this. There were other considerations as well. Ernie was taller but lighter, his arms longer. Whereas Halfus was broad, Ernie was lean. With his greater reach, Ernie could cover more distance with each pull and use less energy in the process. These two advantages really added up over time. Halfus may be better at some things, but Ernie reminded himself that he was at others. Climbing was one of them. The thought was reassuring.

The better man won. That was nonsense. He had just been feeling down on himself. The truth was he was just as good a man as Halfus. And just as deserving.

He could see Halfus tiring as he neared the top. Ernie spoke words of encouragement. "Almost there. Just a few more pulls."

Then Halfus was within Ernie's reach. "Let me give you a hand," he said. He reached down. Halfus took the hand, and Ernie pulled up. Halfus, now half-in and half-out, let go of the rope with his other hand as it fished for a place on the rim from which to push himself up. Then Ernie let go, and his friend plummeted back down into darkness.

The way he would later remember it, Ernie's hand had opened before his mind was aware that he was doing it. The realization only occurred to him in the same split second that his eyes met Halfus', seeing the momentary look of surprise before he was gone.

Ernie stood. His knees wavered. The same panic that he had experienced less than an hour earlier flowed over him again. He trembled, staring at the gaping mouth of the pit. He forced himself to take a step toward it.

"Halfus?" he said. His voice sounded weak. "Halfus?" he called, louder. There was no answer.

He was dizzy. He stepped back from the edge, lest he fall.

Ernie closed his eyes and shook his head. *What do I do now?*

He could think of nothing. He could not think at all. *It doesn't seem real.* Sometimes he was like this, unable to think for himself. *It's not fair. The others always know what to do.*

He sat down and closed his eyes. It did not help. Soon he began having trouble breathing, as well.

Calm down, Easy, a voice said. *Let's think this through.*

Halfus? Rich? Doc? It did not matter. He could function as long as he imagined someone else doing the thinking for him. Slowly the panic receded.

He went back to the dais. He would retrieve the pack, and the rope. Then he stopped himself. It had to look like an accident. *It was an accident.* But taking the rope would be suspicious. If he made it back to camp before anyone woke up, he could proclaim innocence. It would seem like Halfus came down alone. For that, the rope and pack needed to stay.

He left Halfus' flashlight where it lay, illustrating the scene of Ernie's betrayal. *It wasn't betrayal. It was a mistake.* Lighting the way with his own flashlight, he stepped carefully past the pits to the entrance of the room. Then he started to run.

There was a hint of daylight coming through the small hole. Ernie realized he had not looked at his own phone since before he went into the pit, and Halfus had not told him the exact time when he had last checked. How long had Ernie stood there, immobile, unthinking? He realized he honestly had no idea. It seemed to have been seconds, but it could have been much longer.

Panic washed over him for a third time that night. The others would be up. His plan would have to be scrapped. They would know the two of them came down together. Ernie might be in serious trouble. Two men had gone in, but only one returned. They had to believe him. They had to know it was an accident. If not, his life would be ruined.

As he climbed up this last rope, the tears on his face were genuine.

PART II

Outbreak

7

AFTERMATH

MODERN TAXONOMY CLASSIFIES *four types of germs in the world: fungi, bacteria, viruses, and protozoa. The term germ denotes pathogen, which is an infectious agent that causes disease. Of course, not every fungus, bacterium, or protozoan is harmful. Some are benign or helpful, and many bacteria are even critical to human health. This leads to an important distinction—all germs belong to one of these four groups, but not every member of these four groups is a germ.*

Fungi may seem like plants, but they are actually categorized as an entirely separate kingdom. There are over a million types of fungus in the world, but only several hundred are known to cause disease in humans. Familiar examples of fungi include mushrooms, yeasts, and molds. Lichen is a curious amalgam—the technical term is mutualistic symbiosis—of fungus and algae. Common diseases resulting from fungal infection include candidiasis, ringworm (of which Athlete's foot is a subset), and cryptococcal meningitis, which is particularly threatening to AIDS sufferers.

A protozoan is a single-celled subset of the protist kingdom. There are tens of thousands of species of protozoa. Some are symbiotic, but many are parasitic. They commonly prey upon algae, fungi, and bacteria. Some play a role in digestion for various members of the animal kingdom. Others cause diseases such as malaria and sleeping sickness. Protozoan infections are extremely contagious, as they can be transferred by either direct contact or the exchange of blood through a third agent, such as a mosquito.

Bacteria, like fungi, are a taxonomic kingdom unto themselves. They are microscopic, bountiful, and hardy. Bacteria were probably the first living organisms on Earth, and can prosper in any environment imaginable. Like the protozoa, bacteria exist in symbiotic and parasitic forms. Each human being alive today lives only through the divine presence of trillions of bacteria residing on the skin, in the gut, and throughout the body. It is not hyperbole to say that man is 90% microbe and 10% human. They are an integral part of human biology—which is not to suggest that all bacteria are beneficial. Anthrax, cholera, botulism, diphtheria, leprosy, Lyme disease, syphilis, scarlet fever, tuberculosis, and typhoid fever are all caused by bacterial infections.

The final germ type is unique. The virus is the one member of the list that is always a pathogen. It cannot live and propagate on its own, but is capable of replication only inside the cells of other living organisms. These hosts include not only animals, but plants and fungi as well. There are even viruses that infect bacteria, known as bacteriophages. Viruses contain genetic material with which they hijack the cells of others, generating a vicious expansion at the most basic level of life. Cells are literally transformed into something new, their original function subordinated to the good of the invader. Smallpox, rubella, rabies, hepatitis, herpes, influenza, and Ebola are all viral diseases that plague mankind.

Some scientists believe viruses are a unique life form, while others insist they are not. Viruses do not have a cell structure of their own, and therefore do not qualify as life based on some definitions. Yet if they are not life, what exactly are they? Why the same drive to reproduce experienced by real life forms? Could there be more to them than meets the eye?

In this and other ways, the existing classification is not without controversy, and subject to periodic revision. As scientists continue to delve deeper into our natural environment, they are sometimes forced to jettison tenets that were previously held dear. Already one of the four types of germs, protozoa, is falling out of usage in some circles. It turns out that life is really quite complicated. The more we learn, the less we know.

They were called Angel's Trumpet. It seemed an appropriate name for the lovely pendulous pink flowers. Ahmed and his wife had first discovered them while on vacation in Argentina six years earlier. They had packed as many activities as they could into that two-week trip. Hiking, snorkeling, horseback riding, and shopping in Buenos Aires. One day after another of fun and adventure. Each evening they retired, exhausted, to the quiet cabana away from the commotion of the city. They would sit, hand in hand, admiring the lush bounty of nature, forcing their senses to enhanced levels of perception. Together they discovered wonderful new colors, sounds, and smells.

Anjali had noticed the flowers first. She guessed they were the source of the delightful aroma that permeated the refreshingly cool air of the enclosed patio where they spent each evening, laughing over the day's events until the musical soundings of birds and bugs soothed them toward sleep. It was that setting Ahmed hoped to recreate when he discreetly inquired about the flowers before the couple departed the tropical paradise. He learned that the plant was genus *Brugmansia*. It was all but extinct in the wild, and those at the cabana had not gotten there by happenstance.

It had taken no little time and effort, but he had been able to surprise Anjali with a beautiful specimen of the plant on her fortieth birthday. She had known immediately what it was, as well as the memory Ahmed was conjuring for them both. She had spent the next five years lovingly attending the flowers. Since her death last year, Ahmed had taken that responsibility upon himself. It was a lot of work to keep the plant pruned and nurtured, the soil moist and fertilized. Neither the climate of Iraq nor Ahmed's busy schedule was conducive to maintaining a tropical plant, but Ahmed had made a promise. He could still picture Anjali in the hospital, twisted and shriveled from the cancer treatments, clutching his hand, asking him to carry on her work. She need not have asked. Every time he looked at the flowers, he saw her face. Each evening, when their scent filled his patio, he felt her presence calling to him. Angel's Trumpet, indeed.

He was on the patio tending to them again this morning, but his mind could not stay focused on the task. It made him irritable, because this was a labor of love. It was a daily ritual that had become a sacred observance. Nothing else brought him closer to those deeply treasured memories, and any memory of his wife deserved his undivided attention. Today, alas, he was distracted by recent reports of rebellious activity in the countryside around Mosul. Ever since the American invasion had driven any conspicuous signs of unrest from the city, Mosul had lulled itself into a mood of peace and normality. Now, as the bulk of the occupying forces were withdrawing from the country for good, that lull was appearing ever more illusory. The U.S.-trained Iraqi Army still maintained a secure hold on the immediate vicinity of Mosul, but beyond that perimeter the signs of discontent were increasing in intensity and frequency.

It pained Ahmed to admit it, but the primary reason for the unrest was sectarian. The predictions that Sunni and Shia could not get along in the absence of a severe, punishing authority were turning out to be true. The Sunni minority in the country was indignant at the loss of power following the fall of Hussein. It was hard for any man, or group of men, to accept a sudden loss of respect and influence. Although ostensibly a part of it, Ahmed had to admit the Shia regime in Baghdad was not helping matters with their heavy-handed, one-sided decisions.

A scant few years ago, the country had been close to a full-fledged civil war. Areas that had been mixed Sunni and Shia for decades suffered the most. Ahmed had heard of something similar happening in Bosnia during the collapse of Yugoslavia. Friends and neighbors who had gotten along all their lives suddenly turned against one another. The quickly shifting loyalties were not always voluntary. Regular people were placed in a position where they risked their lives and families if they failed to support their side with sufficient vigor. Whole neighborhoods went from diverse to homogeneous in a matter of months. In Iraq, Shia militias were the primary instigators, driving people out of their homes in many cases, killing and looting in others. But the Sunnis were not all victims during this episode. They formed their own militias and committed their fair share of atrocity. Moreover, there were also tribal warlords throughout the country who saw opportunity in the crisis, consolidating their own power at the expense of civilians who had the bad luck to live within these petty fiefdoms.

The Americans had responded by increasing their own troop presence, a move they entitled their "Surge." Admittedly, it tended to work in the areas they kept garrisoned. But the Surge came with its own set of problems. The first was that Iraq was a big country, and the Americans could not be everywhere at once. A second was that while such a show of force tamped down fighting in the short term, it also added to the levels of resentment and animosity already felt by many Iraqis. Those hard feelings would naturally remain after the troops left. To make matters worse, the Americans had dealt with the insecurity in regions outside their control by paying off the warlords. Once again, it was a sound plan in the short run, but Ahmed feared those same warlords would use the money and supplies to strengthen themselves and turn against the authorities as soon as they smelled weakness.

The outbreak of civil war in Syria had momentarily provided a release valve for the pressure building up in Iraq. Many of the most belligerent fundamentalists left the country to join the fighting in their troubled neighbor. As a result, the past few years in Mosul had been blissfully calm. But the border between Syria and Iraq was porous at best, and now the Syrian conflict was turning into a double-edged sword. Many of the fighters were coming back, better armed and more experienced.

All this was happening as the Americans were withdrawing from Iraq. Ahmed was thoughtful enough to understand that the U.S. had its own political agenda, but it seemed to be blind naiveté for the new American President to pull out now. The U.S. was, of course, blaming the pullout on the Iraqi Prime Minister. Contrary to American perceptions, however, the sticking point was not that the Iraqis did not want America to leave troops in the country. It was that the Americans wanted their troops to be immune to the law. While Ahmed could understand the American reluctance to be subject to Sharia law, allowing troops legal immunity was never really an option for the new government or the Iraqi people. Especially in light of some of the incidents that had occurred during the occupation.

He wished he could talk about the troubling situation with someone. Lonely is the head that wears the crown, and Ahmed was the highest-ranking official of his department in the governorate. In years past, he shared his innermost thoughts with Anjali, who had been even more intelligent and well educated than he. He also used to speak to his neighbor, Jalal. They had grown up together in one of the most affluent areas of Basra before moving to Mosul at the same time with positions in the newly formed Iraqi government. Jalal's young wife Merat had gotten along swimmingly with Anjali, and the four of them had spent many an evening conversing out here on their adjoining patios.

Ahmed looked at Jalal's patio now, remembering the last time they had discussed serious politics. It was several years ago. An American missile had struck what was supposed to be a meeting of insurgents, but had turned out to be a group of civilians. One hundred twenty-three people had been killed, many of them women and children. Ahmed had been furious. He grieved for the families, of course, but also for the difficult position it put upon his superiors. He understood that it was an honest mistake. The Americans had not deliberately killed civilians. Unfortunately, honest mistakes in a war zone had tragic consequences. When over a hundred innocent civilians die in one push of a button, people were naturally going to get upset. Moreover, the Americans did themselves no favors with the manner in which they handled the aftermath. There were repeated denials of eyewitness accounts, until the accumulated evidence had forced the U.S. Army into admitting fault. It would have been much better for everyone involved if they had simply apologized up front. Instead, they led many Iraqis to feel that they were covering up because they had something to hide.

Jalal had talked Ahmed down from the ledge that day. He had been willing to submit his resignation as a gesture of protest, but his neighbor always had an eye for the greater good. Casualties were tragic, but inevitable in the process of getting rid of a monster like

Hussein. When it came to the changes happening in the country, the good far outweighed the bad. No longer would only the privileged few have access to the education and opportunity that the two of them were blessed with. A day of new liberties was dawning, and Iraq would be the better for it. Rather than being so critical, Ahmed should be grateful for the chance to play a role in the change. It was the crux of what Ahmed believed as well, but he had not fully appreciated it until hearing his friend say it aloud.

That conversation had led into a happier one. Merat joined her husband on the patio, her skin radiant and her face beaming with pleasure. Jalal had swelled with pride as he told Ahmed that she was pregnant with their first child. "May it be the first of many," Ahmed told them. Anjali had regrettably been unable to get pregnant, and so the two of them made plans to spoil Jalal's children as though they were their own.

That was before Jalal and Merat were killed. The young woman had gone into labor prematurely, and Jalal had raced her toward the hospital in a thoughtless panic. He either forgot or ignored the new checkpoint the occupying troops had set up not far from their home in response to a botched attack on a local police station. It was simply one more honest mistake. Ahmed had met the young man who pulled the trigger as the car ignored his signal to stop. The boy seemed genuinely affected by what he had done. These types of accidents happened in a tense occupied zone between people of different cultures. Ahmed understood this. He simply wished others did, too, instead of this endless cycle of blame and accusations that perpetuated more violence and death. He took some comfort from knowing that Jalal would feel the same way.

That was a conclusion he had come to only after a great deal of thought, however. He had not been so accepting at the time. On that horrible day, Ahmed's convictions had been brutally tested by reality. Again, he might have resigned, not so much in protest of the Americans as at the futility of it all. But it had been only days later when Anjali was diagnosed with an advanced case of ovarian cancer. During the painful months that followed, Ahmed did not have the spirit to do much of anything, let alone make a stand. He was glad his position with the government was largely a ceremonial one. Never had he felt like such a useless human being, no more capable of doing his job than he was of willing a cessation to the spread of the evil inside his wife's body.

Then one day, something had clicked within him. He was not only able to return to work, but with newfound energy and purpose. The sensation had an odd mixture of dedication to improving Iraq without the hindrance of caring about anyone or anything else. The invitation that led to the Schwarzvogel Expedition had been one of many bold ideas stemming from that brief spurt of industriousness.

He heard his doorbell ring. Ahmed set down the paper towel he had been using to wipe the leaves of the *Brugmansia* plant, then went inside to answer.

It was his assistant, Tariq. It was unusual to see him here, at Ahmed's residence. For that matter, it was unusual to see him so early in the morning. He normally showed up for work each day somewhere between several minutes and several hours late. Tariq was not what Ahmed would describe as a dedicated member of the Cultural Ministry, having received his appointment through connections and his Sunni affiliation. A year ago, Ahmed received an order from above to fill positions with an eye toward diversity. It was a noble idea, prompted by American coercion, that functioned poorly in reality. Employees like Tariq were often so impudent as to be more trouble than they were worth. Ahmed would have to look into dismissing him as soon as he could find a suitable replacement.

Tariq delivered his message. The more Ahmed heard, the greater his displeasure. It seemed that Herr Doktor Schwarzvogel had contacted the ministry yesterday afternoon. He had asked to speak to Ahmed, who had taken the day off but made it clear that he was available if needed. When asked why this message was just now getting to him, Tariq merely shrugged. Ahmed should have emphasized to his staff that any communications from the dig site were to be given the highest priority—although judging from Tariq's slouching indifference to his reprimand, he doubted whether it would have made any difference.

Ahmed kept Tariq waiting while he made a few phone calls. He informed Yasin and Naji, his security escorts, that they would be taking a trip out to the site today. Only after overhearing that order did Tariq think to tell Ahmed that Schwarzvogel was already in Mosul.

"What?" Ahmed said in surprise. He was becoming increasingly irate with his incompetent employee.

"Yes. He is waiting at the ministry." Despite Ahmed's obvious aggravation, Tariq appeared unperturbed.

Ahmed considered. He had orders to have his security attachment with him whenever he left his home. Throughout Iraq in recent years, no less than a dozen officials of varying importance had been murdered by insurgent attacks. Still, Ahmed had long since accepted the risks that came with a job in the new government. This would be neither the first nor the last time he traveled without his escort. He would call them back to have them meet at the office.

"Tariq, take me to the Ministry, now. I have calls to make on the way."

By the time Herr Doktor Schwarzvogel finished his narrative, Ahmed had regained his composure.

"So, the rest of your team remains at the site?" he asked.

"Herr Müller came here with me. Fräulein Stimpel is with the Americans at the dig."

It was interesting that Schwarzvogel was distinguishing the Americans from the Germans. Ahmed had always considered the expedition to be a single team, but clearly the group's own leader did not see it that way.

"I see. And you have no idea what is beneath the ruins?"

"No. I considered it paramount to inform you and go through proper channels before proceeding."

"That was wise. Rules are in place for a reason. Thank you for your diligence." He glanced at Tariq, seated beside the little professor, as he said this. He hoped the message would be received by both men, but his subordinate seemed to not be paying attention.

Schwarzvogel was rigidly sitting up in his chair. His back did not appear to be touching the padding behind. He was small, but his perfect posture increased his aura of authority. He seemed like the type of man who would have tight reins on his project. It was therefore surprising that he seemed to be distancing himself from the largest contingent of his team. Ahmed knew from experience that Americans came across as less disciplined than Germans. So did Iraqis, Englishmen, and everyone else, for that matter. Had something happened in the past week that led to the Herr Doktor's disapproval?

Another thing he wondered about was the man's lack of excitement over this most recent discovery. One would expect such a find to be the pentacle of an archaeologist's career, yet Schwarzvogel spoke of it in the same droning tone that he used for everything. Did he believe the find would turn out to be nothing? Or did he simply have such control over his emotions that he revealed no outward signs of the enthusiasm boiling within?

Ahmed did not have time to let this worry him. There were more pressing considerations. "In any case, your decision to pull the team out was correct. I am afraid we are receiving reports of increased activity from several directions."

Schwarzvogel nodded but said nothing. Apparently, the thought that his decision might be mistaken had never occurred to him, so he felt no relief about Ahmed's affirmation.

Ahmed leaned forward in his seat. "As soon as my own team arrives, we will all go to the site. We will do what we can to secure things until this difficulty blows over." He could only hope it would be that simple. First, pacifying the province might require a show of force from the Iraqi Army. He shuddered to think what damage a mass of soldiers might do to the dig site, especially if they had any suspicion that something valuable could be down there. Second, now that Schwarzvogel had brought this discovery into official channels, Ahmed would have to send it up the food chain. That meant politics would be involved. It might be years before any progress was made, and even then it would be likely to take a form that enriched the ruling families. Despite what he had said earlier, part of him wished the expedition had just continued on its own and told him what they found later. But that, of course, was not Herr Doktor Schwarzvogel's way.

The door to the meeting room opened. Ahmed looked up, expecting to see Naji or Yasin. Instead, it was another Ministry employee. A new one. Ahmed tried to recall the name. *Amid? No, Alim.* The young man had a message in his hand and a troubled expression on his face.

"Excuse me a moment, Herr Doktor." Ahmed stood and left the room with Alim. Then he glanced at the message. It was brief and to the point. He felt his arms go weak. "God help us."

From the first moment she woke up that morning, Wendy was angry. She had waited half the night for a visit that never came. Not knowing how Lisa might react to a revelation about Halfus, Wendy had tried to go about her usual routine the same as every night. She changed into her pajamas and climbed into her sleeping bag as though she had not been bursting with anticipation. She feigned sleep but kept both ears alert to the slightest noise outside the tent. Halfus would be discreet and wait for her to join him, so she needed to be ready. There was no danger of her falling asleep prematurely—her mind raced with excitement and desire. They could not risk more than a few minutes together, but that would be enough. She had not appreciated until now just how empty her soul had felt without him.

In her agitated state, it was difficult to keep track of the lapsing of time. It must have been hours before anticipation turned to disappointment and disbelief. She tried to tell herself that something was wrong, that he wanted to come but could not do it without being caught. But she was unable to convince herself. With Schwarzvogel away, there was literally no one at the camp whose disapproval would be enough to stop him. That left only the appalling possibility that he had changed his mind. Their encounter in the afternoon had been sudden and confusing. He had certainly seemed receptive enough at the time, but may have had second thoughts as the hours passed. Perhaps he needed time to think about it. Halfus often thought about things too much for his own good. As the night crept on and on, possibility had turned to probability.

Wendy audibly groaned at the notion, causing Lisa to stir in her slumber. Wendy was annoyed at herself, then immediately shifted the blame back onto Halfus. Everything was his fault.

After her discovery yesterday, when he had said he was proud of her, Wendy had felt that she might burst with happiness. She had been so certain that things were turning a corner for the two of them. Now that thought only made the disappointment much harder to bear. Last night she had cursed him for getting her hopes up. She had finally fallen asleep regretting the kiss entirely. She somehow felt embarrassed.

As she went about her morning rituals, Wendy's anger only intensified. She emptied half a bottle of water into a small bowl that served as a washbasin. She dipped a cloth into it and rubbed irritably wherever she felt dirty. She decided there was really no question how she would react at their first contact this morning. She wanted to tell him that it was no big deal, that she had second thoughts herself. But she could not bring herself to do that. She was just not made to keep her emotions bottled up, and her anger and frustration were too overwhelming. She would give him the cold shoulder as long as she could. Then, when he came to her with some lame explanation, she would let him know how poorly he had treated her. He liked to pretend that he cared about the feelings of others. It was high time he learned to show it to her.

She did not know exactly how or when this would transpire. They would all be terribly busy this morning. They had to pack up everything that could reasonably be extracted from the camp. Last evening they had already brought down what they could from the dig itself. Now came the time to finish the packing.

As the group assembled for what would be their final breakfast at the site, Wendy suddenly felt herself overcome with mixed feelings. She simultaneously wanted to see Halfus and dreaded the first eye contact. More than anything, she just wanted to understand.

Lisa was serving up the warmed leftovers of yesterday's oatmeal. The sight of it reminded Wendy of the incident with the finger, and her rage boiled anew. She absolutely hated feeling jealous, and she especially resented Halfus for making her feel that way. She deliberately avoided looking in the direction of the tent where he and Ernie slept. It was a little surprising that he was not already out. He was usually up before she was. Wendy took some consolation from the notion that perhaps he, too, had experienced a difficult night.

Rich said good morning to her as he emptied an excessive number of sugar packets into his bowl. Wendy forced herself to smile back at him, then thanked Lisa as the other girl handed her a serving. Their eyes met for just a moment, and Wendy felt that those blue orbs were staring into her soul. Lisa was sharp. She must know, or at least suspect, what was happening. Wendy found herself wondering what her would-be rival thought about it. Did she approve? Disapprove? Think less of Wendy for taking both Halfus and Ernie? It was hard to read much from the girl's expressionless face.

Then that face broke into a smile as Lisa looked toward a newcomer. "There you are, you little skulk," she told Mahmoud as she spooned some oatmeal for him. "I wondered if you were hiding around here somewhere." He flashed his mischievous grin as he accepted the bowl.

"Rich, check on Halfus and Ernie, please," requested Doc. His voice sounded more tired than she could ever remember its being. The past week—and especially the past day—had clearly been a strain on him. Although none of them had spoken about it, it was obvious to everyone that he did not get on well with Herr Doktor Schwarzvogel. *At least he will finally get a break from it,* she thought with some small relief.

"They're not here," Rich said a moment later.

Wendy looked up in surprise, as did the others. Rich had unzipped the tent and now held the flap up for them to see inside. Then he dropped it and stared up the ridge, toward the dig site—and the discovery. *Oh, Halfus, tell me you didn't.*

But clearly he had. Suddenly she understood why he had not come to her last night. The temptation to explore would have been irresistible for him. The realization did nothing to abate her anger. He had chosen exploring some stupid hole in the ground over her.

It was a little curious that the two guys were not back already. She was certain they would not have wanted to make the others worry. Most likely, they would not have wanted the others to even know. Maybe they found something to bring back up, meaning the rest of them would find out in any case. If so, it had better be pretty damn impressive to be worth standing her up. She could visualize the others marveling at whatever dusty old relic the two guys brought into camp. The tense disapproval of this moment would be forgotten, as would be the fact that the discovery was Wendy's to begin with. And Halfus would smile innocently and bask in the praise. She hoped he was proud of himself.

Wendy saw Doc and Rich deep in discussion. They were probably weighing options. She felt a momentary impulse to join them, believing she should cover for the guys. Angry though she was, she did not want them to get into any real trouble. But then Doc would think she was in on the little stunt. Why should she risk implicating herself, after what Halfus had done to her?

"There's one of them now," called Lisa.

Doc and Rich stopped talking, and they watched the solitary figure walk slowly down the ridge. Whoever it was seemed to be in no hurry, as though deliberately heightening their anticipation of whatever discovery he was coming to announce. Wendy was growing impatient. Then the figure stumbled, and instead of getting back up, stayed down on his knees.

Wendy found herself running along with the others. *Please, please, please,* she thought, without really knowing what she was hoping for. Her pace only increased when she saw that the figure was Ernie. He regained his feet and took a few more steps toward them, and she saw that he was really struggling. Was he hurt? She could not see any obvious injuries from here.

Rich was much faster than Wendy, and reached the spot first. He wrapped an arm around Ernie to hold him up. Lisa ran to his other side to help, and Ernie draped an arm over each of their shoulders. Lisa said something reassuring into his ear and used her free hand to brush his dirty, sweaty hair back from his eyes.

Wendy was unaware of what the other girl was saying. She had stopped as soon as she saw his face. He, too, seemed unaware of the German girl. He was looking directly at Wendy with wet, pleading eyes. That horrible look of despair was wholly for her.

Wendy had never liked those girls who reacted to shock and horror by screaming. She had never understood why they did it. It certainly did not help solve whatever crisis confronted them. Now she discovered why they screamed. It was unavoidable.

"He was never good with heights," Ernie said. "But he was stubborn. He wanted to be the one to go down into the pit."

Ernie was sitting on a crate back in camp, his red, swollen hands clutching an untouched bowl of oatmeal. Instead of eating, he had simply stared into it while he recounted the events of the night. Lisa had draped a heavy blanket over his back, but his body continued to shiver despite the rising temperature.

Wendy was sitting some distance away, sobbing as she listened. She visualized Halfus doing exactly as Ernie described. She knew from her own experience that Halfus was too stubborn for his own good, and he would not ask Ernie to take a risk on something that he would not do himself.

"He was so slow," Ernie continued. "But he made it down okay, so I thought he was fine. He must have been tired, though. He was even slower coming back up. He almost made it to the top. Then I saw him stop. I tried to encourage him, but...he couldn't hold on any longer. He just let go. I watched him fall into darkness."

She wanted to stop crying, but could not help herself. It was not helping in any tangible way, but it was very slightly cathartic. Her heart ached painfully, and the tears were the only thing that made it tolerable. It was too cruel a twist of fate, to go from the promise of yesterday to the anguish of today. It seemed surreal, and she knew she had not fully taken it in. And yet she was aware of an unbearably immense loss. All she could visualize was his face, happy and longing, just after their kiss. Yet it was something she would never again see for real. It did not seem possible. *Please, God, make this go away.*

"I should have stopped him, anyway." Ernie now seemed to be speaking to himself. "I couldn't think of a way to convince him." The pain in his voice echoed her own.

"Doc." Something in Rich's tone made Wendy look up. Two dirty beige vans were driving up the road toward the camp. Wendy put her head back down. They could be full of rebels coming to kill or capture them, for all she cared. Maybe they would put her out of her misery.

They were not rebels. Schwarzvogel was back. With him were Michael, Ahmed, and the two men whose names she had never learned.

Wendy gave them only a cursory glance as they stepped out of the vehicles. All she really wanted now was to be alone. She paid little attention to the hurried questions and answers that ensued between the newcomers on one side and Doc and Rich on the other. She was only vaguely aware that the conversation was animated, even heated. She wondered which one of them was going to go down to recover Halfus' body. And whether she wanted to be around when they did.

"Shut...up!" bellowed Ahmed. That got her attention. She looked at the little congregation again and noticed a few things that she had not before. Michael seemed to be standing back, not wanting any part of the argument. Ahmed, Schwarzvogel, and the other two seemed to be aggressively surrounding Rich and Doc, who appeared cowed. Not without good reason. Wendy just now noticed that Ahmed's two companions were holding large, ugly-looking rifles.

"Everyone listen to me," said Ahmed in a volume somewhere between normal and shouting. "Everyone is getting into these vans right now. No questions, no discussion."

The second part of his command did not register in Wendy's mind. *He wants us to leave, now? What about...?*

"We can't just leave!" she found herself saying. "We have to get him out of there."

She expected an argument. Her brain was already formulating rational responses.

"Wendy." Doc's voice sounded almost pleading. But she was not looking at him. She was focused on Ahmed, who was clearly in charge here. He looked like he was on a very short fuse, but she believed she could get through to him.

"Listen," she started.

"Yasin." Ahmed barked the word like an order, and one of the two armed men stepped toward her. He was an ugly man, a terrible man, with savage brown eyes and a beard that ran full down his neck. But Wendy did not back away from him, even as he grabbed her by the shoulder and yanked her to her feet.

"Take your hands off me!" she shrieked as she tried ineffectually to pull away.

She had lost track of Ernie during her crying spell. She had assumed he was still sitting with Lisa, some distance away. Suddenly Wendy saw him step up beside her and shove her assailant back. Neckbeard let her go as he stepped back a pace. With all her strength intent on pulling away, the sudden loss of his hold caused her to take two stumbling steps backwards before falling onto her side.

Emboldened by the man's limited retreat or some internal sense of chivalry, Ernie positioned himself between her and Neckbeard. He raised his fists. "She said—"

The man quickly jabbed the butt of his rifle into Ernie's nose. There was a crunching sound, then Ernie crumpled to the ground beside Wendy like a puppet whose strings had been cut. Neckbeard spun the weapon around and aimed the barrel at the two prostrate students. She ignored him as she rolled over to Ernie to examine his injury. The nose was almost certainly broken, and a stream of blood gushed from both the bridge and nostrils. She wiped the blood away to see how bad the wound was. It was not more than a minor gash. The amount of blood made it look worse than it was.

"Enough!" Ahmed barked. "I do not have time for this. You will forget your friend. You will forget this discovery of yours. You will get into these vehicles immediately."

"Herr Müller, Fräulein Stimpel. Come," Schwarzvogel said, and the two of them obeyed like docile pets. Michael stepped into the back of the first van, and Lisa began to follow.

Then she paused with one foot in and glanced around. "Where is...? Never mind." She seemed to think better of whatever she was about to say, then climbed in. Herr Doktor Schwarzvogel stepped in with them and closed the door. Wendy was not sure whether he wanted to speak to his own students privately or wanted to completely separate the Germans from the Americans. Either way, the division was palpable. Her group was on its own.

She looked at Doc. Events had clearly overtaken his sense of authority. He met her gaze, then looked down. "Okay. Rich, Wendy, Ernie...we'll talk about this on the ride."

One of the armed men—the one who had not struck Ernie—was getting into the driver's seat of the first van. Ahmed was standing by the passenger door of the same vehicle, but he did not yet get in. He was watching them. Wendy wished he was close enough to spit on.

"Wendy." Rich's voice was calm and tender. He held his hand out to her. "It's all right. We'll get through this."

"I can't leave him like this, Rich," she said. She started crying again, weakly.

She meant it, but Rich's voice was always persuasive. "Shh. It's all right." He lifted her up and put his arm around her. He was taking over now, and her mind began to shut down. It was far easier to let him do the thinking so she could get on with the grieving.

She became aware that Ernie had his arm around her as well. He was rubbing her back in commiseration, and she did the same for him. All together, the three of them followed Doc into the van.

As soon as the two vehicles were out of sight, Mahmoud emerged from his hiding place inside the tent. He told himself that he had not really been afraid...he just had not wanted to be a participant in the ugliness that had taken place. Besides, he could not leave yet. He had unsettled business to take care of.

Fortunately, the expedition had left behind nearly all the supplies. Mahmoud did not know where to look for the things he needed, and he realized this might take quite some time. This day was not going to be at all what he had expected when it started.

He wondered whether he should tell his family what he was doing. If he was not back by dusk, they would worry about him. His father would be particularly angry. He had already castigated Mahmoud several times for spending so much time with the foreigners. It was only when Mahmoud explained how much he was learning that his father had finally relented. The two of them were very much alike in their natural curiosity and desire to learn all they could of the world. Yet for reasons that Mahmoud did not fully understand, his father still admonished him to not let himself be seen with the research team.

He grabbed a few tins of food and stuffed them into his pockets, then thought better of it. He would not be able to heat anything down below. He put the tins back and grabbed a few bags of peanuts and packets of crackers instead. Then he looked to see if there was any more rope, just in case he would need it.

A few minutes later his hands and pockets were overloaded. He needed to make more room for the essentials. With no small hesitation, he took out his new iPod with all its wires and placed it gingerly on a crate where he could find it later. Beside it he placed the item he had intended to give to Halfus today. It was a small piece of cedar, cut away from a larger chunk that Mahmoud's father had brought back from Lebanon. Mahmoud had spent the past few evenings carving upon it a single word, 'Akhi'. He would not be needing it now.

He spent quite a while looking for something that he could use as a pulley device. There were no trees in the area from which he could find a suitable branch, and everything scattered about the camp was too small or too square. He was beginning to feel mounting frustration when his eyes drifted to the campfire. He had completely overlooked it. Months ago one of the Germans had fashioned a large iron rotisserie from a number of steel rods. Mahmoud looked it over, considering. He was not sure that it would be sturdy enough for his purposes. He could use the rope itself to widen the diameter, but he might need to figure out a way to extend the handle to increase torque. He would also need to find a way to secure it. Still, it looked like his best bet. He was confident he could figure everything else out when the time came. After all, he had inherited his father's engineering mind.

He spent a little while familiarizing himself with the assembly. It would not do to disassemble it here without knowing exactly how to put it back together again. It did not appear to be very complicated, however. It was simply a matter of knowing which rods were which. Then he got to work.

He tried not to think too much about what he was feeling. Part of him was excited about going down to explore. Part of him was busy reviewing what he would need to do when he got down there. He could get a loop around the torso and under the arms. With a tight enough knot he should hopefully be able to avoid too much slippage. He focused on breaking everything he was going to do into small, manageable tasks. But the last part of his mind kept interfering. He had already visualized the moment of first sight, and instinctively knew how upsetting that would be. Mahmoud ignored the thought as much as he could. He kept his hands and then his legs in constant motion. That way, it was easier to stop them from shaking.

He was already at the dig when he realized he had not brought any water with him. That could be a problem. But had not the tall man, Ernie, said something about finding water inside? Mahmoud could not really remember. Most of the story had been confusing. Even though he had attended an English-speaking school for years, there were still times when the dialogue of the Americans was hard for Mahmoud to follow, and Ernie's account of the night had seemed rambling and incoherent in parts. Not that it mattered. Regardless of how thirsty he got, he was not going to turn back now. He wanted to get this over with. It might not mean much now, but it was all he could think to do. It was one final favor for his friend.

Ben was very disappointed in himself. If he wanted to be brutally honest about it, he had been since the start of the trip. Perhaps even before. He had never reached the point where he was comfortable with their preparations. He had experienced that moment of panic at the embassy when he thought he had messed up something vital. Even the relief at learning he had not was short-lived, because Adolphus had dominated his thoughts ever since.

He thought the first few days of the project had gone well. How quickly the two of them had fallen back into a first-name basis. Ben's students really pulled their weight at first, and even Adolphus seemed impressed. Not in front of them, of course. That was not how he behaved. But he had paid Ben a single compliment about their conduct one evening as the two of them ate dinner alone in their tent. Ben had been so delighted that he asked his peer for a recommendation to Harvard. He felt like he was back in school again as he said it, and immediately regretted the request. But Schwarzvogel had not said no, and the allure of the man's good word clouded Ben's judgment in the days thereafter. Now he wondered if he had mentally sacrificed his students in the process. *All for naught.*

There was no question of getting that recommendation now, and he frankly did not care. The tragedy of Halfus' death overshadowed everything else. Ben felt that he was responsible, although he did not know what he could have done differently. He had placed his trust in Halfus, along with Rich, yet his student had betrayed that trust by directly disobeying orders. And had gotten himself killed in the process. But Ben was not angry at the boy. He was just incredibly, inconsolably distraught.

It seemed as though his whole world was crashing down around him. Brenda's engagement. Schwarzvogel's disapproval. His students failing him, and he failing them. And now this. Whatever *this* was.

They were not calling it arrest, but that is how it felt. The two vans had taken them back into Mosul, then gone in separate directions. Ben had no idea where Adolphus or his students were now. The van with the Americans had delivered its passengers to a facility that seemed to be some sort of converted hotel. They had marched with nary a word into the building and through a disused lobby, then down a poorly lit corridor to the rooms they now occupied.

Ben was in one all to himself. He believed the others shared a room. Considering the relatively tiny dimensions of his own, he hoped theirs was larger.

They had been here for a few hours now, and all he could do was wait.

If this was a hotel, it must have been a poor one. There was a single-sized bed with a clunky mattress. He really hoped they would not be staying overnight. The sheets did not appear to have been slept on, but were dusty as though cleaned and placed here months ago. It had a blue blanket that he would sleep on top of, if necessary. There was no other furniture in the room, unless he counted the grimy toilet in the tiny adjoining bathroom as a chair—which was all he hoped to have to use it for. The only window in the room was boarded up, but he could see thin wisps of sunlight shining through the cracks between boards, illuminating the hovering specks of dust. Those teasing hints of sun would be his only means to discern when day faded into evening. His phone, like all his other possessions save the clothes on his back, had been taken from him.

Ben had never dealt well with boredom. Not that this was exactly boring, per se. There was simply nothing to keep his mind from obsessing over all that had happened that morning. He did not know what was coming next, but resolved to take it like the man he believed himself to be. He had failed one of his students already, but he had three more that he was still responsible for. At the moment, he did not much care about himself. But he swore that he would do everything in his power to get the others back home as safe and soon as possible.

. . .

He judged it to be early evening when he finally had a visitor. It was Ahmed Shalhoub.

"Please take a seat," Shalhoub said calmly as he entered the room and shut the door behind him. Ben had been sitting on the bed, then stood when the door opened. He remained standing, determined to be defiant.

"I'd offer you a chair if I had one," he told the minister.

"I am sorry that your accommodations are so meager." Shalhoub's tone was measured, neither pleasant nor hostile. "The authorities are in some disagreement as to your disposal."

Ben became alarmed. The fear must have shown in his face, because Shalhoub immediately made a gesture of apology. "Forgive me, I did not mean 'disposal' in the way you think. What would be a better word? 'Processing.' The authorities are discussing how to process you." The look of relief must have been too obvious, for Shalhoub became more severe as he continued. "Do not be at ease, Doctor Appelstein. You and your team will most likely be arrested very soon."

"Arrested? What for?"

"For attempting to steal some of Iraq's precious treasures, of course." He cut off Ben's protest with another gesture. "Please stop, Doctor. It makes little difference whether you intended to or not. What matters is what we think. Quite frankly, we have little inclination to give you the benefit of the doubt."

Ben was disturbed. This was all wrong. There was no chance that Halfus and Ernie had intended to steal anything. Even if that had been the intent, nothing had been taken once Halfus had the accident. But Ben could appreciate what the minister was telling him. The people of Iraq had put up with a lot during the American occupation. Might they seize an opportunity to strike back? Clearly they were divided on the matter. Which side would win out? Which side was Shalhoub on? Ben tried reading the man's face. *Is he for us or against us?* But the man was a statue, as far as Ben could tell.

"It gives me no pleasure to bring you this news, Doctor. It will likely be several days before a decision is made. You should prepare yourself for a long wait."

Surely the American authorities would help as soon as they heard about this. It could be an international scandal. He hated to put his students through that, but it would be better than rotting away in this makeshift prison.

The minister had turned back to the door. The meeting appeared to be over. "Mister Shalhoub, wait. Please. Is there any way I can resolve this quickly?" Ben wondered whether a bribe might work. He had never committed a bribe in his life, but he had seen it done during his trips to Egypt and Jordan. He knew there must be corrupt officials in Iraq, as well, but had no way of knowing whether Shalhoub was one. Something about the man led him to doubt it.

The situation felt preposterous. He did not understand this desire to point fingers. He could not imagine what conceivable benefit the Iraqis would derive from an arrest. Had the Americans not already paid a high enough price? One of them was dead...

Perhaps *that* was the problem. He turned things around in his mind. Might the Iraqi government be looking for absolution? It was no small thing for an American civilian to die in their country. Perhaps the Iraqis simply did not want those fingers of guilt pointing at them.

Ben decided to meet them halfway. "Could I take responsibility? If I confessed, would you let the others go?"

Shalhoub stared at Ben for a very long time. He appeared to be considering. Ben became hopeful. Then the minister shook his head. "I'm sorry, Doctor, but you did not go into the ruins yourself. I don't see how you have anything to confess."

Ben was simultaneously disappointed and relieved. He believed he would have done it, just now, the way he was feeling. Yet at the same time it felt like it might be the end of his life, professionally if not literally.

"Unless..." Shalhoub seemed to be pondering another possibility.

"Anything. I'll do it." Ben spoke quickly, before he could lose his nerve.

"It would not be your confession we need. But if you will attest that the boy who died was acting on his own behalf...if you condemn this act...perhaps my associates will be satisfied that justice was served."

This was not something Ben had even considered. It felt very wrong. Halfus had been a good kid, and did not deserve this. His reputation would be destroyed. Ben knew nothing of his family or loved ones, but surely they would suffer unjustifiably. On the other hand, perhaps Halfus did not even have any close family. In any case, was his reputation and their peace of mind more important than the reputations and livelihoods of the other three who were counting on Ben? Besides, Halfus really had been wrong to go exploring against explicit instructions not to. He had let them all down.

Ben needed to put the other students first. What would they want him to do? As soon as he thought about this, he had his answer.

"I'm sorry, Mister Shalhoub. I can't do that. I know Halfus was innocent. Of that, at least." He hesitated as he saw disapproval register on the man's face. "Figure out a way for me to take the blame, and I'll do it. But I won't sell out one of my students."

Shalhoub paused a moment, then bowed. "As you will. Enjoy your stay, Doctor." With that, he left the room. Ben heard a key turn, locking him back in. *Did I do the right thing?* he wondered. Only time would tell.

Things changed dramatically a few days later.

Ben had eventually allowed himself to sleep when the strain and stress turned to exhaustion. Each day since that first had been the same. With morning and evening came his "room service"—a spartan meal that tasted like stale airline food. Each afternoon he was visited by Shalhoub, whose growing insistence on the plan to indict Halfus made Ben more and more certain he had made the correct decision.

At every opportunity he asked to see his students, or speak to a representative at the American embassy. To the former he was flatly denied. To the latter, he was informed that the embassy was well aware of the situation. Shalhoub told him bluntly that their one and only concern was to avoid a scandal. Ben was not sure whether to believe that, but he was certain that it would be a consideration, if not a priority. As the days passed without a change in information or circumstance, he began to despair.

This was the fourth day of his captivity. He had long since finished his unappetizing breakfast, and now waited impatiently for Shalhoub's visit. Eagerly was perhaps the better word, for the longer Ben went without any other social contact the closer he was drawn to the dour Iraqi.

He heard words outside the door and stood up expectantly. *He is early today*, Ben thought with some enthusiasm. But it was not Shalhoub, after all.

"Wendy. I'm glad to see you."

She did not look particularly glad to see him, however. She appeared haggard and careworn. Still very pretty, but tired. Her hair was tangled and matted, suggesting she, like Ben, had not bathed since their arrival.

"We've been asking to visit you for the past few days," she told him. "They finally let me come, but they said I only have a minute."

"Who is they?"

"That Ahmed."

So Shalhoub has been talking to them, too. It did not come as a surprise.

Wendy wore a pained expression. He hated to think how hard these past few days had been for her, and not only because of their confinement. He knew she and Halfus used to be very close. Clearly her feelings for him were still very strong. Tragically so.

"Are you hurt, Wendy?"

She winced a little, but shook her head. "No, I'm fine."

"How are the others?"

"Rich is okay, but...Ernie's sick, Doc." The inflection in her voice told him it was serious. "I mean really sick. It started the day after the...accident." Her voice broke momentarily. Ben waited patiently for her to recover her composure and continue. "He could barely sit up and his skin started breaking out with these little black spots. Rich kept pestering the man who brought us food to get a doctor, but we don't think he speaks English. Ernie told us not to worry, that he was feeling better. But he didn't look better.

"Yesterday we feared the worst. We had trouble waking him up, and when we did he was delirious. His nose was oozing and he...well, we didn't get him to the toilet in time. Rich really started yelling at the guy who brought breakfast. He pointed at Ernie and tried to make the man understand, but he just gave us our stuff and left like he always does. Then last night, he came back with Ahmed and a doctor. At least, we assume it was a doctor.

"The doctor took his temp and a blood sample and gave us some pills. He told us to give one to Ernie every morning and night. He didn't tell us what they are, and the container doesn't have a label. We're worried that it could be...well, we don't know what it is."

Wendy told Ben all of this in a voice that was almost a monotone, as though she was forcing herself to be unemotional. But now she looked at him with real feeling. "Doc, he needs more than some pills. He needs a hospital." Her face expressed something that her words did not. *I'm afraid he might die.*

"I see. I'm...doing what I can, Wendy."

"Do more. Do you want to lose another one of your students?"

Ben flinched, and she immediately apologized. "Doc, I'm sorry. I'm just...really worried about him. And I don't know what's going on. Do you?"

"They want me to sign something that says Halfus was attempting to steal from that tomb."

"What?" She somehow managed to look even more upset. "Doc, you can't. He didn't—"

"I know." Ben tried to calm her. "I wouldn't do it. That's why we've been here for days." Now it was his turn to convey a deeper message. "That's why we're still here, Wendy. That's what they're waiting for."

She understood him. He saw conflict and indecision in her

reaction. But she began shaking her head. "Doc, you can't. Please tell me you won't do that."

And if Ernie dies? He considered asking her that question, but stopped himself. He did not intend to burden her conscience with this decision. It was his alone to bear.

She had held herself together quite well to this point, but she must have reached her breaking point. He saw tears well up in her eyes, and she dropped her head to hide them.

He put a hand on her back, wanting to comfort her. He felt her body begin to shake as she started to sob.

"It's all right, Wendy." She did not resist his touch as he feared she might, so he put both arms around her and held her tight. She wrapped her arms around his back and cried softly into his chest. He wondered if she had been holding it back these past few days. If so, there must be a river waiting to pour out. That was fine with him. This was the first time in days he felt even marginally useful.

The door opened. Ben looked up to see Shalhoub standing there. He stared at them, saying nothing. Ben assumed that her time was up, but he believed he might hit the other man if he tried to intervene. Ben looked at their host and shook his head emphatically. Shalhoub stared a moment longer, then closed the door without coming inside. He was allowing them this moment of privacy, for which Ben was immeasurably grateful.

Not long after Wendy finished crying and took her leave of Ben, he received another visitor. As usual, when he heard the voices in the hall he assumed it was Shalhoub. For a second time he was mistaken.

This time he did not have the strength to bother standing when the door opened. Thus the man's first words were, "Please stand up, Doctor Appelstein."

"Mister...McGammon, correct?" Ben obeyed the request because his mind was too tired to protest.

The representative from the embassy was, if anything, even less personable in Mosul than he had been in Baghdad. He was wearing a wrinkled dark suit with a loosened tie, and his previously pristine hair was now sweaty and ragged. The long lecture that he delivered to Ben made it clear that he considered this trip an extreme inconvenience, and that he held the professor personally responsible for it.

Ben was in no position to argue, had he even wanted to. As it was, he could not have cared less how annoyed the man was. He listened patiently as McGammon vented his frustration, waiting for the monologue to turn into a discussion. With luck, a discussion about getting out of here.

"And I understand that you are refusing the Iraqis' request to bring a resolution to this matter?" McGammon said at last. *There it was.*

"I am not refusing a resolution to this," Ben replied with the strength of conviction. "I *am* refusing the particular resolution they have in mind." If this was going to turn into another attempt at bullying, Ben was ready for it.

McGammon sighed. "Doctor, I understand your hesitation. The resolution is not exactly ideal, by any means."

"Not exactly ideal?" Ben repeated, agitated.

McGammon continued as though he had not been interrupted. "But you do not see the big picture. How could you?" The man seemed to be asking himself a rhetorical question as he started pacing around the small room. "There are more factors at play than you are aware of."

"Such as?"

McGammon stopped pacing and looked at him earnestly. "I will not beat around the bush. It's not pretty. There are things happening outside..." He pointed toward the wall, but Ben was unclear whether he meant outside the shabby hotel, outside the city, or outside the country. He wished McGammon would get to the point.

He did. "There is unrest in this region. No, not unrest. Revolution. An army is forming. This province is going to be the first to go."

"But—"

"Please don't keep interrupting me, Doctor. Yes, the Iraqi Army has a strong presence in Mosul. *Had* a strong presence. Four battalions went out to fight these upstarts just two days ago. There was some actual fighting, but not much. Those battalions just...dissolved. Some soldiers came back. Most dropped their weapons and ran. And, apparently, a lot of them joined the rebels. Who are now marching on the city.

"Let me be clear, Doctor. Mosul is not safe. Not for its residents. Not for anyone. Most especially, not for foreigners.

"We're getting reports of some of the same sick shit we saw in Syria. Torture. Beheadings. Cutting off body parts. These people are zealots. They're not people, they're more like animals. They'll chop you in half just for believing in a different successor to Muhammad. What do you think they'll do to Christians and Jews, Doctor?"

McGammon had gotten a little emotional, and now he calmed himself a bit. He tightened his tie, and the professional statesman regained control. "I can appreciate your predicament, Doctor. You're trying to protect the reputation of yourself, your students, and your school. But you can see there is more than reputations at stake here."

He pulled an envelope from the pocket of his suit jacket. "Now we can paint this as one bad apple and you can all go home, or you can refuse and hope for the best." He opened the envelope and pulled out a single sheet of typed paper. He held it in one hand while he fished out a pen with the other. "Which will it be, Doctor?"

8

BEDRIDDEN

IT IS WIDELY BELIEVED that humans experience five stages of grief: denial, anger, bargaining, depression, and acceptance. These stages are based on the Kübler-Ross model, developed by Swiss psychiatrist Elisabeth Kübler-Ross in the 1960s. Despite its general acceptance, however, the model warrants a little more scrutiny than it generally receives. Kübler-Ross' studies were initially focused on subjects dealing with a terminal illness, then subsequently expanded to encompass other types of personal loss. Many theorists question the model's broad utility, and follow-up studies have not been able to substantiate her findings. This does not mean the model is necessarily wrong, but simply that it should never have attained the unassailable status in which it is regarded by much of society.

While some people may in fact experience the exact five-stage progression, many will not. Kübler-Ross herself stated that not everyone will go through each and every stage, nor will those stages always happen in the same exact order. Nevertheless, although not the end of the story, the model is certainly a step in the right direction toward understanding how humans grieve. The identification of these five stages provides an anchor of understanding for many sufferers of loss as well as a framework for future analysis.

Looking beyond mere grief, it is estimated that more than a quarter of the population suffers from clinical mental distress of one form or another. The distress can take on many forms, ranging from anxiety disorders to manic depression and schizophrenia. While some may feel that simple anxiety is not a real condition, few still deny the existence and consequences of Post-Traumatic Stress Disorder. Over seven million Americans suffer from PTSD, and far too often their lives are ruined or prematurely ended as a result of the condition.

Acute stress disorder, related to PTSD, is a condition that strikes many victims of trauma such as rape, vehicle accidents, and natural disasters. Symptoms include emotional detachment, derealization, and depersonalization. In essence, people affected can feel completely disconnected from the world around them, or even from themselves.

It is fair to say that, for all our modern marvel, study of the human mind remains in a nascent state. Yet this avenue of research is both immensely rewarding for those who engage in it, and immeasurably valuable to society at large.

Wendy was in mourning. That much was clear.

The two of them met at the fountain on campus. It reminded Matt of the last time they had talked like this, just before the group left for Iraq. The weather was once again perfect, with a clear blue sky and refreshing breeze to keep the rising summer heat at bay. Such breezes were blessedly common on the mountain this time of year. It was nearly August, summer nearing its oppressive peak, yet Matt was able to wear his lab coat over slacks and dress shirt without discomfort.

In one sense, Wendy looked terrific. She was not even dressed up —quite the opposite, in fact. She wore a pair of faded jeans and the same white short sleeve top he remembered from that last lunch they shared here. Not that she was heavy before, but she had definitely lost weight during the trip, so he was more distracted than usual by her figure. Her hair was pinned up in a haphazard bun, single strands hanging loose and glistening in the sun. He always liked her appearance better like this, when she seemed unaware of it. It was

ironic how often a girl could be most attractive when she was not trying.

Her attractiveness was not the important thing today, however. She looked terrific, but she did not *look* terrific. She wore light makeup, but it failed to mask the puffy redness around her eyes. She clearly had been crying a lot. Matt was not surprised. He had known —probably better than the two of them did themselves—how much she and Halfus belonged together. Seeing her like this broke his heart. He wished he could say or do something to make it even a little better. All his life he had been driven to help others, leading naturally to his study of medicine and illness. He had every intention of curing some diabolic disease as part of a long, successful career. But today, with her, he was completely helpless.

After their initial hug and greeting, Wendy got straight down to business. "Tell me how it went with Mom," she said. She was clearly in no mood for pleasantries.

Matt hesitated. He was reluctant to answer any questions about her mother until he was certain she was all right herself. He did not want to upset her even more, although he knew he would have to soon enough.

"In a minute," he said, taking a seat at the fountain. He made room for her to sit beside him. "Wendy, please tell me what happened on the trip. I heard bits and pieces from the news coverage, but there's got to be a lot more to it. Frankly, I don't believe most of what I've heard."

The story had been big in the local news for several days, but the reporting was mostly sensationalist. There seemed to be little or no background research done, just an official statement from the State Department and a brief, unflattering bio on the dead student. There were no actual facts presented to support the story, simply a repetition of the terms "falling accident" and "attempted looting."

Wendy looked reluctant. "I know you don't want to dump your burdens on me," Matt continued. He hoped his face did not betray his thoughts, for rarely had he spoken a more blatant untruth. Wendy seldom hesitated to dump on him at every opportunity. It was the cornerstone of their relationship. But he was fine with that. He took great pleasure from her companionship, and believed strongly in making small sacrifices for the sake of friendship.

She showed no reaction to his statement, which was not surprising. Only heaven knew where her thoughts really were at the moment. He supposed the chances were high that she was barely listening to him. Nevertheless, he pressed on. "But this is something you need to talk about with someone. You can't just internalize this. Now is the time to let your friends help. You know I'm always here for you."

It sounded cliché to his own ears, but Wendy seemed to accept the offer graciously. She nodded and gave him a pained smile. "I know, Matt. You always have been. And I've always taken advantage of you." He saw tears welling in her eyes as she said it.

He moved quickly to stop them, if he could. Self-reproach was not something he was used to seeing in Wendy, and it did not suit her. "No, you aren't. This is what friends do for each other. I know you'd do the same for me." He tried not to think about whether she really would. Right now, that was beside the point.

"You're too good to me. I don't deserve you." What hell she must have been through to come back like this, he wondered. She looked down, and he knew she was crying. He reached out and pulled her in, and she accepted his hug without returning it. It seemed that she was reluctant to. He wondered whether, even after all this time, she worried about leading him on. Despite their friendship, they were not immune to the natural draw of men and women. With Halfus now permanently missing from her life, maybe he was the next best person for her. But he forced the thought from his mind. She was clearly very vulnerable, and he refused to take advantage of that.

"Thanks. I'm better," she said, sitting back up. Then she started into a lengthier rundown of all that had happened in the past month. Once she got going, Wendy settled into a comfortable rhythm. Talking seemed to be cathartic for her, as Matt had known it would be. She stumbled a little as she described the last day and night at the dig, but she recovered as she recounted their captivity and Ernie's illness and recovery. Matt was particularly interested in this last topic. He asked a few questions, attempting to formulate some idea of exactly what malady had struck their friend, and how on earth he had gotten it. Sadly, her answers were vague and unhelpful. He stopped pressing her for fear of irritating her or taking things too far off topic. She was clearly straining under the pressure of all she had been through, and this lengthy narrative seemed to take a lot of energy and effort.

She and the others had gotten back last night, but she had waited until today to call and let him know. Now that he saw how affected she was, he could not blame her. He could imagine what the past week had been like, and last night would have been her first chance to be alone. When she called him this morning, he had already been at work. He had immediately taken the rest of the day off in order to be with her. Only now he was realizing she probably did not want his company—or anyone else's, for that matter. It was inconvenient to drive from Baltimore to Catoctin just for lunch, but he could accept that. She was strong, and would heal in her own way. Besides, she had things to do now that she was back. Perhaps caring for her mother would actually help take her mind off Halfus' death.

With that in mind, Matt steered the conversation in that direction. "About your mom..." He saw renewed interest in her eyes. "I checked in on her twice a week, like you asked. I can continue to do so more or less often, if you want my help."

"Does she need it?"

"I'm afraid so. I usually cooked meals for her when I was there, and I always put enough leftovers in the fridge so she would have something to eat on the days I wasn't. Even so, I'm concerned that she isn't eating enough. Sometimes I threw out some of the leftovers because she didn't eat them, and once or twice it seemed like she hadn't had any of them at all. I didn't weigh her or anything, but she looks like she's getting thinner. And she doesn't have that much weight to lose."

Wendy nodded. She seemed to be taking it well, so he continued with the rest of it. "Also, she spends a lot of time in bed." *And by a lot, I mean all of it.* "And her coughing has gotten worse. She says she isn't having trouble breathing, but she's clearly uncomfortable. I...thought about calling a doctor, but she didn't seem to want me to. And it's not really my place. But it's something you might want to consider."

"Mom hates doctors. She has since Dad died. She would throw a fit if I called one."

"I see. I'm not surprised. She can be a stubborn old broad." He smiled, hoping Wendy would appreciate the humor.

It did not work. Her brow furrowed. "I'm sorry, Matt. I know she can be a handful. You did a wonderful favor for me—"

He raised a hand to stop her. "Nonsense. I really enjoyed getting to know her. She's a lot of fun to be around. She loves to talk, even with the coughing. She told me stories about your childhood."

Matt stopped. What was he was seeing in Wendy's reaction? Surprise? Panic? Fear? Whatever it was, Miriam had told him nothing to justify it, so it must be something Wendy preferred to keep secret. It surprised him and hurt his feelings, for he had thought she told him everything. He believed he had earned that much. He briefly considered asking her what was on her mind, then dismissed the idea. If she wanted him to know, she would tell him in time. And if she did not... Well, he did not much like knowing secrets anyway.

Wendy clearly was not going to tell him anything today. She cut the conversation short. "I should probably go see her as soon as I can. I should have done it last night, but...I guess I just wanted to be alone." She looked down, not meeting his eyes, which was unusual for her. "Anyway, thanks for meeting me today, Matt. And for helping with Mom. I'll see you again soon, right?"

"Any time you want."

Wendy did not look forward to her visit with her mother, and for more than one reason. Seeing her unwell was always troubling. Wendy had always heard about how the bond between parent and child led to a mother's distress when the daughter fell ill. Yet it seemed to Wendy that it worked both ways. She had hoped her mother's condition would improve during the past few weeks, but now it seemed the opposite had happened. Wendy would see for herself and, if necessary, make arrangements for a doctor's appointment.

But the real reason she dreaded this visit was giving the news about Halfus. Her mother had always been very fond of Wendy's ex-boyfriend, at one time even calling her foolish for breaking up with him. More than anyone else she knew, her mother understood how complicated people could be, and she had urged her daughter to give him more time to come to his senses. That being said, she had also understood completely when Wendy explained how painful it was to compete with the memory of a dead girl, and it had not taken long for criticism to turn to unconditional support.

But Wendy suspected her mother had always harbored a hope that they would get back together. It was a hope that Wendy had harbored herself, despite long months of self-denial. And it had very nearly come true. *No, it had come true, just for a moment.* It made her feel a little better to think they were, in fact, a couple again when his accident occurred. And thinking that way put her squarely in the shoes he had worn when Shauna died. Wendy had newfound appreciation for what Halfus had gone through. Not that it did her any good now.

She pulled up to her mother's building. Before getting out, she searched through her handbag. She realized that she was developing quite a headache, but it was difficult to tell how severe. Oddly, she had become so accustomed to emotional pain that it was impossible to discern where that stopped and the physical started. She found a container of aspirin and popped four into her mouth, then washed them down with lukewarm water from a bottle that had spent too long in the car.

Then she stared at the building's ugly edifice. Just seeing it brought the feeling of being back in her real life again. The ordeal in Iraq was over. But if this was a return to normalcy, it was an empty one. She tried to tell herself that she was no farther behind where she was at any other point this past year. Unfortunately, that was not much relief. She had been then and still remained single and unhappy, full of worry about the future.

She steered away from that line of thought, making an attempt to stay positive. In the interest of self-defense, she tried to examine her situation logically, the way Rich might. She told herself that she was ahead of where she had been. For one thing, she would be starting an exciting new job soon, giving her one less thing to worry about. And it was a bit of a dream job, where she could make a real contribution to the world. Or at least she intended to work her way up to a place where she could. She had tremendous confidence in her own abilities and moral compass. She would succeed in a way she could be proud of.

For another thing, she had not been back with Halfus long enough to make it really feel as though they were together. She had not regained that level of attachment and intimacy that long-lasting couples developed. It hurt to lose him, but she had spent the last year believing she already had, so in this respect it was easier to accept. And, as terrible a loss as it was, it was in some small way compensated for by the improvement in her relationship with Ernie. She had been used to thinking of him as Halfus' sidekick, but now she was very fond of him in his own way. He had been wonderfully attentive to her during the trip, and she felt good about being able to return some of that attention while caring for him during his sickness. He had said he owed her one, and it was comforting to know that someone genuinely appreciated her. Especially someone as appealing as he.

Wendy frowned. She knew the truth was more complicated than that. She could not go down this path without having mixed feelings. Was she really considering him as boyfriend material? She liked him, but did she like him enough? Or did she simply want to find someone to take her mind off Halfus? She knew that most women would jump at the chance to reel Ernie in. He had many appealing qualities—tall and handsome, funny and intelligent. And brave. She remembered how he had tried to shield her from the brute at the dig site. Ernie had received a broken nose for that. He owed her nothing. At best they were even. But in reality she believed that she owed him.

He was also clearly crazy about her. And how exactly had she handled all this? She had used him to make Halfus jealous. Not that she had done it deliberately, nor even seen it that way at the time. But looking back it was as clear as day. It had worked, for Halfus had come back. And look where that had gotten her. So maybe she owed it to both Ernie and herself to give things with him a chance.

She dismissed the thought for now. Now that she was walking in the shoes Halfus had worn when they failed as a couple, how could she turn around and do to Ernie what had been done to her? It would not be fair to either of them.

It felt like the right decision. She liked Ernie a lot, but she was not really ready to look at him, or anyone else, in a romantic light. There was no spare room in her heart, no matter what her mind might want.

One thing she could be sure of was how much relief she felt that he had gotten better. The skin blemishes, messy eliminations, foul odors, and delirium had been unlike anything she had seen before. A few days into their confinement she had been really worried, even to the point of fearing they would lose another member of their group on that awful trip. She had expressed her concern to Doc, which had no doubt influenced his shameful decision. Then, almost miraculously, Ernie had been conscious—even upbeat—upon her return to the room. He was hardly aware of the hellish effects his sickness had had on his own body and the morale of his friends. His skin looked clearer, his nose had stopped running, and he smelled much better after just a simple washing. His only complaint was a little queasiness and a strange feeling on his tongue, and even those things disappeared by the time they evacuated the hotel the following day.

Now her concerns for him were replaced by those for her mother. It seemed to Wendy that her life was turning into one bad break after another. No sooner did she get through one crisis—for better or worse—than she was confronted by another. Curiously, however, she actually found herself having a hard time getting as worried about her mother as she had been about Ernie. She believed that the illness was real. Her mother would not make something like this up out of nothing. But Wendy was so used to the woman's histrionics that she doubted it was as bad as Matt made it sound.

As she left her car and entered the building, she considered a second reason for her relative calm. At this point, her mind was simply too frazzled to stress over anything more. It was as though she had a finite amount of emotion and too many problems to spread it among. It was somehow easier to take one more in stride.

Matt was right about the leftovers. Wendy took a few minutes emptying the refrigerator of the remnants of the last meal he prepared. He had taken the time to put each item in a separate container—chicken, mashed potatoes, gravy, and corn all had their own piece of Tupperware. Now they were spoiling, so Wendy dumped them one at a time into a small trash can she kept by her feet. *What a waste of good food.* As she went about her business, she noted that Matt appeared to be a pretty decent cook. Probably better than she was. It was an appealing trait in a man.

When she rinsed the containers and placed them in the dishwasher, she noticed an absence of any dirty utensils or dishes in the machine. Either a load had very recently been processed and emptied, or her mother was flat out not eating. It was hardly worth doing a load with so few items, so she hand-washed the Tupperware instead.

It was boring work, but Wendy took her time, drawing it out as long as she could. She was trying to settle her mind. Seeing her mother had been more disconcerting than expected. Wendy had never seen her look so small, pale, and feeble. And she was completely bedridden. Matt had been right about that, too. The same went for the cough, which was not only persistent but louder than before. Each repetition was like a boom that sounded louder than that failing body should have been able to produce. By contrast, her voice was as weak as a mouse's.

But her mind remained strong, as did her determination to not see a doctor. This is what upset Wendy the most. Her mother seemed not only accepting but resolved. *If God is ready for me, I am ready for him,* she had said. Wendy did not like the messianic talk. It had always made her uncomfortable in the best of times, but now it sounded like an excuse to stop trying. Yet if her mother took comfort in her faith, Wendy could not bring herself to ruin it for her by arguing.

Another comment stuck in Wendy's mind. *I miss your father. I want to see him again.* Left unspoken was a reference to her brother, but she knew that her mother was thinking of him, as well. Now that Wendy had experienced overwhelming loss herself, she had a newfound appreciation for all that her mother had gone through. Her parents had been married for twenty-five years before her father's death. How much worse her mother's situation than her own.

But this lying around, waiting to die, did not sit well with her. She needed time to think of a way to make her mother want to live.

With the leftovers disposed of, she thought about making something the older woman might actually consume. She hoped that a snack of tea and cookies might be more acceptable than a meal. In any case, she could go for some herself. She found some Oreos in the pantry and unfolded the legs of a TV tray to take back to the bedroom. Next she put the much-used teapot on the stove. She filled it with water and began rummaging through the cabinets where her mother kept the packets of tea. There was usually a range of flavors to suit every occasion. *Which one was for despair,* she wondered despondently.

Her mother had always had a preference for loose leaf teas, and Wendy had inherited the same taste. She decided that a fruity tea might lighten their moods. She found a pomegranate cranberry and emptied it into the pot. As she tossed the empty packet into the trash, she saw Truman sitting on the edge of the can, skillfully balanced to lick the tasty morsels on top without falling in.

"Get away, you stupid oaf." Wendy reacted without thinking, pushing the cat off the trash can, then moving it beneath the sink.

Unfazed by the reprimand, Truman jumped onto the kitchen counter, working his way up from floor to chair to TV tray to countertop. There he remained perched, watching her with interest.

She felt mad at herself. She was frustrated and upset and had taken it out on the innocent pet. "I'm sorry, buddy," she told him.

She began rubbing his soft gray fur. "You caught me at a bad time." He looked up at her face affectionately, then pushed his head against her hand. She scratched him behind the ears, and he yawned complacently. Clearly, he held nothing against her. At times like this, Wendy wished she could have the relaxed disposition of an animal.

The teapot whistled, and she poured out two cupfuls. She carried the tea and a plate of cookies on the tray back to the bedroom. She set it down where her mother could easily reach, then seated herself on the side of the bed.

"Thank you, Sweetie." Her mother lifted her cup with both hands, then took a minimal sip.

"Don't burn your mouth, Mom."

"Mmm, delicious." Her mother set the cup back on the tray. It still looked full to Wendy. There was an awkward moment of silence. Then her mother smiled. "You make the tea so much better than your friend."

"Matt?"

"Yes, Matt. He tried and tried, but I don't think he had ever made tea before. Honestly, how hard is it?" She chuckled. It sounded like a croak that changed into a cough. "Anyway, he is a dear. Did everything I asked and more. He kept me entertained as much as he could. We played Scrabble. And he listened to me and my old stories."

"Mom, you didn't tell him..."

"No, I didn't talk about Billy." Wendy cringed at the name of her brother. It was a painful memory. "That's a hard subject for both of us, Sweetie."

There was another awkward silence, then her mother picked back up on the subject of Matt. "So your friend..." Cough. "He found out I like orchids. I told him all about the ones your father and I kept in the old garden. The next time he came over, he brought me this beautiful bouquet of purple Dendrobiums."

Wendy laughed. "That's my Matt. Where are they?" She looked around.

"Oh, Truman knocked them over. Made quite a mess."

"Mom, that cat is a constant hazard. You need to teach him some boundaries."

"No, no. He keeps my life exciting, that's all." Cough. "Matt made a joke about it. He said he will make sure the next thing he brings me is unbreakable." Cough. "He's so thoughtful. He reminds me a little of Halfus. You always have such good taste in boys."

Wendy looked away, fighting for composure. She did not want to cry for this. "Mom, I have something to tell you."

During the time with her mother, Wendy had forgotten all about her headache. Now it was back in full force as she drove home. Adding insult to injury, her nose would not stop running. It had started, naturally, when she and her mother both cried during her account of Halfus' death. Although the crying had stopped, the runny nose had not. Now she was forced to drive with one hand so she could constantly wipe with the other.

Fortunately, McGahey was a small town and it did not take long to get home. She was absolutely exhausted. It was not even dinner time, but she felt that she might just skip eating completely and go straight to bed. She had slept for ten hours last night, but apparently her body still had a lot of catching up to do.

She let herself into the apartment and plopped down on the couch, gathering her strength. She resisted the impulse to go crash on her bed. Having just gotten back after several weeks away, there were still too many nagging little things to do. Before she could get to any of them, however, she found herself racing to the bathroom.

She emerged a few minutes later, feeling a bit lightheaded. That had been sudden and unexpected. Wendy was as regular as a person could be, and her bowel movements always came first thing in the morning. This one had not only been abrupt, but irrepressible and malodorous. Thank goodness it had not happened a few minutes sooner, when she was driving.

She sat back down on the couch, less for comfort than out of necessity. She wanted to believe that the stress of recent days was catching up to her at last. But she had to admit there was a better explanation. First Ernie, then her mother, and now her. She was getting sick.

She had no groceries, and no medicine besides the aspirin in her bag. Suddenly the thought of going back out for either seemed overwhelming. She thought about calling Matt. He would come over right away, of course. He was always there when she needed him. Yet he had already done so much, she hated the idea of asking him for more. Besides, he lived too far away. But did she really have any other options? She had many friends, but few close ones, and fewer still that she would feel comfortable letting see her like this. Was Matt really her only choice? The thought made her sad.

With some effort, she reached over to the bag where she kept her phone. She had put it on silent mode during her visit with her mother. Now she saw that she had a message. She thumbed a button and listened.

"Wendy, I...was thinking about you. I just wanted to make sure you're okay. Call me if you feel like talking. That's all. Bye."

It was a coincidence too strong to ignore. He was offering just what she needed. She thumbed another button to call him back.

An hour later she was lying on the couch with a blanket wrapped around her. Ernie carried a small tray with something on it in from the kitchen. He had come over right away and taken charge, making her lie down while he went about preparing some comfort foods.

"I saw you have oatmeal in there," he said as he set the tray beside her. "I thought about fixing that, but decided we've had enough of that in the past month."

"Yeah, I don't think I'll ever eat oatmeal again in my life." She looked at what he had brought instead. There was a cup of hot chocolate and a little dish of coffee-flavored ice cream. She smiled at him. "This is perfect."

"It'd better be." He laughed. "Those are pretty much the only things I could find in the whole kitchen."

He watched her take a sip and then a bite. She found herself rather enjoying his gaze. "The ice cream feels soothing," she said. "My throat is starting to get sore."

He nodded. "I thought about that. That happened to me, too." He got serious. "I'm afraid this is your repayment for taking care of me. No good deed goes unpunished."

She shook her head. "I was glad to do it. We needed to stick together." She hesitated a moment, considering. "We still do."

He nodded, but said nothing. This was getting close to awkward territory, so she lightened the mood. "I'm just glad to know you got better. Means I will, too."

"Yeah, but I have to warn you...if it's anywhere near as bad as mine, you're in for a rough couple of days."

The thought troubled her, but she took no small comfort from being back in civilization instead of suffering through the conditions he had. She also felt better knowing he was there to help.

Then another thought troubled her. "Ugh. I'm sure I look like a mess. I don't usually let people see me like this."

"You look great to me." He said it nonchalantly, which she was thankful for. He started looking around. "You need groceries. I'm going to run over to the store and get some. You're going to be stuck eating whatever I make for the next few days. Any special requests? And anything else you need me to get while I'm out?"

"No. I'm in your hands."

"Never tell a guy that," he quipped. He kissed her forehead and stood up. "Be back soon."

It was just after dark when he returned. He asked what she wanted for dinner, but she was not at all hungry. Besides, she was not sure she would keep down any solid food she put in her stomach. She thanked him but politely declined.

"Well, if you don't mind, I'm going to make a little something for myself."

"Knock yourself out," she replied. *"Mi casa, su casa."*

They chatted intermittently while he cooked. He called out loudly from the kitchen, and she mumbled responses that he could not possibly have heard. Nevertheless, he seemed about as happy as she had ever seen him. She assumed he was behaving that way on purpose, to keep her spirits up. If so, it was working. She was very quickly becoming increasingly fond of—and dependent on—her charming new friend. She did not resist the feeling. It was somehow comforting.

He came back out a short while later with another little dish and a devilish smile. "I know you said you don't want anything, but you have to try just one of these." He held out the dish. It was peanut butter fudge, still warm and sliced into small cubes.

She loved peanut butter. She faked a groan. "Oh, if you insist." She plopped one into her mouth, where it seemed to melt. "It's delicious. Thank you."

He sat down by her feet. "I don't want to smother you, so I'm going to head out. You have food and drinks in your fridge now, so I think you can survive the night. I'll be back in the morning to check on you." She nodded along to everything he said. "I only live a few minutes away. Please call me if you need anything." He sounded sincere.

"Thanks again, Ernie," she told him. Her stomach did a little flop over the piece of fudge, but she ignored it. If she needed to vomit, she could hold it off until she was alone.

"My pleasure." He began to stand up.

On impulse, she reached out and touched his arm. "Don't go yet, please. There's something I need to ask you."

He sat back down. "Sure. Anything you want." He looked hopeful. Helping people clearly suited him.

Part of her regretted doing this. He was being so kind to her, and she felt so much gratitude that she did not want to hurt his feelings. But she was willing to risk them over something she just had to know. She wanted to believe she and Halfus were together again before he died. It meant everything to her. The idea made the rest of this terrible ordeal a little more tolerable. But she had not been with him in his last hours. Ernie had.

"That night...before the accident. What did you and Halfus talk about? Did he say anything to you?"

Ernie's expression had gone blank, unreadable. It was one habit of his that she did not like. Then his face formed a confused smile. "He said lots of things. About the tomb—"

She shook her head. "Did he say anything about...girls?" she asked clumsily. She could not bring herself to come right out and say it. This was already not going the way she expected. She had assumed that Ernie would immediately catch her drift, nod, and say something reassuring. But his very hesitation was giving her troubling second thoughts, like warning bells sounding off inside her mind. Maybe it was better to have a kernel of doubt than to get an answer she did not want to hear.

He opened his mouth, then looked away. She seized on it. "He said something, didn't he?" When Ernie would not look at her, she summoned the energy to sit up. She grasped his arm pleadingly.

He shook his head. "No. Not really." She thought his voice seemed on the verge of breaking.

She went from grasping his arm to rubbing it, soothingly. "I'm sorry, Ernie. It's okay. I know that night was hard on you. It was inconsiderate of me to ask."

She watched him wipe two fingers over his eyes. "It's all right," he said. "You just...brought back that last moment really vividly. I guess I blocked it from my mind."

"I'm so sorry I asked."

"I'm all right," he said. He pulled away from her, just a little. She noticed and let his arm go, feeling angry at herself.

But he had something for her, after all. "He did yell a word as he fell. A name." He paused a second. "Shauna." He shook his head sadly. "I guess it's tragic and poetic that they died the same way."

She closed her eyes as a wave of sickness rushed over her. Never before had she felt so weak.

"Wendy, are you okay? Do you need me to—?"

"No. I mean, yes, Ernie, I'm okay. Thank you. That helps." It did, in a painfully perverse way. She now realized that she could get on with her life. A cord that she had been clinging to with all her strength had just been brutally severed.

"I can stay if you need me to," he offered.

"No, you've done everything you can. I just need to get through these next few days. Then I'll be good as new."

"You'll be better than new," Ernie told her. "You'll feel like a million bucks. I promise." He kissed her forehead again. "I'll see you in the morning. Sleep well."

"You, too."

There was light above and dark below, and he was trapped between. It was a horrible sensation, suspended between the two, not fully in either, unsure what his fate would be. Light and dark. Happiness and anguish. Life and death.

The light transformed, becoming images. An open sky, a single bird soaring majestically high above the bountiful earth. A beautiful landscape. Mountains, canyons, rivers, beaches. The landscape became a painted canvas, one display in a collection filling a museum hall. A museum with more than just paintings. Statues. Artifacts. The collected works of mankind. Libraries of books. Knowledge. Understanding. Philosophy. Debate. The images moved faster. Many friends together, sharing an interest in the human condition. Laughter, dancing, and singing. Faces radiant with pleasure. Then one in particular, framed by a golden aura of curls that metamorphosed back into the light.

He wanted to go up. He tried and tried, but could not move. He was in a purgatory that was indistinguishable from Hell. Then, when he finally did move, it was in the wrong direction. Down, toward the darkness. Slowly at first, then faster and faster. This was no longer just a dream. It was a memory. In those brief terrible seconds, three distinct things flashed through his mind. Regret, for all he was about to lose. Understanding, of the mistake he had made. Then, finally, fear. The light diminished with distance. He called out to it, for someone to save him. He yelled her name, a cry for both help and forgiveness, knowing neither would come. The acrophobia seized his mind, a nightmare manifest, rendering him mute and inanimate. Then he struck bottom. It was the end of a short life, like those of Odin's fallen soldiers. He readied himself to ascend to the heavens, accompanied by a dirge of mournful trumpets and pounding drums. The trumpets trailed off but the drums remained, sounding off in a ceaseless, ominous barrage.

Halfus woke to the sound of gunshots in the distance. Yet the sound of shooting, disconcerting as it was, immediately became relegated to a lower priority. The left side of his body screamed with a dull aching pain, augmented by occasional bursts of sharp stabbing agony. A thin sheet stretched over his body, all but weightless yet somehow heavy and smothering on top of his wounds. It prevented him from seeing the damage, but his ankle, leg, hip, arm, and shoulder all felt as though they had been repeatedly struck with a sledgehammer. He did not know how he would stand much more of this torment, and his mind longed for a return to blissful oblivion.

Unconsciousness did not come, but he slowly adjusted to this new normal. The pain remained omnipresent and overpowering, but he began to feel that he could bear it without going mad. His mind moved on to the next dreadful concern. He could not imagine that he would ever walk again, let alone box or climb or undertake any of the other activities that made life what it was. But at least he was alive. He supposed he should be thankful for that. He did not know how or why, but he appeared to be stretched out on an uncomfortable cot in someone's home.

The room he was in was small. The walls were a rough white stone, with a single square window cut into one side, through which he saw idyllic blue sky. The window was uncovered, and a not unpleasant scented breeze wafted through the room. A small wooden stool sitting in a corner was the only other furniture, and a colorful woven rug hanging on one wall the only decoration. The room appeared to have no entrance, until he saw the hanging rug ripple in the breeze and realized it covered an otherwise open doorway.

He could barely move. Not that he wanted to, for he quickly found out that the slightest movement drastically increased the pain shooting through his side. But he was too curious to just lie there in ignorance. He managed to lift the sheet with his right hand enough to see that his left arm and leg were both bound tightly to heavy wooden splints. He had fallen fifty feet or more, and could only imagine how many fractures his bones had suffered. He would have preferred to wake up in a hospital, and did not understand why he had not, but at least whoever had rescued him had taken some basic steps to help his broken body repair itself. Halfus tried to be thankful for the little things, but the whole situation was so surreal that he could not yet grasp simple emotions like gratitude.

He felt as though he had been in this room for some time—several days or more—although he had no idea how he knew that. His surroundings looked oddly familiar to him even though he had no memory of this place. He guessed that he had slipped in and out of consciousness these past few days, without ever being sentient enough to think. He looked forward to solving the many mysteries plaguing his thoughts, but for now he groaned and dropped his head back to the mattress as a wave of nausea and dizziness washed over him.

He closed his eyes and waited for the wave to pass. It took far longer than he hoped, and he gained a terrible new appreciation for just how much healing his body needed before he would be able to perform even the simplest of tasks. There was a time when he would have had the determination to push through this setback, to get back to the closest approximation of normal he could find. He was no longer certain he could muster up that drive. Life had given him some pretty nasty punches in recent years. They were like body blows that had an accumulated effect on his will to keep going.

He heard the faintest hint of a sound and rolled his head to face the doorway. There stood the most adorable little girl he had ever seen in his life. She had pulled back the rug and stood with it draped across her tiny shoulders. Dressed in white cotton pajamas covered in a pattern of little red flowers, she looked about five years old, with an olive complexion and unruly black hair. She clutched a teddy bear tightly to her chest as though protecting it from him. He imagined what a frightening spectacle he must be. In contrast, she was a sight for sore eyes. She was such an unexpected vision of innocence that simply seeing her made him feel immeasurably better.

He tried to show her the warmest smile he was capable of. Her eyes widened, but she did not smile back. Since he probably looked like a monster, he decided that a smile was perhaps not the best approach. He counted his blessings that she had not simply run away. Despite the discomfort that followed, he forced himself to move a little. "Peekaboo, I see you," he said, using his thin pillow to hide his eyes before showing them again. This time the girl did run away, and he collapsed in another wave of disequilibrium. He regretted losing the opportunity for human contact, even though the girl almost certainly did not know English. He really hoped he had not seen the last of her.

Then he heard running sounds inside the dwelling. He weakly turned his head again, facing the entrance, curious as to what he would see. Wendy, he hoped. One of the others? A doctor? Armed soldiers? Any of these things seemed possible, and nothing would surprise him. A moment later the curtain lifted, and Halfus was filled with a mix of relief and joy.

"Hello, my friend," Mahmoud told him, his impish grin as wide as ever.

9

PLAGUED WITH GUILT

TWO BASIC HUMAN FUNCTIONS, *digestion and metabolism, are often confused with one another. Metabolism comprises two distinct and opposite processes. Catabolism is the process whereby matter is broken down into its constituent parts, releasing energy. Anabolism is the process whereby energy is consumed to form compounds out of constituent parts. Digestion itself is partly, but not entirely, an act of catabolism, and therefore overlaps with the much larger function of metabolism.*

When meat-eaters asks vegetarians where they get their protein, it is generally because the questioner associates the protein content of meat and other animal products with the proteins of the human body. Similarly, when an athlete consumes a high-protein diet, it is with the assumption that protein consumed will automatically become protein in his or her body. These beliefs are not wrong, but there is a little more intricacy to the story.

Obviously, the food one eats is not absorbed, untransformed, directly into the body of the consumer. Instead, digestion breaks that food down into smaller parts so they can be absorbed through the intestinal wall into the bloodstream. From there, the body's metabolism reassembles these pieces into new, usable compounds. In the case of proteins, amino acids combine to form peptides, which in turn combine to form proteins. So it is true that protein eaten can become protein again, in whole or in part, but only after the body effectively breaks it down, absorbs it, and reassembles it that way. Some foods are not digested efficiently, while others can have their components reconstituted in surprising ways. Meat is generally rich in proteins that are broken down into the many types of amino acids. But many plant foods are also rich in amino acids and, depending on whom one asks, might be an alternate or even better source of protein. So the age-old expression should not be, "You are what you eat," but rather, "You are what you metabolize."

Proteins are created from peptides through a process known as protein folding. Sometimes the folding process goes wrong and misfolded proteins called prions are formed. Prions are a fifth type of pathogen. Unlike the other four—viruses, bacteria, fungi, and protozoa—prions contain no genetic material and are indisputably lifeless. They can be thought of as accidents of nature, although in some cases the accidents might seem willful. They are sometimes formed from the corruption of another vital process. One example is feeding to cattle the decaying remains of other cattle, which in rare instances leads to bovine spongiform encephalopathy, or mad cow disease. Other prion-induced diseases include Creutzfeldt-Jakob Disease in humans and scrapie in goats and sheep.

An interesting, and frightening, characteristic of prions is in the way they attack the brain. Mental disturbances such as memory loss, speech impairments, depression, paranoia, personality changes, psychoses, and hallucinations can all be caused by prions. Prion diseases are quite rare— thankfully, because they have one other shared characteristic. They are one hundred percent fatal.

Rich began feeling weak on his second day back in Maryland. He was at the McGahey hardware store, examining a new model power drill, when he suddenly felt a swell of dizziness that left him barely able to hold the heavy tool. It was not the sort of thing he cared to risk dropping, so he lowered the drill to the nearest rack and pressed both hands against the display wall to steady himself. Within a few seconds the sensation passed, but Rich was not foolish enough to assume it would be an isolated event. Already his mind harkened back to the bug Ernie had caught in Iraq, and Rich assessed the likelihood that it had been passed on to himself and others. That had been some nasty business. If it was going to strike him, too, he did not want it to catch him out in public. He decided to cut his errands short today and spend the afternoon at home, just in case he started to feel worse.

He went ahead and bought the drill and some other supplies for the modest kitchen refurbishing he was planning. He counted his blessings that the dizziness did not return during the brief drive back home. He saw an open parking space on the street in front of the house. He backed into it, shut off the engine, and stepped out with his purchases.

Rich had been fond of this home ever since he moved in, but never had he been as happy to see this quaint little dwelling as he was these past few days. The trip to Iraq had taken a toll on all of them. The return to Catoctin and McGahey had felt like a blessing of rest and decompression. Just looking at the front door of his home brought Rich an enormous sense of relief.

He was less comforted, however, to see his neighbor's wife, Jeannie, standing by her car a few spots ahead of his. He had not noticed her when he pulled up. She must have been inside the vehicle. He intended to say hello as he walked past, but had no expectation that she would return the greeting. Although it was Jim and not Jeannie who insulted him, he assumed she felt the same way her husband did.

Then he glanced at her a second time and had a change of heart. Jeannie was not even looking at him. Instead, he watched her pop the hood of her car and raise it with her hands. She stared at the engine with an expression of complete bafflement. Rich hesitated, considered, and set down his package. It was not in him to ignore a person in distress.

"Engine trouble?" he asked, stopping a few paces away. He did not want to get too close for fear that she would back away like a skittish animal. As it was, she still looked a little frightened of him.

Then she nodded. "It won't start."

Progress, he thought. Funny that it required a crisis for her to acknowledge his existence.

"What's it doing?"

"Nothing."

"It's not turning over?" She looked at him blankly, so he tried again. "Is it making any noise at all?"

She shook her head.

"It's most likely a dead battery," he told her. "Mind if I take a look?"

She said nothing, but stepped back to let him inspect the engine. He saw nothing visibly wrong.

"Hang on," he said. "I have a tester in my car."

She showed no sign of stopping him, so he retrieved the tester and verified his hunch. She waited silently while he pulled his car back onto the street, parked it close to hers, turned off the engine, and popped his own hood. He fetched some jumper cables from his trunk and carefully connected the two batteries with the red cable, positive side to positive side. He attached one end of the black cable to the negative side of his own battery and the other end to the head of a bolt on her car. Then he restarted his own car, revved the engine a few times, and climbed back out. He was not sure how comfortable she would be with his getting inside her car, so he gave her a basic explanation. She listened and obeyed. At last he double-checked the cables and nodded to her. As soon as she turned the key her own engine started, and she immediately broke into a wide smile. It was the first time he had ever seen her look happy.

Rich disconnected the cables carefully, black before red, making sure not to let the ends touch until everything was clear. He glanced at her one time, saw her looking at him, and flashed her a thumbs-up signal. He was putting the cables back into his trunk as she pulled out of her space. He expected a simple thanks, but she drove off without a word.

He had no time for disappointment. He quickly moved his car back into its space, retrieved his package, and hurried inside the house. He could feel his bowels loosening before he even got through the door, so he dropped everything on the countertop on his way to the bathroom.

Rich was curled up in bed when, just before sundown, he heard a knock on the door. His first inclination was to ignore it. He was not curled up by choice. The cramps in his stomach were forcing him into contorted positions to relieve the discomfort. It felt as though a vise was clamping down on his abdomen, squeezing and releasing with dreadful regularity.

His body seemed to be purging from every orifice all too often. The sudden bowel movement when he walked in had only been the first of several. He also had vomited more times than he could count, and his urine had turned unnaturally thick, dark, and odious. Curiously, he began to taste cigarettes in his mouth, even though he had not smoked in years.

When the knock sounded a second time, he forced himself up to answer. He guessed it could be Wendy, or possibly Kevin. The two of them, plus Halfus, were the only friends to ever visit Rich at home. Clearly, it was not Halfus, so that narrowed it down. Then another thought occurred to him. He got his hopes up. It could be Tre'Andre. It would not be the first time his boyfriend surprised him by coming to town unannounced. Rich really hoped he was doing so again. It would be quite a relief to have someone keep him company just now.

He opened the door with a modicum of optimism. But it was not Tre'Andre.

"Jeannie," he said, trying not to sound as surprised as he felt.

"I, uh, wanted to thank you for helping me this afternoon." She was clearly nervous, and he cringed at the realization that this was a stressful encounter for her. "I brought you some lasagna. I made two today. One for us, and one for you. I, uh, thought you might like it."

The thought of lasagna brought bile to Rich's throat. At the same time, he was touched by the gesture. For one of the few times in his life, he did not know what to say. He stared at her blankly. She stood there, holding a casserole dish out to him, her slight confidence waning with every second that passed without his acceptance. Her plastered smile began to fade.

Then his mind clicked back into function, and he took the heavy dish from her. It was still warm. He could smell the sauce wafting through the aluminum foil covering. It made his stomach flop, but he forced himself to smile back. "Thank you for this."

Concern was crossing her face. "Are you feeling okay?" she asked.

"I'm all right. Just a little bug." He would have told her he was perfectly fine, but he imagined that was too obvious a lie considering his crooked posture and labored speech. "Please forgive my manners. Would you like to come in?" He tried to sound welcoming, but he really hoped she would turn him down.

She did. A different look of concern showed on her face. "No...I, uh, need to go, actually." She sounded conspiratorially guilty.

Rich could guess why. "Jim doesn't know you're doing this, does he?"

"No."

"Don't worry. I won't say a thing." She looked relieved. "I will have this tomorrow, when I can enjoy it properly," he told her. "I'll hang onto the dish until you can come over and get it."

She smiled at him, more genuinely than before. "Thank you." She took a step back from the door and began to turn away.

He started to close the door, but then she stopped and looked back. "I'm, uh, sorry, Rich."

He nodded. "Me, too." Then he did shut the door and put down the lasagna. The bathroom beckoned once more.

"And so we've decided to place you on mandatory leave until further notice, pending review of your case."

"I see," Ben replied meekly. Then, exacerbating his sense of inadequacy, he instinctively added, "Thank you, sir." *Yes, thank you for ruining my career.*

"Good day, Doctor Appelstein. We'll be in touch."

Ben nodded to each of the other three gentlemen and showed himself out of the university president's office. He assumed it would be the last time he was ever in the august chamber.

"Ben, wait." He turned to see the Dean of the School of Graduate Studies, Avram Paltrow, following him into the hall.

"I'm sorry about this. I advocated for you, but the school is concerned about the bad publicity." Ben's associate wore a friendlier smile than seemed justified, given the circumstances. Ben believed what he said was true. The embarrassment to one of Avi's professors also reflected poorly on his department, so he had a vested interest in minimizing the damage. If possible, he would have kept this quiet to protect his own career, regardless of the effect on Ben's.

That was not entirely a fair assessment, he realized. Avi had been a friend ever since Ben had joined the faculty. The two of them seldom socialized outside of college events, but he had no reason to believe the other man only looked out for himself. It was hard not to be disappointed in the university's decision on this matter, but it was wrong to hold that decision against the one of the three who had the least influence on it. Nevertheless, Ben was not happy, and Avi was the nearest representative of the school. Ben could not bring himself to act friendly toward him. He stood and waited for the man to speak his piece.

Taking Ben's silence for understanding, Avi continued. "I'm pretty sure we can get you reinstated when the press dies down a little."

"But with a permanent black mark on my record."

Avi's smile disappeared. "Perhaps in time...we'll see what we can do."

"I'm going to go clean up my office. I'll see you later." He turned his back and walked away from the dean. It was perhaps the strongest act of insubordination Ben had ever displayed, and he was not sure how he felt about it. At least for the moment, he did not much care.

The first thing he did in his office was retrieve his painkillers from the top drawer. They were like an old friend, there to provide moral support as much as pain relief. Oddly, he had not thought of them much during the time in Iraq. Perhaps it was the fresh air or incessant activity, but he could not recall a single headache during the entire trip. He had carried a supply of pills with him but never taken a single one.

Not surprisingly, he felt a headache coming on now. Maybe he was allergic to the school. If so, he supposed he would not have to worry about that any more.

He peeled off a tablet and plopped it onto his tongue, then held it there while he searched around for something to wash it down. Normally, he always kept a bottle of water on his desk for just such occasions, but he had not thought to get a replacement in the short time he had been back. His thoughts had instead been focused on the review board and their choice of reprimands for his failure.

He found a half-filled, month-old mini water bottle in one of the lower drawers, and gulped it down with urgency.

"Ben?"

He lowered the bottle with an air of embarrassment. He did not like for others to see him taking pills. He should have closed the door of his office, but had not intended to be here for more than a few minutes.

Now Brenda stood in the doorway, looking at him with concern. He did not particularly wish to talk to her. There were too many other things on his mind. But politeness was an ingrained habit, so he invited her in.

She took a step forward but did not sit down. "I know you probably don't want to see me right now," she started. She paused a moment, as though giving him a chance to contradict that statement. He said nothing. Then she looked down as she went on. "I just wanted to say that I heard. I...think you deserve better than this."

Well, that was fast. He supposed news traveled quickly in a small institution like Catoctin.

She looked up again, into his eyes. She seemed more resolute. "Look, I know you're a great teacher. And a great scholar. This is really rotten luck, but keep your chin up."

He let out a half-hearted laugh. Never would he have imagined himself getting a pep talk from Brenda, of all people.

The laugh made her seem even more determined. "You'll get through this. I know you will." Then she paused. "Ben? Are you okay?"

He hurriedly pulled the waste basket out from under his desk. Then he vomited violently into it.

She came forward, putting a hand to his back, trying helplessly to comfort him. He vomited a second time. He gasped to steady his breathing, his gaze looking down at the mess he just made. He saw the undigested remnant of the pill he had just swallowed resting on top of the disgusting liquid mixture of which his stomach had just emptied itself. He felt sweat building at his temples, his headache transforming from a dull tapping to a pounding hammer. Then his stomach flipped over a third time, and with nothing left to purge he found himself retching nothing but bile and air.

"Lie down," Brenda commanded, motioning to the couch and practically pushing him onto it. He obeyed, his mind wondering at the oddness of this situation. She had driven him home personally, helping him walk from the class building to her car and again from the car into the house. He had regained his senses enough to direct her here, a place where she had never been despite his many months of pursuing her. Now she was inside, searching through his personal belongings for things to make him more comfortable, behaving with no greater sense of immodesty than if she owned the place herself. He would have found humor in the irony if he had not felt so wretched.

She went to the kitchen and returned with a tall glass of water, which she placed on the coffee table beside him. "Where are your linens?" she asked. He pointed to a closet, and she retrieved from it a heavy blanket and crisp clean pillow. The latter she puffed and placed under his head, and the former she shook out to cover his body. Then she sat on the couch by his midsection and rubbed his shoulder comfortingly. "I think you'll live," she said with a smile.

He weakly smiled back. "Thanks, Brenda. I really appreciate the help."

She brushed a strand of sweaty hair away from his brow. "It's no problem, Benji. I'm glad I was there."

"Me, too." He noticed her use of the old playful name she used to call him, back when they were far closer than they were now. It brought back a mild sense of nostalgia, tinged with regret.

"Any idea what brought this on?" she asked.

"Yes, I can make a decent guess. One of my students became deathly ill on the trip, just before we returned. It's likely that he passed it on to me." He thought about his own limited contact with Ernie compared to that of Wendy and Rich. "And maybe others. I should find out if anyone else is sick."

"Later," she told him. "You just get some rest for now. I should call Trevor, to tell him I'm going to miss dinner."

"You don't need to do that, Brenda. I'm much better now," he lied. He still felt horrible. The terrible nausea had passed but was replaced by a host of other uncomfortable symptoms. "You've done more than enough. You should get back to your life."

She hesitated. "Are you sure?"

He studied her expression, unsure of how to interpret her behavior. In other circumstances, he would try to figure out what she was not telling him. But as things were now, he preferred to be alone. There was not only the sickness, but a whole host of other problems bouncing around inside his head. Ben was a thinker. He was not comfortable doing much of anything without thinking it through multiple times. Now was a time to focus on himself—he did not have the leftover energy to think about Brenda, too. "I'm sure."

"Okay, if you say so." She stood up. "Call me if you start feeling worse, Benji."

Ernie's promise had come true. It was three days following Wendy's first symptoms of illness, and she felt terrific.

When she was in high school, Wendy had gone through a health-nut phase. She experimented with assorted cleanses and diets, each of which promised to improve her life in some form or fashion. Whether it was filling her body with nutrients or emptying it of toxins, she tried every one that made the slightest bit of sense and even a few that did not. Most of them had no noticeable effects on her body or mind, but a few did. A juice fast made her headaches worse, while one cleanse with magnesium oxide made her stools long and rubbery. She had experienced some of the same things during this recent bout of illness.

Now she not only felt good, she had never felt better. She knew that everything was relative, so she could not be certain whether it was anything more than being normal again after a particular bad spell. But it seemed to her that there was more to it than that.

Another thing she had tried during her health-nut phase was dry skin brushing. Each morning before showering she used a special brush to gently rub every inch of skin on her body. She remembered those brush strokes vividly, circular motions that stimulated the lymphatic system and opened surface pores to release more toxins. It was one of the few practices that really did seem to have an effect. The first few days were uncomfortable as her skin adjusted to the sensation of all that stimulation, but then she got used to it and even came to enjoy the brushing. Plus the effect on her skin was remarkable. It became super-smooth and naturally radiant, the little spots and blemishes winking out like dying stars.

Wendy had forced herself to repeat the process every day until it became routine. It took only five minutes each day, and seemed to have become a permanent part of her life. Then, sadly, she visited a friend the following summer and her routine changed. Just as easily as she had built up the habit, she lost it again. She had not picked it back up in all the years since. Five minutes a day no longer seemed so insignificant.

The way her skin felt today reminded her of the dry skin brushing. The best thing about it was that it took no time or effort to accomplish. And it was not only her skin that looked and felt better.

The booklet that had sparked that whole health-nut phase was entitled "Paradise Health." It was all about the optimal human condition if each system in the body worked at full efficiency and in perfect harmony. Energy levels would be higher and the body would age more slowly. She could eat less because she got the most out of her food, which in turn made eliminations cleaner and less frequent. The little hallmarks of poor health that everyone became accustomed to—things like gas, bad breath, headaches, heartburn, constipation, and weight gain—would all fade from life like so much discarded trash. People would not only live longer, but lead happier lives in the process.

It seemed that booklet had been describing the way she felt now. She hoped the feeling could stay this way a little longer. But because she had done nothing to achieve this heightened state, she had not the slightest idea how to maintain it.

She was looking forward to talking about it with Matt. No one knew more about health and the body than he did. For that reason, she had called him this morning and asked if he wanted to meet for lunch. Of course he agreed. He had limited time available to him, so they picked a quaint little coffee shop in the outskirts of Frederick. It had a nice outdoor patio where they could enjoy the clear day.

She was proud of herself for not relying on him at all during her sickness. She looked forward to telling him about it in the past tense. No doubt he would be thankful for having been spared.

She was already there and standing by the entrance when she saw his car pull into the parking lot. He parked beside her car and waved.

She gave him the traditional hug, then beamed at him. She just knew what he would say.

"Wow, you look great." She decided that hearing those words never got old.

"Thanks. I feel great."

"I only have a little while, and I'm thirsty. Shall we?"

"We shall."

She let him hold the door open for her, and they got in line. Luckily, there were only a few patrons ahead of them.

"So, you look happy. Going to tell me what's up?"

"Do I?" She realized she could not stop smiling, but she did try to tone it down a notch.

"Ma'am?" asked the man behind the counter. He looked like a high schooler, not terribly interested in his job.

"Let's see...I'll have the Rainforest Nut. Venti."

He pushed a few buttons on the computer screen in front of him. "Sir?"

"Just a regular coffee. Black. Large." Then Matt caught her staring at him. "What?"

"Nothing." She giggled.

They grabbed their drinks and walked out onto the patio. There was no one else there at the moment. Wendy thought this was a travesty of American culture. No one went outdoors anymore. A place like this should be wall to wall people. Kids should be playing, kicking and throwing balls around the field behind them. Instead the view was nothing but parked cars in one direction and tall grass in the other. To make matters worse, there was a 'Keep Off' sign posted on the grass. It made her think of that Talking Heads song, *Nothing But Flowers*. It had been one of Halfus' favorites. Wendy quickly forced him out of her thoughts, an act made easier by recent information.

They sat at one of the round tables and she blew on her steaming hot coffee, helping it to cool to a drinkable temperature. Matt was doing the same. Wendy braved a tiny sip. She made a face. "This coffee tastes funny."

"Of course it does. You ordered Tropical Monsoon Crunch."

"It's Rainforest Nut, silly. I've had it before. It's too sweet. Here, try it."

"It's too sweet all right. No argument there."

"Grr. You're no help. You drink that black stuff. I don't know. Maybe I'm just imagining it."

He shrugged. He seemed to be disinterested in the sweetness of her flavored coffee. She found that a little annoying.

He took a few sips of his own, then set it down. "So, tell me why you're in such a good mood."

Well, I was in a good mood, she thought. "Remember the illness that Ernie had, in Iraq? I just had it, too."

"Okay, I can see why that would put you in a good mood," he said sarcastically.

"Be quiet. The illness sucked, quite a lot. But apparently when you recover you feel really great."

"Yeah, that's pretty normal."

"Not like this. I've never felt so good. I mean it. I can tell a difference. I have tons of energy. My skin feels smoother. My hair looks better. I'm never hungry. I eat only for the enjoyment. My hearing is better. I...just feel so alive."

"I'm glad your skin feels smooth, Wendy, but I don't see how—"

"I know this sounds crazy, but I really think the illness had something to do with it. It's like my body worked so hard to fight off whatever was inside me, it got stronger in the process."

Matt frowned. "It doesn't really work that way." She thought it sounded fairly condescending.

She was getting more irritated. She was trying to share good news with him, and he did not seem to believe her. She should have known. He always was so skeptical about things.

"Fine, don't believe me. But Ernie thinks the same thing." She sat back and crossed her arms.

Matt glanced at his watch. "How's your mother?" he asked. She assumed he was just giving up on the other conversation. *Fine. His loss.*

"Just as you said. I haven't been able to visit her in the last few days. I'm worried about her."

"Me, too."

"I'm going over there after this." She looked at her watch, too, as though she was on a schedule. "Right now, in fact. I just...I was glad to feel better and I wanted to share it with you. It's silly, now that I think about it."

A cloud of bitterness had fallen over their conversation, but now she tried to sound conciliatory. He seemed willing to meet her halfway.

Her hand was resting on the flimsy grilled tabletop. He reached across and covered it with his own. She resisted the urge to pull hers away.

"I guess it's possible the antibodies in your system might be the reason you feel so good." He still sounded skeptical, but at least he was trying. "Anyway, I'm glad you're feeling better, Wendy." The condescension was gone. She heard genuine empathy in his tone. It was what she had come to expect from him. Perhaps that's why his earlier reaction had been upsetting.

He leaned back again. "I could take the afternoon off, if you want me to go with you to your mother's." He almost sounded hopeful.

"No, that's okay."

He looked away. "Well, tell her I'll visit soon."

"I will."

The faded carpet in the foyer of her mother's building reminded Wendy of the one in the natty hotel in Mosul, and her mind drifted to a place where she did not want it to go. Those were the four worst days of her life, and she had no desire to think about them any more than she had to. Particularly now that she knew all that grief had been for nothing. Even after their kiss at the dig, even after her amazing discovery, even after saying he was proud of her, Halfus had still been obsessed with Shauna to the end of his life. Wendy refused to shed one more tear for him.

After her disappointing meeting with Matt, it seemed that only one person really understood her. Ernie was a godsend. It felt as though he had come from nowhere, but ironically had always been right in front of her eyes.

In the hall outside her mother's apartment Wendy met the family who had moved in next door. They were an attractive young black couple with a cute little boy. Don Planter was on a knee, tightening the knob of his door as Wendy came out of the stairwell. He stood, smiled, and shook her hand as he introduced himself. She asked what brought him to town, and learned that he was starting an administrative position at the college. He asked if she was a student there. She told him she was a graduate student, and to let her know if he had any questions about the campus or town.

The two of them were joined by Don's pretty wife, Kiara, and their eight-year-old son, Samuel. Kiara was as open and friendly as her husband, but Samuel was a shy little boy who seldom spoke and would not meet Wendy's eyes when she tried to engage him. It was a quality that only made him more endearing to her. Husband and wife asked her a few polite questions, which led her to inform them about Miriam's condition. Kiara gave Wendy their cell phone number along with an invitation to call if there was anything they could ever do. She was touched. It was reassuring to discover there were still people like this in the world.

Then she checked on her mother, who was now sleeping peacefully, although it was only the early afternoon. Her face was tranquil, but signs of the illness remained present. Her quiet breathing was intermittently broken by a struggled gasp, mild cough, or agitated movement. She seemed to be nothing but skin over bone, and that skin looked paler than ever. She looked so tiny, so fragile. It was heartbreaking to behold, so Wendy walked out of the bedroom to spare herself the distress.

She decided to fix herself a tuna sandwich. She was not at all hungry, but she needed something to distract her troubled thoughts, and she knew her mother always kept tinned tuna to feed the cat as a treat. The sandwich did not taste good, however, so she found herself throwing most of it into the trash. And, a moment later, chasing Truman away from it. She filled his food and water dishes and cleaned his litter box before going back into the bedroom.

This time her mother was awake. Their conversation was brief and troubling. Wendy tried to think of a pleasant subject, so she talked about how she was looking forward to the start of her new job. It was still several weeks away, but she had already begun to fill out the preliminary paperwork. She had also called Sandy Kesmet again, and this time came away with a more positive impression.

"I'm so happy for you, Sweetie," her mother said. "I just know you are going to make your father and me proud."

Wendy excused herself, went to the bathroom, and burst into tears. She did not know whether her mother was confused and thought her father was still alive or was already counting herself among the angels, but either one was equally upsetting. It did not seem fair that she felt so alive yet was forced to watch her mother diminish with each passing day. She wished there were a way she could give a piece of her own health to the sick woman.

Truman entered the bathroom and brushed up against Wendy's leg. She bent down to scoop him up. He allowed her to clutch him to her chest like a baby. She stroked the fur of his belly as he looked up at her appreciatively.

"Truman, what am I going to do?"

The cat closed his eyes and purred contentedly.

"Thanks a lot. A fat lot of help you are."

There was no malice to her words. Quite the opposite. He had been a better companion to her mother than Wendy herself. In the last few years since they moved to McGahey, she had spent so much time avoiding her mother. Now she wished she could have every minute of it back. She was beginning to appreciate just how important companionship was. People needed to feel love, and have it returned, or else they were missing out on the vital essence of life. She regretted that it had taken her so long to understand this one simple rule of humanity.

Two things were happening to Ernie, marvelous and dreadful, a pair of prevailing currents overwhelming all others.

He unquestionably felt better now than ever before. Which was ironic, considering that a week ago he had been staring at death's gate. The sickness that he had gone through—which had seemingly come from nowhere—was probably the second worst experience of his life. Yet within a few days there remained nary a trace of it. And then the natural high that he associated with recovery just kept going, taking him higher still. It was simultaneously exhilarating and scary, like soaring through the sky with no idea how to land. He believed he was a pioneer entering a brave new world, walking a path untraveled by any man before him. The only reassuring thing about it was knowing that Wendy tread this path with him.

He had never before known anyone like her. She seemed to be layer after layer of complexity and contradiction. Brilliant and charming when she wanted to be, selfish and cruel when she did not. Knowing her was like riding a roller coaster, and he had jumped aboard this ride with both feet. He knew he had never felt this way about anyone before. She was no longer just a conquest for him. She was more of an obsession.

Which led into the second thing happening to him—he was utterly consumed with guilt. Every decision he made and every act he performed seemed devoted to a single purpose—possessing her—and it was taking him further and further from the man he wanted to be. He did not know exactly how he had become so manipulative. Being charming was something that came naturally to him. That fact had been a delight to discover during those first few months at Catoctin, when guys and girls alike had been drawn to him, and all things seemed possible. His behavior had never seemed as sinister then as it felt now.

Sure, he had seduced the girlfriends of other guys, but he believed they had always wanted to be seduced. Now he looked at those episodes in a different light. There were real relationships at stake, something to which he had never given much consideration. He thought of a girl he met at the *Bluff* the night he learned about Iraq. *What was her name?* Laurie. Her boyfriend had bought her a necklace for Valentine's Day, yet Ernie could barely remember her name. She talked about spending her life with that guy, but she had spent the night with Ernie. What caused a person to do that? How upset would that boyfriend be if he found out?

Laurie was the friend of Deanna, who had gone for Halfus. Ernie had been less interested in her, until it looked as though she had captured Halfus' eye. Then Ernie had suddenly found her much more appealing. Without understanding why he was doing it, he had encouraged Halfus to bring her out more often. Ernie wanted to believe that he had his friend's best interest in mind, but how much of his motivation had stemmed from a desire to seduce her for himself?

He told himself that he was not doing anything that was not already happening in every country, culture, and household around the world. People were people. It was not just that they became attracted to each other, even after finding a mate. It was more that they actively tried to attract each other. Doing so provided a critical impulse of pride and delight needed by every social being. Then, where attraction sprouted, temptation bloomed. Some temptations were resisted, some were not. It was the way of humankind. Perhaps some animals were made to be monogamous, but clearly humans were not. Ernie was not alone in this.

But there was one thing others did not do. They did not kill their best friend. Ever since the moment it happened, Ernie had wanted to believe it was an accident. His hands had been sore, his muscles tired. He had spent a great deal of time and effort telling himself it was not his fault. But the truth had never left his subconscious thought, and now it was inescapably back in his conscious. He had been jealous. All the lies since then, to himself and others, could not block out that terrible understanding. It was tearing him apart from the inside.

He believed he was still a good person at heart. In order to save himself, he needed to start acting like one. He had to bare his soul to someone, to beg for forgiveness. If he had been a religious man, he would have sought absolution from a priest. But in Ernie's mind, there was really only one person he could tell. It had to be Wendy. She had been affected by his actions more than anyone else. At least, anyone else alive. He had thoughtlessly manipulated her all along. And it had completely failed; she was never going to see him as more than a friend. She belonged to Halfus. She always had and always would. It was time to accept that one simple truth. There would be other girls for him. In time, another one would enthrall him as she had done.

But what would he say? That he had murdered her lover? That was out of the question. A confession like that would do more than end his chances with her. He could wind up in prison, his entire life in ruin.

Besides, murder was not the right way to describe what had happened. The reality was much more complicated than that.

He could at least admit that he had made up Halfus calling out to Shauna. Wendy might hate him for it, he might lose her friendship, but at least he would not wind up in jail. Yet he did not know how to express even this small thing. Would he say that he simply was not sure? That the yell was unintelligible, and so he had made an assumption that may not be true? But this would only be another lie. Halfus had been unnervingly silent as he fell. How could Ernie purge this guilt with more deception? He could claim that he lied to Wendy for her own good, to help her get through the grief. That was closer to the truth. And more likely to earn her wrath.

The more he thought about it, the less he knew what to say. Yet he had to say something. He felt that he might go mad if things continued on the same course. Perhaps the words would come to him when the time came. He was good at reading cues. Hopefully, she would give him one.

The uncertainty of his thoughts did nothing to calm his nerves as he let himself into her apartment. He had visited her at least once a day since the afternoon she got sick. She had even given him a copy of her key. There was no need for him to ask to whom it had last belonged.

As he entered, Ernie could tell immediately that something was wrong. Wendy was in the living room, her back to him as she stared out the window. He had made enough noise that she must have heard him, but she did not say hello.

It was not an auspicious beginning, but he was resolved to go through with this. He approached her. He gently reached out to put a hand on her shoulder. "Wendy, we need to talk." He felt her body tense. She turned around to face him. She looked upset.

"Are you all right?" he asked.

She nodded affirmation, but her face gave a different message.

He instinctively wanted to help. "Is there anything I can do?"

She stared at him for a frightening moment. There was a storm brewing inside her, he could tell. When she spoke, he realized how very painful this was going to be. "You've done enough already."

I wanted a sign, he thought. *Well, here it is. Somehow she already knows.* He took a cowardly step back. His heart started racing, his mind becoming jumbled with words. He forced some out, just wanting to get this over with. "This is hard to explain—"

"Oh, Ernie," she said. Her voice seemed as agitated as his own. She was shaking her head. "Will you forgive me?"

He was confused. "What?"

She stepped toward him. He froze, fearing an attack, yet unwilling to defend himself. He had no defense. He was out of excuses.

"For making you wait?" she said. Her face was incredibly sad, and incredibly beautiful. She wrapped her arms around him. He put his around her, timidly, torn between disbelief and a suddenly rising hope. Had he gotten the signs wrong, after all? He had to force himself to not look away. She stared up at him, those blazing blue eyes drawing out all the ache in his heart. Then she stretched up and kissed him. And did not stop. He held her tighter. A wave of emotion washed over him, head to toe, a new sensation utterly foreign to everything he had been feeling for as long as he could remember. It felt like salvation.

This was the third day since Halfus first woke up in Mahmoud's home and the seventh that he had been there, according to what the boy told him. As always, he spent the first few minutes of morning consciousness with his eyes closed, clenching his teeth, settling his mind into accepting the intense pain from the left side of his body. So far there was no appreciable diminution of it. He told himself there would be, in time. It was a mantra he repeated multiple times per day. Then he opened his eyes toward the window and another pristine Iraqi sky.

He heard movement and turned his head to the other direction. There was the second beautiful sight of the day. Amelia, Mahmoud's little sister. Many times he had caught sight of her peeking in on him, although she had not yet been brave enough to enter the room. He played peekaboo with her each time, and each time she ran away.

But this morning she smiled instead. She had a gap where a baby tooth had recently come out. Nevertheless, that smile won him over instantly. She hid her face behind the hanging rug until he hid his behind the pillow. Then he lowered the pillow quickly and caught her looking again. "Gotcha," he said. She squealed with delight and ran off.

Halfus lay back, breathing heavily. That little exercise had taken a toll on him. But he would not have traded it for the world. *Well, maybe for a beer.*

So far his only real communication had been with Mahmoud. The boy spent a few hours with him each day, answering questions when he felt like being helpful and acting deliberately mysterious when he preferred to be mischievous. Halfus was starting to believe that mischief was Mahmoud's go-to behavior when he did not know or was uncomfortable with an answer.

There was plenty to be uncomfortable about. Halfus was alive, but under no illusions about the uncertainty of his situation. Apparently a civil war was being waged in northern Iraq, and it did not sound as though the forces of security and stability were winning. The rebels were anti-Baghdad, anti-Shia, and anti-foreigner. As an American and Christian, Halfus' life was almost certainly forfeit if he were discovered.

Which led to an even more immediate concern. Going back all the way to the first evening at the dig, Halfus had been told that Mahmoud's father was opposed to the boy spending time with the expedition. Now Halfus understood why. His very presence in this house put the entire family at risk. If the insurgents found out that they were sheltering him, their own fate might be as dreadful as his. It was no wonder that Mahmoud's father had never so much as checked in on him a single time. Halfus' being here was undoubtedly a sore spot for him, a source of persistent worry.

When Halfus had asked Mahmoud why then the man had accepted him into his home, the response was more of the boy's frustrating evasions. It was clear that Mahmoud adored his father, yet was at the same time aware of the man's disapproval. Halfus actually hoped that Mahmoud did not fully appreciate the danger they were all in. Hopefully he would never find out. And if he did because they were caught, there was no reason to make the horror last any longer than necessary. *Please God, don't give the rebels a reason to search this place.* If the father were put in a position of choosing between protecting his family or harboring Halfus, there was no question what the outcome would be.

But he gave the man credit. Halfus had no right to ask for even as much consideration as he had received, and it appeared that this family had gone through the effort to make his accommodations as comfortable as possible given the circumstances.

Halfus had no illusions about exactly how dire those circumstances were. He was incapacitated, unable to speak more than a few words of the language, living at the mercy of a man of indeterminate loyalties. He was in a constant state of agony and fear, his nerves pushed to their limit. Perhaps that was why he relished the trivial moments with Amelia so much.

That afternoon was the first Halfus saw of his host. During each midday thus far, Mahmoud had brought in a few bites of food, leftovers from the family meal. A few bites was really all Halfus felt like eating, so he actually looked forward to these times more for their social component. Today, however, it was an older man who brought him a small plate with a scrap of meat and thin piece of pita bread.

"Thank you, sir," Halfus told him as he accepted the plate. He had no idea how much English the man understood, if any, but politeness seemed to be the appropriate behavior considering what they were doing for him.

The man looked down on him disapprovingly, saying nothing. Halfus met the man's intense eyes for a moment, then caught a movement from behind him. He smiled. "Hi, Amelia. I see you." She peeked out from around her father, then squeaked and ran off. The entire time, the man never took his eyes off Halfus. He seemed to be deep in contemplation.

Halfus took a bite of the meat. Goat, he presumed. "Delicious," he said, as much to himself as the visitor. He dipped the pita bread in the meat's juices and took a bite of that. He swallowed. "My compliments to the chef."

The man turned and walked out.

Halfus finished the meager meal and set the plate on a stand by the bed. He heard more gunshots in the distance. They were not an infrequent occurrence, but they still caused a knot of tension in his stomach. This time they were followed by a booming sound. Artillery. He had no idea whether that was a good or bad sign. It could be the rebels gaining ground, or it could be the Iraqi Army fighting back. Either way, he worried that each day the sounds seemed to be inching closer.

Halfus closed his eyes. He rarely prayed, but this time he could not help himself. *Please, Lord, protect this family. Do not let me be the cause of their destruction.*

Mahmoud came to see him at nightfall. He apologized for missing most of the day. Apparently he had been running errands for his father and their neighbor, a man named Hassan.

"Does Hassan know I'm here?" Halfus asked.

Mahmoud was sitting on the bed beside Halfus. He shrugged. "I guess so."

This isn't an 'I guess so' question, Halfus thought. He did not appreciate the ambiguity. But he was not going to say or do anything to upset Mahmoud, nor any other member of the family. He owed them more than he could possibly repay. The least he could do is behave like a respectful guest.

He moved on to the next question. "Mahmoud, what is your father's name? I'd like to address him respectfully."

"Ammar," came a voice from the hall. A hand brushed open the rug, and Mahmoud's father entered the room. He barked a few words in Arabic. Mahmoud hopped up and left them alone.

"Ammar," Halfus said. "Thank you for—"

The man shook his head. He appeared to be in a foul mood. "Forget these empty courtesies, Mister Halfus." His English was excellent, with barely a trace of accent. Halfus should have known. "I understand that you wish to be respectful, but this is not a time to concern yourself with such things. You are putting my family's lives at risk."

"I know," Halfus said. He did not try to deny it. "I wish it were otherwise. If I could walk away from here so your family could be safe, I would do it this minute."

"Would you, now?" The man seemed amused.

"Yes, I would. I'm not deaf. I hear the fighting. I know it's getting closer. I am as frightened as I have ever been. I don't know where I would go or what I would do, even if I could walk. But I would never wish someone else to suffer on my account."

Ammar paused. Then he started a new line of conversation. "You are an archaeologist, Mister Halfus?"

"Please, just Halfus. If you don't wish to be so familiar, you may call me Mister Lonagon. I'm a student. I study ancient history and languages. I was here to help translate Assyrian script."

"And how do you like my country so far?"

"I love it. And hate it. I guess it's possible to feel both."

Ammar nodded. "As do I. Did my son tell you what I do?"

Halfus shook his head. "No. He avoided telling me much about you, although I asked him many times. His English—and yours—is better than I would have expected, though."

"I was an electrical engineer. I worked for American companies in Bahrain and Dubai. My son went to an English school. We returned to Iraq just before the Americans came to bring democracy and capitalism to this country. Many American companies are now here. There is great demand for engineers in the new Iraq. What do you think I do now?"

Halfus could guess, but he waited. The man clearly needed to vent his anger.

"I am a goat farmer. I speak three languages. I studied two years in London. I am an electrical engineer. And they do not want me. All the jobs are given to Americans and Europeans."

Halfus had no response to this.

Ammar went on. "You come here to fight terrorism. Islam is the new bogeyman. Like communism was when I worked for you. You come to fight terrorism," he repeated. "And what happens? There are more terrorists than ever. They are all around me and my family. They walk by my house whenever they please. Don't you see? The very thing that you came here to fight you make worse."

Ammar began pacing the room, his agitation needing a physical release. With some discomfort, Halfus turned his head to follow his movement. "You see yourselves as victims because many died on Nine-Eleven. All of us were with you then. But you don't even understand that you are not victims anymore. Now you are the cause of death and suffering and I am tired of it. I have learned to hate Americans."

He stopped. Halfus wondered how long the man had needed to say all that. Halfus was not without sympathy, at least for the parts he understood. There were things about the war and the process of rebuilding that he would have changed if he could. But he was no political expert. He was sure there were reasons behind the decisions that were made, and complexities unknowable to the two of them in this room. He also had no idea what to say to this man. What could he? This was a smart man, an educated man, perhaps a potentially great man. Yet his potential was denied him by things beyond his control. Nothing Halfus could say would make any of that better.

But he had to try. He feared this man was about to throw him to the wolves. "Ammar, you don't hate Americans. You are too smart to lump us into one group. You hate what's happened to your country, and so do I. Maybe you hate my government. Most of us do, sometimes. But you don't hate Americans. Not all of us."

Ammar shook his head emphatically. "Perhaps not all. But I hate you, Halfus. For putting my family in danger."

He walked out.

Halfus became aware of the surging pain in his side. He had been sitting up through most of the tirade. Now he lay back down, clenching his teeth. As the surge tailed off to normal levels, he began to shake his head. He wished he could dig a hole and bury himself in it.

For a short while, Ahmed had felt a little guilty about the way he treated the Americans. He had behaved more ruthlessly than he thought himself capable of. First there had been the bullying to get them into the vans. The girl had been upset, and Yasin had needed to hit the boy to end their resistance. That was regrettable, but it had to be done. They had needed to get away from the area as quickly as possible.

Then came the manipulation. Ahmed had never experienced an interrogation before, but he had heard enough about them to pick up a trick or two. He used those tricks on Doctor Appelstein, all in an effort to get him to betray his own student. There had been more fire in that man than Ahmed expected. He respected that, even as he saw it as a problem to be overcome by any means necessary. He had enlisted the aid of the liaison from the US embassy, and together they got what they needed from the professor. It felt wrong, it felt harsh, but this too had to be done. It was because of Ahmed that they were alive and back in America. And not here for this. He could take some small satisfaction from that.

Tariq punched him again, a solid blow to the jaw. Ahmed fell to his knees for a second time. He was momentarily dazed, his brain fighting for equilibrium. He found it and steadied himself, then looked back up at the face of his employee. Make that former employee. Ahmed would have struck back had he been able, but the two men standing above him kept his arms restrained. He would have to be defiant with words alone.

For several days, he had known this was coming. When the security situation worsened, Yasin and Naji had wanted to move into Ahmed's house to provide round-the-clock protection. He had refused them. This house had always been a refuge from the troubles of the world outside. A place of happiness, comfort, and finally mourning. Now he was glad the two of them were not there today. If they had been, they would almost certainly be dead. He hoped they were getting away from the city entirely, now that it was being overrun.

No one had believed that Mosul could fall. Certainly not so quickly. There were more than ten thousand soldiers stationed in the region, compared to only a handful of insurgents. Intelligence estimates had numbered them in the hundreds. Now that count appeared to be disastrously low. Even so, there were not more than a few thousand. The army, trained and supplied by the Americans for the past decade, should have had no difficulty winning any contests on the battlefield. Yet that had not happened.

Will and discipline. It always came down to will and discipline. One side was doing a job. The other wanted to fight.

Tariq paced around like a little general. He was enjoying his sudden rise to prominence. He did not understand, as Ahmed did, that his moment in the sun was likely to be brief. Tariq was too lazy and insubordinate not to anger some higher-up in the not-too-distant future. He would most likely wind up another casualty of this conflict, the same as Ahmed.

The spiteful young man stopped in front of the Angel's Trumpet. "I hate these fucking things," he announced. "How many times did you make me wait like an asshole while you watered these flowers?" he asked with annoyance. Then he shoved the large pot off its perch. The clay shattered, showering the white stone of the patio with black, green, and pink. Ahmed's heart tightened. *Anjali, I'm sorry.* He choked back a sob.

"Allah will punish you for this, Tariq. This is not Islam."

His captor ignored him, instead turning to the other men. "Pick him up," he told them, still basking in his newfound authority. They obeyed wordlessly. Ahmed stood on his own, but they would have to drag him from here. He would not be a docile captive.

"Follow." Tariq walked into the house, and the men dragged Ahmed along behind. Tariq nonchalantly broke a few small items on the way to the front door, then led them all outside. Tariq's car and two vehicles Ahmed did not recognize were haphazardly parked in the street. It was over two miles to the police station the rebels were using as their jail, but Ahmed's captors did not put him in any of the vehicles. It seemed they would walk. He dragged his feet uselessly for the first hundred feet, then realized that was only going to make things more painful for himself. He reluctantly began walking, matching their slow pace. He was on display and all of them knew it. He tried to tell himself there was no reason for it, but he felt shame nonetheless.

Several rows of palm trees separated Ahmed's neighborhood from the nearby commercial district. They passed a few blocks before anything began to look out of the ordinary. It was a quiet morning, with few pedestrians on the streets for obvious reasons. Those who were carried automatic rifles or larger weapons such as rocket launchers. By themselves these sights were not uncommon in Mosul and throughout Iraq. But everyone was aware that a new power was taking over the city, and every reasonable civilian was staying indoors until the shift was complete. Ahmed heard birds chirping from the wires above, and there was almost no visible sign to indicate that a revolution was in progress.

Then they walked past a small but gruesome scene of destruction. Someone had recently opened a new storefront against Ahmed's advice. The owners sold clothing and trinkets emblazoned with American slogans and insignia. Apparently the business was booming in Baghdad, so they had sought out new markets and greater profits. Such was the way of businesses everywhere. It was a ghastly mistake to open such a store here, however. Even during the lull of recent years, when Iraq had seemed at peace with itself, Ahmed had known the store was a bad idea and warned the owners that they were inviting trouble.

Mosul was not Baghdad. The resentment of invasion was stronger here, the government presence weaker, the religion more intolerant. The first signs of rebellion had started months ago, and Ahmed again warned the owners. Rather than suspend operations, they had hired contractors to protect the building. Ahmed was seeing those contractors now. Two bodies hung suspended upside-down, arms hanging down to the pavement, their heads brutally mangled. As he passed by, Ahmed saw that one had the tattoo of a dragon running the length of his arm. These poor guys had found themselves fighting against hundreds of rebels. Yet they had fought, and died, when so many of Iraq's own soldiers had fled despite much better odds. It made Ahmed want to weep for his country, its past and its future. As much as he wished Western values on his society, he better understood that war was seldom the way to a brighter age.

As they walked on, Tariq called out in a loud voice, recounting Ahmed's sins against the country, the people, and their religion. Most of it was totally bogus, although some was merely a perversion of the truth. In any case, he barely listened. It made no difference what they accused him of. There would be no fair trial forthcoming.

He now envied the death of his friend and neighbor, Jalal. How much better it would be to die quickly in a hail of gunfire. A life extinguished abruptly, without the opportunity for reflection. Ahmed did not wish to think now, but he could not help it. It was fair to say the new Iraq was not turning out quite the way the two of them had hoped. They had praised the end of an extremist, a dictator who deserved to fall. They had even been willing to turn a blind eye to atrocity and corruption. Now extremism was not only back, it was worse than before. *That's a job well done,* he thought sarcastically, then snorted.

Tariq heard the noise and looked over. He saw the rueful grin and was angered by it. He punched Ahmed again, hard in the gut. Ahmed crumpled to his knees, unable to breathe. And he knew this would not be the worst of it.

He had never experienced an interrogation before, but he expected to face one now. It would be the last thing he ever experienced, at least on this Earth. He told himself he would be with Anjali soon. That, at least, was some small comfort.

They lifted him back up and held him as he struggled to get his feet back beneath him. They began moving again before he was ready. Then he was able to find his stride. He looked up, and saw the converted police station just a few blocks ahead. He swallowed weakly. He was suddenly very thirsty. He felt a rising urge to fall on his knees and beg Tariq for a few more minutes. With great difficulty, he suppressed it. He walked as slowly as they would let him, looking around, trying to take in all the sights and sounds of the peaceful community he had called home for the last eight years. He tried to memorize every line and curve. Once he went inside that station, he doubted he would ever come back out. He would meet the end with as much dignity as he could muster. But he knew that, in time, they would take that from him, as well.

10

SCIENCE AND DEATH

ANCIENT HISTORY TELLS *of a disease called hydrophobia. A man bitten by an animal would, on occasion, develop an irrational fear of water—not of drowning, but of drinking. His mouth would develop an overabundance of saliva, which in turn made the act of swallowing painful and the thought of swallowing anathema. Within days, the sufferer would be beset by fever and dementia on the short road to a tortuous death.*

Prions are not the only pathogens to affect the brain. We now refer to hydrophobia as rabies, caused by a virus of the same name. In an unvaccinated individual, the rabies virus causes inflammation of the brain leading to such side-effects as fever, fatigue, hallucinations, excitability, uncontrolled movements, and the aforementioned fear of water.

For most of modern times, rabies was widely accepted to be one hundred percent fatal if untreated. With treatment—in the form of a vaccination that can be received within the first week of exposure—the disease is one hundred percent curable. Then, in 2004, an American teen survived a case of rabies without receiving a vaccination. She was induced into a coma so that her brain could avoid the overstimulation caused by the disease until her body's immune system had time to overcome the virus. The patient heroically survived the procedure, but was forced to begin a long journey of recovery to relearn basic human functions like balance and walking.

Brain infections are labeled according to location affected. Meningitis is an inflammation of the membrane surrounding the brain and spinal cord, encephalitis is an inflammation of the brain itself, and an abscess is a collection of infectious material inside the brain or spinal canal. All of these can be caused by viral, bacterial, prion, or fungal infections.

Polio is caused by a virus. The disease decays the central nervous system until leading ultimately to paralysis, coma, and death. Thanks to the polio vaccine, it has been all but eradicated from the world, although several hundred people in a few unfortunate countries continue to suffer. Rubella is a viral infection that causes in newborns a litany of terrifying defects such as heart trouble, deafness, and mental retardation. AIDS patients often suffer from a form of dementia characterized by behavioral impairment. Even everyday measles and mumps are viral infections that affect the brain. They can cause meningitis or encephalitis if complications arise, developing into seizures or deafness.

Even in the twenty-first century, each year there are tens of thousands of cases of rabies and other brain diseases caused by pathogens, inducing symptoms across the spectrum from behavioral changes to permanent paralysis. That so many mental disturbances can result from something so simple as a dog bite or eating an unwashed vegetable is testimony to an important basic tenet of human biology. The brain, like the body at whole, is extremely vulnerable to microscopic threats, unseen and often unimaginable.

"Matt, you're wearing yourself out. Please tell me you aren't going to pull another all-nighter." Tammy stood behind him, rubbing his shoulders while he peered into the microscope.

He would tell her no such thing, so he deflected. "Not everyone has your social life, Tammy."

He could sense her smiling. She liked being flattered. Once he had learned that simple truth, it had been easy to hit it off with his coworker. And hitting it off was essential, because Matt had initially been overwhelmed by the halls and laboratories of Maryland State Medicine. Tammy showing him the ropes had been the only thing that saved him from losing his confidence. It felt good to have her on his side.

Plus, she was cute, with lightly tinted red hair and emerald green eyes. She reminded him a bit of Wendy's friend Tracy, although her hair was not the same deep fiery shade. The two redheads shared the same happy disposition and jovial mannerisms. Tammy was also the one person who knew about his extra-curricular project. Because they worked together almost every day, he would not have been able to hide it from her even if he wanted. So he told her up front. The two of them got along well, and he did not think she would turn him in. In fact, he suspected she rather liked being his partner in crime.

"Seriously, though, you look like shit. I might report you just so they send you home to get some sleep." She let go and returned to her own work. She was kidding, of course, but the thought still caused him a slight shiver. He could not afford to lose this job. He was exactly where he had dreamed of being all his life.

Maryland State Medicine had a policy strictly forbidding the use of their facilities for anything other than sanctioned research, so Matt had gone rogue on this project. Whatever his friends had carried back from Iraq was too insignificant to show up on the company's radar screen. But Matt had a personal interest in this one, and he believed that it brought with it a lot of potential for academic recognition. Not that recognition was his primary motivation. He had now been conducting personal research for several weeks, and he was becoming increasingly convinced that this as-yet unidentified pathogen had the potential to be far more dangerous that it initially seemed.

It would have been nice if he could have employed the full resources of the organization. Unfortunately, Maryland State Medicine, like all the other major disease control centers in the country, was focused on more high-profile cases. The lion's share of research and field operations were currently devoted to the Duck Flu epidemic, which had captured the imagination of the public and remained officially listed as the number one biological threat in America. The total volume of cases had topped the one hundred thousand mark in mid-July with little sign of slowing down, although fatalities remained reassuringly low.

So Matt worked on his own. He was breaking the rules of the company, but he made sure to get all of his own assignments completed on time and spent only after-hours time on this side project, which eased his own guilty conscience. He was juggling anxieties, and he hoped that he had found an acceptable balance.

The night after his last meeting with Wendy, Matt had been unable to fall asleep. Something had nagged at him. His discomfort had something to do with the way she had spoken about her recovery with such ebullience. What she said was only part of the message he received from her. The other part was what she did not say. Even as she spoke of her health in such glowing terms, he could see that she was holding something back, as though she were actually toning down her description for the sake of believability. Which was ironic, since it had not been believable at all. She had come across as a little too fervent, like one of those crazies who belonged to a cult. She had wanted to spread the good word to him, and had taken offense at his resistance.

On the following morning Matt did something he had never done before. He called Rich. Matt had intended to ask a few questions about her, but instead he learned that the imposing black man had also been sick. He, like Wendy, had recovered in less than forty-eight hours. And he, like Wendy, felt even better than before. Rich was forthcoming with information, and Matt had quickly found a pen and notepad and started taking notes. As they concluded the call, Matt asked if he could take a sample of Rich's blood. He had been reluctant to ask, because he had not wanted to alarm his friend. He could almost hear an "are you trying to tell me something is wrong?" reaction before it came. But Rich had been perfectly willing. Unbeknownst to Wendy, Matt had driven to McGahey at his first opportunity and thus started his unofficial research.

That was two full weeks ago. Even working part-time on the project, Matt had learned a lot. The first step was always to identify some kind of foreign agent at work. The problem was that he was getting to Rich's blood during the recovery period. The invader, whatever it was, might be gone, in which case Matt would have to work backward by examining the antibodies Rich's immune system used to neutralize the menace. Those antibodies were normally found in abundance after a sickness like this. Even if Matt had been unable to find the invader itself, he still might have been able to make an educated guess as to its identity.

If by chance he still found existent forms of a foreign agent, the next step would be to isolate and inspect its structure. In nearly every situation like this, the invader was a known quantity and it was simply a matter of finding a match. However, when Matt had started his research, a part of him hoped that he was discovering something completely new. If that were the case, he would need to categorize it and look for comparisons to other pathogens. That meant a lot more work. It also had the potential to be worse news for his friends. Far better for them that it be a simple infection the world already knew how to deal with.

Thus it was with a mix of emotions that he had prepared and examined the first slide. His first reaction had been confusion. He thought he had made a mistake with the blood. He saw nothing wrong. Nothing out of the ordinary. No invader, and no antibodies.

The first day had been a waste. It was not until the second day, when he resolved to repeat the entire process with another drop of blood, that he made progress. He had been extra careful, making sure to meticulously follow every step of the procedure. He looked into the microscope again, and saw the same thing. Rich's blood looked normal. But this time Matt kept looking.

The power of electron microscopes allows for some amazing discoveries. Using accelerated electrons with much smaller wavelengths than visible light, an electron microscope provides magnification millions of times beyond the naked eye. The tiniest cells become live wall paintings, every pattern and movement easy to discern. Looking at a blood cell was like watching a primitive dance. Matt had stayed focused, watching, studying. And then he had seen it.

He was repeating the process now, as he had done for several hours every day since his initial discovery. There was so much that he still did not understand. All he could do was watch, take notes, and hope that inspiration struck.

He knew he was looking at a virus, or something that looked like one. Other than that, things did not make sense. Normally, viruses attach to regular cells, penetrate the cell wall, and inject their own genetic instructions. They hijack the cell, telling it to cease its original duties in order to make more copies of the virus. Then, when the cell dies and splits open, those copies spill out in search of more cells to corrupt. The human immune system fights back by using antibodies to kill viruses, block them from attaching, or prevent them from replicating.

Matt could see the invader, a tiny spider-like anomaly perched predatorily on the cell membrane. But only on some of the blood cells. Most seemed to be uninfected. And he saw no replicated copies. Even the infected cell was going about its normal business, seemingly unaware of the intruder. Whatever the virus had injected into the cell, it had not dramatically altered its function. Matt had been spending days and days trying to figure out exactly what it *was* doing.

Matt saw no antibodies because there were none. For whatever reason, the immune response had not been triggered. This, too, was confusing. It did not match up to the facts as he knew them. Ernie, Wendy, and Rich had all gotten sick. Many of the common symptoms of illness—runny noses, sneezing and coughing, frequent urination, and the like—were not caused by an invader directly, but were instead part of the body's attempts to clean out the contamination. So why had the patients manifested these symptoms if the immune response was not triggering?

Some viruses, such as herpes, could experience a latency period. This allowed them to remain in the body without actively attacking it. Matt had been operating under the assumption that this was what was happening here. But it still did not explain their illnesses. Something was not adding up, and it was driving him crazy. The blood cells Matt was examining were not replicating on their own. Red blood cells never divide. But if the cells were not dividing on their own, and the virus was not forcing replication, where were all the infected cells coming from?

"I'm heading out, Matt."

He looked over to see Tammy watching him. She had removed her lab coat and he saw the chic semi-casual outfit she was wearing. He guessed she had plans to go out dancing. Or perhaps on a date. He had no doubt she was popular.

But her next words nixed that thought. She paused, a little awkwardly, and asked, "Care to come with me? We could get a cup of coffee." He decided that she was adorable when she got nervous.

He shook his head. "Next time, maybe."

She looked disappointed, but unsurprised. "Okay. Well, see you tomorrow, then?"

He shook his head again. "Probably not. I'm visiting a friend for lunch. I probably won't be back in until after you're gone."

"Oh." She paused. Then she smiled. "Okay, well, have a nice time."

"Thanks. You, too."

He watched her leave, reconsidering. She was asking him out, and he could really use the break. Besides, he liked her company. Matt felt a moment of indecision. As if right on cue, his stomach growled. He could stand to put something in it. It would take a minute for her to reach her car, and he could easily catch up to her. A cup of coffee and carefree conversation was very appealing right now.

But he was going to see Wendy tomorrow, and he wanted to have a lot more to tell her than he currently could. Since he would be in McGahey, he also planned to see Rich, to tell him what progress he was making due do the other's generosity. Matt felt a clock ticking, and this needed to be priority one. The next time Tammy invited him out, he would accept. Assuming there was a next time. *If I had a dime for every bad assumption I've made...*

Matt looked back into the microscope. In moments, all thoughts of hunger and socializing were lost to his research.

.   .   .

From the corner of his eye, Matt saw a few rows of overhead lights come on in the corridor outside. That would be the maintenance staff, who made daily rounds at six in the morning.

Was it morning already? He had been at this all night, but it seemed that hardly any time had passed. He had pulled another all-nighter without even noticing. The notion did not completely displease him. It made him feel productive.

So did the thought of the progress he had made. There was still a lot that he could not explain, but he had formulated a pretty good theory for what was happening. If the theory was accurate, it was simultaneously fascinating in design and frightening in implication.

He needed to take some time away from the microscope and the computer screen. His eye was strained, his facial muscles tense. Besides, it would take several hours to copy his notes into a form that he could present to others. That was the next step. Matt had taken this as far as he could go on his own. He felt strongly that there was enough substance here to raise some much-needed attention.

His moment of revelation had come last night when he came across a blood cell containing the virus DNA but *without* the tail and fibers that attached to the membrane. He was seeing cells already containing the genetic material of the virus, apparently without ever having been injected from the outside. That meant the cells were being created with the infection already inside them. Red blood cells were formed in the bone marrow. Matt believed he would find that the marrow was likewise infected, but needed to test a sample to be certain.

Which led him to worry about stem cells. Stem cells were a generic form of cell that the body converts to a specialized purpose. Muscle cells, for one. Brain cells, for another. Adult stem cells were created in specific parts of the body, including the bone marrow. If the marrow were infected and producing contaminated blood cells, it might also be producing contaminated stem cells. That was a sobering proposition, because those stem cells could go anywhere. The virus could corrupt any part of the body, including the mind.

For this theory to hold water, Matt needed more answers. For stem cells to be having such an immediate impact on the health of an infected patient, the body's use of stem cells would need to be highly accelerated. And the virus had to have infected the bone marrow to begin with. These were big unknowns that could only be verified through more research. But it seemed like a good working model to move forward with, because it was the only thing he could think of that fit all the facts.

The virus was not causing reckless duplication inside cells, but nor was it latent. It was not following the usual process of reproducing copies of itself until the host cell exploded. He was seeing new cells created that already had the virus. Or not exactly the whole virus, but the most important part—its genetic material. Instead of creating more viruses to leak into the bloodstream and infect more cells, it was able to accomplish the same objective by causing new cells to form with the DNA already inside. It was able to go around the body's immune system. But for what purpose?

He believed the virus was not attacking the body directly, but in some unseen way. Unlike most pathogens, which damaged their host, this one seemed to coexist with it peacefully. Perhaps more than peacefully. Based on the description given by Rich and Wendy, perhaps the virus was functioning symbiotically with the body in certain respects. This was a method for the invader to continue growing inside a body without triggering the immune response in the process.

If the virus were capable of coexistence in blood cells, how was it affecting other types? If it were somehow accelerating metabolism or strengthening the immune system, Matt might actually have the answer to the mystery of the sickness. The period of illness might actually be nothing more than detoxification on a massive scale, as though the person had somehow undergone the perfect cleanse. It was like weeks of fasting, exercise, and a change of diet all rolled into one. If the body were forced to suddenly purge itself of every contaminant within an abbreviated time span, he would expect to see some of the exact things they had all reported. Assuming the body survived this period of extreme overload, it could make a real difference to their baseline health. Although some people were healthier than others, no one functioned on a sustained basis at full capacity, without the strain of some interference or handicap on their system. Perhaps this virus changed that paradigm. Depending on how effective this new virus truly was, Rich, Wendy, and Ernie might be the healthiest people on the planet.

Many types of bacteria worked symbiotically with the body, allowing both organisms to thrive together. Along those lines, Matt could see the ostensible benefit of a virus that actually made the host healthier. That gave it more time to perform any other action it was programmed for. It could even potentially affect the ability of the host to help it perform those actions. Nine times out of ten, that action was the multiplication and propagation of the invader.

Matt guessed, without knowing for sure, that this symbiosis was happening here. But it was likely a false symbiosis. The virus still wanted to reach out to the world, expanding its influence through deception rather than frontal assault. If its only immediately noticeable effect on humans was to make them healthier, Matt worried what the reaction would be. People were fond of quick, easy fixes. He thought of Wendy and how defensive she had gotten about her robust condition. Never mind that months, if not years, of study were needed to determine the actual efficacy and side effects of this germ... Put it into pill form and it would fly off the shelves.

The r nought of an infection was a number representing how many people, on average, one patient would go on to infect before themselves succumbing to the disease. The best case scenario was an r nought less than one, which meant that the volume of cases would trickle down on its own. When the r nought was higher than one, the disease would continue to spread without human—or divine— intervention. The perverse benefit of some of the most horrible diseases like Ebola was that their deadliness worked against their own spread in two important respects. First, they killed patients so quickly that they had less opportunity to pass on the affliction. Second, by the very nature of the horror it inflicted, a lethal disease entered the collective consciousness of the population and induced people to take precautions to avoid its spread.

Matt was more than a little worried by the potential implications of his discovery. A disease that took its time to develop inside a patient, while still being infectious, pushed the r nought higher. Add to the equation an agent that gained a reputation for being helpful, and the number could be astronomical. Instead of society taking steps to avoid exposure, he could imagine the opposite happening. A virus clever enough to trick people into acceptance was the perfect disguise. Thankfully, it was only a worst-case scenario. It seemed a little too far-fetched to take seriously.

He was making too many guesses—educated or not—and he knew it. To solve these mysteries and find out if there were any truth to his theory, Matt needed to continue doing research with a lot more than what he currently had. He needed more samples, and not from the blood. And he needed to enlist the help of other researchers. They needed to study what effect this thing was having in every type of cell. He was worried about vital organs like the liver, heart, and—most importantly—the brain. The latter was such a sophisticated instrument, far more complex than the most powerful computers created by humans, that the slightest alteration could have unfathomable consequences.

Viruses predated humans on Earth. They were primordial, prehistoric. Primal. Whether one believed that a virus was alive or not, its purpose was indisputable. It not only sought to exist, but to expand. Usually that happened at a primitive, cellular level. What Matt had discovered was a little different, but there was no reason to believe it was strictly benevolent. This pathogen had something up its sleeve. If it did not reproduce through sheer volume, it would find another way. It might not be obvious, but it would most certainly still be primal.

Copying out the notes was taking much longer than anticipated. The activity was boring, and Matt's brain was tired. He had trouble formulating his ideas in the right way to impress the higher-ups. USAMRIID was only a short distance down the road, and this sort of thing was right up their alley. Perhaps he could pull some strings and get an audience with them. But USAMRIID was military, and he had no idea how best to appeal to the military mind.

He was not even halfway through his notes when he glanced at the clock and realized he needed to go. He had promised to meet Wendy at noon, and he still had to run home for a quick shower and change of clothes. The two of them were going to see her mother Miriam, which was something Matt had been unable to do for weeks. He looked forward to it, and had even offered to do the cooking—although Wendy had jokingly made him promise to let her brew the tea.

It was also more important than ever that he see Rich. Matt hoped to talk him into being even more of a lab rat. Obtaining bone marrow samples was no pleasant procedure, but Matt believed his friend would do it. But first Matt needed to call and schedule a time to meet. And he was already running late. McGahey was an hour away. Adding the shower at home meant he needed ninety minutes. It was already past ten-thirty. And before he left, he had one more thing to do.

He wrote a note to Tammy. *Breakthrough! No more all-nighters, I promise. Next time coffee is on me.* He left the note on her chair where she would see it first thing. He then paused, wondering if he really wanted to open himself up for possible disappointment. He might very well have misinterpreted her kindness. He considered toning it down a notch, by taking out that last sentence. Then he considered turning it up a notch, by being even more obvious. Finally he decided that he was much too tired to worry about it, and left it the way it was.

It was early evening in Iraq. Each day was a scorcher, but today had been worse than most. Now a light breeze brought with it the incentive to get up and move.

Halfus sat on the edge of the cot, contemplating whether this was a good idea. He had two major concerns. His sense of balance was incredibly rusty. Even sitting upright was making his head swim as though he was spinning on a merry-go-round. He also worried about just how much weight his left side could support. If he fell to the floor, he might make his injuries worse.

At the same time he was pleased to have gotten this far. His splints were off, his limbs looked relatively good, and the agony of those first days had dulled to a tolerable soreness. It was quite remarkable, really, the speed at which his body was healing. By his count it had been three weeks since the fall. He had never suffered through something quite like this before, but he had worked through any number of smaller injuries in the course of his life. Enough to give him a sense for the rate at which his body recovered, leaving him no doubt that his body had healed faster from this than he had any reason to expect. He had no idea why, but he was not going to complain.

Nevertheless, he still had a long way to go. Even sitting up was exhausting. His energy was fading rapidly, so if he were ever going to try this he needed to do it soon. The dizziness did not seem to be going away, and he wondered whether it might not be better to simply lie back down. He could give it another go tomorrow. But the stubborn streak inside him egged him on. Self-improvement always meant pushing the limits of comfort. He would be very disappointed in himself if he did not at least try.

Halfus inched closer to the edge of the cot. In another moment he would lose its support, forcing his legs into action. Then he would find out if he could stand on his own.

He stopped as a swell of nausea overpowered him. A sudden throbbing in his left side told him to hold off for another day.

The hanging rug lifted up, and little Amelia stepped quietly into the room. She had with her the same teddy bear he had seen her holding the first time he laid eyes on her. Rather than clutching it protectively, she held it in her hand, swinging it backward and forward in short little arcs. Then her eyes grew wide as she saw Halfus sitting up, locked in indecision.

She put the stuffed animal down on the floor and stepped closer to him. She gently reached out and took his giant right hand in her tiny left. She held up her right hand, waiting for him to take it. It was a good twelve inches away from his left. To reach it he would need to get off the cot.

Darn this little girl, he thought with amusement. He liked her more and more with each passing day. He would have grinned if he was not already in so much discomfort.

She waited patiently as he eased forward. He stretched his right foot down first, then placed more of his weight on it until it, and not the cot, was keeping him up. Then he placed his left foot and timidly tested it. *So far, so good.*

Then he stood up. He stretched his left arm out to her hand. She slowly pulled it farther back, her gaze intently following his legs. *Oh, you little devil, you.* He took one truncated step, then another. He felt some small pain, but his worry that he would collapse like a rag doll now seemed unwarranted. *I can do this.* He reached out again and took Amelia's other hand. This time she allowed him to take it. He squeezed with perhaps more pressure than he wanted, overcompensating for his imprecise balance. She did not seem to mind.

He was breathing heavily from the exertion, but proud beyond any reasonable measure. She looked up at him and showed him her silly gap-toothed smile.

"*Shokran*," he said. She giggled, most likely at his butchered pronunciation.

Then Mahmoud came in and joined them. He looked happier about the accomplishment than Halfus was himself. Mahmoud had seemed to take a personal sense of pride for every fractional improvement in Halfus' condition. *And why shouldn't he?* Halfus thought. The boy was single-handedly responsible for getting him here.

Without warning, Amelia let go of his hands to bend down and recover her bear. Halfus momentarily feared that he would fall over, but the moment quickly passed. The dizziness faded completely. He still was putting almost all of his weight on his good leg, but it still felt great to know he could get up and move around. Even a marginal freedom of movement did wonders for his outlook. *Things are starting to look up*, he told himself reassuringly.

They heard voices outside. Four or five of them, from the sound of it. He had grown familiar with a few voices, but now he heard several that he did not recognize. It was not a welcome change from the norm. He felt a cold chill run down his spine. He suddenly needed to urinate.

"Mahmoud, help me," Halfus hissed. He cocked his head and lifted his arm. The boy ducked under it and helped him move awkwardly toward the window. He looked out from an angle that would conceal him from most outside observers.

For the first time he was seeing the terrain around the homestead. The ground was flat and dusty, with patches of vegetation and stretches of fencing. A few date palms were scattered here and there, looking lonely and sad. Halfus could see about a dozen goats milling about. Some distance away an old faded blue sedan sat parked beside a meager dirt path. The path ran from the vicinity of the home into the distance. It was difficult to discern, but he believed he could just make out where it intersected a wider road about a half-mile away. It was along this dirt path that three men carrying automatic rifles were approaching.

Ammar and another man stood a few dozen meters from him, their backs to the house. They were watching the three visitors. Halfus had boxed enough to read a man's muscles like an open book. There was an unmistakable tension in Ammar's neck and back. The newcomers were not friends.

One of the approaching men barked a few words. Halfus really wished his Arabic were better than it was, but he and Mahmoud had never gotten beyond a few simple phrases. On the other hand, he decided maybe he was better off not knowing what was being said.

The man beside Ammar responded. The same soldier said something else. Ammar's companion replied again, this time with more animation.

"That's our neighbor, Hassan," Mahmoud said in a louder voice than he should have used. Halfus felt a jolt of panic that the men outside would hear. He forced himself to not look away.

Hassan began gesticulating. Halfus could see just enough of his face to make out that he was smiling, but his words sounded more belligerent than calm. The mixed message was confusing. Then he pointed at the house, and three sets of eyes followed.

Halfus ducked away quickly, leaning his back to the wall. His heart was now pounding cruelly. The urge to urinate was gone. His body was too tense for that, all of his muscles clenched uncomfortably tight.

He could no longer see, but he heard movement outside. He heard Ammar call, "Mahmoud!"

Mahmoud met Halfus' eyes. They were wide and full of fear. The boy understood the situation perfectly well. "He's calling me," he said to Halfus, this time in a whisper. Halfus nodded, and Mahmoud ran out of the room.

Halfus looked around and saw that Amelia was gone.

Whatever strength he had felt in his legs had completely drained away. Halfus let his sagging body slide down the wall into a sitting position on the floor. He realized he was gasping for breath, and forced himself to try to breath more calmly. It was not working.

The voices were louder now, and it sounded as though all five of them were talking at the same time. They kept growing in volume as each one tried to talk over the others. Then one voice dominated for a minute. He believed it was Hassan's, but he did not dare look out to verify. It was not worth the risk, even if he had been able to get himself back up to a standing position, which he doubted he could do. His entire body felt uselessly weak.

He looked around desperately, but he already knew there was nowhere to conceal himself. The closest thing to a weapon was the stool in the corner. Perhaps he could break off one of its legs. But he would have to get to it to use it. Right now it might as well have been a mile away. He could only hope that things would not come down to fighting.

An angry voice interrupted Hassan. Then a second. Halfus held his breath and hugged his knees, as though he could make himself smaller. This new voice sounded like it was just outside the window. Halfus knew it would be possible to see him here just by looking in and down.

He closed his eyes, as though that would help. *Peekaboo, I see you.* He felt himself shaking.

All five voices were going at it again.

Holding his breath had been a mistake, because now he needed to breathe and was afraid that gasping for air would be too loud. *Breathe through the nose, Halfus. You can do it. Nice and easy.* He could not do it. He gasped and immediately held his breath again.

He was not hearing the voice outside the window any longer. In fact, the voices seemed to be slowly receding.

His chest was heaving. The adrenaline pumping through his body was making both temples pulse demonstrably. He opened his eyes again. Then he dropped his head back, staring at the ceiling. He let himself gasp again, swallowing for air as hard as he needed to. Then he covered his eyes with his hand. Ever since Shauna's death, Halfus had not been able to let himself cry. But this was a close approximation. His body shook uncontrollably.

He was vaguely aware of Ammar coming into the room. The man looked down on him for a moment. Then he bent down and wrapped an arm around Halfus' back. "Come on," he said.

Halfus draped his good arm over Ammar's shoulders. Together they got his body up and back to the cot. Ammar lowered him down onto it, not ungently.

Ammar, I'm so sorry. I'm so sorry. Halfus waited for the anger and accusations. But the older man kept his peace. He pulled the sheet back over Halfus' body. Then his stern face looked down, and his expression seemed to soften. There was sympathy here. Or perhaps pity. Halfus hated himself for putting his weakness on display.

Ammar nodded. Halfus had not said a thing, so it must have been a response to some internal dialogue, a gesture meant for himself. "Rest for now. They are gone," he told Halfus, patting his shoulder. Then he, too, was gone.

~

Wendy was early. She had a few more minutes before Matt would be meeting her, so she decided to call Ernie to pass the time.

"Hi, Curlicue." His voice sounded cheerful. "How's the first day going?"

"It's over. It was only an orientation, remember? I have the rest of the day off."

"Oh, that's right. I remember you telling me." Wendy doubted that he did, but she let it slide. "So, how was orient-tion...orientation?" he asked, correcting himself.

"All right, I guess. What I expected."

Actually, it had not been what she expected, nor was it all right. But she did not feel like talking about it at the moment. She was trying to keep things all sunshine and roses with her new boyfriend. She forced herself to smile, even though he was not there to see it. She simply believed it was easier to stay upbeat with a smile on her lips.

"Do you have any plans for the afternoon?" he asked. She searched for hidden meaning in the question, but detected none. She thought he might want to do something together. She would have had to turn him down, but it still would have been nice to receive the offer.

"I'm meeting Matt for lunch." She nearly added, *We're going to go see Mom*, but she decided to leave that part out. Then she listened for any hint of jealousy on Ernie's part.

"Okay. Tell her I shed hi."

Wendy's smile faltered. She waited for him to catch himself again.

"Grr. I mean, tell her I *said,* 'Hi.'"

"Her?"

"Him. Tell him I said, 'Hi.'" For this final repetition, Ernie forced himself to speak slowly enough to carefully enunciate each syllable.

"Will do. Love you. Bye." She felt a little embarrassed about saying it. She looked around. The street in front of her mother's building was deserted. She breathed a little easier.

"Love you, too. Bye."

There were so many things nagging her about that conversation.

She was trying so hard to construct a perfect life for herself. Why did reality have to keep throwing obstacles in the way?

She knew that the speech mistakes were a minor thing. She had never before spent as much time with him as in recent weeks, so she could not be certain, but it seemed as though he had more trouble speaking now than he used to. She wondered if he had a speech impediment growing up that he had overcome. Perhaps there were certain triggers that brought it back out of him. The mistakes were trivial and infrequent. He would occasionally misuse a pronoun or mispronounce a word. The first time she noticed was when they were out at a bar, so she thought he might have been drunk. But since then she had noticed the lapses at other times and places. He seemed as annoyed by them as she was, and although she usually let them pass without comment, she believed that they made him seem less intelligent than she knew him to be. In that sense, they were a disappointment.

But the real truth was that the mistakes were just one of several things bothering her about their relationship. In fact, the relationship itself gave her pause for thought. She still had the troublesome feeling that she was getting into this for the wrong reasons. She genuinely cared about Ernie, and was generally happy when she spent time with him, but there was still a forced quality to her behavior. She had said she loved him faster than she had ever done with anyone before, and yet she still felt uncomfortable telling him about even her basic doubts and worries.

Her first day of work was an example. Her office manager, Sandy —the very woman who had hired her—clearly did not like her, and Wendy had no explanation as to why. Whatever the improved impression she had of Sandy from their last phone call had been wiped away as soon as she entered the office that morning. The broad-shouldered, heavyset woman had shown her around with a curt demeanor that bordered on low-key hostility. The looks on the faces of the other three coworkers were equally confusing. They looked at Wendy as though they believed she were a troublemaker. She knew she could be argumentative, and she wondered if that reputation had somehow preceded her. She made it a point to be on her best behavior for the foreseeable future, get to know them, and then get to the bottom of this.

It was a simple, every-day anxiety. Why, then, was she reluctant to share it with Ernie? Did she really think he would only stick around for the good times? Did she think he would leave her for someone more fun? Nothing he had said or done gave her any reason to expect that.

Perhaps she had simply compartmentalized her feelings. Happiness was for Ernie. Drama was for Matt.

Speaking of which, he seemed to be running behind schedule. She glanced at her phone. Ten minutes late. That was very unusual for him.

She was sure he would have a good explanation, but she did not appreciate having to wait. She decided to call him.

He answered after several rings. "Hello? Wendy?"

"You're late," she told him. It sounded more accusatory than she wanted, so she forced herself to soften down her manner. "I'm sorry, that came out wrong. Is everything all right?"

"Yeah, I'm sorry, too. I worked all night, lost track of time. And the lunch hour traffic around Frederick is heavier than I expected."

"It can be, yeah. Should I get started without you?"

"No, I'll be there in fifteen."

She started thinking out loud. "I might anyway. I...have some things I might do before you get here."

There was pause. "What things?"

She heard the suspicion in his voice and realized she had hinted at something she really had not intended to. "Nothing. Forget it."

"Wendy." Now his voice sounded more like a demand.

She did not need to explain anything, she told herself. At the same time, she had nothing to be ashamed of. Besides, he had been the one who gave her the idea.

"I feel like I should do something. Anything is better than helplessly watching her die."

There was silence on his end for a few seconds. She could

practically hear the gears of his brain in operation. When he spoke, the disapproval was evident. "I hope you're not thinking what I think you are."

"You said the antibodies in my system are what's making me feel so good—"

"Wendy, listen. I've been doing research...that's what I was...Rich gave me his blood. He doesn't have antibodies. They're not doing anything." She heard him take a breath and start over. "Okay, let me explain. Antibodies are what fight a virus. But your body doesn't think it has a virus. So it's not that, it's...well, I think maybe it's stem cells."

He was not making any sense. She realized he must be very tired indeed. "Matt, what are you talking about?"

He groaned in frustration, either at her for not understanding or himself for failing to explain. "Okay, let me try again—"

She cut him off this time. "Matt, you shouldn't be talking on the phone while you're driving anyway. You can tell me when you get here."

"You were the one who called me," he defended himself. Then he sighed. "All right, fine. Just...wait for me to get there, okay? I really need to—"

Whatever he had been about to say was interrupted by a horrible screeching sound followed by a deafening bang. Wendy reflexively jerked her ear away from the phone. Then she brought it back, uncertainly. "Matt, that was really loud. Are you all right?"

There was no reply. Instead, Wendy heard more rending of metal followed by the sound of yelling. The voices sounded upset. She kept listening, frozen in place. The voices were getting louder. They were coming closer to the phone.

For once in her life, Wendy's voice was meek. "Matt? Please say something." There was still no response from him, although the other voices were now intelligible. She deliberately tried not to hear what they were saying. She covered her mouth with her hand. *Oh, no. No, no, no.* She remembered a similar sense of dread from the not-too-distant past. She felt her body begin to shiver.

Then she heard the sound of a hand pounding on metal. "I can't get him out," one panicked voice said. It sounded like a frightened woman.

No, no...

"I don't think it matters," said another. An older man with a tone of resignation.

Wendy hung up.

She felt that she was living in an absurd reality, some surreal alternate dimension. It was just too much, too fast, to be believable. So it was not happening. Not really. It could not be. This was not her life, this was a dreamy approximation.

She put the phone away and walked into her mother's building.

She bumped into Kiara just outside her mother's apartment. The petite woman was just stepping through her own door into the hallway.

"Hi, Wendy!" The woman flashed a brilliant smile with dazzling white teeth. Then, a second later, her happy expression changed to concern. "Wendy, what's wrong?"

"I...think my best friend just died." The part of Wendy that was still cognizant, still controlling her, was amazed at how calmly she could say this.

"Oh, my God. Come here, girl." She wrapped her short, skinny arms around Wendy's unresponsive body. "Oh! You're shivering." She raised her voice. "Don, come here!"

"Kiara? What is it? Oh, my—"

"Don, help me. She's in shock."

Wendy allowed herself to be led into their apartment and onto their couch. She admired their taste in furniture and the room's sensible decor. She became transfixed by a small painting of a white lighthouse overlooking a violent sea. It was a simple image—the constructs of man versus a willful nature. "I like your picture," she told them.

Kiara looked at her husband. "I'll call a doctor," he said.

.   .   .

"I'm fine now," she told the compassionate couple. She put down the half-consumed glass of water Kiara had given her.

Don and Kiara looked at each other. "The doctor said—"

"I know. I'll get some rest, I promise."

The truth was she had been in their living room for almost an hour, and now she needed to be alone. Or at least with her mother, which was almost like being alone. "I'll be next door. If I feel any worse, I'll let you know."

She wondered where their son was. She had not seen him once during the entire time she was there. Apparently, he was still too afraid of her to let himself be seen. That was probably just as well. She was not exactly at her best at the moment.

She thanked the two of them profusely for their kindness and went next-door. She quietly peeked into the bedroom. Her mother was sleeping in her bed, blissfully unaware of the turmoil that was threatening to bring down her daughter's world. Wendy thanked God for small favors and sat down on the living room sofa. She did not turn on the television, nor look at her cell phone. She wanted no distractions. She just wanted to think. When the cat walked by and purred up at her, she did not even notice. He wandered off.

Five minutes later she had come to a decision. It seemed that her life was collapsing all around her. Her mother, her friends, her job. Well then, she would fight back.

She went to the kitchen and turned on the stove. She rinsed out the tea kettle and filled it with water, then placed it on the burner. Then she searched for an appropriate flavor of tea. "What flavor goes with death?" she asked the empty room. She grabbed the nearest packet without reading the label, ripped it open, and emptied it into the pot.

She opened a drawer full of measuring utensils. It was the wrong drawer. She closed it, then opened the next. Eating utensils. She pulled out a serrated steak knife. She hesitated. Would boiling water be a problem? She decided to wait a minute for the kettle to whistle, then she removed it from the heat.

She held out her left hand and quickly drew the knife across her thumb. She flinched a little, but did not really mind. She put down the knife and used her right hand to squeeze her wounded thumb so the blood flowed. She let ten heavy drops drip into the teapot, paused to consider, then dripped in another ten. She did not want her mother to get suspicious, but Wendy doubted that the woman could taste much of anything at this point.

She sucked on her thumb for a minute as she continued her preparations. She pulled out the television tray and placed the pot and two cups on it. Then she opened a cabinet, found the half-empty package of Oreo cookies, and poured a few onto a saucer. She added the saucer to the tray. Then she inspected her wound. It would not do to leak blood where her mother would see it. But she need not have worried. The cut had already stopped bleeding, as she had expected.

Would it work? She did not know. God would decide.

She picked up the whole spread and carried it back to the bedroom.

"Good, Mom, you're awake. Ready for a little snack?"

11

THE EDEN AFFLICTION

THE MOST VENOMOUS *animal in the world is the box jellyfish—or box jelly,
as it is more accurately labeled. A human stung by the creature is unlikely to
survive unless treated immediately. Most victims die in the water, either by
drowning or heart attack, as the deadly toxins released by a sting attack the
nervous system and send the body into shock. Box jellies are found in the
waters of Australia and Asia, and have accounted for thousands of deaths in
the last half-century.*

*The most poisonous animal in the world is the poison dart frog, found in
Central and South America. It is so named because of the natives' historical
use of the frog's poison to coat their blowdarts. A single inch-long specimen
contains enough poison to kill ten human adults. This poison is found on
their skin, thereby affecting anyone or anything that touches or tastes them.
From the frog's perspective, the poison is less of a weapon than a defense
mechanism.*

*Although often used interchangeably, the terms venomous and poisonous
actually have significantly different meanings. The distinction is based on
delivery method—poisons are ingested, while venoms are injected. Thus, a
spider is venomous while a mushroom is poisonous.*

*Crocodiles and snakes are the deadliest reptiles on Earth. Crocodiles
employ a powerful bite in conjunction with a rolling maneuver capable of*

ripping entire limbs off. If that does not kill their victim, being dragged and held beneath the water usually will. Snakes, on the other hand, kill with an equally unpleasant variety of methods. Many are venomous, others use constriction to crush their prey, and some swallow their living victims whole. Crocodiles kill thousands of humans per year, and snakes many times more.

Excluding humans themselves, the deadliest mammals are lions, buffalo, hippopotamuses, and elephants. Many of them seem peaceful and most are herbivores, but all of them attack humans on a regular basis, making Africa a unique location to witness the peculiar capriciousness of nature. Each of these animals is responsible for mere hundreds of deaths on an annual basis, serving as a reminder that the lethality of a monster is not directly proportional to its size.

On the opposite end of that spectrum, the deadliest animal in history is, by a wide margin, the mosquito. Of course, it is not the bite of the insects that inflicts so much suffering on humankind, but rather the diseases they transmit. Malaria is the biggest culprit, but mosquitoes carry a whole host of others including dengue, yellow fever, and West Nile virus. Humans are also not the only victims—dogs and horses are plagued by other afflictions carried by the ubiquitous pests.

Mosquitoes account for the deaths of roughly one million people per year. The only creature that even comes close to matching this total is humans themselves. However, try as they might, people manage to kill each other at only half the rate of mosquitoes. Perhaps in time, with sufficient diligence and ingenuity, humans can scratch and claw their way to the top of the list.

Rich was surprised to see how out-of-shape most of his teammates were. They had just completed their first practice of the new year, and guys who had been able to run all over the field all day long just a few months ago could now barely handle a few wind sprints. He saw a lot of hands clutching sides, a sure sign of cramping. His fullback Joey even bent over as though he wanted to vomit, although it was just a passing bout of fatigue. Coach Schneider ended practice early in frustration.

He blew the whistle shrilly to get their attention. "All right, ladies, go ahead and hit the showers. This was pretty pathetic today. I want to see a lot more effort tomorrow, or there will be changes the day after." It was a serious threat, because those changes might be to the starting lineup. Every single man on the team was competitive. It was the reason they were playing collegiate sports to begin with. And no one wanted to suffer the embarrassment of getting benched.

Certainly, Rich did not. He was not particularly concerned about it, however. He felt that he had had a pretty solid practice. He was certainly in better shape than the guys who now struggled to walk normally. Unfortunately, his job was less about endurance and more about reflexes. And, for the first time since he joined the Catoctin squad, he had real competition.

Justin was a tall, lanky freshman with a face of fresh pimples and peach fuzz. He looked terribly ungainly as he strutted about, with an awkward, squeaky way of speaking that matched. But stand him in goal and he transformed into a terror. Those clumsy limbs moved with astonishing speed, and he had displayed more than one tremendous save during the day's practice. It was the mental part of Justin's game that needed work. Rich believed he could help him with that. He could mentor the kid into a fine replacement for next season, when Rich would be gone.

A small crowd, mostly friends and relatives, had turned out to watch the first practice of the year. Several of Rich's teammates stopped to talk instead of heading straight to the locker room. Rich frowned. The coach did not consider practice over until everyone was showered and changed. Sometimes he liked to catch them all in the locker room, away from prying eyes and ears, to discuss strategy and tactics for upcoming games. He would almost certainly have something more to say today.

Rich looked around. He saw the coach engaged with two of his assistants, both new to this year's staff. So far he had not noticed anything.

Rich viewed part of leadership as doing what was best for the others, even if they resented it. He headed over to the stragglers, feeling a little regretful. He intended to apologize to whatever family members he would be interrupting. Then he saw that the guys were actually deep in conversation with a trio of attractive young ladies. Suddenly, Rich felt less regretful and more annoyed.

"Ethan, Joey...come on. Coach will want us all together in a few minutes." The two of them looked at him with expressions that conveyed their own annoyance. Joey's eyes flashed him a silent reproach. *Come on, man, not right now.*

"Who's your cute friend?" asked one of the girls, a tall brunette in an emerald top that matched her eyes.

"Uh, this is Rich," replied Joey with a mix of hesitation and displeasure. When he saw her stepping toward the newcomer, he started to continue. "Don't worry, he's cool. But, he's—"

"Hi there, Rich." She smiled flirtatiously and offered her hand. Rich could see that she was attempting to manipulate him and wanted to ignore it. But instincts proved too strong.

He shook her hand, once. "Hello...?" He raised his chin as he drew the word out, converting the greeting into a question.

"Danielle," she said. "You can call me Dani." Her eyes flashed mischievously. *You're chirping at the wrong bloke, little bird.*

"A pleasure," he said politely, in a tone that suggested it was *only* polite. She did not drop his hand, so he dropped hers. He looked away from her. "Guys, wrap it up quickly, all right?"

The girls tittered. "Ooh, Dani, I love his accent," said one of the others, a much shorter blonde.

Rich ignored her and kept his eyes on Joey and Ethan. They nodded. Rich tried to overlook how amused they looked.

"What do you three think you're doing?" came an angry voice. Rich turned to see Coach Schneider jogging toward them. "This isn't some frat party. You're not out at the *Bluff*." His face was a little pink. He rarely yelled, but this looked as though it might become one of those times.

Rich spoke before anyone else could. He trusted himself with excuses more than these other two nitwits. "Coach, we were ginning up some fan support for the big game. It never hurts to have a loud crowd on our side."

Coach gave his bubble gum a few hard chomps while he looked over the six of them. "So? Are they coming?"

"You betcha," said a voice behind Rich. The other two girls giggled again.

Coach looked at Dani and then back at Rich. Then at all six of them together. "You've got two minutes. Hurry up and get their numbers and get your asses up to the showers." Then he turned and jogged off.

Rich looked at his teammates. Their expressions suddenly looked a lot less annoyed. "All right, you boners," he told them. "You heard the man. Hurry it up, okay?" They nodded at him.

Rich turned back to Dani, intending to politely bid her adieu. Before he could, she was already stuffing something into this hand. He looked down at it in confusion. A small folded piece of paper. He did not bother to unfold it, realizing what it was. He simply nodded. "Nice to meet you, Danielle."

"You, too, Rich." She matched his tone with mock sincerity. He was not sure whether she was teasing or still flirting. Either way, he was uncomfortable. He nodded again and jogged after the coach.

"I won't say this is the most important game of the year, because every game is important." Coach Schneider paused. "But it's the most important game of the year. You can look at this two ways. It's our bad luck that it's the first game, so we don't have as much time to prepare as we'd like. But they don't have as much time to prepare as they'd like, either. In any case, I plan to give them a run for their money. They were lucky to escape here with a win last time. None of us want that to happen again."

As luck would have it, the first game of the fall season was against none other than Bowie State. Whereas the last had only been an exhibition game, this one counted. It was only a few short weeks away, and they had their work cut out for them. Bowie State was not only picked to finish first in the conference, but had climbed into the Division II national rankings. They had achieved this lofty status off the shooting foot of Tre'Andre Bryant, which simultaneously filled Rich with pride, bitterness, and embarrassment. He was happy for his boyfriend's success and recognition, but the competitor in him was eager for some payback. That had been a particularly dispiriting loss in the spring, and the memory still lingered. He wanted a win not just for himself, but for the team. Plus Rich felt a particular responsibility when it came to Bowie State, for he was guilty by association. His coach and teammates never said a word about it to him, but it had to be on their minds nonetheless. Winning would wipe away any and all hard feelings.

Coach finished speaking. Rich looked around to see how his words had gone over. There was general agreement amongst the guys. No one wanted a repeat of the last time they played. Whether they put the effort into practice, however, remained to be seen.

Coach and the assistants went into the office to discuss their respective preparations. Absent the presence of authority, the mood of the players lightened. They began to discuss non-soccer-related topics. Classes. The summer's activities. Rich hoped no one would pry into his trip to Iraq. A few of them knew about it, which meant everyone would know—if not now, then soon.

Instead, they began talking about girls. Which brought the discussion around to the three succubi at today's practice. To hear these guys talk about them, they were the hottest girls on campus. Rich would not have gone that far, although even he had to admit they had been a bit dishy.

"And how about that brunette?"

"Oh, man, I know."

Rich allowed the conversation to get his attention. He heard Joey inform the others, "That brunette was all over Rich." He looked over and caught Rich's gaze. "Wasn't she, buddy?"

Rich shrugged. "I suppose." But he had to fight not to break into a proud grin. It was a rather pleasant feeling, this camaraderie. He could see why it appealed to so many men. It was all a matter of respect. He was finding out that self-esteem stemmed in large part from the esteem of others. He had their respect, and more than just that. He now had their envy. It was probably the first time he had ever felt it from straight men, and it felt better than he expected.

But Joey was chuckling now. "What a waste," he said, and slapped Rich on the shoulder. The other guys giggled, too. Rich clenched his teeth and forced himself into a pathetic smile. They were laughing at his expense without realizing that it was hurting his feelings. He was glad when the conversation broke up and no one was watching him any longer. His smile changed to a grimace. *No, this is not me. I will not let this bother me.* This particular kinship with his teammates would have been nice, but he reminded himself that it had always been just an illusion.

"Rich, may I see you in my office?"

He looked up to see Coach Schneider calling him in. He nodded, then noticed several of his teammates looking back and forth between him and the player who was just coming out of the office. It was Justin.

Rich's heart sank. He read the expressions of the others, then realized himself what was coming. The kid had looked good, of course, but Rich thought he had played well enough himself to keep his job. Now he looked at it from a different perspective. This was his last year. Whatever foundation the coach was building for the future, he would not be a part of it. Justin might not be as good right now, but all he needed was experience to develop. And playing time was the best experience. It made sense for Rich to give up playing time to the younger keeper. The question was how much.

He knocked on the frame of the coach's open door. "You wanted to see me?"

Coach looked up. He let out a deep breath. "Yes. Come in. Close the door. Have a seat." He leaned back in his chair and crossed his arms. He seemed to be studying the player in front of him. Then he exhaled deeply, and his eyes looked away. "Rich, this is a little awkward."

Rich had never seen the man like this. Coach was a straight-shooter who never got flustered. He was not exactly flustered now, but there was definitely something off about his behavior. Rich actually felt a little spark of satisfaction that the coach cared enough about him to feel awkward about this moment. He instinctively tried to make things easier for the man. "It's all right, Coach. You can say it."

Coach Schneider took a deep breath. "Are you juicing, son?"

Well, this is...unexpected. "Am I juicing?"

"Just answer yes or no. I'll find out either way, so just give me the truth."

Rich was still struggling to catch up. He opened his mouth to say something, then realized that stammering would only make it seem like he was hiding something. So he took a moment to collect his thoughts. "Coach, I am not juicing. Emphasis on not." He thought of a way to explain things without lying or sounding like a madman. "I...focused on my conditioning this summer."

"I see..." The man still looked skeptical. "Well, then, how would you feel about taking a piss test?"

"No problem," Rich responded without hesitation.

At that, the invisible pressure seemed to lift off Coach Schneider's shoulders. He smiled for the first time. "Thank God. You have no idea how relieved I am."

Rich hesitated. "So...I am not being benched?"

"Benched? Good Lord, no." The coach seemed amused. "Did you pay attention to how you played today? I don't think you allowed a single goal during the whole practice. If you play that way during the games, we could surprise a few folks this year." He paused in reflection. "Hell, the school might even extend my contract," he snorted.

Then Rich did something he seldom did, and never with the team. He laughed.

A few weeks had passed since The Scare, and his nerves had slowly returned to normal. Of course, normal for Iraq was something quite a bit different from normal in Maryland. Just because The Scare was no longer looming ominously over everything, that did not mean it ever left his mind completely. But Halfus was also aware of an upside. He had never lived so in the present as he did now. He found himself appreciating all the little things far more than ever. Every moment was precious. Each day was a new day, a brighter day, with gradually growing hope.

He lifted his left arm, then rotated it in slow, tight circles. It moved remarkably well, all things considered. He had been forcing himself to engage in a little light stretching once each afternoon, after his blood began flowing and his muscles loosened up. Each session brought a little more range of motion, and a little less discomfort. He felt confident that he was healing nicely.

"Halfus!"

He watched Amelia run in and hop on the bed. She immediately sat up on her knees and held her hands out in front of her, palms facing him.

A few days ago she had looked in while he was going through his stretches, moving his arms in random motions. She had watched with curiosity, so he motioned her into the room and tried to communicate exactly what he was doing. She had not seemed to understand, so he dispensed with the effort. Instead, he made a game of it, getting her involved. He thought of it as pattycake, although it was really only a bastardized version of the children's game. Or so he assumed. He had never learned to play it as a little boy. Why would he? Growing up, he certainly never thought he would find himself in this situation. So he simply followed the movements he could visualize from his memory, and made up the rest.

The two of them sat cross-legged on top of the cot, clapping their hands every which way in no particular order. She laughed happily all the while, and he contented himself that this was actually good practice for both his muscles and his hand-eye coordination. It reminded him of jumping rope during his boxing workouts. One could derive all sorts of benefits from simple everyday playing around, if he applied himself hard enough.

Oftentimes, he and Amelia would be joined by Mahmoud. Halfus hoped it would happen again now. In recent weeks, he had been spending a lot of time with the boy, trying to improve his Arabic. Unlike the recovery of his body, learning the language was not going well. Halfus was a bit confounded by the setback, considering that studying languages was one of his specialties. He had never struggled with Ancient Sumerian and Akkadian the way he did with modern Arabic. It seemed that he had learned more in the week before his accident than he had in all the time since.

But this afternoon, he and Amelia were joined by someone other than Mahmoud. Ammar entered the room bearing his usual gruff countenance. He looked once at Amelia, who wordlessly hopped off the bed and ran away, still giggling from their game. The two men watched her go, feeling a similar appreciation for her gaiety in the midst of a war zone.

Then Ammar faced Halfus. He nodded at the arm, which Halfus was back to stretching. "How is it?"

"Good. The leg, too. I can move around quite a bit better." Halfus almost added something else. *I could walk out of here, as soon as you kick me out.* He thought of it as a joke, but left it unspoken. He was afraid Ammar would take him up on the offer.

The man nodded again. "Good. That is better for all of us." He seemed to be speaking more to himself than to Halfus. Then he caught himself and their eyes met. "My family would like you to join us for dinner this evening. Do you think you're up for it?"

Halfus was so pleased that he almost laughed. He had been waiting for this. Or perhaps more hoping than waiting. He had been healthy enough to join them long before now, but he understood why they kept him inside this stodgy little room. The more he left it, the more likely he was to be seen by anyone approaching. And the more that Ammar's family got used to his moving around, the more they would let their guard down. In fact, Halfus had actually resigned himself to staying inside the room until the very day that Ammar deemed him fit enough to leave. So the invitation came as a pleasant surprise.

Then Halfus hesitated a moment. This offer could very well be a test. If he accepted, he might be signaling to the man that he was ready to go.

It did not matter. One way or another, he was ready to get on with his life. Whatever remained of it. And the temptation to be treated as a human again by this family to whom he owed so much was too much to pass up. "Of course. I would be honored."

Ammar nodded yet again. It seemed to be his standard response to everything. He turned his back and took a step toward the exit. Then he stopped. "I'm sorry for saying I hate you, Halfus."

He was gone before Halfus could reply.

The woman seldom spoke. When she did it was only to bark commands at her two children. Yet her eyes were friendly, her countenance soft and pleasant, and even those commands conveyed the warmth she felt for her family. Halfus wished he had thought to ask her name earlier. He did not want to do so now that he was in her presence.

He thanked her as she served a portion of rice to him. He was unaware of their customs, so he said little and tried to follow his host's behavior as much as possible, not wanting to offend her. He was similarly unsure how much she understood of what he said. He had given up on Arabic entirely. Even the few words Mahmoud had managed to teach him sounded painfully inarticulate to his own ear.

In the same vein, he wondered how much she was listening to his conversation with Ammar. In this, also, Halfus did not want to be impolite. So he allowed Ammar to dictate the conversation, which in the early going comprised only pleasantries and descriptions of the food. Halfus had never really regained his appetite since his fall, so he limited himself to a few bites of every item. There was rice infused with an unknown but savory spice, fresh pita bread, a soft cheese, and two meat dishes—both of which he assumed to be goat, flavored in different sauces. One was mild and one spicy. The latter was actually hard for him to keep down, which was surprising. He had never really gone out of his way to eat spicy dishes, but neither had he avoided them. He did not remember ever getting an upset stomach from them such as he was now.

Discomfort aside, Halfus genuinely enjoyed everything he tasted. So he felt no qualms about praising each dish, directing his words to Ammar but hoping they would be understood by the woman of the house. Periodically, he watched her from the corner of his eye to gauge her reaction, not only to his compliments but to some of the more serious topics that came up as the conversation grew heavier.

Mahmoud ate with the men, although he spoke very little for a change. Amelia did not eat with them. She sat off to the side of the main room, her attention divided between her mother's cooking and the discourse of the men.

Halfway through the meal, Ammar began filling Halfus in on current events. It was not good news. In fact, it was so bad that Halfus had difficulty believing it. What had been either an insurgency, a civil war, or both—depending on one's definitions—was moving into a new phase. Battle lines were beginning to stabilize, which was discouraging. The longer the rebellious state remained in existence, the more people would come to accept that existence. It was now calling itself an Islamic state, which he also interpreted as a bad sign. The way he understood it, this nascent Islamic state spoke about seizing Baghdad for its own. But that was just talk. The claim was merely a useful rhetorical and recruiting device. No one inside the state or out genuinely expected it to happen. And as long as it did not seriously threaten to topple the legitimate government of Iraq, it would be easier for the United States to treat the aspirant state as a mere nuisance.

Halfus had allowed himself to entertain a lingering hope that if word was somehow given to the American embassy in Baghdad, a rescue effort would be forthcoming. That had been the easiest way to view his recovery—just get better, and salvation would come shortly thereafter. He now allowed that hope to be extinguished. It seemed America was already fighting against the enemy with as much earnestness as was politically viable, and even so was making no headway. The northern region of Iraq in which he found himself was squarely behind enemy lines. If they could not even bomb the rebels into submission, there was little chance that they would drive in and extract him.

Moreover, Halfus was now apparently a bit of an embarrassment for the Americans. They would benefit more from his continued death than his sudden rebirth. This was the most depressing of all the news Ammar dumped on him like some malevolent television anchor.

Either the rebels needed to be pushed back on the battlefield, or Halfus needed to escape on his own. The former did not seem likely to happen for the foreseeable future. Which left him with...

"Halfus, I am sorry to say this. You need to go."

Halfus pulled away from his rush of thoughts to meet Ammar's eye. Then it was his turn to nod. This was sudden, but thankfully he was already coming to the same conclusion. "I know. Will you allow me a few more days to prepare?" He felt guilty asking anything further from this man. He hoped it would sound like a reasonable request, because the thought of heading out was still a little overwhelming. He needed time to ready himself, psychologically as much as materially.

To his relief, Ammar smiled. "I will do you one better than that. I will help you escape."

Heaven. I'm in heaven. Ernie still felt guilty, but it had transformed into guilt at how wonderfully terrific things were going. It seemed as though all the karma that he had stockpiled throughout his life had finally paid off at once.

This was how people were supposed to feel, he believed. He was never tired and seldom hungry, his body functioning at peak efficiency. His hopes were high, his spirits soaring. He felt sorry for those who had never tasted these waters.

It felt good to be on campus and back in the swing of things. He had not thought about classes and schoolwork for months. He still was not exactly focused on them, but that would come in time, he had no doubt. He always started semesters half-heartedly. In any case, it was the routine that felt so comforting. As a graduate student, he felt like a big man on campus. Someone to be respected. He walked with an air of self-importance, breaking his regal countenance only to smile at the pretty coeds he passed. They generally smiled back. It made him feel good about himself.

Not that he really needed to worry about that. Things were going quite well with Curlicue. Better and better with each passing day, it seemed. Ever since Matt's funeral they had gotten much closer. He could feel it, and he imagined she could, too. Before then he had sensed a certain hesitation to her behavior, as though she wanted to maintain a slight distance between them. Not ready to give her all. He did not blame her, considering how quickly everything was happening. Nor did he press her, believing it was far better for her to move at her own pace. After Matt's accident, however, she had drawn closer to him than ever. And he was glad that he could be there for her. Being there for one another was beginning to be a habit.

For a few days, things had been tense. She was grieving and confused. There seemed times when she wanted to tell him something, but held back. She spent a lot of time at her mother's apartment, enough so that Ernie had briefly worried she was pulling back away from him. But when he tried to address the topic, she simply explained that her mother's condition was worsening. Ernie assumed the woman was dying. He flinched away from the prospect of suffering through it, but he had offered to go over with her if she wanted his help. And he had concealed his relief when she turned down the offer.

But her mother had not died. Now she was apparently feeling better than she had in months, and Wendy's own outlook improved proportionately. She began to spend less time at her mother's and more with him. And he made sure she enjoyed it. He had taken to spending more nights over at her place, which was something he had rarely done with other girls he dated. He used to feel a little uncomfortable being where they felt most comfortable. Looking back, he realized that was a flaw in his own personality, and he was glad to have gotten past it. For her part, Wendy had certainly made him feel welcome.

Overall, Ernie could not remember seeing her as happy as she had been in recent weeks. It made him feel good to believe he was having a positive effect on her.

They had not made firm plans for the evening, so he decided to have a home-cooked meal ready for her when she came home from work. He glanced at the time. Just after three in the afternoon. He could head home, put on something a little more swank, swing by the grocery store, and let himself into her place before she got back.

"Hey, Ernie!" He looked up to see Kevin and Tracy heading his way. It was the petite firecracker who had called out to him, and now she was waving. He waved back and waited for them.

He and Kevin exchanged quick greetings before Tracy gave him a great big hug. The last time he had seen them was at the funeral, where they had not had much time or inclination for meaningful conversation. Now that they could, he found himself wondering what he could say if they asked about Iraq. No doubt they knew the basics already. He rather hoped they did not try to delve any deeper.

Fortunately, Kevin had other obligations and hurriedly excused himself after a few words. "See you, babe," he said to Tracy. She gave him a kiss and watched him go.

Then she turned back to Ernie. "So...you and Wendy, eh?" Her smile was contagious, and Ernie found himself grinning along with her. He hoped it did not look quite as scandalous as it felt. Sure enough, Tracy began to pry into his personal life. He replied with vagaries and deflections. All the while, his mind operated on two levels, as it always had. He was good at communicating on autopilot while his brain remained one step ahead, planning out where he wanted to lead the discussion. He was relieved that it still could function this way when called upon, despite the worrying little defects that had been creeping in as of late.

Tracy looked great, he noticed. Better than he had ever seen her. Ernie began to appreciate just how lucky a man Kevin truly was. She was grinning at Ernie mischievously while they walked toward the parking lot. At first, he had assumed that frisky expression was because she knew she was prying into things she should not. Now, he was no longer sure. They had stopped talking about Wendy and Kevin. Now they were talking about themselves, complimenting one another on their looks. Radiant, in her case. Dashing, in his. And still she maintained that impish grin, as though delighting in walking a line. He wondered exactly where her line was.

Then, as though reading his thoughts, Tracy turned the conversation around. "Where is Wendy keeping herself these days, anyway? I haven't seen her in forever."

"She's very busy with her new job." He tried not to let disappointment creep into his voice. He had been rather enjoying the other train of thought.

"Oh, that's right. I forgot. Does she like it?"

"He does. I mean, she does. A lot." He forced himself to focus on what he was saying. Just when he believed his mind was as nimble as ever, it worked to frustrate him. "She's still finding her niche. But it looks like they are trusting her with more and more responsibilities." This last word he had to pronounce slowly and deliberately.

Tracy seemed not to notice. "That's good. She'll do great. She was made for a life of politics. You might find yourself married to a senator."

He nodded silently, only half listening. He was getting irritated at himself again.

"Anyway, the four of us should double-date some time," she suggested. "When Wendy can find the time, of course."

Impulsively, Ernie gave it another shot. "Sure should. Or if that doesn't work out, the two of us should hang out." He watched her eyes.

Tracy seemed a little surprised, then recovered. She laughed. "You're incorrigible, Ernie. You never change."

Apparently, I do. I'm changing in all sorts of ways.

He walked Tracy to her car, parked in the lot across campus from his own. They hugged goodbye and he set out back the way they had come. He no longer had time to do everything he wanted before dinner, but Wendy would not complain if the meal was not quite ready as soon as she walked in the door. As he crossed the campus again, he began to whistle to keep himself distracted. It was an exercise in futility.

Why did I do that? It was a dumb question. He knew perfectly well why he had done it. Tracy was an extremely attractive girl. Today more so than usual. Just the thought of spending time alone with her —hanging out, as he had put it—sent a thrill through him that was alarming in its potency. But not altogether unpleasant. He had absolutely no reason to feel any compulsion. Wendy was already more than fulfilling his desires. From a physical standpoint, they were still in the honeymoon stage of their relationship. He knew from past experience that it would fade in time, but it had not done so yet. If anything, his sex drive was stronger than ever. He wondered if that could be another one of these weird side effects of the illness. He seemed to find more of them with each passing day.

He was not terribly worried about Tracy. She was a free spirit, and would assume he was just paying back some of her own teasing. If it ever came up again, he would pass it off as exactly that. Ernie had absolutely no interest in doing anything to hurt Wendy, or jeopardize his relationship with her. He already had everything he could ask for.

Wendy called it paradise health. Whatever it was, it felt amazing. He hoped this feeling would last the rest of his life.

The many voices of campus swirled around him, blending into a meaningless medley. Then, rising from the din, one sounded familiar. He looked around, searching for the source. It was a male voice, not one he instantly recognized, but one he felt that he should.

He saw the source of the voice, not by recognizing the guy but by the stunning girl with him. Tempest. The one doing the talking was Donny. They had been on the caving trip a few months ago. The other two from that trip—James and Christine, if Ernie remembered correctly—were nowhere to be seen. Instead, Donny had a small audience of five people Ernie did not know listening intently as he told a joke.

"So this guy is spending his first night in prison. He hears someone in one of the other cells yell out, 'Eighteen!' A few seconds later everyone laughs. Then someone else yells out, 'Forty-three!' And a few seconds later everyone laughs. So he asks his cellmate what that's all about. The man says they have a jokebook that's been passed around so many times, they have all the jokes memorized. So instead of saying the whole joke, they just yell out the page number.

"So this guy gets his hands on the jokebook. He finds one he likes, and he yells out the page number. 'Thirty-six!' No one laughs, so he looks at his cellmate again. 'I thought you said I could just yell the page number,' he asks. His cellmate shrugs and says, 'Some people just can't tell a joke.'"

Ernie was staring at Tempest. The white streak in her hair was enthralling. So were her features, and her curves. Then she looked over and saw him. He did not look away, nor did she. He waited a few seconds, then nonchalantly turned away and walked toward the nearest building, a classroom hall he had never been in. He moved slowly, keeping track of her from the corner of his eye. He watched her say something to Donny. Excusing herself. She walked away from the group, in Ernie's direction. He grinned, rounded the corner of the old brick building where they would not be seen by the others, and waited.

Ernie was even farther behind schedule when he reached his car. He still felt good about himself. It was possibly the toughest thing he had ever done, but Ernie had stopped at getting her number. There had been sparks between them, and he felt that his own reticence had only intensified them. For him and for her. She clearly was not used to guys holding back, the way he had done, and had practically thrown herself at him. If suggesting coffee some time was the same as throwing herself.

She had told him to call her, but he had no intention of following through. He had been appropriately insincere about that. He did not even know why he had bothered to enter her number into his phone. But that was as far as he would take it.

He congratulated himself on resisting temptation. It was just a part of his former life creeping back in, but he was a changed man now, too disciplined to make such a foolish mistake. What had just happened simply meant his relationship was strong. He had been worried that his mind was not entirely his own, but this only proved that it was not as bad as he thought.

He was really looking forward to dinner, and resuming his perfect life.

His phone rang as he pulled out of the parking lot. He pulled it from his pocket, glanced at it, and smiled. He answered. "Hey there, Curlicue. I was just thinking about you."

"That's sweet, Easy." He liked that she had taken to calling him by his nickname, now that he had one for her. "What are you up to?" she asked.

"I'm on my way to the store. I thought I would pick up a few things, make my way over to your kitchen, and cook you a delicious dinner."

"Aw, shucks. That's why I'm calling. I have to work late."

"Oh, no," he said. He was surprised at how strongly he felt the disappointment. "Is everything all right?"

"Yeah. Bob...Representative King just asked me to work late. He didn't give me much notice, so I couldn't call you sooner to tell you."

"That's all right. We'll catch up later. I'm glad he's showing more trust in you."

"Yeah. Me, too. So you forgive me?"

"Of course. You can make it up to me this weekend. Do we have anything planned? Maybe we can take a little trip."

"We can't leave. Rich's first game is this weekend, silly."

Well, so much for that. "That's right, I forgot." He allowed more disappointment to creep into his voice.

She picked up on it, as he had hoped. "We'll do it next weekend, okay?"

"Deal." He smiled to himself. "I should go. I shouldn't be on the phone while I'm driving."

As soon as he said it, he wished he had not. There was silence on the other end. He immediately apologized. "I'm sho shorry. I...forgot."

"It's okay." Her voice sounded very faint.

"Call me tonight, okay?"

"Okay." She hung up. He dropped the phone onto the passenger seat.

God...damn it. He felt lousy. She had been through so much. He never, ever wanted to do anything to hurt her. He made a vow to himself. She made him a better person. He needed to be better. He *wanted* to be better. For his own sake as much as hers.

He pulled up to one of McGahey's four stoplights. All four of them stretched along Main Street, where everything from the supermarket to the church and town hall were located. During the brief interlude he looked down at his phone. He contorted his lips in consideration. Then he picked it up. He thumbed through the contacts list until he got to Tempest. Then he thumbed a button.

He pushed himself up from the seat so he could slip the phone back into his pocket. A horn sounded behind him. He looked up at a green light, and pulled forward. He felt better now that her number was deleted.

Ben had mixed feelings about being back on campus. Part of him really resented the school, but he still had associates and students whom he looked forward to seeing. Besides, he was not going to the building where he had worked for these past eight years, and which now haunted his spirits.

He paid the price of admission and wandered along the base of the stands, looking for any familiar faces. The game was not due to start for another twenty minutes, so most of the seats remained empty. He saw no one he particularly wanted to sit beside, so he found a seat halfway up where he could keep an eye out for Brenda and Trevor. They should be there soon.

He and Brenda had been spending more time together since the start of his suspension. There was something ironic about that, considering that their offices had been just down the hall from each other. After taking him home when he got sick, she had dutifully called or checked in on him every day until he was better. After that her attendance had simply continued in a different form. Sometimes they met for coffee, sometimes for lunch, and twice they had even had dinner together. They were becoming friends again, just like old times. He no longer felt the pride of association, and he understood why. Everyone knew she belonged to another man, so no one was jealous of Ben. He had no sense of pride left anyway, along with no peers from which to derive it. He could simply enjoy her company, and that was good enough for him.

All the same, he was pleased that Trevor was finally coming along. So far it had only been Ben and Brenda every time they met, although she continuously talked about the three of them spending time together. She had repeatedly told Ben that she believed he and Trevor would hit it off. Ben had his doubts, but he intended to give it his best shot. Yet it never seemed to happen. There was always some reason why her fiancé could not make it. Ben hoped that the man had not already formed a negative opinion of him, but it certainly seemed likely.

Instead of Brenda and Trevor, Ben caught sight of another couple. It was Wendy and Ernie. He stood and waved to them. They waved back, and he was pleased to see them coming his way. For weeks now he had felt as though Wendy resented him for the way he got them out of Iraq. He believed that he had had no choice, but he was not about to try to explain it to her or anyone else. They had all been through enough. He wanted to move on, and he could only hope they felt the same way.

Thus he was delighted when she hugged him. He shook Ernie's hand as they all stumbled through greetings that would have seemed inane if they were not so heartfelt. Clearly, the time and trouble together in Iraq had brought them all closer together. Ben and Rich had felt a stronger bond of friendship. Now they talked or emailed almost every day. For Ernie and Wendy, it had led to more than friendship. They looked happy together. At least something good had come out of that trip. For himself, Ben was just happy to share in a part of it.

"How is your mother doing?" he asked Wendy. The last he had heard the woman was feeling better, so he watched Wendy's smile intently, hoping to see it remain. To his great relief, it only got broader.

"She's so much better," Wendy answered. The relief was evident in her words, her face, and her body language. Somehow she had gotten past Halfus' death and that of her other friend, but Ben did not want to imagine what would happen if her mother died as well.

"Curlicue, I'd like to sit up a bit higher," Ernie said to Wendy. He seemed to be asking permission. She nodded, then looked at Ben.

"Doc, do you mind?"

"Not at all." He understood completely. He really did not want to be sitting next to two pairs of lovebirds all game, anyway. "I have some friends coming," he added, so she need not feel guilty.

"We'll talk again before the game's over, okay?"

"All right."

He watched them ascend for a moment. He really was pleased to see her doing so well. He had thought about her a lot since their return, so he was pleased to discover that he need not have worried.

"Benji!"

Only one person called him that. He looked around until he saw Brenda working her way up the stands. The crowd was getting larger, and he had not been looking for her, so it was a good thing she saw him.

It was not until she turned in at his row that he noticed she was alone. He waited for her usual hug before asking, "Where's Trevor?"

"He couldn't make it. He had to go out of town."

Ben frowned. "This was supposed to be the time—"

"I know," she said. "Can we just enjoy the game?"

She looked a little annoyed, so he decided to drop it. He much preferred to have a happy companion than an angry one. They took their seats.

The players were taking the field. A few fans stood up and started to cheer. Brenda stood up and joined them. She looked down at Ben while she clapped. "Come on, Benji. Show some spirit."

"I will...when our team comes out."

Brenda snorted, stopped clapping, sat down, and covered her face. "How embarrassing," she said. But she was always the sort of person who could laugh at herself, and did so now.

A horn sounded, and the Catoctin squad ran onto their half of the field. "Now it's safe," he quipped. They stood up and cheered together this time. "You see the player wearing number seven?" he asked. "That's Rich. He's one of my best students." *Was one of my best students,* Ben corrected himself.

"Oh, he looks good," Brenda said, watching as the players took their positions. "Does he score a lot?"

"Not really," Ben replied, unsure just how thick to lay it on. He elected to go with factual, without sarcasm. "He's a goalkeeper. His job is to stop the other team from scoring. He does not shoot on his own."

They sat down, and Brenda covered her face again. "I am just covering myself in glory today, am I not?"

"Not really," he said, and they laughed together.

The teams kicked off. "Do you know much about soccer?" she asked him.

"Quite a lot, actually. I used to love watching. And playing, when I was at uni in England. Sadly, I haven't had much time for it recently." *Until now.*

She nodded, her eyes focused on the action unfolding. He appreciated that she made no references to his job or suspension. He just wanted to enjoy the game without worrying about anything else for a change.

They watched Bowie State get an early scoring opportunity. Ben knew that Rich's boyfriend played for this team, and he quickly identified him as one of the forwards. He made a beautiful pass to a streaking teammate who made a decent, but not spectacular shot on goal. Rich stopped it easily.

"So teach me," said Brenda.

"Excuse me?"

She took her eyes off the field to look at him. "Teach me," she repeated.

He thought about it. He did not see how it would diminish his enjoyment of the game, so he saw no reason to refuse. "All right."

He went over the basics, referencing the action on the field as much as possible. He explained the positions and basic strategies, the subtle ways that coaches placed a focus on offense or defense. As he explained, he noted with interest that both teams today crept a man or two forward as much as possible, indicating an offensive strategy. This came as a surprise. Rich had led him to believe that Catoctin was a defensively oriented team. Ben hoped the change of plans did not backfire, causing Rich to look bad. Casual viewers tended to blame goals on the goalkeeper, but Ben knew that it was usually a mistake by the fullbacks or defensive midfielders that allowed an unchallenged shot.

He enjoyed explaining things. It was a large part of why he became a professor in the first place. It was particularly enjoyable when he was speaking to a receptive audience, and Brenda seemed to soak up his every word. She was not only extremely intelligent, but also a good listener. This last actually took him a little by surprise. He had never noticed that about her before.

Then he noticed something else. She was looking at him with a strange, unreadable expression. "What is it?" he asked.

She gave a funny smile and looked back at the game. "Oh, nothing."

They watched another scoring opportunity by Bowie State. This time Tre'Andre himself broke into the clear and delivered a powerful shot. Ben's heart skipped a beat, and then he breathed deeply when Rich made a fantastic save. *Oh, thank goodness.*

It was nearly halftime already, and the game was still scoreless. The longer that went on, the more the excitement would mount. This was Ben's favorite aspect of soccer. He understood that many people do not like the sport because of the low scores, but that was precisely the reason he did like it so much. In close games, not only every score but every scoring *attempt* became magnified in

significance. In no other sport he could think of was an almost-score
as thrilling as in soccer. It forced a fan to pay attention to more than
just the shooting, because the build-ups were just as important.
Looking around, he saw a lot of riveted faces amongst the fans. They
were feeling it, too. That boded well for an exciting—and loud—
second half.

Brenda slapped her arm. "Ow! Damn mosquitoes," she muttered.
Then she began rubbing the spot. "They're eating me alive out here."

"Tell me about it," he said. "I've been smacking them all afternoon."
He did not really mind, however. His attention was almost solely
focused on the game, so he had barely even noticed the pests. But he
had long since learned it was better to sympathize with a woman than
to downplay her complaints.

Bowie State made one more run of it just before the halftime
whistle. It amounted to nothing, and the two teams ran to the
sidelines with vastly different body language. Bowie State was
favored, yet they had nothing to show for their relentless pressure.
Catoctin, on the other hand, had learned that they could keep pace
with their opponents. Ben noted with fascination how two teams
could react to a tie score in such vastly different ways.

Time seemed to move faster than normal in the second half. Ben
looked at the scoreboard every two or three minutes, only to see that
eight or ten had transpired. The game seemed deadlocked, destined to
end in a scoreless draw. While not exactly ideal, it would be a good
result for Catoctin. As the heavy underdogs, a draw would look much
better for them than for their opponents.

Both teams were clearly getting tired, and the quick attacking
bursts of the first half seemed a thing of the distant past.

Then Catoctin caught a lucky break. A sloppy pass in the midfield
was intercepted, leading to a breakaway for one of their players. Ben
let his hopes rise. He knew that ninety-minute games could turn in a
few short seconds just like this. A defender raced back, one step
behind the attacker, and made a sliding attempt at the ball. Both

players went down, a whistle blew, and just like that Catoctin gained a penalty kick.

Penalty kicks were a tremendous scoring opportunity, but they were far from a sure thing, and Ben had no idea how good the player taking the shot really was. If he had been as good as Rich's boyfriend, it never would have come down to this kick. He would already have scored a clean goal.

"Explain what's happening," Brenda requested.

Not taking his eyes off the field, Ben leaned over toward her. "This is a penalty kick. The player taking the shot runs up and kicks it once at the goal. No one but he and the goalkeeper can move until he does. It's just he and the keeper, unless it ricochets somewhere. In that case, it will be a mad scramble.

"But the thing about a penalty kick is this. A well-placed shot cannot be stopped by even the best goalkeepers. There is too much distance to cover to block a solid kick into the corners. But most shooters don't want to risk it, because there is a fine line between a perfect shot and missing the goal entirely. The only thing worse than having a penalty kick saved by the keeper is having it miss because you shot wide or over the crossbar."

"You said the goalkeeper can move? He looks like he's dancing."

"Yes. There is a certain amount of guessing going on. If the shooter is planning on shooting right, he wants the keeper to guess left. If he thinks the keeper is going right, he might change his mind at the last second, and shoot left. Both guys want to confuse the other.

"Here we go." He took a deep breath. "This is huge," he added needlessly.

The shooter faked left and shot right. The goalkeeper guessed wrong, and the ball hit the back of the net.

Catoctin's players went nuts, while Bowie State's looked deflated. A lot of them sagged with hands on hips, and a few looked around in disbelief. Ben looked at Rich, and saw him hugging his two fullbacks. That was good to see.

The fans were going nuts, as well. The cheering and clapping had escalated dramatically. Beside him, Brenda jumped up and down. She looked at him. "You aren't celebrating," she playfully accused.

"I'm too nervous," he replied, although he managed a weak laugh.

"Why? Didn't we just win?"

"There's still seven minutes left. In soccer time, that's like a month. They're going to go all out against Rich now."

She shook her head at him. But she also stopped clapping and sat down beside him.

Ben was correct. A lot did happen in seven minutes, and they did go all out against Rich. Naturally, Catoctin went into a defensive formation, clogging the passing lanes and getting feet in the way of any potential shots simply by virtue of having so many bodies in a compacted area. It was sound planning, but had a drawback. Without any genuine offensive threat of their own, Catoctin could not burn any time off the clock with the ball on the other side of the field. Instead, there was nonstop pressure on their own end. To make matters worse, Bowie State pulled their goalkeeper up to the midfield stripe where he could act as an additional attacker.

Whereas the minutes had previously flown by, they now seemed to move agonizingly slowly. It was difficult to conceive of how few precious seconds a sustained attack consumed. Ben watched the ball being passed between three or four attackers, then blocked, and finally cleared toward the other side of the field where it was run down by the opposing goalkeeper, who in turn pushed it back up toward Catoctin's goal. Ben was horrified to see that the entire sequence had used less than thirty seconds of clock. Catoctin might conceivably face the same thing six or seven more times before the game was over.

It happened only twice more before Ben's biggest concern materialized. There were so many bodies crowding the box that collisions naturally occurred. One shot ricocheted off a defender and led to a free-for-all, during which an attacker and defender went down together. Ben watched in mounting dread as the referee signaled a defensive foul. Bowie State was awarded a penalty kick of their own. It would be their best chance to equalize the score.

Ben did not need to explain anything to Brenda. She understood both the call and the circumstances. She looked at Ben's face and tried to reassure him. "Hey, our boy will stop it." She shook his knee and showed her winningest smile. Ben forced a smile in return, but he could only wish that he was as confident. Rich had played a good game so far, but it would be All-Star Tre'Andre taking the shot. He was the sort of player who risked those perfect penalty kicks, because he made them.

They lined up for the kick. The fans stood in anticipation, and a hush rolled over the field and the stands. Tre'Andre placed the ball and took a few steps back. Rich did not dance around like his counterpart. He swayed ever-so-slightly back and forth on his heels, knees bent in a crouch, hands flexing. Tre'Andre ran forward and struck the ball. It was a perfect kick, yet Rich stopped it anyway. His stretching hand pushed it wide of the goal by a matter of inches.

It took Ben a moment to let it sink in. He had gotten so used to unhappy endings that this almost felt wrong. But the cheering of the crowd and the reactions of the players told him otherwise. Brenda was jumping and shouting and squeezing his arm. He allowed himself a few whoops of pleasure, pumping his other arm into the air triumphantly. She watched him whoop and started laughing. She moved closer and hugged him. Then she looked up and kissed him.

Ben released his half of the hug and stepped back. She smiled at him once, then went back to shouting and clapping. He could not take his eyes off her, waiting for her to look at him again.

She did. "Is it over now?"

He shook his head. "No. There's a corner kick. And another minute of regulation. And then probably a few more minutes of extra time." *A corner kick. Oh, dear.* He forced himself to focus on the game, realizing that the team was not out of the woods just yet. He watched Rich demonstrably positioning his defenders for the set play. The ball came in, and Rich leapt high to punch it away with a fist. The game turned into another chaotic free-for-all. But now even Ben felt confident that they would win. It was a good feeling.

The fans remained standing and cheering for the final few

minutes. Ben stood with them, continuing to voice his support for Catoctin's victory. But his thoughts were now even more helplessly confused than before.

As the final whistle blew, Rich thought of Tre'Andre. They had spoken briefly before the game, and he knew his boyfriend was feeling the pressure of expectations. It was something Rich had never seen in the confident young man before, and he really had not known what to say. Tre'Andre believed he had a legitimate shot at the pros, but every game would now be under scrutiny. That made it harder to play with the same carefree swagger that had carried him to this point.

And now this amazing ending had to be just as demoralizing to the Bowie State players as it was exhilarating for Catoctin's. Rich wanted to find him through the chaotic tumult, to congratulate him on a game well played, to shake his hand if he was all right or comfort him if not. But there were too many people in the way, and it seemed they were all intent on getting in Rich's way.

What was he thinking? Of course they were. He realized with no small rush of pleasure that he was the hero of the game. At first he had expected William to get the attention, since he had scored what turned out to be the winning goal. But of course that had since been overshadowed by Rich's save. And not just the one. He swelled with pride as he allowed himself to appreciate just how dominant he had been all game.

His fullbacks Joey and Marcus were the first to hug him, but not the last. More and more teammates joined them, forming an unwieldy mass that necessarily toppled over from its own ungainliness. And yet more teammates continued to pile on. Rich was at the bottom, but there was no fear of being crushed. He felt nothing but joy. He had never imagined respect on a visceral level like this. *I could get used to this.*

Coach Schneider had a few nice things to say once they unpiled and recomposed something approximating a disciplined soccer squad.

Rich was relieved that the coach did not single out him or any other player. This was a team win, and it was better that they all looked at it that way.

Not everyone seemed to think so, however. Rich and William were walking together toward the locker rooms when Joey called out to him. Rich looked over and saw his teammate motioning him over. Rich excused himself to William. Then he saw the girls. Dani took one look at him, then ran over and practically jumped on him, as though she wanted to personally repeat the tackling he had received from his teammates.

Rich caught her and put her back on her feet, holding her shoulders at arm's length until he was certain she would not try it again. Her green eyes sparkled with life.

"You're the hero," she flat-out told him. "I had a feeling you would be."

"You did, did you?" He raised an eyebrow skeptically.

"You didn't call me," she said accusingly, changing the subject. She did not sound genuinely mad, however.

"No. About that..." he began.

Passers-by were now interfering with any attempt at communication. "Hey, Rich!" "Great game, brother." "Awesome save, bro." He smiled and accepted their praise, nodding or waving at the faces he recognized. Suddenly everyone seemed to be his friend.

He saw something else in the faces, not only of the passing fans but of his teammates as well. He knew he had their respect for his performance, but now there was more than that. They not only looked at him, but at him and the girl together. They were jealous. Rich was experiencing it again, even more strongly than before. This, too, felt good. It was also very confusing.

Coach Schneider walked by. "I need to see all you boys in the locker room," he told them. There was no harsh authority this time. It might have been a request. Their coach was not immune to the elation of the moment. Rich smiled at the notion.

He turned back to excuse himself from Dani. She and her friends were already gone. *Women,* thought Rich. He did not understand how some guys could like them so much. At least not without going crazy.

His teammates were bragging about the game, which was all right. But they were also putting down Bowie State and Tre'Andre, which was not. Rich had half a mind to castigate them. Then he reconsidered. This was simple, ordinary post-game macho nonsense. They meant nothing by it. He would let them have their fun. Besides, he was not in any hurry to jump off the pedestal on which they had placed him.

"Hey, Rich, are you gonna see Tre'Andre tonight?" Ethan asked.

Rich was not sure he liked where this was going. "Probably. Why?"

"Tell him we said, 'Good game,' that's all."

Well, that wasn't so bad. "All right, I'll tell her."

There were quite a few giggles and snickers before he even realized what he had said. They likely assumed he was making a joke. He opened his mouth to correct the record.

"Hey, Rich," Joey called out to him. "A few of us are going out to the *Bluff.* You want to come with?" Rich examined his expression for sincerity, and decided he was being genuine.

Rich was torn. He was a little surprised at how badly he wanted to go, but he still knew he had to find Tre'Andre. As far as Rich knew, his boyfriend was going back on the team bus with the rest of the players. That left Rich with little time remaining to find him.

"Thanksh anyway," he said. It was boisterously loud in the locker room, so he was not entirely certain he had really committed the error. "I need to shee Tre..." And then he stopped himself. This time he was certain.

"Speech! Speech!" A few of the guys started the chant, then more and more of them chimed in.

Suddenly, and for the first time in his life, Rich became very self-conscious of his speaking ability. Something was wrong, and although it did not exactly frighten him he still did not wish to draw attention to it. He gestured that he appreciated their sentiment, but he shook his head. Several of them continued chanting a while longer before realizing with disappointment that they were not going to get their storybook ending.

Rich waited impatiently for Coach to give them his meaningless parting words. They were nothing but tired clichés about how proud he was of them all. Then Rich ran outside to the parking lot, hoping to catch Tre'Andre. He looked for any Bowie State jerseys, but the only ones he saw were being worn by people who definitely were not players. He saw Catoctin's equipment manager, a pleasant Latino, chatting amicably with another student. Rich approached them. "Hello, Luis. Did you see Tre'Andre around here by any chance?"

"Yes, I did. He was looking for you, *amigo.*"

Rich heard the sound of a bus engine. He knew what it would be before he looked. The Bowie State team bus pulled out of the lot. Tre'Andre would certainly be on it. He had wanted to talk, and Rich had let him down.

He went back inside the locker room. Most of his teammates had cleared out already. Rich found his gym bag and retrieved his cell phone from the side pocket. There were no calls for him, so he would have do the initiating. He pressed a button. It rang four times and went to voice mail. He hung up and tried again. This time it went straight to voice mail without ringing. Rich put the phone back in the side pocket, scooped up the bag, and went back outside.

Most of the crowd was dispersing. But as luck would have it, one of his teammates was still lingering.

"Hey, Joey, does the offer still stand?"

"Hells, yeah. See you at ten?"

"All right. See you there."

"I think some members of my family have gotten attached to you." Ammar eyed Amelia, who was twirling a greasy bone between two fingers, paying no attention to the adults. "It will be hard on her, seeing you go."

"And I've gotten attached to all of your family," Halfus replied. *Even you, you gruff old bastard.* "Going will be hard on me, too. But it's better for everyone."

"Yes. It's better for everyone," Ammar agreed.

Ammar's wife Haifa handed Halfus a small plate with slices of spiced meat. He accepted and thanked her, as always. She nodded and smiled but said nothing, as always. She returned to the table and began stirring things into a wooden bowl. Halfus wondered what delectable dish she was preparing now. Amelia got up from her seat to go watch her mother. *That girl is destined to be a terrific chef,* he thought happily.

He decided that he would regret leaving, if only for the food. It put the primitive meals he had eaten at the expedition camp to shame. How foolish it had been for them to feed Mahmoud from their spartan stores.

Halfus had finally learned his hostess's name, but not whether she spoke English. He continued to watch her for any reaction to their conversations, and she continued to show none. She never revealed the slightest sign of disturbance or amusement, despite the fact that he had said a few terribly witty things in her vicinity. All the signs pointed one way, and yet he suspected that she understood more than she was letting on. He just had a sense that she spoke English perfectly, and was playing a tremendous joke on him.

During each meal he had taken with them, Halfus and Ammar were the only ones who did any appreciable talking. Mahmoud chimed in a few words here and there, but only when prompted by his father. Mother and daughter neither ate nor spoke on these occasions. Halfus felt a little odd having a two-person conversation despite the presence of three other people, but he knew very little of their customs and did not wish to judge. He saw the love and respect that Ammar's family felt for their husband and father, so clearly the man was doing something right.

In recent days, Halfus and Ammar spent the majority of their time planning out escape options. Halfus still believed the best alternative was to get to the Green Zone in Baghdad. From there, the U.S. embassy would take care of the rest, like it or not. The problem with that plan was that the front lines of the fighting were in the way. They would need to traverse the most heavily militarized part of Iraq to get there.

Ammar was in favor of heading east, north, or west. Basically, anywhere but Baghdad. To the east lived the Kurds, who were close allies of the Americans along with having the most success of any force currently fighting the new Islamic state. It was a shorter distance to travel, but again presented the obstacle of passing through a front of the war zone. Turkey lay to the north. There was fighting in that direction as well, but it was less intense than in other places. But Turkey presented an additional problem in that they were less actively opposed to the rebels. Ammar believed the Turks might very well block any entry into the country. He clearly did not trust them, and without any personal knowledge of the region Halfus had no reason to doubt his judgment. Finally, to the west lay Syria, where civil war continued to rage into its third year. Paradoxically, the fighting was least pronounced in that direction, at least until one crossed the border and encountered the disparate warring factions there. Some of those factions were ostensibly friendly to Americans, but the battle lines shifted so frequently it would be hard to know where those groups might be located at any given time. So they were all bad options, which is why Halfus and Ammar spent day after day in frustrating indecision.

No matter where he went, Halfus still had to worry about the reaction of the allied forces to his appearance. It was a difficult pill to swallow to hear that he was persona non grata even amongst the good guys. He was no thief, but he had been branded one. His death was generally perceived as his just desserts. To hear Ammar describe it, he had no friends left outside this poor house. Ernie could have clarified the matter, of course. Halfus had no choice but to laugh at the irony. His former friend was the last person who would want to help. If he got out of here, the two of them had a score to settle.

He was doing everything he could to make sure it came to that. For the past few weeks, whenever he was not planning with Ammar, Halfus was back to studying with Mahmoud. His Arabic was coming along painfully slowly, but at least he had picked up a few more words and expressions. The goal had initially been to be able to pass a cursory inspection, but they all knew now it would simply not be possible. He was progressing too slowly. He felt that he was letting them down. The only hope was that he would not need to speak at all during the escape.

"Hassan believes north is the best route," Ammar repeated for the third time in two hours.

This did nothing to endear Halfus to that option. He did not trust Hassan any farther than he could throw him. In Halfus' consciousness, the man would be forever associated with the first time Halfus had laid eyes on him. He had actually pointed at the house, leading Halfus to believe he was betraying them. Yet Ammar assured him it was a harmless gesture, that Hassan was a good man who had only been bluffing the soldiers. But Halfus relied a lot on his instincts. If that was a bluff, it was a terrible one. It had called attention to the one place they least wanted it.

That scare had been much too close for comfort. Just when his nerves had started to calm down, Mahmoud pointed out that the cot where Halfus had spent weeks was visible to someone standing outside the window. If Halfus had not gotten up when he did, the soldiers would certainly have seen him. The realization had brought back that terrible sense of panic all over again. He still shivered at the thought.

No, he was quite certain that he did not want to rely on Hassan's opinions in this. This was a matter of life and death. Halfus was not happy that he needed to rely on the help of anyone, but the situation required it. That still did not mean he would not be selective in whom he trusted.

"Look, Papa, a man." Halfus and Ammar looked over at Amelia simultaneously. Halfus was not entirely sure he had heard correctly. Then he saw her dainty finger pointing out the window, and the look of horror it inflicted on Ammar's face. He looked terrified.

Halfus was out of his seat and into the hallway faster than he would have thought possible. A pain pulsed through his leg, an insignificant protest that he ignored. He peeked back into the main chamber in time to see Ammar welcome a man into the home. Ammar was smiling, waving the man inside, gesturing for him to sit, calling to Haifa to bring them water and food.

But it was clearly an act. This was obviously a stranger, not a friend. The automatic rifle in his hands and the bandoleer of ammunition draped across his chest betrayed his affiliation. He accepted Ammar's invitation without the same mock pleasantries. His face never once cracked a smile. *How odd*, thought Halfus, *that Ammar's once formidable face seems so friendly by comparison. In fact, the whole man seems friendly to me now.* Had he softened, or had Halfus simply come to know better the man behind the rough exterior?

Halfus quickly fell behind in translating their conversation. The two men spoke in quick bursts punctuated by animated gestures. The newcomer remained even-keeled, assertive without raising his voice. But Ammar's voice slowly grew louder and more irritated. It reminded Halfus of the first time they had spoken, when the older man had lectured him on the Iraqi perspective of the American invasion. Halfus wished Ammar would get himself back under control. It would not be good for things to escalate.

Then Halfus watched Mahmoud enter the room from the outside. He wore his typical happy smile until he saw the stranger. Then he froze in place. Ammar called him over, but Mahmoud shook his head and remained where he was.

Do as he says, Halfus silently urged.

The stranger stood and approached the boy, now speaking in a friendly, almost jovial tone. Mahmoud seemed to relax. Halfus did not. The man put a hand on Mahmoud's shoulder as he spoke a few words directly to the boy. Ammar interrupted. The stranger patiently waited for him to finish, then began speaking again to Mahmoud.

Halfus really wished he could understand what they were discussing. He could sense the tension in the room, despite the measured tone of the soldier. The man's back was mostly turned to him, which meant Halfus could not read his facial expression. But he imagined a counterfeit, perhaps condescending smile.

Mahmoud was looking up, wide-eyed, as the visitor continued to speak to him. Then the man stopped, and a question seemed to linger in the air. The man was waiting for a response. Mahmoud did not answer, but Ammar did. The man ignored him. Mahmoud looked at his father, then back up at the soldier, and shook his head slowly. The man backhanded Mahmoud across the face, sending him sprawling to the floor.

Ammar took a step forward, but the soldier turned to face him. He was now fingering the trigger of his weapon nonchalantly. Ammar stopped, but his hands clenched into fists.

So did Halfus'. They were pressed so tight that the short fingernails made marks in his rough skin. Whether by happenstance or design, Ammar had positioned himself such that the soldier was unknowingly showing Halfus his back.

He could not have asked for a better tactical advantage. His instinct was to step out of hiding and take down this man who had brought violence into the home.

He thought back to the scare of a month earlier, when he had been helpless to do anything but hide. There was a world of difference between then and now. Then there were three opponents, now there was one. Halfus was barely mobile on that occasion, now he was much improved. He remained nowhere near normal, but at least he could move. And his soul ached to avenge that humiliation.

He sized the man up. Halfus believed he could take the soldier, particularly with the element of surprise on his side. He would not even need a weapon. His fists were weapon enough. Once the man was subdued, Halfus could finish the job with something else. And he would have to, because he could not let the man live. Otherwise the soldier would come back, with friends, bringing destruction to this household. So he would have to be killed.

Halfus' arms were straining, his fists clenched so hard that it felt he might never get them open again. He forced them to relax. He had been holding his breath, so he forced himself to quietly exhale and draw in fresh air. His chest was heaving. The overpowering adrenaline rush began to fade, leaving him in a weakened state. He raised a hand to the wall and leaned against it.

He would not do it. He did not believe he could kill a man. He did not *want* to kill a man. Not unless it was a last resort. He could have done it if the rifle had actually been pointed at someone, but so far the weapon had not been raised. Whatever else he was here for, the soldier was not here to kill.

As Halfus' mind calmed, he began to think logically. It became clearer that even killing the visitor would be a mistake. There might be others who knew he was here. The man's disappearance might easily be traced back to this home. Even though he was trying to help, Halfus might have brought about the ruin of the very people he was trying to protect.

Blessedly, the man was leaving. Mahmoud was still on the floor, holding his jaw. Ammar remained standing where he was, head hung. The soldier barked a few last words, turned, and walked out.

Haifa went to Mahmoud, so Halfus went to Ammar. "Should I go after him?" he asked in a hurried whisper. He resolved to do whatever was necessary if his host said yes. That would make it much easier, by putting the burden of responsibility on another. Ammar looked at Halfus with a defeated expression. His shoulders slumped. He shook his head.

Halfus had a second thought. "Should I leave right away?"

Ammar shook his head again. At last he spoke. His voice sounded weary. "They weren't looking for you. They want my son."

They want him? To be a soldier? He's twelve years old. But Halfus did not doubt the truth of the man's words. "What can I do?"

Ammar continued to shake his head. He looked like a man who had run out of hope. "Nothing. They will come back. They will take him. I can't stop them."

"Let him come with me," Halfus said.

Ammar did not respond. *That was half the battle, right there*, Halfus thought. If he did not immediately reject the idea, that meant he would consider it. The thought had just now occurred to Halfus, but it immediately seemed like the right thing to do. The more he turned it over in his mind, the more he was convinced.

But he did not wish to rush Ammar. There was time. *I'll let him sleep on it.* "Think about it," Halfus said, and put his hand on the man's shoulder.

That evening they finalized a plan. They would go east, to the Kurds. That route had its obstacles, but it seemed like the least worst out of four very bleak options. Ammar would drive while Halfus stayed as inconspicuous as possible whenever they ran into other people. They hoped that would be infrequently, for they intended to avoid any but the smallest of roads. Fortunately, the land was relatively flat. Once they reached the rugged hills and mountains in the east, they would already be inside Kurdish territory. Driving cross-country would be much slower, but encounters with others would be significantly less frequent. Just in case they needed to stop and speak to anyone, Halfus would be dressed in local garb and under strict orders not to say anything unless absolutely necessary.

It was not a great plan, Halfus knew. But it was the best they could come up with. There would almost certainly need to be a lot of improvising once they got started. The only good news was that Halfus trusted Ammar as much as he trusted himself. The two of them would find a way. He had to believe that.

They packed enough outdoor survival gear to allow Halfus to leave the car and continue on foot, if necessary. Although different from the modern equipment he was used to, there was no shortage of supplies. Halfus was thankful that Iraqis were hardy, resourceful people. A few nights under the sky were nothing exceptional for them. The same could be said of him. He almost looked forward to the prospect. If he were alone and much closer to his destination, he might have suggested doing this the entire way and leaving the car behind.

But he was not close to his destination. They were fifty miles or more from where they needed to be. It was difficult to be certain because the front lines may have shifted. The news reports that

Ammar received from Hassan were sporadic, vague, and often contradictory. They would be heading into a great unknown.

Halfus also hoped to not be alone. By the time they stopped for the night, Ammar had made no decision on the subject of his son. Halfus wondered how the boy felt about it. But it was not his place to press a family into letting go of their son for what was potentially a very long time. And he was confident that Ammar would make the right decision.

The mere thought of the rebels recruiting Mahmoud made Halfus upset. It also forced him to do some reconsidering. He had always thought of insurgents and terrorists as one and the same. Now he realized that not every enemy combatant was a terrorist. They were not even always willing participants. How many were relative innocents, drawn into the ranks of the warriors by circumstance? How many were children? It was unnerving to think of them fighting beside grown men. A kid with a rifle could kill as easily as an adult. And could die just as easily. There was no way for bullets and bombs to discern the difference. But people could, if they ever learned to stop viewing complex issues in black and white.

Halfus had already learned to hate war. Even so, this cast the conflict in a new light. Being a soldier in a war was scary enough. How much worse to fight for a cause you do not believe in? And how much worse than that to die for it? At the hands of an enemy you never wanted to have, yet who would cheer your demise as a victory? This world was even more broken than he had thought.

Halfus woke the following morning much later than usual. Normally he rose with the dawn, but he judged from the sun and the temperature that today he was several hours behind schedule. It was not a big deal. They did not plan on leaving until late afternoon. They wanted to cover as much distance as possible in the dark of night.

He wanted to share a few words and a smile with each member of the household today. He envisioned them going about their usual routines, pretending to be unaware that today was any different. But he hoped they would miss him after he was gone.

Before leaving his room, Halfus paused and looked around one last time, soaking the sights into his memory. He would miss this place, and not just the people. He would miss the home itself, and especially this room. These shabby white walls had kept him safe week after week, while a world outside tore itself apart. This house had come to seem like a sanctuary for him. He did not altogether want to leave.

He went through his supplies one last time. He had also checked them twice before going to sleep, and nothing had gotten up and run off during the night. He laughed at himself and his own obsessive-compulsiveness. The waiting was the hardest part. With more time on his hands than he usefully needed, his mind looked for ways to keep itself uselessly occupied.

He left his room one last time, eager to get started but sad to say goodbye. That is when the plan started falling apart.

12

CONTRASTING FORTUNES

IN THE YEAR 1618, four representatives of Hapsburg Ferdinand II, King of Bohemia and Hungary and heir apparent to rule the Holy Roman Empire, entered the Bohemian Chancellery in Prague. They were on a mission to revoke the religious tolerance previously granted by Ferdinand's predecessor. A majority of Bohemia's princes and people were Protestant, while Ferdinand had aspirations to restore Catholicism as the sole unifying faith of the Empire. Negotiations between ministers and princes were brief and unsuccessful. As a result, two of Ferdinand's ministers and one of their secretaries were unceremoniously thrown out of the third floor window of the building in an event that came to be known as the Defenestration of Prague. The act was as hasty as it was barbarous, for it precipitated the Thirty Years' War that engulfed most of central Europe and accounted for the deaths of as much as a fifth of the entire German population. Not that Germans were the only ones dying. Protestant Sweden and later, ironically, Catholic France each became the leader of the anti-Hapsburg cause. The Thirty Years' War is widely regarded as the most destructive war in European history prior to the Twentieth Century, and perhaps the largest ever fought in the name of religious intolerance.

The Knights Templar was an order of warriors created in the Twelfth Century in an effort to combine the religious and military functions of the

Roman Catholic Church. This order was officially sanctioned by the Pope within a decade of its inception. It was one of the more effective fighting units of the Crusades, and lasted for nearly two hundred years. The Knights Templar was not the first military order of the Middle Ages, however. That distinction likely belongs to the Hospitallers of Saint James, formed to protect the pilgrims of northern Italy. Nor were these the only two. The Order of Santiago was formed in northwestern Spain, the Order of Alcántara in southern Spain, the Knights Hospitaller in Malta, the Order of the Dragon in Hungary, and dozens of others throughout the continent. Most fought in the Crusades, but some engaged in the Iberian Reconquista while yet others battled pagans located along the coasts of the Baltic Sea.

The Ancient Greeks, Romans, Persians, Egyptians, Babylonians, Goths, Celts, and Indians all worshipped different gods. When these societies interacted, they fought. And when they fought, they maimed, killed, pillaged, and died as much for these gods as any other reason, for the rites and tenets of faith were an integral part of their daily existence. Yet one could easily ascribe other causes to these clashes of civilization. They fought for land, wealth, power, and status. There has always been and will always remain a blurring between religious, political, ethnic, economic, and other lines of conflict. Even wars that are attributed to other causes often contain a religious component. For example, the Yugoslav Wars that led to the fragmentation of that country were primarily political disputes over possession of land. Yet at the same time, one could examine the role of religion in the very definition of the ethnic groups involved—Serbs are Orthodox, Croatians Catholic, and Bosniaks Muslim.

Religious wars have always been with us, as have religious militants. They are as much a norm as an exception. There are significant differences between their modern and historic forms, however. For one thing, much of the world has become increasingly secularized, leading to a fundamental disconnect between philosophies. Today, it is harder for the secular Westerner to understand the mentality that leads others to kill in the name of their chosen god.

Perhaps the biggest difference between the religious wars of yesterday and today is a characteristic common to nearly every modern conflict. The disparity of resources and technology between the haves and the have-nots *has led to a massive increase in asymmetric warfare. Symmetric, or conventional, warfare occurs when two or more sides of roughly equal capabilities elect to resolve disputes on the battlefield. Both sides are willing to risk battle because each has a reasonable belief it can win. Asymmetric warfare, on the other hand, occurs when one side has no reasonable chance of winning in a conventional fight but still considers their cause worthy of bloodshed. Unable to confront their enemy on the battlefield, they resort to unconventional methods. Guerrilla warfare is one example. Insurgency and terrorism are others.*

For most of history, populations fought wars by proxy, selecting a small portion of their number to bear the bloody costs of combat. In this manner, life could continue more or less as normal for the majority of a warring country. Terrorism changes that paradigm by drawing civilians directly into the fighting, both as the victims and, in many cases, the perpetrators of violence. The very dominance of American power is a critical component in the persistence of terrorism. This is not to suggest that it would be prudent for the United States to dissolve its air force or hand out cruise missiles to its enemies. But military planners are aware of hegemony's distasteful effect on an enemy. Soldiers become martyrs. Battle becomes murder. War becomes crime.

Thus terrorism leads to two sides with widely contradictory world-views. One side comprises civilians who cannot understand the particular grievances of the other; who deem those grievances illegal, immoral, or inhuman; and who believe warfare should be left to the professionals. The other side firmly believes in the justice of their cause, and views attacks on civilians as the only practical way to accomplish their goals.

It is no wonder then that both sides describe the other in the vilest of terms, nor why the morality of both sides regresses to a point where the enemy is deprived of basic human rights and protections. There is no solution. The capacity for hatred, cruelty, and violence is already inside each human being. All it needs is a push.

~

Ernie's favorite course of the fall semester was a seminar class entitled *European Encounters With The Middle East*. It covered the breadth of historical interactions between the two regions, stretching from Greece's wars with Persia through the West's recent incursions into Afghanistan and Iraq. He enjoyed the course because it was an excellent forum in which to show off his personal experience. Class met once per week, during which the students would discuss one or more reading assignments on the day's topic.

Class sizes at Catoctin tended toward the low end of the spectrum. It was one of the measures by which the school ranked high on the academic rating charts. Seminar classes were generally even smaller, and this one was no exception. There were only a dozen students enrolled. It had been capped at that number in order to allow everyone sufficient opportunity to speak. Catoctin's philosophy at the graduate level was that students could learn nearly as much from each other as from the professor, whose role in a seminar was less that of instructor and more of facilitator. In the several sessions of class held so far, Ernie had established himself as one of the more active participants. He was discovering that he could keep his vexatious speech problems in check for short periods with careful forethought and concentration. The class discussions were proving to be excellent practice.

Today's class made him nervous, however. He was unprepared. He had not completed his reading assignments for the week on the subject of the First Crusade. It was a topic he knew a little about already, and he had confidence in his ability to bullshit his way through the session, if need be. It certainly would not be the first time he had done so without finishing all the readings for a class, but it would be the first time since his speech irregularities had materialized with worrying frequency. In a class with so few students, it would be difficult to avoid overexposure with two hours of discussion and only twelve of them to divide up the speaking.

To make matters worse, Ernie was becoming concerned that there would not even be the full dozen. The downside to such small class sizes was that more than one or two absent students could disrupt the group's chemistry. In most colleges, students missed class with disturbing regularity. Catoctin avoided the problem through rigorous selectivity. Only young men and women who had demonstrated the discipline to reach the peak of their high school class were accepted at the prestigious college.

Thus it was unusual to see no less than four empty seats as class time arrived. With only eight of them here, Ernie realized he would need to speak far more than he had counted upon. In fact, he began to consider ditching class entirely before the professor showed up. She usually arrived right at the top of the hour. A quick glance at the clock on the wall revealed one minute to go. He needed to make a snap decision.

He was already stuffing a notebook back into his backpack when the matter was taken out of his hands. An administrative assistant for the department came into the classroom to make the announcement that class was canceled for the day. Professor Nichols had called in sick. *Crisis averted.*

It was Ernie's only class of the day, so it gave him a head start on his preparations for the upcoming trip. It was a head start he did not need, and in any case Wendy would not be available until lunchtime to drive him to the airport, so the cancellation was really a waste of his time. He now needed to find a way to use twenty minutes of packing to fill a two-hour window. He did not enjoy having free time on his hands these days. He had too much energy to sit still when he was meant to be out and about, doing things. Staying active.

Which was why he was looking forward to this trip. *The Taylor Allgood Report* wanted to do a segment on their show about his experience in Iraq. The program's producers had invited him to their New York City studio at Rockefeller Center, airfare and hotel stay courtesy of the network. Of all the twenty-four hour news network shows, this particular one would not have been his first choice—it ran a little too liberal for his taste—but he was not about to turn down an offer to be on national television. It was scheduled to be a five-minute slot on Tuesday night. He remembered the warnings the State Department had given the members of Doctor Appelstein's team about what was safe to say and what was not, but the least Ernie could do was emphatically state that Halfus had not intended to steal anything the night he died. In fact, Ernie intended to describe his fallen friend in the best possible light. It might not be much, but it was the least he could do. And it would ease his guilty conscience.

He had received the call from the producers Saturday evening. When he broke the news to her yesterday, Wendy had been as excited as he. She helped him select an outfit that would "bring out his gorgeous eyes." Then she had playfully admonished him not to make any of those New York socialites fall for him. He loved it when she talked him up like that. He knew he had a great many things going for him, but deep down inside he still felt like that timid bumpkin from West Virginia. How different she was from his family, and especially his parents. Ernie felt loved, accepted, and respected here at Catoctin. It was the polar opposite of how he felt growing up. Compliments poured from Wendy's mouth in an inexhaustible stream, while he could not recall hearing a single one from his father. But being on national television certainly could not fail to impress them. He hoped.

It was nearly an hour drive from McGahey to Baltimore-Washington International. Wendy seemed quite willing to do the lion's share of the talking, which suited him fine. At least until she started prying.

"Why does it take three days to do a five-minute segment?"

Ernie shrugged. "Don't know," he replied in a neutral tone. He was a little ashamed to admit that he had requested the extra two days. He hated to remind others, even Wendy, of his uncultured background. This was going to be his first time in New York City, and he wanted to see as many of the sights as he could manage. He would have asked for a week if he had believed the network would agree.

He waited for her to say something sweet. *I wish I could go with you, I'll be thinking of you,* or even just *I'll miss you.*

"Well, I got some big news from work this morning," she said instead. "Looks like I'm going to be having a little trip of my own.

Sandy Kesmet can't go, so Bob...Representative King asked me to be his right-hand-man on a trip to Chicago."

"Oh, what for?" Ernie forced himself to feign a smile. It felt as though she was stealing his thunder.

"He said it was some kind of fundraising deal. Helping another candidate out. Attending rallies. I didn't get all the details, but it's for a few days next week. Should be a big opportunity for me to do some networking."

Ernie tried to be happy for her. Wendy seemed to enjoy her job, but he knew she also felt stifled. She had aspirations for more, and he had no doubt that she would achieve them. He remembered Tracy talking about him someday being married to a senator. He rather liked the sound of that. It should have been easy to be happy for her. Instead, he found it difficult to care.

"That's terrific, Curlicue." He spoke with as much false sincerity as he could muster. Then, to change the subject, he asked, "Do you have plans for the rest of your day off?"

"I'm going to see Mom. I haven't spent much time with her since the job started."

He nodded along, relatively uninterested.

Her tone changed somewhat. "I still need to tell her about Matt. I've been putting it off—"

"I'm sure it will be fine," he interjected. He did not want her mood to turn sour now. They had reached the Baltimore beltway and were within fifteen minutes of their destination. He hoped to keep things light and happy for the duration.

"Yeah, you're right," she replied. She risked a sidelong glance at him and smiled. He smiled back. That was more like it.

Her good mood continued the rest of the way to the airport, where she dropped him off with a kiss. He began the slow crawl through the labyrinthian pretend security measures every airport in the country had instituted. He absolutely hated waiting in line, and walking through metal detectors always made him feel like a criminal with something to hide. It was an hour before he took a seat at his gate, waiting to be called to board. He fidgeted endlessly. At times like this he wished he could have been more like Halfus, who had been able to put in the earbuds of his iPod and slip away into some timeless universe of arias and instrumentals. It was this, his friend's profound sense of calm contentment, that Ernie had admired more than anything. He hoped Halfus found eternal serenity, wherever he had gone.

The thought made Ernie uncomfortable, so he began to pay more attention to his surroundings. Two flight attendants passed before him. They exchanged a few pleasantries with the girl running the desk at Ernie's gate. He hoped they would be working on his plane. Both were lovely creatures. One was slightly older, with lightly freckled cheeks and brunette curls as wild as Wendy's. The other was younger and taller and wore her platinum hair in a fancy bob. She wore a sprightly scarf that matched the powder blue of her tight uniform. He was encouraged when the two of them finished talking to the desk girl and wheeled their suitcases down the same ramp he would soon be traversing. They would make his flight a little more interesting. In his limited experience, flying bored him to tears, but it never hurt to have something other than second-run movies to keep his eyes on.

Within a few minutes they began calling rows. Soon he was boarding. This was one of the worst of many frustrating aspects of flying. The portly woman in front of him seemed to have a difficult time deciding in which overhead compartment to place her little bag. He wished she would hurry up and get on with it, and felt the stationary line piling up behind him. He made an exaggerated face of disbelief as she continued to stand still, oblivious to the roadblock she had created. Finally, he could wait no longer. He forced himself to speak in as reasonable a tone as he could muster. "Ma'am, please allow me." Without waiting for her response, he took the bag from her and lifted it up to wedge it into a bin where a larger suitcase would keep it from moving. She looked at him with an expression of bewilderment. "If you need to get to it during the flight, ask me or one of the other gentlemen around. We'll be glad to help." She seemed to accept that suggestion and twisted awkwardly out of the aisle into her seat. He could not resist a headshake of exasperation now that she was no longer looking at him. As he began to move forward again, he looked up and made eye contact with the young blonde flight attendant. He felt embarrassed until he saw that she looked amused. So he smiled at her. She smiled in return.

The flight was already starting to run behind schedule, and every minute that passed was one he would not have available in the city. It would already be dark by the time the plane landed, but he still intended to cram a few sights into what would remain of the evening. He wanted to see Central Park and Times Square at night. Tomorrow he would check out the Statue of Liberty and Ellis Island before heading to the studio to record the show. That left only one final day for the Empire State Building, Stock Exchange, Public Library, and every museum on his lengthy list. He also wanted to see Greenwich Village and Soho, Yankee Stadium, and about a dozen other sights. It was a little overwhelming, but he was not particularly worried. He was so filled with energy and vitality that he felt certain he would go home feeling satisfied that he had given his all. He was just eager to get started.

Rich was getting tired of the yelling. He continued to tell himself that it was not his problem, but that excuse felt a little hollower with each passing day and quarrel. If only Jeannie would ask for his help. That would make things so much easier.

He had long since grown used to harassment, discrimination, and contempt directed his way. It had been a fact of life growing up as a gay black man in a straight white world. But this, seeing a man mistreat his family, was a different animal entirely. It was abuse, pure and simple. Not only physical but emotional, and Rich was not certain which was worse.

Unable to concentrate, he closed the book he had been trying to read. He glanced at the clock in his little living room. There was still an hour before he needed to leave. Perhaps putting a little food into his stomach would make him feel better. At the very least, the act of cooking would give him something to do.

He went into the small, utilitarian kitchen. He measured out two cups of water and a half-cup of steel cut oats. It was more than he was hungry for, but it was habit, and old habits died hard. He realized this would be his first bowl of oatmeal since Iraq. It used to be a staple of his diet, but now it was the meal he associated with the fateful last morning of the dig. He wondered why he had selected this, of all things, to prepare right now. It was not as though he craved it. He did not crave any food these days. He was never so much hungry as going through the motions, simply putting a little fuel into the engine. A very little fuel. Since the illness, his appetite had never really returned to normal. He seldom ate more than two spartan meals per day, yet always felt satisfied.

But it would not hurt to give himself a little extra energy for this afternoon's practice, the first since Saturday's big win over Bowie State. Rich had delivered one great game, but did not believe in resting on his laurels. He felt simultaneously proud and nervous. He knew he was liked and respected by his teammates and coach, but now it felt that he had broken free of a constraint that he had never really known was there. He had previously been a leader on the field, but that was where the respect ended. Until Saturday night, when he went out with Joey and Ethan and their friends. It was a formative experience of the type he thought were all in his past. It just went to show that people were never too old to change. For the first time he felt that he really fit in with the group, and it was something he wanted to get used to. He needed affirmation that they had enjoyed his company as much as he had theirs.

The timer went off, and he poured the steaming oatmeal into a bowl. As he swirled in a chunk of butter and two heaps of brown sugar, he thought about the drinking games they had played at the bar. Some were new, some he knew, and one he had even taught them. Silly as it seemed, that had been a proud moment.

Rich distractedly blew on the first spoonful to cool it before swallowing. He gagged as it went down his throat. It tasted like pure, unadulterated syrup. He made a face, then quickly poured himself a tall glass of milk to wash out the aftertaste. He had not been paying attention, but he rewound his short-term memory to visualize what he had done wrong. He had not accidentally used far more sugar than usual. He licked a finger and dipped it into the bag of sugar, then tested it on his tongue. There was no question about it. For some reason it tasted far more potent than before. The change was not in the sweetener, so it must have been in his taste buds.

He pushed the bowl away, disgusted. It was not even edible like this. It was a good thing he was not genuinely hungry. There was no time to fix another bowl.

The neighbors were back at it again. Rich could not understand what exactly they were arguing about, but it was pretty clearly Jim who had gotten upset and Jeannie who was defending herself. When the daughter started crying, Rich had to remind himself that it was none of his business. Then there was a noise that could have been a hit, followed by a shriek of pain and redoubled bawling. Rich did not understand how Jeannie put up with it. He supposed that abused spouses were capable of great feats of self-denial. It made no difference. He had heard enough.

With a calm to his stride that belied the excitement building in his blood, Rich walked out of the kitchen onto his porch, crossed over to their half, and knocked on the door. In that moment, he recollected the ironic smile on Jim's face the first time the man had insulted him. Rich now assumed that same sly expression as he knocked a second time, more emphatically. He understood the truth behind the grin in a way he had not before. *Come on, try me. I dare you to. Nothing would make me happier.*

Jim finally opened the door with a look of annoyance. "Butt out, faggot," he blustered. Over his shoulder, Rich saw a scene of distress.

"Touch them again, and this faggot is going to beat the shite out of you," Rich said with sincere enthusiasm. "Try me if you think I am joking." He stood poised in his goalie's stance, waiting for a response in word or deed. Rich was young and athletic and in the best shape of his life, whereas the sad excuse for a man before him was pushing forty and had probably never been half so fit, even in his prime. There was no doubt in Rich's mind that he could take him in a fair fight. And he very much wanted to find out.

Jim's jaw worked up and down, chewing over the same equation. He must have reached the same conclusion. "Try it, and I'll get the cops to chuck your black ass in jail," he sneered. Then he tried to slam the door shut in Rich's face.

Rich had anticipated that reaction and blocked the door with his foot. "It would be worth it," he told Jim. "But I very much doubt it comes to that. One look at that mark on your daughter and the police will take your arse instead of mine. They'll probably give me a medal." Then he pushed the door back open enough to meet Jeannie's eye. "Shame on you, too, Jeannie. It's one thing to look the other way when he hits you, but that girl is helpless. She deserves better than the two of you."

He pulled his foot back, and this time Jim did slam the door.

Rich did not know if he had helped or made matters worse. He expected Jim to think twice about hitting anyone for a while, but whatever fear Rich had put into him would wear off in time. He had just emasculated the man, and pride would demand its payment from someone eventually. It always did. The next few days would mark the time of highest risk. Rich would try to vary his schedule so Jim would not know exactly when he was home.

Rich was angry at himself for what he had done. He was now returning to normal, and was not entirely sure what had caused him to do it. It had been less a compulsion that he could not deny than an instinct that he had not even tried to. There had been no deliberation at all, which was unusual for him. He believed he had done the right thing, but he wished he could feel better about it.

The day was shaping up to be the hottest in weeks, and the pace of practice seemed more sluggish than usual. Many of Rich's teammates looked tired, and two players were absent altogether. One was Ethan, which Rich found disappointing. He had been looking forward to seeing how Ethan and Joey, the two players he had gone out with Saturday night, behaved toward him today. He expected knowing smiles and playful jokes. At least, that was what he hoped for. Now it appeared he would have to judge their acceptance of him based solely on Joey.

But the fullback exchanged neither smiles nor jokes, with Rich or anyone else. He looked exhausted even before the practice began. Rich wondered if perhaps he was hung over. It had been two nights since they went out drinking, but Rich had seen Joey put down so much beer that he would not be surprised if the young man still felt inebriated yesterday. Besides, there was every possibility that Joey had gone out again last night without Rich's knowledge. He tried not to let the idea bother him as much as it did.

Coach Schneider noticed the general lack of energy, not just in Joey but in several others as well. He lectured them about not letting one win go to their heads before kicking off the warmups with two laps around the field.

Rich slowed his pace to jog beside Joey. "You feeling all right, mate? You aren't still hung over, are you?"

Joey shook his head. His long hair was already damp with sweat. "Nah, just tired."

"You sure? You were quite pissed when I left." He caught himself reverting to British slang. Joey would interpret that to mean angry. "I mean wasted," Rich corrected.

Joey snorted. "In your dreams. I can't have you thinking you drank me under the table, can I?" Then he grinned, and Rich was relieved to see he still maintained his good cheer.

"Have it your way. Just don't overdo it, all right? You look like you might shtart vomiting any moment."

"Bite me, Rich." At that, Joey sped up and finished the second lap with a newfound burst of energy. Where he got it from, Rich had no idea. He had watched the kid drink enough to kill a horse. How the body could ever get used to that was beyond comprehension.

One of the drinking games they played Saturday night was Anchorman. Rich had heard of it, but had never played. That was not surprising, since he and his usual friends were social drinkers, while this was a game for guys who went about drinking as though it was an Olympic sport. The girls had looked on while the guys divided into two teams of four. They took turns trying to bounce a quarter into a full pitcher of beer. The losing team became responsible for downing the entire pitcher. In Anchorman, this did not involve filling their mugs. Instead, the team designated an order in which each of them would get one chance to drink as much as possible in a single act of chugging. As soon as the drinker lowered the pitcher from his lips, his turn was over and the pitcher passed on to the next. The last person in line was responsible for finishing whatever his teammates had left for him. It was thus both a great honor and burden to be designated as the anchorman. For reasons he did not understand, Rich had been assured it would bring great disgrace upon one's kin and clan if the anchorman failed to uphold this solemn duty.

As a newcomer, Rich had been designated to go first. He drank as much as he could, but when he lowered the pitcher and passed it to Ethan, it appeared that the volume had barely diminished at all. Ethan did a better job before passing it to Kyle, a friend of Joey's whom Rich had only met that night. Kyle proved himself a Judas by taking only a sip before handing the pitcher to Joey, their anchorman.

"Thanks a lot, you bastard," Joey sneered in good humor. He then preceded to imbibe the remaining three-fourths of the pitcher in one long, impressive feat of endurance. Then he caught the quarter in his teeth and slammed the empty pitcher to the table amid the whooping cheers of teammates and spectators alike.

While Joey basked in the laughter and applause, Rich felt Dani put a hand on his shoulder. She leaned down to speak into his ear, nearly shouting to be heard over the din. "You did great for your first time. I'm proud of you." He thanked her, prouder still. At that moment, he had felt that he truly belonged.

The team was going through its first one-on-one drills now. Rich was in one goal, Justin the other. The assistant coaches were matching the other players up two at a time, tossing one ball randomly onto the field while designating which goal the guys were to attack. The two paired players would chase after the ball and battle it out to get a shot off. Whoever possessed the ball was on offense for the duration of their possession, while the other fought tooth and nail for a steal. There were sometimes two or even three pairs of players involved on each half of the field, so Rich had to pay attention to multiple threats simultaneously. He was watching, assessing, and about to block a shot when he saw Joey collapse.

Most of the other guys were amused at first. Some were even laughing despite Coach's angry shouts, but Rich was immediately racing toward his fullback and friend. The collapse had not appeared intentionally histrionic to him—it looked genuine. Rich was just taking a knee beside the prostrate form when Joey began to convulse.

"Call an ambulance!" Rich shouted. The laughing had stopped. He rolled his friend onto his back. Joey's eyes were open, but there was no sign of consciousness in his face. "Find a stick," Rich barked at the closest teammate without looking to see who it was. A moment later one was handed to him. He wedged it into Joey's mouth and held it there to prevent him from biting off his tongue while the body shook violently.

Rich heard another person arrive behind him, then felt a hand on his shoulder. "It's all right, Rich, the doctor's here." He remained where he was, horrified. In the span of a few minutes Joey had gone from green around the gills to an actual pale green tint. But his skin was more than off-color. Rich recognized the same blotches that he recognized from his own illness. Only much, much worse. He reached down to brush some of Joey's sweaty hair out of his eyes. It was a gesture reminiscent of something else he had seen recently. Something he could not quite place. Or did not want to. He knew it reminded him of death.

"Rich." It was Coach's voice. It was more authoritative this time. "Let the doctor do his work."

Rich just now realized that the athletic department's physician had been nearby. This was his job, and Joey would be best served if Rich got out of the way.

He nodded and stood up. Coach still had a hand on his left

shoulder, and now he felt another teammate put one on his right. Rich hung his head, feeling like crying. Together, they watched the body continue its inhuman dance in the grass.

"Remain quiet," Hassan hissed.

Halfus did as he was told. It was easier than arguing. Or thinking. Panic had seized his mind, and he had all but given up hope. The past eight hours had been a nightmare. Ever since the moment he had said goodbye to his little sanctuary. He never should have left.

He had expected the family mood to be a mix of celebration and sadness. Instead, he found them distressed and distracted. He had expected to spend the midday meal with Ammar, giving their plan a final review. Instead, the plan was aborted before it could even get started. He had expected to receive Ammar's blessing to take Mahmoud. Instead, he had not spoken to Ammar at all.

The man was sick. He knew it from Haifa's face even before he asked. "I am so very sorry, Halfus. My husband is not well. He will not be able to take you anywhere today."

"It's all right," Halfus replied instinctively, even though it was not. "I'll think of something. The important thing is for him to get better." And it was. Halfus was aware that his own desperate status had just been made more precarious, but his overriding concern was for the man who had given him a home and kept him safe for two months. It was only later that he realized Haifa had spoken in English. It was scant comfort to learn that he had been right about her all along.

Mahmoud was spending his time going in and out of the bedroom where his father lay, serving as Halfus' only link to the man his escape was riding on. Halfus had to know whether the plan could be improvised, salvaged in part, or needed to be scrapped.

"What are his symptoms?" he asked Mahmoud. He worried that the boy would find this an uncomfortable subject. Halfus expected him to be as evasive as usual, but Mahmoud remained surprisingly serious throughout the ordeal.

"Vomiting. Weakness. Odor."

"Fever?"

"No fever."

"Thank goodness for that."

"Yes, God be praised." More than anything, the invocation of Allah told Halfus how serious the condition was. By contrast to the sectarian violence broiling around them, Ammar's family seemed positively secular. Yet in times of great strain, a man naturally turned to his faith, be it instinctive or acquired.

If there were no fever involved, Halfus wondered whether there could be a quick recovery. It might be better to simply delay the departure by a day than to throw the entire plan out the window. But every day, every hour, the risk of unwanted visitors increased. Ammar had seemed certain the soldiers would not be long in returning. It was essential that Halfus—and Mahmoud—not be present when they did.

"Is he improving, or getting worse?"

"Worse."

Damn. That was not what Halfus wanted to hear. He began thinking out loud. "I wish I knew how long this was likely to last."

It was intended to be a rhetorical question. To his surprise, Mahmoud responded. "It looks like the same thing we had. If it's anything like you and me, it will be at least two days."

"What? You and me?"

Mahmoud looked surprised. "Yes, our sickness." Seeing Halfus' look of confusion, he continued. "We were both sick, the day after I brought you back from the tomb. I thought you knew."

Halfus shook his head. "No," he said in amazement. He knew he had been out of it for a while, but he had assumed it was simply the fall. "We had these same symptoms, you and I?"

"Yes, for several days. My mother was also sick, after we recovered. But she stayed in the other room. I did not see her, so I do not know if it was the same illness."

"She got sick after caring for you?"

"Yes. And for you, *Akhi.*"

Halfus said nothing.

For a short while, he watched Mahmoud and Haifa move about with deliberate thoroughness. Feeling like an extra wheel, Halfus offered to help in whatever way he could, but there was nothing to do but wait. Mahmoud was everywhere, apparently propelled by a bottomless well of energy. He ran back and forth between this house and the neighbor's, skipping the midday meal entirely and not seeming to mind. Before the afternoon was over, Ammar passed on his decisions to the rest of them through the little messenger. None of it was music to Halfus' ears. The plan would go forward that evening, as scheduled. Hassan would replace Ammar as the driver. Halfus' fate would be placed in the hands of the neighbor he disliked and distrusted. To make matters worse, Mahmoud was indispensable. He was needed here, with his family.

If Halfus were a crying man, he would have done so at this announcement. It had not been unexpected, but it still hurt. He longed for the boy's company now more than ever. The thought of spending the next few critical days alone with Hassan filled him with dread. But more than that, Halfus worried about the fate that might befall the youngster. This was Mahmoud's best opportunity to escape recruitment into the rebel army. If that happened, he would certainly be forever changed, even if he survived. It was heartbreaking.

And so it was with the expected sadness, without the balancing celebration, that Halfus had left this family behind. He knew his heart and mind would cling to them for a long time, but they disappeared from his present to his past. His future was Hassan.

They drove for several hours before the sun began to descend upon the jagged horizon. Until that point, Halfus and Hassan exchanged few words. Halfus allowed his mind to wander. The countryside was barren but beautiful, the many centuries of history rising out of the dusty earth to greet him. He could still commune with the land, the images of armies and kings long since dead reenacting their deeds like some spectral documentary. In time, he pulled himself out of it. As much as he would have liked to soak up every minute of communion, the predicament necessitated his full attention.

He watched the landscape for signs of danger. He saw simple people moving about their homesteads. Periodically, he watched other travelers appear and disappear from sight. But he saw no soldiers, nor any active sign of the war waging inside the country. In fact, the scene reminded Halfus of photos he had seen of roads in the U.S. from the sixties and seventies. If he forced himself not to think about the desperation of his plight he could almost imagine that he was reliving a quiet family drive from his childhood. The landscape was more barren, but there were the electrical towers, phone poles, and quaint simple structures of distant memory.

That was when he had the first warning that the trip itself was not proceeding according to plan. "Aren't you sticking to the road a little longer than we intended?"

"I have to. The terrain is getting rough." He nodded toward the rocks and boulders around the road.

What he said was true. The ground was becoming less flat. Halfus looked ahead. They were approaching the hills much sooner than he expected. According to the map he had carefully reviewed countless times in recent days, the highlands should not have appeared until well after dark. But he could see them off in the distance, and the sun was only starting to set. He considered whether they were simply making much better time than expected because Hassan was sticking to the road.

Only then did Halfus realize the sun was setting not from behind, but to their left. He closed his eyes and cursed himself a fool for letting his mind wander. "Hassan, you are taking the north route, aren't you?"

"It's much better than east, my friend."

Don't call me your friend. Halfus wanted to protest. To argue. But what was done was done. There was no sense fighting about it now, after hours of driving. There was no turning back. His destiny was in the hands of a reckless man of dubious loyalties. His body was sore from sitting still, his mind worn from stress, his spirit deflated from repetitive disappointment. His star was hitched to this wagon, he would just have to ride along wherever it took him.

It was not long thereafter that the danger manifested in a very tangible way. "I see men ahead," Hassan announced. His voice betrayed no emotion.

Halfus saw what the driver was referring to. A quarter-mile ahead, a pickup truck was parked near a ramshackle structure of corrugated metal. There were several men with rifles milling about. It looked like a checkpoint of some kind—exactly the sort of thing Halfus had hoped to avoid by going off-road. The sunset was almost complete, casting the men in shadow, so he could not be sure how many there were. Not that it mattered. He and Hassan had no weapons, and he doubted his companion would fight anyway if it came to that. Halfus only hoped that the man would not voluntarily turn his passenger in. The prospect seemed likely. Hassan would be rid of his burden, and possibly even rewarded. He could then return to Ammar and tell any story he desired.

Now Halfus was panicking. There was no time to hide, so he considered running for it. He had opened his mouth to ask Hassan to slow down. The man had cut him off with the curt warning to remain quiet before Halfus could say a word. His fate would be determined within a matter of minutes, and Halfus was giving up. He had been living on the edge for so long that he felt like a different person. How very far removed he was from the confident young man who had excitedly come to Iraq. He had always liked to remain in control of his circumstances—but now, trapped in a car, sensing Hassan's abrupt hostility, he was certain his short life was about to end. He wanted to go down fighting. Every fiber of his being cried out to do something. Anything. But his mind remained firmly clamped to a single thought, that doing nothing at all was his only chance. Without hope, he put his life in Hassan's hands.

The sun finally descended below the rocks. The air immediately seemed to cool, a drop of temperature that would have been welcome if Halfus had not already been trying not to shiver. However, he was thankful for the sudden pall of night. It would make his pathetic disguise slightly less inadequate.

Hassan slowed the car to a crawl as he approached the men. Two were on the driver's side, one on the passenger. All held rifles before their chests as they walked toward the vehicle. Halfus did not think he could stand to make eye contact with the man nearing his window, examining him menacingly, so he closed his eyes and feigned sleep. His heart was pounding, but he forced his breathing to assume a level appropriate to someone lost in a dream. It even helped to think of this as a dream. The men questioning, Hassan answering, everyone laughing. Halfus visualized spouts of smoke leaking from their nostrils as they laughed, like noxious dragons waiting to spit flames on their quarry. They would pounce on him, holding his feeble body down with their powerful claws as they toyed with him. Then, one at a time, they would bite into his flesh, tossing huge morsels into the air to be roasted then caught in their jaws. They would eat him alive, his final moments a bloody torture.

There was a noise from the hood of the car, the sound of a hand giving it one hard pound. Then Halfus felt the car moving again. They must have told the driver to pull off the road. But he did not feel the car turning. It slowly picked up speed. Halfus opened his eyes. They were still on the road, their speed increasing.

Hassan began to laugh. "Halfus, my friend. That was close. I told you the *burqa* would work."

Halfus felt as though he was going to suffocate. He pulled the *niqab* away from his face and mouth and gasped for air. He wished he could share in his companion's good cheer, but his mind was still digesting the situation. He glanced back. The light of the checkpoint was barely visible.

"Hassan, I owe you an apology. I don't know what you told them—"

"Think nothing of it, my friend. These men may be soldiers, but they are still people. They are bored and lonely out here. They miss their wives and girlfriends and families. They are hungry, so I give them some dates to snack on. They are not placed on this earth just to catch you, Halfus. This isn't the movies, my friend." He laughed again.

Halfus allowed his body to relax back to a sustainable level. Not normal, but a far cry from the paralyzing panic he had just experienced. He felt enormous relief that they had cleared the checkpoint, but he wondered how many others lay before them. He stared up at the shadowy hills rising ahead, the mountains looming ominously beyond. Halfus knew his journey with Hassan was far from over. They were still twenty miles from the border.

Something in Wendy's tone gave Ernie pause for thought. He wished they were face-to-face instead of talking by phone, so he could read her expression and body language. No, on second thought, it was a good thing they were not face-to-face.

She wanted to tell him something, he knew. He hesitated. This was not a good time for that kind of conversation. But he knew it would cause problems down the road if he ignored it now.

"Something is bothering you, I can tell. What ish it, Wendy? Ish..is...it your mother?" He flinched reflexively at his mistakes. They were becoming more and more common.

"Uh-huh. I finally told her about Matt."

He nodded, although she could not see him. It made sense. She just needed to vent a little emotion. Matt had spent quite a lot of time with the woman. Ernie imagined that the talk had been painful for both Wendy and her mother. "I understand."

"No, you don't." Wendy sounded even more upset. "I've been putting it off and putting it off. So when I finally did it today... She didn't get upset, Ernie. She didn't even seem to care."

Ernie felt a tickling sensation on his neck. He brushed it away.

Wendy sounded as though she were fighting back tears. "It's all right, Wendy," he said. "Maybe she was in shock."

"She didn't look like she was in shock."

He brushed away the tickling again. "Well, I'm sure there's a normal splanation for it. I'm shorry I'm not there. We'll talk about it when I get back, okay?"

"Okay." She hesitated, then repeated it. "Okay. I love you."

"You, too."

He hung up. He began to slip the phone back into his pocket, thought better of it, and pulled it back out. He switched it off, then put it away.

"All ready?" his companion asked.

He smiled at Hannah. "Ready," he announced. He decided not to castigate her for tickling him while he talked. She was just one of those playful types, and had no way of knowing the nature of that conversation.

"Girlfriend troubles?" she asked him with a teasing grin. *Then again, maybe she does.*

"Not really. It's minor."

"Come on, let's go cheer you up." Her voice was merry. She sounded a little tipsy from the two cocktails she had gone through already. They had only gotten halfway from the airport bar to the exit before Wendy had called. Now Hannah slipped her arm in his and led him back toward the bar. Apparently she was ready for a third.

Ernie obediently walked with her. He felt the eyes of passersby, full of lust for the sexy flight attendant at his side and envy for him. It gave him mixed feelings.

This was not his fault. They had simply talked a little on the flight. It had not even seemed flirtatious at the time. He had been in line to disembark without a second thought until she approached him. She had invited him for a drink together, not the other way around. This whole thing had been her doing. For once, he had been the passive partner. He had only smiled and nodded to get to this point.

When they had ordered their first drinks, he was still unsure about her intentions. That had changed when the alcohol helped relax their inhibitions. "There's something about you," she told him.

It was true. There *was* something about him. He felt it, too. He liked to think he had always felt it.

"Tell me more," he quipped.

"Buy me another and I might," she replied.

He obliged, and so did she. They had been talking about Catoctin, a college that she had heard of but knew nothing about. So he began describing it for her, attempting to fill her with the same celestial reverence that he felt. She nodded, but had not really been listening. "You're perfect," she told him at his first pause. Her fingernail slowly traced a delicate path along his forearm and wrist. She had not been able to keep up with his penetrating gaze, and looked away. "You almost seem to be glowing."

Ernie was never one to be at a loss for words, but he had no reply to that. From that point forward, he had been completely in her hands. He only needed to follow her lead.

They had one more drink apiece. Three was apparently enough to make her laugh incessantly. The effect on Ernie was less obvious. He felt completely sober, but no more in control of himself than if he had been roaring drunk. He studied her face as she giggled and grinned. This was no mere college student. This was another level altogether. He could not get over how stunning she was, nor the fact that she was with *him*. She had been impressed that he was going to be on television, but he did not think that was her only motivation. She was genuinely attracted to him. It was all too good to be true.

New York City could wait.

PART III

Plague

13
REVERSALS

AMERICAN NOVELIST *and muckraker Upton Sinclair was born in Baltimore, Maryland during the tumultuous post Civil War-era. He had the unique circumstance of growing up in both low and upper class households, splitting time between his father's destitute and mother's affluent families. These formative years endowed Sinclair with an insight uncommon to most Americans: empathy and understanding for the aspirations of the rich as well as the sufferings of the poor. Already a writer, Sinclair worked undercover in the meatpacking plants of Chicago, then used the experience to detail the deplorable conditions of the industry in his 1906 novel The Jungle. The book struck a nerve in its readers. Within a year of its publication the government moved to pass legislation to increase food safety and inspections. The Meat Inspection Act was quickly followed by a series of Pure Food and Drug Acts, the progenitors of today's Food and Drug Administration.*

The Jungle is widely considered one of the most successful examples of literary activism and a triumph of muckraking. There is a problem with this belief, however. When Sinclair wrote of slaughterhouse employees falling into grinders to be mixed with the beef, he was attempting to call attention to the harrowing plight of workers and not to the repulsive quality of meat. He was trying to invoke the outrage of the population in order to enact change in the socioeconomic conditions of the poor working class, not to make people worry about the steaks on their dining room table. In Sinclair's own words, he "aimed at the public's heart and by accident hit its stomach."

Muckraking is a term that conjures either inspiration or outrage, depending on one's perspective. Those who held the reins of power, with a few notable exceptions, tended to challenge muckrakers and dismiss their claims. Franklin Delano Roosevelt called Sinclair a crackpot and his claims absolute falsehoods, until public opinion turned in support of Sinclair and Roosevelt was forced to reassess his stance. As a general rule, authorities dislike challenges to a status quo that placed them in power. They may claim that their actions are dictated by the best interests of their constituents as a whole, and to a certain extent this is true. Economic and social upheaval must be tempered to balance out the rights of all. For every justified accusation of the corrupting influence of special interests, there is equal merit to the claim that public welfare is best served by a thriving business environment. Morality is a nebulous concept. An obvious act of misconduct to one might be easily defensible to another.

It is not the reaction of the authorities but of the majority that is most interesting, providing a reiterative case study on the vagaries of human nature. Whether in reference to inequality, crime, terrorism, or epidemics, public opinion is even more slippery than morality, and nearly impossible to predict. It fluctuates between overreactive, apathetic, self-interested, and altruistic. Those who frame the news exert a modicum of influence over the viewing public, but influence does not equate to control. People seldom behave the way they are expected to.

Historic reactions to pandemics illustrate the point. The Spanish Flu was undoubtedly exacerbated by the indifference of the Wilson administration, which subordinated the welfare of the American public to the war effort the government was feverishly hyping at the same time as the outbreak. Sick troops were shipped overseas to the fighting without the quarantines recommended by doctors. Citizens were caught between a misunderstood illness and a natural instinct for patriotism. Parades and rallies moved ahead as scheduled, speeding the transmission of disease. Precautionary measures were limited and late, and fifty million or more died worldwide as a result.

By contrast, a much later outbreak of the same influenza virus stirred the opposite reaction. The 2009 outbreak of H1N1—commonly mislabeled "swine flu"—led to a much more aggressive reaction. President Barack Obama declared the disease a national emergency after only a few thousand confirmed cases in the United States. Resources inside and outside America were mobilized to mitigate the threat. H1N1 killed less than twenty thousand people around the globe over the course of several years, perhaps due to worldwide efforts to confront the pandemic. Or the disease might simply have been less dangerous than the overreaction warranted.

The crusade to end smallpox, undertaken by the World Health Organization in the 1970s, is the most spectacularly successful campaign of its kind in human history. It is probably the United Nations' crowning achievement, as well as a testament to what humankind can achieve with purpose and dedication. Smallpox not only killed hundreds of millions of people in the twentieth century alone, it continued to afflict an estimated fifty million each year before the heroic efforts of a handful of WHO workers all but eradicated the disease from the planet. Purportedly, the only remaining samples of smallpox are kept in secured laboratories in the United States and Russia.

In recent years, another pathogenic scourge has elicited yet another, highly controversial reaction from the public. Measles has killed hundreds of millions of people throughout history, and even today accounts for hundreds of thousands of deaths annually. The disease was almost entirely eliminated in America by modern vaccination programs in the late twentieth century, but a rising anti-vaccination movement has led to a predictable uptick in the number of cases. This does not mean that all vaccines are one hundred percent safe and effective, or that careful timing is unimportant. Vaccines are created from dead or weakened pathogens, and as such are not entirely without risk. However, for scourges such as measles the benefit of universal vaccination far outweighs the potential danger. Whether philosophical or political in origin, the resistance to these vaccinations is one step toward reversing the trend toward longer, healthier lifespans. For all their many virtues, humans do not seem to be very skilled at threat assessment.

～

"An outbreak of an unidentified illness has one Maryland town searching for answers. But is the disease deadly, or beneficial? Holly Staffer reports."

"McGahey, Maryland. Home of Catoctin College... A strange illness has affected a reported eighty-seven residents and students in the past two weeks. Experts believe the actual number may be even higher. Most patients claim that it feels like a bad case of the flu that lasts for several days. Dozens of patients have already recovered, but one student linked to the illness died during soccer practice, leaving a family and a community to mourn.

"Some reports tie the outbreak to the return of a student from an archaeological dig in Iraq—the same trip that led to the death of another student under mysterious circumstances. A spokesman for the Centers for Disease Control and Prevention stressed to us that the link between this illness and that dig is unconfirmed but is being investigated. The same is true for any correlation between this disease and the death of the soccer player. Meanwhile, other recovered patients actually report an improvement in their overall health following their bout with the illness. One man in his fifties says that he has not felt this good since his twenties. There are even unconfirmed reports of individuals actively exposing themselves to the illness in order to experience the benefits that come after recovery. Investigators are only now beginning to analyze the source of the disease. Until they complete their findings, this town is left with more questions than answers. Holly Staffer reporting for—"

Ernie turned off the television. *I don't know you, Holly Staffer, but you're a bitch. You had better hope we never meet.* He was irritated that the report went into these wild accusations that he brought the disease back from Iraq. They were basically holding him personally responsible for every person who got sick. They might as well accuse him of murdering that kid.

A week ago he had been on top of the world. But the story of his life was once again turning into perpetual failure and disappointment. Even when good things happened, they offered only false hope. The higher he rose, the farther he fell.

He had made himself the face of the Appelstein team by going on that news show. Now he was going to be the face of this disease as well. Taylor Allgood had brought fleeting recognition and pride, but now it also brought lasting ignominy and scorn.

As if Ernie did not have enough problems already. He believed he might be going mad. God was once again playing a cruel joke on him, and there was nothing he could do to stop it.

Ernie boiled with anger and frustration. These days it did not take much to trigger his temper. He noticed that the slightest things could annoy him to distraction, sending his mood into a tailspin. Even more disturbingly, he seemed to have lost his knack for hiding his feelings behind a veneer of affability. It was not so much that he could not pretend to be lighthearted while upset, it was more that he no longer wanted to. His moods were affecting his relationships, and he had a hard time caring.

He wished Wendy were around. Hers was the one relationship he still cared about. He clung to it, in fact. She was his rock, an unshakable anchor in a turbulent sea. Only she could calm him down when he was like this. But she was not here. She was in Chicago with her congressman, pressing the flesh with the country's elite. Soon she would aspire to heights beyond those Ernie could envision, much less participate in. He was a different sort of anchor for her, a tether holding her to earth while she sought only to climb. She would tire of his degeneracy and jettison him like so much ballast. She would let him fall, the same way he dropped his best friend in the hazy past.

Ernie had too much conflicting emotion to remain cooped up inside the apartment. He needed to go out and blow off steam. He stared out the window at the steady rain. He would get soaked, but no longer minded such trivialities. There was still a little daylight left. Perhaps a long walk in the refreshing rain would calm his troubled mind.

Before leaving, he collected a few items from his bedroom. He did not need a coat for warmth, but he did need it for its pockets. He nearly left his wallet behind, then reconsidered. He had no particular purpose or direction in mind, but it would be better to have it and not need it than the other way around. The same could be said of the other item he carried.

He left his stifling apartment behind and headed toward the interior of McGahey. It was a small town to drive through, but seemed quite a bit larger from the perspective of a walker. He did not care. He would wander as long as he needed. There was no fear of getting lost in a small town such as this.

Everything that was anything in McGahey was on or close to Main Street, so that is where Ernie found himself as the shrouded sun began to set. The rain had slackened but not stopped entirely, and there were few other pedestrians moving about. Their absence made the scene outside the church that much more noteworthy.

Ernie saw a small group congregating before the large stone edifice. The church was the oldest structure in McGahey. It sat ten yards off the street, providing ample space for the downtown's most decorous landscaping. Five steps led up from the sidewalk to a white pathway leading to towering red doors, the entrance to the nave. The pathway was straight except where it circled to either side of a small but vibrant garden of red flowers. Standing above the flowers was an eight-foot angel, wings outstretched and book in hand, standing on a platform of polished stone. Beside the angel, an old man was preaching to three unhappy-looking spectators, two older women and a beefy middle-aged man with a prematurely balding pate. Ernie could hear the percussive sound of the raindrops bouncing off that smooth crown. In these surroundings, the man reminded Ernie of a once-childish cherub now grown to adulthood, confronted by the sad misfortunes of life.

Ernie turned his attention to the man speaking. He was not as old as Ernie had originally thought, but lines of worry had carved themselves deep into cheek and brow. He wore black trousers and a white dress shirt beneath a transparent slicker, but Ernie thought he would have been better served to wear the robes of the ancients, for the man was a prophet of doom.

"...this is not the Eden they expected. There may be promises of Arcadia, yes, but look closely and you will see who is making those promises. You see only the garden, but there is a serpent in the grass, whispering in your ear, spreading greed and corruption. This is not paradise, but Gehenna."

Ernie watched in morbid fascination, absorbing every facet of the scene unfolding before him. He saw that the rain was flooding over the flowers. A large pool had collected just below the base of the statue, drowning out the green and most of the red. Was this the false garden of which the man spoke?

"...and those who accept this foul judgment—nay, who embrace it —shall be the first called to serve at Satan's side. You see them now, walking among us, heads held high, full of vainglory, confident in their newfound superiority. They are giants trampling out the meek. But we know the meek shall inherit the Earth. They forget, but we do not.

"They believe they are marked. And they are. They wear the Mark of Cain. They are evil! They must be cast down, destroyed..."

The tone and demeanor of the prophet had intensified dramatically. As his tempo and volume increased, he stabbed the air before him with an imaginary weapon. The speech was having a powerful impact on Ernie, but it seemed to have the opposite effect on the others.

"All right, that's enough," the aging cherub interrupted. "We don't need talk like that." He gestured with his hands while he spoke, waving the aspirant orator down from the platform.

Ernie scoffed. The weak always balked at violence. It was their way. But he knew—as the prophet knew—that there was power in conflict. What had Nietzsche said? *A living thing seeks to discharge its strength.* It was the natural order of things. Humans spent a lifetime repressing their basic desires, and it made them miserable.

"Let the man shpeak," he said, stepping forward to intervene. He stopped the cherub's arm in mid gesture by grabbing it roughly in his hand. For a moment, their eyes met, and Ernie dared the other to put up a struggle. The man withdrew his arm quickly and stepped back.

Ernie looked hopefully at the prophet. He was about to urge the man to continue, but no urging was necessary.

"Here stands before us one of the wicked!" The old man raised a finger and pointed. Ernie felt a flicker of confusion and looked at the others. Then he realized the finger was directed at him, and comprehended what gospel the prophet was preaching. He should have understood all along. He suddenly felt ashamed, and felt his cheeks flush. The man's continuing cries surrounded Ernie, echoing in his head, penetrating his being like barbed arrows. He felt an instinct to run, and then to defend himself. Shame was replaced by anger.

"It is sinners like he who bring the day of judgment!"

Ernie was not even aware that he was lashing out until the man was already on the ground at his feet. Ernie had easily knocked him off his perch, and the man had tumbled into the sloppy garden with an unceremonious splash. Unmindful of the puddle, Ernie went to a knee beside the prostrate figure. He no longer appeared the formidable augur. Instead, he was just a weak old man with mud on his face. Ernie was disgusted at himself for having felt threatened by this creature.

The man tried to push himself up from the dirt, but Ernie easily pushed him back down. The man had no strength with which to compete with his. Ernie held his face down in the puddle. It was important to demonstrate his own superiority, both to his opponent and to himself.

An instinct triggered in his mind. He should be cognizant of other threats. He looked around. The other three spectators were nowhere to be seen, having long since fled the scene. Even better for him, the rain had brought a premature night to McGahey. The rain and darkness provided all the cover he needed to act without restraint.

The man was whimpering now. Ernie continued to press his face to the muddy water with his left hand. With his right he drew the handgun from his coat pocket and pressed it to the old man's temple. It was an elegant Sig Sauer of the same model that he had first learned to shoot with. He had purchased it the day after Halfus and Kevin had taken him to the range, nearly two years earlier. Ernie had been so proud of it at the time, had looked forward to showing it off to them the next time they went out shooting. Now, looking back, he realized that that had never happened. Like so many other things in his life, he had watched pride fade into the ether. But now he was pleased to finally have the opportunity to use it.

The man stopped struggling as soon as he felt the barrel touch his skin. Ernie waited for him to beg, but it did not come. The man trembled and his teeth began to chatter. He appeared to be clenching his mouth shut as though forcing himself not to speak. He was suitably terrified, but he did not beg.

Ernie closed his eyes. He saw a light in the darkness, infinitesimal at first, then growing swiftly in size and brilliance. It was the headlight of a train, barreling straight toward him. To stop it, he needed to pull the trigger. It was a terrible game, this deadly object racing directly at him, compelling him to flinch. It grew larger and larger, until it was almost upon him.

He still possessed enough humanity to resist. He had to slip his finger out of the trigger guard first. Only then could he bring himself to open his eyes, and only after great effort. When he did, he found himself gasping for breath, the gun all but forgotten. He had dropped it to the ground beside him.

It lay between himself and the old man. Ernie felt a moment of panic and an impulse to grab it again. But he saw that the other was making no effort to reach for it. Instead, the man was looking directly at him. The face of the prophet was back, the eyes penetrating Ernie's innermost thoughts.

Ernie felt forlorn. Desperate. He looked back in supplication, pleading with his eyes for direction.

"Kill yourself," the man said. "Before it's too late. While you still have enough control to do it." He put his wet and dirty hand on Ernie's shoulder. He squeezed once in sympathy. Then he picked himself up and walked away.

Ernie remained huddled in the mud, head bowed, until he noticed that the rain had stopped. He looked up and saw the stars coming out. And the moon. The drier air reinvigorated him. He stood up, collected the gun, and walked away from the church. He felt that he had dodged a bullet. These episodes where he felt less and less in control of himself were becoming more alarming. It was something he needed to keep an eye on. *I'd hate to be the next person who sets me off*, he thought with a twinge of sadness.

The good news was that the rage had dissipated. Perhaps he was learning how to restrain himself. He needed to find a healthy release, preferably more constructive than this one had been. But he took comfort in the knowledge that it was over now, and no one had been seriously hurt. Wendy would be back soon, and that was the key. In the future, she could help him through these out-of-body experiences.

He suddenly felt extremely tired. It was a long way back home.

"The rain looks as though it's letting up," Ben said. He felt foolish even as he said it. *Here we are, two college professors, and all I can think to talk about is the weather.* But it was the first thing that came to mind that he felt comfortable saying. The warm, wet air was also laden with romantic tension. He could feel it clearly, and was certain she did as well. It made him uneasy and overcautious.

Naturally, she smiled at his discomfort. She ignored his comment and changed the subject entirely. "Benji, thanks for taking care of me."

"It was my pleasure." He smiled agreeably as he looked down on her lovely features. "It was symmetry."

They had been walking in McGahey's quaint little park, peacefully watching the clouds roll in. It took less than an hour to walk the park's perimeter, even at a leisurely pace, so they stopped for a while to sit side-by-side on a pair of children's spring animals. Brenda sat on a dinosaur and left Ben to take the yellow duckling, which promptly compelled her to take a picture of him with her cell phone. He did not mind. She had been in a good mood, laughing at the silly spectacle he made of himself, and her mood had a contagious effect on him. They had rocked gently and talked until the rain forced them to dash under the roof of a pavilion. Then they watched the rain, shoulders pressed together, each of them deliberately enjoying the moment without stating the obvious. They spoke of banal matters until evening became night, neither of them wishing to leave.

In some ways this was like a dream come true, but only if he forced himself to ignore the elephant in the room. Brenda was engaged to another man. Ben supposed he might be deluding himself when he thought she was romantically interested in him. Other than their momentary kiss at the soccer match, nothing physical between them had transpired at all. It was quite possible that she viewed him more like a best friend or an older brother. But he did not think so. As they watched the last of the evening showers taper off, he fended off the nearly irresistible impulse to hold her hand. He felt certain that she would willingly accept it. Yet he held back, focused on a single overriding thought. *Why now?*

It was possible that she felt a sense of gratitude for his nursing her through the illness. When she had asked for his help, he had given it without reservation. He had been excited to do it, which should have been his first warning. Once he realized it was too awkward to ask why he—and not Trevor—was caring for her, he knew that his intentions were not entirely innocent. Eventually he had forced himself to ask anyway, and learned that her fiancé was not only out of town, but sick with the same illness. Somehow, that made Ben feel less guilty.

It had all begun a few days after the soccer match, close enough that Ben now believed he had passed the sickness on to her. He had not thought so at the time, for his symptoms had long since disappeared and he had not known he was still contagious. But the most recent news reports about the disease told him otherwise. As the volume of cases increased beyond the level of general apathy, the CDC had reluctantly assigned a few resources to get to the bottom of the mysterious new illness. What they found was neither alarming nor reassuring. The virus was unidentified, but appeared to be relatively harmless, at least when compared to the continuing Duck Flu epidemic.

The CDC had passed responsibility over to USAMRIID, the United States Army Medical Research Institute of Infectious Diseases.

The transition made sense considering the institute's geographical proximity to Catoctin. USAMRIID was based at Fort Detrick in Frederick, just twenty minutes down the road. It had local doctors who could visit McGahey and the college while still living at home. Recently, Ben had overheard that the World Health Organization might also get involved, depending on the similarities between the outbreak in Maryland and similar ones happening in Europe.

All that was neither here nor there as far as he was concerned. The only relevant news was that they were now reporting how patients remained contagious long after their symptoms disappeared. In fact, it seemed that the longer a patient carried the virus, the more infectious he or she became. It had something to do with the body's failure to produce antibodies. The same condition complicated any attempt at a vaccine, as well. It was all a little confusing to Ben, who had too many more important things to occupy his attention. All he knew was that he felt great, physically and emotionally. And now Brenda said she did, as well, so he found it hard to feel particularly guilty about passing a two-day bug on to her.

Especially when the consequences had brought them closer together than ever. He had been fortunate to have so much free time, providing him the opportunity to attend to her all day long during her bout. Their time together did not diminish even after her recovery and Trevor's return. Ben presumed the other man in her life felt tremendous resentment toward him at the moment. But this, too, he had difficulty feeling guilty about. There had been so many times that Ben found himself feeling rejected by Trevor's last minute excuses that he felt nothing but contempt for his rival. He honestly wondered what Brenda saw in such a man. Ben had to remind himself that he and Trevor had only met a few times, and those a long time ago. His impressions were being developed at a distance, and thus were susceptible to distortion.

He told himself that it made no difference what he thought of Trevor, nor what Trevor thought of him. All that really mattered was what Brenda thought. She was the essential factor in this equation. All the time they were spending together was the best thing going on in his life, and he did not want to jinx it through overanalysis.

"The stars are coming out," she said.

"Make a wish," he replied jokingly.

"Starlight, star bright, first star I see tonight, I wish I may, I wish I might, have the wish I wish tonight."

He wanted to ask her what she wished for. But if he remembered correctly, telling him would ruin it. Besides, he thought he had a pretty good idea.

She leaned her head on his shoulder and sighed contentedly.

On the first day back from Chicago, Wendy quit her job. It was a painful act to perform. If not exactly giving up on a budding career that she had striven to achieve for as long as she could remember, resigning now was at the least setting her back for the foreseeable future. At best, she would lose a much-needed reference to get her foot inside someone else's door. At worst, she would be blacklisted and shut out from doing political work entirely.

Painful, yes, but not difficult. Others might not see it the same way, but she believed the decision had been made for her, when an inebriated man gave voice to his motives in the unfamiliar confines of a hotel room, safeguarded from prying eyes and ears by a thousand-mile buffer. Just like that, Wendy understood the suspicious attitudes of her coworkers, along with the brutal truth about how she had gotten the job after a single spontaneous appeal. To say nothing of the reason a position was available in the first place. A brief inquiry revealed that she was not the first to be placed in this position, although she suspected she was the first to reject him. Others might wonder why she did not grit her teeth and put up with it. She was hardly the only person to be harassed in an office, and others had found ways to go on doing their job despite the interference. But there were two reasons that Wendy did not even give it a second thought. First, the Congressman's wife had apparently intervened in the affair with Wendy's predecessor, and Wendy would not live under the constant scrutiny of a scornful spouse. Secondly, she could not escape the shameful conclusion that it was not her intelligence and talent for which she had been hired. She wanted to be the respected woman who thrived despite the persistent attention of men, not because of it.

Although the decision had been forced upon her, Wendy was not without regret as she left the office that afternoon for what she assumed would be the last time. She came in that day not only to officially give notice and pack her few personal belongings, but to apologize to Sandy for being the source of so much unwanted anxiety. Wendy felt no animosity for the woman. She was simply trying to do the best job for her employer, to whom she no doubt felt considerable allegiance. Sandy had simply accepted the letter and nodded, but Wendy believed she could read the woman's thoughts. *It's for the best. You were always going to be a temptation.* It was so frustrating to discover that men and women could not work together professionally without so many human foibles getting in the way, but she did not know what other conclusion to draw. In this case, it was doubly frustrating because Wendy still respected Bob King as a politician. Just no longer as a person.

She needed to talk to someone about it. She wished that could be Ernie, but it simply was not in the nature of their relationship. He did not seem like the kind of boyfriend who could help with matters like this. Perhaps she had waited too long to share her private thoughts with him, or perhaps he would have been this way regardless. For whatever reason, her reluctance to vent her doubts and fears on him had stubbornly persisted. Now it seemed to be a fundamental parameter of their relationship. She told herself that it was all right. Every relationship had unique constraints. She simply needed to appreciate the other qualities he brought to her life. She reminded herself of how alone she had felt before accepting him. From that perspective, this minor complaint felt like nitpicking. For the hundredth time she told herself that she had known what she was getting into when she rushed into his arms.

Regardless, she needed someone to talk to. She missed Matt. So much, in fact, that she suddenly wanted to cry. She kept an eye on the edge of the road in case the water works started and she needed to pull over. She would forever be a more cautious driver because of what happened to him. The irony was that she was the beneficiary of that deadly lesson, yet the accident had been more her fault than his. Life could be so cruel, and her own problems paled in comparison to the fate of those she cared about. She questioned whether God was punishing her or trying to make her a stronger person. If it were the latter, she was afraid that it would be a wasted effort. On the other hand, if it were the former, it was working. She really hurt.

As she turned off Route 15 and headed into McGahey, she steered the Toyota toward her mother's apartment. She had not seen her mother since well before the trip to Chicago. Her last visit had been upsetting, to say the least. She hoped to erase those sour memories and replace them with something better. What she really wanted was one of their old fashioned mother-daughter heart-to-hearts. They had not had one of those since Miriam's health problems began, many months earlier. It would feel good to have one again.

"Mom?" Wendy called as she let herself in. She had high hopes for this visit, as she had seen open curtains from her vantage point below. *Good moods welcome the light.*

"Back here, Sweetie," came a cheerful voice from the bedroom. It was another positive sign. The past few times they had spoken together, her mother had been acting strangely. It was a relief to catch her on a better day.

"I'm going to make some tea, okay? We need to talk."

Wendy tossed her bag onto the couch and headed into the kitchen. Her mother may have been in a good mood, but her housekeeping had clearly not recovered the way her health had. The smell in the kitchen informed Wendy's nose that the trash had not been emptied in quite some time. She sighed. She could take a load to the chute down the hall while the tea was boiling. It would not be the first time she had done something her mother could easily do herself. She just hoped it was only a token of forgetfulness rather than a sign that her mother's independence was coming to an end. Wendy loved her mother dearly, but the thought of living together in the same home filled her with panic. When she had gone to Iraq while her mother was bedridden, she had briefly contemplated such a move on her return. After that, she had gone directly from believing her mother would die to watching her make a full recovery, so the idea had been laid to rest. She sincerely hoped she would not have to consider it again for many years to come.

Wendy produced a flame on the stove, then opened the cabinet where the tea kettle was stored. It was not there, so she looked around and found it on the counter by the sink. She filled it with water and set it on the burner, then went to another cabinet to sift through the flavors. There were fewer choices than she remembered. Apparently, her mother was back to making tea on her own. Wendy made a mental note to pick up another box or two the next time she was grocery shopping.

Which one goes with unemployed? she wondered. She did not feel like thinking about it, so she grabbed the most colorful packet she saw, tore it open, and emptied it into the hot water. She tossed the packet into the trash can. Then she jumped back and covered her mouth with her hands, her heart suddenly pounding like a jackhammer. Truman lay on the floor beside the trash can, unmoving, his paws stretched out in a macabre, unnatural leap. His head rested at an abnormal angle, the neck clearly snapped. Now Wendy recognized the smell in the kitchen for what it was.

She heard the water of the tea kettle boiling in the background. She stepped gingerly around the dead animal as though it were a land mine, then pulled the kettle off the burner. Her hand shook as she poured out two cups. *Just get through this, Wendy. You can think about it later.*

But it was impossible not to think about it now. What had happened? Was it an accident? If so, how did her mother not notice the carcass and take care of it? Could she be so devastated that she was blocking it from her mind?

Wendy wobbled unsteadily as she carried a tray with two cups back to her mother's room. Even as she pushed open the door, she did not know how she would broach the subject.

Although it was mid-afternoon, her mother was still wearing the white and blue nightgown she used for sleeping. She was not in bed, however, but rocking contentedly in an antique chair while gazing out the window. "I saw you pull up," she announced with a grin. "My eyes are as sharp as ever."

Wendy set the tray down carefully. She was unable to keep this feeling bottled up a moment longer. "Mom...what happened to Truman?" she asked tentatively. She had to ask, but she was not sure that she wanted to hear the answer.

"Oh, that. He was being a real nuishance. She knocked over the trash can. I warned him. I even hit her a couple times, but he did it again." She continued to rock at the same leisurely pace.

Wendy forced herself to remain calm, although she wanted to tear her hair out. Clearly, they were not going to have the heart-to-heart Wendy had looked forward to. She would not be talking to her mother about quitting her job. Or anything else. It was all she could do not to scream. "I'm sorry to do this, Mom, but I have to run. Something came up."

Her mother did not react. She was already looking back out the window. She seemed completely disinterested in her daughter.

Wendy backed out of the room. She closed the door noiselessly, not wanting to attract her mother's attention. She needed a place to think, and it had to be away from here.

Wendy grabbed her bag and let herself out of the apartment. She walked halfway down the hall to the stairwell, then stopped. She turned around and went back in, making her way to the kitchen as quietly as possible. She opened the cabinet where the garbage bags were stored, shook one open, and grabbed some disinfectant spray from under the sink. She filled the inside of the bag until the sides ran heavy with liquid.

She placed the bag on the floor, top held open, then used a dustpan to lift Truman from the floor and gently place him inside. She tied the bag off at the top, twice. Now she could finally leave the apartment for good.

Her first thought was to throw the bag down the chute, just to be done with the whole sad tragedy. But Truman had been a loving pet to her mother through many troubled years. Wendy would figure out a way to give him a proper burial, even if her mother would not be there to participate.

The limitless energy that Wendy had begun to take for granted decided to abandon her for the time being. She felt tired and sore and dreaded even having to drive, much less what would come after. She did not really know where exactly to drive to, but she knew she needed to get the hell away from this place. She pulled away from the curb and drove for five minutes, paying no attention to where she was headed. Finally, she decided she had put enough distance between herself and perdition. At last, she could pull over and think.

This was a quiet residential neighborhood that she did not recognize. She got out of the car and walked around it. Feeling light-headed, she stopped and stood still, wondering whether she might faint. She did not, and the feeling slowly passed.

Her cell phone began to ring. At first she ignored it, uncertain whether she was capable of conversation right now. Then she wondered if it could be her mother. Maybe the woman slipped in and out of lucidity. Wendy thought this might be her best chance to get some answers.

Dazedly, she pulled out her phone and brought it to her ear. "Hello?"

"Hello, Wendy?" It was a man's voice. Her hopes sank. *Whoever you are, please take my mind off this.*

"Who is this?" she asked.

The man on the line sounded hesitant, as though he were gulping air. "Wendy, this is Halfus."

She did not reply. Instead she sat down, right on the curb. She felt faint all over again.

He gulped again. "I know this is probably..."

She was vaguely aware that words were continuing to be spoken to her, but she had no idea what they were. They might as well have been Russian.

She closed her eyes, pressing the lids down hard. She was trying hard, but she did not know how to stop it. The effort was too great, and after she felt the first tear run down her cheek, she stopped resisting.

She realized she was missing words. Valuable words. She pressed the phone hard against her ear and tried to soak in every sound. Not just what he was saying. She wanted to hear him breathe.

He paused. "Wendy, are you crying?"

"Yes. Oh my God, yes." She was also shaking. She rocked herself forward and back. Somehow that seemed to help. She recollected her thoughts into something coherent. "Can you...start over?"

He chuckled. That sound was wonderful to hear. But his next words were not. "Listen, I don't have time to repeat everything I just said. They want me off the phone now. I just needed to hear your voice."

"Wait!" she cried. "Where are you?"

"Ankara. I'm coming home as soon as I can. But I don't know when that will be. They have lots of questions for me, believe it or not." She found herself smiling. Her tears were abating. She had no idea what he had been through, but was sure it must have been hell. Just hearing him make a wisecrack was a welcome relief.

But this whole conversation hardly seemed real. She was not sure she was not imagining this. She needed more. She could not just hang up and wait. Somewhere in the back of her mind, she was aware that she had things to talk about. Halfus would be the perfect person to talk to. This was divine intervention, a rare blessing from a whimsical God.

"Halfus, don't go. I...there are so many things I need to talk to you about."

"I know. Me, too. We'll talk about everything, as soon as I'm home. I promise."

No! Not yet. "But—"

"I've got to go. I'm sorry. I'll see you soon, Wendy. Goodbye."

"Halfus, I..." She stopped. The call had already ended.

She had wanted to tell him she loved him. It came out of nowhere. She was not sure why she had wanted to say it, except that he was about to hang up and she wanted to keep him on the line so they could go on talking and she did not know when she would speak to him again and it was true.

Oh, dear Lord, Halfus is alive. There was a warm glow filling her from the inside. Strength was returning to her body. *He is alive, and he needed to hear my voice.* The amount of comfort she took from that one statement was disconcerting in implication.

She felt the same way she had after they had kissed in Iraq. The intervening months had not happened. She had not gone to sleep angry, he had not disappeared from her life, Matt had not died, she was not with Ernie...

Ernie. Shit. She could not love both him and Halfus, could she?

No, she could not. It was so simple, now that she allowed the thought of Halfus to reenter her mind. She simply did not love Ernie. Not at all. She had wanted to. She had tried to. She had pretended to. But she never had. And she did not have to go on pretending now.

It was a second lease on life. She was aware of a million problems that should be overwhelming her right now, but for the moment they faded to the background. It felt as though things were going to work out, after all. *Right?*

She got back into her car, turned the ignition, and cringed as a terrible noise reminded her that the engine was already on. She needed to calm her frenzied mind. She pulled away from the curb and headed toward home. Then she had another thought. She changed direction.

She needed to tell Ernie. He would be so thrilled to find out that Halfus was alive. They were practically best friends. He might be nearly as happy as she.

Except that she had two things to tell him. *Halfus is alive, Ernie. Oh, and I am leaving you for him.* This was going to be a mess.

She considered changing course yet again. But she could not do that, she had to see him. She was simply getting a little ahead of herself. She had no idea what was going to happen with Halfus. She even had a vague memory of a reason she was supposed to be angry at him. She needed to approach this logically. She would share the good news that Halfus was alive. She would not deny Ernie the same moment of celebration she herself had felt. Then, in coming days, she would ask for space in their relationship. That would spare her the difficulty of pretending she loved him any longer than necessary. What excuse would she use for space? Perhaps trouble with her mother, the typical default.

Oh, God, my mother. The horror of the afternoon came flooding back to the forefront of her thoughts. She looked over at the passenger seat and the heavy package lying there. She had needed to talk to Halfus about the nightmare that had happened, but they had not had time. She did not think she could handle it alone. Perhaps Ernie would help, after all. She would soften him up with news of Halfus, then ask for a huge favor when he was feeling happy.

She saw his Jeep as she pulled up to the apartment. *He's home. That's good. I think.*

She left Truman's sad remains in the car as she walked up the steps and let herself in. He had given her a key as soon as they started dating. He had wanted this relationship to work just as much as she did, Wendy realized. Perhaps this would be harder than she assumed.

He was sitting at the small table that functioned as his kitchen, dining room, and office. His head was down on his arms, buried. She could hear a faint muffled sound. He was crying.

"Ernie?" Her voice was not much more than a whisper.

He looked up. His face was forlorn. She felt an instant pang of sympathy. *Oh, Sweet Ernie, what now? How could I have thought of hurting you?* She stepped closer to him. "Ernie, what's wrong?"

Her nose told her before his words. "I pooped myself," he said. Tears welled in his eyes anew. He seemed pitifully helpless, and she threw her arms around him.

"It's okay, Easy. Shh. It's okay." She hugged him and stroked his beautiful black hair.

He shook his head. "No, itsh not. I don't know whatsh shappening to me, Wendy." His voice sounded scared. Genuinely scared. She had never heard it like this before. Even with everything that had happened in Iraq. "I feel like I'm turning into an animal."

She had no idea what to say, so instead she simply hugged him as hard as she could. She wanted him to know she was there for him. And she resolved that she would be. She could set aside her own selfish problems for a while in order to focus on him. She did not know what else she could do.

"Shh. Shh," she said reassuringly. "Just rest tonight. Tomorrow we'll decide what to do."

She decided not to say anything about Halfus. For now, she wanted Ernie to be less excitable, not more.

There were so many things to do tonight, none of them enjoyable. She would clean him up, put him to bed, and make sure he fell asleep. Then she would go back to her car and give Truman a proper farewell. Only then would she let herself think about anything else. This was her chance to help other people for a change, and she intended to give it all she had. If God was trying to make her a stronger person, he was going all out. It was going to be a very long night.

14

CONFUSION AND ANGER

THERE IS no single clinical distinction between psychopathy and sociopathy. The terms are often used interchangeably, both amongst professionals in the field and the public at large. In most cases, even those who see a clear divide between the conditions recognize that they share several similar characteristics: a lack of empathy and respect for the rights of other people; disregard for society's laws and conventions; an inclination toward aggressive, often violent behavior; and an inability to feel guilty afterward.

For those who see a separation, sociopaths are capable of emotion and at least some level of identification with and attachment to others. They are often visibly troubled, and thus more easily identified. Psychopaths, on the other hand, have a complete detachment from others and act solely in their own self-interest. They are perfectly aware of laws and expectations, adapt their behavior accordingly, and often come across as charming and intelligent. They can be exceptionally skilled at concealing the condition, both as a matter of survival and gain.

Sociopathy and psychopathy are not the equivalent of insanity, at least in the legal definition. Legal insanity requires that defendants be unable to understand the illegality of their acts at the time they performed them. In contrast, sociopaths and psychopaths generally have a clear understanding of *what constitutes right and wrong in the eyes of the law. Insofar as they obey the law, they do so only to escape punishment, not as a matter of concern for the good of society.*

The American Psychiatric Association lists both psychopathy and sociopathy in the category of antisocial personality disorders. These disorders are defined by some of the same identifying characteristics listed above, plus a number of others including impulsivity, irritability, irresponsibility, and certain age requirements. At an international level, the World Health Organization has separate but similar criteria for identifying dissociative personality disorders. In both cases, these definitions also encompass a wide range of other, generally milder illnesses.

Because of the variance between definitions, multiple tests have been used at different times in an attempt to identify sociopaths and psychopaths. Due to the difficulty of testing the general population, prison populations have often functioned as case studies. The results are highly questionable at best, making it extremely difficult to extrapolate numbers for society at large. However, many experts believe the projections are surprisingly high. Depending on the methodology employed, estimates place the number of people afflicted with these conditions at approximately one to two percent of the population. There is a high probability that everyone knows, or is even close to, at least one sociopath or psychopath without necessarily being aware of it.

The causes of these disorders, like the definitions themselves, are subject to debate. Psychopathy most accurately fits the characterization of a genetic illness. No amount of good parenting will cure a child born with an absolute disregard for rules, morals, and the welfare of other people. Sociopathy, however, may stem in whole or in part from a troubled upbringing.

The impairment of brain functioning as a result of physical changes in the brain is called dementia. There are many types of dementia, although the vast majority of cases belong to a single illness: Alzheimer's disease. Other types include Parkinson's disease, Huntington's disease, and vascular dementia, which is often caused by strokes. Less common is Creutzfeldt-Jakob disease, the human derivative of mad cow disease, caused by an infection of prions. Other conditions such as frontotemporal dementia may cause personality and behavioral changes and language difficulties.

Recently, brain disorders have come under increased study, largely due to the frequency of football-related head injuries and the popularity of the sport. Many parents are becoming appropriately concerned about the potential long-terms effects of brain trauma, and prohibit their children from playing football and other contact sports. Whether this is an overreaction to dangers real and perceived is up to the individual, but the increase in scrutiny can only lead to much needed improvements in our understanding of the body's most complex organ.

Joy. Pure, absolute joy. Ben felt that he was bursting at the seams. He needed to speak to someone, and he wanted it to be in person.

Without breakfast—without even showering—he pulled on a sweatshirt and jeans and hopped in the car. It was not yet dawn, but it would be soon. He felt confident that Brenda would be up by the time he arrived. But even if she were not, she would understand once he explained things to her.

As he drove, a second reason to be excited joined his first. This was a break from the usual routine for him and her. This was the first time he was taking the initiative. Ordinarily, she initiated their meetings. She liked having everything go exactly according to her own plans. This morning he would surprise her, and maybe even catch her at a moment of weakness. If so, maybe he could glean a clue as to how she really felt about him. One way or another, that was the next step in their relationship. Perhaps an impromptu visit could be the sign she needed to express her feelings once and for all.

He was assuming that her feelings were stronger than the simple friendship they had renewed. He did not understand how or why it had happened, but he was not going to look a gift horse in the mouth. If she wanted him, he would not push her away. But if it happened, it needed to be her decision. He felt guilty enough already about having feelings for a woman engaged to another man. He knew that feelings were all it took for some people to act, and commitments be damned. But he was not one of them. Humans were emotional *and* logical animals. It might not always be quite as much fun, but he had spent his entire life letting logic dictate. He could not change who he was now.

It occurred to him that she might not be happy about his showing up unannounced. Even worse, Trevor could be there. The couple lived apart, but they likely spent some nights together. Ben felt a pang of unwanted jealousy. He quashed it. He was getting ahead of himself. She was not his—at least not yet—so he had no business feeling possessive. He was hopeful that things would work out, but he told himself that he could accept his fate if they did not. There were other things to carry him past any possible disappointments this morning. In that sense, this was an ideal time to force the issue.

Ben was blessed with a splendid sunrise as he parked the car on the street in front of her house. He practically skipped up the walkway through her postcard-perfect front yard, framed by trimmed hedges and elegant peonies. Still bursting with exuberance, he knocked on the door instead of ringing the bell.

Brenda opened the door in a sleek silk robe. It clung to her narrow shoulders, making her seem smaller and more vulnerable than he was used to seeing. He distractedly glanced at her slender calves, then caught himself and looked back at her face.

She detected the brief glance and grinned amusedly. "I suppose you want to come in."

"I do indeed."

"Well, then, come on in." She held the door open wider, invitingly.

Oh, glorious day, he thought. This was the happiest he had felt in ages.

She led him into the kitchen. "Benji, what is it? You look positively jubilant." She put her hands on her hips, a thought clearly occurring to her. "Did they end your suspension?"

Ben paused. Of course she would think that. He had not even considered it. What had happened was even more important.

"Better."

She raised an eyebrow. "What could be better than that?"

"Remember my student who died in Iraq? He just turned up in Turkey. He's alive."

She stared at him in silence. She looked thoughtful for a moment. Then her face lit up in pleasure. "That's wonderful. How?"

Ben nodded, then shrugged. "I don't know. But he's at the U.S. embassy in Ankara. Apparently he's been there for days, and they are just now getting around to telling me." He shook his head. "Never mind. I cannot begin to tell you how happy it makes me." But of course he did not have to tell her. It was obvious from his behavior. He could not stop smiling.

"Well. It's about time." She approached him. "I've been waiting weeks to see your brilliant smile again." She stepped into him, forcing him to wrap her in his arms, and she made his smile disappear with a brief kiss. He held her shoulders, lightly, in case it should turn into something more. But a second later he was letting her go and staring at her back as she walked toward the bedroom.

"Let me put something on," she called back to him. "Then we'll celebrate. Be a doll and find us a nice bottle of wine, will you?"

He had two glasses of white poured out for them when she joined him in the kitchen a few minutes later. She looked much more stylish than he. She wore a thin red sweater and designer blue jeans that showed off her hips even more than the robe had. It appeared that she had also put on a hint of makeup. He took that as a good sign, although he reminded himself that it did not necessarily confirm anything.

She flicked on a small radio that rested on the kitchen counter, nestled behind some expensive white crockery. Ben read "Sugar" and "Flour" on the sides of the largest two pieces.

"Music or news?" she asked.

He shrugged. "What do you normally do?"

"I like to get the news while I make breakfast." She left it on the station it had already rested on. He recognized it as WAMU, from American University in Washington.

She picked up her glass and lifted it toward him. He took the other and waited.

"To happiness," she said.

"I can drink to that," he replied. They clinked their glasses and sipped.

"So, tell me—" she began.

"Just a second." He made a quieting gesture and cocked his ear toward the radio.

"...*Organization today confirmed another outbreak of the Schwarzvogel virus in Frankfurt, Germany. This is the second German city, after Stuttgart, to report cases. So far, Germany, France, and the United States are the only countries with confirmed outbreaks, but officials point out that because symptoms are often confused with the flu there may be more cases going unreported.*

"*In America, USAMRIID spokeswoman Colonel Gloria Horvat stated yesterday that they are increasing the number of resources devoted to testing patients and studying the illness in all areas so far affected. Representatives are in the process of being dispatched to New York and Atlanta and are already on location outside Frederick, the source of the American outbreak. She requested that patients self-report to these representatives, or to contact the institute via the front page of their website. She also asked that friends and family of patients take precautions not to expose themselves to the blood or saliva of the infected, and emphasized that no one should voluntarily expose themselves to the virus until researchers have time to study its long-term effects. Although there has only been a single death linked to the Schwarzvogel virus, Colonel Horvat emphasized that the infected are at risk of other unwanted aftereffects.*

"*When asked about the rumors that the Schwarzvogel virus has a regenerative response on nerve damage and other conditions, Colonel Horvat repeated that research is needed to evaluate what effects, alleviative or harmful, the disease produces. That research will be conducted as swiftly as possible, and until then people who voluntarily expose themselves are only putting their own health at risk—*"

"Seems a little late to be warning people away," said Brenda.

Ben agreed. He flinched whenever he heard the term "Schwarzvogel," for the name was wrapped up in a tangle of unwelcome associations for him. But the name on the street for the virus was even worse. Americans had trouble pronouncing the cumbersome German name, so they had found a much easier and more descriptive term for the bug. It was called the Eden virus, both for the part of the world in which it originated and for the glorious effect it had on the way one felt after the initial, awful purge. It was catching on faster than a drug. Plus it was perfectly legal, free of cost, and brought no uncomfortable withdrawal symptoms.

At least that was the popular impression. Ben was starting to have second thoughts. Personally, he still felt wonderful. Apparently, the same was true for Brenda. But in his recent conversations with Rich, he detected that the student was experiencing some unusual problems with his speech and personality. Ben had no idea whether these things were related to the bug they brought back from Iraq, but the timing was certainly suspicious. Rich had always been a brilliant speaker, which made the occasional misuse and mispronunciations of words all the more striking. Even more disconcerting, Ben had noticed the young man becoming increasingly irritable. Only time would tell how long these effects would last. Ben felt sorry for his friend, yet could not fully identify with him, as he himself had experienced no issues whatsoever. He was thankful for that, of course, but he gladly would have taken them in place of his student, if that had been possible.

Ben supposed that since he had no children of his own, he perceived his students as surrogates. Maybe one day he would start a real family—perhaps even with this woman before him—but until then Rich was the closest thing he had to a son. And he hated to see the boy suffer in the slightest. Rich was one of the most exceptional people Ben had ever known, student or professor. He had the potential to make a real impact on this world, and Ben deeply regretted anything that might hinder his progress.

But today was not a time for regret, he reminded himself. He was with a beautiful woman who seemed as charmed by him as he was by her. He sought to turn the conversation away from sickness and disease and back onto her. Onto *them*. "I know you need to go to campus today, but perhaps we can celebrate over dinner...?"

Her response was a thoughtful sigh, as though she were

considering. He was immediately reminded of her other commitments, so he quickly interjected. "Unless you and Trevor have plans, of course. I wouldn't want to intrude." *Any more than I already have.*

She sighed again. "We do. He wants us to meet with some of his work associates." Then she smiled. "But I can probably get him to reschedule."

Ben found this all just as confounding as ever. His heart was in limbo, and he craved some indication that he should stop hoping and move on with it, one way or the other. On a whim, he did the one thing he did not want to do. He forced the issue.

"If you reschedule, the three of us could have dinner together."

Perhaps forced was too strong a word. He nudged, then watched her reaction carefully to glean some insight into her perplexing thought process.

She scoffed in exasperation. Then she shook her head. "For being such a brilliant man, you're really dumb sometimes, you know that?"

He nodded. Her words did not sting. In fact, he felt the opposite. His heart swelled in hope. He believed that he understood her meaning, but he still harbored one last doubt. There were two possible explanations. The one he wanted to believe was that she was choosing him over Trevor. But she also might simply mean that Trevor loathed Ben too much to ever join them for any activity. That, too, would explain the half-dozen last minute cancellations.

Ben decided to play dumb. He had to hear the words from her. "He hates me that much, does he?"

Brenda scoffed again. "He doesn't hate you at all. He barely knows you exist." She showed Ben a conspiratorial smile. "Maybe I just want you to myself."

This response was confusing. Instinct told Ben to stop there, to let the matter drop. But a cord was struck in the back of his mind, where his misgivings resided. "I don't understand. How is that possible? Even after all the times he said he was going to join us—"

Brenda shook her head at Ben. She still looked amused. "And I worried that I was being so obvious." She laughed at her own expense. "I suppose I have a confession to make. He didn't cancel all those invitations. I never invited him." She smiled widely at Ben. "I just wanted to be with you."

Ben knew he should have felt flattered, but instead he was disturbed. This changed everything. The man he had been feeling such animosity toward suddenly seemed like a hapless innocent. Ben had trouble collecting his thoughts. He struggled to arrange them in a logical order so that he could express them.

She was already stepping toward him, obviously intending another kiss. He caught her shoulders and stopped her. He needed to say something, but his brain was stuck in slow motion again, just like the old days. "How...?" was all he managed to say.

Her smile had faded. Now she studied his face the way he had been studying hers. She looked uncertain. It had always been an unfamiliar, unflattering expression for her, and her beauty diminished significantly. Then she took a step back. "We agreed to maintain a degree of independence. We both think it's better for a relationship."

"This?" he blurted out. "Look at what you're doing. How could *this* be better for your relationship?" He heard the cynicism in his own voice. He did not intend to sound preachy, but he was too upset to calm himself.

She flinched. For the first time, she looked away, unable or unwilling to meet his eyes. "I thought you would be pleased. I...really care about you, Ben." The volume of her voice steadily diminished. "What do you want me to do?" she asked feebly.

"I want you to think things through," he told her, this time without the bitterness. His thoughts were catching back up to events. He was calm again.

He boiled things down to a simple equation. "Do you love him?"

Brenda's shoulders sagged. She took a moment to answer. "I...don't know." She looked back at Ben. It seemed that she was looking for guidance.

He did not want to say it, but he forced himself to. He even allowed himself to smile as he did so. He put his hands back onto her shoulders, willing his message to penetrate through her cloud of confusion. "Look, you're just nervous about getting married. It happens to almost everyone, and some more than most." It felt odd to be lecturing her about something he had never experienced for himself, but he did it anyway. "It's a big deal, spending the rest of your life with someone. Your whole existence is going to change. You're simply having second thoughts, nothing more."

Her eyes bounced back and forth, scanning his face. He believed she was trying to read his sincerity, so he took a moment to make sure he believed it himself. He did, so he tried to convince her with a little humor. "You're just lucky the guy you chose to share those doubts with is a good and decent man, and not some scoundrel."

He hoped for a laugh, or at least another smile. She did neither. Instead, she continued to read his face with a look of gravity. "What about you, Ben? How do you feel?"

Ben had a feeling that he could still change course, if he chose to. He could tell her he loved her, and she would probably still fall into his embrace. "I want you to be happy, Brenda. Think back to when you accepted his proposal. Did that make you happy?"

Slowly, she nodded.

Ben smiled. His hands were still on her shoulders. He drew her in and kissed her forehead. "That's good enough for me." It did not feel good, but it did feel right.

He felt her arms circle around his waist, tentatively. He hugged her back, not without mixed feelings. Perhaps today was a day for regret, after all.

Ernie was angry again. And this time, he did not think he could stop.

It did not help that he was left to sit for hours on end, simmering in the juices of his own indignation. He needed to vent himself in an act of cathartic fury. He was waiting for his victim to walk in that door. This time, Wendy would not be able to help. This time, she was the object of his anger.

He did not want to hurt her. Or perhaps he did. He wanted to lash out at her, his friends, and everyone else. They had made a mockery of his life. Or perhaps they had not. He had done it to himself, with his own vile actions. He had wanted to be someone worth being. Instead, he had disgraced himself.

Ernie reverted from rage to sorrow and back again, over and over, as he had done all day since hearing the news.

He was barely aware of the door opening, of Wendy's greeting as she came inside. She was momentarily tangential to his struggle. He remained seated, stationary on the couch. She set a bag down on the countertop between kitchen and living room, withdrew a box from it, and approached him. She stood, box in hand, looking down on him. She blocked the sunbeam that had illuminated the room, and his face was bathed in shadow. Only then did he look up.

"I brought you something," she said pleasantly. She held the box out to him.

He stared at her, making no move to take the gift. He was not sure if he wanted to attack her or not.

Wendy stopped waiting for him. She opened the box herself. "It's a watch," she told him, lifting it out of the packaging. "I had it engraved to say—"

He slapped her hand, hard. Viciously. The watch flew across the room until it collided with the wall. He paid no attention to it. His eyes were on hers. She suddenly looked terrified.

"When?" His voice sounded rough even to his own ears. He realized he was breathing too heavily to articulate complete sentences. "Were...you..." He forced himself to hold a breath. "...going to tell me about Halfush?"

Her face went white. It was all the proof he needed. Ernie's anger intensified.

Wendy tried to take a step back, but he grabbed her wrist. He was not gentle about it, but she did not cry out in pain. Instead she simply cringed, as though expecting a blow to follow.

"I didn't know how to tell you," she gasped. "I was going to, and then you were so upset, and I wanted to calm you down, and since then I've just been so worried—"

"Worried? Or ushing me?" he accused. "You were jusht going to ushe me until she wash back. Then what? Laugh at me? Together?" He was working himself into a frenzy. He could not think straight, and the accusations simply poured out on their own. He stopped trying to focus on speaking correctly. He no longer cared about that.

"No! Ernie, no." She sounded desperate.

"Didshyou ever care about shme?"

"Ernie, of course I did. I...that's all I've done all week. Care about you. I tried to do everything I could think of to help you." She sniffled. "And I cried every night when I went home."

Hearing that did not make him feel better about his prognosis. But he wanted to believe her. Ernie eased his grip slightly, ready to clamp down again if she tried to pull away.

She did not. Instead, he watched a tear roll down her cheek. She went on. "I've felt so helpless, watching you fight with...this, whatever it is. Watching you suffer. So I bought you a watch. I thought it would look good on you. I wanted you to feel good about yourself, even if only for a moment."

He let her go. He felt his anger abating again. Part of him wanted to hug her, like he had done before, to wallow in his own misery from the comfort of her soothing embrace. But he resented that part of himself. He feared it. It was weakness. All he knew was that when it took over, he felt wretched. Things were better when he was angry.

He was getting better at controlling his emotions, but not in the way he used to hope for. He found it easier to force himself to stay mad. "You are such a bitch," he growled, trying to convince himself. "You come into my home and try to make a fool of me."

She slapped him. It did not hurt in the slightest, but he stopped talking nonetheless. He did not need to. The mission was accomplished. He stared at her, wild-eyed. He wanted to strangle her.

She looked scared. She took one step back, then another.

His breathing was much calmer now. Controlled. She seemed to be moving in slow motion. He could pounce at any moment. He had no fear of her. He could pounce and then he could...

Ernie stopped himself from acting. He forced himself to remain still as long as he could. He trembled from the effort. He became aware that he was clenching his hands so tightly that the nails were hurting his palms. He glanced down at them. A minute flow of blood dripped from the vise-like grip. He attempted to relax his fingers, but was unable.

He looked back up. Foolishly, Wendy was still there. She had noticed the same thing as he. He watched her eyes as she stared at the trickle of blood. Then she looked back at his face.

A second later, she turned and ran, straight into another room. His bedroom. He watched the door slam shut. He imagined that she was just behind the door, pressing her back to it, holding it closed in case he pursued.

He stayed exactly where he was. He willed himself not to budge from this spot until he had regained some semblance of control. He judged that would be when his fists unlocked.

He waited. Time passed. He recalled a lesson someone had once taught him. Who was it? Halfus, naturally. Ernie closed his eyes and thought of a beach. Nothing but sand and waves. He inhaled as the waves rolled in, filling his lungs, then exhaled slowly as the water receded. Repeat. Sand. Wave. Inhale. Exhale.

When he opened his eyes again, his hands were open. He took one last deep breath. Then he went to the door. He knocked calmly, nearly too soft to hear. "Wendy?"

There was no answer. Ernie reached for the knob, prepared to encounter resistance. She might be holding it from the other side. He twisted, and it turned smoothly. He pushed unhurriedly. The door opened a crack. No one was blocking it. He pushed it open fully, prepared for an attack.

She was standing by his bed, looking down at a case that she had placed on it. She stared, trance-like, at the object inside. It took him a moment to look from her to the object, then another to understand what she had found. It was his gun.

He stepped into the room. She did not look at him. She simply started speaking. "This has been here...all along? While I've been here? While I slept here?"

He nodded. She waited, then looked up. He nodded again.

"Do you not know how much I hate guns?"

This time he shook his head. Speaking was so very difficult. He might not ever do it again. Even thinking was becoming a challenge. He waited for her to explain.

The distress in her face was apparent, even to an observer in his condition. "I never would have set foot in this apartment if I knew this was here. The very sight...the very thought of guns brings back horrible memories. I...watched my little brother die from an accident with a gun. He was nine years old."

Then her expression changed. She looked at him with cruel judgment. It reminded him of the Prophet of Doom. "You shouldn't have a gun, Ernie. You're so angry. You lose control. You're going to kill someone. Maybe you'll kill me."

He could not deny it. It seemed likely. It even seemed imminent. *You need to leave, Wendy. Now. Please.* But he still did not speak.

"You're turning into a monster. Don't you see that?"

He nodded. He did see it. He had been watching it for days, if not weeks. He felt immeasurable sorrow, for the loss of a promising future. Then despair, for the inexorable fate that awaited him. Then fear, of the unknown. Finally, that too began to fade. He looked down at his hands. The fingers were curling again, of their own volition. The anger was returning. He doubted he would stop it again. He doubted he would want to. It felt so much better than the other emotions. "Run away," he croaked. Or at least thought he did. Part of him hoped so, its final impulse. The rest of him did not care.

He backed out of the room, dropped onto the couch, rested his elbows on his knees, and watched his hands. He was transfixed. The fingers were moving through no will of his own. Soon his hands were fists again, though they no longer felt sore. It might have been seconds, it might have been minutes. He was ready to fight. He had a lot of venom within, ready to release.

He stood back up, then approached the bedroom. He looked in, but the female was gone. He did not worry. He would find others to hunt. They were everywhere.

~

The ringing of the doorbell turned into a knocking on the door. It also become more persistent.

"Ignore it, Baby," the girl whispered.

"I wish I could," he said regretfully. It had been more than a week, but the run-in with his neighbor still weighed heavily on his mind. He imagined that he was about to have another. In a perverse way, he looked forward to it.

Rich got up from the bed and scooped his clothes off the floor. The pants he pulled on first, the rest he managed while going down the stairs. He finished buttoning his shirt before opening the door.

It suddenly did not feel so awful to have an enemy, he thought. Strange how he had changed. He had always considered violence to be the fool's version of debate. Yet now it had a certain appeal. He supposed it was the only message some people understood. Besides, there was a thrill to the thought of putting fist to face. Perhaps he would break the man's nose, the way he had seen that soldier do to Ernie. *That* had definitely won the argument.

He opened the door with an unfamiliar sense of anticipation, but the man on Rich's doorstep was not his neighbor. Tre'Andre had chosen an inopportune time for a surprise visit. Rich felt a sick twisting in his gut. He had not seen his boyfriend in weeks, and they had rarely even spoken by phone. Rich had assumed he was still in a petulant mood about the game. He would have been glad to find out otherwise, but this was hardly the circumstance he would have chosen.

For all his annoyed knocking, Tre'Andre seemed in fine spirits. "Surprise, Handsome." Then his eyes gave Rich a quick once over. "Rough night?" he chided.

Rich became flustered. "Tre?" It was the nickname that Tre'Andre frowned upon, but Rich had always been allowed to get away with it. It had become a sort of pet name for their more intimate occasions. Rich had always been pleased that Tre'Andre did not accept it from others. It was something special, reserved just for him.

Tre'Andre chuckled. He was clearly aware of Rich's embarrassment and found it comical. "Are you going to let me in, you jackass?"

At all costs, Rich had to stop that from happening. "This is a bad time, Tre'Andre."

For the first time, Tre'Andre's smile faltered. "Is something the matter?"

"I have an appointment. I'm tutoring a student." Rich relaxed as he felt the plausibility of the lie. "He's supposed to be here any minute." *She.* He had meant to say *she.* Not that it mattered. "I thought you were him." His biggest concern was that Tre'Andre would want to hang around the house while Rich tutored. There was really no reason why he could not, if the story had been true.

"Oh, I'm sorry," Tre'Andre said. "I can come back a little later."

That was a relief. "Thanks. Lessons last an hour."

"I'll give you two."

"You don't need to do that. Come back in an hour. I want to spend all the time I can with you," Rich added, suddenly feeling much better.

Tre'Andre flashed him that smile again. "Cheers, Rich." He turned to leave.

"Cheers, Tre." Rich closed the door. His pulse was returning to normal. He had dodged a bullet. But he was not out of the woods just yet. He needed to get Dani out of there. Now he began to worry that she would put up a fight. She seemed like the type who would not take kindly to playing second fiddle.

He was relieved to see that she was already dressed and waiting upon his return to the bedroom. "Is it safe?" she asked nervously. Clearly, she sussed the situation's importance.

Rich nodded. "I'm sorry about this." He felt like a fool. He would not blame her at all for being upset with him.

She smiled, then kissed his cheek. "Don't worry. I know it's confusing."

He walked down the stairs and ushered her out. He was tempted to kiss her goodbye, and would have if she had asked for it, but she simply waved on her way out the door. He turned around and headed back toward the stairs. The first priority was to shower. He needed to get any trace of her scent off his body. Tre'Andre was perceptive, and Rich was thankful that their conversation had been brief and outdoors. Inside the house the smell would be stronger.

He made it as far as the upstairs landing before the pounding on the door began. Rich froze in place, his shoulders slumped. His pulse quickened again. The pounding continued. He retraced his steps back to the door, then pulled it open. It was Tre'Andre again, looking more irate than Rich had ever seen him.

"Tre—"

The punch caught him by surprise. Even with his enhanced reflexes, Rich was unable to avoid the blow. It rocked him back, momentarily stunned. The soles of his shoes stuck to the rug and he lost his balance. He went down with a hard crash.

"You fucking bastard. Get up."

Rich pushed himself up. His jaw stung, but he did not give that another thought. Physical pain right now meant nothing. His brain was in overdrive, searching for the right words. He was a world class debater, he had confidence he could think of something. He wanted to explain all the reasons this had happened. His illness, and the changes that had followed. The respect of his teammates. Her magnetism. His loneliness.

It would all mean nothing to Tre'Andre. So Rich did not waste time in foolish excuses. Instead, he stood up to take his medicine.

He stared at his boyfriend, aware that insults and recriminations were spilling from his lips like a wound disgorging pus. It was a part of the healing process. It needed to happen. Rich did not listen to the words, but he watched the face. He would react only when he saw that Tre'Andre had gotten the poison out of his system. Only then would Rich have a chance to salvage their relationship.

He considered whether that was something he even wanted to do. Tre'Andre had been his partner for two years, ever since they first met on the soccer pitch. It had not taken long to fall in love. Rich had other friends, but no one else who made him feel as special as Tre. Rich realized now that for some time, he had been living with the assumption that they would remain together after college, and perhaps for the rest of their lives. They had never spoken of marriage, but he had assumed it would happen at some point, whenever it felt right. With Tre'Andre, there was no need to hurry. There was no need for discussion. There was just the comfort of easy companionship. Rich had taken it all for granted.

Life as a gay black man had not always been easy. Race and orientation aside, life without a partner was not always easy. Rich had always believed that when the right person came along, you bent over backwards to keep them. The effort, hardships, and infrequent anger were nothing compared to the emptiness and uncertainty of being alone. Couples who were meant for each other made each other better people. That was how he felt with Tre'Andre. Until he had forgotten it. Of course Rich wanted to salvage their relationship. He would do anything to do so. It had taken this debacle for him to understand.

Tre'Andre's animus was reaching an end. His shoulders, which had been raised like a prowling predator's, now slumped in weariness. Rich used the opportunity to apologize. "I'm sorry, Tre. I made a mistake."

Tre'Andre's teeth began to grind. The apology clearly had not dispelled the anger and resentment. "How long?"

"A few weeks."

"How?" Tre'Andre appeared to want to say more, but could not. Rich understood the question regardless.

He nodded. "I'll explain. You want to come in?" He pushed the door open wider.

"No."

Rich flinched. That was a bad sign. Then he composed himself. He wanted his voice to come out steady and reassuring, as though the man on his doorstep was a nervous animal that might bolt away. Rich had been experiencing some trouble speaking, but he had learned to take his time and focus on each word. He actually rather liked the slower, more deliberate cadence. To his own ear, it sounded more distinguished.

"It was after our match. I went out with the guys from the team. We drank too much. She flirted with me, and I...liked how it felt." He waited for Tre'Andre's reaction to that, but saw only continuing disgust. "Not only her attention, but the way the blokes looked at me. She kissed me that night, but I stopped her. I thought of you. I liked the attention, but I believed I could find a balance. I thought she would go on chasing me as long as I resisted, and the guys would still look up to me.

"Then Joey died. I needed to speak to someone. I tried to call you, but you were still angry. I'm not blaming you, it's just—well, it is what it is. She called me. We talked. We *only* talked. Then she got sick, and we both thought of what happened to Joey, and she got scared. I wanted to help her. Then it just happened." Rich did not feel the need to go into any further details. They were baffling and embarrassing, and would only irritate Tre'Andre further.

There was no response to the brief narrative. Rich could not tell whether the explanation had made a dent in his boyfriend's anger. He decided to bare his soul all the way. "I...weird things have been happening to me. I don't understand them. It's worrying. And confusing. I feel like a different person, Tre."

At last his words got a reaction, although not the one he wanted. "Don't give me that bullshit. And don't call me Tre. In fact, don't call me anything. I'm out of here." He turned away.

"Don't, Tre. Please come in, so we can talk."

Tre'Andre stopped with one foot on the step and one on the walkway. He turned back. "I'll never step foot inside there again, Rich. I don't care that you're confused. Some things can't be forgiven."

Rich watched him get into his car and drive away. He wondered whether he would ever see him again. Somehow, he doubted it. The thought filled him with grief, greater than he had ever felt. He was suddenly very weak. He closed the door and found a seat on his small couch. The room was silent, but he could hear the ubiquitous chatter of his neighbors. They sounded as though they were arguing yet again.

Rich did not like feeling so very helpless. He had used truth and reason to solve his problems, and did not like where it got him. Why had Tre'Andre not understood? Why had he not been more supportive weeks ago, when Rich first started feeling different? Instead, he had been petty and angry and withdrew from Rich's life at the point when he was needed most. Now he blamed Rich for everything, when he was really as much to blame as anyone.

Rich felt anger replacing the helplessness. It was invigorating. It made him feel stronger. It was another tool with which to solve problems. Why had he never seen that before? He was a man of words and thought, but men were also creatures of passion and aggression. He had denied this half of himself for far too long, and it had made him less of a man.

The racket from next door was becoming more irritating. Several times since he had warned his neighbor, Rich thought he heard the sounds of hitting. But he had never been sure. Now he believed that Jim was at it again. Rich felt compelled to act. At the very least, he could warn the man again. If he saw any fresh bruises, he would do more than that.

Rich walked outside and pounded on their door. He told himself that he did not want to see bruises. Except that part of him did, because that would give him the excuse to act. He knew that was the wrong way to feel about it. It would mean that the abuse was still going on. He hated the thought of the little girl—or even the wife—being hit by that brute of a man.

The door opened sooner than he expected. "What do you want?" Jim bellowed. He seemed to be puffed up, arms held out wider than usual, as though he could intimidate Rich. The scene struck him as comical.

He wanted to hit Jim then and there, but was still capable of restraining himself. He would put a little scare back into the man. Renewing the threat should reset the peace timer. It would buy the family another few days or weeks of relative tranquility.

He opened his mouth to speak, then stopped. Things would have gone fine, if Jeannie had not come into sight behind her husband. She, and the large red mark around her eye.

"I warned you," Rich said as he pushed the door open wider. Jim's face lost the look of belligerence. Now he suddenly looked scared. He took a step back. For the next few moments, everything was a blur to Rich. He fought on instinct, knocking his opponent down, pinning his arms, disabling his ability to fight back. Then he attacked to inflict pain. It would not do to go through all this without making the point so obvious that even a simpleton like this could understand. Rich's knuckles were cut open, but the sting only pumped him up more. It made him feel certain that he was achieving his goal.

The female starting pulling at his shirt. He shrugged her off once, delivered one last punch, then eased up. She tugged him again, and he hopped back up to his feet. She shoved him toward the door. She was too weak to propel him on her own, but he was ready to leave in any case. "You're welcome," he said as he stepped out. The door closed behind him.

He paused a moment on the porch the two households shared. There was a scent in the air. He recognized it as blood. He did not know if it was his own or the other's. Either way, it was invigorating. He felt as alive as he ever had.

The physical release had also calmed his mental turmoil. He no longer felt so angry. He began to feel guilty instead. His neighbor had deserved the beating, there was no question about that. But Rich was unhappy about the way it had happened. He began to see the attack for what it was. Naked aggression. For most of his life, he had always rationally weighed his options and selected the most efficacious. This time, he had reacted without thinking. He was doing that sort of thing more and more often these days. He shuddered to realize that this time it might get him in trouble.

He thought of the illness. Eden, they were calling it. Plenty of people had gotten it by now. Were others feeling the same mental effects as he? He knew there were doctors in town, taking samples, studying the disease. He wondered what they had learned so far. It was time to start doing some research of his own. Presuming the police did not show up and drag him off to jail.

The next few hours were anxious ones for Rich. By evening, however, he felt reasonably sure that he was not going to jail. With that worry assuaged, he decided to go out for a walk. He wanted to do some reconnaissance.

15

THE LESSER OF EVILS

THERE ARE *certain parallels between war and disease. Anyone unfortunate enough to be caught up in either should take all appropriate precautions, but it is an inescapable truth that there will always be a certain amount of uncertainty involved. Just like a soldier on the battlefield, the fate of the afflicted often comes down to simple blind luck. Diseases can be notoriously fickle in selecting how and when to strike, who is infected and who is not, who lives and who dies.*

The deadliest outbreak of Ebola in history started in West Africa in 2014. This disease is especially dangerous not only due to its high degree of lethality, but because its transmission is aided by the very customs of the affected region. Traditional local funeral practices require contact with bodies literally overflowing with virus. Yet somehow, not every person who interacted with contagious bodies caught the disease. Some family members of the sick contracted Ebola while others did not, with no discernible variance in their levels of exposure. Medical workers from all over the world selflessly volunteered their time—and risked their lives—to help contain the raging epidemic. Naturally, these workers used every available protection to defend themselves while combating the disease. Nevertheless, many workers contracted Ebola despite those precautions, even while some unprotected villagers in frequent contact with the disease escaped unscathed.

Every infectious disease has an incubation period, which is the length of time between infection and the manifestation of symptoms. During the incubation period, infected individuals are often unaware that they have been exposed. Some diseases—such as the flu, cholera, scarlet fever, and Ebola —can have a relatively brief incubation period, when symptoms begin almost immediately. Others, like chicken pox, take weeks to show. Some have a narrow window of only a few days, meaning that someone with the disease will definitely show symptoms within this thin sliver of time. For example, when individuals do not show any signs of the flu within a few days of exposure, they may breathe a sigh of relief. Other diseases, however, have a relatively wide-ranging incubation period. Most Ebola patients exhibit symptoms within a few days of exposure, but some rare cases take more than a month.

The incubation period is distinct from the latency period, which measures the time between infection and infectiousness. Infectiousness marks the term when a patient is capable of transmitting the disease to others. In some cases, the incubation period is longer than the latency period. In other cases, the reverse is true, and in still others the two are the same. Oftentimes, diseases are simplified by equating symptoms with infectiousness, but one should not always assume this to be the case.

The incubation and latency periods are defined by the total range of recorded behavior, and thus are necessarily imprecise. At the point of exposure to most diseases, a doctor cannot tell a patient exactly how long it will be before he or she will start experiencing symptoms. Nor can a doctor say exactly when that patient will start and stop being contagious to others. For all of modern medicine's effectiveness in combating disease—which is considerable—there remains sufficient unpredictability to frustrate every step forward.

Perhaps the biggest hurdle to further advancement is the propensity for germs to evolve. Wherever mankind develops drugs tailor-made to fight a particular pathogen, there is a risk that a new drug-resistant strain will figuratively crawl forth from the primordial ooze. Not that diseases need drugs to compel them to evolve, for it happens perpetually. Mankind has witnessed numerous strains of influenza throughout the years, and will likely encounter more in the future. Ebola has several variants, each named for the region of Africa where it first surfaced. There is even an Ebola Reston variant which struck Northern Virginia in 1989, killing dozens of research monkeys but failing to take hold in humans, for reasons unexplained.

As recently as February 2015, a new virus was discovered in Kansas. An unfortunate man was bitten by ticks while working outside his home. Within a few days he fell ill and checked into a hospital. Sadly, he died less than two weeks after exposure. The CDC conducted testing on his blood and announced the existence of a previously unknown virus, named Bourbon. Scientists continue to expand their knowledge with unrelenting efficiency, but diseases will likely always remain a step ahead.

Ben was no longer the only local professor without a teaching job. Catoctin College had suspended classes for an indefinite period. In so doing, they merely made official what had already become reality. The last few classes held by determined professors were sparsely attended by students. Those who had not yet been infected with Eden were afraid of exposure, while those who were became preoccupied with more pressing concerns. The human race seemed to be evolving—or devolving, as seemed more accurate—right before their eyes.

The residents of the dual communities—the college and neighboring town—did not seem to know how to behave during the crisis. More and more people shuttered themselves in their houses and apartments, although a significant number fled the area to stay with friends or relatives. Many of the students returned home to their families, despite the request of authorities to remain at Catoctin until they were tested and cleared. For most people, the incubation period between infection and symptoms was a brief one or two days. For a rare few, however, the first symptoms did not manifest until weeks later. Until they did, there was no easy way to identify an infected patient. USAMRIID had developed a blood test that was quick and accurate, but the announcement that they intended to systematically test everyone in the community only triggered a substantial exodus. A sensible appeal was made "for your own safety and that of the community," but few seemed interested in listening.

Some people neither sheltered themselves nor fled. They continued to go about their lives as though nothing were out of the ordinary, despite the many visible signs to the contrary. Spontaneous, nonsensical assaults were becoming an everyday occurrence. Violence, it seemed, begets more violence. The frequency of incidents had increased at an astonishing rate in just the past few days, as a collective pall of distrust and anger enveloped McGahey. There were news reports of "muggings" where nothing was taken. A day earlier, right in the center of town, two youths had accosted a woman, then beaten to death the man who sought to intervene. His body had lain on the street for hours from fear of exposing the ambulance crew to virus or attack. Now the residents were justifiably scared. Many local businesses stayed closed, service appointments were canceled, and incoming deliveries postponed. Nevertheless, a few deniers treated these occurrences as minor, temporary inconveniences and scoffed at those who panicked over what they proclaimed to be an insignificant bug.

Ben marveled at the levels of self-delusion his fellow man was capable of attaining. There were now far too many reports of Eden's third phase to ignore. The first phase was the day or two of extreme sickness, during which the body seemed determined to expel every unwanted contaminant at once. The second phase was the continuing physical revitalization that every patient felt to a greater or lesser degree, and which had served to draw so many willing volunteers to experiment upon themselves. Ben had heard this stage likened to exercise-induced euphoria. Thus far, Phase Two never seemed to end. But there was now an apparent overlapping third phase affecting an undetermined number of patients. This phase started with speech impairment before progressing to more severe symptoms such as aggression and hypersexuality. As far as he knew, the doctors still did not have a name for this last stage, but the street did. It was being called feralization, the unfortunate souls suffering from it now colloquially known as *ferals*.

No one knew how long this phase would last. The populations where the outbreaks were occurring had become a human science experiment. Moreover, if the researchers knew what percentage of Eden patients progressed to the third phase, they were not saying. Ben took that as a bad sign. If the number were low, they would be more inclined to share it in order to calm down the growing panic. And restoring a little calm was now very much needed. There was a sense in the air that events had come to a precipice. He had seen this happen several times in his life, and on each occasion the world saw fit to pull back from the edge. Some shift would occur to make the defeatists feel foolish. He was still waiting for that to happen now.

Until it did, he liked to think that he was one of those rare individuals who had found a happy medium. He acknowledged the existence of the danger and took rational precautions, without allowing his entire life to shut down. He had already contracted the virus, so there was no sense worrying about the surgical masks and rubber gloves that so many people had taken to wearing. He suspected that some of them already had the virus themselves, and their superfluous protections were simply a byproduct of misinformation and wishful thinking. Ben was under no such misconceptions. He worried only about the rising rate of violence. He still allowed himself to venture out, but only when necessary.

Today was one of those times. He had not been one of the masses who made a run on all the bread, milk, and toilet paper in the corner market at the first sign of trouble. He believed that sort of behavior was classic overreaction. Unfortunately, it now put him in the position of needing to head farther afield to get what he needed. Not that it was excessively inconvenient. Since both small groceries in McGahey were closed, he simply needed to drive to Frederick, which was only twenty minutes away. Instead of an hour, his errand might take two.

There was a door leading from his kitchen to the garage. He locked it while the automatic garage door opener was operating. Then he climbed into his tan Camry, started it, and checked the gas gauge. The tank was just over one quarter full, more than sufficient to get him to Frederick and back. He pulled out of the garage, blissfully unaware that he would never set foot inside his house again. He had no precognition of the storm that was coming.

For the past month, the presence in McGahey of the United States Army was barely noticeable. A few weeks earlier Ben had met one doctor, a petite young woman with a pleasant face, and her assistant. The two of them stood out because of their army fatigues, but the impression they conveyed had been polite and professional rather than overtly military. He knew there were several such teams dispatched to the town, and he would occasionally see them moving door-to-door or on the road to and from Fort Detrick. He did not know whether it was the result of a conscious decision, but the army presence had so far been unobtrusive, with little effect on the town's rustic pulse.

Now that pulse had changed of its own accord. There was no sense maintaining a low profile any longer. Ben wondered whether the authorities would get more involved. As much as he would have liked to say otherwise, he believed McGahey was in need of some intervention. Divine would be best—but failing that, perhaps the government would help.

It was not long before he had his answer. There was only a single road leading out to Route 15, running parallel to the edge of the woods and the creek just beyond. He turned out of his small neighborhood onto this road, feeling a bit silly about obeying the usual stop-and-start rules of driving. There was a near-total absence of other vehicles to contend with.

As he left the eastern boundary of town he saw something new, a large military tent erected between the road and tree line. Beside the tent sat two camouflage-colored Humvees, while perhaps as many as a dozen soldiers milled about the area. Ben noticed that these men and women, like the medical personnel before them, wore the ubiquitous masks and gloves. He also noticed that they, unlike the medical staff, carried what appeared to be strange-looking rifles. This was the first he had seen of these odd weapons in McGahey. Although he supposed others might not react the same way, the sight of these guns did not frighten him in the least. If anything, he was relieved. Armed soldiers was a clear sign of authority, and a little authority might restore some order to the town.

Ben slowed as he neared the encampment, turning his head to stare as he passed. Thus he did not see the young black soldier step in front of his car, waving him to stop. It was only a last-second yell that impelled him to brake, just in time to avoid a collision. His heart fluttered at the close call as the young man came to his window.

Ben was emphatically sorry, but the soldier only pulled down his mask and grinned. "No harm, no foul," he replied to Ben's earnest apology. "But I'm afraid I'm going to have to stop you here. Orders are to keep the road closed for the time being." He spoke with a Texas twang.

"Are we being quarantined?" Ben asked, more curious than worried. He glanced at the name on the uniform. Grimes. Ben supposed it was Private Grimes, but he did not know how to decipher military insignia.

"I can't answer that, sir. Our orders are to keep the road closed until we hear otherwise. They did not say how long that would be." His tone was friendly and convincing, even though it sounded to Ben like a typical half-truth. If they had indeed decided to officially quarantine the town and campus, they probably would not go around announcing it. It might be the right decision for the country, but it would not go over well with the locals. They would find out eventually. People were already tense, and this would only add to the strain and uncertainty. The tension would build like a volcano, and God only knew when and how it would erupt.

"May I ask about your rifle?" Ben asked sociably. He felt no resentment toward these soldiers. He did not know where decisions like these were made, but he was certain that it was miles from here.

The soldier held the weapon up for presentation, although he kept it out of Ben's reach. "This is an FN three-oh-three non-lethal riot gun," he said. "It fires a fin-stabilized round designed to incapacitate without damaging the target."

"Like a Taser?"

"More like a paintball gun, except ten times more powerful."

Ben was relieved that the soldiers were not carrying deadly weapons, although he suspected there must be some nearby. He did, however, wonder whether these nonlethal guns were for the soldiers' protection, or another purpose entirely.

This, too, was answered in short order. Ben was curious to learn how many forces were currently deployed to the area, and how many more were on the way. He was not certain that Grimes would be forthcoming with that information, so Ben decided to lead to the question in a roundabout manner. "What unit are you—"

"There's one!" called out a voice nearer the tent. Everyone turned to look at the soldier who had yelled, then in the direction where he was pointing.

Ben saw a young man, most likely a student, sprinting across a field about thirty yards from the road. The student was wearing gray shorts and a brown-and-white Catoctin Bears tee. As he raced across the grass at a breakneck speed, his pale skin flashed through several tears in the shirt. Ben saw two soldiers raise and aim the funny rifles, and his heart leapt into his throat. *They're going to shoot that kid.* Then he heard several loud popping noises, and he remembered that these guns were nonlethal. The boy continued running, now directly away from the squad of yelling soldiers. The shots must have missed. Ben saw one of the Humvees pull out in pursuit, and he realized the motor must have been kept running for just this very occurrence.

Grimes was still standing nearby. "Private, was that...a feral?" he asked.

The black soldier nodded. "Yes, sir. An aberrant infected. That's the third one since we've been here."

"Will he get away?"

"No, sir. We have a perimeter around the town. We're picking them up as they come out."

Grimes did not seem particularly affected by the escape attempt.

His mask was still resting below his chin, and Ben could see him smiling in a nonverbal exchange with some of his comrades. Unsure quite what to make of it, Ben put the Camry in reverse to begin a three-point turn. Then he stopped again.

"Excuse me, Private Grimes?" Apparently, he had guessed the rank correctly, or else the soldier had not seen fit to correct him.

"Sir?"

"How long have you been here?"

"Since oh-seven-hundred."

Ben had been expecting a day, not a time. "You mean today?"

"Yes, sir."

Three, just this morning. That seemed like a lot to Ben. It also raised two more questions in his mind. Had any escaped before this perimeter was established? And how many more were still in town? The town he had just been directed back into.

He drove more slowly than usual as he reentered McGahey. His nerves were more on edge than they had been on the way out. He knew the safest thing he could do would be to return home and wait out the quarantine from the relative safety and luxury of his house. He was low on supplies, but he would not starve. He had canned and frozen goods that he could make last for several more days at the least.

Ben did not feel like waiting this out, however. His Ancient Studies team had brought the bug back with them, so he felt connected to this outbreak. Interwoven, if not directly responsible. He needed to see if he could help in any way.

He steered toward the town center where the city hall, middle school, and Catholic church were located. If any sort of community organization were occurring, that was the area to look. The problem would be noticing it from the street. Given the level of paranoia gripping McGahey, any meetings would necessarily be held indoors.

He need not have worried. The middle school had been converted into a medical clinic, and the signs of occupation were obvious from a distance. He did not know when the conversion had happened. Clearly, he had not paid close enough attention to what was happening in his own community. There were several handmade signs directing sufferers to the makeshift hospital. Ben could guess which ones were old and which were new. He saw a few large ones with friendly invitations written in curvy red lettering. They reminded him of childish "Car Wash" signs of yesteryear. He half expected to see glitter on them. Then he saw the smaller, strictly functional ones. Black lettering on white background, the word "Clinic" with a single arrow pointing the way.

The building's small parking lot was full of cars, not all of them parked legally. The same was true of Main and the side street nearest the clinic. Ben parked a half-block away. He scanned the vicinity, saw no one nearby, and stepped out. He took a second glance around as he locked the Camry, then began to walk toward the front entrance. He had one alleyway to cross and then he was on school grounds, still a few hundred feet from the doors. He quickened his pace. He scanned the area once more, saw nothing out of the ordinary, and forced himself to slow down to a natural speed. Then he thought of the feral student—the aberrant infected—that had raced by the checkpoint just a few minutes earlier, and broke into a run.

Every time her phone rang, Wendy hoped it was Halfus. She wished that habit would end, because it only led to disappointment. Sadly, it was not the sort of thing she could will herself to stop. She had felt a small measure of genuine hope for the first few days after their ephemeral talk, but that hope had faded a little more with each passing day. The conversation itself seemed more and more distant and surreal, like a pleasant dream with no basis in reality. Given her current state of mind, she could not rule out entirely the possibility that she had imagined the whole thing. *Wouldn't that be a cruel joke?*

Her phone was ringing now. She glanced at the display. An unexpected name appeared, and she answered in pleasant surprise. "Hi, Tracy."

"Wendy, it's Kevin. I'm using her phone." He was breathing heavily, as though having just exercised.

"Oh. Is everything okay, Kevin?"

"No, it's not. Not at all. It's pretty fucking far from okay, actually."

Alarm bells sounded off in Wendy's head. She feared the worst, but did not want to ask. She did not wish to vocalize the images that began to appear in her mind's eye, for fear that it would give them form. "Where is Tracy?" was all she asked.

"She's in the bathroom now. She's not letting me in. She's crying her eyes out, Wendy. She thinks she is turning into an animal."

Wendy's entire body sagged. *Not Tracy, too.*

"The past few weeks have been really hard, but I'm trying to tell her things will be okay. She doesn't believe me. She sees what is going on all around and...I don't really know what else to say to her. Then I thought of you and Ernie. I know he was having some issues. I thought maybe you would have a suggestion—"

"You need to get the hell away from her, Kevin." Wendy was surprised at how assertively the command came out.

Apparently, Kevin was, too. There was a moment's pause. "I can't do that. She needs me."

"I thought that, too, with Ernie. There's nothing you can do. I'm really sorry, but—"

"I can't leave her. She needs me," he repeated. Wendy heard a sense of desperation in his voice that she never thought to associate with him. She knew exactly how he felt. Watching this happen to someone was the most helpless feeling imaginable. She was no longer focused on Tracy, she was focused on him. One was a lost cause. The other was not—but he was at risk. She had to say something that would get through to him.

He was still speaking, but the words had become unintelligible. He was at the point of breaking into tears. She recognized that as well, having experienced it many times herself.

Through the phone, Wendy heard a banging sound. Kevin's voice grew clearer but more panicked, informing her what was happening. "Oh, God. She's pounding on something in there. I'm afraid she's hitting her head against the tile." He stopped speaking to Wendy and started calling to his girlfriend. "Tracy, don't. Tracy, don't!"

"Kevin—listen to me. Tracy is gone." Wendy tried to sound decisive and unemotional. Authoritative. It was the opposite of how she felt, but she wanted him to stop thinking for himself and follow orders. Exactly what she wished had happened for her. Having someone tell her what to do would have made her own trials so much easier. "You can do nothing for her. I know it seems like you should try, but you shouldn't." She thought of her last visit with Ernie. "Trust me, it will only get worse."

She knew this to be true. She had witnessed, up close, what the disease did to a mind once it got a hold on it. It was probably the worst thing that a person could suffer. It was torture, both for the ones going through it and for those who cared about them.

A thought occurred to her. Kevin needed to hear more than what *not* to do. He needed to hear what *to* do. "We should meet. Come over here." He had stopped talking, so she assumed he was listening. The more she thought about it, the more she liked the plan that was forming in her mind. "We should round up as many friends as we can. Share our experiences. Figure out how to get through this." It would give them a sense of purpose. Something to do besides watching in hopeless turmoil as their loved ones went crazy in front of their eyes. "Each of us should get at least one more person. Can you do that, Kevin?"

"When?" he asked, and she breathed a sigh of relief. He was not only listening, he was considering it.

"Tonight. Six o'clock. I have...something I need to do first."

She thought that he would be too distracted to hear the hesitation in her voice, but she was mistaken. "What is it, Wendy?" She wondered what it was about guys that made them more comfortable worrying about a woman's problems than their own.

"It's nothing. I need to help out my mother."

He had calmed down noticeably. "You shouldn't go out alone." If nothing else, at least she had gotten him thinking clearly again.

"It's okay, I'm meeting Rich. I'll invite him to join us tonight."

Kevin breathed easier. "Yes, that's a good idea. He'll know what to do. Okay, see you at six."

Now it seemed that he was in a hurry to get off the phone, and alarm bells sounded in her mind again. "Kevin?"

"Yes?"

"Promise me you're leaving there right away."

There was a pause. "I can't do that, Wendy. It sounds like she's calmed down. Maybe I can get through to her."

"No, Kevin, I—"

"Goodbye, Wendy. See you tonight." He hung up.

So she had failed, after all. She thought she had gotten through to him. She thought he was going to follow her directions. Now she wondered if her words had any effect at all. *Some leader I am.*

There were two other cars in the parking lot when she pulled in. When the school had suspended classes, all sports and other activities were shut down with them. The soccer field, bleachers, and concessions buildings were all as still as a cemetery. The seller had wanted to meet in an out-of-the-way location where they would not be bothered by others. Wendy did not know if he was more worried about ferals or the authorities. She worried about both.

She recognized one car and pulled up beside it. The owner was seated inside, waiting for her. He saw her and nodded, and the two of them got out at the same time.

"Thanks for helping me, Rich."

"It's no problem, Wendy."

They hugged, timidly. She supposed neither one of them felt quite as amiable as normal, given the circumstances. "Shall we?" she asked.

"Let's get this over with." He spoke slowly and calmly, and she immediately drew strength from his presence.

They were several hundred feet from the field itself. They walked quietly at first, then her nervous energy got the better of her. "You have no idea how much I appreciate this," she told him, just to fill the silence. When he said nothing, she added, "You can always tell who your true friends are when things get rough. Times like this bring out the best in people."

Again Rich did not reply. She glanced over at him, and was surprised to see that he looked pained. It seemed so out of character. Then he caught her looking and smiled reassuringly. She often wondered what was going on inside that brilliant mind. He was so prone to keeping his thoughts private that it was easy to forget he even had feelings of his own.

They were walking down the slope between the lot and soccer pitch. In the distance, she saw a solitary figure standing in midfield. She assumed this was the seller.

"Ah, the scene of my greatest triumph," Rich said. Wendy was a little taken aback by the sadness in his voice. This, too, was out of character for him. He was always the even-tempered, unemotional one of their group. But she could not blame him. Things were hard on everyone.

They approached the figure, and Wendy formed a different impression of him than what she had expected. He was young and bespectacled, with a comical outgrowth of undergrown muttonchops. She guessed that he had attempted to grow a beard, been frustrated with the result, then settled on this ridiculous substitute. He wore an Iron Maiden tee shirt that looked as though it had not been washed since the band was popular. She had expected someone young, but not quite like this.

They stopped a few yards away from him. "You're Lenny?" Rich asked.

"Ya." The kid looked at her. "I'm guessing you're Wendy. Who's the fucking narc?" He sounded as though he was pretending to be a tough from some sophomoric cop show.

"Back off, mate," Rich said aggressively.

Lenny spit onto the grass. Although young, he did not appear to be nearly as nervous as Wendy felt.

She noticed he had a backpack resting by his feet. That was where the stuff would be, she realized. Along with his proceeds. Thousands of dollars worth, perhaps more. The thought of all that money made her uncomfortable. So did the thought of the pills themselves. A few years ago, she had once tried smoking a single blunt of weed before discovering that it only gave her a headache. That had been her last foray into the seedy realm of illegal substances.

Rich looked at the boy suspiciously. "So, what, you're a chem student? You cook this stuff up yourself?"

Lenny shrugged. "My methods are my own, Holmes."

It was Rich's turn to shrug. "Have it your way." He paused. "Aren't you taking a risk out in the open like this?"

"Not really. The authorities have their hands full."

"I don't mean from the authorities."

Wendy could not help glancing around. Lenny, however, was dismissive. "Nah. I'm packing heat." He lifted the front of his shirt. A handgun was tucked inside the waistband of his jeans. Wendy gasped and stepped back.

To her immense relief, Rich changed the subject. "How much?"

Lenny dropped his shirt, and the gun disappeared from view. "Five hundred."

Wendy was shocked to hear the number. "For one pill?" It was far more than she expected.

Rich, however, did not seem particularly perturbed. "We heard it was two hundred."

"That was days ago," the kid snorted. "It's five hundred today. There's an ATM up in the cafeteria on campus. I can wait if you need to tap it."

Wendy would need to. She did not have that much money in her purse. "Rich, we—"

Rich shook his head. "It's okay. I anticipated something like this." He withdrew his wallet. He began slowly counting bills as she watched. She was equal parts embarrassed and relieved. She did not want to be here any longer than necessary. She was more thankful than ever that Rich had agreed to help her out.

He spoke while he counted. "Your prices are high, mate."

"My prices are what the market will bear. Supply and demand."

"That's fairly callous, it is."

"It's free enterprise, Holmes. It's the bedrock of our country."

Wendy was disgusted. She had no problem with people making a buck, but this felt wrong in all sorts of ways. "You're profiting off the misery of desperate people," she blurted out.

Lenny looked at her, amused. "I am an entrepreneur providing a valuable service."

"You're a lowlife."

"I'm a businessman."

Rich turned to face her. "Wendy, why don't you wait for me back at the cars?"

It felt like a dismissal, and her instinct was to protest. But one look at Rich told her that he was bothered, too. He was simply trying to help, to put this burden on himself so she would not have to. In other words, he was being Rich.

"Are you sure?" she asked, hoping he did not change his mind.

He nodded. "It's all right. I'll take care of it."

"I'm sorry. This whole thing just bothers me."

"I know. It's fine."

She turned and started back toward the parking lot. She really did not want to spend another moment around Lenny. *So much for the best in people*, she thought with bitterness.

As she entered her mother's apartment building a few hours later, Wendy marveled at her own relative composure. She suspected part of it was Rich's steadiness rubbing off on her. But she believed there was more to it than that. This was her first time back here since the terrible night she had found and buried Truman, and although she had two brief and disturbing phone calls with her mother since then, the thought of seeing her again was incredibly upsetting. In fact, everything about this visit was. Yet her nerves were calm, her thoughts focused. She supposed this was the net effect of two long months of continuous distress. There was a hole in her heart through which all feeling had leaked out. The residue left her immensely unhappy, but at least she was taking control of her life.

That did not mean she was not afraid, however. She felt very vulnerable inside her mother's apartment building. At first it was eerily quiet—or at least absent of normal, everyday sounds. There was nothing to remind her of the humdrum activities of life. The desk in the lobby was unmanned, and nowhere did she hear the usual ubiquitous sounds of televisions and conversation. As her ears adjusted to the unnerving stillness, she became aware of other noises instead. Noises she did not immediately recognize, causing her imagination to run wild. Each sound seemed inhuman for a split-second before her mind could attribute it to something mundane. She heard the hard breathing of a predator in the distance, before identifying it as air passing through old vents. Next she heard a sudden buzzing from behind her and turned back to the lobby, feeling the approach of something unseen and ominous. Then the rare bus rattled past on the street outside, headed toward who knew where, and she stopped holding her breath.

She realized she had been all but tiptoeing her way around the building. Now she took the opposite approach and dashed into the stairwell and up the stairs as quickly as she could. She raced up six flights and came out on her mother's floor without breathing heavily. She sighed with relief when she reached her mother's door without encountering a soul. Then she thought about the occupant and realized her trials were only beginning.

Wendy unlocked the door and let herself in, attempting a stealth entry. She still had not decided how she was going to go about her task, and she wanted to avoid a confrontation with her mother for as long as possible.

"Wendy, ish that you?" Her mother was sitting on the sofa in the living room. The window was curtained, the lighting faint and shadowy. Wendy had not seen the figure until after it had spoken.

She forced herself to sound normal. "Hi, Mom. I wanted to check in on you. I haven't seen you in a while."

"I know, Shweetie." Her mother's voice sounded like a croak. "I've been waiting for you to come back."

Wendy panicked for a moment. But when her mother made no

aggressive movement, she decided that it had not been a threat. It was simply her overactive imagination again.

She began to instinctively put her bag down where she always did, then remembered that she needed it. She stopped in mid-gesture and hiked it back up over her shoulder. She spoke cheerfully, hoping not to sound as guilty as she felt. "Mind if I put some tea on?"

"Help yourshelf."

As Wendy's eyes adjusted to the low light, she saw her mother's face. It appeared to be utterly devoid of emotion. The woman was speaking to her daughter, but her heart was not in it. Wendy remembered how her mother had been the last time, and wondered if she had been in this same state ever since. Over a week without a human's capacity to feel? That was a fate worse than death, and it made Wendy feel better about her task.

She went into the kitchen, where things seemed about the same as she had left them. Perhaps a little messier, but nothing as terrible as her last discovery. Only after she started making tea did she begin to consider how she would get her mother to take the pill. Wendy considered cooking some treat and hiding it within. However, if her mother's tastes had changed along the same lines as her own, the thought of a sweet dessert would be repellent instead of appealing. In fact, Wendy recalled how her mother had barely any appetite even before getting Eden, which had a dampening effect of its own. There was an excellent chance she would not want to eat anything her daughter prepared.

Wendy considered whether she could dissolve it in the tea, then realized she had not even examined the pill. She did not know whether it was a tablet or capsule. One would dissolve, the other would not. She reached into her bag for the small candy wrapper Rich had given to her back at the cars. She unraveled it. It was a large white tablet, like an oversized aspirin.

She could put it in the tea, but now she wondered if that was a good idea. She had heard that these things had a smell, so it was possible her mother might detect it. Wendy could not smell anything now, but she did not want to get her nose close to it. In any case, the smell might be much stronger once it dissolved.

In the end, Wendy decided not to hide it at all. She retightened the wrapper and put it back into her bag. Then she carried a tray with two cups of tea out to her mother. She set it down in front of the sofa, then took a seat beside the woman who had brought her into this horrific world.

She reached over and stroked her mother's hand. She expected it to be soft as tissue paper, but instead she found it warm and vibrant. Although painfully thin, her mother looked as healthy as she had in years. "Mom, how are you feeling?"

Wendy expected another flat response. Instead, her mother looked right into her eyes. "I'm worried, Shweetie. I feel...different."

It was a sign of life at last. And it bothered Wendy more than she could have known. She had resigned herself to the knowledge that her mother's mind was gone, and reconciled herself to the thought that at least she was not suffering. This, however, was the worst of both worlds. Wendy could not afford to let herself be dissuaded, however. It had taken an act of will to come this far, and she knew she would never get another chance. She thought of everything that Ernie had gone through. She could not abide the thought of her mother going through that, as well.

"I know," she said tenderly. She had intended to remain detached throughout the ordeal, but now, in a spontaneous rejection of her own self-defenses, she reached out and hugged the woman tightly. "I know. I love you, Mom." There was no reply. Her mother's arms hung limply at her sides.

Wendy let go and forced herself to smile. "But I have good news. I brought something that is supposed to help." She let go of her mother's hand and turned back to her bag.

This is the point where I'm supposed to cry, she thought. As recently as a week or two ago, she would have. Now she was dry, incapable of tears. But there was more to it than that. She had been living with one catastrophe after another for as long as she could remember. Her brain had learned to go on functioning without purgation. She felt a new injection of sadness, but she no longer needed catharsis.

She came up with the candy wrapper. "Here," she said, holding it in front of her.

Her mother did not look at it, nor at Wendy. She was back to her stupor. Wendy unwrapped the pill and set it down on the tray. She picked up one cup of the tea and placed it in her mother's hands. "Drink," she instructed. Her mother complied, and Wendy breathed a sigh of relief. This could be done.

She took one of her mother's hands and opened it, then picked up the pill and placed it in the palm. She was about to instruct her mother to swallow it, but the woman plopped it into her mouth on her own, then washed it down with another sip.

Wendy waited, transfixed. She had no idea how long this would take. She cursed herself for not doing more research. All she could do was grasp her mother's hand and hold it tightly. If any part of Miriam Weald was there, she wanted it to know it was loved.

Her mother showed no reaction. Wendy began to wonder if she had paid five hundred dollars for a placebo. It seemed like exactly the sort of scam that damn punk Lenny would pull.

Wendy corrected herself. It was five hundred dollars Rich had paid for the placebo. Wendy had told him she would pay him back right away, but he had simply dismissed the comment. "Don't worry about it," he told her. Well, she did worry about it, and she intended to pay him the next time she saw him. At least she would not have to come up with it today, because he had apologetically turned down her invitation for tonight.

Her mother started to shake, pulling Wendy back into the moment. The woman began to gasp, and Wendy gripped her hand tighter. Her body went into convulsions. All Wendy could do was repeat, *Please let it be over, Please let it be over*, again and again while she watched. She had no sense of time, but eventually the shaking ended and the woman lapsed into unconsciousness. Wendy let go with one hand and checked for a pulse. It was there, but feeble. She remained in that position for what seemed an eternity. Finally the pulse stopped. For a long time afterward, Wendy could not bring herself to let go.

As she stepped back out into the hallway, the uneasy silence returned to her awareness. Wendy closed and locked the door, surprised at the steadiness of her hand. Her imagination was not playing tricks on her any longer. She doubted anything was about to ambush her. Right now, she really did not care if it did.

She dropped the key into her bag and started back toward the stairwell. Although she wanted to be gone from this place, soon and forever, she did not run.

"Lady? Can you help me?"

She turned around to face the speaker. It was the little boy, Samuel, standing with one foot in the hall and one inside his door. She was surprised to see him, recalling how he had been afraid of her the day she met Don and Kiara Planter. Pleasant as they were, she desperately did not want to visit with them right now. She found herself at a loss for words.

"Lady? Can you help me?" he repeated, and she became aware of an urgency in his tone. "Mom and Dad are scaring me."

In an instant, Wendy reprioritized everything. She walked briskly back toward the boy, simultaneously motioning him to join her in the hallway. He obediently came out to her. Considering his prior reticence, she took this as proof that he was truly uneasy.

She spoke in a voice just above a whisper. "Are they inside? Don't say anything, just nod your head."

The little boy nodded. She took his hand and gave it a little squeeze. "It's okay, Samuel." She resolved not to let go of him again until she knew he was safe.

She cautiously peeked around the open door. She saw the apartment that Samuel's parents had graciously welcomed her into on the day of Matt's accident. She saw the couch where the doctor had evaluated her, and the picture on the wall of the steadfast lighthouse and tempestuous sea. Then a shape crossed in front of the picture, and she yanked her head back in a panic. It had been Don. But was no longer. She could tell from the wolfish gait and hunched posture, even from one brief glimpse. It moved silently and deliberately, as though prowling.

Wendy did not know whether Kiara was in the same condition, and she had no way to find out without putting herself at risk. Samuel had said 'Mom and Dad,' so she assumed the worst. She wondered how long the child had been in there with them like that. It was a miracle that he was alive.

She squatted and looked into his face. He appeared anxious, so she attempted to inject as much confidence as possible into her whisper. "Listen, Samuel, but don't speak, okay? Good boy. I'm going to look after you for a while. Your parents would want me to. Is that okay?"

The boy nodded. Wendy felt an immense sense of relief. This would have been impossible if he had been taught not to go anywhere with strangers. Perhaps he had been taught, but was clever enough to appreciate that circumstances had changed. Or perhaps he did not see her as a stranger. She really hoped that was the case. It would make everything easier.

"Good boy," she told him again. "We're going to leave the building and go out to my car. We're going to be as quiet as possible, okay? Good boy. Don't let go of my hand, okay? Good boy."

She considered closing the door to his apartment, but was worried that the slightest sound might stir a reaction. She decided to lead him straight toward the stairs. Her ears once again became acutely aware of every minor sound, and she had less success keeping her imagination at bay.

She led him a few steps and then hesitated. Another worry joined the others. It was a growing congregation. She knew she would not be able to come back here again, so they had to get everything the boy needed right now. She crouched again. "Samuel, do you have any medicines you need?" She prayed the answer was no. If not, one of them would need to go into the apartment to get them.

He was staring at her, wide-eyed and obedient. He shook his head. She stood back up.

They reached the stairwell and began to descend. She did not like the sound their footsteps made on the uncarpeted stone. In the ambient silence, she thought she could hear them echo. Then she stopped and gripped Samuel's hand. He stopped beside her. She did hear an echo. But the sound continued, which meant it was not an echo at all. It came from below.

She and Samuel were caught on the third floor landing. She did not want to go back up, in case whoever or whatever it was heard them. Already, she made out muffled sounds from below, and worried that she and Samuel had given themselves away. She quietly led him into the hallway of the third floor. She considered running as soon as their feet were back on thin carpet, but instead she elected to hide. There was a small space near the opening in which they could crouch and keep an eye on the opposite wall, where the light from the stairwell cast a shadow.

She motioned Samuel into the space and pressed herself close to him. "If I tell you to run, I want you to go as fast as you can all the way until you are outside. Okay?" She worried that she was whispering too quietly for him to hear, but he nodded again. She squeezed his hand once in lieu of another "Good boy."

She held her breath as a shadow appeared. It resolved into the shape of a person, moving slowly up the stairs. She could barely hear its footsteps, which made her even more anxious. She told herself it might simply be a person being cautious, as she had done on her way in. But it could just as easily be a feral. The image of Don was fresh in her mind. He had looked as though he was stalking someone.

A second shadow, just as silent, joined the first. The first continued up the stairs. The second paused, and Wendy tightened her grip on Samuel's hand. The shadow grew larger, and she realized it was coming into the hallway where they crouched. She clenched, trying to make herself smaller. She prepared to push Samuel away if they were discovered. She was ready to fight, and hoped she could buy him enough time to escape.

The shadow stopped, and the ogre-sized silhouette of a man

lingered threateningly on the far wall. She heard her named spoken in a tempered hiss. "Wendy?"

"Kevin?" She peeked around the corner and saw him. "Kevin," she repeated, louder than she intended. "Oh, thank God!" she cried as she stood.

She looked down at Samuel. He was staring up at her, alert, ready for her direction. "It's okay, Sam," she said joyfully. "He's a friend."

Then she looked at Kevin suspiciously. He wore a large bandage on his cheek, and his gaze burned with an intensity that she had never seen in him before. But he was still a sight for sore eyes.

"What are you doing here?" She had told him where she was going, but he had never been here before, as far as she knew. How had he found her? "Did you follow me?"

He shook his head. "A friend knew where to come." He nodded his head back at the stairs. She looked and saw a second person, shrouded in shadow, walking back down from the floor above. He stepped into a slanting shaft of sunlight, and she recognized him. It was Halfus.

Rich made one more stop on the way back home. Although many shops were closed these days, he was not particularly worried that this would be one of them. As expected, he found the liquor store open for business. The one constant through good times and bad was the human desire to drink, for celebration or escape.

He came out with two bottles of scotch, which he assumed would be enough to get him good and drunk. He was not a heavy drinker, although he enjoyed the occasional pint with the mates. He thought of himself as a social drinker, then remembered the night he played drinking games with Joey and Dani. How many of his problems today could he trace back to that one night? How much could he blame on the booze? Had any single substance inflicted as much sorrow on humankind as alcohol? If so, he was not aware of it—and he knew a lot about history. There was clearly a self-destructive instinct in man.

Humans were an endlessly fascinating species. He wished he could have five lifetimes just to study them.

It had not been a long day, but he still felt weary. Buying the potassium cyanide from Lenny had been a gut-wrenching experience. He wondered if Wendy had dosed her mother yet. It was a horrible thing to have to do, but he understood perfectly well where she was coming from. He believed she had made the right decision, assuming she had gone through with it.

The transaction itself had been stressful, but he was glad to have seen the soccer pitch again. It was the scene of many of his fondest memories. He wondered if the field would ever be the site of another game. It was hard to imagine the community recovering from this catastrophe.

He considered spending a few minutes on his perch by the creek, then decided against it. He had had enough of quiet reflection. Instead, he drove straight home.

Unlike the soccer pitch, Rich's house had not seen a lot of action. But it was still one of his favorite places. This was the first home that he thought of as his own. It was old, cozy, and adorned with the vestiges of a forgotten era. Perhaps his favorite of these was an antique cast iron clawfoot bathtub. He rarely used it, but loved the idea that it was there. Most of the world was in such a hurry to modernize, and not without reason. The modern world had done a lot to make lives longer and more fulfilling. But every once in a while Rich liked to be reminded of where they all had come from.

As soon as he walked through the front door, he pulled the first bottle from the bag and set it on the kitchen counter. He peeled off the wrapper, opened the cap, and filled a juice glass. He took a sip and set the glass down, forcing himself not to spit the disgusting liquid back out. He was not exactly sure why he had settled on scotch. Once upon a time, he thought of it as a classy drink that sophisticated people enjoyed. It fit the conception of himself that he sought to attain, so he had tried to develop a taste for the liquor. The attempt was unsuccessful, and he had gone back to beer years ago. Yet today he decided to go with scotch once again, mostly because beer was not quick or powerful enough for what he had in mind.

He was losing his mind, and it tormented him. He had always been a thinker, and so it was with profound regret that he realized he could no longer bear his own thoughts. At first, he had viewed these intermittent sojourns into another mind as though they were somehow separate from him, an out-of-body experience to be studied like a textbook. The beatdown of Jim had been a turning point, however. Rich could no longer pretend that the episodes were not affecting his life, directly and disturbingly. They became more frequent. And the more he learned of the other afflicted, the more he accepted that the deterioration was irreversible. It was irrevocable, unrelenting, and merciless. He was on a speeding train to a destination he had no desire to reach.

At first, he had looked for information online and in the local news coverage. Then he had decided to go see more for himself. Rich was far less worried about his own safety than everyone else he knew. He had gone out into the streets, watching the other afflicted. Some cases were not as far advanced as his own. Others were noticeably worse. Or perhaps those people simply had less self-control. He saw the behavior of humankind shift right before his eyes. He had witnessed more than one attack, finding himself caught between a desire to intervene and a desire to join.

Perhaps the worst part was that sometimes he rather liked where things were going. There was a wild, raw appeal to it. This part of his mind often took over at times of stress, when he was least able to focus. This was going to be one of those times, and that was what the scotch was for.

He forced another gulp down, then another. It tasted even worse than he remembered. He chalked that up to one more effect of Eden. His taste buds had changed dramatically, leading him to give up everything from sweeteners to peppers. Anything stronger than a weak onion was now much too potent for him.

He forced down another gulp with renewed sense of purpose. He was in a hurry to get bombed. It had to happen quickly, before the primitive version of himself took over and stopped him from acting. He finished the first glassful, then poured another. He carried it with him up the stairs.

The logical Rich knew there was a very simple calculus. He could tolerate a certain amount of anguish so long as he retained a certain amount of hope, that most precious of commodities. Recent days had given him a lesson in just how little hope was required to keep himself going. It did not take much. He began to understand how people could experience unthinkable levels of pain and suffering and go on with their lives. All that was needed was a light at the end of the tunnel.

He started running the water in the bathtub, plugged the stopper in the drain, and returned downstairs to the kitchen. He finished his second glass of scotch and poured a third. His brain was already woozy, so he hoped not to need the second bottle. He scooped his cell phone off the countertop and went back upstairs.

He tested the temperature of the bathwater with his finger. He liked it good and warm. This felt just right. He shut off the faucet and removed his clothes, letting them drop to the floor by the tub. He put his phone down on top of his shirt to keep it from getting wet in case any water spilled onto the floor. He took another sip of scotch, then inspected the glass clumsily, his muscles and mind now moving in a slower gear. There was about half a glass remaining. He set it down on the floor next to his clothes, then carefully climbed into the tub. It felt delightful to submerge himself shoulder to toe.

He held his right arm above the water, keeping the hand dry. With it, he reached down to the phone. He pulled up Tre'Andre's number and called it again. This had been a daily routine for him since their breakup, but his ex-boyfriend never answered. Today was no different, so Rich thumbed the call off. He thought he had already given up on hope, and was surprised to discover that he could still manage to feel disappointment. Then he reached down to his pants and lifted them closer. He held them with one hand while using the other to fumble inside the pocket. He came out with the second candy wrapper he bought from Lenny. It sounded loud as he unwrapped it, his sluggish fingers struggling to get a secure grip on the ends. He tugged and the wrapper came open. He had pulled too hard, and the pill fell out. He drunkenly jerked his hand in an attempt to catch it. At least some measure of his speed and dexterity remained, and he snatched it out of the air just before it was out of reach.

More carefully, he picked up the glass of scotch. He tossed the pill into his mouth, then washed it down with the remaining liquor. This time, it did not taste nearly as bad.

16

SHIBBOLETH

In 1937, Dominican Republic President Rafael Trujillo bemoaned the depredations of Haitian immigrants crossing the border into his country. He came up with a uniquely creative, and uniquely evil, solution to rid his nation of the problem. He sent soldiers into the communities along the border to ask residents one simple question. The soldiers would hold up a sprig of parsley and ask what it was. Those who spoke the word perejil *with the proper Spanish trill were spared. Those who said the same word without the trill, which Creole speakers had difficulty pronouncing, were deemed immigrants and executed. As many as several thousand people were slain in an event that came to be known as the Parsley Massacre.*

During the Second World War, American soldiers in the Pacific Theater used the word lollapalooza *to distinguish between English and Japanese speakers. The premise rested on two assumptions. The word itself is a colloquial term that non-Americans would have difficulty speaking, even in unaccented English. Moreover, Japanese speakers often confuse the 'r' and 'l' consonants. Similar distinctive constructs were used in other locations throughout the war.*

The term shibboleth refers to words or phrases that are used to identify members of a group, or more commonly to identify non-members. The word is Hebrew in origin, and its use is derived from a passage in the Old

Testament. The Book of Judges describes a war between the Gilead and the tribe of Ephraim:

"And the Gileadites took the passages of Jordan before the Ephraimites: and it was so, that when those Ephraimites which were escaped said, Let me go over; that the men of Gilead said unto him, Art thou an Ephraimite? If he said, Nay; Then said they unto him, Say now Shibboleth: and he said Sibboleth: for he could not frame to pronounce it right. Then they took him, and slew him at the passages of Jordan: and there fell at that time of the Ephraimites forty and two thousand."

Naturally, shibboleths are not used only in conflict and war. Today, the term is widely ascribed to cultural customs and values that distinguish members of a group. Written dates are formatted differently by Americans and Europeans. So are the ubiquitous decimal points and commas used in counting numbers. The first floor of a European building coincides with the second floor of its American counterpart. Rubbers, biscuits, hookers, and fags all mean something completely different on opposite sides of the Atlantic.

Groups do not always correspond to nationalities or ethnicities, however. Shibboleths are sometimes used to separate experts and amateurs in a particular field. The term "spelunking" is used by amateurs, for example, while experts generally prefer the term "caving."

Shibboleths can even be used to characterize a member of a particular age group or social circle. Children who grew up in the decade of the eighties might easily identify with a particular song, movie, or dance style that would merely elicit shrugs or headshakes from others. These familiarities are used for social bonding as much as any other purpose. How else could one describe such frivolous phenomena as the Safety Dance *and* Who Let the Dogs Out?

In the context of the broad definition of the term, the list of shibboleths is endless. Each item on it is used consciously or subconsciously to pass judgment and sow confusion. Shibboleths—like racism, nationalism, sexism, and homophobia—represent a part of humankind's boundless ability to

*subdivide itself, bonding through rejection, aligning through differences, and
uplifting the few through repression of many.*

The last time Ben had been in a medical clinic was six months earlier,
when the college had sponsored a blood drive. That clinic had
operated out of a mobile trailer. There had been three nurses and two
cots for patients. It had taken most of the day to process a few
hundred volunteers.

By comparison, this was a much larger operation. There were
dozens of people in the converted lobby of the middle school, with
eight or nine cots and numerous pieces of medical equipment. Only a
few of the cots were occupied, and most people were standing or
sitting. There looked to be six medical personnel, who stood out by
the fatigues they wore as well as their protective gloves and masks.
That left at least twenty civilians. Most were huddled in small groups,
although there were a few loners standing about, looking lost.

Judging by the quantity of vehicles outside, Ben had expected there
to be even more people than this. Perhaps there was more going on in
the area than just the clinic.

He took a minute to get his bearings. The patients in the cots
looked to be suffering from Phase One symptoms. Each of them lay
prostrate and had a large bucket nearby. Ben did not need to look into
those buckets to know what was in them. Thankfully, an antiseptic
smell was the dominant odor in the room. All of the other patients
appeared to be more or less normal. They carried on conversations
with the workers or each other, and some of them seemed to be
helping out with menial tasks such as cleaning and distributing snack
food and bottled water. Very little remained to remind him that he
was inside a middle school. The only noticeable indicator was a large
shelf of trophies encased in glass, which he presumed to be bolted to
the wall.

A young man in fatigues walked by. Ben got his attention. "Excuse me. I'm new...but I'm not a patient. I'd like to assist, if I may. Who should I talk to?"

The man looked toward a pair of workers talking some distance away. Ben recognized them as the doctor and assistant he had dealt with back when USAMRIID first came to McGahey. "Major Schlepp," called the man Ben had just spoken to. The woman looked over, nodded, said a few final words to her companion, and came over. Her eyes met Ben's, and he remembered that she had a disquietingly intense manner about her.

He swallowed and tried not to stutter. "Hello, Major. We met once before," he told her. "I'm—"

"Doctor Appelstein," she said. "I remember you." She held out her hand.

He shook it with relief. Knowing who he was would save him some time.

"What can I do for you?" she inquired.

"I'm hoping I can do something for you."

She raised a thin eyebrow. He saw her cheeks shift, and believed that she was smiling beneath the mask. "So, you're interested in helping out?" she asked, sounding hopeful.

"If I can. I'm not a medical doctor, though. I'm a doctor of—"

"Ancient Studies," she finished. "Everyone knows who you are, Doctor."

He did not know whether that meant he was famous or infamous. Logic told him it was the latter, but her smile seemed to indicate no ill will. Quite the opposite, in fact. She seemed quite friendly, considering the unfortunate circumstances.

"That's quite all right," she assured him. "We have plenty of things you can still help with, assuming you're willing to get your hands dirty. Figuratively, not literally. We actually prefer that you keep your hands clean."

He forced a smile. Laughter did not seem appropriate in this environment.

She wiggled her finger, motioning him to follow. She led him toward a pair of interior doors. He followed her through and into a corridor. From here, the building was once again recognizable as a school. In the distance, he saw rows of lockers. Above hung signs for the auditorium and cafeteria. He thought of the food distribution he had witnessed happening in the lobby, and wondered why they were not using the cafeteria instead. Perhaps there simply were not enough people to warrant it.

Just inside the hallway, Major Schlepp turned to face him. "Do you have any open sores or wounds?" she asked.

"Not that I know of," he replied.

"Let me see your hands," she ordered. Her tone was commanding, but not belligerent. He held his hands out. She grasped and inspected them, top and bottom. Then she released them and looked into his face. "Say, 'She sells seashells by the seashore.'"

"What?"

"Please do as I ask." Her tone became more assertive.

"She sells seashells by the seashore."

She breathed a sigh of relief. "Good man," she told him. He felt immeasurably relieved himself. For some reason, he did not want to be on her bad side.

"Was that to determine whether I'm turning feral?" he asked.

She nodded. "It's imprecise, but it's the best we can do for now. We have a blood test to indicate whether a patient has been infected, but we already know you have. What we can't tell from the blood is who is progressing from Phase Two to Three. And that's a problem."

"How many are?" he asked bluntly. This disease was partly his responsibility. He wanted to know just how bad it was.

She paused, considering. Then she sighed. "Doctor Appelstein—"

"Please, call me Ben."

She paused again, staring at him. *She has pretty eyes*, he thought. They were big, brown, and perceptive. He wished he could see her without the mask. He recalled her being not unattractive. Now he thought she was probably quite lovely when she had a mind to be.

"Okay, Ben. You're going to find out soon anyway. Follow me."

She led him down the corridor. He noticed they were following the directions to the cafeteria. They rounded a bend, and he saw two soldiers armed with the same nonlethal rifles he had seen at the checkpoint outside of town. These two men, however, also wore hip holsters with pistols. Those were not nonlethal. *For emergencies*, he assumed.

"We're going to take a quick peek inside," she informed the sentries. They nodded and pushed the doors open.

She stood in front of Ben, but was short enough that he could see over her head. Now he understood why everyone was not eating in the cafeteria, as well as where the owners of all the other cars had gone. There were easily twenty or more people inside the large chamber. Many of them were engaged in conversation just like those in the lobby. But many were not. Some of them were pacing in agitation. Others were simply staring at the open doors, as though considering a run for it. Some of them looked to have torn their clothing. Some seemed utterly oblivious to their surroundings. One man sat at a table with his head buried in his arms, sobbing.

Ben looked away. The scene was painful to behold. The major nodded again, and the sentries allowed the doors to swing closed.

He felt a hand on his shoulder. He saw her looking up at him, concern in her eyes. "I'm sorry, Ben," she said. "You seemed like you really wanted to know."

"I did," he confirmed. "That's everyone who's going feral?"

She shook her head. "The worst cases have been taken away already. We've been averaging three or four a day recently. But the number keeps going up. I might send as many as ten later today." She motioned with her head, and they began slowly walking back toward the lobby.

"I'm sure you've done the math," he said. "What percentage are we talking about?"

"It's a small sample size, of course," she replied. "But early estimates are seven in ten."

He winced. "Is there anything you can do to help them?"

"Yes, a little. We've been issuing anti-psychotics. They take a little while to ramp up, but if we start them off right as the language difficulties begin, it seems to slow the pace of deterioration. That's only for the people at the clinic, however." She sighed. "Despite all the people who came here, I'm afraid the lion's share are out there trying to deal with this on their own. All we could do was make requests. We can't force them to come in."

"What about now that the extra troops are here?" he asked. "You could get a little more heavy-handed. It might be better for the town if you did."

She stopped walking. They had not yet reached the lobby, and he realized this conversation was intended to be private. He was surprised to see her close her eyes. When she opened them again, he thought he could see the faintest glimmer of wetness. "You picked a strange time to show up, Doctor. No...the opposite is happening. We're pulling out. With the quarantine, we can't easily get more supplies in. Our usefulness is coming to an end."

That did not seem entirely correct to him. "You're the Army. You can get more supplies in here if you want to."

Major Schlepp reached up and drew her mask away from her mouth. She lowered her voice. "The food and water isn't the problem. It's the drugs. We're burning through them quickly, and...they're needed elsewhere."

Her eyes seemed to be burning into him. This was how he felt the first time they had met. It was unnerving. "Elsewhere?" he asked. "The other outbreaks?" She nodded, so he continued. "How many other outbreaks are there now?"

She lowered her voice even more. "A lot."

"I see." The latest news reports had mentioned two other cities in the U.S. He now got the distinct impression that was an understatement. It was a sobering thought.

"You understand that this is sensitive information, correct? The news will get out eventually, but it will be better for everyone if we control how and when. So please don't tell anyone yet, all right?"

"All right. Under one condition. You tell me your first name."

She smiled, and at least some of the worry in her face took a temporary leave of absence. "It's Kimberly. My friends call me Kim."

"Kim, I wish we could have picked a nicer day to meet," he told her.

She winked as she pulled her mask back up. "Day's not over yet. I need to get back to my duties. Join us when you're ready to start work." Then she turned and walked back through the lobby doors.

Seven in ten. That was very, very bad. He was worried about all of humanity, naturally, but he was even more worried about his team. There were six of them. He knew Ernie was suffering, and he suspected Rich was as well. But that was only two. Had they beaten the odds, or was another shoe going to drop? He decided it was time to get back in touch with his students.

For the first few minutes, it felt strange being back inside Wendy's apartment. Halfus struggled to calculate exactly how long it had been since he was last there. So many things had happened—his months of incapacity in Iraq, his harrowing escape, the dig itself. But he had to go back even further. The two of them had broken up a year earlier, and although they continued to see one another in and out of classes, Halfus could not remember visiting her home in all the time since.

It was not long, however, before the sense of abnormality faded and he slipped back into old habits. He had spent quite a lot of time in this apartment when they were dating, so he knew exactly where everything was. She told him and Kevin to make themselves at home while she set Samuel up watching cartoons on the small television in the bedroom. Halfus took her instructions to heart and retrieved a bottle of beer for each of them from her refrigerator. He did not see a bottle opener, but he found he could twist the caps off surprisingly easily. It was light beer, which was not his preference, but it was refreshing nonetheless. The tension of the day eased somewhat, though he still felt on edge.

When she rejoined them, Halfus gave them the broad brush stroke version of his story. Kevin had already heard fragments, but Halfus rehashed everything from beginning to end for her benefit. Unsurprisingly, she had questions. She particularly wanted to hear more about the night he and Ernie had explored the tomb beneath the ruins. Halfus quickly got the impression that there was some critical piece of information she had heard from Ernie that she wanted to verify. But without coming out and telling him, he was not exactly certain what she was driving at.

He tried to handle the entire Ernie situation in one fell swoop. "I think it's safe to assume that anything he told you was bullshit. There are probably pieces of truth to his story, but it would take too long to weed them out. He had to cover up what he assumed was murder, after all." Halfus paused a moment, sorting out his emotions. "He and I have a few things to discuss. I'm *really* hoping I run into him."

"What a fucking little weasel he turned out to be," snorted Kevin in disgust. "He got what he deserved."

"No," Halfus disagreed. His gaze kept returning to the bandage on Kevin's cheek. His friend had said Tracy's fingernails tore it open in a frenzy of rage. It must have been horrible, and not because of the pain. "No one deserves this. Besides, I think he only did it in the spur of the moment. It's partly my fault. There were plenty of signs that he would be jealous. I made a mistake. I should have been a lot more aware of his feelings."

Wendy reacted with surprise. "You're not going to apologize to him, are you?"

"No, I'm going to kill him. You cannot imagine what he put me through."

No one said anything for a moment. Then Wendy glanced at the clock on the wall. "It's five. Time for a news check." She scooped the remote control off her coffee table and turned on the television set.

Halfus remembered Wendy being a bit of a news junkie. She seldom watched sitcoms, dramas, or sports, but she could keep these twenty-four hour news networks on constantly. He supposed it was driven by her interest in politics, although he wondered whether he had the cause and effect backwards. Most likely, it was a self-reinforcing loop by this point in her life.

She generally only watched the liberal hosts, but he seriously doubted it made any difference which channel she put on now. In recent days, the only thing any of them covered was Eden. And they were all terrified.

For the next fifteen minutes, the three of them watched the television broadcast without discussion. For his part, Halfus watched disinterestedly. He knew the limits of what television news would tell them, so he doubted they would learn anything new. But he could understand her desire to hear every tidbit, snippet, and morsel about the progress of the epidemic. Few people had their lives more affected by this disease than Wendy. He could not blame her for clinging to the hope that a breakthrough would be forthcoming. He had his doubts, but he kept those to himself.

The news program had four guests who spent time spewing their thoughts and trepidations. None of these talking heads seemed to know anything more than Halfus and his friends, although they liked to pretend that their opinions were somehow worth listening to. At last the program cut to a press conference for Carol Hunt, a Pentagon spokeswoman with the impressive title of Assistant Secretary of Defense for Health Affairs. She provided the only real insight into the progress of the disease, and even this Halfus knew to be filtered by political considerations.

The spokeswoman acknowledged outbreaks in more American cities—Boston, Richmond, Chicago, Columbus, Jacksonville, and Tucson. She neither denied nor confirmed the existence of the virus in a dozen others with suspected cases, and she referred questions about London, Amsterdam, Brussels, and Barcelona to the World Health Organization, which was responsible for worldwide containment. Halfus wondered why the reticence to confirm these rumors. He knew from his own recent travel through Europe that Germany and France were no longer the only countries dealing with Schwarzvogel. Surely, that would be common knowledge by now, at least outside this country. Americans themselves were notorious for their lack of interest in the rest of the world when they had problems at home.

Frankly, he had greater confidence in the U.S. Army's chances to bring the disease under control than he did the international community's. His respect for the military—for the entire American government, in fact—went up dramatically in the wake of his ordeal in Iraq. He had been worried that they would see his survival as a thorn in their side, but instead he encountered genuine goodwill. He met with representatives from both the military and State Department who had scoffed at his concerns. One Colonel listened to his harrowing tale and simply shook his head. "Next time, just let us know, Son." Halfus had spent all those days of planning and fretting about his escape route, when what he really should have done was find a cell phone or Internet connection. They would have found a way to come and get him.

He knew many others did not agree, but he saw nothing sinister in the decision to place the Eden outbreaks under army control. They were simply better equipped to handle it than anyone else. The hysteria and paranoia were already out of control, and were getting worse by the day. In less than forty-eight hours back in the country he had already listened to predictions that the army was going to kill everyone who caught the virus, as well as speculation that the whole thing was a bioweapon project gone bad. He had not bothered to tell these fearmongers that he had been at ground zero of the outbreak. They never would have believed him. He knew from experience that most people believed only what they wanted to.

The television briefing ended on a particularly sour note. The spokeswoman admitted that the progression of the Schwarzvogel virus was causing certain individuals to commit acts of violence, against strangers, friends, and loved ones. The most frequent manifestation of this violence was happening behind the wheel of a car. Road rage incidents were skyrocketing, according to law enforcement data. Less frequent, but even more disturbing, were rising statistics on suicides. These were more difficult to directly attribute to the virus, but Ms. Hunt acknowledged that some people were overcome with remorse at their own behavior following bouts of violence. She then evaded every attempt by reporters to probe deeper into the topic.

At the first commercial break, Wendy turned off the television.

None of them spoke for a long moment. They were each lost in his or her own disturbed thoughts.

Kevin finally broke the silence. "That little bugger moves fast."

"I don't understand," said Wendy. "How did it start spreading again?"

Kevin took a guess. "I think it never stopped. They just weren't telling us. Reporting is usually a step behind reality. Maybe they didn't know. Maybe they just underestimated it. They probably thought that public panic was worse than the virus itself. I think it's safe to say that we weren't very well prepared to tackle two different diseases at the same time."

"But if it only gets transmitted by blood and saliva, that shouldn't be hard to control."

Halfus joined the conversation. "You might be surprised how much blood and saliva get exchanged. People get little cuts on their fingers without even realizing it. They rub their eyes and noses and mouths. They don't wash things as much as they should. They drink after one another. In a lot of other countries they kiss like we shake hands."

"And apparently people everywhere like to have sex with each other. A lot," Kevin added.

Wendy still protested. "But the masks and gloves—"

"Are annoying," Kevin finished the sentence for her. "People wear them when they're afraid, but then nothing happens for a while, so they lose some of that fear. They get lazy. They take shortcuts."

"Not if you know you're going to catch it if you stop being careful."

"If I stuck you in the finger with a poison needle, then told you the only way to save yourself was to cut off that finger right away, would you do it? Would you really believe me? Or would you hesitate to believe that it could really be as serious as I said? Obviously, chopping off a finger is different from wearing protective clothing or not kissing anyone, but it's the same principle. Fear is a good motivator. It can push you to do a lot of things you normally wouldn't. But at some point human nature kicks back in."

"People are people," Halfus said.

"People are people," Kevin agreed.

Wendy changed the subject. "Kevin, your bandage needs replacing. I'll go get some gauze." She got up and left for the bathroom. Halfus hoped she was not too upset. She was holding up quite well, he thought, all things considered. The Wendy he used to know would have started an argument. Now she seemed as intent on solutions as he and Kevin. The irony was that he had sneaked back into McGahey to try to help her, only to find out she was doing well on her own.

She came back out with a first aid kit. She immediately set to work on Kevin's injury while he sat as stiff as a statue. His cheek had a trio of ugly gashes. Tracy's fingernails had really done a number on him. Halfus had not been there when it happened, and Kevin was not sharing specifics. But it was clear that she had attacked him, given him those wounds, and sent him into the worst mood Halfus had ever seen him in. Kevin was ordinarily one of the happiest people Halfus knew, but now acted as though he hated the world.

It was not surprising. Halfus understood at least part of his friend's turmoil. The way Kevin had watched Tracy decline conjured memories of Halfus' own experience with Shauna. Staying at her bedside day after day, hoping things would change, feeling utterly helpless. The images were years old but still sprang vividly to mind. The hospital room, the collective anguish of her family, the ironic expression of contentment on her unforgettable features. She had remained lovely to him despite the need for her beautiful brown hair to be shaved off for the operations. Operations that had ultimately done no good at all. But it was her spark that had enraptured him, and without that she began to seem like a different person. That had been the cruelest blow of all, having the memories of the vivacious Shauna slowly replaced by those of this inferior version. Sometimes it was better to say goodbye quickly than to watch your hope slowly drain away like sand through your fingers.

Wendy leaned over Kevin and mercilessly ripped off the old adhesive, then taped a new pad in its place. While she worked, she got them started on a plan of action. "Let's set some ground rules, okay? The three of us should decide on a few things before we start getting others involved."

"Such as?" asked Kevin cautiously, trying not to disturb her work.

"Such as are we staying, or leaving?"

"Town?"

"Town." Her tone left little question where she stood on the issue.

Halfus was not sure what they would accomplish by leaving. The army had presumably set up the quarantine for a reason. They were trying to get the outbreak under control. He was of a mind to give them a chance to do so. "If the disease is spreading, what would be the advantage of leaving? There are more resources here than other places—"

Kevin stopped him. "Begging your pardon, but you haven't been here, watching the people you love go crazy right before your eyes. Part of me wants to stay to see if I can help. But most of me knows I can't, and I'll go crazy too if I don't get out of here."

Halfus saw Wendy nodding along. "You feel that way, too?" he asked her.

She nodded. "This town has nothing but bad memories for me now."

Halfus gave it one last try. "You two know that just leaving isn't automatically going to make everything better, right?"

They both nodded. Then Kevin clinched it. "I don't know what's coming, Halph. But I know I'd rather face it anywhere other than McGahey."

"All right," Halfus conceded. "I can probably sneak a few of us out the same way I came in. There are patrols, but the ones I saw were low-tech. I didn't see them using night vision. If we go after dark we can probably slip through."

"That's one decision," said Wendy. "Here's another. We don't take anyone who has started turning. Agreed?"

Again, Halfus hesitated. That seemed overly harsh to him. Then again, he had not watched a person turn feral the way the two of them had. He looked at Kevin. "What are your thoughts?"

Kevin was less adamant about this decision. "I don't know. I can understand the point, but even someone who's just speaking poorly? It takes a little while for the bad stuff to happen—"

Wendy chimed in. "Remember what Halfus said about there being resources here. That's what they're for. To help people who are turning. Not people like us. We're just caught in the crossfire, trying not to become collateral damage."

Kevin nodded again. "You're right. Okay, no partials."

He looked at Halfus, who accepted their decision. "All right."

Then Kevin brought up a topic that Halfus had hoped to avoid a while longer. "We need weapons. I have a friend who left town a week ago, but gave me a key to his place. He's got a couple guns there, I think—"

Knowing how Wendy felt about the subject, Halfus wished he had had a chance to warn his friend. But the redhead was not paying attention to the stricken expression on her face.

"Kevin, please don't."

"I'll be fine. Just a quick run in and out."

"Not that. It's just...no guns, please."

Kevin either did not notice the pleading tone in her voice, or did not let it dissuade him. He defended his position, coming down pretty hard on her in the process. "What? You don't want to hurt them? You yourself said they aren't really people anymore. I mean...the person you knew is gone. Now they're just animals. I should have listened to you about Tracy—"

"Haven't we all seen enough killing?" she begged.

Kevin saw she was upset and moderated his tone. "Look, I'm sorry about your mother, but you did what you had to do. I understand what you're going through."

"I'm not talking about my mother." Wendy looked at Halfus, and his heart went out to her. This was one subject he had learned to stay away from throughout their relationship. One time he had called her irrationally emotional about guns, and she admitted that her brother had died in a childhood accident. Horrified, he had not wanted to cause her any more grief, and had never brought up the topic again.

He tried to intervene, to protect her from talking about it. "Kevin, drop it. We'll—"

"I killed my brother when I was ten years old." Both men stared at her, totally stunned into silence. She faced Halfus. "I told you he accidentally shot himself. He didn't. He and I were playing with my father's gun and I thought it would be funny to scare him by pointing the gun at him and I shot him." A single tear rolled down her cheek as she continued. "I've had to live with it every day of my life. It's with me wherever I go, whoever I'm with. I always feel like the worst person in the room."

Halfus would have given anything to cure her of the pain he knew she was feeling. But he was not a gifted talker. He could only say the first thing that occurred to him. "You're not," he said. He went to her and touched her shoulder, unsure whether she wanted the contact or not. She took his hand, slipped her fingers between his, and leaned her head forward. He did the same, pressing his head to hers, whispering. "You're not. You've punished yourself enough. You saved a boy's life today." Then they shared a moment with nothing but their touch and the sound of their breathing.

He was ready to wrap his arms around her if the tears kept coming. Instead, she needed only a minute to settle herself. Then she squeezed his hand once, released it, and forced out a weak smile. "Thank you," she said. She looked at Kevin. "If you want to take a gun, I won't stop you. But I'm not taking one."

Kevin reached out and touched her shoulder, too. "I won't use it unless I have to, okay? But if I need it to save you, or Halph, or that boy in there..." He nodded his head toward the bedroom.

Wendy resigned herself to the argument. "If it's to save a friend." She sounded defeated. She turned away from the two of them. "Speaking of which, I'm going to check in on him." She walked away, her face hidden. Halfus understood that she wanted a minute alone.

He and Kevin got to work discussing people to contact. By the time Wendy rejoined them to announce that Samuel had fallen asleep, they had come up with a couple of names to start with. Halfus had no phone, so Wendy allowed him to borrow hers. He did not have phone numbers memorized, but most of his friends had their information posted on social media. He booted her laptop then switched on her phone, which had been turned off.

"Wendy, it looks like you have a few messages," he announced.

"I'll check them later," she replied.

He was about to make his first call when her phone rang in his hand. He looked at the name that appeared on the display. It happened to be one of the names already on the list. He smiled as he answered.

"Hello, Doc. Guess who?"

"I'd know that voice anywhere," came the cheerful reply. "How are you, Halfus?"

"I'm all right, all things considered. You want to talk to Wendy? I can get her."

"You'll do just fine. I just want to see how everyone is. I'm...getting worried."

"You should be. I'm sorry to say it, but there it is."

He spent the next few minutes filling in their professor on the status of each of his students. Doc had already known about Ernie and was saddened to hear about Tracy. No one seemed to know much about Rich, but Halfus was distressed to hear that Doc believed their esteemed colleague was doing his best to hide the advance of his affliction. Halfus assured the professor that they would check in on Rich. They wanted him to join their impromptu conference anyway.

"Which reminds me," Halfus said. "We were about to call you. We'd like to add you to this little meeting, too."

"Thank you for thinking of me, but I'm helping out at the clinic downtown."

"I'm sure they'll let you take a few hours off," Halfus suggested hopefully.

"I'm sure they would, but...I want to help them. Things are bad here. There are some...problems."

Halfus became alerted to a cautionary note in Doc's voice. "Is there anything you want to tell me?"

There was a brief pause. "No, not really."

It sure seemed as though the professor was troubled by something. Halfus considered forcing the issue. Then he decided against it. Doc would tell them if and when he was ready. "All right. You're a good man, Doc. Call us back if you think of something. And don't try to be a hero over there, okay? Help those you can, but don't take stupid risks. If things are as bad as they sound, find a secure location and hole up until help comes."

He heard the man chuckle. "You don't need to worry about me being a hero. That's for you young folk."

Halfus grinned. "All right, then. Not sure when we'll talk again. Good luck."

"Halfus, wait."

"What is it?"

"I thought of one thing I can tell you. Over here they're using a shibboleth to detect Phase Threes."

"Oh? What is it?"

"She sells seashells by the seashore."

"Makes sense. Should have thought of that one myself."

"I had the same reaction."

Halfus saw that Wendy and Kevin were beginning to look impatient. "Thanks again," he told Doc. "I hope to talk again soon."

There was another hesitation. "One more thing, Halfus. Do you forgive me for throwing you under the bus?"

"Shit, Doc, I'd have done the same thing in your position. I screwed up pretty bad. No one feels more guilty about things than I." He sighed. "Anyway, don't waste another thought on it. We'll see you again when this mess gets cleaned up."

They ended the call. He looked over at his companions. "He's worried about Rich. Says he's been hiding his speech problems so we wouldn't know."

Wendy looked puzzled. "I just saw him earlier today. He seemed fine." Halfus watched her lips twist the way they did when she was concentrating. Then she frowned. "No...wait. Maybe he didn't." She looked troubled. "I can't be sure."

"We need him," Kevin stated matter-of-factly.

Halfus agreed. "Well, we have to start calling folks anyway. Let's put him at the top of the list."

"Okay, who else? The more the merrier, or do we keep it small?" Wendy asked.

Halfus thought of the difficulties organizing a large group in the best of circumstances. Trying to get them past an army patrol at night was asking for trouble. "I suggest we keep it small," he said. "Each of us nominate one person to call. Plus Rich, and Doc if he changes his mind. That's about all we can manage."

"One more thing," he added. "The three of us are in charge, right? In case any disagreements break out. This isn't a time for democracy."

Kevin took it a step further. "I suggest Wendy calls the shots from here on out. There needs to be a single leader, and I think she's earned it."

Halfus nodded. "Suits me fine." He looked at Wendy. "All right with you, Chief?"

She looked taken aback for a moment. Then she nodded.

They began to toss out names. It took several minutes to narrow the field down to three. Wendy decided to place the calls herself and put the two guys in charge of other preparations. Halfus could think of a dozen things he would have liked to have. He wished he could go home for them, but he had no home in McGahey any longer, much less the gear that used to be inside it. He thought of an alternative, however.

While Wendy started on the calls, Halfus asked a favor of Kevin. "Can I get a ride from you?"

"Sure. Where to?"

Halfus glanced over to make certain that Wendy was not listening. "Ernie's."

Kevin raised an eyebrow. "You think you'll find him there?"

"Probably not. I'm going to make use of his Jeep, if it's there. And a few other things that might come in handy for the trip."

"You're going to steal his car?" Kevin did not sound particularly bothered by the notion.

"He stole my girl. I think it's only fair, *n'est-ce pas?*"

"I've got no problem with it."

Halfus waved goodbye to Wendy, who was holding the phone to her ear. He hated the thought of leaving her, even for a short while.

He had been through a lot to get to this point, and so had she. They belonged together. But it would be for only a few hours...he hoped.

Kevin pulled open the door, but she held up a finger in the gesture to wait. The two of them stopped. She shook her head and hung up. "I tried Rich twice. He's not answering. Can one of you go by his place?"

"I'll do it," said Halfus. "I want to double-check the way out of town while we still have some daylight. I'll swing by and look in on him." The back route out of town that he was thinking of would pass within a few blocks of Rich's neighborhood.

"Good idea," said Wendy. "Maybe seeing you will make him change his mind about joining us. Are you going, too, Kevin?"

"I've got a few things to pick up, myself," added Kevin. He did not use the word "guns," but Halfus assumed that was what he meant.

"Good luck, guys. Come back safe," she told them. "And soon."

Kevin dropped him off in front of Ernie's apartment building. "Want me to come in with you?"

Halfus shook his head. "Nah. I'd rather handle this on my own."

"Want me to wait out here?"

Again, Halfus shook his head. "I see his Jeep over there." He climbed out of the passenger seat. "I'll meet you back at Wendy's." He closed the door and tapped the roof. Kevin pulled away, leaving him alone on the quiet street.

He stared at the building. It was not much to look at, just two rows of four doors with a window by each. Ernie's apartment was on the second floor, accessible by a stairwell in the rear. Halfus did not worry about getting in. It was what he might find inside that occupied his attention. If Ernie was not there, Halfus would help himself to a few of his ex-friend's belongings. If he was, they would just have to deal with things here and now.

Halfus hoped he was there.

The street may have been quiet, but in this case that did not equate to peaceful. Everywhere he looked, there was discarded trash and damaged property. He wondered how much of the destruction was caused by ferals, and how much by regular people. He suspected a little of both. Sometimes it seemed that people did not need much of an excuse to slip off the constricting leash of civility and slide into barbarity. Not that he was passing judgment. Sometimes people had a reason.

He found a decent-sized chunk of cinder block lying between the sidewalk and the front of the building. He scooped it up on his way toward the stairs. He ascended, rounded the building to the front, and heaved the block through the glass of the window. It made less noise than he imagined it would. He spent a minute kicking away all the remaining projections of glass from the frame. He raised a foot to the window, ready to climb through, then hesitated. He brought the foot back down, went over to the door, and turned the knob. The door opened.

Halfus sighed at his own stupidity. He had just unnecessarily alerted anyone inside to his entry. It was a sign that his brain was too rattled to think calmly before acting. He was in for a long night unless he got that problem under control.

He pushed open the door and quietly stepped inside. The sun was declining and the room was in shadow. It took his eyes a few seconds to adjust, and in the meantime he focused on his ears. There were no signs of life. No sounds and no movement. He left the front door open in case he needed to make a hasty retreat.

Not much had changed since the last time he was here, months earlier. He recognized the placement of furniture and assorted objects. He knew where to look for the things he was here to collect. But first, he had to find out if the owner was home.

Halfus moved cautiously from the living room to the hallway. He glanced sideways into the kitchen as he passed, then moved toward the bathroom. The door was open, the room empty. The faucet was dripping, slowly, each rhythmic beat echoing like a drum in the stillness of the apartment. The noise distracted him all out of proportion to its volume. He could not resist the impulse to shut it off.

At last Halfus tiptoed to the bedroom. The door was cracked open just enough to see a floor littered with clothing. He made a fist with his right hand and pushed the door open the rest of the way with his left. The bed came into view, then the dresser, then the entire room. No one was home.

Halfus stepped into the bedroom and inspected the container on the bed. It looked like a gun case. He glanced inside and saw that it was empty. He had no idea if ferals could still use guns, but the thought of Ernie roaming about with a pistol sent a shiver down his spine.

Halfus flicked on all the lights and began to rummage through the apartment for equipment. A few years earlier, Halfus had taken Ernie to REI and loaded him up with camping and hiking gear, including a Coleman tent and dependable North Face daypack. These things were his primary objective.

The place was a mess, but it was impossible to determine how long it had been since anyone had been there. One whiff of the rancid milk in the refrigerator told him that Ernie had not been living here for quite some time. A quick search of the pantry revealed some Clif bars, which Halfus tossed into a bag. They were quick and easy food for an emergency. He also grabbed a waterproof jacket and a pair of ill-fitting heavy boots, just in case. He thought it was likely they would have to leave their vehicles behind to make it past the perimeter, so he grabbed a few items to help in the dark—a flashlight, some road flares, and a caving helmet with attached lamp. He found the tent and a sleeping bag, but was disappointed to see no sign of the backpack he remembered. In its absence, he found a simple old canvas rucksack to throw everything into. The last thing he grabbed were the keys to the Jeep, hanging on a hook inside the kitchen.

There was not much daylight left as he left the apartment. At least he did not need to worry about traffic. He would hurry over to Rich's and convince him to come along on the reconnaissance. It would be dark by the time they reached the outskirts of town, but he was not particularly worried about tracking the patrols. On his way into town, he had noticed that they were not attempting to be inconspicuous. All he needed to do was note their path and timing. Compared to what he had gone through in Iraq, escaping from McGahey should be a snap.

He breathed a little easier leaving Ernie's apartment behind. He had not really expected his false friend to be home, but his nerves had been strained nonetheless. He felt himself relaxing. Now that he had done the hard part, he could look forward to seeing another of his true friends.

Afternoon was turning to evening when the clinic experienced a disturbance. At Kim's request, Ben was hunched over a cabinet with clipboard in hand, counting the remaining inventory of mundane medical supplies. The door to the hallway was nearby. It was seldom used, and only by a single staff member at a time. It had taken on a measure of taboo in his mind, so he remained aware of it from the corner of his eye even when he tried to ignore it.

Now, without warning, it opened from the other direction. A soldier walked through the lobby toward the exit, his eyes never veering off-target. He was followed by a long line of patients, flanked by two more soldiers and followed up by a fourth.

There were several dozen patients in the line. Most of them stared down and away from prying eyes, but Ben recognized a few faces from the cafeteria. He wondered whether this was all of them. Then, toward the back of group, he saw one more face that he actually knew.

"Avi!" he called. The college dean looked his way with an expression of confusion that quickly turned hopeful.

"Ben," he said. He stepped out of the line and reached out for a handshake, as though they had just happened upon one another at a social function. Ben shook it instinctively while his mind pondered the significance of this exodus. He was about to inquire what his associate knew about it, but Avi eliminated the need. "You have to help me. They're taking us away."

"What? You?"

"Yes, they think I'm a feral. They're taking all of us out of here. We're being disappeared, like this was some kind of Chilean *junta*."

"They think you're a feral?" The thought was perplexing. "Why?"

"I don't know. I'm perfectly fine. You've got to help me."

Ben looked at his colleague thoughtfully. He seemed perfectly normal, other than being understandably anxious about his fate. Ben considered the tongue twister. It would be impolite to put his boss through that discourtesy. On the other hand, it was better to be safe than sorry.

Then Avi was pulled away before Ben could respond. The man was thrust toward the others by the rearguard, a soldier with a surly expression who Ben had no desire to irritate. He elected to find out what was going on from someone in charge.

He followed the group outside. The sun was setting behind the base of the nearby mountain. The air was already getting cooler. There was a lot of activity in the parking lot. Two military trucks were sitting nearby, their engines still running. In addition to the patients and guards from the procession, he saw a handful of other soldiers. He looked for one person in particular, and found her between the two trucks.

Kim was engaged in an animated conversation with another officer, an older gentleman with short salt and pepper hair. Again Ben's ignorance of military insignia frustrated him. He did not know which of the two of them was giving orders. He waited for them to finish. Behind her, Ben saw patients being loaded into the back of the first truck. He got impatient, and considered interrupting the discussion. Then she saluted the other officer before turning away. She began walking toward the truck's cab.

"Kim," he called out. She looked his way and stopped as he approached. "What is happening?" he asked.

"I'm sorry, Ben. We're pulling out."

"All of you?"

"Yes." Her tone was crisp and professional, but he thought she looked upset.

"And you're taking all these patients with you?"

She nodded.

"I thought you said you were taking ten."

"Plans changed. Orders are to take as many patients as possible, starting with the advanced cases."

"How many in total?"

"We're hoping to get everyone from the cafeteria, plus the staff."

"That still leaves a lot of patients behind."

"I know." She did not sound happy. She looked away from his judgmental gaze. "Give me a day to talk in the ear of my superiors. Maybe they'll let me come back."

"What are the rest of us supposed to do?"

She looked back at him. "Go home. Stay safe so I can see you again." A horn sounded behind her. She became agitated. "I've got to go. I'm sorry."

He watched her dash to the front of the truck and hop inside the cab. It began pulling away even before the door was closed.

Everything about this seemed hurried. He wondered what they knew that he did not.

The second truck was still loading. Half of the patients from the cafeteria remained. They were now being herded into the back.

Ben saw Avi amongst this group. He was lingering in the rear, delaying his turn as long as possible. He looked genuinely scared.

Ben looked around at the soldiers. Perhaps there was a way to help his colleague. Then he saw one more face he recognized.

He stepped forward and called to the young soldier. "Private Grimes. May I—"

The soldier glanced at him, then back at the line. "It's Specialist Grimes. I overlooked it before, but enough is enough." The face was shrouded behind the mask, but it was clear that the friendliness was gone. This was a man with a tough job to do, and he was clearly not in the mood for interference. He was hurrying the patients into the back of the truck with quick, hard shoves. Avi's turn was coming up.

"Specialist Grimes, this man is not a fer…an aberrant infected."

"Look, I don't have time for this."

"But this is a mistake."

Specialist Grimes gave out a sigh and met Ben's eyes. Ben sensed an opening. "Look, if you can just listen for a minute—"

Then Grimes suddenly grabbed Avi's arm, pulling him closer. He twisted it roughly while he pulled up the sleeve of his shirt, exposing the skin. "See that? Tell me again this is a mistake." His tone sounded both challenging and impatient.

On the wrist, Ben clearly saw the letters "AI." They were smudged, as though Avi had recently tried to wipe them off, but whatever ink had been used to write them had proven resistant.

"Please," Avi pleaded. "I was sick a month ago. I just mispronounced a few words yesterday. It doesn't mean I'm a feral."

"Yes, it does," Ben told him. He looked at Specialist Grimes. "My apologies, Specialist."

The soldier looked as though he wanted to say something else, but stopped himself. He dismissively pushed Avi into the truck. A few yards away, two other soldiers had turned to watch the exchange. Grimes began to shake his head. "Just step back and let us do our—"

Ben saw movement behind the soldiers, but his flustered mind processed the data too slowly to help. By the time his mouth opened to shout out a warning, it was already too late. The feral—a middle-aged woman with wild eyes and long brown hair—covered the last ten yards and pounced on Grimes, her claw-like hands gripped on his shoulders, teeth sinking like a tiger's into the side of his neck. At the same time, her knees impacted his back and staggered him. Grimes went down with a grunt, then a scream. Ben reflexively stepped backwards, horrified.

One of the other soldiers raised his rifle. Ben became aware that this was a real gun, and not one of the nonlethal ones, only when the loud reports sounded off like a thunderclap and the feral woman was knocked off her victim. Ben could not look away from Grimes, who was clutching his neck and pushing his feet around as though trying to run. They wiggled in the air uselessly.

Ben dropped to his knees by the young man's side. He clamped his own hands over the wounds. "Hold on," he barked. "We're right beside a clinic. You'll be all right."

He heard yelling and more shots. He looked up to see one of the other soldiers collapsing from the weight of a giant man in overalls. It had taken him down in the same method as Grimes' attacker, except from the front instead of behind. And there was no one there to knock this feral off. The other soldier was being dragged away by two more attackers, each gripping an arm while he jerked about, trying unsuccessfully to pull free. He disappeared from view, and Ben forced himself to look back at the giant. Just in time to see his mouth come up from the neck pulling a bloody hunk of flesh and tendons.

Ben was horrified. For an instant, the two of them made eye contact, and the sensation of a thousand icy needles pricked all over his skin. Ben realized he was not looking at a *he*, but an *it*. There was nothing human left behind those eyes.

The roar of the truck's engine momentarily drowned out the yelling. Then the truck was gone, leaving him feeling alone and exposed. One feral was dead, but another stared back at him with grotesquely bloody visage. Then he became aware of others, rising up out of the night like zombies from a graveyard. They had been waiting, watching the first wave, apprehensive of the soldiers and their weapons. Now they were emboldened.

Ben felt a tight grip on his wrist. Grimes clung to it with his own bloody hand. He looked desperately afraid, but managed to blurt out an order. "Go... Run!" Then he released Ben's wrist.

Ben looked back at the onlookers who had emerged from the clinic to watch the trucks being loaded. Few of them remained, and those few were backing toward the entrance of the school. "Help me!" Ben yelled to them. He saw them continue to back away. He turned his attention away from them and back to Grimes. He slipped an arm under his back and lifted. "Can you stand?"

Not waiting for an answer, Ben pushed himself up. The soldier was much too heavy for him to lift on his own, but Grimes apparently had a little life left in him. Together they managed to get to their feet. From there, Ben was able to support most of the specialist's weight as they staggered toward the doors. They were much too slow to outrun any attempt to run them down, and Ben gritted his teeth in anticipation. He expected an attack to land on his back at any moment.

Then Grimes' legs gave out. He became dead weight, dragging Ben back down to his knees. They were still a dozen yards from the entrance. Ben kept the soldier's arm around his back, which gave him the leverage to try to get them back up and moving again. He strained unsuccessfully, feeling the young man start to slide down. He was losing the leverage, and panic began to set in.

Then a woman was beside them. "Grab his other arm," Ben ordered, and together they lifted Grimes enough to stagger the rest of the way to the building. Without looking back at the ferals, simply appreciative that they had not been attacked, Ben continued to carry the soldier toward the nearest cot until a dozen strong and willing hands took over.

Released from his burden, Ben finally looked back. He saw several faces staring at him expectantly. "You two, clear a table and barricade the entrance." They followed his instructions without a word.

He looked around for signs of anyone in command. "Did any soldiers come in?" he asked out loud.

"Just the one you brought," someone replied.

Ben went back to Grimes. When he had felt the body go limp, he worried that he was carrying a corpse. At the time, he had not wanted to think about the possibility. Now he allowed himself to look down on the face. Grimes was unconscious, his breathing shallow, his neck completely coated in blood. But at least he was alive. The bleeding appeared to have slowed.

"Will he survive?" Ben asked no one in particular.

"He's lost a ton of blood," came a reply. Ben looked at the speaker. It was the woman who had helped Ben carry the body. On second glance, woman was not the right word. She was barely more than a girl. He doubted she was old enough to be one of the college students. Her pink shirt was decorated with the image of a pony that was once white, but now mostly red. She looked down on Grimes with an expression of concern.

"What's your name?" he asked.

"Samantha."

"You were a patient here?"

"Yes. Me and my mother." She still did not look back at Ben as she spoke. She was gently wiping the soldier's neck, dabbing up a little of the blood but not daring to risk reopening the bite. Then she held a huge pad of gauze over the wound. "Help me," she said, nodding toward a roll of surgical tape. Ben taped the bandage while she carefully held it in place.

"Is your mother here now?" he asked as they finished.

Samantha shook her head. She still did not look up at him. "She was on one of those trucks."

A feral, or becoming one. Ben did not know what to say.

Ben felt a hand on his shoulder. "Excuse me...buddy?" A young man was getting his attention. Behind the man stood three or four others, all looking at Ben.

"What is it?" he asked. "Is something wrong?"

The man looked either frightened, confused, or both. "We were just, uh, hoping you'd tell us what to do."

Ben looked around the clinic. There were still more than a dozen people present. Only two of the cots were occupied by incapacitated patients, including Grimes. Everyone else looked relatively healthy, but terrified. By now word of the attack would have been passed around to those who had not witnessed it firsthand. They had a right to be scared. But he was uncertain why they were looking at him. Perhaps they had seen enough of his interaction with Kim to think he was a doctor.

I am a doctor. Just not the kind they're looking for. He was about to tell them that, then hesitated. Of all of them, only young Samantha had helped when he asked for it. She was the closest thing to a leader in this bunch, and Ben doubted the others would follow a teenage girl. That left only him.

He pointed to a middle-aged man and woman. He had no idea if they were a couple, or even if they knew each other. "You two. Find out how much food we have. In fact, you're in charge of dinner. Make some for everyone here." He looked at the man who had gotten his attention. "You. Pick one other person and look around the school. We may need to defend ourselves. See if there is any way we can secure this room. Maybe by barricading a few of the corridors. Or anything else you can think of."

"The rest of you sit tight until we get some food in our stomachs. Then we'll reconvene and figure out a plan. No one is to leave this building for any reason. Scratch that. No one is to leave this room, unless I give orders to. Understood?" There were a few nods, but most of his audience simply looked spooked.

He glanced back at Samantha. At last, she was looking back at him. He lowered his voice a little. "How did I do?" he asked.

"Not bad. Any idea what you're doing?"

"None at all. Keep my secret?"

For the first time since the attack, the faintest sliver of levity crept into the room. She smirked. "What's in it for me?"

"How would you like to be an honorary doctor? I'll put you in charge of medical services."

Her smirk became a grin. "Deal."

Wendy did her best to keep the five of them focused and productive while they waited for Halfus to return, but she wished he would hurry up. It was not that this group of people made her feel particularly uncomfortable. Quite the contrary—she felt as confident and in control as she had for a very long time. She simply felt better with him around. She had spent a year trying to convince herself that was not the case, then one day knowing it was, then a few more months trying to forget it again. Now that he was back, she did not want to spend another moment apart.

She forced a friendly smile as she served drinks and snacks to the newcomers. Kevin had gotten back from his errands first, carrying a large gym bag heavy with things she did not wish to talk about. Thankfully, they had not had time to. His return had been followed a moment later by the arrival of the other three, and all the time since had been spent getting them up to speed.

Aaron was the only person she called to have both been available and interested in doing something about the crisis unfolding in McGahey. She had not told him on the phone that their plan was to leave. She knew how quickly rumors, like viruses, got passed around. And she did not want any uninvited tagalongs.

She knew Aaron from her time together with Halfus, when he had been a frequent companion on the hiking and caving expeditions they all seemed to enjoy. She saw a particular irony in that, considering that Aaron came across as a bit of a nerd. Before now, every time she had seen him he wore pressed trousers and a polo shirt buttoned to the top. Tonight he presented a different image. He was wearing torn jeans, a long sleeved tee, and a baseball cap. It was a different side of him, making him seem less stuffy. In any case, he was an unbelievably nice guy, and a talented musician. He played the viola, if she remembered correctly. She wondered why he had stayed in town after classes had been suspended. She suspected it had something to do with the woman beside him.

His girlfriend, Mindy, was also a musician, although Wendy did not know which instrument she played. She was a cute, plump Chinese-American girl. Wendy did not know her nearly as well as Aaron, but she was happy to welcome both of them to the little assembly.

She did not, however, feel the same way about their companion. Mindy's friend Anna was ordinarily the prettier of the two, although she did not look it at the moment. Today she wore no makeup, and lines of worry were straining her otherwise attractive features. Wendy remembered her being quite a chatterbox, although this characteristic was also not currently on display. Yet the memory of it brought back the hint of resentment Wendy felt toward those who were compelled to always be the center of attention. She repressed that resentment. They were allies now, and the girl was clearly in a state of distress. Wendy wondered if she, too, had lost someone close.

Wendy had started to introduce the three to Kevin, but he shook his head and looked away, as though distracted. Aaron explained that they already knew each other. She first took that to mean they were already friends, but something about their body language since told her otherwise. The two guys never seemed to speak to each other, only to her. She quickly reached the conclusion that they did not get along.

The whole thing made for a strange atmosphere. Despite the low-key hostility from Kevin, Aaron was in a good mood. He sat on the couch beside his girlfriend, spinning his ball cap on his finger. When she had spoken to him on the phone, he had been thrilled to learn of Halfus' miraculous survival. That mood had apparently lingered, and now he was anxious to see his friend in the flesh. Mindy was as pleasant as always, although Wendy had to assume that at least part of it was an act. No one could be chipper all of the time, let alone while a catastrophe was befalling her home and school. Still, the two of them made Wendy want to rise above the depressing gloom of the day, at least when Anna and Kevin were not bringing her crashing back down to earth.

Never had she seen Kevin so angry at the world. She wondered how badly his experience with Tracy had scarred him, and she worried that he might not ever recover. He seemed like a completely different person from the jocular classmate she used to know. This disease changed people. She understood that more than anyone.

There was a quick knock on the door, then it opened before she could stand up. In walked Halfus, and Wendy's spirits lifted like a kite in the wind. Just as Kevin had done, he came in carrying gear. Wendy wished his eyes would meet hers, but instead he looked around for a place to put down his burden. Then he went straight to scanning the faces of the others. It almost seemed that he was deliberately avoiding meeting her gaze. He appeared to be troubled. Kevin had informed her of where they had gone, and her heart skipped a beat thinking that something had happened. Had Ernie been home after all?

Then Halfus broke into a wide smile as Aaron popped out of his seat and went to him. Wendy was surprised to see the two of them hug. She had not realized Halfus and Aaron were that close, nor did she think Aaron was the man-hugging type. Then she remembered who she was thinking about. Halfus had this effect on people once they got to know him. It was sometimes maddening to see him win people over without seeming to try. She had to suppress a smile in spite of herself.

Halfus let Aaron go, then greeted Mindy and Anna. At long last, he turned to Wendy. "Sorry I'm late," he said. "Scouting was tougher than I expected."

"Kevin told me you went by Ernie's place. You shouldn't do that sort of thing without telling me."

He gave a smile that seemed more relief than pleasure. "Beg pardon."

"Did you get a chance to talk to Rich?" Kevin asked.

Halfus shook his head. "No answer at home," he said, turning back to the rucksack he had brought in. "But the trip wasn't a total waste. I scrounged a few things that might come in useful. Courtesy of the dude who tried to kill me."

He spent a few minutes showing them what he had. Some of it caught Wendy by surprise. She had expected them to drive out of town. Even if they were forced onto back roads, they could be in Frederick in no more than an hour. Now Halfus was talking about hiking all night. She stopped him with a quick objection. "Can you explain why you think we'll need all this?"

Halfus took a breath and nodded. "You're right. Let me back up. The Army—I don't think it's just USAMRIID anymore—they set up a perimeter. It's heaviest along the roads, but they patrol in a circle around the town. East then south to Frederick would be the quickest way out, but it's the most heavily guarded. East then north to Emmitsburg or Pennsylvania is probably second. That leaves the mountain, north, and the back roads south and west. I don't see any reason to climb up the mountain. 'Because it's there' doesn't really apply at a time like this. That leaves the back roads. There's only one way to get to them, and they have that blocked, too."

"If it's blocked—" asked Wendy.

"Let me clarify," said Halfus. "The road is blocked, before it branches out west and south. But there are fields around, and some of them are commingled with woods. My Jeep and Aaron's Santa Fe can go off-road a bit. We can go around the checkpoint. They'll still be patrolling, but if we keep the trees close behind us, we have a chance to cover some distance in the cars. But we'll have to go slow, without headlights. At some point we'll lose the woods as cover. If there are any patrols around, that means hoofing it.

"Heading west on foot makes for a long hike to civilization. We can't trust strangers along the way, so it basically means walking to Hagerstown. That's a dozen miles as the crow flies, over rough terrain in the dark. We'll be lucky to get there by daylight tomorrow. Just in case we need to stop, I'm bringing a tent, along with some other things for whatever unknowns crop up. Make sense?"

Aaron raised his hand. "Can someone tell us what the heck is going on? This is the first we heard about leaving."

Shit, Wendy thought. She forgot that no one had told them yet. "We decided that before you came over. Is it a problem? You don't have to join us, if you don't want. Just don't tell anyone we're—"

"Hell, no," Aaron grinned. "We were already thinking about leaving. Then this quarantine came down before we could make up our minds. Now...I think I speak for all three of us..." He glanced at his two companions. "...When I say we're on board." He grinned at Mindy. "We like hiking anyway, don't we, Hon'?"

Wendy found his good humor engaging. She grinned, too. "Now that that's settled, there is another thing I forgot to tell you. It's healthy people only. We're not taking anyone who's started going feral. They're better off here, where the authorities can help them." This was a statement she had memorized back when she expected there to be more of a crowd. It felt a little silly saying it now, with so few of them. It seemed more like a formality. "Are all three of you fine?"

Aaron and Mindy exchanged a look. Then Aaron said, "Yeah, we're fine." Based on his reaction, Wendy worried that she had just needlessly come across as a stone cold bitch. Knowing how well he and Halfus got along, she wished she could take it back.

She tried to win him back with her most disarming smile. "Sorry, I just had to ask—"

"Wait a minute," said Kevin. Wendy saw him looking directly at Anna. She doubted if he knew the girls at all, and he clearly was not fond of Aaron. Of course he would have no reason to trust them. Plus he was in a foul mood. She wanted to apologize for him. She opened her mouth, but he spoke first.

"Your name is Anna, right?" He sounded calm, not belligerent. Perhaps she had been too quick to judgment.

The girl nodded timidly. Wendy could not see even the faintest hint of the brash girl that she had once disliked.

"Anna, are you fine?" The question was not spoken without compassion, but all eyes were now on her. Unlike the attention seeker that Wendy remembered, this girl seemed to wilt under the spotlight. She nodded again.

Kevin was about to say something else, but Halfus stopped him. "Go easy, bro."

"Halfus, she flinched when Wendy said—"

"I know. I've got it." He faced the anxious girl. In a tone that matched Kevin's, Halfus said, "Anna, will you say, 'She sells seashells by the seashore?'"

Anna burst into tears. Mindy put an arm around her friend, comforting her. The rest of them looked at Aaron. "I'm sorry, buddy," Halfus informed him. "I understand if you want to reconsider coming along. But she can't go. She's better off here. Hopefully they'll figure out a cure soon." Wendy was thankful that he was defending their decision. She hated to feel as though this was all her fault.

Aaron nodded. "I understand. Give us a few minutes to talk it over ourselves, okay?"

"Sure. Not too long, though," Halfus replied. He looked at Wendy and Kevin. "We leave in an hour."

NIGHT OF TRIALS

THE DEADLIEST BATTLE in American history was fought at Gettysburg on the first three days of July, 1863. Total casualties from the battle numbered approximately fifty thousand out of the one hundred sixty thousand men participating. Of the more than one hundred generals commanding forces there, nine were killed. There were sixty-three Medals of Honor awarded for actions taken during the battle, proving the age-old adage that the worst of times can often bring out the best in people.

The butcher's bill was fairly evenly spread among the three days of fighting, each of which ranks in the top fifteen bloodiest days of the war. The distinction for the single bloodiest day of the war belongs to September 17, 1862, the day of the Battle of Antietam. The casualty count was a staggering twenty-two thousand men generated from twelve hours of ceaseless combat. Much of the fighting was performed at extremely close range, with opposing lines less than a hundred yards from each other, at a time when tactics involved thick lines of men standing still and upright while firing and reloading.

"Casualties" is not synonymous with dead, however. The term encompasses anyone killed, wounded, captured, or gone missing during an engagement. Thankfully, the count of the actual dead is often the lowest of

any of these columns. In the American Civil War, only one in seven wounds resulted in death.

One interesting historical sidebar involves the geographic proximity of Gettysburg and Antietam. The two battles occurred within thirty miles of each other. They are divided by the eastern rampart of the Appalachian Mountains. At the midway point where the bird flies between the two historic battlefields lies the forested heights of one prominent peak. Gettysburg is located fifteen miles northeast, Antietam fifteen miles southwest, of Catoctin Mountain.

Contrasting with other wars in which the United States has participated, the Civil War ranks highest in these casualty tolls in large part because both sides were American. By way of comparison, the morning of the D-Day landings on the beaches of Normandy resulted in seven thousand American dead and wounded, in addition to several thousand more suffered by British and other Allied forces. For further comparison, at dawn on the morning of the Battle of the Somme, the British army lost nearly sixty thousand men within the span of a few hours. Fifty thousand Romans were killed or captured by Hannibal in one day during the Battle of Cannae, during an epoch when populations were but a fraction of those today. The bloodiest single-day battle of all time, with an astonishing eighty thousand casualties, was at Borodino just before Napoleon's Grande Armée reached their beguiling objective of Moscow. With respect to the appalling arc of warfare, Americans have been relatively fortunate.

As costly as battles like Gettysburg and Antietam were, they pale in comparison to the single biggest killer of the Civil War. Fully two-thirds of the soldiers who lost their lives in the war died from the ravages of disease, not wounds. But disease is a slow killer. In a contest to inflict the greatest number of deaths in the shortest period of time, natural disasters are the clear winners.

The deadliest single-day event in the history of the U.S. was the Galveston Hurricane of 1900. Before the storm, Galveston was home to thirty-six thousand residents. The highest point on the island was less than nine feet above sea level. On September 8, the storm waters surged fifteen feet, inundating the entire island and leveling nearly every building. On the

day and night of landfall, perhaps as many as twelve thousand people were
killed. More recent hurricanes such as Katrina and Andrew cost far more in
property damage, but appreciably less in human lives.

For all of humankind's proficiency and propensity for killing one another,
sometimes Mother Nature deems it necessary to remind us that when it
comes to death and destruction, she still reigns supreme.

"I want each person to say your name, something about yourself, and
why you're here. I'll go first. My name is Ben. I worked at the college, I
love soccer, and I came here to see if I could help." He decided not to
tell them his full name, nor that he was the same Ben who led the
team that brought Eden back from Iraq. He was not ashamed of it, but
people were not always rational in times of stress, and this was not the
time for an argument about culpability.

He nodded to the woman beside him. She was the first one he had
given an order to, when he had put her in charge of dinner. If she or
her partner had protested his authority, the whole situation would
have been much different. But she had not, and he was more grateful
than she could possibly know. She sheepishly introduced herself,
looking about nervously while she spoke. "I'm Alexa," she started.
"I...work from home." Ben assumed this was her way of saying she was
unemployed. Although jittery, she seemed fit and able. She had done a
fine job of getting a tasteless but soothing cup of noodle soup to each
person remaining in the clinic. It was a shame she was not in a
situation to feel more confident about herself. "I'm just here because I
was bored," she admitted. "Like him...I thought maybe I could help."

"You have," he told her. She smiled briefly and looked down. Then
the next person began to speak.

It was a simple team-building exercise he used frequently in his
classes. The hardest part of overcoming shyness was speaking those
first words aloud. When participation was volunteer-only, some
people naturally faded into the background. But get them used to

talking, and often they would open like a flower. He doubted that would happen with anyone in this particular group, but the last thing he wanted was a bunch of people as scared of each other as they were of the creatures outside.

Ben tried to remember as many names as possible, but there were a million conflicting thoughts in his mind and he had difficulty focusing. His primary take-away from the introductions was the diverse reasons these people were here. Some hoped to find supplies at the clinic in the absence of any open stores. Several, like himself, just wanted to help. Some were clearly scared and sought the peace of mind that came from being with others. A few came in because they had convinced themselves they were getting worse, only to be told otherwise. Two of them, including Samantha, had lingered because they knew someone in the cafeteria. No matter the reasons, all of them had managed to be caught in the wrong place at the wrong time.

The three who stood out in Ben's mind were Samantha, Alexa, and Percy. This last was the young man whom Ben had instructed to secure the clinic. An electrician by trade, he was one of those guys with natural good looks and no need for the pretentious hairstyles or fancy clothing that were so ubiquitous among college students. His hair was long and unkempt, and he wore an old flannel shirt with rolled up sleeves. Ben guessed he was in his early thirties.

Percy may not have come out to help him carry Grimes, but since then had displayed no lack of courage or discipline. Like Alexa, he had accepted Ben's commands without question and carried them out without hesitation. In times of difficulty, it was always good to identify those people who could be relied upon. Ben hoped Percy and Alexa would set the example that others would follow. He would need it for what came next.

He waited for the last introductions to complete. "Now that that's out of the way, I have an announcement. We have to leave the clinic." He waited for the gasps and protests, but those were not as pronounced as he had expected. He saw a few worried looks exchanged, but no one immediately challenged the statement.

Nevertheless, he felt compelled to explain his logic. "We have the front blocked, but there is no easy way to secure the interior doors." He hoped this would be obvious to all. Most of the doors around the building were loose, swinging doubles. "And we can't block all the ways in and out of the whole building. Most classrooms have lots of windows. Percy reports that some of them are already broken." He needed to let this sink in for effect, but not so long that they would think ahead to the next terrifying question. *Are there ferals already inside the school?*

"Where would we go?" asked a woman.

"The church," Ben replied confidently. "It's close. Maybe a hundred yards. It's solid. There's only the front doors and one side door. Those can be blockaded, if they're not already. It's the most likely thing around to be occupied already, so someone can let us in." He did not voice his final reasoning, because he did not want to open the Pandora's box of distrust. *It's the least likely place for them to refuse to let us in.*

"What about those who can't run?" asked someone. This was the middle-aged man who had helped Alexa with dinner. The two of them were not beside each other now, so he presumed they were not a couple, after all.

"The cot mattresses can be used as stretchers," Ben replied. "I'll take one end of one, so I need three more stretcher-bearers. We're not leaving anyone behind."

"I'll help," volunteered Percy. Ben had a feeling he would. It was a good sign. Hopefully, it would spark others to follow suit. However, Ben intended to turn the offer down. He had a different favor to ask this man.

"Alexa, will you round up three strong men for me?" he asked. He turned away from her before getting a reply, not wanting to give her the option to refuse. "Percy, I appreciate that, but I have something else in mind for you."

The young man stiffened. He suddenly appeared suspicious, as he had every right to be.

Ben did not sugar coat the request. "I need a runner. Someone to go ahead to the church. To let them know we're coming. We can't have a group stuck outside, pounding on the doors, waiting for someone in there to open them." *I need someone to be convincing.* "I think you're the right person to get over there safely. And to explain what's happening. To get them ready, so that when the rest of us get there, the doors will open right up for us and close again as soon as we're through."

Percy just stared back at him. Ben would not order the man to do this against his will, but neither did he want him to take a long time thinking about all the things that could go wrong. "What do you say? Should I ask someone else?"

"No," came the reply. "I'll do it. When?"

The sooner he goes, the less time he'll have to work himself into a panic. "Can you go now?"

Percy swallowed. He looked terrified, but the fact that he was agreeing to do it anyway restored Ben's natural belief in the basic goodness of the human soul.

They walked together to the front doors. A third man slid back the table that was blocking them. Percy stared at the doors as if willing them to magically lock. Then he looked at Ben. He held out his hand. Ben shook it. "Good luck, son. But you won't need it. You'll be fine." Ben gave a reassuring smile. Percy nodded and pushed a door open. Then he began to run.

Ben put his foot to the door, keeping it cracked open so he could watch the man's progress. The steeple of the church was just visible, a block up Main Street. The entrance was not, but Ben had a clear line of sight most of the way. He watched Percy sprint, white soles of his sneakers flashing, then turning gray with distance and shadow, until Ben could no longer hear his footsteps. He watched a few seconds longer, then lost sight of Percy completely. He listened for a moment, but heard nothing but the stillness of a frightened town. Ben closed the door. There was nothing to do but pray that he made it the rest of the way.

He turned back to his tiny community. Alexa was nearby. "How are we on the stretcher-bearers?" he asked hopefully.

"Okay," she said, then lowered her voice. "But there's a different problem."

"Oh?" He continued to try sounding confident. He wanted them to think there was no challenge that could not be overcome.

"Some of them don't want to leave," she said quietly. She looked away from his eyes. "Some of *us*, I mean."

"How many?"

"Four."

Damn. He could guess who the other three were. They were the ones milling about the far side of the room, deliberately not looking his way. He had seen enough students trying desperately not to be called upon that he recognized the signs of embarrassment.

"Alexa, listen to me. We're going to make it to the church. Percy just went over there with no problem." *I think.* "It's a short run and then we're safe. Much safer than here." She still did not look at him. He steeled his heart. "All right, then. Thank you for your help so far. I hope you change your mind. We're leaving in two minutes."

He turned to the others, most of whom were watching him with expectant faces. He was pleased to see Samantha standing in their forefront. "Right then. Who are my other stretcher-bearers?" Ben hoped Alexa had not lied about this task being taken care of, but he was past the point of asking for volunteers. He would pick the three biggest men, if necessary.

Four men stepped forward, and Ben relaxed. "Thank you, gentlemen, but I only need three." *Always better to have too many than too few,* he told himself.

One of them cleared his throat. "We, um, thought it would be better that you not have your hands full. We'd feel better if you were able to pay attention to, um, everything going on."

Ben almost felt like laughing, he was so relieved. He had been worried that they would all see that he was not a real leader. "Thank you again, but it's only a quick run down the block."

"All the same."

Ben smiled. "Have it your way, gentlemen. Are you ready?" They nodded, then split up to lift the cots and collapse the legs. He looked at the others. "You all ready?" More nods. Then he looked down at Samantha. "You ready?" She flashed him a thumbs-up.

He glanced to the back of the room. He could tell that Alexa and the three others were watching, but only from the corners of their eyes. He noticed that her designated helper was one of them, and he once again wondered if they were together. He also wondered if he would ever find out. He thought of giving them one last chance to change their minds. Then he thought of telling them he would send assistance at his first opportunity. Instead, he said nothing. Neither statement needed to be voiced.

"All right, let's move," he said. He pushed the doors open and led the way out.

At ten in the evening, two cars breached the ethereal town limits of bedeviled McGahey. Halfus was in the lead, driving Ernie's commandeered Jeep. It was a 2006 Wrangler, painted a showy silver with black trimmings. Once upon a time, Halfus had liked the color, but now he found himself wishing it were black in its entirety. Or any other dark shade, for that matter. Anything that blended into the darkness better than silver. But tonight the moon was obscured by cloudy sky, so at least there would be little light to reflect.

Aaron followed in his SUV. Of all that were available, these were the two vehicles best suited for the off-road digression Halfus had planned. He had not been thrilled about the idea to leave town, but once the decision was made he put everything he could into his preparations. He knew that the success of this, like most plans, would come down to details. He had tried to consider and mitigate all the risks that he could, but there were far too many out of his control. He could not escape the persistent nagging feeling that he was leading them all into danger. They were trusting him, and he desperately did not want to let them down.

Especially the woman beside him. It was disquieting how much a part of his life she had become. Rather, it would have been disquieting, if he were not so confident that she felt the same about him. The savage severance and the months apart had only seemed to fuel their need for each other. When he lost Shauna, he believed he would never allow himself to feel this strongly about anyone again. Now he understood that allowance was not something he had control over. Love had overtaken him, like it or not.

He peeked over at her. She was staring into the backseat, a thin smile creeping onto her beautiful face. He glanced into the rear view mirror. Samuel had fallen asleep in the back, the span of the seat just wide enough to fit the whole of his tiny body. Now Halfus understood Wendy's expression. The kid was unbelievably adorable, in appearance and disposition. He reminded Halfus of Amelia. It was reassuringly pleasant to see him so peaceful. Halfus was glad that at least one of them was not overcome with anxiety. He hoped that the next time the boy woke up, the trip would be all but over.

Seeing the two of them looking so content contrasted painfully with his own inner turmoil. He detested lying about anything, and he had particularly hated lying about Rich, but now he was glad that he had done it. The scene that awaited him inside his friend's house had been dreadfully upsetting for him, and he had no desire to inflict the same horror on her. She had been through so much already, he wanted to protect her from any more burdens.

His eyes still in the rear view mirror, he glanced back at the car behind them. Aaron and Mindy were in the front seat, with Kevin in the back. Halfus would have felt better with Kevin in the Jeep, but knew it was better this way. The redhead had returned from his foraging with a shotgun and handgun, and Halfus did not want the weapons in the vehicle with Wendy and Sam.

He wondered how the two guys were getting along back there. Wendy had told him about the hostility between Kevin and Aaron, and it brought back some vague recollections of arguments from years ago. It was a strange fact of life how not everyone could get along, even those who seemed like they should. But he was not overly concerned. They were both grown men, and truly decent at heart. He felt certain they could force themselves to get along for one night.

As the buildings around them became fewer and farther between, he turned off the headlights and slowed his pace. Now came the hard part, when they needed to be deliberate and discreet. Speed was unimportant. He was less concerned about distance than he was about detection.

Ahead, he saw the ramshackle barn that he used as a landmark. He turned off the road onto the field between it and a line of woods. The ride became noticeably bumpier. Slowing the pace even more, he continued alongside and as close to the trees as he dared.

Somewhere to the left, unseen at this distance, was both the army checkpoint and the fork in the road. One branch led south and the other west. It was the western road that Halfus hoped to reconnect with once they cleared the perimeter. Whether that would be in the vehicles or on foot remained to be seen.

He kept the Jeep in the lowest gear as they crossed the hardened earth. They passed within yards of a recently harvested cornfield. He could make out large cylindrical bales of hay scattered periodically across the shadowy horizon. The two vehicles continued for nearly a mile before coming to the first point of concern.

As they neared the top of a shallow ridge, Halfus came to a stop. He put the Jeep in neutral well back from the crest, pulled on the hand brake, and glanced over at Wendy. "Be careful," she whispered. He nodded and stepped out to scout ahead on foot. He did not like leaving the relative safety of the vehicle, but they could not risk being seen in profile coming over the top by anyone on the other side.

He crouched down as he moved forward for the last few dozen yards, then went to a crawl as he reached the summit. He wiggled his way behind a rock before daring to look out. The field below stretched for another quarter mile before ascending again to another low ridge. He would have to repeat the process there, and every subsequent rise, until he knew for certain they were past discovery.

He took his time scanning the area before him. His heart was not exactly racing, but he was aware of a certain acuteness to his senses. He thought he saw movement, and stopped scanning. He waited, focusing on the spot, searching for anything that might have caught his eye. Eventually he decided that he had been deceived by a trick of the light and an overeager imagination. He reversed his motions, crawling then crouching his way back to the Jeep.

As he climbed in he saw Samuel awake and watching him. He winked at the boy, then settled behind the wheel and pulled forward again. A few minutes later he repeated the routine. This time he stopped next to a copse of trees that provided limited camouflage to the two vehicles. Cover was getting thinner, and soon would be gone completely. At that point, he would need to make a judgment call about whether they had passed the perimeter. If so, he would lead them as quickly as possible back toward the road and hope for the best. If not, they would need to decide whether to abandon the vehicles. He suspected they would all defer to his choice, which did nothing to ease his burden.

He put that decision out of his mind for the moment as he reached another vantage point. He focused on the immediate. This time he saw not the tiniest flicker of movement. The world seemed wholly asleep but for the six of them. He did not allow himself to relax, however. He knew he would see a patrol sooner or later. He simply hoped to see them first, before they saw the vehicles. He stared ahead and saw another copse suitable for cover on the third ridge. He returned to the others and led the way in that direction.

In another few minutes he was looking down from the third ridge. Initially, he saw nothing different. His inclination was to stop taking so much time at each station, but he forced himself to be patient. A minute saved now was worth nothing if they were spotted.

On his second scan of the fields ahead he saw something out of place. It looked like a glint of metal in the weak moonlight, sixty or seventy yards away. He wished he had binoculars, but there had been no way to acquire many of the items he would normally have brought along. The stores had been closed, and he was not one to go looting. He considered crawling closer. Instead, he gave his eyes a minute to study the obscure shapes. He could not be certain, but he thought they were bodies. Perhaps four or five of them. He was not without curiosity, but he decided that the best thing to do was steer clear of them. He would not even mention them to the others, and hopefully they would not...

One of the shapes moved. It appeared to be trying to crawl. Halfus closed his eyes and sighed deeply. In an instant, their entire escape plan had to be discarded.

He went back and pulled Wendy and Kevin into a hushed, impromptu conference. He noticed that Aaron stepped out of the Hyundai to listen, but did not opt to voice his thoughts. Halfus explained what he saw, then volunteered his own opinion. They could not leave someone who was hurt and needed help. They were not equipped to do much themselves, but they had room for one more in the cars. He suggested using the back seat of the Jeep for the wounded figure. If these bodies represented the patrol, which was his assumption, then the six of them no longer needed to worry about detection. They could drive back onto the road and make for Hagerstown, where there was a hospital.

He looked at Wendy, trying to gauge her reaction, but her face was difficult to read in the dim light. She did not reply. Instead, Kevin did. "That's not a good idea, Halph." Halfus' hopes sank. He thought he would have Kevin on his side, and that Wendy would be the one to require convincing. "You've got Sam in your Jeep," Kevin continued.

"He can move up front," Halfus replied, but Kevin shook his head. "Why don't you let us handle this one? Aaron and I can get this. Can't we, buddy?"

They all looked at Aaron, who nodded. "Of course," he replied eagerly. Halfus wondered if perhaps the two of them had bonded during the short stressful drive. It would not be surprising. Danger could do that to people.

Halfus opened his mouth to protest, but Wendy cut him off. "That's what we'll do. There's more room in the SUV anyway." She met Halfus' eyes. "You put me in charge, remember?"

He gave in. But he was not done making suggestions. "Aaron, you pull up to them. If you see one moving, make sure it's not a feral before getting out of your car. I'll pull close and shine my headlights on the area. We need to see what we're doing, and I think the risk of detection is now low enough to warrant it."

They returned to their respective vehicles. Everyone knew they were taking a risk, but Halfus felt as though they really had no choice. He was pleased that no one had suggested leaving the wounded to their fate.

Headlights on, they drove over the crest and down toward the bodies. Halfus stuck his arm out to point, then swung the Jeep around in a loop. He stopped about twenty yards from them so that his headlights illuminated a wide area while Kevin and Aaron worked. None of the bodies were moving now, and Halfus had no way of knowing which one he had seen crawling. He could, however, see what exactly they were dealing with. There were five bodies total. Two of them were soldiers. The other three appeared to be regular people dressed in ragged clothing, two older and one likely a student. Those appeared to have been shot repeatedly. The soldiers had bloody wounds of a more primitive variety.

Halfus looked over at his passengers. He preferred that Wendy not look, but the more important consideration was Samuel. He was relieved to see her keeping the boy's attention focused elsewhere. She was pointing to the moon, barely discernible behind a ghostly wisp of cloud. Halfus watched her a long moment, lost in a cobweb of emotions. He could go on staring at her for hours, if there had not been serious work to be done.

He turned back to the others. Kevin was bent over the body of one of the soldiers, and Halfus saw that he was holding the man's hand. Aaron stood nearby, spinning his keys on a finger as he watched. Beyond Aaron, in the distance, Halfus saw more movement. He shifted his gaze that way, and felt his body go cold. Their lights and commotion had attracted something after all—just not the Army.

"Kevin!" he yelled. His friend looked over, saw Halfus pointing, then looked in the same direction. There were at least four human shapes running toward them, already less than half a football field away. That they had gotten so close before being seen was the tragic consequence of a moment's distraction. Kevin half-dragged, half-shoved Aaron toward their car. Halfus doubted they would get away in time, and Kevin apparently reached the same conclusion. He reached inside the window and withdrew a long stick-shaped object. He flipped it around in his arms, and Halfus recognized the shotgun.

Halfus hoped that the sound of gunshots would sending the ferals fleeing. He knew he had a decision to make. But it was really no decision at all. He faced Wendy. "Take the wheel. Get out of here. I've got to try to help." He did not wait to see her reaction, fearing it would be disapproval.

He turned back toward the others. He saw Kevin drop to a knee and fire off three blasts from the shotgun. The harsh booms shredded the stillness of the night. If the evening had thus far been a whispered silence, it now thundered like a storm. The first of the ferals spun around and crashed clumsily to the grass. The others did not scatter as Halfus had hoped.

He began to run toward his friends, but only made it a few steps before the other three ferals got there first. Aaron was standing by the door of the Hyundai, reaching inside as Kevin had. He swiveled around with a pistol in his hand, then fired at a feral man that was already leaping toward him. One shot appeared to hit its shoulder as they collided. Then they both went down to the grass. Aaron's arm was outstretched, pinned at a useless angle. He fired again, the report merely muffling his cries of pain.

Kevin fired the shotgun once more into a feral that was mere feet in front of him, coming on at full speed. It went limp as their bodies impacted, dislodging the weapon and sending it flying through the air in Halfus' direction. Still running, he veered for the area where it landed. He went into a baseball slide and came up with it in his left hand. He used the momentum of the slide to pop back up onto both feet, just as the fourth feral bore down on him. From this close range, Halfus could make out the features of a pudgy, pug-nosed man. His face was twisted in a snarl. Halfus jabbed out with the butt of the shotgun. It crunched the tiny nose, and Halfus felt bone break. The man lost his inertia and stumbled down onto a knee.

Halfus felt a momentary surge of relief. He took a step away, swinging the shotgun back into a firing stance. He hoped he would not need to use it.

The man regained his feet and came right back at him. Halfus winced. *I'm so sorry,* he thought. Then he pulled the trigger. He felt the painful kickback in his chest and realized he had not positioned the gun well. But a bruise was the least of his worries.

The fat man was down, but Halfus saw more figures racing toward them from the same direction as the first wave. Considering all the noise the guns were making, they were probably attracting every feral for miles. He looked at his friends. Kevin was picking himself up, having pushed off the corpse of the one he had shot. The fourth feral was ignoring them for the moment. It was still biting into the neck of Aaron, who was unmoving. The amount of blood soaking into his shirt told Halfus that he would stay that way. Halfus took a step toward them, raised the shotgun again, and pulled the trigger. Nothing happened. It took him a moment to realize that it was out of ammunition.

He heard a noise, and looked over to see Mindy jumping out of the passenger seat of the car. She began running clumsily, back in the direction from which they had driven. "No! Mindy!" he yelled, to no avail. The feral on Aaron saw her, too. It sprung up and went after her.

Halfus looked at Kevin, then beyond. Several more ferals were coming from another direction and bearing down quickly.

He shoved the shotgun into Kevin's chest. "You have any more shells for this?" Kevin grabbed it and nodded. He unzipped a pocket of his cargo pants and reached inside. Halfus hoped to buy him a few seconds to reload. He raised his fists, wishing they did not feel quite so inadequate. The two ferals were almost upon them. Both looked like wild students after a night of binge drinking.

He hoped to hear Kevin behind him, telling him to step aside. Instead, he heard a horn sound off in one long, sustained blast. It got the attention of the ferals, as well, who stopped and faced the oncoming vehicle. The Jeep crashed headlong into the two of them, sending them flying like broken ragdolls. Wendy let off the horn and jerked the wheel, but clipped the rear corner of the SUV and ricocheted off. The Jeep spiraled wildly, its wheels still spinning, attempting to propel the car forward even as it careened about. Then the wheels stopped as the engine stalled and the vehicle came to a choking halt. Halfus saw Samuel in the back, clinging to the bar. He looked neither particularly scared nor excited, leaving Halfus to marvel at how the child seemed to take everything in stride. He was probably not old enough to understand how terrifyingly abnormal all of this was.

They heard screaming and looked toward it. Three ferals were on Mindy, her arms and legs thrashing about wildly. Wendy held a hand over Sam's eyes, rather pointlessly by now.

"Come on," Halfus ordered. He wondered how many more creatures were bearing down on this location. He glanced at the front seat of the Hyundai, saw that the airbags had deployed, and felt his heart sink further. He pulled Wendy out of the Jeep while Kevin lifted Sam and set him on the ground. Halfus grabbed the rucksack, then realized it would slow him down at its current weight. He spent a few seconds hurriedly tossing the heaviest items from it. Then the four of them began running.

He knew where they were, but the knowledge seemed as though it would do them little good. There were no buildings nearby, and even if there were he doubted they could secure it from a mob of savage adversaries. Besides, with the mindset of paranoia that had seized the community, any residents were likely to shoot them on the approach. So he simply focused on distance, hoping the ferals would remain content to linger at the scene of the wreck. What motivated them was anyone's guess. They were not normal predators, and did not eat their prey. With no idea what drove them to violence, he had no notion of how to escape their warpath.

Nevertheless, when a minute passed without hearing any pursuit, he began to think they had given up after all. Halfus led his companions up another low rise and, nearing the summit, allowed himself to look back. His hopes sank yet again. There were at least ten shapes behind them, just now starting up the slope. They were simply not making any noise. The ferals did not announce themselves like a pack of hunting dogs, much to his disadvantage.

He tried to coax some extra speed from the others, but everyone was already moving as fast as they could. This was simply not a race they could win. Samuel was the weakest link. He ran with his hand in Wendy's, and she was moderating her pace to match. Halfus would have to do something about that. He knew the boy felt an affinity for her, but was not certain whether it would extend to him. He was certain, however, that he had to try.

He ran a few steps ahead of Sam, then stopped. He adjusted the rucksack from over his shoulders into his hands. "Climb aboard," he called. If there was any hesitation, he decided he would have to toss the sack to Kevin, scoop the boy up, and carry him for as long as he could.

Sam practically launched himself onto his back at full speed. Halfus felt the thin arms close around his shoulders and neck. "Hold tight!" he called, then took off running again.

Now they could move faster, but he worried it still would not be fast enough. Having both the kid and the rucksack was definitely slowing him down, but even so the weak link was now Wendy. Halfus just now noticed that she was running in sandals. He wished he had warned everyone to wear better footwear, but he had not envisioned their lives coming down to a footrace. They were simply not going to get away at this rate.

Once again, Kevin reached the same conclusion. He was running with one hand holding the shotgun by the barrel. Then he stopped and faced Halfus.

"Keep running. I'll catch up."

Halfus did not argue. If anyone could pull this off, it was Kevin. "Keep going this way, through the next set of woods. Then follow the road."

Kevin nodded, but was already turning to face the other way. Halfus silently wished his friend good luck as he and Wendy ceaselessly ran on. He began a silent count as they went, attempting to gauge just how close their pursuers were. He guesstimated that he would reach thirty. Any less than that and the three of them would be losing ground. Any more, and they would be gaining. If Kevin could slow them down even longer, perhaps their pursuers would give up.

He reached eleven, then heard three loud shots in rapid succession. Followed by a fourth. Halfus pumped his legs harder. Then he heard a fifth. He hoped to hear another, indicating that Kevin had reloaded. But no more came.

He led Wendy through a thick cluster of trees. From this angle, it appeared that they were heading straight into the woods, but he believed that was an illusion. Unless he had his lost his bearings—a not unlikely possibility—he believed this was a shortcut to a twist of the road.

Wendy followed him in without question. He was glad for her trust, even as he wondered if it were foolishness instead. The trees were thicker than he expected. No moonlight shone through, and the beam of the flashlight he pulled from the sack was a paltry substitute. The risk of confusing his direction was exceeded only by the danger of twisting or breaking an ankle. There was no clear pathway here and he was forced to go where the undergrowth was thinnest. "Slow down a little," he warned Wendy. "Get behind me and try to follow my steps exactly. Until we reach the other side. Then run like hell again."

The brambles tore at their legs. They were fortunate to be wearing jeans that protected their calves, but Halfus thought of her sandals and worried that her ankles were being mutilated. She did not complain, however. Branches swiped at their bodies and faces. Halfus did his best to shield Samuel from them, but he had no doubt the boy was being struck by a few. Yet Samuel, too, remained silent.

Halfus attempted to set a pace that balanced the need for speed with that for caution. But he had to admit that he was only guessing. If they made it through without mishap, it would be more through luck than competence.

A minute later he saw the break in the trees, ahead and to the left. He aimed for it, and they came out of the woods and onto the road. They were more or less where he expected. He shifted Samuel back up, felt the small arms clench tighter, and struck out a course alongside the road, where the grass was softer than asphalt yet unblemished by the ankle traps of field and wood.

Wendy ran alongside him. She asked if he wanted her to take Samuel for a while, but he shook his head. He was amazed that they had been able to run for so long. He still did not feel tired. He was also pleasantly surprised that his left leg was not bothering him in the slightest. He was just now appreciating how wholly remarkable were the full effects of Eden. If their lives had not been in such danger, it would have been exhilarating.

All the while, the back of his mind had been grasping for a plan for deliverance. Something—anything—other than running until they were overtaken. Now he experienced an epiphany, as though some mark on the roadside landscape triggered recognition in his brain. He knew how to get them to safety. At least for the night.

The idea sparked a second wind that he had not realized he was lacking. He began to run faster and encouraged Wendy to do the same. "One more mile!" he called.

"To what?" she asked, sounding as though she were flagging.

"A cave I know," he replied.

"How is our patient doing?" Ben asked.

Samantha was bent over Specialist Grimes, examining the fresh bandage she had just placed over the wound in his neck. She had wisely brought a package of medical supplies over from the clinic. He glanced into the cardboard box in which she had transported them. It all appeared to be fairly basic: scissors, thermometer, stopwatch, blood pressure meter, and a few syringes, along with cotton swabs, rubbing alcohol, gauze pads, tape, and even a box of regular Band-Aids. There were even a few bottles of pills tossed in for good measure. Seeing them brought back memories of the Vicodin he used to take on a regular basis. He actually felt a pang of longing for them. They had served as both a pain and stress reliever, and it was the latter need that cried out for attention now.

He believed that he should have felt more comfortable than he did. They had made the crossing without mishap. No one had so much as seen a feral person, and Percy had the doors ready to open as soon as they arrived. Ben felt more secure now that they were inside the church, and he believed most of the others did, too. He could not help thinking about Alexa and the others in the clinic. He hoped they were all right. It would be worth a little embarrassment to find out that fleeing the school building had been unnecessary. He doubted anyone would hold it against him.

When they arrived, there had already been four other people inside the church. The count was now almost twenty, and a few more seemed to join each hour. He had asked Father Confoy if they could ring the church bells to let others in the area know this was a safe haven. He had envisioned someone needing to climb up some dusty, cobwebbed tower to pull on a rope, but the priest had merely stepped into a side room and pressed a switch. That had been two hours ago. It was now well after midnight, and although they continued to ring the bells each hour, Ben doubted there would be many more newcomers.

He felt safe from the ferals, but he still had a nagging feeling in the back of his mind. Someone had started the rumor that the Army had a plan to exterminate the residents of the town. It sounded absurd on the surface, but he knew sometimes people—including authorities— reacted strangely in times of great stress. He remembered irresponsible Congresspeople calling for humane execution of Ebola patients during the recent outbreak of that disease, and this was ten times scarier to the American public than that had been. He thought about Avi and the truckloads that had driven away. That had had something wrong written all over it. If the military had decided to dispose of the patients, they would do it exactly like that—out of sight to avoid alerting the others. Was it really so far fetched that the authorities might sacrifice the few for the good of the many?

Even if the rumor were incorrect, it could do severe damage to the morale of these survivors. He particularly hoped the gossip had not reached Samantha, whose mother had been on the trucks. He wished he could say something uplifting to her, but she seemed lost in a world of her own thoughts. Any attempt at pleasant banter would seem inane.

Ben wished he was tired enough to go to sleep, as some of the others had done. Many of those who remained awake were now praying. Ben even felt like it himself. He doubted that God would mind a prayer from a Jew coming from inside a Catholic Church. But he did not wish to give the impression to the others that he felt desperate about their situation. Instead, he went around sharing a few words with each person who seemed open to conversation.

He left Samantha to her rumination and headed toward Percy. He was sitting beside a slightly older woman who probably would have been quite pretty if she had not looked so worn out. Ben stopped before interrupting them. He saw Percy make a joke and the woman laugh. They were doing just fine without him. His company would only derail whatever was happening between them.

They heard gunshots outside, and all internal conversation came to a halt. There were three quick reports, followed by a lengthy interregnum of profound silence. Then a few more shots. These sounded closer. Now people began looking at each other. Ben saw a lot of anxiety on these weary faces.

"It's fine, everyone," he called. "The Army is probably securing the town." He was not only just saying it to calm them down. It was, in fact, his best guess as to what was happening.

"He's right," agreed Father Confoy. "You are all safe in here."

Judging by the exchanged glances and worried stares, the others did not seem to believe it.

The gunshots continued in brief bursts. Ben went to the door and asked the man there to open it a crack. He hesitated, then nodded. They peeked out together. Ben scanned Main Street, seeing nothing unusual at first. Then a few more sharp cracks erupted in the darkness, and his eyes were drawn in that direction. He saw the front end of a vehicle pull into view. It was an army halftrack with several men positioned on top. One of them was stationed at a frighteningly powerful-looking machine gun, but that was not the source of the noises. The others held standard issue rifles and were sweeping them left to right in precise arcs. As Ben watched, one of them fired off another quick burst, although Ben could not see what target—feral or civilian—he was aiming at.

They closed the door, hearts beating faster. The church was a conspicuous building, but perhaps the soldiers would pass it by. Ben suddenly had no interest in getting their attention. He looked around the room and guessed that others felt the same way. Then his eyes noticed a figure far away. It was Father Confoy, stepping back into the side room.

No! Ben nearly yelled out. It was too late anyway, for a second later he heard the sound of the church bells.

He took a few steps away from the door, staring at it. He half-expected to see bullet holes appear, the projectiles tearing through the thick wood and slicing into the church's occupants. He forced himself to calm down, then looked around at the others. They were clearly as frightened as he.

"Everyone take a few steps back," he told them. "I'll take care of this." He turned back to the door and waited.

He noticed two others come up to join him. They stood to his left and right. One was the priest, an innocent smile plastered to his face. The other was Percy, whose bravery had been on a sharp incline ever since his initial failure.

There were more gunshots, and Ben tried not to flinch. The three of them continued to wait, shoulder-to-shoulder. Someone began thumping on the door, three hard knocks then a pause, followed by three more. Father Confoy stepped forward and opened the door.

Two soldiers stood outside, clutching rifles aimed downward. Their expressions were dreadfully serious. The one in front looked to be about Ben's age. He reminded Ben of an actor he had recently seen in a paint commercial, and he had to suppress a hysterical giggle.

"You're here to kill us, aren't you?" asked Percy.

The man looked at Percy in confusion. "What? Heavens, no. We're here to help." His shoulders were rigidly formal, somewhat belying the intended comfort of the statement. He gave Percy a look of disapproval. "Now, who is in charge here?"

Ben looked at Father Confoy, but the priest was looking back at him. So were the others, he realized. He stepped forward. "That would be me."

The soldier nodded. The name on his uniform read Walsh. Ben assumed this was an officer, but he had given up trying to guess ranks. He motioned with his hands. "Come in. I imagine we have a lot to discuss."

"Yessir," the man replied. "Private, keep an eye on this entrance while this gentleman gets me up to speed." The other soldier nodded, and only then did Ben realize they were not wearing masks. He did not know if that was good or bad news. Walsh briskly stepped to the side, where Ben joined him.

Before they started talking between themselves, Walsh took in the interior of the church in one glance. Suddenly his shoulders relaxed, and his entire posture eased. "Don't worry everyone. You're all safe."

The body language had a more dramatic effect than the words. Ben felt his own muscles relax, and only then became aware of how stiff he had been throughout the confrontation.

Walsh looked at him. "What's your name?" he asked.

"Ben Appelstein."

The man raised an eyebrow. "*The* Ben Appelstein?" Then he shook his head. "Forgive me. Tell me everything you can in two minutes."

Ben did so, starting from the point where the trucks pulled away from the clinic. He assumed that would be where the gap in the Army's knowledge started.

Walsh listened silently. At the end, he asked, "You have a soldier here? This Specialist Grimes? How is he?"

"He's unconscious. We're worried about how much blood he lost."

"Don't you worry. We'll get a doc in here ASAP." He looked around at the others. "These are all the people from the clinic?"

"Mostly. A few were already here, and a few more joined us since." Ben hesitated, hating to make an admission. "And a few stayed behind. Please check out the clinic as soon as you can."

Walsh nodded as he took a silent count of those in the church, his finger repeatedly jabbing the air. Then he met Ben's eyes. "I need to go back out, but I'll leave Private Torres here for protection. You mind staying in charge a while longer?"

Ben shook his head. He was not sure how to feel. Mostly just relieved, he supposed. The ordeal seemed to be coming to an end.

Walsh put his hand on his shoulder. "You did well, Ben. I'll see you again soon." He turned and headed for the door.

Ben felt something else mingle with the relief. He tried to fight it, then stopped. It had been too long since he felt pride. Perhaps a little of it would do him some good.

"How is he?" Halfus asked as Wendy returned from deeper inside the cave, bringing the flashlight with her.

"Asleep," she replied. "I don't know how he can do it in here, but there it is."

The flashlight in her hand and the few lit candles on the floor provided all the scant illumination inside this chamber. He wished he could see her face better. She sounded as though she was happy, and he genuinely wished it were so. The events of the night had been brutally tragic, but now the three of them were safe, and the resulting exaltation superseded all else. Instead of admiring her face, he settled for squeezing her hand. She squeezed back, and they shared a moment of mute companionship.

Halfus finally broke the silence. He dropped her hand and bent down to the rucksack. "How on earth is he sleeping?" he wondered aloud. He had seen children fall asleep in the oddest contortions, but a cave was just about the most uncomfortable place imaginable. "Is his head right on the rock, or is he lying on his arms?" He was distracted as he asked, and paid little attention to her reply. He spoke partly just to keep their minds off the events of the past hour, partly just because he liked talking to her about Sam. It was one topic she always enjoyed.

"No," she replied. "I found an old backpack that he's using as a pillow. What are you doing?"

He was pulling several items from the sack. "I need to set some flares outside."

"What?" Her voice was raised in surprise, and the echo filled the air of the cave for a few seconds. They were in the Gatehouse, not far from the entrance to the pipe. He had let her take Sam down to the Wash so they could talk without disturbing him, but Halfus dared not take them down any of the deeper tunnels. This cave was too easy to get lost in. Besides, he needed to stay close to the entrance.

"For Kevin," he replied, not looking at her. He really hoped she did not come out and say what they were both thinking. *You're risking the living for someone who's already dead.*

To her credit, she did not. Instead, all she said was his name with a hint of concern. He knew she wanted him to think things through for himself and realize that this was folly.

He tried to assuage her concerns. "I'll be guarding the entrance. If any of them come, they won't get through." She did not respond, so he continued. "I have to try. If he's still alive, I can't leave him out there." He wished his voice sounded a little more confident and a little less hopeless.

Wendy reached out and rubbed his back. "I know. Just be careful." She rested her hand on his shoulder comfortingly.

He had expected more of an argument from her, but she actually seemed supportive. This was not the same Wendy he used to know. He had already been crazy about her, and it was only getting stronger. He put his hand over hers. "I love you, you know." He gave it one more squeeze.

"I love you, too." He knew she was smiling, and that meant a lot to him. He scooped up the flares, left the flashlight with her, and headed back into the pipe.

He felt immeasurably better with the two of them safe inside the cave. It meant that he had only himself to worry about. He had no idea whether the ferals had located the cave or not. He did not know how they thought or hunted. It seemed unlikely that they could track by scent, given the underdeveloped sense of smell of humans in general. And ferals were themselves human, so their own scent would cause confusion. He assumed they remained vision-oriented beings, just as they were before their descent into madness.

He stopped at the end of the drainage pipe and peeked out for a minute. The tunnel was terribly dark, lit only by the faintest reflection of the flashlight behind and the moonlight ahead, so it took no time at all for his eyes to adjust to being back outside. Seeing no movement or shapes around to merit concern, he stepped out.

The first order of business was fashioning a weapon. There were fallen branches near the tree line, twenty yards from the road. He picked up the thickest and straightest one that he could find. It could function as a poor club in a pinch, but what he really hoped was that he would not need to use it.

He returned to the road. He withdrew one of the flares from his pocket and pulled the cap off. He struck the end of the flare against the coarse surface of the cap, igniting it like a match. Then he tossed it onto the asphalt. It shone insanely bright in the night.

He walked some distance away to a white oak tree that stood alone in the tall grass. He sat and perched his back against its bark, keeping his eyes on the vicinity of the flare. Now there was nothing to do but wait. He was not certain how long road flares lasted, but he had only brought four of them with him. He had a feeling they would not last through the night. It made the whole exercise seem pointless.

He was not willing to give up hope for Kevin, however. Not out of any sense of probabilities. To do otherwise was simply too much to take in so short a time. He had led Aaron and Mindy to their deaths. He had been trapped in a war zone where atrocities became commonplace, and yet the worst thing he ever witnessed turned out to happen here in his own backyard. He had not wanted to leave McGahey. He had had a feeling it was a bad idea. Even so, he had not expected this outcome. He had done his best to lead them, and half of them were dead as a result.

His guilt went beyond that, however. The entire pandemic was his fault. If only he had not gone exploring with Ernie, none of this would have happened. Wendy was upset about her brother, and rightfully so. But she had not been responsible for anywhere near as much tragedy as he.

The flare looked as though it was already starting to burn out. It seemed as though it had only been a few minutes, but he admitted that his sense of time was hopelessly warped. He stood up and pulled out another flare as he walked back toward the road. At this rate, there definitely would not be enough to last the night. He supposed he should be thankful that he had any at all. He had grabbed that rucksack from the Jeep based purely on instinct. He had no idea at the time what was in it that would turn out to be useful.

I found an old backpack that he's using as a pillow. Halfus stopped, his brain only now thinking through what she had said. Where would she have found an old backpack in the middle of a cave?

He dropped the flare and began to sprint. He went straight into the drainage pipe and through it as fast as he could manage with his back hunched and his legs bent. "Wendy!" he called out.

He was halfway. He yelled again. Three quarters, and he could see the light of the flashlight ahead. "Wendy!" he called, with slightly less volume, as he reached the end of the tunnel. He badly wanted to hear her chastise him for making too much noise. He stepped from the pipe into the cave.

"Halfus," he heard her say, and he started to relax. Then his mind noted the pleading tone of her voice, and he stiffened again. His eyes were still adjusting to the light, but he made out two adult-sized figures in the chamber. He raised the makeshift club threateningly. "Get away from—"

The shape was coming at him, impossibly quick, and he instantly changed tactics. Rather than using the branch as a weapon, he was forced to hold it before him as a shield. It took some of the impact out of the crash, but he was still knocked backwards and down. His back landed on the hard stone with a painful crack, made worse by the realization that his own body was cushioning the impact for his assailant. The feral was on top of him, its own hands on the branch, attempting to tug it away. Halfus resisted, and they jerked back and forth for a few excruciating seconds.

The feral arched its back as it pulled, and Halfus got a look at the face of the enemy. It was Ernie. Suddenly, Halfus' opponent changed the pull to a push, and the branch came crashing down into his forehead. It was worse than any boxer's punch he had ever experienced, and he was momentarily dazed. All he could do was continue to cling to the branch, but now it came down hard against his face. He felt his skull cracking against the stone below, so he twisted his head. The branch went up and down again, smashing into his cheek and eye socket, and Halfus lost sight in his left eye.

He struggled to regain his senses. The most dangerous part of the fights he remembered was not the physical damage, it was the disorientation that prevented one from fighting back effectively. He felt Ernie pulling back on the branch again. Halfus let go, and the club suddenly flew into the air before clanging against the cave wall.

Halfus threw a punch with his right hand. It connected solidly, giving his knuckles that rewarding tingle of pain. He did it again. Then Ernie reacted, pinning Halfus' arm with his own left hand. Halfus lost whatever small advantage he had momentarily gained, and his mind scrambled for a new plan.

Unarmed, Ernie turned to his teeth. With his one good eye, Halfus saw him coming at his neck in the same manner he had seen happen with Aaron. He twisted his shoulder to protect himself. Ernie bit into that instead. It was painful, but nothing compared to the alternative. Then Ernie twisted his head, expanding the wound, and Halfus felt strength draining from his left arm. He was already at a serious disadvantage. He had enough experience to know when he was losing a fight, and right now he felt that he had no chance at all. A feeling of panic flooded over him, sapping much of his remaining vigor.

He urgently needed to do something to reverse the course of the confrontation. He grimaced and shoved out with his right hand with all his remaining power. Ernie's mouth came up bloody. Halfus flexed his left hand into a fist. The arm was weak, but he had to hope that one solid punch might buy him a little more time.

A noise like an explosion pounded his eardrums. Ernie flinched to one side, and Halfus felt the momentum shift in an instant. Then a second bang drowned out the echoes of the first. This time a small splash of blood spilled from Ernie's chest. Halfus felt his opponent go limp, and he pushed the heavy weight off him. He rolled away from Ernie and struggled to lift himself into a sitting position.

He looked over at Wendy. She was on her knees holding a pistol in both hands, but it was no longer aimed at anything. This time, Halfus was glad he could not see her face. He could not imagine the horror she was feeling. He had no idea where the gun had come from, but it had certainly saved his life.

He heard a noise from Ernie. The feral was pushing out with its arms, attempting to move.

"Wendy, he's not dead," Halfus croaked. She made no response whatsoever. He used his right arm to pull himself up. His left shoulder was in terrible agony, but it was nothing compared to the damage to his face. He wondered if he would ever see out of that eye again.

He slowly moved toward her. He did not want to spook her—she still had the gun in her hand. "Wendy," he said. He tried to add a small measure of urgency to his voice. "Wendy."

Ernie was still writhing. He was making choking noises. His lungs were likely filling with blood, Halfus figured.

Halfus crouched next to her. He lowered his voice to just above a whisper. "Wendy, he's in pain."

Finally, she looked up at him. He gently pried the handgun from her hands. Counterintuitively, they dropped limply to her sides when relieved of the weight.

"Cover your ears," he said. She obeyed.

Halfus made no ceremony of this. He crouched by the maddened animal that was his former friend, held the barrel six inches from his temple, and fired. The body stopped moving. Ernie was out of his misery.

Halfus returned to her. He rubbed her shoulder. She was sobbing.

"It's going to be okay now," he told her. She looked at him, listening. "You didn't kill him, I did. All you did was save me. I'm rather glad you did."

She did not smile, but she did stop crying. He decided the best thing was to give her something else to occupy her mind.

"Will you do something for me?" She nodded. "Check on Sam, okay?"

She nodded again and got to her feet.

Halfus tucked the pistol into his waistband at the small of his back. Then he tucked the shirt in behind it. He felt woozy, so he took a moment to force in and out a few deep breaths. Then, head throbbing and muscles aching, he began to drag Ernie's body out of the cave.

1 8

SUNRISE

THE TOBA supervolcanic eruption occurred approximately seventy thousand years ago in Sumatra, Indonesia. It was over two thousand times more powerful than the recent eruption of Mount St. Helens, the deadliest in the history of the United States. Toba launched so much magma and ash into the sky that it caused a global volcanic winter for ten years and cooled the Earth for one thousand more. Some scientists believe that it may have killed off sixty percent of humans living at the time, and one controversial theory posits that it caused a genetic bottleneck that actually slowed down the evolution of humankind.

A supervolcano is one capable of erupting with at least one thousand times the mass of normal volcanoes. There are known to have been a dozen supervolcanic eruptions in the Earth's long history. Toba was not the strongest, but it is the most notable because of its coexistence with humans.

An extinction event is a dramatic spike in the decrease of life on Earth. Species are constantly breeding, evolving, and dying out in the normal course of affairs, but an extinction event causes a massive increase in death, thus throwing off the ratio. There have already been many extinction events in the history of the world, although there is disagreement as to what exactly constitutes such an event, and so the exact number is in dispute. Ninety-nine percent of all species of life that have ever existed on Earth are now extinct.

The rate is once again rising. Scientists estimate that as many as two hundred species of plants and animals become extinct every day, possibly the fastest pace since the disappearance of the dinosaurs.

Extinction events have occurred for a variety of reasons, including volcanic eruptions, oxygen levels in the oceans or atmosphere, flooding and drought, climate changes, and possibly asteroid impact. Some of these are clearly related, and therefore many extinction events are ascribed to more than one cause. The most recent increases in extinction rates are attributed to human behavior.

There is an overlap between an extinction event and global catastrophic risk, which by definition would cripple or even destroy all human life on the planet. Not surprisingly, the latter topic is a subject of frequent research and speculation, as well as a great deal of heated debate. No one knows with any certainty just how likely an extinction or near-extinction of humans in the short-term really is, but there are reasonably good projections of risk. One recent study at the University of Oxford suggested a one in five chance of human extinction in the next century, although most previous studies place the chances much lower.

There is a handful of potential human extinction events, some natural, others man-made. Some seem the stuff of science fiction, such as nanotechnology or artificial intelligences running amok. Others, like unlimited warfare, are more like long-abiding companions. Many causes, such as nuclear technology, are able to cause extinction either through war or peaceful means, in the form of scientific or industrial accidents.

The impact of interstellar bodies such as asteroids or meteors is already commonly believed to have led to one extinction event, and the possibility remains that it could happen again. The odds are quite low compared to most other scenarios, however.

Climate change is a slower and steadier potential risk. Some theorists believe that the current trajectory is leading the Earth toward an exacerbated loss of biodiversity, a diminishment of habitable portions of the planet, a decrease in the world food supply, and an enhanced environment for the spread of diseases.

Pandemics are an under-appreciated potential source of extinction. There is some truth to the belief that diseases cannot truly eradicate all human life on the planet, because a host must generally be alive to continue the transmission of a pathogen. The deadliest diseases often burn themselves out the fastest. However, there remains cause for concern. Biowarfare leads to the engineering of "better" diseases with which to plague our fellow man, and natural mutation shows the tenacious propensity of pathogens to figure out a way around our best defenses.

A worst-case scenario is a highly infectious disease that kills slowly, or has other long-term debilitating effects. Fortunately, humans have thus far managed to dodge this particular bullet.

Shortly after sunrise, Captain Walsh returned to tell them that they were evacuating the town. Everyone in the church would need to be ready to go in an hour. The officer did Ben the service of letting him know first, thus allowing him to break the news to the others.

It felt as though they had passed a significant milestone. They had made it through the night. Their ultimate fate was still in doubt, but the dawning of a new day brought a renewed spirit and sense of hope.

Ben was feeling good about things. He had accepted temporary responsibility for the lives of others, and now that time was drawing to a close. The moment had come to pass that responsibility on to those who were more used to and better equipped for it. At the same time, he could take some satisfaction from the knowledge of a job well done.

While he had his attention, Ben had a few questions for the captain. He was not certain how much information the man would be willing to share, but he saw no harm in inquiring.

He asked how they would be evacuated, and learned that a convoy of trucks was on the way. The parallel to yesterday's debacle was not encouraging, but he decided not to dwell on that. Next he asked where they were being taken.

"We've made arrangements with two hotels in Frederick. They will accommodate you as long as necessary."

"Two hotels? For the entire town?"

"All the civilians," replied Walsh. He paused, his face assuming a look of stoicism. "There are fewer of them than you probably assume."

Ben wondered just how few there were. He was aware that many residents had left town well before the quarantine, but over two thousand people normally called McGahey home while college was in session. He thought back to what Kim had told him. *Seven in ten.* If he extrapolated that across the whole population, then there were probably only several hundred "normal" McGaheyans remaining. Along with possibly twice that number of aberrant infected, many of them well into Phase Three. It was a sobering thought. No wonder the night before had been so harrowing.

Sensing the end of the discussion, Walsh excused himself and stepped away.

Then Ben had another thought. He called out to Walsh with one more question. "Captain, I forgot to ask...did you check in on the people at the clinic?" The officer turned back, then nodded.

That told Ben nothing. "How are they?"

Walsh shook his head. "I'm sorry." Then he turned away and headed back out.

Ben's earlier optimism winked out like a dead bulb. He had been right after all, but he wished he had been wrong instead. There was some solace from knowing he had saved most of them. But he had failed four. He wished he had tried harder to bring them along. He almost certainly could have forced them.

He felt a hand on his back. He looked over to see Samantha, her face full of sympathy. "It was their choice," she told him. He tried to tell himself the same thing. If only he could believe it. But he did not. He believed that real leaders could stop bad things like this from happening. The truth was that he had not possessed enough faith in his own capacity to lead to impose his decisions on others. Just like Iraq, he had left people behind.

He spent the next hour doing his best to make sure everyone would be ready when the trucks came. He spent a few minutes with each person, trying to remember names. He would always feel connected to this small community of survivors. That included

Grimes. An army medic had arrived late in the night with a few bags of blood and hooked up an IV. Now the Specialist was conscious and grateful. He had deliberately embarrassed Ben by informing the medic and everyone else within earshot how Ben had saved his life. It was uplifting to see the man in high spirits so quickly after his brush with death. Ben felt some of his faded optimism returning.

If only he could also be more optimistic about the containment of the virus. He had hoped that the absence of masks on their rescuers indicated that some cure had been discovered. But there was no such luck. The answer was much simpler than that. "For this operation, they are only using those of us who already have Schwarzvogel," Private Torres told him during one of their brief talks. It appeared that the world had not yet stepped back from the edge of the precipice. But neither had it gone completely over yet. In which direction the world tumbled remained a matter of uncertainty. That question would have to be decided another day.

They continued to hear sporadic gunfire in the street. Although they no longer feared that innocent civilians were being gunned down, it was still disconcerting to hear. Every aberrant infected killed was one more person who would never be cured. The reversion to the use of conventional rifles clearly indicated that the nonlethal weapons had proven ineffective, or that the magnitude of the problem was greater than originally anticipated.

He wished his college team had discovered a virus that reduced or eliminated humankind's natural aggressiveness, rather than unleashing one that made it worse. But he supposed that type of virus would be much less likely to thrive. Humans, like other animals, needed to possess an aggressive instinct in order to survive. It made sense that a virus which took advantage of that fact would be better positioned than one that did not. Darwin's theories applied to germs as much as animals. It seemed likely that hostility and competition would always be a part of human nature.

His mind drifted back to one of the legends he had read during the expedition to Nineveh. It involved one of the old kings of Assyria. The legend was all about aggression and conflict, but this king had somehow overcome his instincts and saved his empire at the cost of his life. There had been warnings there, if Ben and the others had known where to look. He could now see connections between the Schwarzvogel virus and the events of that narrative. Most good legends were based on a kernel of truth, shrouded in layers of ignorance and imagination. The problem—which was insurmountable—came in knowing which parts were which.

Army personnel were now coming in and out so frequently that one of the doors remained propped open all the time. At first, it clearly made some of the church occupants nervous, but they quickly got used to it. The presence of so many soldiers made everyone less uneasy about the likelihood of an attack.

Through the open door, they all listened then watched as the convoy of trucks arrived. There was no cheering or other celebration from the few tired souls in the church. They simply grabbed their few belongings and resignedly filed out of the building that had shielded them through the night. As their designated leader, Ben stood by the door and nodded to each as they passed through, then brought up the rear. Thus as the truck pulled away, he had the last seat in the back. It provided him with the surreal last look at the gallery of buildings as they scrolled by, receding like the scenes of a dream. The town that he had called home for almost a decade was diminishing before his eyes.

He felt a tap on his shoulder. It was Percy. "You look like you're about to fall out of the truck," he told Ben with a jovial smile. Ben had to admit that he felt completely worn down, both physically and emotionally. The young man pointed at the bench they were seated on, then gestured to the others to move down. They did so without objection.

"Megan brought a blanket with her," Percy went on. "She's not using it, though. Why don't you take it?" He reached out a hand and someone threw a thin blue blanket to him. He shook it out and held it up invitingly.

Ben smiled. He had taken care of them, so it was nice that they were now trying to return the favor. It made him feel respected, a sensation that had been far too absent from his life recently. He accepted the blanket, but instead of covering himself he crumpled it into a ball to use as a pillow. Then he lay down on the stretch of bench that they had cleared for him. It felt quite pleasant to finally close his eyes again. Within seconds, he was asleep.

"Dear Mom and Dad, I'm sorry for turning out the way I did. I'm sorry I wasn't the son you wanted. Everything I did was to make you proud of me. But everything turned out the opposite of how I hoped. Every time I thought I was happy, I was really just climbing up for the next big plunge. I understand now what you were trying to teach me as a child. The only joy in this life is a trick. I guess it's fitting that it ends this way.

"I almost killed an old man today. I wanted to and I didn't want to at the same time. He told me I should kill myself. But you always taught me that killing yourself is a sin, that people who do can never go to heaven. I'd really like to go to heaven. I don't know if I still can, but I don't want my last act to be what keeps me out. I want my last act to be something good for a change. Maybe that will be something you can be proud of.

"I'd like to think that I'm a good person who made mistakes. Every mistake I made, I tried to make up for. I tried to be a better person. I think I was a better person, until I wasn't any more. I hope that people will learn that this disease made me into what I am, not that I was a monster all along. But that is what I am becoming. I didn't kill that old man today, but I will kill someone some day soon. I can feel it.

"I can't leave yet. I want to be with her as long as I can. I know she doesn't love me, but we have been happy together. When we stop being happy, then I will find a way to leave. I won't kill myself, but I will find a place where I cannot hurt anyone. They'll find me some day and at least you'll know I died to protect the ones I care about from myself. Then let God do with me as he will. Love, Ernie.

"P.S. Tell Jackie that I'm sorry I didn't call. I wanted to wait until he would be proud of me, too. I just waited too long."

Wendy lowered the letter. They had found it tucked inside the backpack.

"I liked it better when it was easy to hate him," said Halfus. It did not feel good to be reminded that the creature he had just killed was once a sensitive, loving human being. Ever since returning to Maryland, he had been driven by a personal desire for revenge. A few hours ago it had seemed fitting that things ended the way they did. Now he simply felt sad.

At least he still had Wendy at his side. They were sitting together beneath the oak. The sun was just beginning to rise. It would have been a picturesque scene under different circumstances.

"I never did," she admitted. "Hate him, I mean. I was afraid of him, but I never hated him."

"Is that why you kept his gun?" he asked. "Because you were afraid of him?"

"Yes and no." She shook her head sorrowfully. "I ran out with it that day. I don't think I could have used it then, though. I just knew I wanted to keep it away from him. Then I forgot I had it. Well, maybe forgot isn't the right word. I pushed it out of my mind. It wasn't until yesterday, when Kevin talked about getting his guns, that I remembered it. Then he said he would kill to protect the people around him. That's when I realized he was right. I hate guns more than anything. But sometimes the world forces us to choose between two things we don't want to do."

"You've got that right."

"I'm glad I shot him," she said, and Halfus wondered whether she was speaking more for her own benefit than his. "It meant I got to keep you."

"Bah. I had him right where I wanted him." It still hurt Halfus to talk, but it would have hurt more to give up on humor.

Wendy grinned at him, then leaned over and kissed his forehead. He had a huge knot on it, to go with the cuts and bruises all over the left side of his face. His left eye was still too swollen to see out of. He hoped to get to a hospital soon. Later that day, with any luck. But he felt no particular hurry to leave this spot. Here, they were within a quick dash of safety. Once they started out again, they would be vulnerable. It led him to wonder how far out the ferals were roaming. For that matter, how many parts of the country were beginning to experience feral problems of their own? Was the disease still spreading, or receding?

He realized it had been only yesterday that they watched the news report. It seemed more like a week ago to his rattled brain. Suddenly, he was not in a hurry to learn the answers to his questions. Things were more likely to get worse before they started to get better. Someday they would turn, however. History taught him that they always did.

"Samuel, don't wander too far away, honey," Wendy called.

"I won't," the boy replied. He was scrounging around the fallen branches, not far from where Halfus had picked up his club.

"He'll be all right," Halfus assured her. "He's such a dear kid. Are we going to adopt him?"

Wendy grinned at him again. "Getting a little ahead of yourself, aren't you?" Then her smile faded, the expression replaced by concern. "You look terrible, Halph."

"I feel all right," he lied. "That's the important thing."

Her mouth curled up the way it sometimes did. It meant she was dubious. She leaned back against the tree. They silently watched Sam play for the next few minutes. The boy had been unhurt last night. He heard the commotion but stayed hidden until it was over, to the immense relief of both Halfus and Wendy. They both considered his safety their most important objective.

She yawned. Neither of them had gotten any sleep all night. It was a wonder he was not even more tired than he felt.

"You know, if you really wanted me to go caving with you, all you had to do was ask," she said.

He chuckled. It was slightly painful, but felt good nonetheless. "I'll keep that in mind."

"I never asked you, but I've always been curious. How did the two of you become friends, anyway? You were so different." There was no need to ask who she meant.

"He had a spark. It was hard to see at first, but it was there. He had so much potential. It was so obvious that his family wrecked him. I guess I hoped I could fix some of the damage." He sighed remorsefully.

"You did, Halfus. He thrived while he was your friend."

"I think I helped. For a while. But it's hard to overcome a childhood of abuse. I can't blame him entirely for his mistakes."

"We all make mistakes," Wendy agreed. "You know, my father always blamed herself for having that gun."

"It would be hard not to. Sometimes accidents are really, truly horrible. But they're still accidents. Not everything that goes wrong needs to be blamed on someone." He was saying it less to defend her father than to plant the seed in her own mind. And maybe in his own.

As if reading his thoughts, she said, "My mom got sick because of me, you know that?"

"Wendy, nearly everyone in town got sick. She would have, too."

"Maybe. Maybe not. I shtill feel guilty. I...never mind."

Halfus felt tension in every muscle of his body. Painfully so. He had to force himself to keep breathing. He tried to think of something banal to say. But his mind was utterly fixated on a single word. *No. No. No. No. No...*

She had stopped talking, as well. Had she noticed? God, he hoped not. *Please, not yet.*

He was finally able to unlock the jam in his brain. "I guess we should start moving out soon. Let's have a delicious breakfast of Clif bars first. You hungry?" He looked over at her, forcing fake enthusiasm. The mood had certainly shifted, but he tried to will back the lightheartedness.

She was staring directly ahead. "Halfus, I'm scared."

"I know." He dropped the pretense. He took her hand, holding it between both of his. "It's probably nothing."

He watched a lonely tear roll down her cheek. "I'm afraid to talk," she said. Another tear rolled down on the other side.

Halfus sank back against the tree, pressing himself closer to her. He wrapped both arms around her shoulders. "Shh," he whispered. "It's nothing. We had a rough night, and you haven't slept a wink." He leaned his head into hers, trying to reconnect as they had the day before.

She clung to one of his hands. She turned her head into his chest and sobbed. "I don't want Samuel to see me," she begged.

"He won't. He's not watching." Halfus was in completely foreign territory. He had no idea what to say to make her feel better. He settled for rubbing her back.

She did not cry long. Within a minute she had calmed herself. She was able to pull her head up and wipe away the tears with the back of her hand. Then she met his eyes and showed him a smile that looked as forced as his own.

"Why don't you try to get a little sleep?" he suggested. "There's no rush."

She nodded. Then she leaned in and kissed him. He put his hand on her cheek and stroked her hair. He wished they could keep doing it indefinitely, but she pulled back and sighed, then stood up. "Come on, Samuel," she called. "Come with me." She held out her hand. The boy ran over and took it, and together they climbed back into the cave.

Halfus watched them disappear from sight. He wished she had left the boy outside so Halfus could watch him. There was something inherently soothing about the child.

He waited another minute. He wanted to be sure she was not coming back out. Then he sank battered face into sore hands, and wept.

Why was this happening now? Why was it happening at all? She was one of the very first people to get Eden. She had gone this long without Phase Three. If she were still vulnerable, then all of them were. Halfus himself could wake up tomorrow and turn feral. It did not seem real.

He was not worried about that, though. He did not care what happened to himself. He would have given everything for that speaking mistake to have happened to him instead. This was just too unfair. He had gone through emotional hell before, with Shauna. It had nearly ruined his capacity to feel. He had not really been living, but simply existing. Now that he could live again, he absolutely could not go through that hell once more. He would lose his mind, with or without the disease.

Is there any good in this world? Or is it all just a trick? Maybe Ernie was right.

The intensity of the pain in his face and shoulder seemed to have doubled. He was not at all sure he could force himself to hike ten miles today. Maybe they could get to Smithsburg and catch a ride. Surely some passerby would see him and take pity. Relying on the aid of strangers, once anathema to him, showed just how low his spirits had fallen.

He heard a rustling in the woods, not far away. He still had the pistol tucked into his waistband. Yesterday he balked at the thought of killing another human being, even a feral. He felt no such qualms today. He felt anger at the world. Perhaps this would even be therapeutic.

He drew the weapon, slipped off the safety, and held it aimed at the sky, his arm forming a perfect L. From the sound of the rustling, it sounded like one or two creatures. An entire group might have worried him, but he had a hard time getting worked up over this. Perhaps it was not even a feral, but a deer or elk. But he doubted that. It was making too much noise to be a being of nature.

"Shit!" came the curse, followed by an increase in the disturbance. Whoever it was, he was having a heck of a time clearing this particular tangle of woods. Halfus lowered the gun and slipped the safety back on. He watched the figure finally break free and stumble into the open. It was Kevin.

"Need a hand, bro?" Halfus called out. He stood up. His head was pleasantly dizzy. It was no wonder. Somewhere along the way, the world had started to spin off its axis.

Kevin looked up and saw him. There was a moment of stunned surprise. Then his face slowly broke into an enormous grin as glorious as the morning's sunrise. He began to climb the short rise between them. "A word of advice," he said, speaking in a deceptively calm voice. "Never try to run through the woods in the middle of the night."

Halfus tucked the pistol back into his waistband. Kevin waited patiently, then the two of them hugged. Kevin's squeeze was harder and longer than expected, but that was all right by Halfus. He noticed that his friend no longer had the shotgun. That, too, was all right. He had had enough of guns for a while.

He saw that the bandage had come off of Kevin's cheek, and several new scratches had joined the terrible gashes on his face. Judging by his expression, Kevin did not seem to mind.

Thank you, world. I'm sorry for doubting you.

Kevin took a step back and glanced around. "You're not alone, are you?"

Halfus shook his head. "See that drainage pipe?" He pointed. "Believe it or not, there is a cave in there."

"Oh, yeah...I've heard of it." Kevin nodded, then shrugged, then nodded again. He looked giddy, almost hysterical. "God damn, Halfus," he said, "You have no idea how good it is to see you."

"I think maybe I do."

Halfus felt all the anger, self-pity, and physical pain drain right out of him. He believed he could walk fifty miles today, if he needed to. Carrying Sam the whole way, and enjoying it. It was truly remarkable just how much influence the state of the mind and spirit had over that of the body.

Kevin seemed to be looking at him earnestly for the first time. "Jesus, Halfus. You look like shit."

"I know. I bumped into Ernie last night."

Kevin's mouth formed an unspoken *Oh.*

"He's at peace now. Let's not talk about it in front of Wendy and Sam." Halfus paused thoughtfully. "In fact, there's a few things I need to tell you." His high was coming back down now. *Find some balance, Halfus. That's how you'll get through this. Balance.*

"Me, too," said Kevin. "It was quite a night."

"That it was. Here, kick up your feet by the imaginary fire so we can swap stories. Then I want to take you inside and show Wendy that miracles can happen. We're in need of one right now."

Kevin looked at him quizzically, then nodded. He glanced up at the sky. "I've discovered that I love the daylight. It looks like it's going to be wonderfully sunny today."

"I hope you're right. I really do."

Slowly and awkwardly, like a pair of decrepit war veterans, the two friends seated themselves under the oak. They were quickly lost in animated discussion, as oblivious to the rising symphonic resonance of nature as it was of them.

THE END

I have a favor to ask. Small for you, but huge for me. If you enjoyed this book, please leave a review.

Alas, I am not a household name, nor do I have the power of a big publishing house behind me. I am a new author trying to make a name for myself, and the only way I can do that is if readers who enjoy my books share that with other readers.

I would be very grateful if you would spend a minute leaving a review on the book's Amazon page. It can be as long or short as you like, as long as it's honest.

Thank you,
Michael

KINGS CLUB

If you enjoy my writing I invite you to join the Kings Club. Members receive bonuses to supplement the *Empire Asunder* series, currently including a free full-size, full-color version of the map and a free copy of *Empire Unveiled: The Complete Atlas and Sourcebook for the World of Empire Asunder.*

The sourcebook grows with each novel and contains background information about the characters, places, and culture that fill the Empire of Twelve Kingdoms.

The map is available as PDF and the sourcebook in both PDF and ebook formats.

Kings Club members also receive monthly announcements from me about special offers, the progress of the series, and are invited to join my Launch Team, who receive copies of each novel before publication and are an important part of each book's launch.

www.MichaelJasonBrandt.com/Offer

ABOUT THE AUTHOR

Michael Jason Brandt is a specialist in history and geopolitics. Born in Washington, DC, he has lived, worked, and studied in the US, England, and Spain. He received his first degree in business from Shippensburg University of Pennsylvania. After a decade in the corporate IT world, Michael returned to academia and received degrees in International Relations from George Washington University and The London School of Economics and Political Science.

Now dedicated to research and writing, Michael is a co-founder of Casus Belli Books. He currently lives in Maryland.

His first novel, *Plagued, with Guilt*, is the story of five friends confronted by war, disease, and the end of humanity. The *Empire Asunder* series, inspired by his time in Europe, is his second writing adventure and first sojourn into fantasy.

ALSO BY MICHAEL JASON BRANDT

The EMPIRE ASUNDER medieval fantasy saga, featuring political intrigue, turbulent warfare, and star-crossed romance:

Book 1: Three of Swords

From humble beginnings is greatness born...

With one fateful decision, the Empire of Twelve Kingdoms drifts from tenuous peace toward limitless conflict. Emperor Eberhart's unexpected abdication creates an absence of power just as the land most needs strong leadership. Kinship, unity, and hope give way to ambition, conspiracy, and tragedy. Royal families, once allied, now fight for the throne, heedless of a rising threat from abroad. All the while, an ancient, sinister presence looms in forgotten corners, awaiting an opportunity to reclaim a world it once enslaved...

Yet some stars shine brightest on the darkest nights. An unheralded prince places honor and conviction above privilege and prestige. A quiet soldier's unwitnessed heroism has the potential to save a kingdom. A common servant boldly confronts the face of supernatural evil. And the unlikeliest of love blossoms in the midst of hatred and violence.

Book 2: Hearts of Fire

Three conflicts. Three heroes.

As the cards predicted, three conflicts tear through the once-mighty empire, and three heroes rise to confront the challenge.

Prince Nicolas finds himself at the center of a civil war he regrets more than anyone, and the centerpiece of his father's plans to become the new emperor. Separated by cruel politics from the princess he loves, surrounded by enemies on every front, he learns that ambition and survival are one and the same.

As death and darkness overwhelm his village, Housethrall Jak leads a small band of survivors on a desperate journey through an underground nightmare. Along the way, he discovers the knowledge to fight back against demon and devil. But will he lose himself and all he holds dear in the process?

Surviving impossible odds to warn the kingdoms of invasion from abroad, Soldier Yohan seeks only a brief respite from the fighting and some time to repair his wounded heart. Yet even as new companions provide an unexpected joy for life, he finds that in the Empire of Twelve Kingdoms, love and tragedy are not so easily escaped.

Book 3: Shield and Crown

Some champions rise, some champions fall...

From prince to king, commander to general, Nico's rise from obscurity to power has launched him closer and closer to the seat of the emperor itself. But he is still a young man, untrained and unprepared for the countless pressures of ruling a land at war. Will the struggle to protect his people, help his friends, and preserve his love for his enemy's princess become too much for him?

Fed up with the endless sacrifices of friends and loved ones, housethrall Jak begins a personal quest to bring down the mysterious devils that hold the empire in their malicious grip. As he seeks to find safe refuge for his companions, however, he discovers that they are not so willing to let him go on alone. Soon he learns that he needs their aid, and that from unexpected new friends, to have any chance of success. And so he must risk more sacrifices from the very people he wishes to save...

The ravages of war have left soldier Yohan bereaved and bereft. Left only with one unwanted companion and a heart full of anger, he begins the hopeless quest to rescue two women from the enemy tribesmen terrorizing the empire with surprising impunity. Outnumbered and exhausted, rejecting friendship in favor of revenge, he faces a personal battle as much as an external one. Does his transformation into a single-minded killer make him as evil as those he hunts? Will he rescue the women he loves, or will he lose them along with his humanity?